BEWITCHING MONSTERS

THE COMPLETE SERIES

YVE VALE

BEWITCHING MONSTERS

THE COMPLETE SERIES

YVE VALE

Published by Entraverse Publishing

Sedona, AZ 86339, USA

YveVale.com

AUTHOR'S NOTE

The Bewitching Monsters Series is a dark yet often humorous paranormal monster why choose romance.

The female main character will end up with more than one of the love interests. Group scenes are on the agenda.

This series also has male/male romance within the group that will occur with and without the female present.

But there's no cheating.

If you believe love is love, you enjoy having some laughs too, and of course, some spicy times, then please charge forward!

This series also contains elements that some readers may be sensitive to. For more information, visit: ValeRomances.com

BEWITCHING HER MONSTERS

BEWITCHING MONSTERS BOOK ONE

YVE VALE

AUTHOR INTERRUPTED

JADE

Attempt number three:

*G*oliath pulls me to his broad chest and growls, "You are coming with me, menace."

I twist and scramble to get away. But some part of me wants him —a very needy part between my legs.

"No, you... brute!" I kick to make him drop me.

Not a smart move since he's carrying me over treacherous and rocky terrain.

His clawed feet are the only things keeping us from slipping down the mountain and plummeting to our deaths.

"Stop, Nora," he orders, clasping my head to his shoulder and trying to comfort me. It's the first time he's called me by my name. This should settle me somewhat, knowing I'm not just some nameless sacrifice to him.

But the toxin in my system is making clear thoughts impossible. I *can't* settle down. My actions might get us both killed. I don't want that.

After a few more minutes of scrambling over the mountainside to escape our enemies, Goliath sighs with relief when we see a narrow entrance to a cave ahead.

Once we are at the mouth of the cavern, Goliath sets me down. "Don't move," he warns in a whisper.

For the first time today, I listen to him. If there's an animal out here that is bigger and scarier than his beast, then we are fucked. His monstrous bearlike form is four feet taller than my height. I have to crane my neck backward to see his face. Holy crap, he's big.

I shiver with the thought of how big his other parts will be. I believe I'm about to find out.

After a quick investigation, he returns, apparently having deemed the cave safe for me to enter. He picks me up and carries me inside. Just enough light filters in to see it's previously been used as a shelter. A flat, smooth rock the size of a small bed is clear of debris at the far end. He sets me down.

Without an ounce of hesitation, he rips off my jacket and shirt, yanking them over my head and revealing my breasts. "I need to be inside you," he says roughly.

I try to cover my chest, but he won't let me.

"Mine." He circles his massive arm around my waist and pulls me closer. His claws dig into my flesh.

I can't control the whimper that leaves my throat, and it causes his enormous member to inflate. He presses it against my stomach.

He sweeps my legs from under me, and I fall backward. But his large hand catches me and sets me on my back gently. The rough stone beneath me scratches my sensitive skin, and I try not to squirm as Goliath rips my pants off and spreads me open for his viewing pleasure.

His long tongue sweeps out, taking his first taste of my slick center. He groans with approval and strokes his hardening length.

"You can't claim me," I protest.

"I have won you in combat. And you want me," he argues, flicking his tongue out to brush against me again. "Don't you?"

"But—"

"No. You are mine. And I am yours... finally." His eyes glint with mischief. "Do I need to make you ready for my cock? Is that it, my treasure?"

I can't say anything as I stare at the threat to my vagina's health and well-being. Even with proper and thorough preparation, that thing will destroy me.

I nod my consent. I might as well get a couple of orgasms out of this before it's death by dick.

He feasts on my center. His long, thick tongue slides through my folds and plunges into my channel.

It takes next to no time at all before my body quakes with an impending orgasm. He shoves two giant fingers into me, and I scream. When I stop trembling, he lines up the baseball bat sized appendage he calls a cock, and I...

Wait, wait, wait... This monster has a *baseball bat*-sized cock?

And doesn't he have claws???... *In* her vagina?

Come on now...

He really *is* going to kill her. Ugh. Author problems.

Nora is dead by dick, and I'm not even past writing chapter four.

Frustrated, I lean back in my chair and stare at my computer screen.

Can I call him a monster if he can retract his claws while they're fucking?

How big of a monster cock is too big?

Age-old questions.

Knowing I need some outside opinions, I open up a chat with a couple of fellow authors and begin asking them what they think.

They are all for the biggest dick imaginable...

> Mere: A knot the size of a grapefruit and a wine bottle size dick.

All I can think is, ouch.

My FMC's poor cervix. But this is a fantasy land where all things are possible. Maybe women there have truly magical pussies, and they won't get their organs rearranged by a monster-sized cock with the girth and length of a wine bottle.

> Clara: You could be vague about how big is big.

> Bekka: There is no limit but our imagination.

They're right. I just need to lean into the fantasy.

Sighing, I rub my face and realize my muse is a bit broken. I don't really like Goliath or Nora. I won't get anywhere without an inspirational boost.

Oh, well. Time for my ritual to get the magic flowing again.

Off to my little kitchen, I steep my tea and glare at the herbal blend as I wonder if this is what's failing me. Maybe I need a change. Maybe I need a *lot* of changes.

However, I know the true culprit of my writer's *malaise* (Never call it a block. It gives it power). I haven't been the same since Rob. Perfect name, really, since he's the thief that robbed me of my muse.

For comfort, I head to my support group in the other room. They're my hostages, who I keep for their happiness as well as mine. My fur babies.

"I have a confession. I'm a romance writer who doesn't believe in love at the moment," I whisper to my guinea pig. "Sorry. I shouldn't confess that to anyone. Not even you. If I don't get inspired here soon, your food is on the line."

As a paranormal romance author, I should believe in magic and love, if only in my imagination. And usually, I do. But right now, I don't believe in tiny magical moments in life.

Sure, I have my favorite crystals and know their metaphysical properties. I've researched all the mythical creatures. I tell myself it's all in the name of research. But deep down, I want magic to be real. Sometimes I wish my grandmother wasn't crazy, and I was a genuine witch, as she's claimed.

Maybe it wouldn't be *Hogwarts'* level of magic. But I *have* seen miracles and the power of positive thinking. I just haven't felt it in a while.

It seemed 'magical' when I first met my ex-boyfriend. But apparently, that kind of magic doesn't last. Maybe it was only magic lust.

The weird part was that I wasn't really attracted to Rob.

So if it was magic that I felt when I met him, it was a black magic spell.

2

WALKS INTO A BAR

ADE

Slamming my teacup down a little too hard onto my banged-up writing desk, I curse my continued writer's *detour*.

I shuffle out of my writing cave and into my bedroom, flopping onto my disheveled queen bed with a grunt. I pull the tangled blanket over part of my body and give up on the effort it will take to completely cover myself up.

Maybe I should make my bed once in a while?

But what's the point in keeping it tidy when it's just me here now? Besides, I take about five to ten power naps a day, anyway. Sometimes I believe I must be a damn cat trapped in a human body.

Now I'm wondering about the various animal shifters and what combination of fancy peens I could use in my next book.

Speaking of animals, I need to feed my horde of rescues. Groaning, I lift myself off the bed to slip into the spare bedroom, where I have my odd collection of friends.

My guinea pig squeaks as soon as he sees me. He's one of the extra fluffy breeds, reminding me of the 'Trouble With Tribbles' episode from the first Star Trek series—a mop of fur with feet.

I open up Trouble's cage and lift him out to give him plenty of affection, holding him to my chest and placing several kisses on his little head. "How are you doing today, buddy?"

Trouble makes his chirping sounds again, and I swear in my head I hear him tell me he's fine, but I get the mental image he wants food. Sometimes I wonder if it's just my imagination or if I'm really picking something up.

Animal whisperers are real… right?

I blow off this thought as nothing more than my overactive imagination. I've always had a crazy mind. It's why I'm an author.

However, when I was a kid my abuela told me stories that she was a powerful bruja—a witch. She passed away when I was little, so unfortunately, I never had the chance to know her as well as I would have liked. From what I remember, she was an intense character, beautiful and strange. My mother often said I inherited my grandmother's eccentric ways. Since she hated her mother, she wasn't happy about that.

But my mother isn't wrong that I'm an oddball. When I was little, I believed I could see all kinds of crazy stuff. I thought I saw auras, glowing strings connecting people, and swirling energy in the air.

I believed sometimes I could see what people were really like on the inside —glowing eyes, fur, and even monstrous faces. No wonder I used my imagination to make up stories for a living.

When I was around eleven years old, my mom screamed at me, trying to convince me I couldn't see what I was seeing. She cursed and ranted for an hour straight, telling me that she wasn't going to allow me be a crazy witch like her mother.

So, from that day on, I forced my wild imaginings to stop. Mostly.

But also I was just distracted by my hormones at that point in my development too.

I'm brought back to the present as my rabbit does zoomies around her cage, trying to get my attention. Without a voice, she usually rampages around to communicate her need for attention.

"Sorry, Sage."

I set Trouble down in his habitat with a last pet, and give him a healthy serving of food and an apple slice for a treat.

Sage stands on her hind legs and scrambles to take the raisin I pass over the wire fence. Her soft furry lips brush against my fingertips. She is always gentle, no matter how excited she is to get her goodies.

I open the door to her cage and give her the evening dose of attention, snuggling her and rubbing her soft ears.

I glance at the clock and realize I've wasted the entire day sitting at my desk and not writing much at all. However, I did get some edits completed on my other book due to be released next month.

And… I forgot to eat all day, and it's close to midnight.

After giving my fur babies their food and love, I wander into the kitchen and find I have nothing much for a human in the fridge.

I haven't exactly been taking care of myself since Rob left. And if I'm being honest, I wasn't great at it when I was with him. It's not like he kept me balanced. He wasn't the best guy to rely on for… well, anything.

Without someone to remind me to take a break, I get so deep in my tunnel-vision that I forget the world outside my stories exists. Hence, the hunger pangs right now.

I know my chronic self-neglect has got to be addressed—*mañana*.

Left with very few choices this late at night, I'll go to the bar down the street with a limited after-dinner hours menu. Then I'll grab a few items at the 24-hour market on the way back for tomorrow's meals.

Wham, bam, thank you, ma'am, problem solved.

I look down at my outfit and realize I'll have to put something else on. A dirty and now fur-covered sweatshirt and pajama bottoms won't cut it, not even this late at night.

I change into yoga pants and a clean sweatshirt. Yeah, I know it's not a big step up, but I at least *appear* cleaner than I did a moment ago.

I grab my e-tablet for notes, hoping the odd characters who often frequent my neighborhood bar might inspire me.

Slipping into my well-loved and aged green '69 Mustang with my engine purring, I drive the short ride to the bar. Yes, I did buy it because it was a sixty-nine.

From the parking lot, I see that the dive bar is busier than normal. Despite that, I easily find a table with a good vantage point to watch the other patrons.

Jimmy, the old barkeeper, nods to me as I sit down. He's an odd duck but registers as relatively harmless on my douche-o-meter.

The long bar is filled with regulars. Most of them are guys in their mid-thirties and forties. They don't bother with me anymore since I've turned them all down at some point. They aren't a bad lot, but I have to have some spark for a potential date. And even though a couple of them are attractive and seem nice enough, I felt nothing for them.

The floor server, Lora, brings me a hot herbal tea set up without needing to ask if I want it. "The usual tonight, Jade?" she asks with a big grin. Lora doesn't mind me taking up space for hours since it isn't often busy this late at night, and I always leave a generous tip.

"Sure, thanks," I say, glancing around the dimly lit room as she walks away.

My attention instantly darts across the sea of tables to the entrance. It's as if gravity has become a vortex, and I'm falling into its well. I think I may have stopped breathing.

Four men—no, these are not *mere* men—file in the door and sit down, mostly facing me in the large, round corner booth. These guys seem to have walked right out of one of my novels. They're so good-looking that I have to turn away since it's like staring directly into the sun.

Their sheer hotness has burned my retinas.

My skin flushes. My mouth goes dry as something else gets wet. My clit perks up, begging for attention.

To distract my body from any more inappropriate reactions, I slurp my tea.

Crap! It's too hot, and I scald my tongue and choke.

I'm waving at my face to stop my freak out. If they look over at me now, I may just die. My obituary will read: "She died horny, survived only by her closest friend, her vibrator, Mr. O'Mygawd."

I take a deep breath, turning my gaze out my window and do my best to ignore the romance cover models, who are (weirdly) in some neighborhood dive bar in the middle of the night.

Light bulb!

This is perfect for my writer's *hump*.

An avalanche of questions hit me. But the first one is: *what* is the hot squad doing *here*? *Of all places?*

As I sip some water, I casually glance around the room, skimming my eyes over them again.

Damn. Their presence feels like an electric shock to my body every time I look in their direction. I thought that only happened in books. And yes, I confirm my earlier assessment... they are perfection incarnate.

I power up my tablet and take notes on their appearance.

On my third slow perusal, I go deeper with my assessment. It helps that I'm becoming accustomed to their stupidly ridiculous attractiveness.

I need to continue staring to desensitize myself, right?

The first guy sits on the edge of the circular booth, looking as if he's ready to bolt out the door. His strong jaw is clenched, and his knee is bouncing with frustration.

The word *alphahole* pops into my mind. Got to have one of them in the story.

He has short, dark brown hair sticking up as if he's been running his fingers through it in agitation. His golden-brown eyes seem to glow with passion and intensity. Roguish stubble covers his strong jawline. He's wearing a black t-shirt that strains against his muscular chest and biceps.

And *fuck me…* gray sweatpants. *Really?*

Of course, he has on the SoCal standard—flip-flops. He's lucky he's in temperate, near-coastal Southern California, where it seems to be the footwear of choice, even in winter. He must be close to six foot tall, maybe taller. With all that muscle, I assume he has a physical job, or he hits the gym as frequently as I take naps.

Although he wears sandals and exhibits anxiety, he still radiates total dominant alphahole energy.

I'd say he's in his early thirties, but I would also guess he has had a rough life. Something in his eyes suggests that he's had his share of grief. And grief recognizes grief. But right now, he looks downright upset.

I wonder why.

A breeze sweeps over me, and a shiver runs up my spine. Inspiration is here.

A scene filters into my mind.

These four have lost someone important recently… maybe a day or so ago. Mr. Alphahole was close to their fifth *missing* buddy. They're worried they will be targeted next. And they should be worried—

Someone barks out a laugh at the bar and I'm distracted, losing my train of thought. So I move on to the rest of the guys to see if they will inspire me, too.

The man (or should I say beast) next to him looks to be four inches taller and bulkier than Mr. Grumpy. Almost matching his skin tone, his hair is an unusual color that reminds me of light-colored sand. His eyes are fair too—maybe a pale gray?

I wish it wouldn't be weird for me to go up and see.

His features are bold, and everything about him appears massive. He's the human equivalent of a tank. But this one has stoic, somber vibes and appears to be made of beautifully sculpted stone compared to the alphahole next to him. I want to crack his calm persona and see what's underneath that cool exterior.

The third hunk is all that and a side of *oh-damn-me-to-hell-for-what-I'm-thinking*. He's the tallest of the four of them, but not much taller than Mr. Stoic. And if anyone was born with extra muscles, it's him. He has short black hair and a definitively masculine face. His obsidian eyes lock onto whoever is speaking with an intensity that could make lesser beings crumble. He's fuming too, but he's better at concealing it.

Finally, the guy on the other end is the smallest and sleekest of the oversized bunch. He scans the room every few minutes with a smoldering mien with ice-blue eyes. This one might be able to *literally* light my panties on fire.

I watch them as discreetly as I can while eating my grilled cheese sandwich and a side salad. Imagining them as some super elite spies isn't completely ridiculous, although they would have a hard time blending in with their disarmingly good looks, not to mention their immense size.

From my understanding, the best spies blend into a crowd with their mundane appearance.

I wouldn't be a horrible spy. Well, except for everything it entails—like coordination and finesse. I imagine running would be involved in that line of work, too—not my jam either. Now, if I could briskly walk away from a threat, then I'd be good with that. In addition to my aversion to real-life danger and running, I'm just this side of kooky and would attract unwanted attention. And I'd likely blow my cover since I'm not the best liar, even though I make up stories for a living. I've been told my face is far *too expressive*.

Okay, on second thought, I'd make a terrible spy. But I can write about being one, so I'm not going to cry about it.

Covertly as possible, I take a picture of the guys with my tablet's camera. Sure, maybe it's not ethical, but it's not like I plan on sharing it anywhere. It's for… *research*.

But when I look at the picture, it's fuzzy. Their figures are there, but blurred, and they have strange auras around them. I wipe the lens clean, because I'm sure I must have put my greasy hands on the lens.

I try again—blurry. Figuring it must be the tablet, I pull out my phone and snap a few shots. When I study them, the pics are still blurry and flared with colors. Well, damn. I guess I will just have to commit these guys to memory using my tired brain.

Frowning, I stare at them. I wonder if I'm blowing their attractiveness out of proportion. Am I just that much of a thirsty bitch? Maybe I only *want* them to be hotties since I've been alone the last few months.

And maybe not everyone would think they are damn fine.

Lora wanders around the tables and checks on them. Then she makes her way to me. "How are you doing tonight?"

"Mostly good." I shrug, being honest.

We've chatted quite a bit over the years. Enough to know we are both around the same age. I'm about to hit forty, and she had her fortieth birthday last month.

"Is it just my romance brain and hormones, or are those guys stupid-hot?" I ask.

"Yeah, they could change my oil anytime," she jokes.

"If only it were as easy as making an appointment for a lube job." I smirk.

"I'd tell you to go flirt with them, but they seem tense."

"I picked that up." I shake my head. "Nah, I'm good. My FMCs always have better luck than I do in the boyfriend department, so I'll focus on setting those guys up with my characters for now."

"Make sure I get a copy." Lora smiles. "Need anything else?"

"Not tonight, I suppose. Can't take those guys in a doggy bag."

Lora takes my card to run my tab. And I jot down some other observations about my new harem… for my next book.

When I glance up again, all their eyes are on me.

Oh, shit. They must have caught me staring.

Blushing as bright as Barbie's Corvette, I quickly drop my gaze, pack up my stuff, and rush to Lora at the register. I sign my receipt and bolt before I can further embarrass myself.

After stopping by the 24-hour corner market to grab some food for tomorrow, I head home.

I feel another wave of embarrassment over being caught staring by those guys.

They obviously had more important things to deal with than some middle-aged, horny author leering at them. My skin flushes pink again as I pull into my driveway and cut the engine.

When I get out of my car, I realize I've forgotten to check my mail the past few days. As I approach the curb to open my mailbox, I see a shadowy streak fly down the dark road. It appears to be a gigantic dog.

I hurry to my porch. Out of the corner of my eye, I see him hide across the street, tucked in the shadow of my neighbor's house.

His eyes lock onto me.

I go inside briefly to set my groceries down just inside the door, returning to the porch to see if he will come closer to my house, seeking safety.

Yeah, I know. I'm *that* person, the one who rescues every lost animal I see. But I can't leave him out there.

I bend lower to make myself seem less threatening. Not that I'm all that intimidating with my five-foot-five inches.

"Hey, gorgeous, are you lost?" I ask.

Yes… I *do* talk to animals as if they're humans. And maybe plants too.

The beautiful, giant dog raises his brows and turns his head to look behind him to see if I'm talking to someone else.

Hilarious. He's a smart one.

He dips his head downward and doesn't move forward.

I lean all the way over, trying to look smaller and less intimidating to the big lug. Whoops, my cleavage is on full display. At least I didn't subject those hotties at the bar to a desperate play like that.

"I have special treats for *good* boys," I say sweetly, trying to tempt him into the house.

He coughs, which sounds more like he choked. I hope he doesn't have some kind of lung infection. *Poor thing.*

"Come on. I have a warm place for you." I slowly walk backward toward my front door.

Some dogs don't like it when you seem too eager to snatch them up. Of course, he's too beautiful for me to let him live rough. Life on the streets is no good for any dog, but something draws me to this one. He's special.

So I'll have to play it cool to snag him.

3

DOGGY RESCUE

ARRAN

$\mathcal{T}$he crazy witch leans over to lure me in with her luscious, hypnotizing breasts. Then she tempts my wolf-half with treats.

I have to stay strong.

"*You're* the one who was following me, remember?" She places her hands on her hips. "And now you're going to play me like this?"

I'm shocked that she's just calling me out. It's a damned challenge, is what it is.

But my wolf is intrigued and right now, he wants nothing more than to dive into her cleavage with his snout.

Down, boy!

Dammit, it's been far too long since we've had a nice rut. But this witch might kill me. My wolf's arguing it might be worth it.

"I guess you think you're pretty smart," the woman sasses me. "Well, we'll see… you know, you'll be more comfortable inside. Come on, I have something soft and warm for you to rest your head on."

I can't help it. My brows rise, wondering what's up with her. Is she really trying to seduce me? Is this a trap? Some part of me wonders if she is actually clueless about who she's dealing with. She must be. Otherwise, she's either crazy brave, crazy powerful, or just plain crazy.

The witch casually spins and saunters back toward her front door.

And now she's playing hard to get?

With a shake of her head, she peeks over her shoulder and says, "Poor skittish baby."

Skittish baby!

I slowly stand up and follow her. I have to know why she was watching us at the bar. Thankfully, she didn't live far away. I wasn't thinking it through when I shifted and chased after her car.

"You want something to eat? You want some of my meat?"

What the actual fuck? But my legs carry me after her.

She opens the front door and keeps it wide after she slips inside, waiting for me to decide to fall into her devious trap or not.

I am *not* a skittish baby, so to prove this, I trot inside confidently and glance around, sniffing the air.

Now that I'm within biting distance, I pause and stare up at her.

Slowly, she shuts the door, allowing me the chance to bolt instead of attacking her. But I cautiously watch her as she does. The witch won't intimidate me.

In the full light of the house, her eyes widen as she sees how massive my wolf really is.

I'm huge, even for a wolf shifter. I could give a mastiff a run for its money.

"You *are* a *big* boy, aren't you?" She chuckles, mostly to herself. "But I'm sure you get that all the time from the girls." She waggles her eyebrows. "You can stay as long as you'd like, but don't cause any trouble," she warns me. "I have some other hostages here who I'd rather you be friends with if you're going to be my new friend."

I chuff with that. I cannot believe the set of crystal balls on this witch!

"Oh, sweetie! Would you like some water?" the witch asks with genuine concern. She hurries toward her kitchen with her groceries and tosses them in the fridge. She gets out a dog water bowl, fills it with filtered water, and sets it down in front of me.

Huh?

My wolf almost accepts this offering.

But I remind him she might have poisoned it.

He disagrees. Why the fuck is *he* on Team Witch? He usually hates witches —and for a good reason.

I don't drink. Instead, I give her my best approximation of an indignant look.

She frowns and glances at my neck. "I don't see a collar, but it could be lost in your thick fur."

Why she keeps joking about me being a dog, I do not know.

The witch places her hands on her hips again. "Are you going to tell me your name?"

I give her a quizzical look.

"Yeah, I know you can't talk. But fair warning, I'm going to touch you. Okay?" She cautiously reaches out for my neck, likely to curse me or put a magical chokehold on me.

I give her a low growl to back off.

"Fine." She pulls away. "I guess any touching will have to wait until we get to know each other better."

I blink at that comment. She *is* a strange one.

"Let's get something in you, since you look like you want to eat me." She shrugs and heads for the fridge. She bends over, rummaging through her stuff, and gives me a marvelous view of her full, juicy ass. "Do you like it raw?"

I cough again.

What is it with this woman and her sexual innuendos? Does this game ever work?

Shit. It probably does. If she were a supe and not a freaking witch, I'd be all over that plump ass. As it is, I want to take a bite out of it for several *conflicting* reasons.

She takes her sweet time bending over and pulling stuff out of her fridge.

What would she do to me if I were to shift and grab those wide hips from behind? Would she let me rip the seam of those tight leggings and slam home?

Focus!

I sniff the air for magic…

She must have activated some sort of lust charm for me to be thinking like this.

Sneaky little witch.

But oddly, I don't scent witch magic in the air. That makes little sense. Why would she allow her enemy into her home without protections in place?

And other than the random and *uncharged* crystals on shelves, there's nothing that screams this is a witch's house. Is this even her home?

I trot around the small but cozy place, sniffing the cushions and inspecting a few photographs. From the scents in the room, I can tell this *is* her home. She's been here for a while. Tucked behind a bunch of other framed pictures, there's one of her with a guy and some other friends.

My wolf snarls when he sees the male has an arm around her waist.

Maybe he's a warlock who is truly evil, since my wolf can't be this possessive over a freaking witch.

I admonish him, *You can't like a witch.*

"Hey now, whatcha doin'?" From the kitchen island, she lifts onto her toes to see over the couch and what I'm up to. "Oh, don't get bothered by him. He's out of my life... mostly," she whispers the last word.

Hmm. Maybe *he* is the one who is making her spy on my friends and me. I study the picture again to memorize his face. My wolf is agitated and aggressively bumps it with his nose. The frame falls to the ground, and the glass shatters.

"Oh, no." The witch quickly yet calmly approaches me. "Step back. I don't want you to get your feeties hurt."

My feeties?

Does she *really* think I'm a dog? She must. Either that, or she's incredibly condescending and has a death wish.

She looks at my front paws to make sure I don't have any glass on my fur. Picking up the bigger pieces of shards, she piles them on top of the broken frame to collect them. "I don't know why I kept this picture. Maybe because it reminds me of when I believed Rob wasn't such an alphahole."

I have a name for the man. Good.

But *alpha*hole? Was she dating a jerky wolf shifter? Maybe that's why she works for the Witch Council as a spy—for revenge.

I have so many questions.

Is that why she's so comfortable with me in my wolf form? Maybe she has already dated one?

Her eyes water, but she doesn't let the tears fall. Turning her face from me, she brushes away the moisture and stands.

"Why don't you come over here and eat?" She motions me over to the kitchen.

I don't follow. Rather, I continue my inspection of the living room, intent on figuring out what this witch is up to.

The witch doesn't force me to go to the kitchen. Instead, she sweeps up the glass with furtive glances my way. She's trying to figure me out, just as I am trying to understand her.

I suppose I should just shift and interrogate her.

"Do you have anyone who will miss you?" she asks, sounding sad.

That's a fucking threat if I've ever heard one.

And the sadness? I suppose she regrets that she needs to eliminate me. Perhaps she is one of the few witches with a conscience.

Just as I'm about to snarl and show her I won't go down without a fight, she stops me cold.

"I'll call animal control in the morning to find your humans. I'm sure someone is worried sick about losing such a beautiful dog." She looks about ready to cry again.

Holy crap. She *really* does think I'm a regular dog.

She must be a magically weak witch and can't sense I'm the supe she was watching earlier.

She might know nothing about the four of us. And they sent her on a reconnaissance mission without many details about her targets. Maybe the council only picked her to watch us because of her proximity.

I sniff the air again and only get a faint hint of witch magic, but I don't know why it suddenly appeared now. So she doesn't practice her craft—much. Or she doesn't know how to use it. I almost didn't scent her muted magic at the bar either. But oddly, the magic was stronger there while she was watching us.

The witch pulls her computer tablet and phone out of her purse. But after she glances at me, she shoves it back inside and takes all her personal belongings with her as she heads toward the bedrooms. "There's food in the bowl if you get hungry. I hope you don't mind staying out here alone. Oh, and please don't eat my sofa. I'm going to bed. Don't worry, we'll get you sorted in the morning."

4

HAUNTING DREAMS

JADE

*T*his dog is the most intense animal I've ever encountered. And I've dealt with some animals I was sure had human souls. I have a couple of highly intelligent brats in my spare room right now.

I leave the huge canine to check on my little ones. When I open the door, they look at me like I've disturbed them. "We have a visitor, so don't get freaked out. Kay?"

They obviously don't reply, because, yeah, they're animals. I'm not that weird.

I suppose I talk to my furry friends because it's a bit of a lonely life, writing all day long and promoting stuff online. And I often go days without human contact—physical human contact. Sure, I network online and interact with my author friends there. I make comments on their posts and support them as much as I can. And that's rewarding, but it isn't the same as physically touching or talking with a living person in front of me. Sometimes I miss seeing a friend's smile and the crinkle of their eyes when we joke around or hug each other. Maybe that's why I go to the bar at least once a week—to experience humans.

I carry my purse into my bedroom and shut the door behind me. I don't think my new friend will chew up my stuff, but I don't want to risk having to go through the hassle of replacing my credit cards, ID, phone, and tablet.

I don't hear him whine or bark, so I relax and lock my bedroom door. It's an instinct now. I do it out of habit. Lessons learned and all that.

Using my ensuite bathroom, I brush my teeth and wash my face.

The bed invites me to a good time. And I pull back the covers, *real* slow. Okay, maybe those hot guys tonight worked me up a bit.

I pull my vibrator, Mr. O'Mygawd, from the side table drawer and imagine my new harem picks. I wonder which one of them I would choose first. The intense leader? The stony giant? The smoldering player? The broody bad boy?

A shiver runs up my back. The room feels like it dropped a couple of degrees. *Odd*.

There's no reason for the drafty breeze. I didn't hear the dog crash through the window or—I chuckle to myself—open the front door.

I'll need to make my noises quietly, since I don't want to upset the dog. He might think I'm being hurt in here when I come. I'd hold off, but the urge to rub one out is overwhelming. It's like I still feel their eyes on me. And I envision a world where they are interested—one where *all* of them are interested.

Ha! Fat chance, but it's my job to dream this shit up.

Got to fight the good fight. Research and all.

I feel my pussy wet with just the thought of them closing in on me. Each of their muscular bodies presses closer and closer until they tower over me.

Taking up all the oxygen in the room, they all reach out and caress me. A kiss on my neck. A hand on my breast. A firm cock against my ass. Another against my stomach. I feel dizzy with need and I sway.

"You are ours now," the dominant one claims me. "We are going to stretch you with our cocks, and then our cum will fill you so full you'll be leaking for days."

They tear the clothes off my body, and I cry out, "Yes, claim me."

Each of them tears off their own clothes and frees their cocks, stroking themselves with their massive hands. Not that they need the extra stimulation to get hard.

Strong hands push me down and I go willingly. On my knees in front of them, I open my mouth, understanding what they desire from me. What I desire from them.

One after another, their thick cocks face fuck me, rammed down my throat.

But it's only the last guy, Mr. Blue Eyes, who comes in my mouth. I swallow him down as he shouts, "Drink it all, my pet."

After he withdraws, I'm lifted into the dominant one's arms, and he spears me with his enormous cock, stretching and filling me beyond anything I have ever experienced.

Grumpy Alphahole comes up behind me, fists my hair, pulling my head back so he can plunder my mouth with his fingers, wetting them.

Then he slips his wet fingers down over my ass crack and slides two into my ass.

Bouncing me on his massive dick, Mr. Dom rams into me, keeping a brutal pace.

The quiet one squeezes my tit.

And the fantasy overwhelms me…

"Fuck!" I shout when the orgasm crashes into me.

I blush for some reason, even though I'm alone. It's not like the dog is going to judge me—probably. Although *he* might, since he seems way too smart.

Maybe I feel a bit smutty because I'm using real people to jerk off to?

Whatever. Another strange, cool breeze skims over my naked flesh, and I decide to throw on a long t-shirt before falling asleep. I have the unnerving sensation that I'm being watched. But that feeling just might be because I have a new presence in the house in the form of a highly intelligent dog.

But even with that feeling, I fall asleep, content with the knowledge I have found some inspiration. Now that I have my new characters, I just have to come up with the beginnings of a plot.

I can't wait to play with these guys some more…

***

I fall instantly into a strange dream…

"Hey!" A huge red demon runs directly at me, but I'm not afraid.

In this dream, I'm supposed to know him. His large horns curl above his head. Blood covers his hands and soaks into his shirt.

I realize he looks very much like one of the hot squad from the bar. Maybe this is actually one of my own dreams and not one that I've picked up from some stranger.

Yeah, I sort of believe that I *might* dream other people's dreams.

"Are you alright?" the demon asks while he studies my body for injury.

My avatar glances down, and I see from my build and bulging pants I'm a man. I'm also splattered with blood. "I think so. Let's leave before anyone else shows up."

"Let them come! I will rend them apart too." The demon flexes his muscles, and his eyes flare with a spark of fire.

I notice there are bodies and body parts strewn about in the dark alleyway. A distant streetlight makes the wet blood gleam.

My heart pounds, but not from fear.

I grab the demon's horns and pull him in for a possessive and passionate kiss.

Our hips grind against each other, and I can feel his hardened length, ready to be unleashed. We've been worked up from the adrenaline of violence. *Righteous justice.*

Pulling back, I curse. "We need to find the others. These bastards would have attacked them too."

The demon rests his forehead against mine. "When this is done, I'm fucking your ass so hard that even you won't recover."

"Promises, promises." I chuckle, but it's a sad thing. "If we survive this night, I'm going to fuck you all, even Blockhead."

The demon roars with a laugh. "I don't think he'll be pleased with that."

I chuckle too. "Maybe not, but it will be fun to watch him squirm when I tease him."

Now, this is getting interesting…

Then a voice whispers in my mind, *"Who are you?"*

Abruptly, I wake up and shiver. My skin is goose-bumped. And a wave of cold air washes over me. What the hell?

I believe in ghosts, not that I give it much mind… usually. I always assumed they were like energetic echoes of someone from the past. However, now I sense a presence, one that feels aware of me.

"Leave me alone!" I state firmly, and I feel the energy fade away.

I shiver. It's one thing writing about the paranormal and supernatural worlds and ideas. It's another thing to be living in them.

With how violent my dream was, I wonder if a spirit was influencing my dark nightmare. I'm not comfortable with that.

Well, I was okay with that panty-melting kiss. But everything else? No, thank you.

Maybe I'm losing my mind?

That's what Rob would tell me when I recounted my strange dreams.

5

WITCH PLACE

ARRAN

This witch must really think I'm only a dog. Why else would she allow me free rein over her home while she slept?

I hear her brushing her teeth and readying for bed, so I wander back to the room where she keeps her hostage-friends. They smell like small animals, but I wonder if she's somehow trapped shifters in there. That's concerning.

With my enhanced ability, I hear her slip into bed. I shift into my human form and open the door to her menagerie.

"Who the fuck are you?" an angry-looking guinea pig demands with a hiss, when I step naked into the room.

"No. What the fuck are *you*?" I growl, my voice low.

He scrambles backward into the corner of his cage, surprised I've heard him, I think. But that is a talent of mine—hearing the thoughts of magical creatures. Less than half of the shifter population can hear these unique animals' thoughts or the thoughts of other shifters.

The little thing glances at the other animals in the room, back at me, and toward her bedroom. "Don't hurt the witch," he says threateningly.

"Why shouldn't I?" I tower over his cage, wondering if he might shift into a human form. But I don't scent shifter magic on him. "Are you going to fight me?"

Instead of answering me, he pees. Fair enough. He probably expects that I'm going to eat him as an appetizer before the main course, the witch.

When my mind thinks of sneaking into her room and making her a meal, I imagine feasting on her pussy instead.

Goddess, I need to get laid soon. I've never been this distracted on a mission before.

"Tell me what you are doing here?" I demand.

"I'm a magical creature. I like to think of myself as her familiar, but—" he trails off and sighs.

"But what?"

"Jade doesn't know I can speak. She can't hear me like you do."

"She's really that stupid that she allows both of us into her home?" I rub my face, because now it seems unfair to kill her.

"Not stupid," the furry pig explains defensively. "I don't think she knows much about magic. But then, other times… it seems like she does. Like she might hear me, but not really."

This little twerp doesn't seem too bright either.

From down the hall, I hear a strange humming sound.

Is she casting a spell?

Giving up on her magical creature, I sneak down the hallway to investigate and press my ear to her bedroom door.

She's making little mewling sounds, and my dick twitches as a whiff of arousal leaks through the door's crack.

Is she trying to lure me in like a siren? Because the scent is intoxicating. It must be her witch magic.

Does she intend for me to shift, race in there, and fall into her trap? Maybe the whole ignorance angle is a guise of getting me to lower my guard.

She shouts out what sounds like an orgasm.

Fuck.

My cock is not immune to her dangerous seduction. I press my palm against my length, hoping to calm my raging boner.

Within moments, her breathing evens out, and she sounds to be asleep. Still, I wait another half hour before trying her door to sneak in.

Locked.

Interesting. The witch must have a clue as to what I am. Why else would she lock her bedroom door to keep out a regular dog?

I debate crashing through her locked door and torturing answers out of her. But that won't likely work out well for me, since her grip on my libido is overwhelming.

I imagine pinning her down, demanding the truth, and my hand

27

wrapping around her fragile throat. However, I'd end up as the tortured one as my cock would throb with the sounds of her whimpers and pleas.

Instead, I decide to check out the other rooms down the hallway. There's a guest bath, but the other one is an office.

Traces of her magic are strongest in here. I wonder why. It doesn't appear to be a witch's casting space.

The walls are lined on three sides with bookshelves filled with books—not old creepy witchy books, but modern paperback novels. I pick one up and see it's some magical fantasy romance. After a quick perusal, I find most of them are, except for a few classic fantasy books like the *Lord of the Rings* trilogy. I'm not much of a reader anymore, but I recognize that title and a few others.

I don't see any family grimoires passed down through generations lying about, not that I'd expect witches to leave their spell books out in the open and unguarded.

But with how reckless this witch appears to be with her life, I wouldn't have been surprised to find them next to these romance novels.

I glance at another title. Uh... *Monster Lovers' Manual*?

What the actual fuck?

Is this witch into screwing monsters? Or is it just research for her seduction magic?

Either way, the true beast inside me perks up.

The more I discover about this woman, the more confused I am. I rub my forehead to ward off the severe headache coming on.

Waking up her laptop with a touch of a key, I'm happy to find that she doesn't have a passcode to log on. I do my best to bind my magic so that I don't fuck up her electronic device. I have to see what information she has on us.

Most low-powered witches and warlocks are able to use computers with minimal issues. But almost all supes have some problems, if not actually blowing them up. Since my magic is more tied in with my shifting and not as active as other supes, I can usually use electronics sparingly. That ability fails if I get riled up or otherwise engage my limited magic.

I scan her desktop files and see a shared user folder labeled 'BAR GUYS' and today's date. I click on it and skim through her notes.

She has described all four of us in detail. Also, she was trying to figure out what we were talking about. And she isn't far off, but her language is a bit flowery for what I'd expect from a spy or assassin. I skim over most of it, because she goes on quite a lot about our bulging muscles and strong jawlines.

She describes Flint as *stony*, I'm an alphahole, Maxum is hot as hell, and Calder has *smoldering* eyes. I chuckle at that.

There's no way she's not on to us. But why she would take weird notes like *this* is beyond my comprehension.

I glance at the romance books on the shelves. But if *lust* is her magic, then maybe it does make sense. I've never run across a lust witch. However, my hardened cock very much wants to learn more—much, much more.

I shouldn't be having this lustful reaction right now. Yesterday, I lost the one person who meant the most to me in this world. My heart is broken—so my physical response to her *has* to be a manipulative spell she cast around us at the bar.

The smart thing to do is to take off now and warn the others. But I don't want to risk losing my position here, where I can spy on her without her knowledge.

Besides, I need to know if she's the one who killed Osen.

6

INVITED

JADE

*M*y sleep is restless and filled with strange dreams. I'm not sure if it was the late-night greasy cheese sandwich or the new animal energy in my home.

Still in bed, I stare at my ceiling, allowing my mind to wander and dream up some more details about my new characters. I find some of my best ideas come when I'm in the in-between headspace somewhere before falling asleep and just after waking up.

Half-awake, I groan when I hear a knock at my front door.

This flipping early!

Checking the clock, I see it's past noon. Oh... so no longer morning. I suppose I can't be this indignant about a midday visitor.

I can't believe I slept this late. Not that I usually get up at the crack of dawn. Being single and fueled by inspiration and manic writing episodes, I've become unreasonably flexible with my sleeping patterns.

I figure whoever is at the door is just here to save my naughty soul. So I close my eyes, hoping they will realize it's a hopeless cause, and move on when I don't answer their call to salvation.

I'm fairly certain that upon my death, I'm going to the Underworld and chatting up Tartarus about writing smut.

The knock comes again. Hmm. Maybe I ordered something that needs a signature? I didn't think 'Living The Smut Life' stickers would require that level of security. But what do I know?

I slide into my comfy sweatpants, since last night I've felt weirdly underdressed wearing only tight leggings around my new dog. I pull up my long, gray-streaked brown hair into a messy bun and check myself in the mirror. Not horrible for forty, but too many of my younger years had been wasted on Rob and other ex-jerks. It's time I wish I hadn't wasted.

Shrugging off the negative thoughts, I rush out to the living room. Realization dawning on me that I probably shouldn't be running since I have a new, skittish dog here now.

The dog is standing at attention, watching me closely, but doesn't seem overly spooked by my sudden appearance. He must have expected me with the door knock. Clever boy that he is.

I appreciate he didn't automatically and incessantly bark at someone on the porch. If no one claims him, I might keep him if he can play nice with my other fur babies. Oh, damn, I need to let him out to go to the bathroom if he didn't already use a rug in my house. Ugh. I'm not used to having dogs.

Hearing scuffling feet at the door, I remember I have someone waiting for me. I remind myself to let the dog go out to the fenced backyard after I deal with this intrusion.

I spy through the peephole and see the stupidly handsome dominant guy from the bar waiting for me.

I spin and slam my back to the door as if to brace it closed. Or brace me from the panic I feel. I pant with nerves. My body heats.

Is this a hot flash? Nerves? Arousal? Check all the above?

"Fuck," I murmur to myself. "How did he find me? And what is he doing here?"

I suck in a breath to calm down and count to five to clear my head. My hand clasps the 'protection' pendant hanging around my neck that my abuela gave me.

The dog watches my whole chaotic display with interest.

Studying the canine, he seems like the type who would attack this visitor if this guy is a bad dude.

I swing open the door and plaster on a fake smile. "How can I help you?"

The man's eyes narrow on me, and he doesn't immediately respond. Finally, he tilts his head as if he's confused. "You look familiar."

My face burns with a blush. He knows *exactly* who I am. Stop bluffing, dude. "We might have both been at the bar down the road last night."

He grins, and his dark eyes trail down my body, taking me in—not in a creepy way, but *not not* in a creepy way either. "Ah, yes, of course."

He has a hint of an Irish brogue, but there's something else that I can't yet place.

His quiet attention is disarming. Hell, *he's* disarming. And he looks like he could literally remove my arms with no effort.

He must stand a foot taller than me, at least six-foot-five inches of sculpted muscle, highlighted by his form-fitting long-sleeve shirt and expensive-looking jeans that hug him in all the right places.

Eyes up, Jade! On his face! Be a good girl... Ugh. Don't say good girl right now.

"Did you need something?" I ask and sort of hope he'll growl and tell me it's me he needs. Then he'll throw me over his massive shoulder and carry me off to ravage me.

Keep it together, naughty girl.

He smirks as if he's read my mind.

Shit, my face probably gives me away. I don't think I can get away with casually checking my mouth for drool. Even if he can't read my face, I'm sure he just assumes that's what's going on in my mind. This man exudes barely bridled masculine power.

He's ruggedly handsome with a strong brow, perfect black hair, and the darkest brown eyes I've ever seen that look like volcanic obsidian.

I'm ready to fall into his gaze when he finally answers me.

"I'm looking for a lost... canine."

I'm suddenly protective of the mutt and close the door enough to block this man's view into my house. "Yeah? What does this dog look like?"

"Much like the one I just saw sitting in your living room."

Whoops. Too late. I'm not great at being covert.

"Is he yours?" a bit of loss seeps into my voice. I don't want to let the grumpy dog go. I was hoping we could go for a walk before I reported him to animal control. If no one claimed him, I wanted to adopt him. Make him feel safe.

The huge male pats his pant leg, and commands, "Heel."

The dog looks unimpressed.

"He's a friend's," McHottie confesses. "I was hoping he would come with me."

Reluctantly, I step back so the dog can feel free to join his owner's friend.

"Come with me, now," he says. His voice has a tinge of irritation.

"Does he run off a lot?" I ask, giving the dog time to warm up to the idea of going.

"Enough."

When the dog doesn't move, I ask, "Does the dog know you very well?"

"He should." McHottie studies me again. "But apparently, he prefers your company. And I can understand why."

I laugh heartily because this guy is so far out of my league, and I'd guess at least ten years younger than me. The thought is so absurd, and I think I snort at one point. "Uh, yeah. Okay. Well, I offered him free meat." I blush again because now it sounds naughty.

"Beautiful women don't usually tempt that beast. So it must be something about you."

I glance around this guy's massive body to see if someone is filming me for a prank video.

He turns to see what I'm looking for. "What's wrong?" His hand goes out as if to block someone, protecting me from an attack.

Odd. Maybe he's a cop or something? I could see him in a uniform—military or otherwise. Although, I doubt he would be low ranking with his dominating presence.

"I was looking for the prank camera," I admit.

When his dark eyes turn back on me, all I read is confusion. "Prank?"

"Umm… Well, it sort of sounded like you were hitting on me. Which is ridiculous."

"It is?" He frowns. "Why? Are you involved with someone?"

"No."

"Good." He smiles, and his whole face lights up, blinding me with his perfection. "Would you like to go out with me tonight?"

"That's funny." I shake my head.

I know I'm not ugly. But this guy? There's no flippin' way he's into me, especially how I look right now. No makeup, crazy messy bun, and dumpy oversized clothes—guys can't really like me like this. Currently, I don't even qualify as a hot mess. I'm just straight-up messy.

Rob didn't appreciate how I looked. He called me a sloppy pig. But whatever. I don't care.

"Oh, yeah. I suppose it *is* last minute." He nods like that's the reason I'm laughing and smiles again. "If you aren't busy now, I'm not doing anything since I've found my friend's beast."

"Beast?" I glance back at the dog, and he appears to be giving McHottie the stink eye. "Is that his name? It seems fitting. But he seems like a smart one."

"He's not *that* smart," McHottie says with a chuckle. Then he rubs the back of his neck nervously and shows off his humongous arms. I swear they are thicker than my thighs. And that's saying something since I'm not thin.

"So, how about that date?" he asks quietly, his voice a deep rumble that vibrates through me all the way to my clit.

I cross my arms defensively. Then I realize I've just pushed up my ample breasts with no bra on and in a thin t-shirt. "So, are you into older women or something?"

McHottie clears his throat. "Or something." Then he steps closer, and his shadow looms over me.

I'm equally turned on and a bit intimidated by his size. I think he might be an oxygen hound since I can't seem to get enough air.

"I'd like to get to know you. Is there something wrong with that?"

"Nope," I squeak. I'm tempted to take a step back... or maybe a step closer, and see what he does. But I'm starting to think he might actually be into me. "Uh. But I just rolled out of bed."

"Hungry?"

Oh, god, yes. I want to say for some sausage, but I don't. "Yeah. Can you give me a minute or several to get ready?"

"Sure." He retreats to the edge of my porch. "I'll be right here."

I shut the front door and quietly lock it, because, yeah. I don't know this guy. And I want a quick shower. I can't trust the new weirdo dog to protect me if this guy has ill intent.

Not that I expect McHottie to be a dildo, but I've learned the hard way not to let down my guard even with—especially with—people I'm attracted to.

When I turn, the dog looks at me with raised eyebrows.

As I stroll by him, I grumble, "What? I don't get asked out on dates. Not my problem if you didn't want to go with him first."

I give myself a quick rinse in the shower—no need to shave or primp. This pussy isn't going for a spin over brunch. Any guy who expects that within the first hour of knowing me and after hash browns isn't going to get to eat my dessert taco. I've been there and done that, and it doesn't work out happily in real life... at least, not for me.

Honestly, dating never works out great for me. Maybe that's why I retreated to the world of romance books. I'm safe within the pages. I always get my happily ever after or my happy for now.

No one can break my heart.

Okay, that's not necessarily true. Sometimes, I cry like a baby with some scenes I read.

But I don't plan on falling for this sexy cougar-chasing fuckboy.

However... I plan to enjoy myself and flirt. I will make notes so I can use our conversations for my book inspiration.

I don't usually wear much makeup, but I put on some blush and tinted lip gloss. He's already seen me at my worst and asked me out anyway. Playing it up now seems freaking silly and pointless. Fortunately, I've been blessed with naturally dark eyelashes, so it already looks like I'm wearing eyeliner or mascara.

I slip on some comfy jeans and a lightweight sweater. Quickly, I make sure all my fur babies are fed and watered.

I frown when I see the dog didn't eat any of the steak I chopped up. Or the kibble I threw in there. I open the back door to see if he will go outside and relieve himself, but he doesn't take the hint.

As I saunter by the dog, I say, "Don't wait up." And I give him a saucy wink.

He goes from lying down to sitting up and glaring at me.

"Fine. Do what you like, just don't eat the furniture. Or my friends. If you're good, I'll get you a doggy bag."

I want to reach out and pet him goodbye, but when I step closer, he ducks his head and trots away. So not as standoffish as last night, but close. We have a way to go, but I don't expect I will have him long enough to win him over. His owner will come to claim him soon.

7

BRUNCH MISTAKEN

MAXUM

*W*hen I hear her shower running and the sound of her stepping inside it and water crashing over her naked body, I take a brief moment for myself and imagine the hot water pouring over all those tantalizing curves. Down the slope of her—

Snapping out of my lust-filled thoughts, I rush across the small porch. Crouching down, I peek in through her living room window. I motion for Arran to come closer.

His wolf shakes his head at me.

What in the ever-living fuck?

I want to mind-dive him to find out what the hell he's thinking, but I promised him and the other guys I wouldn't do that. I can't break their trust. I can't even cheat. They would know I was invading.

I wonder if the witch would sense it was me if I did. I suppose I could just scramble her brains and call it a day.

Instead of fucking up Arran's brains with a mind dive, I mouth the words: *"What are you doing in there?"*

His head flicks in the direction of the witch's room.

Yeah, no shit, asshole.

I wave him closer again so that even with a low voice, we both can talk through the glass window because of our exceptional hearing.

He trots up to the window and shifts to his human form. With how I'm crouched down at his waist level, I get an eyeful of wolf shifter dick.

Ugh. I can't deal with his crap right now.

I glower up at him and say in a low voice, "What the fuck are you doing?"

He squats down and answers, "Investigating." The bastard has the audacity to look perturbed with me.

Out of anyone in our group last night, I'd have thought he'd be the last to willingly infiltrate a witch's home. And he's probably the last one who should. I'm surprised that he hasn't turned into his true beast and attacked her.

But I suppose he hasn't learned his lesson yet. He will, when either this woman or some other mortal magic weaver kills him.

I don't sense any wards around her house, but I'm tempted to risk being zapped just so I can storm in there and wring Arran's damned neck for being so reckless.

"Does she have you under a spell?" I ask. *"Trapped?"*

He shakes his head but looks unsure. "I think she really believes I'm a dog."

I picked that up too. I didn't dive into her mind. But from what I was able to pick up from her on the surface, she doesn't seem to know his true nature.

However, I don't trust a casual assessment. She could be skilled at blocking her thoughts and be able to project only innocent ones.

Although the few stray thoughts I caught on the surface might not be categorized as entirely *innocent*. She seems to be attracted to my physique— not that I blame her. Most find my body pleasing. Even without my glamour to make me appear human, I look almost the same.

But I need my glamour because without it, I have crimson skin, horns, and some other special bits that must be hidden from norms and witches.

She might not be so inclined to fuck me if she saw the actual complete package.

Wait! Why do I care if she wants to fuck me?

I shouldn't be sliding down this line of thinking.

But this crazy witch who invited a wolf into her home intrigues me. Even if she doesn't get that he's a shifter, Arran is a fucking huge beast of a dire wolf. And she just let him in and *protected* him. From me.

The witch doesn't appear to be dumb, so why is she behaving this way? She allowed herself to be caught spying on us last night. She invited Arran inside. And now she is going on a brunch date with me.

What's up with this woman?

I have to know. Hence, the date…

I hear the floor creak as she moves out of the bathroom to likely get dressed. Arran shifts and sits down to appear casual, waiting for her to return. I quickly return to the spot on the far side of the small porch and attempt to appear calm.

However, I'm anything but relaxed. I've lost my best friend and occasional lover, and this woman is already under my skin and inside my head.

I sense an insignificant amount of power coming off her. I wonder what sort of affinity this witch has. Is she a green witch—tied to nature and the elements? Is she into potions? Or is she more powerful than I understand and is able to hide it from me?

I have to stay alert.

The witch flings open the front door with her eyes wide, looking upset.

I hate to say that my first instinct is to protect her. I remind myself that she's likely my enemy.

She covers her face in embarrassment. "I can't believe I agreed to go out with you, and I didn't even find out your name!"

"Maxum," I answer truthfully. If she is a spy, she already knows my name. It's probably why she *forgot* to ask me.

"I'm… uh, Jade—" she then mutters, "Uh, never mind me."

Curious now, I ask, "Do you have more than one name?"

Ironically, *I* have two names, my sacred summoning demon name and my common use name that everyone calls me—Maxum.

"Uh, yeah." She locks her door behind her.

I grin to myself at her safeguarding measure. She already has her enemy inside her home.

"I'm an author," she explains. "I've been so immersed in that world and marketing that I forget my other name sometimes."

"Would you like me to use your real name?" I fish.

"Let's see if you earn it." She playfully quirks her full lips.

And… my heart flutters. *Flutters!*

That hasn't happened to me in… six hundred years, when I was just a teenage spawn. Not even Osen's power used to make me feel this ebullient attraction.

For the second time today, I am lost for words in front of this witch. This is not something I am accustomed to.

"I like my author name better anyway." Jade glances up and down the street. "Did you bring your car? And where are we going to eat? Do you have any special dietary restrictions?"

She looks ready to ask me another series of questions when I answer the first. "My car is back at the bar on the corner. I was canvassing the neighborhood," I lie. "Should we take your car?"

Nervousness plays on her face. She bites her lip. She points to her sensible tennis shoes. "Maybe we can walk down to the place just past the bar? It's not far."

"You're a smart woman." I nod appreciatively. "You don't know me. I'm glad you take precautions and don't give in."

Why does it please me that she knows how to claim her boundaries?

"I've learned that being polite can get a woman in trouble." She cocks a brow at me. "Are *you* trouble?"

Even if she is ignorant of my true identity, deep down, she must instinctively know that I am dangerous.

"I suppose anyone can be trouble." Giving a shrug, I take a step toward the sidewalk. "A walk sounds perfect. It gives us time to talk and get to know each other on the way."

Her eyes travel up and down my body, cautiously appraising me. Does she sense how much potential danger she is in being around me?

If I wanted to, I could scramble her brains right now until she didn't remember her own name. It wouldn't be the first time, and I doubt it will be the last. I had to do it for an old acquaintance just the other day.

I take up most of the sidewalk with my bulk, so I move as far toward the street as I can to give the witch some space. I want her to feel safe... for now. Once I determine what her intentions are, I'll likely have to destroy her.

But until then, she gets the nice, charming Maxum.

"Should you call your friend?" the witch asks as she nods to my pocket, thinking that I have a mobile phone.

"I don't have a phone."

She stops in her tracks, eyes widened, and places a hand over her chest. "Someone *your* age *doesn't* have a phone?"

I chuckle. Someone *my* age never even dreamed we would have cell phones. Sure, we had magic mirrors to communicate hundreds of years ago, but those are becoming rare and now don't work over long distances because of the failing magic in our worlds.

"That's surprising, huh?" I cock my brow and study her.

Odd. It shouldn't be surprising to her. She *should* know that a supernatural being's magic kills electronics.

Hmm. Is she really that oblivious of that basic fact?

"I figured you'd be some social media celebrity posting thirst traps every day."

Now my eyes widen. *"Thirst... traps?"*

I've heard of a lot of magical traps, but not these. The only traps I've had to worry about are demon-summoning circles, since they can trap me if someone knows my sacred name.

She doubles over with laughter. "Your face! You really don't know what I'm talking about?"

"Explain." I want to be angry with her for mocking my ignorance, but my lips can't help curling into a smile instead of a snarl.

Jade covers her face and blushes. "You know... when an attractive person posts themselves all sexed up to get attention."

I turn and stand directly in front of Jade. Towering over her, I ask in a low voice. "Do I look like someone who seeks attention?" My hands itch to touch her soft skin, but I keep them firmly at my sides.

Her mouth opens into a little O shape, and I want to fill the tempting opening with my tongue, then with my cock.

She sucks in a breath and gulps, maybe reading my mind as easily as I can read others. Her voice is soft with awe as she says, "No. You seem like you should have plenty of attention just by existing."

I resist the strange urge that overcomes me, making me want to pull her toward me, seat her on my growing cock, and claim her. My attraction might be a lust spell, and I won't fall for another one of those. It's one of the few magics that work on a demon other than a demon trap.

With blown-out pupils indicating her attraction, her hazel-green eyes drop to my lips. Then she snaps out of her naughty thoughts and locks gazes with me.

Surprisingly, she doesn't back down or avert her eyes.

I want to run my fingers through her gray-streaked hair and fist it while I claim her delicious body. I admire that she doesn't hide her silver as it reveals her hard-won life experiences. But since witches hardly age over their mid-thirties, I idly wonder how old she really is to have earned her gray. Not as old as I am.

I'm so close I can feel the heat of her luscious body. And I'm sure since I run much hotter that she must feel my heat caressing her curves. All I have to do is reach out and touch her, and I could destroy her—with my mind or with my body. It would be an easy thing to do.

But right now, I want to destroy her pussy with my cock.

Focus! Has it really been that long since I've been with a woman that I'm succumbing to the first female in my proximity?

Yet, I haven't been attracted to a female in years.

It must be a spell. Although, I can't deny what she offers on the surface isn't tantalizing all on its own.

I step back and raise my mental shields again.

Jade exhales, and her knees shake. Is she scared or turned on? Or both?

Worrying that she might actually be as innocent as she projects, I say reluctantly, "Sorry. I can be—"

"*Intense* as fuck?" she finishes for me with a bit of humor and relief in her voice.

"Yeah, that." I bite my lip and turn my face away as I walk again. Why does she have to be so damned… *cute*?

"So… no phone," she continues, as if my show of dominance never happened. "Are you anti-technology? Or just don't like to be tied down to a phone?"

"Technology and I don't really get along."

"I hear you. I remember the days when you weren't on someone's shit list because you didn't call or text them back within ten seconds. And since I'm an author and I work from home, people in my life don't always respect that I might be working on a scene. But if I were at some corporate job, it would be okay that I'm not answering for basic chitchat."

Okay, I'll bite. She's claimed this author's persona as her cover. "What sort of books do you write? Would I know your work?"

"Uh…" Her ears turn pink. Her heart beats wildly, more so than when I was looming over her. "I don't think you've read my stuff."

"Because I don't look like I can read?" I deadpan.

"Oh, geeze, no!" She covers her mouth in embarrassment. "I just… I write romance. You don't really seem like you would be into that."

"Because I don't look like I enjoy romance?" I joke but continue my serious tone.

She turns bright red now. "No! Oh, man, I'm turning this conversation into a shitshow. It's just… my audience is ninety-nine percent women, so I don't expect you to have heard of me or the genre I write."

"Is it… what do they call it?" I ask. "Steamy?"

Her eyebrows rise with surprise that I know something about romance books. "Uh. Yes, there are *detailed* and explicit scenes." Her aura tightens around her body, and she seems agitated.

Why is she nervous now?

"I didn't know you would be ashamed of your writing," I offer. "We can move on from this subject."

"I'm not ashamed of my work," she says, straightening up. "I just don't talk about it with people I only met five seconds before. And being a guy, I thought maybe you'd belittle me somehow."

"Does that happen a lot?" An urge to rip body parts off anyone who has mocked her rushes through my system. What is this protective instinct about?

"Well, I've had all kinds of responses. I've had guys hit on me and tell me they can help with inspiration, then send unsolicited dick pics."

I figure out that reference on my own—modern-day flashing. From this day forward, these dicks will now be burnt sausages.

Jade sighs and wrings her hands.

"But it sounds like there is something else?" I prompt.

"My ex tried to make me stop writing. He was jealous of imaginary guys."

"Truly?" I shake my head.

Humans are so strange.

"It doesn't matter. You don't want to hear about my ex." She brushes it off and changes the subject. "So, what do you do?"

I don't tell her I don't have to work for a living. She doesn't need to know about my finances or that I'm basically a soldier in the brewing war with her kind. So I go with a version of the truth of what I do in my spare time. "I run a disadvantaged youth outreach program."

"No shit." Jade grins. "That's awesome. How does that work?"

"I help high-risk teens to develop coping skills for life." More like teaching them to control their magic and training them in self-defensive combat magic to protect themselves. But she doesn't need to know that either.

"I imagine that would be so rewarding," she says, impressed with my pursuits. "I volunteer at the animal shelter, walking dogs, petting cats, and stuff. But I'm not great with people."

"Really?" I give her a look of disbelief. "You seem like you would be. I mean, you don't appear uncomfortable around me. And I don't necessarily put people at ease."

She frowns as she takes that in. "Yeah, well, I'm definitely not a fan of crowds. But for some strange reason, I feel okay being around you, even though you look like you might break me in two."

I could split her in two… with my cock. *Nope, stop it. Bad dick.*

We walk for a few minutes in comfortable silence.

In my mind, I go over what she's said so far. My senses didn't detect any lies about her feeling okay around me. Which is funny. If anything, her instincts should tell her to run—far, far away.

We get to the restaurant that's located just past the bar where she watched us last night. In the bar's parking lot, I see Flint and Calder sitting in Calder's vintage 1962 Rambler. I step faster to block Jade's view of them and point down the street. "Looks like it's not too busy at the Spud House this morning. That should put you at ease."

She hums her agreement, and we cross the road.

My senses tingle. Someone is watching. I want to shrug it off as if it's only my friend's attention, but I know better. I'm familiar with the weight and texture of their gaze. Maybe her witch associates are now preparing to kill me.

And my friends are probably wondering what the hell I'm doing with our enemy.

Hell, I'd like to know that too.

SCRAMBLED

JADE

*M*axum is probably the most unusual man I've ever met, and that's saying something. He's sexy and intense, but also sensitive. Why he hasn't been snatched up by someone already is beyond me. But perhaps he's just a player who dislikes being tied down. Or, maybe he likes to *tie* people down and torture orgasms out of them. Maybe I'd let *him* play like that…

My mind ponders that kinky scenario for a lovely moment. My wrists and ankles are bound and stretched out. His dark, hungry gaze travels over my body as he calculates how he will make me beg for his cock. How long will he torment my nipples and clit before he gives in and wrecks my pussy?

"Jade?" he calls me as if he's concerned.

Oh geeze, I switched to full fantasy-author mode, zoning out, my eyes likely glazed over. Can he hear my heart pounding in my clit?

"Sorry, author moment," I joke.

He winks at me and opens the door to the cute little restaurant.

It's fine if he's only a fuckboy. This isn't going any further than this awkward brunch, so I can play along for a while as he flirts.

We sit at one of the empty tables the server points us to. This place is nice and cozy, but not fancy. When I'm not feeling like cooking, which is more often than not, I come here or to the bar if it's late and this place is closed.

I don't need to look at their menu already sitting on the table since I've memorized it.

Maxum grins at me, giving me a blast of sexy heat with his perfect teeth. His perfectly white and oddly sharp teeth.

Why did I not notice that before? I must have been overwhelmed by his size and sculpted physique.

His gaze skims over the menu, and he sets it down. His elbows are on the tabletop. He rests his chin on his fists and leans forward. It could be taken as a feminine gesture, but somehow it's all masculine. His corded forearms are huge and end in fists that look like they were made to bash skulls, but are just as ready to pull my hair as he shoves his cock down my throat.

I'm in danger of zoning out and writing a new scene in my head.

Moving my attention from his arms and fists, I look up at his handsome face. It doesn't help my need to fantasize how he would be in bed.

Being caught in his intense gaze throws me off. His eyes are obsidian, with just the palest smokey quartz around his pupils. His raven-black hair is so glossy it seems fake.

And his skin has an undertone of crimson. When I write about his character, I'll say he is a demon in disguise.

Alas, no, he's just an unusual beauty. He likely has a bit of a sunburn under his deep tan and it was probably brought out from walking around the neighborhood this morning.

Breaking my reverie about my gorgeous companion, the server comes up. "Whatcha having today?"

I hand her my menu. "I'll take a coffee and the Mad Scramble."

Maxum raises his eyebrows slightly. Maybe he expected me to appear like I don't have an appetite and order a cute little salad for brunch? Fuck that.

But I drop my hasty conclusion when he says, "The same for me. Thanks."

I fiddle again with my protection pendant and study this guy as he goes right back to watching me.

"So, how did your friend lose his dog?" I ask.

"Oh, sometimes my friend just doesn't think things through. And the gigantic beast got away from him."

"He seems like a well-behaved dog otherwise." Then I remember how he broke my picture frame. "If not a bit clumsy."

"Clumsy? Really?" Maxum perks up. "How so?"

"He knocked over a picture of my ex. Didn't seem to like him either." I laugh to lighten the subject.

"Well, sometimes I think Beast likes to get into trouble."

"He's been no trouble. I'll be sad to see him go."

Maxum grunts at that for some reason.

The server brings over our coffees. I pour some cream and add a spoonful of sugar, whereas Maxum drinks his black.

"When do you think your friend will come and get him?"

He stares at me over the rim of his coffee mug while slowly taking a sip. Then he says, "Beast should be out of your hair by the end of the day. I hope."

That sounds shady. I don't like that he sounds like a neglectful owner. "Uh... Why *wouldn't* your friend come get his dog?"

Maxum shrugs. "He has an on-call job that is sporadic. I'd take the mutt off your hands, but he didn't seem like he wanted to leave just yet."

"Okay." Something's odd about all of this, but I can't put my finger on what it could be. It feels like Maxum is skirting some truth. I wonder if the owner's unavailability has something to do with what made them all tense last night.

I really want to ask him, but I'm worried that might be too invasive, especially over a brunch date. But I think I might be part cat, and curiosity gets the better of me.

"I've never seen you or your friends at the bar before."

His eyes narrow just a fraction, and while he recovers quickly, I still notice. Coming from a volatile upbringing, I'm ever-vigilant for signs that I've displeased someone. Not that it's served me well at avoiding someone's wrath since I don't often stop whatever I'm doing to piss them off.

"I'm not trying to pry." I play off my curiosity. "It's just that I go there all the time. I was only wondering if one of the guys you were with owned Beast."

He takes another sip of his coffee, and it appears as if he's debating how to answer me. Which, again, is so weird. "He's one of my friends from last night," he says cryptically.

I try to lighten the mood. "Let me guess... the guy on the end bouncing his knee?"

Maxum stiffens his shoulders. "And why would you guess it was him?"

"He seemed sort of... upset, distracted," I explain. "If anyone was going to lose their animal, it would be someone who was distracted."

"True," he agrees succinctly.

I can tell now that he's not enjoying our conversation anymore.

"I shouldn't have pried, but I was curious who I should expect to show up on my doorstep."

The server places our plates in front of us. "Two scrambles. Can I get you anything else?"

"I'm good," I say.

But Maxum asks for hot sauce and relaxes in his seat again. "Why were you staring at us last night? Taking pictures?"

Dammit. I was hoping he wouldn't call me out like this.

"Uh. I don't think it comes as a surprise to hear that you are good-looking. And your friends are as well." I clear my throat. I won't be able to eat until I deal with this.

Did he wait until after we got our food to ask me about my gawking? So I couldn't just leave? But if I have to leave without eating, that's what I'm going to do.

However, I feel compelled to explain my behavior. "I feel like the biggest creep. You all are hot enough that you should be on the covers of romance novels. I've been a bit stuck in my writing. And it was as though you were some divine inspiration. I'm sorry if I made you uncomfortable. Anyway, none of the photos even came out!"

I pull my phone out to show him the pics and confirm I have nothing to show my friends or the internet in general. But my phone instantly dies after I show him the first blurry image. "Huh, I thought I charged my phone all the way last night."

He stares at the dead phone, looking guilty, and then gazes into my eyes.

His presence is so big and imposing that I almost imagine that his energy presses into me—into my mind.

I hurry to explain further, "I shouldn't have taken the pics. I wasn't going to share them. Just trying to remember you for inspiration. But I guess that still sounds sleazy, huh?"

Maxum finally blinks, and I fall back in my seat. "And what did you write about me in your notes?"

"Um, just your appearance. Nothing much."

He takes a bite of his scramble and watches me, waiting for me to break and tell him more.

I crumble under his gaze. "Don't be mad. So... as you know, I write romance... well, *paranormal* romance. And I imagined you could be a demon in disguise, and the broody leader of a ragtag group of mythological beings."

He stops chewing, appearing shocked that I've cast him as a monster.

So much for my flirty date!

"But you're a hot demon. A bad boy, but you could also really fall hard for the heroine. Touch her and die vibes. Believe me, it's a compliment in the romance world!" I cover my eyes, waiting for him to get upset and lecture me.

"You're not wrong," he says quietly.

I peek through my fingers. "And you're not mad?"

He shakes his head.

I finally feel settled enough to eat, but while I do, I can't help but wonder why he agreed with my assessment. "What part did I get right? Do you fall hard when you fall in love?"

"I don't know if I've ever been *in* love." He picks at his food with a fork.

"Oh… Then what part did I get right?" I cock my brow and grin. "I see… you consider yourself a bad boy. Or would you be possessive and protective? Or both?"

"All of it." He flashes his dazzling and almost frightening smile.

Is he a psycho?

He has dark red tattoo lines peeking out from under his long sleeve shirt where it pulls up at his wrist. The ink probably covers his arms and chest. He would probably look *fucktacular* if he were shirtless, posing as some promo model for a dark mafia book.

So I pegged him… well, ahem, not pegged. I hop onto that caboose to travel to my imaginary scene and wonder if he'd be into a woman strapping one on and going to town on his perky ass. Fortunately, I quickly jump off the sex train of thought.

Goodness, I'm worse than a teenager.

Where was I?

Oh, yes, I *guessed* correctly. Maxum is a possessive bad boy.

"Good to know." I take another large bite of my eggy scramble.

"And the others? Do you have any *guesses* as to what they are?" he asks. Why the question sounds so loaded, I do not know.

"They aren't guesses, just musings. Creating characters, you know?" I really hope he doesn't make me answer this question. It's not like he doesn't already know I'm a perv. But admitting my list of perversions and kinks to my object of lustful desires is a whole other level I'm not ready for. "Wouldn't you rather we talk about you?"

"No. I'd rather talk about you," he states firmly, with a stern look that makes me want to obey.

He's giving off dominant, master of the dungeon vibes, and my panties are officially flooded.

He continues, "It sounds like getting to know you means understanding your life as an author."

Well, isn't he fucking smart. And dang, he's called me out. I sort of have to answer his question now.

"Don't laugh?" I chuckle. "Okay, at least don't laugh much."

"I'll do my best." He doesn't look as if he plans to laugh. His smile is completely gone as he waits for my answer. His seriousness gives me pause.

Why do I keep getting the odd feeling that everything I say will come back to haunt me? Maybe because I expect the worst from people, especially the love interests in my own life.

I shake off my nervousness. It's so much easier typing this naughty stuff into my computer. "Um. So… the one guy at the end of the booth who seemed agitated? He felt like he'd be a wild animal. So I thought he could be a shifter in my story." Then I realize Maxum might not understand my lingo, so I explain. "A shifter is human and can change into an animal form, but usually they only shift into one kind of animal—most often a wolf, bear, or large cat. However, they don't have to only be these common types. They can be other smaller animals or mythical creatures like dragons, too."

"I get the general idea," he smirks at me.

So at least he's a bit amused with my explanation.

"But your friend can be a bit of an alphahole—a bossy jerk."

"Again. Not wrong."

"The guy with the pale hair and eyes? He was so still that he reminded me of stone. So I went with a gargoyle. I didn't get far with his personality other than quiet and brooding, since he didn't give much away. And the last guy? He confused me, but he was like fire *and* ice. So I thought he might be a cold-hearted dragon in my story? But under all that, he is very passionate about the few things he cares about."

Maxum almost tosses down his fork. "You have to be kidding me." He asks with disbelief and a heavy dose of condescension, "Are you for real?"

I blink. "Huh?"

He shakes his head. "So all that spying on us last night was for your…" Then the jerk has the audacity to use air quotes as he says, *"Novel?"*

"Excuse me?" I sit back and glare at him. "You might not think much of what I do, but people enjoy it. Paranormal romance is a huge and legitimate genre. You don't have to be dismissive." Without another word, I pull some cash out of my purse, throw it on the table, and head for the door.

I will not put up with some punk belittling what I do, no matter how hot. Just because I include magical beings and sexual moments doesn't mean it is worthless drivel. Women have been belittled about their sexuality for far too long. They've been brutalized for it. I'm proud that I celebrate women, and sometimes bisexual men, having choices and claiming their sexual selves. And I will not sit there and make apologies for empowering myself and possibly others.

Fuck him. And not in a fun way.

Am I triggered? One hundred percent.

Storming out of the restaurant feels great until I sense his presence right behind me. I walk faster down the sidewalk. Not that his stupidly long legs can't catch up with my much shorter strides.

"Bugger off," I say over my shoulder.

"*You* were spying on us, remember?" he spits out.

"Oh, I'm sorry that I was looking at you." I glare at him. "Did it hurt?"

"That's what I intend to find out," he mutters.

What in the upside-down-cake hell?

"Okay. Fine. I took some crappy pictures that didn't even come out right. I'm sorry. I get that I'm an asshole. Move along. Date's over... Or whatever this game of yours is."

"Game? *I'm* the one playing games?" he snaps.

I turn and scowl at him, and he stops in his tracks, almost looking nervous. "I'm calling animal control, and your friend can pick the dog up at the pound. Go away now. Bye!"

I spin back around and head toward my house.

As I pass by the bar, I see his two sexy friends in an old car, watching me. This is getting weirder by the minute. Fortunately, Maxum abandons his pursuit and heads toward his friends' car.

Thank goodness, I was worried he would follow me home. And he knows where I live.

I cross the street to my road. Calming myself slightly, I realize I'm still taking stomping strides, so I relax into a slightly less agitated power walk.

What was his deal, anyway? He *really* didn't like some woman watching him and his friends. It seems like a bit of an overreaction. Is one of them famous or *infamous*?

What's he hiding? Did I stumble onto some actual mob meeting?

Is the dog really his friend's?

Oh, shit! What if it was all a lie?

The dog wanted nothing to do with Maxum. If he was truly a friend of his owner, then the dog should have acted like he recognized him.

I glance over my shoulder as I get a few doors from my house. I don't see anyone, but I feel eyes on me.

A shiver races up my back. I run to my front door and unlock it. I crash through as soon as it's open and slam the door shut, locking it.

The dog races over to me, sniffing me. He appears concerned by my dramatic return. At least the dog isn't a complete asshole.

9

PARANORMAL INACTIVITY

ARRAN

*T*he witch crashes into her front door like the demon is on her tail.

Her panic is real. I can smell its authenticity. Fear is flooding her mind. I wonder if Maxum found out something and threatened her.

Everything I found was odd, but not incriminating.

Is he pressing into her thoughts now, bending her consciousness to allow him access to all her secrets?

If she resists, he might scramble her brains. He might do that anyway for fun. The thought of her collapsing in front of me terrifies me. That realization alone is upsetting. I should want her gone just for being born a witch.

But the notes I found don't suggest that *if* they sent her to spy, that she knew anything about us. The only thing that I'm fairly certain about is that she seems to have an untapped psychic gift. This ability is not surprising. Most witches have some sort of psychic ability. Depending on the witch, it can be premonitions, psychometry, mind reading, mediumship, empathic ability, or sensing nature. There are others, but the list is too long to remember.

But that she doesn't even know she has an actual affinity? That *is* unusual.

Thanks to Maxum taking Jade out of the house, I was able to study her computer and tablet in more detail. No longer worried she was in the next room, I could keep my nervous energy to a minimum so I wouldn't blow her computer's circuits.

What I found makes me guess Jade has another gift too—writing. Her notes about us last night from the bar did actually seem to be notes for a book. She does write romance books about shifters and other supernaturals. There are physical copies on the shelves.

If it was a coincidence that she was at the bar, studying us for a book idea, I find it uncanny that she was able to intuit so many details.

However, for someone without training to be able to do this is unlikely.

The whole situation confuses me.

Does she know about us? Or not? And is her writing not just her witchy cover story, but also her day job? Is she a lust witch who uses her powers to sell romance books?

Maybe the Witch Council wanted her to get something more from us? Or she's supposed to seduce us... that definitely won't happen. Well, at least not to Flint or Calder. I am slightly concerned about my resolve. And Maxum released a scent indicating his attraction.

I need to rule out that Jade doesn't live a double life. I need to make sure they have not sent her to kill us off one by one.

I need to know if she killed Osen.

But right now, she appears panicked and leans against the door as if she's just been chased.

I sniff her but don't scent magic, blood, or Maxum's scent. So what happened, and where is Maxum now?

Deciding to lean into the dog cover story, I whine to prompt her to talk... she *loves* to fucking speak to animals.

"It's okay," she tries to comfort me. Fortunately, she doesn't reach out to me. She holds her chest and breathes hard. "I think that guy earlier might be a psycho."

No shit.

I trot over to the window to see if Maxum is outside, but I don't see him. But I get an eerie feeling that someone is watching us.

I slowly back away from the window.

"Oh, my god. Is he out there?" She crawls over to the window and peeks out. "You feel it too, don't you? Like someone's eyes are on you?" She glances back and forth down the streets. "I don't see Maxum, if that's even his real name. Or his friends in that old car."

Hmm. Interesting that she noticed Calder and Flint.

I study Jade while she searches for whoever is after her.

With every interaction, I become more convinced she doesn't know what is going on. If she's acting, she is outstanding—even fooling my senses.

I can smell fear in her. Sure, it could be that Maxum scared the pants off her. He could frighten almost anyone he sets his mind to scare.

Jade mumbles to herself. "I'm pretty sure you aren't even his friend's dog. But why would he come here? Could he be that weirded out that I was admiring him and his sexy friends?"

She really thinks I'm sexy?

After another few minutes, she gives up searching for the source of the eyes on her. Instead of getting up off the floor, she turns and leans against the wall. Her hands cover her face. "What was I thinking? I should have never gone with some random guy. Geezus, the red flags were flying. I should have known he only wanted to be an asshole. I mean, come on..." She looks at me, her eyes filled with hurt. "That hot, young treat? And *me*? Sure, I knew it wasn't going anywhere, but..." She sighs, picks herself up, and closes the curtains to the big picture window facing the road.

She thinks Maxum is young? I have news for you, sweetheart.

One more tally in the she-doesn't-have-a-clue column.

Jade frantically rushes around her house, checking the window locks and closing all the blinds.

"I guess I should call animal control and see if anyone has asked about you."

Jade pulls her phone out of her bag and curses. "Why does this thing need charging? Great, I need a new phone too."

Agitated, she pulls a taser and a can of mace out of her purse.

Part of me approves she was prepared for her date with Maxum.

But I'm stopped short when she draws out a small gun.

She tucks the weapon into her pants' waistband at the back.

Well, now... what makes her feel like she needs a gun for protection?

She doesn't live in a dangerous neighborhood. My mind flashes to the Witch Council, then Rob. It's also a wickedly smart weapon for a weak-powered witch to use against most supes.

The witch plugs in her phone and paces the living room. Mumbling to herself about always getting herself in trouble, saying this is why she's a homebody, and people aren't worth the pain.

I get it. My heart softens toward her just a little.

Jade shivers and glances at me. "I hear animals can be sensitive to spirits. Can you see anything? Because I swear, it's not just you witnessing me lose my mind."

I lie down and attempt to look innocent because, no, I can't feel spirits.

Maybe if I could, I would talk to Osen, and I'd find out how one of my best friends died.

Her phone dings, and she races over to use it. She calls the pound, but no one has been looking for a huge-ass wolf. Big surprise.

After a disconcerted frown, she sets the phone down, checks on her critters, and sulkily sits in her office. She stares at the computer screen for a long beat.

"That's weird," she mumbles. "I didn't think I had that file open on here."

Whoops. I fucked up Spy Craft 101: leave things as you found them.

A moment later, I hear her clicking away on her computer. It occurs to me she might communicate with the Witch Council, so I quietly enter and sit where I can read the screen. She gives me a soft smile of welcome and turns back to her computer.

She's on some social media website… Facebooked? She has a screen open and is telling other people how she had a weird day. And she might have a new creeper boyfriend.

One of her associates says to be careful, but to channel all her nervous energy into her new book. Another friend tells her to fill it with smutty good times.

And she does… I watch in amazement how she twists the events of the last day into a completely new story.

She probably thinks I'm the weirdest dog ever for reading over her shoulder. But so far, she's been lost in the words and hasn't paid attention to me.

Hours go by, and Jade finally slumps in her chair. She yelps when she feels the gun in her pants pressing into her back. She pulls it from her waistband and sets it on the desk.

Then her gaze lands on me, and she grimaces.

I'm nervous for a moment. If she's ready to end this charade and she uses the gun, I'm likely a goner.

Instead of popping a cap in my ass, the witch opens a drawer and sets the gun inside. "We don't want you to knock it off and hurt yourself, do we?"

Don't worry. I'm not fond of guns.

She feeds her animals and gasps. "Oh no. What the hell is wrong with me? I just realized that you haven't needed to pee or poo in a whole day! God, I hope you aren't sick." She gets on her knees in front of me, and her hand moves to touch my belly. "Please, I just need to see if your stomach is bloated. I'll have to take you to the vet if there's something wrong."

Oh, crap, *literally*. I had used her toilet when she was gone.

I move back and then hurry to her front door. She follows me out and shakes her head. "No. Out back." She opens the door and points. "It's fenced."

I race outside and pretend to pee to make her happy. I trot around and pretend I like the outdoors. I do, but that's beside the point. What I need is for her to leave me alone out here. I'm not taking a dump as a wolf while she watches.

Oh, Goddess. Am I going to shit in her yard and make her clean it up?

There is no chance of redemption after I do this.

Where has my life taken me?

I've made poor choices.

I did not choose wisely…

Hanging my head as I come back inside an hour later, I shuffle past Jade through her back door by the kitchen.

"Good boy," she coos when she spots my *gift.*

I'm strangely conflicted by this praise. My wolf loves it, but I'd rather get that while I was between her legs.

I'll show her who's a good boy.

When I was outside, I found Maxum had left my discarded clothes behind a bush in her yard. I suppose he didn't find Jade too dangerous if he allowed her out of his sight and didn't come back and demand I go with him.

So the verdict is still out.

"Will you eat for me tonight?" she asks sweetly.

I am fucking hungry. I probably will eat kibble if she offers it to me.

Please don't offer that crap to me…

"I had to throw out the bits of steak I gave you last night. I suspect you didn't like the dry food mixed in? Maybe you are used to a different brand?"

I'm seriously going to need to go on a bloody, vicious hunt after this is over to heal my bruised ego.

"How's this?" She places a measly amount of chopped steak in front of me on the floor. I sniff it but don't scent any poison or potions.

I understand her offering me a small portion. She doesn't want to waste food if I refuse it again.

Fuck it. I close my eyes and imagine I'm tearing the meat from the bones of my enemies and not out of a bowl on a witch's kitchen linoleum.

She squeals happily when she sees me eating.

My wolf pants happily and smiles.

Ugh. Why do I crave her approval already? She must be messing with my emotions, and I just can't sense how she's delivering the spell.

Jade chops up some more meat and waits for me to finish before dumping the rest in a clean bowl. "I'm so happy you're okay. I was getting worried."

I stare into her hazel-green eyes and truly wish she wasn't born a witch. Even if she doesn't know she is a witch and isn't aware yet that we are enemies, she *is* our enemy.

She *will* turn on us.

Jade says goodnight and locks herself in her room... again.

I sniff the door to scent for magical warding to prevent my entry, but I don't sense a thing.

A lock won't help her much if a supe or witch, or even a strong human wishes to get inside. It might slow down an attacker for a moment, but that's all the time Jade will need to grab her gun and put a bullet between someone's eyes.

I remind myself that I likely wouldn't heal from that.

She gets ready for bed, but I don't smell her arousal tonight. The witch must be done with her lust games, or, if she's innocent, isn't in the mood.

My wolf is rabid with the thought that Maxum scared her the way he did. Logically, I know I shouldn't be upset. But she has ignited protectiveness in me. Perhaps it's just my recent loss that makes me want to protect. Maybe I shouldn't have gotten this close to her.

But my wolf doesn't seem to believe she killed Osen, and I have a strong inclination to agree. She might know nothing about Osen, even if she is a pawn for the Witch Council.

Or...

I shiver... if she's part of the ASO—the Anti-Supernaturals Organization. Their goal is to get rid of supes by brainwashing supes to kill their own kind. No one knows who runs it, but our money has always been on an underground movement of fanatical witches and warlocks.

Witches are bad enough without being part of the elitist crowd. Supes had hoped that at one point, we had a tentative peace brewing between our kind. And on the surface, it appears the Witch Council was playing nice. But we know they aren't as friendly as they like to pretend.

The terrorist group, ASO, is likely who killed Osen. And the Witch Council is probably pulling their strings through secret channels.

Thank goodness the supernatural disappearances have stopped. But now we know some of the missing weren't from that horrendous magical scheme.

No, from what we understand, ASO uses unwitting supes against their friends. Osen had been investigating along with my small group of friends—the same friends that Jade was spying on.

I wonder if Osen didn't submit to ASO's brainwashing techniques and died because of it.

If that's true, it means he died to save our quirky little family.

Standing outside of her bedroom door, I contemplate what to do next. I've already snooped as much as I can in the house.

Convincing myself that it's only because someone was watching her, and I might catch them if they come after her, I stay close to her room. I can also hear if she communicates with someone during the night.

Dozing in her hallway, I wake to hear her whimpering. I immediately know this isn't the same sound she makes when she's climaxing.

Right now, she sounds scared. But I can't scent or sense anyone else in the room with her.

Is it a nightmare? It must be.

Even so, I stay alert, just in case someone is able to fool my senses.

The Witch Council might have come after Jade, thinking she has been compromised by my continued presence and Maxum taking her to brunch.

Her breathing becomes ragged. She's more panicked. She's reliving a painful moment.

I hear her drop from her bed with a thud. Then she crawls along the floor.

What the fuck? Is she being attacked?

I still don't scent anyone. She sounds as if she's crawling into the closet.

I almost break down the door so I can understand what's happening, but this will only blow my dog cover. Shifting instead, I race into her office and grab a thick paperclip to pick her bedroom lock.

Within seconds, I unlock her door and crack it open. I shift back into my dog... ugh, *wolf* form, before fully entering.

Goddess, has this woman domesticated me already?

As my animal, I crawl on the ground army style, making myself a smaller target, as I don't want Jade to shoot me. I don't see her, but the door to her walk-in closet is open.

The entire room is laden with the scent of fear so potent it burns my nose. It smells as if the person knows they are about to die. But not yet pissed themselves.

When I get close to the closet with my 'night' vision, I can see Jade curled up on her side. She's shivering, no longer whimpering, but is grunting in agony, like a soldier might do after being shot.

Relieved that I don't see her gun in her hands or on the floor, I glance back and see it's on her nightstand. Odd. If she had woken up and been frightened, she would have taken that with her. She must have been sleepwalking.

Without the threat of the gun, I venture inside the tight space and peer down at Jade's face.

It doesn't quite look like her—much like how actors can change how they look from role to role by engaging different muscles in their faces.

She's holding her stomach as if she's been injured. She has her knees drawn up protectively, from what, I am not yet sure.

Her eyes pop open. The irises are now a dark charcoal, no longer their pretty hazel-green.

"Arran? Is that you?" she asks, her accent and tone much different as well.

Is she possessed? And who has taken control?

"I can barely sense anything. Are you there?" they ask. "It feels like your energy."

I'm in my wolf form, so… not answering. And I'm not sure if I should.

"Arran… It's me… Osen."

What the fuck? No way. It can't be. Can it be? But this is impossible.

"Tanil is after me. She fucked me up real bad." Jade-Osen moves their hands as if to show me the damage. "She dosed the wound with iron. Help me?"

I shake my head in disbelief. This is an echo of exactly what happened almost fifteen years ago. Tanil was an evil witch Osen had fooled around with. Of course, he didn't know she was evil at the time. She seemed to be a sweet and kind witch, but she had seduced Osen and then tried to kill him.

It's just another horrific example of why I resist trusting Jade's innocence.

Which makes me wonder if this is some trick.

Is this really Osen's spirit? And is his soul stuck in the past?

But supes don't connect with the spirit world and work through mediums. We don't see or communicate with ghosts. Although hellhounds, a particular race of demons from the Underworld, can capture souls.

But witches are a different sort of magical being. Communicating with spirits is a talent witches sometimes have. However, most aren't spirit *mediums*, able to host a disembodied soul. Now, I suspect Jade might also have a talent for mediumship.

Yet, I had never heard of a witch channeling a *supernatural* soul before—only humans and other witches.

This is suspicious.

"Arran?" they call again.

Risking my cover, I shift into my human form, now on my hands and knees next to their side.

"Osen?" I whisper.

They jerk and look at me, squinting to see me in the dark closet.

"Goddess, I'm so happy to see you," they say, grabbing me around the neck and pulling me to Jade's chest.

I almost pull away. But the magic behind the touch feels faintly like Osen's energy, so I allow myself to sink into the embrace.

"What happened to you?" I ask, my voice cracking. I missed the jerk.

"Tanil," he says with confusion.

"No," I sigh. "You went to check out the old foundry building. You didn't..." I don't finish and remind him I found his dead body, stripped of all magic, even the usual residual amount that clings to a corpse. Bizarrely enough, there were no physical marks to indicate how he died, either. Nothing to tell us what happened. Only a void of energy.

"Foundry?" Osen asks, then he shouts as if he's being attacked.

Jade's arms and legs flail, and she vibrates.

Suddenly, I realize Osen is being expelled from her body, and I quickly shift back to my wolf.

With no hesitation, Jade clings to my furry neck, crying into my fur. For a moment, I worry she's cursing me with her tears.

But the emotion I scent on her is pure terror and fear.

A few minutes pass, and she pulls back. I'm guessing she realizes I shouldn't be in her room.

"Beast?" she whispers Maxum's name for my wolf. Her eyes widen, and she slowly removes her hold, a lingering worry in her eyes that I might bite her. She glances around the closet and rubs her eyes. "What happened? And how did you get in here?" Frowning, she looks at my foot that touches her leg. "Why are you allowing me to touch you?"

She doesn't expect answers. But I wonder if she is a medium, a psychic, if she could pick up my thoughts. I send her an image of her shivering form in the closet.

"You were worried about me?" she guesses, sounding uncertain. "Thank you. But we should get out of here, but... uh, I don't want to upset you by moving into your space again."

Looking at our surroundings, I find I'm blocking the exit.

I take the hint, trot out to her bedroom, and sit near the foot of her bed.

Jade climbs out of the closet and stands. Noticing that I didn't crash the door down to get to her, she shakes her head in confusion. "I swear I locked it." She bites her full lower lip. "I suppose if I got into the closet without remembering, I could have unlocked the door, too."

I'll say one thing about her rambling mouth. I don't ever have to wonder what she's thinking.

I follow her closely when she goes out to the kitchen and drinks a glass of water.

Her hand shakes as she lifts the glass. With her other hand, she holds her forehead as if she has a headache. "I haven't had an episode like that for... well, since I was dating Rob." She sighs. "Maybe it's because I had a messed up day? I'm sorry I upset you, Beast."

When she returns to her bedroom, I stay at her side. She allows me entry, but shuts and locks the door behind her. "Thanks for coming to my rescue." She offers her limp hand for me to sniff and accept.

I do because I need her to trust me. And I'm beginning to trust her.

That trust will probably bite me in the ass.

10

WAKING DREAMS

JADE

*L*ast night was one of my more intense *episodes*.

Episodes... such a light and fluffy word for feeling like someone or something is invading my mind. Sure, I often dream what feels like another person's dream. Heck, I've used some of it in my stories.

But these episodes are more than the unusual dream of places and people I've never seen before. I've had odd dreams my whole life. But the intense episodes started almost two decades ago when I turned twenty-one.

The severity of the nightmares has made me wonder if I should be on medication for what feels like a paranoid delusion.

I rarely remember what happens to me and why I ended up somewhere odd... in this case, my closet. Another time, I ended up in my backyard. Once, I even woke up while walking down the sidewalk.

One day, I expect it's going to get me hurt or killed. I'll set my house on fire or I'll wander into traffic, and bam.

This time, though, I remember more than I usually do.

In this dream, I watched as a woman threw a curse at me, or more accurately, the person I was supposed to be.

Then the woman poisoned me with powder and terror hit me when I recognized what it was: ground-up iron. For some reason, I was afraid of the iron.

Thinking about it now, I had read that fae are supposed to be allergic to the stuff. Myths and legends. I wonder why I'm dreaming of fantasy beings. Especially since this vision felt all too real.

Then I recall another strange part of my vision.

"You want to hear something odd, Beast?" I ask as I chop up some more meat for the huge lug.

Beast is finally warming up to me after my episode. It's sweet that he was trying to comfort me when I was scared. Animals can be wonderful that way.

At my question, he stares up with his strange golden eyes that sometimes seem to glow, waiting for me to continue.

"Last night, I must have been really desperate for some hunky snacks. I thought you were one of the guys from the bar... He was holding me—shirtless, no less." I shake my head, amused. "But fortunately, I realized it was you right away."

Beast seems to visibly gulp. I swear this dog isn't normal. Maybe he does have a human soul.

"Don't worry, sweetie. I know better." I wave off the projected concern I've assigned to the poor animal. "It's just... I felt so at peace in his arms, like I belonged with him. And not just because he's hot, I mean, it definitely doesn't hurt. Anyway, I wonder if that's what genuine love will feel like. The feeling like I've found my true home. Safe. Cherished." I sigh dramatically, brushing away the few tears. "Oh, well, of course when I woke up it was just you, a dog. And even you will probably leave soon, out of my life in a day or so."

After I fill his bowl, he stares at me for a long beat, watching me. Perhaps he senses my sadness. But finally, he eats.

I show him out the backdoor so he can enjoy the pleasant weather. "I'll be writing for a few hours. But if you need anything, be sure to bark."

He bumps my hand, and I pat his head softly. My heart warms with his acceptance of me. Like I've won the skittish doggy lotto.

"Maybe if you let me put a leash on you, we can go for a walk later." The uncomfortable memory of someone watching crashes back over me. It can't be Rob again, could it? "Or maybe no walking. Maxum or whoever might still be lurking. I won't risk you getting hurt, too."

After letting him out, I settle into my office and begin to write.

The story pours out. It's a continuation of the one I started about the guys. There are some baddies who want to kill supernatural beings. And my harem are trying to stop them.

Witches show up in the story.

I often write about witches and warlocks. They can be morally gray at worst, but now, some witches in my story are downright evil.

Not to say that shifters and other magical people aren't also jerks.

In my mind, I see that there's a war on the horizon. It's over magic, and who should wield it. Neither side trusts the other. Both sides have legitimate reasons for their hatred and blame the other faction for the loss of magic. But my gut tells me the loss isn't about either side. Something cosmically is afoot.

Leaning back and stretching, I take a breather from writing… and let my fingers rest. Checking my email, my blood runs cold, and my heart rate picks up.

Rob emailed me.

It's his only mode of communication left since I've finally blocked him on my phone and social media.

My first instinct is to delete the damned thing without opening it. But with my strange interactions lately, the sensation that I have a stalker, and my nightmare episode—which I haven't had since Rob was around—I open it up instead.

It reads simply: "You should be more careful who you go on dates with."

Yeah, no shit. Like you, for one.

Then my second reaction is to freak the fuck out.

Has he been watching me? Or did he just happen to see me walking with Maxum? He doesn't live that far away, so maybe it's just a coincidence?

Perhaps someone from the neighborhood ratted me out and relayed what they saw?

No matter how he found out, he has no right to email me and tell me who I can and can't go out with. It gives me creeper sicko vibes. But unfortunately, he didn't do enough that the police would take an interest in my complaint. He's smart enough to never document any of his actual threats outright. This could be seen as 'friendly' advice.

Cursing. I'm pissed that I have nothing on him. He's been extremely careful to never get caught doing anything to me in public or in front of our friends.

I soon realized our friends were truly his when we broke up. All of them sided with him when we split. He painted me as the neglectful girlfriend who only cared about her career. Well, someone had to care about my career.

Staring at the sentence on the screen, I cycle through all the emotions, finally landing on wariness. He's watching. He's still invested in me—feels he owns me.

If I hadn't already shuttered all the windows, I would have done so now.

I hate how unsafe I've felt over the last day, ever since… Maxum's date.

Too bad my dream man from the closet hadn't been real. The actual guy is likely a jerk, just like Maxum. But at least I'd have someone's hand to hold and assure me that I'm not crazy for being worried.

I've been through worse. I can face this alone too. Whatever *this* is.

11

NO GO

MAXUM

Since Jade stormed off from the restaurant, I've been incapable of getting the feisty, curvy seductress out of my mind.

I offended her. I truly upset her about her writing.

From my mind-reading affinity, on the surface of her thoughts, I picked up that she really didn't understand my snarky insinuations about her spying for the witches and their nefarious plans to eliminate our kind.

She might actually be oblivious to everything.

So what the hell is Arran still doing snuggling up in her house? Has he found something I didn't? Is he falling for her wicked yet sweet smile and her dirty mind?

And *who* was watching us?

I was so preoccupied with her anger that I couldn't pinpoint the source.

For some blasted reason, I hate that she's pissed at me. Which isn't like me.

I usually revel in pissing people off.

It's a professional-grade hobby. After hundreds of years, one does get bored with the day-to-day, even with a war or two thrown in for shits and giggles…

I certainly wasn't bored yesterday.

She intrigues me with her protectiveness over Arran's wolf, then she draws me in with her passion for her career. Her ability to stand up to my gruff and her naughty mind sealed the deal.

I've been casing her house throughout the night and most of today.

Fortunately, Ms. Jade lives on a corner, and I've just watched as she lets Arran outside so he can take a dump.

Oh, this is precious.

When I sense she's moved away from the back of the house, I stroll up and can easily see Arran's wolf over the fence.

He snarls at me. Defensive much?

I want to taunt him about his new lifestyle choice, but I need to convince him to get out of there while I don't sense anyone currently watching.

Arran perks his ears up, confirming Jade has walked away. Then he shifts and glares at me.

He's naked and has his hands on his hips in defiance. And while I would enjoy having Jade walk out to see his glory displayed in her backyard, it occurs to me she might not find a naked man in her yard as funny as I do. But I don't doubt she would check out his package and muscles before she called the cops. Maybe take some of those *thirst trapping* photos.

"What do you want now?" he growls.

Something in his tone concerns me. "Does the witch have you under her spell? Why are you still here?"

"No, she doesn't even know what she is. But there is *something* going on."

"I know. Come on, put your clothes on, and jump over this fence. Someone has eyes on her, and conveniently, I don't sense them now."

"Dude," he huffs. "Slow down."

Ugh. I hate SoCal lingo.

Arran continues, "I think she's a medium."

"Big fucking deal. Stop sniffing her panty drawer, and let's go, you idiot." I turn toward Calder's car down the road.

A pile of shit hits the back of my head.

What. The. Fuck?

I slowly turn back, wondering how I will kill him and how fast I should make it happen.

"Was that *your* shit?" I ask. "Did you crap in her yard like a common dog?"

His face is red with embarrassment. I didn't think he'd stoop so low as to actually shit in her yard.

Oh, oh... this is too much... I can't take it. This is hilarious. No longer mad at his tantrum, I roar with laughter, knowing that I'm going to roast him for decades over this. "You took a shit in her yard like a pet, and then you threw it at me like a damned monkey in a cage? What happened to you... *dude*?"

Arran paces the yard. "I don't know. But I can't leave her. She channeled Osen."

"No way." I wave him off, but I am worried he doesn't feel he can leave her. "Supe spirits don't speak through witches."

"But Osen did. And you know he was... special." Arran's voice is soft.

He's not wrong. Osen captured all of our hearts at one point. And he was powerful, even for what he was.

"So... what?" I shake my head. "You're going to be her sweet puppy from now on? We don't know where her allegiances lie. She's a fucking witch, for fuck's sake."

"I don't think she knows she is. Even her pets don't think she knows."

"Her pets?" I scoff. "So, has she captured other dumb shifters like you? Does she keep a menagerie in her basement? You want to join her collection?"

I should know better than to antagonize him. He's unstable and a legit monster when he's really pissed. Right now, he *should* be riding, or at least close to crossing that line with my comments.

He's proven in the past that he can't cope when one of his pack dies. And he considered Osen his pack, even if he wasn't a wolf.

Idly, I wonder if Jade's presence has calmed his beast. Stranger things have happened. She is unusual.

"Not shifters. It's a magical creature—a guinea pig. He fancies himself her familiar."

"A guinea pig familiar?" I blow out a puff of air. "That's it. I've heard everything."

Arran turns serious. "Something even bigger than Osen is going on here... which in itself is pretty big. By the way, I'm not happy with you. You frightened Jade out of her mind after your date yesterday." Deep in his throat, a growl rumbles. He really is becoming attached to the magic mortal. "What the hell did you say to her?"

"She was rambling on, claiming she mysteriously guessed all sorts of stuff about us. *My flaming red ass.* She knew I was a demon, and you were a shifter, and she pretended it was her imagination."

"She isn't playing. She believes that's where the stuff in her books comes from."

"She actually writes?" I rub my chin, pondering our brunch conversation in a different context. "It doesn't matter. Get your clothes on and let's go."

"No." He snarls at me. His skin ripples with his monster. "I'm not leaving Osen."

I cross my arms, highlighting my brawn. He won't make me cower, not even with his berserker beast.

"Did Osen's alleged spirit tell you who killed him?"

"Not yet," he admits.

"Did you ask?"

"I think he was having a hard time possessing her. He didn't seem to grasp that he was dead. But he might next time. I have to give him at least another night to see if he can remember."

"Fine. One more night. But if you aren't out of there after that, I'm dragging you out of her house and melting her brain if it comes to it."

"Shut the fuck up. You aren't hurting her." His beast's teeth elongate, and fur erupts over his body.

"Oh, yeah?" I step menacingly toward the fence.

We both know a fight between us does not end well. For either of us.

Pulling back his beast and losing the fur, he glowers at me, daring me to lie. "Yeah. Don't try to hide it, you like her too. My wolf scented it."

I give Arran a deadly glare that makes him take a step back. "I'll end her if I have to. Don't think I've gone soft just because I can play nice. She isn't part of our pack. Understand?" I jab my finger toward the house. "But for some confounding reason, you're pack to me, asshole."

Arran shakes his head, shifts into his wolf, and barks at the door.

Well then, I guess I've been fucking dismissed.

Angrily walking back to the car, I almost rip the passenger door off its hinge and slam it shut after shoving myself in the passenger seat with a huff.

"What's up with Arran?" Calder asks. "Did he find something?"

"Osen, supposedly," I grumble.

They both come to attention. Funnily enough, my violent car entrance did not even faze them.

Flint frowns at the house and asks in a low, rumbling voice that sounds almost like granite churning, "How?"

"Arran claims the witch is a medium." I hold up my hand so I can cut off their arguments. "Yeah, I know. Can't happen. Arran claims it did. I don't know if it's wishful thinking. Or maybe she's actually psychic and picked up on some memories Arran has of Osen? I don't fucking know. But I'm allowing him to have another night there to prove me right. That this is a hoax. Then I'm dragging him out of the house. Consequences be damned."

"We all might be damned." Calder scowls at the house like it's offended him personally. A bit of flame simmers in his ice-blue eyes. "My senses are confirming what yours picked up before... things are going to get ugly real soon."

And if anyone can sense when death is near, it's a phoenix.

1 2

GHOSTING

JADE

*B*east was more friendly with me today, following me around and letting me rub his soft ears. He's no longer giving me indignant glares when I offer him food or let him out to use the yard to stretch his legs.

It's cute that he enjoys being in my office and watching me write. I tease him and ask if he likes my latest plot twist or what a character did in my dreams. I swear he's reading over my shoulder and sometimes looks scandalized by some of the sex scenes.

But perhaps he can just read my nervous energy. I see his owner in some of the scenes and feel guilty about including the hunk of perfection.

I do love that I combined Beast and his owner into a wolf-shifter, though. It feels right, as if I'm just plucking these characters out of the ether, and they've always existed.

However, it troubles me that Beast has a hard time trusting me. Did his owner neglect or abuse him?

But if he's a wolf breed mix, or an actual domesticated wolf, as I'm beginning to suspect, they can be standoffish with strangers or anyone who isn't their alpha.

So I'll defer judgment about his owner's behavior until I know more. Perhaps it isn't his current owner who might have mistreated him.

When it's time for bed, Beast trots after me, so close he's almost on my heels, into my bedroom. He has his head cast downward as if he expects to be kicked out. But his solid presence brings me comfort, so I'd rather he stay.

I don't know if I want him on the bed. He strikes me as the type who will claim the entire space. So I grab an old, soft blanket and place it at the foot of my bed on the floor.

"Here you go, buddy." I kneel down by the makeshift dog bed and pat it, trying to entice him to use it.

He glances at my bed, then his offering, and concedes. Stepping onto the blanket, he sits and rests his head on my shoulder. His sweetness is almost enough to allow him on my bed. I sink my fingers into the thick fur at his neck and give him a nice massage. Apparently, I'm growing on him.

"I wish you didn't have to return to your owner." I give him a quick ear rub, and he settles down on his blanket.

When I walk away, he stares at me as if he wants to say the same thing. Boy, my imagination has been running wild lately.

I change into my sleep shirt in the bathroom. Mainly because no matter how I brush off my anthropomorphizing as my intense imagination, it still feels like there's a human inside that dog. The dreams about him being the guy from the bar haven't exactly helped.

Sometimes, I think I can see that man behind Beast's eyes.

Ugh, it's just that I'm writing and dreaming about that idea.

As soon as I crawl into bed, Beast abandons his spot and hops up, curling at my side.

But I don't mind the company, so I sigh and close my eyes. Between Rob's alarming email and Maxum being a jerk, I could use the comfort of having someone nearby.

Would Beast help me if shit were to go down? I don't know, but maybe just his presence would deter someone... especially Rob.

I become lucid in my dream state, which is a fairly common occurrence for me. I'm often aware I'm dreaming in my dreams. Most of the time, it's because they don't seem like my dreams at all. Sure, it could be that I just read a lot and have picked up random scenes and scenarios. But if I do have a magical ability, it would be this... I'm almost convinced that I dream other people's dreams.

Now, I'm currently in a strange landscape that feels like hyperrealism. The colors are more vivid and brighter. It looks like a painting of a fairy world.

The sun sets, and a portal opens in front of me. The alphahole from the bar and Maxum walk through the portal and shake my hand.

I glance down and see my hand looks to be masculine. I'm tall, but not as tall as Maxum, but really, few people are over six-foot-five.

"Did the witches see you?" Maxum asks.

"Nah. I think we're good," my persona says with a deep voice that reminds me of whiskey pouring over ice. "The tracking spell should lead us right to their hideout."

"Perfect." Then the broody alphahole wolf-shifter warns me, "Don't go by yourself to check it out. Okay?"

"Sure," my avatar says, but even I can hear his lie.

The scene fades, and I'm outside of a large mansion. Not sure why it feels familiar, but maybe it's the sense I have in the dream. I'm supposed to have been here before.

Then the male voice I used earlier speaks directly into my mind. *"Who are you?"*

"Excuse me?" I've never had someone realize I had invaded their dreams. "Who are you?"

"Answer my question, witch," he says with a firm tone. By the way he spits out the witch nickname, it's obvious that it isn't meant to be cute. It sounds like a curse.

"Might as well just level up and call me a bitch, because I'm not answering you until you answer me."

"You don't want me rummaging through your mind. I won't make it pleasant."

"I'm in your dream. Not the other way around." I wave my/his hands around at the scene.

"This is… no. This isn't a dream. It's a memory." He sounds disoriented.

I feel bad invading his mind, especially if I've made him confused by my presence. I sweeten my attitude and suggest, "Hey, I'll help you out if you help me. Okay?"

"I won't betray my friends or my kind for the likes of you or your kind, witch," he snarls.

It seems his favorite curse word is *witch*.

I don't want to keep dreaming about this irritating guy and his drama, so I try again to smooth things over.

"Listen, I don't want to hurt anyone. As a measure of good faith, I'll help you work out your dreams, and then we can come back to you telling me why we both know Maxum."

"Yes…," he says, as if he's straining to remember. *"You were spying on them."*

"I didn't mean anything by it. They were just hot!" I grumble.

"As if the witches or ASO didn't send you to kill them."

"Is this part of your dream? What is your trip with Wiccans? Are you sexist?"

"Wiccans?" He sighs. "Witches, you witch!"

Well, this is lovely.

"I'm picking up some signals that you don't like witches, and you believe I'm a witch," I say dully.

"How else do you explain you are speaking to a spirit?"

"Because I'm dreaming that you're dreaming you are a spirit," I reason.

"I can't get back into my body. So I'm dead."

I decide this conversation thread isn't getting us anywhere, so I surrender. "What do you want me to do? Tell me how to help you so I can end this dream and escape this nightmare!"

"Tell me who you are."

"My name is Jade. I'm a romance author. That's it, buddy. No top-secret dossier. No coven membership. Just Jade."

He grunts at that. *"Was it the witches or the ASO who killed me? Or are they one and the same?"*

"You don't know who allegedly killed you?"

"Was it the Witch Council? Is that why they sent you to follow my associates?"

"I don't know any witches! And I don't even know what ASO stands for. And when you say your associates, do you mean Maxum and his buddies?"

A shadow circles around my throat, closing in around my neck. A shadowy ghost of a figure stands in front of me. *"Did you kill me?"*

"No..." I wheeze.

Why does it feel like I'm really being choked?

"Are you tasked with killing my friends?"

"No... I'd never..."

He loosens his grip around my throat, having heard the truth in my words.

"I saw Arran. Why is he in your house?"

"I have a new dog in my house. He's supposed to belong to Maxum's friend."

He chuckles at that. *"Do you not remember what happened before? In your dream, with the 'dog'?"*

"I had a nightmare of being hurt, stabbed, and poisoned with iron. And then the scene changed, and I dreamed the dog was a man in my closet," I say softly, wondering how fucked up my mind really is. "But this is all just a dream. My dream, right?"

"It's not."

"But—"

"Time to go to sleep, witch," he says ominously, and everything goes black.

13

NIGHTMARES

ARRAN

"*A*rran?" Jade's voice comes out gruff and masculine.

It's not her…

Where I rest next to the sleeping witch, I shift into my human form. Crawling closer to her face, I look into their eyes.

Similar to the closet last night, her sweet hazel-green eyes, have been replaced with Osen's dark charcoal ones. "Osen?"

"What the fuck are you doing here?" he snaps. "With a filthy fucking witch!"

"I'm talking to you, you asshole!" I growl. "You can't figure out why I would be here?"

"But I'm not the only reason, am I?" Jade's small hands grab my throat. "By the way, she's going to put it together. She might be playing innocent about my murder, but she has enough hints to realize what you are now. You need to kill her while you have the chance—while you have the upper hand. Or you'll be next on her hit list."

"No," I argue. "I'm certain she's ignorant of all this—her gifts, supes, witches."

"Listen to me, you reckless fool." He clasps the sides of my head and presses our foreheads together. "I don't know if I can hold her back much longer. End this now."

"I said no." My anger rises. My beast is being tested by his request. He doesn't want to see the witch dead either. Hoping it will jar the memory loose, I demand, "Tell me who killed you, and then I'll leave her alone."

"I don't know. It took me watching you all at the bar to even realize I had died. All I know is that I was alive, and then I wasn't. I don't know who killed me." A thumb brushes over my cheek, just like Osen used to do when we were together.

"How are you able to speak through her?" I ask.

"Maybe because of what I am?" He shrugs. "I'm getting stronger the longer I'm connected to the *witch*." He spits out the last word.

"I think Jade could help you. Could help us."

"Why are you going soft on me? Now?" Shaking his head, he collapses back on the bed. "Fuck... She's fighting me. I have to go."

"Stay close to her. There must be a reason for this connection." I cling to him, not wanting him to fade.

"You were never much for fate." He chuckles lightly, and his eyes close. "Torture her, get the information you need, and avenge me."

"Don't leave," I whisper.

My instinct is to kiss her mouth and maybe call him back. But that's a no-no. It's bad enough that I'm an uninvited naked male in her bed.

Jade lazily flutters her eyes open, and she catches sight of me hovering over her. She must be more than half asleep because she smiles instead of screams. "Arran, is it?"

I return her smile but don't answer. I'm afraid my voice might be enough to break whatever spell this is over her mind.

Her hand reaches for my face, and her soft fingertips graze the stubble on my chin. "You're very handsome for a man, or even when you're the dog... *wolf*," she corrects herself.

Gazing into the depths of her green eyes, I wish things were different.

The desire to kiss her is more than I expected in my human form. I wouldn't have expected it to be so overwhelming without Osen's presence to lure me in.

However, at any moment, this beautiful exchange is going to degrade into chaos.

She will come to her senses, find her gun, and shoot me.

And I won't stop her. Sure, I'll run, but I won't hurt her for protecting herself.

I've seen she's been in battles of her own—personal battles.

Her fingers trail over my bottom lip. "It's too bad you only exist in my fucked-up head. I'm probably just feeling up my pillow like a pervert in my sleep."

I haven't moved other than my smile. But I'm tempted to suck on her fingers and see what the steamy romance author would do with that.

Would she pull me down for a kiss? Would she reach down and stroke my hardening cock? Would she open her legs and attempt to take my knot? Would she let me bite down on her delicate neck and claim her?

Goddess! Snapping out of my fantasy, I find I'm practically on top of her, my mouth ghosting over hers.

She closes the distance and presses her sweet lips to mine.

Keep it chaste, asshole!

I have to go before she asks me to fuck her. Because she believes this is a dream. And it wouldn't be right.

But would it?

No, bad dog! WOLF! Ugh.

I let the kiss linger before pulling away slowly.

Jade's hand skims down my neck to my chest. Her eyes are half closed, looking as if she will fall asleep any second.

If she feels me up, is that my fault? Because her hand on my body feels so amazing that I'm tempted to let her explore.

Would she wrap those lush lips around my dick? Would she ride me, her big tits bouncing in my face, and come when I rubbed her clit? Would she take all four of us at the same time? Would she let us fill her up with our seed?

Whoops… I shouldn't have read her why choose romance. *Naughty witch.*

Sleep, my sweet. I give her a kiss on each eyelid, and she drifts off to sleep.

I shift into my dog form and rest my head on her shoulder, staring at her pretty face.

She snuggles me closer, her fingers tangled in my fur.

I fall asleep peacefully. It's the first time I've had a good night's rest in years.

I wake to Jade's groan and gasp of surprise that I'm basically on top of her—in my wolf form, unfortunately.

Her eyes are shadowed. I'm worried that Osen harmed her with his possession. Is his spirit draining her life force?

"What a weird night," she moans. "Sorry if I made out with your nose last night. I thought you were someone else." She chuckles to herself, but sounds depressed. "I had some strange, upsetting dreams."

I don't want to move away so she can get up. I want to snuggle with her longer, because today, I'm supposed to disappear from her life.

My mind scrambles to find any excuse to stay. But Osen doesn't remember his death, and Maxum will drag me out of here, and in the process, possibly hurt Jade. I can't have that. Besides, the longer I stay, the more likely she will catch me. She won't be happy with me. I'm betraying her trust by being here. And I'm beginning to feel guilty.

"Beast?" She gently strokes my neck. "Are you okay? You aren't usually this clingy."

Realizing I'm acting the fool Osen accused me of being, I stand up and jump off the bed.

She stretches, and her sleep shirt lifts up, revealing her belly. When she walks to the bathroom, her tiny sleep shorts highlight her full ass.

How I want to sink into that soft heat.

I'm falling for a witch? When the fuck did this happen?

Does it count against me when she doesn't know she's one?

When I hear her groan at her reflection, I'm upset by Osen's behavior last night. He had always skirted the morally gray area, but now? Maybe death changes a person.

What am I saying… it does.

Yet, Osen was always anti-witch, ever since he was a young man and had been tortured by one. That was well before he had fully come into his powers. He let his guard down again with Tanil, and that backfired. I don't blame him for being anti-witch.

I have my own painful history with witches. But Jade doesn't seem like she would ever hurt me... not on purpose, anyway. She really is different.

Wondering what I should do about Osen, Jade, and all these lies, I contemplate leaving and coming back in my human form to date her. But I'm afraid Maxum fucked that up. She won't trust me after he upset her. Nor should she.

Besides, she definitely won't trust me if she finds out about the supernatural world and realizes I've been masquerading as her pet doggie.

I'm screwed.

If that weren't enough, I can't trust my monstrous beast to leave her unscathed—physically or mentally. She might read and write monster fucking books, but that doesn't mean she actually wants to be in danger.

And she would be in danger.

Jade comes out of the bathroom, freshly showered, with only a small towel wrapped around her voluptuous body. I contemplate tugging on the cloth. She slips into the closet and wisely shuts the door. Her instincts must sense something isn't quite right with me. After all, she does *dream* that I'm the *alphahole* from the bar.

Fully dressed, Jade comes out of the closet and heads to the kitchen. "I have to run some errands and get some food for all of us." She snatches up her keys and purse and opens the back door. "Be a good boy, and I'll bring home some yummy treats."

As soon as she closes the door behind me, I realize what I need to do.

Beast must run away.

14

DOGGIE DADDY

JADE

*H*eading out my front door to my Mustang, I feel a tingling, and not in a good way.

Someone is watching me.

Casually, I glance up and down my street to see if I can spot Rob's car, Maxum, or his buddies. No one.

My car rumbles to life. I briefly wonder if someone put a tracker on it. My spy slash writer's mind is hyperactive again.

Yet is it so far out of the realm of possibility? Not really. I received an ominous email from Rob. I had the sense that someone was watching me, even before that.

My first stop is the pet shop. I grab some special food and treats for my little guys. Then I picked out a masculine black leather collar for Beast. It has a bit of a BDSM vibe, which makes me grin and my mind wanders.

Would Arran look hot in this? Duh, he'd look good in anything, I'm sure. Well, if Beast refuses to wear this, maybe I can find a guy who will.

As I head over to the grocery store for some human food, I have that same unnerving sensation of being watched. While at the store, along with some of my own food treats, I buy a long-handled mirror.

After driving off, I find a quiet residential cul-de-sac and wait several minutes to see if someone follows me here. Again, no one shows.

I hop out of my Mustang and use the mirror to check under the car frame to see if there are any tracking devices. Nothing.

I sit back down in my bucket seat. Then I allow my vision to blur, staring into the distance through the windshield. Wistfully, I wonder why I can't just have a normal life where I dream up fancy peens all day without interruption.

Starting up the engine and driving home, I worry Rob will escalate to violence. Again.

Oh, well, maybe it's time I sell my house and move. But I can't really afford the time off to deal with all that—not with my packed book release schedule.

However, if things get any crazier with Rob, I will just have to disappoint fans by pushing back my release dates. Hopefully, they'll understand.

Driving down my street, I see a man on my porch, facing away from me and waiting.

My heart thumps wildly in my chest, because my first thought is that it could be Rob.

I slide my gun into my pocket for easy access, because I don't know what's going on.

But as I get closer, I can see clearer. The man turns, and I quickly recognize my gentleman caller. Now, I'm even more freaked out.

I grab my frozen food bag. It's the lightest bag for ease of movement if I'm attacked. Besides, I need to bring them inside after my tracking device check detour. This is partially self-defensive and ice cream-melting defense.

I am woman. Watch me multitask.

I glare at the man as I slowly approach. "What do you want?"

The male I've dreamed up the name Arran for, stands with his hands in his pockets and his head dipping down, looking timid. "Uh, hi. I heard you had my dog. I'm sorry for showing up unannounced, but I didn't have a number to call."

I huff that this guy shows up *after* I finally buy Beast treats and a collar. It shouldn't piss me off, but it does. Not to mention how long it took him to make his appearance.

But honestly, I just don't want to let the big lug go. We bonded last night. Emotions well up in my chest.

Ugh... do *not* cry in front of the hot guy. Shove the pesky feelings down, Jade.

He will probably just tell Maxum all about my breakdown.

Stiffening my spine, I brush past the man and eye him the whole time I unlock my door. Fortunately, he is conscientious enough to stand back at the edge of my porch. "Just give me a second to put my food in the fridge, okay?"

"No problem." He nods. "And thank you for taking him in. That was kind."

I don't respond to that. Let's see if Beast wants to go with him any more than he did with Maxum. I quietly lock the door behind me as soon as I'm inside.

Tossing my food into the freezer, bag and all, I hurry to the back door and expect to see Beast standing right there as he had done every other time. But he's not there. I step out and scan my small backyard.

"Beast?" I call. But the bushes aren't big enough to conceal his massive size.

My stomach drops.

He ran off because I left today. I glance at my six-foot-tall fence and see scratch marks. I thought it would have been high enough to contain him. I guessed wrong. Maybe for a Shih Tzu or medium-sized dog, but for Beast, it was a small hurdle.

He left me. Why does that hurt just as much as a boyfriend abandoning me? Maybe I really do need to find someone to love.

Getting over my pain, I remember that his owner is here. Crap.

Will he believe that Beast ran off? Or will he insist that I've hidden him and demand him back? Will he storm into my house, searching for his beloved pet?

Take a breath, Jade.

Sometimes my author-mind gets away from me, contemplating every scenario.

I race throughout the house, checking to be sure that I didn't imagine letting him out before I did my errands.

Centering myself, I head out the front door and step out onto the porch, but on the opposite end from this man, so he can't easily push me back inside. For all I know, he's been the creeper watching me.

His eyebrows rise in confusion, reminding me of his dog.

"Uh. While I was out…" I wring my hands. "Your dog escaped. I'm so sorry!" I start waving my hands over my face as I heat up with nerves. I'm worried for Beast, and I'm concerned about what this guy's reaction is going to be. *Is* he an alphahole? "He might still be in the neighborhood. I'll put the rest of my food in the house, and I will make the circuit with my car. We'll find him. God, I hope he's okay!"

"Hey," the man says softly. "It's not your fault. He does this. He's a bit of a free spirit and takes off. He's probably headed to my place. I don't live that far away."

"You believe me?" I ask, sort of shocked he took my claim at face value. Especially considering how his friend Maxum acted so suspicious of me.

"You seem like a caring person." He comforts me, even though it's his animal missing. "I don't think you would steal someone's animal."

"Tell that to Maxum," I grumble under my breath.

"Maxum?" The guy shakes his head. "He can be… intense. And sometimes distrustful. I'm sorry if Maxum bothered you when he saw you were taking care of Beast."

I chuckle lightly. At least I'm not the only one who thinks Maxum's a bit much. Unfortunately, it doesn't diminish how sexy he is.

"Beast was pleasant company. I'm sad to see him go," I confess.

"If you give me your number, I can give you a call and let you know when he shows up at my house."

"How about my email?" I counter, because I don't like how stalkery things feel in my life right now.

"Is it odd that I don't have an email account?" he asks.

"Yes. Yes, it is." I crinkle my brow. "Are you and Maxum part of some anti-technology movement?"

He smirks, and damn if it isn't a classic book cover model pose. The dominant mafia man is here to rock my world, and maybe tie me up and teach me how to be a good girl.

And… I'm a goner again. I imagine his strong, rough hands gripping my hips as he thrusts into me. He tells me I'm his and demands I come around his cock over and over.

Returning to the real world, he says, "We just don't jive with the computer fad."

"It's a damned cult, really," I agree with a laugh. "I'm sure the whole technology gimmick will blow over any day now."

"Exactly." Mr. Fuckolicious chuckles. "But we aren't anti-tech fanatics or anything." He shrugs casually.

Then he studies my face like I'm the most fascinating thing on the planet.

Did I accidentally fall into a vat of pheromones this week? I try to sniff my armpit casually, but abandon the attempt for later.

"Oh, I don't even know your name." I grab my other bags and carry them to the door.

He reaches out to help me.

I check in with my douche-o-meter, and I sense he's just trying to be helpful. But I pull back anyway. "I'm good."

"Of course, sorry." He takes a step back. "I'll let you be. But could I have a pen and paper? I don't have one on me. I can give you my number in case you want to check in about Beast or if he shows up again. My number is a landline, so don't text it."

"Uh, sure. Give me a sec." I rush inside, put my groceries down in the kitchen, and check the backyard on the off chance Beast has returned. Nope.

I snatch a pen and slip of paper out of my office.

Once again, I'm struck by his gorgeous features as I return. He has the kind of face that sucks my breath away.

Why do I feel like I could sink my fingers into his dark brown hair and he'd let me?

Centering myself, I offer the pen and paper to Mr. Hunky, who is waiting patiently outside. I don't know why he's being so insistent about this. Maybe it's because Beast might return. Or he's being considerate that I took care of his pup.

When he hands me back the paper, I see that he's written 'Arran' on it.

My world spins. I'm sure Maxum never mentioned his friend's name. How is it that I guess his name?

I stumble back a step, my heel snags on a plank, and Arran catches me as I fall. A surge of electric heat travels from my back, where he's touching me, to my heart, then immediately to my clit. Dammit. And that's just from a hand on my back?

What pleasure could he bring me without clothes and time to explore?

Geeze, is this guy a walking radiator? Heat pours over my body. I'd like other things pouring all over my body...

Arran pulls me upright and hesitates before letting me go, but he doesn't step back. Instead, he towers over me, with his amber eyes, much like his dogs.

That's weird, right?

I've heard people often look like their pets, but this is next level shit.

Do men have amber eyes outside of romance novels? I'm pretty sure they don't.

"What's wrong?" he asks, his voice soft, as if he's worried he will spook me.

"Your name is Arran?"

"Do you hate the name? I can change it." He jokes.

"I don't hate it. It's just... I don't remember Maxum mentioning your name, but strangely enough, it's the name I associated with you." I shake my head. "I must be losing my marbles. I'm sure he said it, and I must have forgotten. I'm not *that* psychic."

Arran still is all up in my personal zone. "Just a little psychic?" he asks, teasing, but also with interest.

"Nah. Intuitive at best." Reluctantly, I step back, making sure not to trip again.

"What does your intuition say about me taking you out tonight for dinner? I want to thank you for taking care of my Beast... urm, my dog." His voice is full of innuendo. That must be accidental, though. Right?

I remember how Maxum behaved. Do I want another Mr. Hyde situation?

"I don't know if that's a great idea. Your friend was..."

"Maxum screwed up my chances, didn't he?" Arran steps back too, now realizing he's not getting anywhere with me.

"It's nothing personal. You seem cool enough, but I've been having other issues, on top of Maxum. You don't need to risk having problems just for a thank you dinner."

The eerie feeling of someone watching again crawls up my spine. I glance around the neighborhood to see if I can catch my voyeur.

Arran turns too. "Do you have someone bothering you? Because I've been getting the vibe I have eyes on me. I thought maybe it was only a nosey neighbor. But you appear unsettled."

For some reason, I feel like I can confide in him. Like I know him already. "You shouldn't take me to dinner because I think my ex has been watching. It's nice of you to want to thank me for Beast, but I don't need it. He was no trouble," I confess instinctively.

I move toward the door to end the conversation and get out of sight. I don't want to linger on the porch with Arran, fearful that whoever is watching might get angrier. Knowing that if it is Rob, he will just get crazier.

Arran moves with me—not blocking, but not letting me just dismiss him, either. He drops his voice low. "Are you in danger with your ex?"

How much do I tell a stranger? And does this random hot guy really care about my problems? "I appreciate the concern, but—"

"Call me if he shows up." He grimaces. "I'm guessing the cops don't do much to deter him if he's still bothering you?"

"Not really. But I'm not going to drag you into the middle of it."

He presses closer again. Not invading my space, but damn near. "It's what I do. I'm a personal bodyguard... mostly on-call."

"Oh." I wave my hand toward his huge, muscular shoulders and arms. "That explains all this."

Preening, he flexes ever so slightly. Guys are so cute when they get a compliment.

Not giving up, he asks, "Maybe you can meet me at the bar tonight at seven? We can casually run into each other. We could sit at the bar so it doesn't look like a date?"

"Do *you* think it's a date?" I ask, my eyes wide. "I thought it was a thank you."

"It's a '*thank you slash I want to get to know you better*' date?"

I never thought I would feel this drawn to someone. But maybe it's a sign from the Universe that I'm meant to go out and have a bite with this guy. What are the odds that I would see him at the bar *and* his dog would follow me home? Also, that I would dream up his name?

"Fine." I grin. "It's entirely conceivable that I might drop into the bar for a drink tonight."

His handsome face lights up with a smile. It does things to me. Specifically, my nether regions.

"Then I look forward to *maybe* running into you." Looking victorious, he skips away down the street in the bar's direction.

As I put my groceries away properly, I'm in a daze.

How is it that I'm going on a second date this week? I usually don't leave the house that often.

Finally, I get to sniff my underarm. Nope. Same smell. No magical pheromones. I check my reflection in the chrome toaster. No, as per usual, I'm the same warmed-over mess.

I could write off Maxum's interest that he was paranoid about me watching him and wanted to prove a point.

But Arran? It didn't seem like the case. I sure hope that isn't what this is.

Now that I've been around a couple of attractive guys, my crotch engine is idling hot, waiting for a spin around the block.

15

WITCHES GONE WILD

ARRAN

"What in all things unholy are you thinking?" Maxum growls.

The entire bar goes silent with Maxum's commanding energy. When I laugh it off, everyone relaxes and returns to their drinks. I need this dickhead demon to take the hint and take a hike.

I hiss my answer. "I need to get closer to her."

"Osen told you to back off," he says, using my own report against me. I knew I shouldn't have told the guys about that. They always blindly followed Osen's orders. I sometimes did, but I knew he was fallible. I'm fairly certain his stubbornness and obsessive need to fight the Witch Council is what got him killed. He had tunnel-vision when it came to them, and they likely used it against him.

"Osen's dead." I lower my voice. "And if I can still talk to him, then maybe we can work this out. He was getting stronger. Maybe he'll eventually remember something."

"So, you are going to use this woman to get close to him?" Maxum huffs and pounds his whiskey. Not that the human-made stuff could affect him. "That's fucked up. I know we hate witches, but *if* she is as innocent as you believe, then that's not cool."

"It's not like that," I grumble. I don't want to admit that I want to get into her bed for a whole other reason. That I'm falling for her.

"So it's *not* like you are going to fuck around with her, risking your beast killing her, then wait until she falls asleep, and talk to your former lover? I swear I thought I was the most fucked up one of us during our date." He scoffs and rubs his face. "Not even close."

I grip my glass so tightly I'm dangerously close to shattering it in my grip. "I want her. Okay?" I confess. "Even if Osen never comes back, I want to be with her. But if he does return, I can help her understand what's going on. Maybe if I got him to work with her instead of fighting her, he could think clearly. Besides, I think Osen's power is messing with her—draining her. And there is something else..."

Maxum perks up when he hears my hesitation. "What's that?"

"Her ex sounds like a jerk."

"Has your wolf claimed her as part of his pack?" He raises an eyebrow.

With a heavy sigh, I lean back in the booth and check the clock. I have five minutes until my witch is supposed to show up for our non-date date. "No, my wolf hasn't technically claimed her... yet." I glower at him. "You don't have to control every aspect of my life. Can you just fuck off and let me be for once?"

"Well, I *could* just chain you up and fuck your ass." He leans close. "Make you forget her pretty face."

My cock responds despite my frustration. "Wait. You are attracted to her too. That's why you want me to back off!" I glare at him. "You know, we could both pursue her. If her books are any indication, she might be up for a three-way, four-way... I don't even know how many ways. One book she wrote had six guys for only one woman. Some guy-on-guy stuff, too. So she's probably cool with that... as long as we are open with her."

"Just because she—*allegedly*—writes that doesn't mean she wants us all sticking our dicks in all her holes, filling her up with our cum."

The vision of that very scenario gives us both pause. Our eyes glaze over with lust at the image of the four of us and her.

As we abruptly shake our heads to bring us back to reality, Jade clears her throat and walks up to the table.

Did she hear Maxum's comment?

My face turns red. Almost as bright as the demon in his natural state.

She icily stares at Maxum for a long beat. It impresses me that she can handle the intensity of his gaze. Even after all these years, I can barely do that.

Then she dismisses him with an eye roll and says to me, "I think I'm going to pass on accidentally meeting up now or in the future. Good luck with Beast."

I scramble to stand up and stop her, but she has already spun on her heel and is walking toward the door. "Wait!" I rush after her. "Maxum was just leaving."

Jade gives a cold, calculated glower that travels up and down my body, as if inspecting my worth. Goddess, I hope my erection isn't too obvious. With the combination of imagining her taking all of us, Maxum's dirty mouth, and what I know he can do with it, I'm impossibly hard. I'm quickly deflating as I see my chances of tasting Jade's lips dwindling with every beat of my pounding heart.

Jade crosses her arms and glares at the huge demon, daring him to fuck with her. I'll give her props for sheer boldness. Not many would dare to do this, whether they know his true form or not. He's intimidating no matter what.

Maxum stands up slowly and locks eyes with our witch the entire time he walks past her.

Jade doesn't even blink.

Damn, when it comes down to it, she's a fucking badass. It's making me hard again.

When Maxum finally turns away and heads to the door, Jade looks at me with a cocked eyebrow.

Over her head, I see Maxum nodding his head in approval. He likes someone who isn't easily quelled.

She would fit in nicely with our group. If she doesn't run screaming for the hills when she discovers what we are, that is.

I hate that this dive bar is our first official date, but I wanted to pick a place where she felt comfortable.

"Sorry about him. He doesn't mean to be an ass," I say.

"Oh, so it just comes naturally to him, does it?" She grins as she slips into the booth where she had watched us that first night. Her eyes widen when she feels the heat of the seat Maxum left behind. He runs even hotter than I do... usually.

"I'd say a bit of nature *and* nurture." I flag down our server with a quick wave so we can get Jade settled with a drink. "Not that I'm defending his dickishness, but he's not always quite this paranoid."

Thankfully, the server comes up to interrupt our conversation, so Jade can't ask more about his paranoia and why he is especially touchy lately.

"Hey Jade, what can I get you tonight?" The server's eyes are alight with mirth.

"Paloma," she orders.

"You want another whiskey?" the lady asks, eyeing my empty glass.

"Yeah, since my friend drank mine." I chuckle. Maxum is such a dick.

The server hurries off after a little wink at Jade that I pretend not to notice.

"So, how's Beast?" she asks. "Did he turn up?"

"Hmm?" I take a beat before I remember her name for my wolf. "Oh, yeah. He was right where he was supposed to be!" I shake my head with a grin like he's a scamp. And right now? I fucking feel like one.

"Oh, good. I was worried about him today. Missed him too." She frowns, picking at her nails.

"I hope you don't mind shared custody, because he's likely to come knocking at your door at some point again."

Jade chuckles at that. "As long as he doesn't break into the house if I don't answer the door."

I can't promise her we won't do that.

When our drinks arrive, she raises her glass and looks me in the eye when we clink glasses together.

"To new connections," I toast.

She echoes me with a wry grin and peruses my defined, broad chest. "So, a bodyguard, huh? I might have to quiz you on that so I can write a bodyguard trope."

"Is that a romance thing?" I rub my face in embarrassment. "Uh, I guess it makes sense. Feeling safe and protected is something people want and need." I laugh. "Too bad it isn't as sexy as in your books."

Her face flashes with surprise. Whoops. I hope she doesn't quiz me about romance books. I only know how steamy her stuff gets because I peeked. And wow, she described things that made me blush.

"Well, that's the job of the author, isn't it?" She rubs the condensation off her cold glass. "We must take a mundane relationship or situation and heighten it until it's extraordinary. Life is messy. It's not like passionate romances with happy little bows at the end happen all the time. Most of us don't get scorching sexual tension that winds up being amazing, earth-shattering sex with synchronized orgasms with a perfect partner that completes us, heals our emotional wounds, and makes us better people."

I study her for a moment. "You're not wrong. But you're not completely correct either."

She laughs heartily at that. "Oh, boy, I know what you're going to say."

"Do you?" I lean forward, drawing her in with my intense gaze. She unconsciously leans toward me. "Tell me then," I dare her.

"You were going to say something like passion and romance happen all the time, and it's not that bleak." She lifts her glass, points with her index finger, and waves it at me, as if it gives weight to her argument. "But I'm sure you get all kinds of whirlwind hookups and torrid nights of passion. Except, not all of us have the supermodel thing going on. Or are we extroverted enough to go out and stumble upon someone who wants to be with us. Some of us are introverts. And we don't go outside where all the people are."

I nod my appreciation for her compliment. "Thank you for the vote of confidence concerning my sexual prowess, but I'm not getting laid every time I walk out the door—"

She interrupts, "Just every *other* time."

Laughing at her playfulness, I explain, "I was going to say… we can *easily* find romance in books, but that doesn't mean we can't have the same passion in our lives. Or true love. And yeah, sometimes love is messy. But when you find someone to connect with on a soul level, it's…"

Jade sets her drink down, waiting for me to finish my thought, but I can't. It's too much to think about Osen being gone. Or about my other loves who hurt me. I don't want to think about how she'll react when she discovers my lies, my secrets.

"You've lost someone?" she asks softly.

"Yeah, but enough of that. I'd rather talk about you." I try to change the subject. "On that note of the past, I wanted to ask if you're okay. Is your ex still harassing you?"

"It was just a one-sentence email." She waves me off, and I watch her energy tighten and shrink.

"Don't dismiss your feelings," I encourage her to arm herself with her natural Goddess-given gifts. "Your instincts and intuition are there for a reason. My instincts tell me that you are more worried than you are letting on."

"I've been getting this vibe lately that I'm being watched. All the time," she confesses, glancing over her shoulder. "Rob must have seen me walking with Maxum, because he said: 'You should be more careful who you go on dates with.'"

I sit up and go on alert. His language might suggest that he knows exactly who and what Maxum is. "Anything else?"

"No. He's always cryptic in his threats, so I can't use it against him with the cops or the courts."

"Is he a physical threat as well?" I dare to ask… on a fucking date. So much for fun banter.

Jade bites her lip, and it's all the confirmation I need. He's hurt her in the past, and he will die. I'll make sure of it. That will solve the stalker problem.

"Rob was more connected than I realized. So no matter what my complaints or reports I try to file, they all seem to be ignored or disappear into thin air." Jade rubs her temples like a headache is coming on. "I wish I never fell for his nice guy act."

He sounds like someone who can put a spell on the authorities. My best guess is he's a warlock. But the guys and I will find out for sure. It behooves us to follow him as a lead, since he might be our enemy. Besides, if I know what he is and how to end him permanently, it will be easier for me to remove him from the realms.

"Would you give me his full name so my security buddies can run a background check? I don't like leaving this alone."

"Just a background check. I don't want you entangled with this." I nod, and she acquiesces, "Robert Holden. He's forty-one. Lives in the city." She waves her hands in a stop motion. "Okay, enough about him. I never go out, so I'd like to enjoy the little time we have left together."

"That statement sounds ominous. Are you about to whack me?"

"Whack you?" She blushes. "Do you mean to smack, jerk off, or kill?"

I smirk, running both my hands through my short dark hair. I enjoy her playfulness. There's been so little in my life in the last decade I have enjoyed. She is the sunlight after a never-ending storm. Sadly, Osen was often part of the storm.

I lace my fingers behind my neck, flexing my arms a bit to highlight my musculature.

Her eyes dilate, and her breath quickens.

My cock hardens, knowing I am tantalizing my witch. "What would you *like* to do to me?"

She eyes me seriously for a moment. "Can we circle back around to that after the evening is done?"

"Fair enough." I chuckle, drop my arms back to the table, and take another sip of my whiskey. "How long have you been writing?"

"Since I was a kid. But I've been an indie author for about ten years now."

"Does indie mean you publish your own stuff?"

"Yeah. It also means I'm responsible for everything: from book covers to editors to constantly promoting. It's a list so long you don't want to hear it. And if the books don't sell or people pirate our books, we eat all the costs of production and ads. On top of that, we can get our books banned on the online bookstore gods, if someone steals them and puts them up on pirate sites. I've been lucky to eke out a semi-comfortable living. But it's always a hustle. I work twelve-hours a day, every day."

I know that's true. I've seen her spinning all her metaphorical plates. She doesn't have time to be a spy.

"Sounds like you could do with some relaxation." I waggle my eyebrows playfully.

Jade chuckles.

I ask, "It sounds like a lot, so why do you do it?"

"Because I love creating new worlds, new characters, and I love getting lost in my own stories. And when a reader connects with my work, it's the best feeling. It sounds silly, but reading is true magic. When someone reads a book, they join me in my world. I tell them there's a handsome man with a cocky grin sitting across from me, and they are there with me. They get to fill in everything else about you. In a way, the reader and I can become co-creators in that world. And then the characters really take on a life of their own. They become real. In a way."

"It does sound magical." I find her choice of words interesting. "The way you explain it, the mundane can transform into a mystical experience."

When she sees I understand her, Jade's smile lights up the room.

We talk for hours about life, her writing, and how she has a habit of rescuing strays.

It feels like she's rescued me. Is that what we are searching for? Someone who will truly see us and take us in—into their hearts—and accept all the broken pieces.

When we finally walk out to the parking lot to our cars, she is practically dragging her feet, like she doesn't want the night to end.

"Would I be able to buy one of your books to read?" I ask.

Or maybe I should have asked to borrow one, so I have a reason to come back.

"Uh, yeah." She unlocks her Mustang's door, and I have to admit I'm a bit jealous. My old 1980s Toyota pickup is no muscle car.

"I suppose you could follow me to my place, and I can give you one," she suggests.

"Perfect!" I say with a bit too much enthusiasm. I jump in my car and follow her on the short way home.

She rushes inside and meets me back at the front door by the time I get up to the porch. She has two books in her hands. "One is steamy. The other is very steamy. Which would you like?"

I lean against her door frame, moving in close so that our bodies are brushing, and I pretend as if I'm studying the covers. But I'm watching her.

With my proximity, her skin flushes with arousal. Her heart rate increases.

She's gripping the books as if they are ropes, and she's dangling off a cliff. I can scent that I turn her on.

I have to say I feel the same way, but I don't have something to hold on to… yet.

"What would *you* like me to read?" I ask suggestively.

She finally turns to look up at me. We are so close that I only have to drop my head just a few inches to kiss her.

She glances at my lips and then back to gaze into my eyes.

I wonder if they are glowing. I feel like my whole body is glowing.

This is the moment where everything can change… the moment of possibility. Or the moment she destroys my hopes.

"May I ask you something?" When I nod, she presses her lips together briefly. "Why does it seem like you're hitting on me?"

"Because I am," I answer simply, but tilt my head in confusion. "I know I'm rusty, but I thought my flirting skills would be sufficient enough for a romance author to do something with."

"So, is this part of your thank you for taking care of your dog?" she asks with a smirk.

"No. I like you… a lot. You're beautiful. Smart. Kind. Sexy." I lift my hand to cradle her cheek. "If you need a reminder of all you have to offer, then I'll make it my mission for the foreseeable future."

She gulps at the word *future*. My witch thinks this is just a fling for me.

"I don't have casual one-night stands," I say. "So if you like me too, and you want to take this slow, I'm good with that."

Jade drops her books to the ground with a thud. She grabs the back of my head and pulls me in for a passionate kiss that makes my dick inflate instantly. Damn, her alpha assertiveness is making my wolf perk up and howl.

My introverted witch continues her boldness, grabbing the front of my shirt and pulling me inside.

I kick the door shut and flip the lock, but I don't dare break our kiss while I do.

Her tongue tangles with mine. She wraps her hands around my waist, then slides them up my untucked shirt. Soft fingers caress my back as I guide her slowly to the couch. I don't presume I will get her into bed tonight.

Nor should I.

If I'm correct, she doesn't know about supernaturals, so she definitely doesn't think that dick knots are real.

I'm also afraid of my beast—my true beast. Not the one that Maxum jokingly called my wolf… no, the monster I now become when my emotions are riding too high, or when I'm in the throes of passion. All because of that evil witch from my past.

I'm honestly surprised I haven't shifted into my berserker with the weight of everything I've been feeling. Osen's death. Walking into a witch's house. Finding out she's my mate.

Is she my mate? Fuck, I think she is.

There's a light on in the hall from when she went to grab her books, but the living room isn't bright with ambient lighting. However, if I shifted into my monster, there would be no hiding it.

Do I risk taking this further than kissing?

I capture her head and waist as I settle her back onto the long couch. Placing one leg between her splayed thighs, I hover over her, caging her in.

Her hand skims down my muscled abdomen, and she hums with approval. Fingers slide along the edge of my waistband, testing me.

The beast inside wants to burst free and claim her.

My kisses become more frantic. Soon, I'm biting and sucking along her jawline. Jade's body undulates, grinding her sex over my thigh that is wedged between her legs.

Her fingernails claw up my back. Just that alone is enough to make me unravel.

I pull up her shirt and suck in a breath when I see her ample breasts heaving and ready to burst out from her pretty bra. I know this is the sexiest one she has. I've checked. I'm a perv.

My cock swells even more, knowing she wore the pretty item for me. Maybe she was not expecting this, but she wanted to feel sexy because she hoped this was a date and not just a thank you for the dog.

The dog… I almost growl that I can't tell her yet. That I can't fuck her as I want to.

I gently bite the soft flesh of her breast. My teeth are sharper with a barely contained shift.

She gasps, but arches her back to encourage me to continue with my play.

I pull down the edge of her bra to reveal her large but rock-hard nipples—perfect for sucking.

I run my tongue over each nipple, then blow gently over them.

Jade is biting her lip, watching me like *I* might be magic.

Staring into her hazel-green eyes, I suck on her tit harder and harder until she squeaks. With one hand, I massage the other breast, teasing and plucking the nipple.

Her heart is pounding, and I smell another wave of her arousal—blackberries and a hint of lilacs.

Maybe I *could* fuck her if I flip her over just before my beast is unleashed?

"I need to taste you," I rasp, kissing her sweet mouth again and hooking my fingers at her waistband. I wait for her consent. I watch for any hesitation, but I see none.

"You sure?" she asks, like this is some sort of task for me.

But her thumbs hook at her waistband, and she helps me pull down her pants as she lifts her hips.

"Babe, you don't think I want to taste your sweet slick and savor every drop of you?" I ask as I fling her pants away, grasping her ankles and throwing a leg over each shoulder.

"I, it's just Rob never wanted to, and he wasn't the only one..."

"Then you've been with all the wrong males," I growl. "And I don't think I want to hear about those imbeciles right now."

I leave a trail of kisses down her inner thigh, torturing myself by delaying our gratification.

"Good plan," Jade agrees, but doesn't open fully.

Assertively, I pin her legs open and gaze upon my prize. "Fuck, that's perfect. You're perfect." I lean in and swipe my tongue over her wet, soft flesh, and she whimpers.

"Fuck, that is... yes." She allows her legs to relax as I explore her folds, and then I suck on her clit. Her body arches, and she grabs her own tits, pulling on her nipples. Now that is a sight I never want to forget. "Yes, Arran. Please."

My fingers slide over her wetness.

She cants her hips to encourage me when I near her entrance.

I dip one, then two fingers inside her and delve in slowly, licking as I take her pussy. I work her with my hands and mouth. Exploring and discovering all the places that make her light up. I watch every twitch and gasp, every flutter of her cunt. I will make it my mission to learn every inch of her body. Even if all I can ever do is lick and touch, I will willingly sacrifice my own release to bring her pleasure.

I will exist only to worship her body.

She's on the edge of an orgasm that I keep working her toward. I rub the spot inside her that makes her tremble and palm one of her breasts with my other hand.

When I bite down on her clit, she bucks and cries out.

"Come for me," I command.

"Oh, god!" Her body flails, and she shakes.

I watch as her mouth opens, and she makes sweet groans and whines. I keep her climax going until she finally returns to the room.

Jade smiles at me with mischief glinting in her eyes.

"Come here," she calls me, clasping my head to bring me up to kiss her on the mouth.

I brush my slick-covered lips over hers and then delve my tongue into her mouth.

Her small hand cups the front of my pants. "Would he like to come out to play?" she asks.

Fuck. I have to be careful here. She wants to reciprocate, which I definitely want. But I can't with my monstrous self, and even if I didn't have that issue, I have a knot at the base of my cock. I know she thinks this is only some sort of mythological penis in her books, but it's very real.

She will freak out when she realizes supernatural beings are real. A blow job on a first date is no way to find out all that. I don't think we should have sex, because even if I agreed, I'd have to ask her to turn off the lights.

I don't want her to think it's because I don't want to see her luscious, naked body.

"I want to take this slow," I say instead.

"You just consumed my soul through my vagina. How is that slow?" she jokes, but I hear the concern.

"It brings me pleasure to give that to you. I didn't do it to get payback," I explain.

"I wasn't suggesting that you were. But I wouldn't mind sucking your cock or fucking your brains out."

I close my eyes to center myself so I don't jump her bones from her direct and sexy words.

"As much as I want to do both of those things, I promised myself that I wouldn't fuck on the first couple of dates with anyone. But I have something more intimate in mind, if you are okay with it. Can we do that here for a bit?"

"Uh?"

"I want to hold you." I feel the heat of a blush on my cheeks. "Snuggle."

She grins. "As long as you do it with your shirt off." She pulls a soft blanket from the back of the couch.

I stand and pull my shirt off. Jade's eyes drink me in, and she licks her lips. "You sure about that no-fucking rule?"

I chuckle. "Not really. But I need your shirt and bra off you, too."

She slips the shirt off, and I unfasten the bra and groan when her beautiful tits tumble free of their hold.

I slip my hands around her and pick her up easily, and she squeals with joy. I flop back down on my back with her on top of me.

"I haven't had anyone pick me up like that in a long time." She feels up my arms. "You did that with no effort," she says with awe. "You're strong."

I puff up with that compliment. Then I pull the throw blanket over us so she doesn't get cold. Not that she is likely to get chilly with my shifter body heat. We always run hotter than most.

Content, we both sigh together as if we had planned it.

I pray to the Goddess, let me have this. Give me one chance at happiness.

Let Jade forgive me for my secrets.

Please, let us move beyond our differences.

And if she accepts me, give me the strength to keep my beast at bay so I can bond with her how she deserves—with my complete mind, heart, and body.

16

POSSESSED

JADE

*P*lastered over Arran on the couch, I can feel by the enormous bulge in his pants that he enjoyed snacking on my pussy very much.

It's sweet that he wants to take things slow, but my author's mind is now imagining what terrible event happened in his past to make him want to take it slow.

Guys usually like to take it fast.

Hell, most people don't take things slow.

Unless someone has hurt them badly enough to make them cautious.

Speaking of which, I should be cautious and slow things down too. I know better than to fall so fast.

My pussy got away from me.

I breathe in Arran's cozy scent of lightning storms and sage. It reminds me of his dog, Beast, since he has the same earthy scent.

Arran hums happily as I run my hands up his sides. Under his silky skin, I feel muscles that flex with my touch.

My hand drifts up to his hair, and I tangle my fingers through his dark locks.

He moans and then sighs contentedly.

This is actually nice. I forgot how much I enjoyed snuggling. Rob wasn't much of a snuggler or one at all, really.

I still wonder why I was with him and for as long as I was. Objectively. Rob is handsome, but otherwise, he doesn't have many redeeming qualities—physically or emotionally... or at least none that I found particularly attractive.

Maybe I was just lonely enough to put up with his shit. I wouldn't be the first person in the world to stick around a jerk because I was more tired of being alone.

Arran's strong arms cinch around my body. He pulls me tightly against him as if he can sense the dark road my mind is traveling down, and he wishes to protect me from the memory of my ex.

I tuck my head under Arran's chin, and his naked flesh warms my skin. I feel more protected and cherished by this stranger than I have in my entire life.

I have no idea why.

Maybe it's the whole bodyguard vibes he gives off.

Could this be the beginning of something real? Could he really like me? Could I really want to be with someone again?

He's been funny, intelligent, and protective. He ticks all my boxes for a partner.

And some boxes he checks twice... such as his gorgeous physique, personality, and talented tongue.

He makes me feel good—not just attractive or desired, but in my heart, as though I'm at peace. I can't remember when a man elicited that feeling from me.

But am I someone he sees a future with?

It's not like younger guys don't date older women. I never expected it to happen to me, not when he looks like a cover model for a fitness magazine.

I suppose we will have to see.

Comforted in his embrace, inexplicably feeling safe, my mind drifts into sleep...

I'm embodying the mystery guy again, the jerk from the nights before.

This recurring situation is so odd. I rarely dream I'm the same person twice.

And never have my dreams been so visceral. It's as if I'm actually living these moments, not just the vague, ethereal quality of most dreams.

Maxum and Arran are beside my avatar. We are storming through a dense forest at night, searching for something… or *someone*?

My eyes catch a gleam of light-colored stone in the distance.

"There!" we all say in unison.

Our steps quicken, but my head swivels back and forth, constantly looking for a threat or a surprise attack.

When we get closer, I realize it's Arran's friend that was at the bar that first night. He's the giant, quiet man with sand-colored hair and light gray eyes.

Lying twisted on the ground, he's mostly on his side. He appears to be nearly undressed, but wearing pants and a strange-looking robe glued stiffly to his back. His eyes are closed, but he doesn't look to be sleeping. No, this is far too consuming to be sleeping. He appears frozen solid. But it doesn't feel cold out here.

My avatar's heart races, and even Maxum looks concerned when I glance up at his face.

The crimson-skinned, demon-like version of Maxum crouches down and sniffs his friend.

"This is a witch or warlock's magic. He's stuck in his stone form," Maxum informs us.

I curse and spin around, scanning our surroundings for our enemy.

"We should get him out of this realm," Arran says, pacing back and forth and pulling on his short, dark hair.

Both my avatar and I want to reach out and soothe him. My male voice says, "We can't move him like this. He weighs too much, even with all of us helping."

"Someone needs to stay behind and guard his body while he's under the spell," Maxum suggests.

"What if he doesn't come out of this curse? What if it's fucking permanent?" Arran growls.

"I haven't seen a witch or warlock powerful enough that they could cast a spell that could make a stone form permanent in several generations," Maxum says, shaking his head but still looking worried no matter his assessment. "I doubt this will last more than a day."

"But that's long enough for them to distract us while they murder our entire crew. Or what's left of it now," I say. "Maxum, can you sense Calder at all now that you are in this realm?"

"No. He's not on this plane." Maxum stands up and gazes into the distance. "I will search for him in the Underworld."

"No. That's too risky to do alone," I argue.

"And who would I take?" Maxum challenges. "They've already killed anyone who would survive on that plane."

"Fine. Just go." I wave him off. "You're right. But be safe."

"Nowhere is safe... or haven't you been paying attention," Maxum grumbles and then waves his hand, chanting a few words under his breath.

A portal opens, and, unafraid, he steps through to an even darker place.

The doorway snaps shut, and I turn back to Arran. "Are you going to be okay?"

"If you are asking about my beast? No. I don't think we're okay." Arran palms his face with both hands and then rubs his eyes. "I'm on the verge of losing it. He wants to go on a wild, indiscriminate rampage. You may have to kill me."

What the fucking hell? Please don't make me watch Arran get hurt...

Feeling my shock and fear, my male avatar becomes aware that I'm dreaming with him again.

"Witch?" he asks in my mind.

This feels like something different from an ordinary dream. This doesn't feel like my dream. Or even a dream, really.

The scene fades until I'm only in complete darkness.

I would almost believe my avatar was a spirit possessing my mind and body.

"What's going on?" I ask, because now I fear that might be exactly what is happening.

"How are you able to channel my memories?" he asks, as if I had any answers to this craziness.

"This actually happened to you?" I ask. "But... it can't be. There's no such thing as realms, portals, and warlocks that can cast people into stone."

"Are you really that ignorant?"

"Are you really this much of an asshole?" I ask.

"Yes." He chuckles at his own answer.

"Well, thank you for being honest. And for my part, I don't know why I'm dreaming I'm you. Or what the hell is going on. I wish it would stop."

He hums to himself as if he's finally taking my word for it.

I feel pressure gathering around my mind.

"You don't seem to be lying. But you might also have been trained to compartmentalize your thoughts."

"I doubt my mind power skills are to the level you are estimating. I'm barely able to remember what I was supposed to be doing after I leave a room. But I appreciate the vote of confidence," I sass.

The pressure around my mind lessens, and I'm starting to believe that something paranormal is really happening in my life.

"I don't know if I can stop you or your people from hurting mine, but just know if I believe you will hurt them, I will do everything in my power to stop you."

"If I'm going to hurt someone unprovoked, then I don't blame you. But if you are talking about the guys from the bar… I like Arran. A lot. Maxum was a bit of a jerk, but I'm not planning on talking to him anymore. And I have nothing against the other two. But if they attack me, I will defend myself. Not that I'm likely to win, since they are all huge guys."

"Guys?" he chuckles again. *"They are more than mere men."*

"So they *actually* are demons, shifters, and gargoyles?" I laugh.

"You really don't know you have witch blood?" he asks, disbelief ringing in his voice.

"My grandmother claimed I was a witch like her. But my mother told me to ignore it. Said that she was crazy and dangerous. So I never took the claim to heart."

"So, you have no powers other than the channeling of spirits?" he asks.

"If that's what I'm doing right now, then I didn't even know I could do that. I half believed I could dream other people's dreams, but that's a far cry from being a medium."

"You have dream magic?" he asks with renewed interest. *"Fascinating."*

"If you really are a ghost, and you need me to get a message to someone, I could help." I say the next part primarily to myself, "If I had a validated fact, it would prove that this isn't just a dream."

"Unfortunately, I don't feel I can trust you not to betray me."

"Okay. Then how can I win your trust? For that matter, how can I trust someone who is supposedly invading my body and mind?"

"We can't trust each other. You are my enemy. Your kind hates my kind. We don't get to be friends," he answers, and I feel him fading from my consciousness. *"Actions always speak louder than empty promises. And all your kind has ever handed out is lies."*

I can't disagree with him about actions speaking louder than words.

I open my eyes and see the morning light filtering through the cracks of my closed blackout curtains.

And I've literally drooled on Arran's spectacular chest.

It's a chest that should be bronzed for posterity. Okay, ouch. Maybe not actually bronzed, but take a mold casting of it and make thousands of replicas. It should then be placed on display for others to drool over. But jealousy pinches my heart at the thought. I don't want to share.

Shockingly, this Adonis is still snuggled up with me.

Man, does he run hot. He's like a furnace. And where our bodies are pressed against each other, I've also sweated and now have moisture-stuck myself to Arran skin to skin.

I feel like wet velcro as I carefully pull away from him.

But he catches me as I try to lift myself off and presses us back together again. He gives me a sweet kiss on my forehead.

Finding that stupidly cute, I return his kiss under his chin.

"Where were you sneaking off to?" he asks playfully.

"Pee. Coffee. Clothes. Fur babies. Work," I list off.

"Would you like food?" he asks.

"It will probably be on the agenda at some point today."

His hand slides down my side to palm my hip. "How about you take care of your bodily functions and fur babies, and I can make you some coffee and breakfast?"

"Don't you have to go?" It sounds harsh, but I don't mean it like that.

I'm just a busy person, and I assume others have a full day too. Besides, I'm not used to the attention. Rob never wanted to hang out and make my meals. Often, I felt like an irritating obligation. As if he was forced to put in the minimum required time to get his pension package.

"I have the day off, but if you want me to go—" he says with a tint of sadness.

"You can stay… But I thought maybe you'd want to do the walk of pity this morning."

"I thought it was the walk of shame?"

"Well, you have nothing to be ashamed of. Your performance last night was five stars. It's a *pity* since I didn't get to return the favor."

He pulls me back by the shoulder and looks me in the eye. His brow crinkles. "It wasn't a *favor*. I thought it was more than that."

I get this guy is more sensitive than most. But he acts like I've known him for days, and we have a developed relationship beyond our date last night and some fantastic cunnilingus.

Normally, I would take this as a red flag, but I feel our connection, too.

Is this the comfortable feeling people talk about when they say they found their person? And dare I say it and jinx myself… my true love?

"Okay. Sounds good. Coffee and breakfast. Stat!" I say with a grin and snag my throw blanket and wrap it around me as I race off to the bathroom.

I pee and splash my face with water to wash off my sleep drool.

Why does Arran have to be so sexy and sweet? With my track record, I'm nervous that I'm going to be broadsided by some horrible, dark secret.

I remember my crazy dream last night. And I wonder if it really is only a dream. Or is it a warning he might be a raging maniac underneath a kind facade? Or am I just trying to talk myself out of falling for him? Am I just damaged from all the jerks in my life—including family and boyfriends?

I pick up my phone and open my messenger app for my small author chat group. I update them quickly about my situation.

Me: "He was eating my taco like it was his interview for his dream job."

Mere: Proof of dick?

They want pics. Not really. Well, I *hope* she doesn't want me to send pics of my boyfriend's dick. Boyfriend? Can I call him that? Are we dating now?

Does Mere want a ransom's style 'proof of life' picture with a dick next to a newspaper with the date showing to prove this is a current penis situation?

Me: Do you mean a picture to prove my hunky boyfriend is real? Not his actual dick, right?

Nanette: These things are not mutually exclusive.

Bekka: Send us whatever you got.

I laugh and close the app when I smell coffee brewing. I walk out to see a shirtless Arran scrambling some eggs. My heart pounds in my clit. Nobody has ever made me breakfast before, and definitely not looking as good as he does.

Can I keep him as my human hostage?

Do I have it in me to be a sugar mama? I'd need to write a few more books a year, and then I should be able to afford to pay for his membership to whatever magic gym he goes to.

Arran turns around and gives me a brilliant smile that instantly makes my clit, I mean, my heart pound too hard. He might be the death of me.

But damn, I could get used to this. Forget fucking. If he does the dishes, I think I might spontaneously orgasm.

He returns his focus to his cooking as I walk over to him. I spot scars barely visible on his back. They look more like scratches. For a second, I worry I scratched him that hard. But no, when I get closer, I see they are old, faint lines. It appears as if he were sliced several times with a knife. Did one of his bodyguard jobs get ugly? Was he tortured?

Ignorant of my wild ride down imagination lane, he says, "I hope an omelet is okay."

"Perfect." I get out two mugs from the cabinet and set them down to fill them up. "Do you take anything in yours?"

"No coffee for me, thanks." He smiles and grates some cheese for the omelet.

"All for me?" I nod approvingly.

But I'll switch to my 'writing' tea for the rest of the day. It's time to channel all this craziness into my book.

17

WALK OF PITY

ARRAN

$\mathcal{I}$ cannot believe I was able to lick her pretty cunt and keep my beast at bay. Jade is a miracle. What if she is the cure for my curse that I've been looking for?

But I'm worried I will press my luck if I go any further with our explorations. I can't test my theory that she might help me control my monstrous curse.

Not yet.

Not until she understands what she is.

What I am.

I've been awake all this morning, basking in the bliss of having her naked flesh on mine.

I worry she had another unpleasant dream—if her grunts and whines were any indications. But just as I was ready to wake her or dare to call Osen's name, she settled in my arms.

I wonder if his soul still lingers around her, or if he has passed on through the veil.

Yet, I'm no longer here for Osen.

I want her. I want to protect her. My wolf wants to claim her.

He likes the ear scratches and tells me he wants to be around her again.

It's difficult explaining to your animal self that it's not as simple as all that.

I tell him soon, but I worry I shouldn't show my wolf until I confess my sins. I spied on her and pretended to be a dog to discover her secrets. She might not forgive me.

As she wakes, her cheeks turn pink when she realizes she's drooled on me. Beast loves it. Honestly, we both find it charming.

After convincing her to let me stay to make breakfast, she rushes off to freshen up. I hear her giggling before she comes out. Probably texting her friends about me.

I'm half-tempted to spy again and see what she says about my performance last night. From her facial expressions and body's reaction, I seem to have got the physical part right.

But does she see me as someone she might want for more than a few nights of fun? I felt her distancing herself already.

And last night, she appeared baffled that I would want to snuggle rather than get my dick sucked.

It would have baffled me as well, if I had been just a regular guy. However, I'm not a regular guy. I have a beast inside me. Besides, I secretly lived a dog's life in her house for the last couple of days. I can't take this too far without confessing what I am and what I've done. But first, I want her to get to know the person behind the supernatural curse and all my deceptions.

I start some coffee in her stovetop percolator. I love that she has an old-school coffee maker. Opening the fridge, I find there's enough ingredients to make an omelet, barely—dangerously close to expired eggs and a chunk of cheese.

This woman really needs someone to grocery shop for her. She can strategize an entire series plot line, but not what to eat for the next three days. There are tortillas with nothing to put inside them. Not much in vegetables, except for the stuff she purchases for her pets. Her frozen dinners are all she has for full meals. However, she's fully stocked with ice cream... and chips.

I realize she probably eats out regularly.

My alpha instinct to protect and care for my pack extends to making sure she has whatever she needs. And right now, she needs good food. Not that I think she needs me to help her, but she needs *someone* to help her. I want it to be me.

When she emerges from her bedroom, she wears a loose t-shirt and leggings. Both look soft, and I fight the urge to find out if they are.

I don't want her to think I'm clingy. She already accused Beast of that. I'm guessing she isn't used to a lot of physical attention... even when she has a significant other.

She's surprised I don't want coffee, but shifters can't usually stomach it. Not that I'm telling her that reason. She'll assume I'm a health nut, which isn't completely wrong.

"I'll be a few more minutes with the omelet if you want to check on your pets."

Jade raises her eyebrows and remembers telling me about her fur babies. "Good idea," she saunters off, sipping her coffee.

When she returns, we have a nice, simple breakfast filled with talking about her animal hostages, as she likes to call them. I laugh like it's the first time I've heard this joke. And I admit, it's funny now that I know she isn't *really* keeping abducted shifters.

"What are you doing today?" I ask.

"Uh, I've been goofing off too much lately, so I need to get my word count in."

"Is that your not-so-subtle hint for me to get lost?"

She finishes her omelet and clears her throat. Nothing good ever comes from a throat clearing when relationship topics are in play. "Look, I really enjoyed last night, but you said we should take this slow."

"Physically… sexually," I correct.

"Well, I suppose I need to take it slow *emotionally*." She looks me in the eye and waves her hands in my direction. "You seem serious about wanting to date me, which is lovely."

"*Lovely?*" I laugh without humor.

"I'm guessing I'm close to a decade older than you."

"How old are you?" I know this, but she doesn't know I do.

"Forty," she says with defiance, crossing her arms.

"I'm older than you," I tell her.

Her mouth drops open. She won't believe me. I know I don't look my age. Most supernaturals and many witches don't look their ages.

She gives me a distrustful glare and says, "That can't be. You don't look over thirty."

I grin and shrug. "It's true."

"Well, you look like a player—at whatever age you really are."

"Like I said before, I don't have flings." This is turning sour fast. She can't understand why I like her? She just has to look in the mirror. And her personality? I fucking love all her quirkiness. I frown and sigh. "Look… if you don't like me, then just say that. Don't make excuses. Tell me if you aren't interested in me. But please, don't assume I'm a player. I don't make a habit of what happened between us last night. I can't remember when someone has captivated me the way you do."

It's true. Not even Osen grabbed my attention as she did.

"You are very attractive, and… I like you… a lot. Probably too much." Jade rests her elbows on the table. She gives me a sad expression of grief and weariness. "I barely got out of a terrible relationship alive because I let him get too close too fast. I'm not even sure why I allowed it to happen."

"With Rob?" I ask.

"Yeah." She studies her fingers, unwilling to look at me while she shatters my dreams. "So even though I'm actually very attracted to *you*, I don't want to fall into another situation. I thought I was into him, but it quickly felt like he had tricked me. I'm not accusing you of that, but…"

This Rob person concerns me even more now. "You make it sound like you weren't very attracted to Rob."

"I wasn't… His looks, personality, and energy were all wrong for me." She shrugs. "I'm not sure *why* I was with him. Even the sex was bland and pointless."

I barely fight back a growl. I don't want to imagine Jade fucking that male.

Instead, I turn the growl into a hum, considering what she confessed. Rob is sounding more and more like a warlock.

"And it appears he's stalking me. I'm sorry, but it wasn't smart of me to let you stay last night. Or even hang out at the bar. You might have been dragged into my drama already."

"I'm not being dragged. I walked into this with you willingly. And if something happens, I want to be there to help you."

She hears the sincerity in my voice and clasps my hand as I offer it to her over the table. "I appreciate everything you are doing. You're being amazing, but I still need this to go slow. I can't make the same mistake. I hope you understand that."

"Understood." I grin. "So, in the spirit of open communication, I would like to know exactly how slow. When would you like to go out again?"

"Give me a couple of days?" Jade offers, "How about Saturday?"

Reluctantly, I leave Jade to her writing. I plan to meet with the guys at our safe house, which is a few miles from Jade's. She lives on the border of the supernatural side of town, not that she realizes it.

Between all our magical wardings, the safe house is reasonably secure. We don't have much here, as we set this up for emergency use only. But we have a safe place to rest our heads.

I don't go directly to our hideout, since I worry that whoever is watching her could also be following me. I must drive all over town until I'm certain I haven't been tailed.

Pulling up to the single-story large ranch-style house, I appreciate how non-assuming it appears. From the outside, you wouldn't expect some of the deadliest supes reside here. The trimmed yard is basic and unremarkable. The house gives off grandmotherly vibes from the curb.

But inside, it's sparsely decorated and filled with weapons. Maxum invested in the basic furnishing of comfy couches and recliners. All five bedrooms have king-sized beds because we're all big guys, and in the past, we sometimes slept together.

If I hadn't been over at Jade's the last few days, I might have risked bringing more stuff from my house. But as it is, all I have is not much more than what was in my go-bag when Osen died.

When I walk in the wide door, all three guys give me a disappointed look.

"What?" I snap.

Surprisingly, it's Flint, the taciturn gargoyle who lectures me. "What are you doing with her? Your actions are dangerous, no matter how you look at this situation."

"Dangerous for who?" I growl.

"For both of you," he says, his tone even. "You know what your curse can do."

"Jade is in real danger, but not from me," I tell him.

"What do you mean?" Maxum's voice is tight and strained. He doesn't want to admit it, but he's soft for our sweet witch.

"Her ex is a threat. I'm starting to believe that Rob might be a warlock."

Calder throws his arms up in the air in exasperation. "Is she that dumb? How can she really be that ignorant of the supernatural world if she was fucking a warlock?"

I snarl again at the idea of that male's hands on her.

After a deep breath, I suggest, "Maybe he was able to hide it from her just as we can?"

"But why?" Calder prods. "It makes no sense for a warlock to hide his nature, to be with a weak witch. Witches outnumber their male counterparts. He would have his pick. So either your witch is more powerful than you can perceive, or this wanker is nothing but a normal, everyday human dickhead."

Maxum adds, "They're a dime a dozen."

I've been wondering what Rob's angle was in all this. "Perhaps he used her for her mediumship skills? Or maybe she had more magic before he came into her life? We know some supes are able to drain magical beings of their magic."

"Has he threatened her?" Maxum asks.

"Yeah, sort of. Rob sent Jade a message 'to be careful who she dated'… after her date with you. Which means he was somehow watching. It also indicates to me he might have recognized who or what you are."

"That doesn't mean we have to get involved," Calder huffs.

I notice the gargoyle is quiet. He's a protector by nature, so he won't like it if she's in danger. If I can just get him on my side…

"So what the hell are you suggesting, lil' doggie?" Maxum asks and crosses his arms, his classic demon move, closing me off before I can get out my idea.

"That we monitor her… like I've been doing."

"You mean fucking her?" Maxum raises an eyebrow. "You know I can smell her scent all over you."

"I didn't fuck her," I snarl.

"Yeah, I know." Maxum grunts. "Because if you did, I'd smell her blood from you ripping her to shreds, since you can't control your curse."

The guys know what could happen if I have sex.

"If you're going to kill her with your out-of-control dick, can we just get it over with?" Calder groans. "We have bigger fish to catch. We don't have the resources for you to do your pet play kink."

I growl at him.

The fucking phoenix shouldn't be poking me right now. I'm riding the edge with all this talk about me walking away from Jade.

"Does she put a collar on you, then tell you to be a good boy and lick her cunt?" he jabs again.

Maxum laughs and says to Calder, "You're just jealous, little bird."

He's probably not wrong. Calder hasn't been able to be with someone in this incarnation. His last death really fucked him up. Before that? He was a bit of a player.

"Can we just check this guy Rob out to see if he's got magic?" I hand Maxum the paper where I jotted down the information and the half-destroyed picture of Rob I pulled out of Jade's trash. "If he's a warlock, maybe you get to kill him for funsies."

Maxum gives me a wry grin. "And take out your competition for you?" he jokes.

"And your competition," I say to rile him up.

Maxum doesn't want to want her, but I'm not as oblivious as Flint usually is.

That poor gargoyle doesn't seem to understand romance or sex at all.

But he knows loss.

We all do.

Maxum grumbles. "So what? She has a feisty attitude, a fuckable ass, and a fascinating brain I don't want to scramble. That doesn't mean I'm interested in going steady."

I shake my head at his deflection. "I don't think people know what the phrase 'going steady' means anymore."

"It's not my fault the world moves too fast," Maxum mutters and glances at the paper with Rob's details. "I'll investigate this turkey because it makes sense to do that—for us." He becomes serious and stares into my eyes. It's not something he usually does because of my inner monster. "Prepare yourself. She might not be as innocent as she appears."

"I will not let my guard down," I promise.

That's a damn lie.

I've already done that.

18

BACKGROUND CHECK

MAXUM

I have very few mortal human contacts. There are the rare non-supes who are not complete and utter nitwits.

I collect the good ones as if they are golden tickets to a chocolate factory.

Chocolate and brain scrambling are my small pleasures in life—my weaknesses. Deal with it.

After hundreds of years in the realms, I've realized decent and dependable people are like unicorns… so hard to find that they might as well be only a myth.

Almost everyone I've known—supes, witches, creatures, or norms—has betrayed me at some point. It's a surprise when I haven't been ratted out or used. That's why my ragtag group is so precious to me. They might be a pain in my ass, but over and over, they have proven, even through torture, that they are loyal.

That's why I have to discover who killed Osen. I owe him that. It's why I'm allowing Arran free rein to have his *puppy* love, just in the off chance something becomes of Osen's channeling through the witch.

Besides, this Rob sounds like a menace. Warlocks are often a menace.

So, maybe I will get to scramble some magical brains after all if he turns out to be a threat to us… or Jade.

Knocking on the door to what appears to be an abandoned warehouse, I wait impatiently for the humans to answer.

A scrappy-looking young female flings the door open and cocks her hip. Mal currently has blonde hair streaked with a variety of bright colors, making it look like a unicorn farted a rainbow on her head.

She crosses her arms and gives me a perturbed glare. Her big ovary energy is packed into a tiny package. I *almost* find it cute, except for all the smack talk she usually hands out when I swing by. Okay, all of it is adorable, like a sassy little cousin.

Mal knows I'm a supe, but not what kind, how powerful, or what damage I could do to her both mentally and physically without trying.

"What do you want, *orc*?" she asks. Her favorite game is seeing if I'll react to being called different supernatural species.

I give her nothing with the orc comment. So far, she's never guessed demon. If she does, I'll give her the reward of shocking the crap out of her with a full reveal. Well, not the full monty. Her husband wouldn't appreciate that.

"I need to get some info on a potential mark," I say. When she looks as if she wants to turn me away, I explain, "Arran's girlfriend has a bad news ex. I want to know how bad he is before she gets hurt." I don't mention that I might hurt Jade if I discover she's the bad news.

"This isn't about the ASO?" Mal bites her lip. She's a good egg, but she worries about her and her husband getting caught up in this supe-witch drama.

She is not wrong to be worried. If what our supernatural seers have *visioned* is accurate, we will soon be dealing with the renewed vigor of ASO terrorist attacks on supes. And our human allies and assets will become targets.

Just when I thought we could have a moment to breathe with the missing supes situation over.

Mal grumbles, "You know I'm a softie when it comes to jerky exes, so if this is a ploy—"

"Even if it was a ploy, I only come to you when I'm worried. And I don't worry about much."

She looks me up and down—all six-feet-five of me—and nods. "Ugh. Fine." She waves me to come in, and behind us, she locks five different bolts for the industrial door. "Remember to stay away from our gear."

"I know the routine." I must stand almost all the way across the room to keep their computer equipment safe from my magic.

"There are rumors, Maxum," she says quietly as we take the metal stairs.

"ASO is upping their attacks. Osen was probably the first of many supes who will be taken down."

Mal and her husband are part of the small population of humans who know about supes, magical beings, and the existence of other realms. Approximately five percent of the population knows about us, and most of them end up as the supernatural's intermediaries to the mortal realm when we aren't able to cover up our magic. These humans span the cross-section of society—from hackers and thieves to government officials and first responders like cops and EMTs. They help keep the secret safe from the general population.

"I've heard the same rumors," I acknowledge her concern. "Unfortunately, I believe it's true. I'm going to be dragged into another war."

"Shit." She shoves open a door and reveals Dwayne typing away at his console.

"Really, man?" He shakes his head. "You better not have been followed."

"I wasn't, and I have a full payment." I pull a huge roll of hundreds from my pocket.

Mal's eyes widen, then she narrows them. "I thought you said this was a basic background check."

"I don't know how deep it goes," I explain. "I suspect this dickhead might be connected to the supe world or ASO, or maybe he's just a solo dickhead warlock."

I hand her the cash, Rob's name and details, and sit on a worn-out couch, waiting for my answers.

"Maxum." Mal shakes her head. "Is a woman really in danger?"

"Yeah. She's in danger from me if she turns out to be an ASO or Witch Council spy. Or she could be in danger because her ex-boyfriend is an abusive asshat and a possible magic user. I hope she is in danger because she's ignorant of her witchy nature. Because that's an easy fix. I just tell her what she is."

"I don't think that will go over very well," Dwayne says as he takes the note and picture from Mal and types in the info. "Humans don't react well knowing there is all this magic shit."

He's right. I've seen it a thousand times. I can't even count how many times I've outed the magical world to a norm. They deny it no matter how I reveal it to them. I've even removed my glamour right in front of them and shown them my true form. And they somehow block it out or claim it's a trick.

Humans are magical in that way. They can section off their brains to believe any belief they want to hold on to. If it doesn't belong in their worldview, it doesn't exist. They can be amazing as well as frightening.

"Hmm," Dwayne says as he crinkles his brow while squinting at the computer screen. It isn't a small screen, so this piques my interest. "Robert Holden doesn't exist... not in this area. And the ones in this state don't match the picture here. I'm expanding my search country wide. But my guess is that he gave her a fake name."

Arran's photograph has come in handy.

"What about police reports? I believe she filed a restraining order."

"Nada. Zip. He doesn't exist under that name in any local records. I tried all the variations of his name, too."

"Okay. So what now?" I ask.

"Even this picture doesn't help much. Sure, I could run an image reversal search. But that's time-consuming and rarely delivers results without something else to narrow it down. Besides, this picture is half destroyed." Dwayne pushes away his keyboard and spins his office chair to look at me. "It's a dead end until I have something more from you." He grabs the wad of cash I had just paid and tosses it back to me. "No fee for this."

"No. Keep it." I catch the bundle and toss it on the coffee table in front of me before I get up. "Buy some protection spells from my contact. Do whatever you need to keep yourselves safe. If I find something more on this guy, I'll be back."

I storm down the warehouse's stairs and hear the little human female following me with her light steps.

"Maxum, hey?" Mal calls to slow me down since I'm able to take two steps at a time.

"What?" I toss over my shoulder but don't slow.

I'm pissed. Arran was right to be concerned. I hate it when that mutt is right.

He's going to rub it in my face.

Something's off with Jade and her ex. And I need to know if she's lying about her ex's identity or if he lied to her.

I want her to be innocent. Then maybe I can have a taste of the sweetness between her legs as well.

Why would a guy lie about his true name unless he had a big secret to hide?

Hell, *we* didn't even hide our actual names.

"Maxum!" Mal shouts, pulling me out of my thoughts as I'm about to burst through their main entry door.

Whoops. I suppose I should unlock it first.

"What?" I barely keep back the snarl in my voice as I spin to face her.

Mal doesn't even flinch. She's a tough cookie.

"She's important to you too, isn't she?" Mal asks.

"Huh?" I shake my head. "She might be wrapped up in something bigger than herself. But she could easily be at the center of it and is fooling me."

"I doubt many people fool you," she says, worry clear on her face. "When humans lie about their identities, it isn't like the supes... it usually means they are running from the law."

"I've been around a decade or two," I say... more like centuries. I know human games. "But I also haven't ruled out him being a supe yet either."

"Be careful out there. The brewery got hit last night. They think it's ASO."

I hadn't heard about that. I was too busy watching the witch's house with Arran snuggling up with her all night.

I tell myself I was out there to keep Arran safe. But it was also to see who might be watching her. And perhaps I wanted to be there to stop Arran if he were to go into berserker mode. I wouldn't let him hurt her.

But no one showed up last night. If there was someone else outside Jade's house last night, I didn't sense them. It will be interesting to hear if she had any more messages from the ex. It would mean he could slip past my guard.

A lingering thought passes through my mind that she's innocent, and we brought this all down on her head by assuming her a spy, but I let it go for now. There are too many unanswered questions to assume or dismiss any possibility.

Jade still might be our enemy.

I make my rounds throughout the city and hop through a portal to the fae realm to check in with my contacts there. No one has heard more about the incident with Osen or who is behind the ASO.

The Anti-Supernatural Organization has claimed a lot of attacks, but they hadn't claimed Osen for some reason. And nothing at the scene indicated their involvement. Actually, nothing at his death spot made sense. That's why we haven't ruled out the Witch Council and the extremists among them.

If the whispers are to be believed, ASO aren't witches at all, but possibly other supes.

Honestly, I don't think anything would surprise me anymore.

If I didn't know the horrific magical draining operation had been stopped,

I might think it was the people responsible for that who completely sucked Osen's magic from his body.

But he didn't look like how those other victims looked. The others were nothing more than shriveled shells, and it took weeks for the process to kill the victims. Osen was just gone... all of his soul and magic. We even had a hellhound inspect the body to confirm what I felt. Nothing was left but the physical form.

From what Arran said, if Osen is possessing the witch, his spirit was confused and likely didn't know what happened.

As I burst through the front door of our safe house, Arran comes to attention and sits on the edge of the couch, waiting for my report.

"Well?" he asks when I don't immediately give him a news report. I've been dreading this all day.

I pour myself some demon-brewed whiskey. It's the only thing that can give my kind a buzz. Calder and Flint appear from their rooms to join us. After savoring the burning sensation of the liquor, I address my eager audience.

I'm curious about what they will make of this mess. "It doesn't appear that a Robert Holden exists around here."

"She lied!" Calder shouts.

"I don't think she lied," Arran defends her. "Unless she's been acting this whole time, even in her sleep, she doesn't know I'm the dog. And she's afraid of Rob. I can smell her fear, even if she tries to brush off how bad it was with him. She showed no signs of lying when she talked about him. Her heart didn't quicken. She didn't perspire."

"It just means she's a psychopath!" Calder paces the room.

I find it interesting that he's more riled than normal. I would skim the surface of his mind to discover why, but he's the best at blocking me. Besides, he would sense the slightest prying.

Is he also confused about his feelings for the witch, and he's overcompensating?

Am I compensating? Do I like her?

I don't *not* like her.

Focus up, asshole.

"We need more from her about her ex. And I think we should tell her what she is and see how she reacts." I throw out the idea like a grenade, waiting for Arran to panic.

Arran glares at me. "You just want to fuck up my chances with her."

"You've already accomplished that all on your own." I roll my eyes. "You have no chance with her if she doesn't know what you are. What are you going to do if she accepts your beast and forgives you for spying on her? Will you eat her pussy for the rest of your relationship? And hope that your beast doesn't literally eat her pussy with a killing bite?"

Actually, licking her pussy doesn't sound like a terrible way to pass the time.

Flint fidgets uncomfortably. Damn that guy. He needs to get laid. Too bad he never will.

Arran doesn't snap back with a reply. He knows I'm not wrong. He'll want more. She'll want more. And he can't give that to her the way he is. And she won't understand why he's denying her unless she knows about his curse.

"If there were any other way..." I say as my half-ass apology. "But we need to confront her about supes and witches. If she already knows about it, and not her fake book shit, then we can cut our losses. We eliminate her and move on."

"You mean to kill her if she's been lying about her ignorance?" Arran asks.

"Unfortunately."

He glowers at me. "And what if she *is* ignorant?"

"Well, she will know the truth, and she can embrace her magic. Likely, she'll be pissed off at us for everything we've done... like spying on her as a lost doggie." I raise my eyebrow and pour myself another glass of demon brew.

Arran's face turns red at that reminder. She won't want to be with him after that comes out.

"Fuck!" he shouts, and his beast ripples over his skin. He tosses a heavy recliner, and it flies into the wall. "She's going to reject me."

"I hate to tell you I told you so." I down the fiery liquid. "But I told you not to stay with her. Or pursue her."

He whips his head around and stalks toward me. He wants to unleash his beast. It's been riding on the surface for days now.

I can handle his attack. All three of us could survive his beast. It wouldn't be pleasant to feel his claws and fangs, but I heal quickly. Arran would be hard-pressed to hurt Flint. Calder is the most susceptible to his attack if it goes too far, but he would just reincarnate. Unfortunately, he loses a bit of himself each time.

Not that I expect it to come to death blows. But one never knows what to expect from berserkers—that's their intrinsic danger. Unpredictability. Sometimes, we can manage him. Other times, he goes off the rails.

I jut out my chin, inviting him to fight. "Hit me if you need to, but this is why you can't be around Jade anymore."

Arran stops in his tracks. Shame colors his expression.

Without warning, he shifts, tearing his clothes as he does. Surprisingly, he is a massive wolf, and not in his monster form. He races from the house and into the night.

I wish I could ease his pain and give him words of hope. But none of us have been lucky in life or love, so the words would be empty.

And this is just the latest example of life kicking one of us in the balls.

19

NOT AGAIN

JADE

*I*t pisses me off. I miss Arran and Beast. How can they have gotten under my skin so quickly?

I remind myself over and over, like a mantra: *I don't need the peen.*

A casual hookup might be perfect for now.

But shockingly, Arran seems interested in more. He looks like the type who would prefer a young, sexy underwear model on his arm rather than a middle-aged, curvy homebody.

He claims he wants an actual relationship with me?

However, I don't know if I can ever truly trust someone again. How can I let someone inside my heart after the way Rob treated me?

Deciding to go to bed early since I haven't been sleeping enough with these strange nightmares, I crawl into bed. A sense of foreboding weighs heavily on me.

That's never a good sign. I definitely believe in my intuition. I've had too many confirmed instances to ignore it.

Anxiety rises in me, and I know my life is going to be turned upside down soon.

Exhaustion finally takes me after laying awake for too long.

And I have another mysterious dream...

The guy from the bar, with the ice-blue eyes and smoldering gaze, stands in front of me. We are in a cheap motel room with two queen beds. A outdated table lamp casts a dim light around the shabby room.

The place is a mess. It has blankets tossed about. Random stuff, like food packages and weapons, covers all the tables and dressers. Discarded, torn clothes are piled on the bed.

"We can't stay holed up here much longer," Mr. Blue Eyes says. "They'll narrow down our positions soon enough."

"I know what we need to do, Calder," my male avatar grumbles. "But we have to wait for Maxum to show up again. He's the only one who has a secret safe house. Everywhere else has been compromised."

"If he hasn't returned from the Underworld by now, he might never," Calder says. He looks worried and runs his hands through his auburn hair nervously.

"No. Maxum will make it," I stroke his face, soothing him. "He's smarter than any of the shitheads there."

"If he doesn't come soon, we should go after him." Calder gestures with his hand at one of the beds. "Flint is almost recovered."

Hidden in the bulk, I see a massive arm poking out from what I assumed was only a pile of sheets and blankets. His figure was so still, I didn't realize it was a person. From the strange light skin coloring, I assume it's their friend, the one I imagine is a gargoyle. And I had seen him frozen like a statue in my last dream.

Flint—that's a funny name for me to come up with for a being made of stone. The subconscious works in weird ways.

"His recovery took longer than Maxum thought. The witches are getting stronger as we are getting weaker," Calder says.

"No. We are just noticing how weak we've become," my avatar says. "The spells that once would have barely bothered us are now easily knocking us down."

"How are you holding up?" Calder asks, reaching out for me before quickly pulling back. For some reason, he doesn't feel comfortable touching me... but at some point, he has been able to freely touch. Maybe they are no longer together romantically. But I can feel our heart-wrenching ache to reconnect.

My muscular arm reaches out and captures Calder by the back of the neck.

I draw him closer until our lips are only an inch apart. This close, I see the hot blue flames in his irises. Calder is not ice at all, even if he often displays a cold exterior.

He is barely contained passion and a powder keg ready to go off. The blue is not of ice but of the hottest kind of fire.

"As much as I would like to fuck you, I'm not sure you can handle me right now," I say and lace my fingers into the back of his auburn hair, fisting it.

He groans and bucks his hips into mine. His hard cock is apparent as he grinds into me, seeking relief.

"I can handle it," he pleads. "I need you."

Just by his desperate look, I know he's in love with this person I'm supposed to be. I wish someone would look at me like that—just once.

"I love it when you beg for me… for my cock. You know what that does to me." My mouth crashes down on his, and we tangle tongues. I feel I'm holding back some part of me. Some kind of magic power.

Tugging on his hair, I move him away. "Strip. On the bed. Ass up."

Calder strips and snarks. "I know the drill."

"Stop your sass, or you don't get your relief," I threaten.

Not wanting to risk it, he snaps his mouth shut and crawls up the bed, pressing his face into the mattress. He's propped up by his knees, delicious ass in the air.

I unbuckle my pants and pull my dick free, stroking it as I approach.

Oh damn, having a dick is nice.

My dreams or imagination never felt so real before.

From a pack on the dresser, I pull out lube and grease up my cock. Then I drizzle some over Calder's asshole, and he sucks in a breath.

"I'm not going to loosen you up," I warn.

"Goddess, dammit." He tenses and then relaxes. His breathing becomes ragged as I position myself behind him.

I line up my sizable cock to his puckered hole. My vision dims as if my eyes are half closed.

Calder is unusually still as I sink into him. The only reason I know he's felt my invasion is from a moan he lets out.

I finally bottom out, *pun intended*. Grunting my satisfaction, I can't get over the intense realism of this dream.

"You miss this?" I ask. "You miss me dominating you?"

"I'm addicted to your touch," Calder confesses. "Use me if you must. But touch me. Please."

Without warning, I pump into his ass.

Calder remains motionless, with only his grunts and moans to encourage me to continue. My hands skim over his gorgeous flesh—his muscular back, his hips, his chest. I almost feel as if I could consume him with just this simple act. I want to consume him, make him mine completely, but I can't do that.

When I feel my peak is imminent, I release my hold on his hips. One hand brushes down his spine. Calder sounds as if he'll come from that simple gesture.

I wrap my other arm around to his front and finally take his girthy length in my hand.

The residual lube aids in my ministrations as I pump him slowly.

"Do you like that, my sweet bird?" I coo.

As I fondle his balls, Calder whimpers, "Yes."

I pump him faster, and I feel his testicles draw up. His energy swirls around my cock. Something akin to pure electricity tingles up my spine. It's as if I'm empowered by my partner's pleasure.

"Come for me," I command.

He spills his seed with a shout.

I continue to stroke him with the same rhythm as I finish in his ass. He pulses around my cock, milking me with his orgasm.

As I unload into him, my whole body arches back and trembles.

When I'm spent, I fall forward, and press my forehead to his back. In a moment of affection, I give Calder a kiss.

"That was fucking hell," the gargoyle grumbles from the other bed. "Couldn't you get your own room?"

"This is our room," Calder sasses.

"I just wanted to show you what you're missing," I taunt as I unashamedly free myself from Calder's tight ass.

Geezus, I feel bad for Flint. He didn't like this.

The man I'm dreaming I am becomes aware of me again, and the scene freezes in the moment. *"Witch? Did you enjoy the show?"* he asks with an edge to his voice.

"I didn't mean to… I just was here."

"And you couldn't help yourself?" he sounds a bit amused.

"This is my dream. I can do what I want," I argue.

"No. These are my memories, and you are invading my sacred time with my lovers."

"This is so weird," I mumble.

"I'm tired of you poking into my thoughts." He snarls. *"There is only one*

explanation as to why I'm connected to you. And I think I know what it is. You should have exorcised me when you had the chance. Good night, little witch."

Suddenly, I'm kicked out of the motel room and stuck in complete darkness.

I try to will myself to wake up, but I can't.

20

ALL WRONG

ARRAN

I shift and run the fifteen miles to my old house. My wolf gets there faster than I could in my other form. I needed to get out of the safe house. I needed to be alone and anywhere but there. I wanted to run to Jade, take her in my arms, and claim her mouth, her heart, and her body. But with Maxum's reminder, I realize my affections would be rejected when she knew the truth.

Out of habit or instinct, I stop a block away from my home and call upon my senses to see if any witches or supes are lying in wait for me. When I don't sense anyone watching, I slowly approach. My nose to the wind, I'm hoping I don't scent anyone in my space.

Finally, I shift back to my human form as I slip in through the hidden entrance on the side of my home. I double-check my senses aren't on the fritz by peeking in each room. Not that it's a large house. It's only a two-bedroom, one-bath of utter bachelor chaos. As soon as I'm sure I'm alone, I chug a large glass of water.

The fridge reveals that I'm not much better than Jade when it comes to taking care of myself. At least I have a stale loaf of bread in the fridge. I make myself a sloppy peanut butter and jelly and scarf it down.

I feel completely lost as I stand nude, forcing down the crappy meal. The sandwich sits in my gut like a brick. Pacing the tired, outdated kitchen, and I wish I was in my witch's place. But she's already pushing me away, and she doesn't even know all the reasons she should.

I'm pissed at Maxum. But he's right. We need to tell Jade the truth.

She should know about her true nature and about what I am. We all are. That Osen has been possessing her.

I have no right to prevent her from this knowledge, even if it will most definitely cost me my relationship with her. Our future.

I give the safe house landline a call.

Thankfully, it's Flint who answers.

"Can you come get me?" I ask. "I'm at my place."

"You okay?" His deep, grumbly voice carries a lot of concern for me.

I appreciate it and hate it in equal measure. I hate being so damned sensitive right now. But it's as if the threat of losing Jade has me more riled than I've been in years—since I was cursed.

"No. I'm not okay," I sigh. "But Maxum's right. Jade should be told what's really going on."

"I'll be there in a few minutes, brother," Flint says. He only calls me that when I need to be reminded that we're a family—a pack.

I dress in my cheap, tear-away clothes, which are pretty much all I have anymore. It's probably for the best. I have a terrible feeling that I will go into full beast mode and run off when she rejects me.

Flint pulls up in the Rambler. I chuckle every time I see him in a car. He always looks too big to fit inside properly.

Checking down the street, both ways, I put my nose in the air and there's no scent of anyone unfamiliar in the neighborhood.

Sliding into the passenger seat, I grimace at my gargoyle friend.

Flint gives me an empathetic nod. "You should all listen to me. Relationships aren't worth the grief."

I don't argue, because I don't want to get into it with him.

He has his reasons for feeling that way. For myself, I was hoping Jade would be different. That she would be the one who turned my lousy luck around. I hoped, even though she's a witch, we could have moved past that hurdle.

But that was the impulsive part of me that doesn't think things through. To be fair, that is pretty much my whole personality.

Maxum calls me foolish. Osen used to call me reckless. I'd say I'm spontaneous.

We're all correct.

Flint is pulling up behind Jade's green vintage Mustang much faster than I'm ready for. It's later than polite to drop by—nine-thirty at night.

"You sure?" Flint asks. "If she is tricking us and you call out her witchy nature, she might hex you. Or worse."

"If she does, I deserve it. I tricked her into thinking I was a dog. I shouldn't have let the ruse go on like that."

"The problem is you had intimate relations with her before telling her what you are," he reminds me.

I turn my head so I can roll my eyes. This guy and his awkwardness toward sex. But he's called out my unacceptable behavior. "Yeah. I fucked up, and now I'm about to pay for it."

"Should I go inside with you?" Flint asks, his large hand on the door handle, ready to jump out instantly—to follow me into the witch's lair.

"No. It might make her more nervous, having someone there she doesn't know at all."

He nods, but looks a bit disappointed. Is he interested in Jade, too?

Nah, impossible.

Not with his history.

His stubbornness.

Not the 400-year-old virgin.

Maybe he just wants to help me through this.

I knock on her door, but no one answers.

Now that I'm closer, I can peek past the blackout curtains to see that the lights in her house are off. Fuck. I will just have to fret until I come back in the morning. I won't be sleeping much tonight.

Then the curtains pull back briefly as someone checks who is out here. There isn't much light on the porch, so I'm surprised when her door opens without the porch light coming on.

This alone puts me on edge. I don't know Jade very well, but this doesn't seem like a move she would make. Not with her ex allegedly stalking her. Not with how freaked out she's been.

Unless she has her gun pointed at my heart right now.

I realize too late that I should step back.

Before I can react, a hand reaches out from the open door and yanks me inside.

I'm pushed against the wall. The wind is knocked out of me with the force of it. Whoever is attacking me is strong.

I stop panicking and see who my attacker is. I'm in shock.

"Jade?"

She's holding me against the wall with one hand fisted in my shirt's collar.

I quickly glance down, and she isn't holding a gun in the other hand. Thank fuck.

"Nope. Guess again," she answers in a deeper, more combative tone. And a faint accent that I recognize.

"Osen?" I grab her wrist, but not tight enough to hurt her human flesh. "Let go of me!" I snap because the longer he holds his aggression, the more my beast wants to be unleashed. Maybe that's what he wants. "I won't hurt Jade," I promise. "So stop provoking me, dickwad."

He lets me go with a shove, turns away, and paces the room. "This witch is somehow sifting through my memories, searching for names and faces of the people who are working to eliminate the ASO. She's a damned spy, and I'm trapped inside her."

"I don't think she realizes the dreams are real... that they are your memories."

"It's all an act," he says with certainty.

The confidence in his answer makes my heart drop into the acid pit of my stomach. Has he seen Jade's mind and uncovered her innocence as a lie?

But I refuse to believe that about her.

If it's true, she's dead. Not by my hand. I could no longer do the deed. But Calder has been itching for a reason. He would snap her neck in a heartbeat.

"How do you know it's an act?" I ask. "What proof do you have?"

"It's obvious!" he shouts, pulling on her long, silver-threaded hair in angst. "She ensnared my soul. I can't move on. I can't rest. No, she makes me relive all my memories—all my failures."

It sounds more like his own guilt is making him relive his past. I don't see the kindhearted woman I know doing that to him... not on purpose, at least.

"I don't think she means to keep your soul. She's been distressed about what she considers to be dreams."

"She's a witch! That's all we need to know." He charges at me and gets in my face. With his spirit invading her entirely, I can almost see his masculine features overlaid on hers.

He is the most attractive and charming man I've ever known, but he now is downright demented. He was always obsessive... but now?

My heart aches for his condition, but he's not sane. And I won't have him hurting her or convincing the other guys to hurt her.

"Kill her so I can be free," he begs of me. "You'll be safe."

"She may be a witch, but she's not my enemy." I hold my hands up in surrender so he knows that I don't intend to hurt Jade.

"You really care about her, don't you?" Osen steps back, disgust written all over her face. "Enough to betray me? Me?!"

"I don't want her hurt," I agree, my voice soft.

"Even if she wants to kill us?" he asks.

Flint's voice rumbles from the open door. "We don't know that she has any ill intent. She doesn't feel like a threat to me. I would sense that much."

Osen huffs and falls back on the couch, sighing with defeat, giving up the fight a bit. We all know Flint's intuition about threats supersedes all of our senses, even Maxum's. It's built into a gargoyle's basic and primal nature.

Jade's hand rubs her face in a very Osen way. He grumbles, "You sure, Flint?"

"Yeah. There's danger around her, though." Flint steps into the house. "You're hurting the witch—draining her. Aren't you?"

Osen pshaws and waves him off. "Not you too."

"I don't like to see innocents hurting. I feel it in my own soul." Flint frowns. "If you're going to stay connected to her, you need to do so in a way that you don't harm her any more than you have."

Thank Goddess, it's Flint here telling Osen to do this. Because my request wouldn't be so kind and even-keeled.

"How do you have so much control over Jade's body?" I ask, since he barely seemed to be able to move before when he possessed her.

"I... I just took over. I've been feeding off her emotions, I think. It's helping me remember." Osen shakes their head as if confused.

"Then she can help you remember who killed you," I say. "But you know as well as I do that you don't have to hurt her to feed."

"Why should I be gentle?" He huffs. "She was spying on my memories, so I punished her. Pushed her into a corner of her mind."

That doesn't sound good. "She wouldn't be able to see your memories if you hadn't attached yourself to her."

"But *how* am I attached? I didn't do it. Why would I pick some random *witch*?" Osen puts her hands in front of her face and stares at them. "It makes no sense. I can't remember my death, and then I was attached to her. I don't think I *can* let go. I've tried."

"Are you suggesting someone created a bond between you two?" Flint stands in front of Osen, more intrigued by this claim.

"Have you all not been paying attention?" Osen snaps. He's more agitated than when he was alive, which is saying something. He had a temper. "I told you she had a hold on me. She must be lying about her ignorance."

"You need to back off, and we will watch her for signs of her involvement." I doubt he'll listen to me, as he often brushes my advice aside.

He surprises me and agrees. "Yes. To see who is working with her." He nods, thinking I'm devious.

Actually, it's to see who might be *using* her.

My plans to reveal the supernatural world must be delayed. I can't jeopardize our relationship and her pushing me out of her life because I betrayed her trust. She might need my protection. And I need to prove to Osen that she isn't what he believes she is.

I need to stay close.

21

SPLITTING FUR

JADE

I wake up at nine in the morning feeling like I haven't slept at all.

My dreams last night were even more disturbing. I wish I could shake them. But this latest character has taken over my mind and my dreams.

I have no idea why I've created this crazy asshole as the dead friend of the guys from the bar, but I don't always have control over my imagination and muse.

Maybe it's my subconscious trying to justify not developing a relationship with Arran.

I've been lured into a sense of peace over the last few months. I haven't had as many disturbing dreams since Rob left, and I sometimes wonder if he had subconsciously encouraged the horrible dreams by being overly interested in them. It seemed to be one of the only things about me he was interested in.

Now, I know he's just a cruel fuckhead and enjoyed making me suffer.

So I wonder, why have the dreams returned now?

It's been several months since I ended it with him, and he's finally left me alone… or so I thought. But apparently, as his email would indicate, he hasn't completely exited my life.

I sway on my feet when I drag myself out of bed to use the bathroom. My vision spins. I stagger to the bathroom door frame and brace myself. Touching my forehead, I don't feel like I have a fever. And I don't have chills, per se. But my body doesn't feel right.

Am I sick?

I don't get sick often. Well, not until I met Rob, now that I think of it.

Being ill has been so rare for me that I've only been to the doctor a few times for unusual stuff. Although, when I think back on my health, it was only after I hooked up with Rob that I began to have any health issues. Nothing was ever dire enough to go to the hospital, but I was often under a strange malaise.

Why had I not realized that until now?

I suppose I brushed it off as depression from being in a crappy relationship or getting older.

This sensation feels like that funk, but several times more intense.

The fog begins to clear, just enough for me to do my business and wander to the kitchen to make my morning coffee.

I pause when I walk into the living room on my way to the kitchen.

Why does it feel like someone was here? Am I being paranoid?

I had the same eerie feeling after I broke up with Rob. I often had a nagging sensation that he had been in my space when I wasn't around or while I was sleeping.

One night... he came back. Fortunately, I woke up. It's why I lock my bedroom door.

That's why I bought a gun. I needed to feel safe. Not that it did all that much to make me feel safe.

Just because I can whack my side characters and torture my main characters with abandon doesn't mean I could easily pull the trigger if Rob were to attack me. I'd do it if it came down to him or me. But I worry I'd hesitate.

The idea of having Arran as a bodyguard sounds more appealing by the minute. I don't feel I have enough strength to hold a gun or fight someone off.

Yet, I like to think of myself as a strong, independent person. I've never enjoyed relying on people, and I don't want to start now. Jumping into relationships too quickly gets me into trouble. I've learned my lesson.

After I feed and give some attention to my fur babies, I practically fall asleep in there, holding my guinea pig as we snuggle. For some reason, my animals ground me.

Animals have healing in their very souls.

I'm jostled out of my napping with my phone ringing in my pocket. I fish it out of my sweatpants and see it's the number Arran had given me before.

Interesting, I hadn't given him mine. I suppose he was able to hunt it down with his professional security skills.

"Hello?" I answer, sounding curious, like I don't know who it could be.

"Jade? It's me, Arran." He sounds sheepish. "Hey. I'm sorry I looked up your number, but I didn't want to invade your space and knock on your door whenever I wanted to talk."

"So, you invade my privacy in a brand new way?" I'm not that upset, but I need to state my boundaries. It's also a test to see how frustrated he gets with me stating them.

"Yeah. I shouldn't have done it. But I was worried about you," he sounds contrite, so I'll let it slide.

"Why are you worried?" I ask. I get up, head to the living room, and peek through the window, glancing up and down the street to see if he's in his truck, watching me from the street.

"I have a bad feeling about your ex," he says.

I roll my eyes, because that is a sort of weak excuse. "That's been established."

"So, I know you want us to take this relationship slowly. And I want to honor that, but please, will you call me if something feels off or something happens? Anything at all," he asks.

I realize my mistake… I'm putting Arran in harm's way. I need to end this now.

"I appreciate you wanting to look into Rob. But with him emailing me about going to brunch with Maxum, I can't get into a serious relationship right now. I'm sorry. I shouldn't have encouraged something between us the other night. Rob's dangerous. And I don't want to see you get hurt."

"Hey, sweetheart," he says softly. "I understand you aren't ready for a committed relationship. But I just want to be there for you." He sighs quietly. "But you shouldn't let Rob stop you from living your life. And if you wanted to date other people while we got to know each other, I wouldn't try to stop you. Maybe he'll back off if you have me and my friends around."

Where is this coming from?

He almost sounds… *hopeful*. Does he want me to hook up with Maxum or one of his other friends?

Are my dreams picking up on the fact that their group has an open sexual dynamic with each other?

Have I stumbled onto a free-range, all-male polycule?

Have I stumbled upon a sausage queen's dream team?

I grow heated between my thighs, thinking of Arran and Maxum fucking and begging me to join in. "Are *you* with someone else?" I ask.

"Not at the moment," he says with a hint of sadness.

Hmm. I'll wonder what that means later. I really need to pull away from Arran and his friends, so I won't be lured in with the fantasy where I'm spit-roasted by his buddies while he looks on.

Arran clears his throat and says, "Uh, back to why I'm worried... I have new information about Rob. I had a security associate look him up, and..." He trails off as though he doesn't want to tell me.

"And?" I prompt, my nerves vibrating with tension.

"Robert Holden doesn't exist... not with that name. Not in this state."

I collapse on my couch, my mouth dropping open. I cover my face and sit with that plot twist.

"Do you have anything more for me to find out who he really is?" Arran pauses, "Like maybe a workplace? Any relative's names? A copy of his ID, birth certificate, or passport?" He chuckles darkly with the last few suggestions.

"No..." My mind spins back to when I was with Rob. "But... I filed police reports."

"No police reports came up in the search," Arran informs me. "You're right. He must be well-connected."

"Well, shit." I wish Arran or Beast were here with me so I could hold on to them. Both would be awesome.

"Do you remember where he worked?" he asks.

A fog settles over my mind. Details about his past seem far away, as if I should know them, but they evade me. "He... uh, he was a real estate agent," I say, more as a question than a statement. I chuckle uncomfortably. "But every third person in California is a real estate agent."

Arran hums without amusement at my joke. "Okay. What about his last known address?"

"I don't remember going to his place... ever." This fact only seems odd now. "He just always showed up here."

"Friends' names?" he prompts.

When I try to recall his friends' names, I realize now I only got their first names.

My blood runs cold with fear. Am I losing my mind? "How could I not have known anything about Rob? I'm usually too curious for my own good."

"Nothing about his original hometown?" Arran pushes me to remember something he can work with.

"I think he said he always lived in the area." I shake my head, trying to rattle my brain into working. Panic begins to rise inside me, and it's like I can't trust my own mind or senses. What am I doing with Arran? He might be another creep. "Why are details about him so vague?" I ask, mostly of myself.

"I don't know, Jade." He sounds utterly concerned.

Unfortunately, I have a problem to deal with before I can explore things with Arran... and-or his friends. "I should probably call the cops about Rob."

"The cops are probably in his back pocket," Arran reminds me.

"Okay, fine. I'll let you know if something weird happens." I bite my lip, wondering if I should tell him about this morning. "I didn't feel right when I woke up. Like I was up all night partying, but it's been a while since I've done that."

"Oh?" He pauses and then says, "Anything else?"

"My nightmares have been getting crazier." I notice my couch pillow isn't in the spot I left it after cleaning up when Arran left yesterday. But my memory must be failing me. "I have this strange feeling that someone was in my house last night. But I can't believe that's true."

"You shouldn't dismiss your feelings," Arran says with tightness in his tone. Maybe he's worried that Rob is stalking me, maybe even breaking in. "Is it okay if my friends or I are in the area if we drive by and check the neighborhood out?"

"I guess." With him giving my fears validation, my anxiety ramps up more. "You think that's necessary?"

"I'd rather be safe than sorry. I'd rather be inside with you, but I totally understand your need for space... especially after hearing about Rob," Arran's voice softens. "I just want you to be safe. I care about you."

"You were going to drive by my house anyway, weren't you?"

"Maybe." He sucks in a breath, and I can almost hear him squirm over the phone. "I'm not doing great with boundaries because my protective side is being triggered."

"I get it." This sucks. I don't enjoy feeling out of control. But I'd rather Arran have my back than something horrific happens to me. "Is Maxum one of the people who will be swinging by?"

"Is that okay?" he asks, then quickly adds, "I don't expect him to be a jerk to you again. Well, at least not as bad as he was before."

I grin at that. I wonder if Arran told him to back off. Maybe Maxum realizes he was being a wanker.

"It's fine, but let Maxum know I won't put up with his sassy mouth," I taunt.

I hear a deep grumble in the background. Oh, my god...

"Is he there?" I say in a quieter tone.

"He's my roommate, so yeah, he heard. Maxum has exceptional hearing and is just as inquisitive as you are," Arran says with some restrained amusement.

"I wasn't spying," Maxum protests. "It's not my fault she talks so loud."

I know I didn't say it *that* loud.

"My threat still stands." I bluff. "I'll give it right back to him, if he gives me trouble."

"Promises, promises," I hear Maxum mutter.

A chill runs up my spine and into my low belly. But there is no way Maxum is into me too. I hate that Maxum has to be so sexy. If Arran and I end up together, his friends will torment me with their hotness.

There are worse ways to be tortured, though. My mind plays out fantasies of them tying me up and pleasuring me to the point of losing my mind. In a fun way this time.

"Jade?" Arran calls, probably not for the first time.

"Uh. Yeah?" I blush, as if he can read my thoughts.

"Do you think I can come by and see you soon?" His voice is so vulnerable.

Against my better judgment, because of my obviously horrible dating sense and the lingering issue with Rob, I give in a bit. "I'm not feeling great now. Can you check back in with me tomorrow, and maybe we can plan something then?"

"Of course, and be careful."

"Will do," I say and hang up.

Some spidey sense tells me there is much more to Arran, but I can't figure out what that might be.

I don't believe he wants to hurt me though. And that is what matters—for now.

My hopes aren't high that this is a long-term relationship, but he might have come into my life just when I needed a protector.

Whatever runs this universe might be throwing me a bone here—literally and figuratively. I'm going to bite down and hold on for as long as it makes sense.

I stand by the window and peek through the crack in the curtains. The blinding California sun lights up the scene outside. You would think the land filled with sunshine wouldn't have so much darkness, but it seems that there's always a balance.

I wish Beast was with me now. I wonder if he had sensed my need that night, as animals often do, and that's why he found me.

Or maybe humans just put way too much importance on circumstances.

I don't care if I'm doing that, because I like the world a lot more when the crazy stuff that happens has meaning.

After making my chai tea, I head into my writing cave, and the words flow, mostly from the strange dreams I've been having.

Can one plagiarize their own dreams?

I don't know, but I almost feel guilty writing out the hot hotel sex my avatar had with Calder.

22

BETRAYED

FLINT

I won't lie. The odd little witch intrigues me.

She has peeked out several times to catch one of us, or maybe her ex, driving by. But she hasn't seen me, standing across the street yet.

Gargoyles have illusion magic. We can disappear into almost any background—like a chameleon or an octopus. A gargoyle can be so still it seems as though they aren't alive. Most people don't look beyond the obvious human form or movement to catch their eye. So I look to be just another inanimate object while I stand here. And yes, gargoyles can also shift into our actual stone forms when we need to protect ourselves from attack.

Our vision is also better than most supes. Perhaps it's to make up for our diminished sense of smell.

With my visual acuity, I clearly see Jade's hazel-green eyes while they pause their search when she gets to my general location. Can she sense my presence?

Would she panic if I were to drop my camouflage and show her my true form?

Arran and Maxum tell me she reads and writes about supernaturals. But it's one thing to dream up an image and another to have it standing in front of you. She wouldn't want to see a monster appear before her eyes in her quiet neighborhood, watching her.

As our gazes almost seem to lock across the street, she appears to be sensitive, gentle, and perhaps inquisitive enough to want to know a person under their stone.

Few have ever wanted to know me. Even my circle of friends don't know me as well as they think they do. Yes, they know the reason for my refusal to engage in intimate relations. But none of them know the details. No one asks how it feels to be this lonely. They claim loneliness, but they have had the comfort of each other's embrace... of another's touch. The only physical contact I've had in four hundred years has been in battle. And that certainly doesn't count.

My sexual nature, if I have one, has never stirred. But I sometimes crave to feel the soft touch of someone who feels connected to me.

Arran has that same craving with this witch. And I have to admit, I understand his attraction. She has appealing features and qualities.

Her hair looks silky soft with its streaks of silver, and I want to see how it feels in my hands. I never would touch a female... not again. Not even if I lived another four hundred years. I won't do that.

Not that she would accept my touch.

Arran teased me that she wrote about how attractive I was, but she only saw my human glamour. I'm not as pretty as my true self—not at all.

My monstrous appearance would frighten her.

Real gargoyles, living ones, are so rare that they frighten most of the supernatural world. Many supes and witches don't know what to make of my abilities. Most supes prefer the etheric beauty of their own faekind. To them, I'm an abomination.

She is too beautiful for me to claim. Other than her full curves, Jade has the look of a half-fae. She has a beauty that glows. Her clumsiness or the small laugh lines around her eyes and mouth only enhance her attractiveness. She's perfectly imperfect.

Not that I'm interested in pursuing her. It's not like she would see me as a compatible mate anyway.

No one does or should. I don't fit in with witches *or* supernaturals from Fae or the Underworld.

I am *other*.

I had always figured I would never fit in anywhere until I met Maxum.

He accepted me. Then the others did too. We are all outsiders in our own way.

Calder is almost as rare as I am. And Arran is one of a kind with his beast... that we are aware of.

Maxum himself doesn't fit in with his fellow demons, or supernaturals, for that matter. Most supernaturals rarely trust him just because of his species—never mind that he's been a more positive influence in the supernatural community than most. His own demonkind can't understand his desire to make the realms a better place.

If she really is ignorant of her witchhood, then when Jade discovers her true nature, she will probably feel like an outcast too. The witch won't be part of the human community anymore. She won't really be part of the witch world, either. She probably already feels like an outsider, sensing she isn't quite like her human friends.

I don't get the sense she means to be a threat to us, but danger surrounds her. We could be hit with the fallout from the situation going on with her ex.

Arran has entangled his emotions, and I worry for him. But I'm not in danger of doing that, so I must be the one to keep a clear head about her.

Calder claims he doesn't want to be near the witch. However, I believe he finds her form attractive, and that's why he resists her so vehemently. Although, I understand his hesitation to go near her given his traumatic past with a witch.

I've been sitting here the entire day, just watching her place. A few times, I sensed a magical being, but that was in a passing car, but nothing that appeared suspicious.

Fortunately, she lives on a corner lot, so I can also watch her backyard from my vantage point.

No one has attempted to enter her yard or approach the front porch.

One of the guys is due to relieve me of duty for an hour or two so I can go home to eat and rest. I need little sleep or food, but maintaining this level of camouflage has been draining my magic.

Not only am I hiding from the witch so she doesn't get upset by my constant presence, but I'm also making it appear the way is clear to her house.

The setting sun is casting a warm glow over the world. Contentment settles in the hard bones of my primal nature. My ancestors were primarily nocturnal creatures, and most of my kind are still more active at night. I've learned to be flexible with my patterns since I've chosen a pack outside of my kind.

Twilight is my favorite time of day—the in-between time when all things are possible. Magic works differently at twilight and dawn. It's perfect for illusionists like me.

Speaking of illusions... a man is walking up to the witch's front door, using an invisibility spell of his own. A magical cloak around him compels a casual observer to turn away and forget his presence.

I, however, am not a casual observer. I'm a gargoyle. We see beyond that sort of magic. It's Rob, her ex.

Itching to move closer, I want to hear how the witch will respond to his arrival. Yet, if I do, someone might see me lurking. Quickly, I cast my senses out to see if this male visitor has a companion waiting in the wings.

After a brief wait, the witch opens her door. I hear her ask, "Why are you here?"

"We need to talk," Rob says, his voice commanding.

"Then let's talk," she says and opens the door, stepping aside to allow him entry.

Stars and Stone. Why would she do that?

I thought she was supposed to be afraid of Rob. But I sensed no fear from her... none at all.

Something isn't right.

I'm on edge since I can't hear what's being said. I don't think even Arran or Maxum could listen in at this distance.

Is the witch betraying us?

I can't say for sure, but this doesn't look good. And I'm not pleased that she somehow tricked me. I didn't suspect this at all. If she is working for the witches or the ASO, it will crush Arran. She will die, possibly by Arran's hand. Calder would definitely eliminate her.

Just as I'm ready to bolt across the street, Arran's wolf form comes trotting up as if summoned. He's carrying a small bag in his mouth.

"Don't shift yet," I tell him. "I have some bad news."

He tilts his head, indicating for me to explain.

"Some middle-aged average-looking male just was invited inside. He looked like Rob's picture. He wanted to *talk* with her." I frown. "It almost seemed like she was supposed to report what she discovered."

Arran snarls. Ignoring my advice to stay in his shifter form, he steps around the cover of the house behind a large shrub and shifts. "You sure it was Rob?"

"He was using a cloaking spell to deflect attention, but I believe I saw his true face."

"And she just let him in?" Arran growls the question.

"I'm sorry. I really thought she was innocent. But if he was an abusive ex-boyfriend, as she claims, why would she let him inside without a hint of fear?"

"It doesn't make sense."

"No. It doesn't," I say, "Unless—"

We both say it together, "Osen?"

"Or does Rob have some spell on her?" Arran suggests.

"She's compromised… no matter what," I say aloud, so we can solve this riddle. "It was clear that Rob assumed he could just come over. She'd let him in without argument or hesitation. Something nefarious is going on."

When her door slowly opens, I duck behind the corner of the house I've been stationed next to and turn essentially invisible.

Arran peeks around my body.

The guy we assume is Rob shuts the door behind him and hurries away. Not quite running, but only slow enough not to draw unwanted attention.

"Follow him," Arran orders. "I'll check in on the witch."

This doesn't sound good for her.

She's back to being *the witch* in his mind. I hope she survives what wrath his beast intends to unleash.

As soon as my wings catch air, I soar far above the street to keep an eye on Rob—or whatever his real name is.

My first instinct is to rend his arms from his body—perhaps other much smaller body parts. If he is a predator of an ignorant female… as I suspect, that's the least he deserves.

And my instincts are rarely wrong.

I hope whatever Arran discovers back there explains her side quickly and effectively.

I hate leaving Arran when his beast can surface so easily.

Will he take a moment to make sense of things and not just react without thinking things through? My money isn't on that bet. He's too impulsive.

This is when cell phones would be handy for our kind. I could call Maxum and have him check on the situation with the witch. But when it comes to witches, would the demon be level-headed either?

Down the residential street, Rob jumps into a nondescript black sedan on the passenger side. The car pulls into the light traffic. I swing wide so I can dip low enough and see inside the vehicle and memorize the face of the driver.

When I do, I recognize the woman as a known witch rights activist and a likely candidate for ASO membership.

Well, this is a dreadful turn of events.

Jade is indeed involved (in whatever way) with our enemies.

They don't drive far, a few miles away to the business end of the city. They pull into a parking lot. Perched high on a ledge on the opposite side of the street, I watch as they enter a modern office building.

I'm close to our safe house, so I risk losing their trail to alert Maxum and Calder to the current events. If Arran or I were to be incapacitated, they would have no clue. I'm not allowing what happened to Osen to happen to me. He was a cocky bastard who thought he didn't have to check-in. Look where that got us.

He's dead.

And we're in the dark.

I make sure no one tails me back to the safe house and land at our front door.

Barging inside, Maxum reads my aggressive demeanor and is already poised for a fight.

"What is it?" Calder asks, faster than Maxum when it comes to using his voice.

"Rob paid Jade a visit. Not sure what happened inside. My instincts still say she's not behind all this, but perhaps she has been used. Arran planned to check on her. I followed Rob and Galiana Collins to 1020 Main St."

"Rob and Galiana, *together*?" Calder pulls off his button-up shirt, revealing his toned muscular upper body. He straps on his weapons holster that holds his Katana-style blades. The custom holster allows his wings to move freely, if he chooses to half-shift, and use them.

I'd never tell him, but he looks like a badass dressed as a warrior—which he is. Typically, he looks more like a rich, uptight businessman dressed for the weekend.

His back and upper arms have tattoos—wings made of fire—that look a bit too real… because they are.

"You go back to keep an eye on the building," Maxum orders. "We'll pop over to see if Arran's killed the witch yet." He chants and opens a portal in our living room to Jade's backyard. He waves Calder through and gives me a grimace. "Good luck."

"I think you three will need it more," I sigh as the portal closes behind them.

I hope she survives.

23

LOST

CALDER

My fiery wings are desperate to unfurl. I'm ready to enact some vengeance. I've been ready for far too long.

Yet, I will stay my hand—only long enough to confirm that the witch is our enemy. Not that she isn't already *my* enemy by default. But Arran is sweet on her now.

I don't want to make an enemy of him. I've already lost a loved one this week.

I suspect I would be in the proverbial dog house if I kill the witch before he confirms her nefarious intentions.

Maybe he's already killed her himself.

Flint's normally calm exterior was ruffled when he burst through the door. That's no easy feat to rattle him. I don't think he's fallen for the witch's lure. So he's probably feeling what I'm feeling: worry for Arran's fragile sanity.

Maxum opens the portal to the witch's small backyard and waves me through.

My eyes lock on the back door of her house. I don't see any activity, but the blackout curtains are drawn on all the windows. Arran claims she fears her ex. Now, we know she allowed him inside. So it's likely what I thought all along… she didn't want *us* seeing inside.

I can't sense anything inside her home. But most magical beings and supernaturals have a minor magic spell that naturally occurs around their homes. It's where the whole vampires needing to be invited inside nonsense comes from. Just by claiming a shelter as their sacred place, a magical person creates a fragile protective ward around their homes.

Whether she knows it or not, this witch has definitely claimed her sacred place here. Since I'm not one of her chosen friends or family, I wouldn't be able to perceive much beyond her walls.

Maxum's magic works differently, so he could pick up brainwaves and bursts of magic beyond a barrier. He steps through his portal and seals it up. I glance over at him, expecting his quick assessment. He shakes his head, indicating he hasn't picked up anything yet.

I take another step and feel something soft stick to my shoe.

I lift my foot to see it's dog shit.

Without a sound, Maxum doubles over in laughter. His enormous body is shaking, and he points to my crap bombing. "Arran's," he wheezes out.

"You have to be fucking kidding me." I hiss and wipe most of it off in the thick grass. "I... don't have words for this bullshit."

"*Wolf* shit," Maxum corrects. Then he sobers, focusing on the house. "I don't pick up anything from inside. However, I sense Arran at the front, pacing and worrying. So she's likely unscathed... for the moment."

He frowns. I think Arran might be right, the demon has fallen for her charms too. But he's doing his damnest to cover up his interest.

"Why hasn't he gone inside yet?" I ask. But maybe he has, and he's panicking on the porch after ending his woman. I don't envy him. Not that I intend to have another female in my life—especially a witch.

We easily hop the tall fence and rush around to the front. Arran hears us coming, and his expression is one of complete devastation.

"Update?" Maxum switches to soldier mode to snap Arran out of his emotional state.

"She won't answer the door." Arran's half-shifted clawed hands are shaking. He can barely contain his beast. "Probably smart."

"Have you heard her moving around?" Maxum asks.

With this question, Arran focuses on the demon. Then his eyes widen. "No. I don't think I have."

"I'm not picking up brainwaves... not active ones." Maxum steps between Arran and Jade's door. "It could mean anything."

It likely means she's dead, and her brain is sputtering to it's final end.

Arran charges at Maxum, but it's only because the demon is in his way to get to the witch.

"I'm not going to hurt her. Hold on, Arran." Maxum pushes a bit of his mental influence at Arran.

It's not necessarily cool that he is using his ability on Arran, since he's not supposed to use his powers on us, but I'll forgive him for this one. We don't need the berserker version at the moment.

I glance around the neighborhood to see if anyone is witnessing our break-in.

Typically, regular mortal police don't get involved with supes *if* they know about us. But dispatchers will often call the Supernatural Enforcers if we cause a scene. If cops show up right now, we probably won't be able to hold Arran back if he freaks.

"Arran, I'm going to need you to breathe," Maxum says calmly. "I'm going in first since I'm the most resistant to magic. There might be some sort of trap or ward."

He's always risking himself like this. One of these days, someone is going to spring a spell that can take down a demon.

Arran grunts instead of speaking. I don't think he's capable of using his human voice anymore. I'm surprised he hasn't sprouted furry ears and a jaw full of razor sharp teeth.

Maxum takes his grunt as a sign of agreement. He turns around and enchants a spell to unravel any wardings over her front door. The door clicks open.

With his shoe, he pushes it open. When the door swings wide, we see the witch on the floor, face down. It appears as if she was crawling away and passed out.

I clearly sense death now. As confirmation, I don't see her rib cage moving with a breath. I glance at Arran, but he's struck stock-still. Good thing, because Maxum must move forward first to see if the place has been rigged with any spells.

My senses don't pick up any magic, but that doesn't mean a damned thing. I don't have the keen perceptions Maxum has. My ability centers on death and rebirth—and, once upon a time, sexual pleasure. I hate that part of myself has been stripped away by an evil act of a witch.

Despite my hatred for witches, I discover I weirdly care that this woman is hovering near death's veil.

Maybe she put a spell on me...

Nah, it must be my concern for Arran's sanity. I love the jerk. Or that she might be the last connection to my love, Osen.

Maxum slowly steps inside the living room. He scans the entire room for magic traces. When no booby trap attempts to hex him, he crouches to study the witch's condition.

He holds his hand just above her shoulder, then proceeds to turn her over onto her back. "Still no brainwaves." He waves me inside. "Can you check her?"

I won't fucking touch her, but I don't need to touch her to do what he's asking.

Standing near her, I expand my scope of perception. I feel soul energy hovering around us. Hers... and another encasing it, probably Osen's?

"She's disconnecting from her body," I confirm.

Arran is inside the house and on top of her within seconds. He roars, rattling my bones.

Gripping her to his chest, his vocal cords change back so he can call her name. "Jade?" And then he adds, "Osen? Come back."

Energy swirls in my mind's eye, pulling down toward her body.

She sucks in a breath, but it isn't deep.

Arran somehow summoned her back.

"Thank Goddess," he says, lifting her into his arms. "Portal. Now."

Although I see it on his face that he wants to argue, Maxum doesn't. With a huff, he creates a portal back to our safe house.

Apparently, we've adopted a useless, half-dead witch.

Oh, joy.

24

FOUND

ARRAN

On her porch, I work myself up into a frenzy.

I didn't want to intrude on Jade's space again, but I also don't want to leave her alone after her ex showed up.

My gut is telling me his visit isn't what it seems to be.

Thank Goddess Maxum and Calder show up when they do. I am about to lose what I have left of my fragile sanity.

When I see her on the floor, I know. I'm more certain than ever that she is a victim of all this. I don't know if the guys will agree. They might still think she is involved, and the ASO betrayed her. But they don't know her like I do.

Clutching her to my chest and hearing her take in a breath is the sweetest sound I've ever heard.

Stepping through the portal I demand of Maxum, I want nothing more than to carry her to my room so I can be alone with her. I want to symbolically claim her as mine to the males by taking her under my protection. I won't claim her as my mate until I have her permission. Hopefully, one day I can convince her to accept what I am.

Instead of hiding away with her, I settle down on one of our large couches so I can talk with the guys about what to do.

Gazing down at her sweet face, I have an uncomfortable thought. "What if it isn't Jade who returned to her body, but Osen?" I mumble to myself.

How will I deal with him taking her body?

As much as I want Osen alive again, I don't want it to be at the cost of my beautiful witch.

"If anyone could have ousted her soul and claimed her body for his own, it would have been Osen," Maxum confirms my worries.

"What if Osen killed her? Not Rob?" Calder asks.

"What did it feel like when she was outside her body?" I ask. "Did you sense both of them?"

"I did." He frowns. "At first, it felt like he was surrounding her soul."

"To contain it?" I wonder.

"I suppose it could have been like that." Calder pulls on his auburn hair in frustration.

"Osen could have helped her return to her body. His power worked in the astral realms. It's not impossible." Maxum rubs his face and curses. "But I also wouldn't put it past Osen to knock her off if he believed she was the enemy."

"She could have willingly met with Rob. Then Osen attacked her from within, after Rob left," Calder argues, unhelpfully filling my mind with poison.

"Stop it!" I shout. "We don't know a damned thing. We'll have to wait until Jade regains consciousness to find out what we can."

Please wake up. Please.

Maxum clears his throat. "Arran, we have some bad news. Flint followed Rob and saw him drive away with Galiana Collins after he left Jade's house."

"Fuck." I close my eyes to center myself before I go into full beast mode. I'm honestly shocked I haven't yet. "So Rob *is* a warlock."

"Appears so." Maxum shrugs. "Galiana doesn't mingle with humans or supes. So it appears Jade might know more than she lets on."

I shake my head. I hate that they doubt her, but the facts are stacking up against her innocence.

Glancing out the window, I see night has finally come. "Where's Flint?"

"At an office building, last we know. Might be ASO headquarters." Calder stands up and stretches his shoulders. "I'll fly over and see if he's still there, and if he needs backup. You good?" he asks me.

"No. But you know that much." I sigh. "Just don't let her ex slip away. I want to kill him for the hell of it now."

"You got dibs unless, of course, he comes at me. Then I'll take him down. I'm guessing he's the dick who's behind Osen's death, too. Or one of the culprits." Calder glares at Jade's unconscious body, his insinuation clear.

"Rob's probably part of Osen's murder." Maxum cracks his huge knuckles. "Go. Help Flint."

Calder gives us a nod and unfurls his giant red-orange wings from his back as soon as he's out the front door.

"How are her brainwaves now?" I ask Maxum as I stare down at her sleeping face. She almost looks peaceful.

"Getting stronger." With a growl, Maxum launches to his feet and heads into the kitchen to pour himself a demon brew. He downs a generous serving in one gulp, glowering at Jade the entire time.

Is he certain that she's a spy now?

Having her in my arms settles me some. I close my eyes to grab onto the small bit of rational thinking I have left. Even before she wakes up, I need to know what happened to her.

"It appeared as if she was attacked and was trying to get away from Rob," I say quietly, but I know Maxum can hear me. He can hear me across a battlefield, because he has.

"That is how it appears," his tone is flat.

"Can you see if you can pick up what Rob might have used to kill her?" When Maxum doesn't move or respond, I remind him, "If Rob or his friends killed Osen, then he might have tried to use a similar spell on Jade."

Maxum grumbles but walks over and towers over us as I sit, holding her fragile form in my arms. "There's no magic residue around her, but we might have left any traces of that at her house." He grimaces.

"Should we… check her body?" I gulp because I don't want to undress her in front of Maxum. She wouldn't be happy about it. But I remind myself he's practically like a doctor, and she's an unconscious patient in triage after a battle. And we don't have to strip her of her underwear to see if she has any marks to indicate what hurt her. It might still be hurting her because she hasn't regained consciousness yet.

Besides, our inspection isn't sexual. Maxum doesn't want her like that anyway… at least not anymore.

I unbutton her cardigan and pull her right arm free of the sleeve. Trying to hold her and undress her is awkward. Gratefully, Maxum huffs, then helps.

His touch is gentler than I would expect. I wonder if he's doing it for my sake? Or does he realize how fragile her mortal body is?

He holds her arms above her head, and I brace her body as I slowly lift her t-shirt off. She's wearing a flimsy bra that isn't more than a thin, cropped tank top. Her nipples are hard and begging me to touch them.

But I'm not *that* guy.

It's her soft skin that almost undoes me. I want to howl at the moon. I only had that brief, beautiful night with her, and that is likely all I will get.

Maxum gently brings her arms down to her side, then inspects each with care. He brushes her long hair to the side to glide a massive hand down her back. Instead of watching Jade, I observe the demon. He's invested... more than he lets on.

"No curse marks so far," he says. "I don't know what happened to her."

Usually, a hex or curse leaves some energy signature or even a physical mark on a body. I wonder what could have hurt her enough to kill her without leaving a trace.

"Should we?" I nod to her pants.

Maxum grimaces. "We've come this far as perverts. Might as well seal the deal."

We make sure to slide her jeans off without taking her underwear with them.

Maxum does a brief but thorough check, but discovers nothing. He grabs a blanket and places it over her naked form. "You really care for her, don't you?"

"If I thought it was possible to have a fated match with a witch... I'd believe she was my mate."

"Dammit." He flops onto his favorite chair.

He's a sucker for fated mates. It's one of the soft things about him. Although, I'd never say that feeling soul-crushing love for someone was weak. I doubt he believes that either.

We haven't been very lucky when it comes to relationships—especially with females.

"Do you feel a pull to her as well?" I ask, not sure what I want to hear his response.

"I feel... something," Maxum says just above a whisper. Then he crosses his massive arms and sulks. "But we don't know if that's part of her magic. She could have hexed us with a lust charm."

"I'm not feeling lust," I argue. "Well, I feel lust for her, but it's deeper than that. And I think you know that's true for you, too."

"No. Lust never felt this painful."

25

COMING UNDONE

JADE

I don't remember falling asleep, but I must be dreaming.

I'm naked, and my limbs are tied down to bedposts. Arran, Maxum, Flint, and Calder surround me.

We are in a room filled with a soft, warm glow that only serves to accentuate their otherworldly beauty. Currently, they are all shirtless, wearing low-slung pants.

Calder's skin seems to glow orange-red, as if he's about to burst into flames. I might do that too if he keeps looking at me the way he is—like I'm his next meal. I wonder if he will be as skilled as Arran with his mouth.

Maxum has his horns from my previous dreams. His skin is a gorgeous deep crimson. His obsidian eyes dance with fire as his gaze travels up and down my body, pausing at my exposed pussy.

I heat only with his perusal. I'm getting wetter by the moment.

With a predator's grace, he steps closer.

My pussy clenches with excitement.

From the other side of the bed, Arran moves closer. His eyes are filled with more than lust. I see hope within his gaze. His eyes are wild-looking and he appears much larger than I remember in real life. As if he's on steroids... like he's hulked out. His hands look more like monster claws than the human fingers I'm familiar with.

But even with his dangerous monster claws, I crave his touch again.

Will he drag them over my sensitive flesh, marking me with thin lines? Will he use them to pinch my nipples and edge me with a bit of delicious pain just at the right moment?

Arran grins, and I see his canines have elongated as if he's part wolf.

Flint stands in the background. His huge, muscular body leans against a wall, as if he'd rather watch than participate. Maybe he's a bit of a voyeur. The idea turns me on even more. Large bat-like wings frame his broad, thick body. Horns poke out from the sides of his head. He looks like he's made of polished tan-colored marble. Would his cock feel as hard as a stone?

I wonder if he will stroke himself as his friends fuck me. His expression gives nothing away, and I want to know more about him. Who is this mysterious quiet male… *gargoyle*? What's his story? What is his dark secret that he tells no one?

I love that my dream is playing into the characters I've created for them.

Oddly, I wonder where my ghostly avatar is. Usually, it's him that actually interacts with these guys.

"Ghost?" I call.

The four guys glance at each other as if I've said something unusual.

"Are you calling for Osen?" Arran asks.

"His name is Osen?" I frown when I hear how fragile my voice sounds.

"Yes." Maxum leans over, just a few inches from my face. I can smell his smokey scent that warms my insides. "Why did you call for him?" he asks. His voice isn't seductive but demanding… as if I've made some mistake requesting his presence. Maybe I have. Osen seems to tolerate me, at best.

"This is my dream. And I want to know where my ghost is. He's the one to get all your attention." I frown. "I find it upsetting that he's not here, too."

"Why do you care where Osen is?" Maxum cradles my chin, and I feel tension building. His grip is growing firmer by the moment.

I sigh. I hate admitting that I want to know more about him, because he hasn't been the nicest person to me. However, I believe there is a reason for that. We just need to develop a connection, a bond.

Dreaming or not, these guys all love Osen. We must have gotten off on the wrong foot. "Because you care about him," I say simply. "Your hearts ache with his loss. And I want him to stop hating me."

"Why do you want him to like you? So you can pull secrets out of him?" Calder asks.

I narrow my eyes as I look at him and groan loudly. "What the fuck is up with this secret shit? It's all very interesting as a book idea, but I don't care for it in my dreams. I just want to experience the love you all feel for each other. I just want to resolve this tension so I can move on."

Arran's rough hand skims over my arm. "What about experiencing the pleasure we can give you?"

"Yes! I want that!" I nod. "I don't like this idea that we're enemies."

"And if we like to punish our enemies sexually?"

I raise my eyebrows and then grin. "Oh, well, that could work. But I don't want to be really hurt."

"Witch, you need to know this is actually happening," Arran whispers in my ear, but the voice is the ghost... *Osen*.

"But this is my dream," I say. "Or maybe our shared dream."

"It is in a way, but it's also the shadowscape. A very real place. One I can control," Osen speaks through Arran. "I'm a disembodied soul. But what these males do to you now is truly me."

"So you are a ghost... and you'll be fucking me as these guys?" I ask.

"Yes."

I frown. "No."

"No?" His angry voice resonates all around me. "I don't have to ask for your permission. I can take what I want."

"Why didn't you do that then?" I challenge him.

He pauses, then finally answers, resigned. "Because I promised these males I wouldn't do that."

"Why do you want to have sex with me at all? I thought you didn't like me." I ask, "And why are you using their faces instead of your own?"

"Because you're attracted to them." Arran's hot breath washes over my neck. "You want to fuck them. You don't like me."

I squirm with need. "And why do you want me to want them, or you, for that matter?"

"I need your sexual energy," he finally admits.

"Are you an incubus?" I ask.

"How did you know?" His voice is harsh again.

"I write this stuff, silly."

"Oh, that's right." Arran nuzzles into my neck, then his soft lips graze up to my ear. "Do you understand this isn't a dream?"

I feel the pinch of sharp canines on my neck, more real than I've ever felt in a dream.

"Stop!" I gasp. "I... I believe you."

He releases his jaw and licks over the marks. "I always wanted to bite someone like that—as a werewolf."

"Great. Achievement unlocked," I sass. Then I pull back as much as I can and study Arran's face. "Let's just say this is real, and you're trying to seduce me so you can feed off my sexual energy... why do you need it?"

"I've been feeding off your emotional energy for days, but it isn't enough. I need more so I can remember everything. But I had to drain my reserves to save you."

"I was sick..."

"It was more dire than that. If you are to continue to survive, I will need to feed you energy. You might even need outside help."

"I'm that bad?"

He nods. "And I don't like you rummaging through my sexual memories so I can feed."

"I didn't mean to invade your privacy."

He grunts as if he's still not convinced.

"I mean, the scenes were hot as a volcano, but I didn't realize it was real," I grimace. "Sorry."

He studies my face or energy, or whatever, for a long moment. "I sense you are only starting to understand. You really don't know about supes and witches?"

"I didn't... And you need my energy to become stronger?" I ask, nervous to hear his answer.

Osen uses Maxum's hand to wrap around my throat, pinching enough to make me feel how real this is. "Yes, and because your magic isn't enough to protect you."

"Why do you care if I stay alive?" I ask.

"If you die, I won't be able to avenge my death."

"Death goals. I get it." I realize there's more to his game. "Are you planning on taking complete control of my body?"

"I need to confirm you aren't the spy as I had suspected. But if you are innocent, I won't possess you permanently."

"Just for weekends and date nights?"

"You are a sassy one... even though I sense you now realize this is truly happening."

I don't know how I know, but I do... this is terrifyingly real.

He continues, his voice soft and thoughtful, "As long as you aren't the one who killed me, I'll leave when I know my pack is safe and my murder solved."

I feel the truthfulness in his words.

"If you want to sex me up, full disclosure... I hooked up with Arran," I admit, feeling guilty.

"You aren't exclusive, though."

"No, but..."

"I heard his conversation with you. He'd share your love with the rest of us. We all share our bodies. Well, except for Flint," he explains. "Having multiple partners is not unheard of with our kind."

He's right, Arran told me he didn't mind if we were with other people.

"Can you show me what you look like?" I ask.

"You really don't know?" He sounds skeptical. "You have no memory of seeing me?"

"No. When would I have seen you? I only inhabit your body during your memories."

"So you don't remember having something to do with my death?" he mutters, not really a question. Maxum's hand squeezes tighter around my neck.

"No! I could never kill someone."

"You have a gun," he reminds me.

"To shoot them in the leg or wherever I have to hit someone to slow them down, not *kill* them."

"To stop your ex? Rob?" he growls with Arran's voice.

"You know about him?" I'm surprised he is so aware of my waking life.

"That he's a threat? Yes."

"Will you protect us from him?" I worry Rob will hurt me. Wouldn't having an invisible ghost who can help me be a good idea?

"I can help you if you feed me."

"Then show yourself," I demand. "I don't want to be with these guys if it's you touching me."

The four guys disappear. Next to the bed, a dark shadowy figure stands, staring at me, if what looks like eyes are any indication. He is almost transparent, like thick, dense smoke, but in the shape of a man. "This form is much easier to maintain."

"Were you wasting energy on the illusion?" I ask.

"I thought it might work you into a sexual frenzy faster," he explains.

"Maybe another time, but I need to know who you are right now," I say. "If this is really happening, I want it to be between us. Not through them."

He hums thoughtfully, "You are worried it will corrupt your feelings for them?"

"Yeah." Then I pout. "Why don't you show me what you look like?"

"If you want the real me, this is as good as you're going to get until I feed more. In many ways, this *is* the real me. Besides, I don't think I should show you the face my physical form wore yet."

"So, are you made of shadows in the dream world?"

"It's my incubus-feeding body in what you might call the astral plane." His arm reaches down and strokes my cheek. "You sure you want me to fuck you? This will solidify a connection between us. I will see further into your mind. Lines will be blurred."

"Are *you* sure?" I ask, my forehead wrinkling in confusion. "I didn't expect that you would want to bond with me. I'm a disgusting witch, after all."

"I'm looking past that."

I chuckle. "How sweet."

"Do you want sweet? Or do you want me to give you the best orgasm of your life?"

"Door number two," I joke. "If this is an either-or situation."

"When I feed, you will be under my complete control," he warns. "You won't be able to move. You'll only be able to talk, use your eyes, and come for me like a fucking nymph. Starting now."

I gulp. I try to pull on my restraints, tying me to the bed. But I can't move to do that. Glancing to the side, I can see now that my ropes are actually shadows.

My heart is racing. And my body is thrumming with fear and excitement.

I'm about to have astral sex with an incubus ghost. Feels like I might be forging new ground here.

I'm a pioneer.

A trailblazer.

Taking a shadowcock for the team.

Osen drags his shadowhand from my neck and over my breast. He squeezes and pinches my nipple.

"Oh shit," I gasp. I didn't expect the shadows to be so dexterous.

"That's just the beginning, little witch." I can hear the smile in his voice. "Open up to me. Give me all that lust, the desire, and the emotions behind your need."

"That will help you?"

"You actually *want* to help me, don't you?" he asks with awe.

Two shadow tendrils move up from both ankles, slowly climbing up my legs. Again, I try to budge but can't squirm.

"What do you like, little witch?" he murmurs. Now his shadowbody moves around the bed until he crawls up, kneeling between my spread legs. I feel his attention on my wet, exposed pussy. "You want me to fuck this pretty cunt?" The tendrils slide up to pull my labia open, further exposing me to him.

"Oh, god," I blush.

"I'll be your god," he chuckles. "But you should thank the Goddess for my gifts."

The tendrils continue their explorations up my body to my breasts, wrapping around and around each one, covering them completely, and acting as a living bra. He squeezes like he's milking them, and my arousal jumps to another level.

His hand replaces the tendrils at my entrance, sliding through my wet folds, working me higher with his attention. His thumb finds my clit and gently strums it with the rhythm he's now setting with the rest of his shadowy appendages.

"Has anyone fucked your ass?" he asks.

"Once. But he didn't know what he was doing."

"Well, I do. And if the guys claim you, you will know the feeling of amazing anal sex in the physical world."

"Are you going to do that with me now?"

"Let's work up to that, little witch." I notice the hate is dissolving around that nickname and becoming a phrase of endearment.

I breathe out, "Okay."

"Do you enjoy sucking on cock?" he asks. "You like a long, thick dick fucking your throat? Swallowing down a male's cum?"

"Yes."

"Good, because I'm going to take every hole during our sessions."

"Sessions... with an S?"

"Oh, yes, my troublemaker." He leans forward, his phantom tongue slipping over my center.

I cry out because it feels so damned good.

"Feel free to come as many times as you wish," he says off-handedly. This guy is confident. I'll give him that. But I suppose his power centers on sex, so he should be.

I laugh. "Guys rarely make me come, and if they do, it's once. Tops."

"But when you are alone? With your toys? And you don't have bumbling fools in your bed?"

"Well, yeah. But that's different," I argue.

"So am I." His shadowtentacles shoot out from his torso and wrap around my upper thighs, pulling my legs open more and folding me in half. My knees are almost touching the sides of my breasts.

I'm completely exposed to him and at his mercy.

One tendril tickles my asshole. And another fondles my clit. Then I feel a vibration.

I pant. "Are you... *vibrating?*"

Okay, wow.

This whole incubus lover has some serious advantages. All I can do is lay here and take all the pleasure he can dole out. I'm convinced this is only the beginning of what he could do with me.

His tendrils tighten around my breasts, massaging them, and I moan.

Something wraps around my throat and then drags over my lips.

I open my mouth obediently. His shadow feels like a thick cock in every way.

"Good witch," he coos. "Suck my shadowcock. Show me how much you desire this."

I swirl my tongue around the head and give it an experimental suck.

Osen groans with pleasure. Slowly, he presses it farther in until he's blocking my airway. He plays with my ability to breathe, as I feel pressure at my wet entrance below.

With my mouth full, I can do nothing more than hum and moan.

His body comes forward, on top of mine. I open my eyes to see the outline of his face, and a hint of what his human face might have looked like.

He thrusts the cock into my throat deeper. "You like choking on my shadowcock, witch?"

After deep-throating me and ratcheting up the tension, he pulls his shadow out for me to answer.

"Yes, I want more."

"So do I." The large head of his lower cock presses slowly into my pussy. "I need more."

I want to grind against it, make him shove inside faster. But he's in control. There is no mistaking that. With my consent, he means to do with me as he pleases.

"You want me to slam home hard, don't you?" he asks.

"Fuck me," I plead.

He shoves his shadow back down my throat.

A tendril sucks on my clit, and I cry out around the mass.

"I forgot how lovely females can be," he says, licking over the bump where his shadowcock is plunging into my throat.

It's too much. My climax hits me like a freight train.

Immobilized, I can't even move to show how it affects me. I can only feel my pulsing pussy, hear my muffled cries, and see stars behind my eyelids.

When I stop clenching around his shadowcock, I open my eyes to see Osen has a bit more form to him now. Crisper.

I'm helping him. Then I wonder if he's hurting me in the process, but I don't feel drained. If anything, I feel stronger.

"You come on my cock so perfectly. Let's see if you can take the whole thing." He pumps forward, and I feel the burning stretch of my pussy accommodating his girth and length.

The cock in my mouth slides out.

"Tell me how much you want this," he orders.

"I want your thick, massive cock. I need your delicious cum filling me up. I want you dripping from all my holes."

He pounds into me faster, turned on by my words. "I should have been fucking more romance authors all these years."

"The readers would have been a good choice too," I offer.

"And you want to fuck my friends, don't you?" he asks. "I'm going to love watching them destroy this pussy with their huge cocks. They will stretch you and use you so thoroughly that no man will satisfy you again."

"Yes," I shout as his ministrations work me into a fevered pitch.

His shadows are swirling all over my body. They're plucking my nipples, tightening their grip around my throat, and strumming my clit as he rocks into me. He's touching places I didn't know were erogenous zones.

"You're going to take my shadowcum. I'm marking you. You're mine now. My little witch." He hisses, as if he didn't mean to confess that bit.

My bliss lifts me to such heights I'm afraid of the fall. All I need now is a gust of wind, and I'll plummet off the edge.

"Come for me," he commands.

And I do.

A bomb goes off inside me—our energies merging and swirling, like a cascading explosion, echoing out farther and farther until I'm not sure if I'm alive anymore.

Heat fills my core and then reaches my fingers and toes. I'm filled with a strange glow.

A shadow curls around my light.

Osen curses but keeps coming inside me.

Then he collapses on top of my body, and I feel his shadow's weight.

"I wish I could have fucked you with a physical body," he whispers as I drift into total darkness.

Did he just kill me with his shadowcock?

Worth it.

26

REBORN

ARRAN

*J*ade's body is wrapped up in the blanket like a burrito, but she wiggles and squirms in her unconscious state.

It gives me hope that she's returning to us.

However, Maxum's intense glare reminds me we don't know what will happen next. Is Jade working with our enemy, even unintentionally? Was she being used? Was it Osen who hurt her? Or did he save her?

We need answers.

I hold her on my lap and rest my head on the back of the couch. But I haven't been able to sleep.

Calder walks in the front door, returning from checking in on Flint. The phoenix glares at Jade's sleeping face. Then he glances at Maxum and me, reading our energies. He shakes his head in irritation and gives us his update, "It appears Rob and Galiana haven't left that building. Which indicates there might be sleeping quarters inside since it's about three in the morning now."

Maxum grunts quietly, almost dismissively. He doesn't move a muscle, only watching and waiting for a change in Jade's condition.

Perhaps he senses a shift in her brainwaves.

"You two just going to stare at the witch the entire night?" Calder cocks his brow and his hip. Sassy brat.

"Yes," Maxum answers with such resolve and determination that it brokers no arguments to suggest otherwise. Or it wouldn't be wise to comment.

Yet, Calder isn't always smart.

"She obviously betrayed us," Calder says, waving his hands in her direction.

"So why would Rob attempt to kill her?" Maxum asks.

I'm surprised he's the one arguing the point.

Calder huffs, "I don't know, but—"

"But nothing," Maxum cuts him off. "We need answers. And if Osen is still linked to her, we might get the truth of the matter from him. All we know is that Jade was attacked."

Calder softens with the mention of Osen. If anyone was *in* love with the incubus, it was Calder.

I loved Osen as well, but I had ended the sexual dynamic when he became increasingly obsessed. He only cared about fighting the witches and proving who was behind the ASO.

I was invested in stopping the threat, but Osen was a fixated maniac in the end.

Calder sees how I'm clutching Jade protectively to my chest. He sighs and offers, "Snacks while we await the verdict?"

"Sure," Maxum agrees.

"I can't eat," I decline. "Not with her like this."

The phoenix frowns, sympathetic even though he disapproves of how attached I've become. Then he rummages through the kitchen for something to eat. I know he only means to protects us all with his gruff behavior toward Jade, but I can't allow it.

I watch him for a moment, then I turn my attention to Maxum. "Are you picking up anything?"

"She's been dreaming, but the texture of it feels more like a shadowwalk."

I perk up.

So does Calder from the other room. He asks, "Osen? You think he's still in there with her?"

"That would be my guess." Maxum leans forward, watching her like a cat about to pounce.

Jade breathes in deeply and stirs, her head turning toward my chest.

My broken heart soars with the positive sign she will be okay.

But when her eyes open, they are not their normal hazel-green, but charcoal.

"Osen?" I dare to ask.

Jade turns her head and sees Maxum and Calder towering over us.

"Hey, assholes," Osen says.

"It's him." Calder smiles. Then he becomes instantly serious. "What's happened? Is the witch's soul still in there?"

He's asking what I need to know.

Where is Jade?

Calder's likely hoping for a different answer than I am.

I'm conflicted, because I also want Osen to be alive, but not at the cost of my sweet, curvy witch's life. Even if she never forgives me for breaking her trust, I want her to live a long and healthy life.

Yes, even if she knowingly betrayed us.

She doesn't owe me anything.

War is war.

"The witch is still here," Osen says. "I had to pull her soul back into her body, but the act drained my reserves."

"Why did you save her?" Calder sounds completely perplexed.

"It appears that she was under a spell and I need vengeance." Osen looks down at the tightly wrapped blanket around her body. "Worried she's going to hex you?"

"Should we be?" Maxum asks in a neutral tone.

Osen jerks in my arms and closes his eyes as if fighting off a pain.

Her body goes limp.

Then Jade's eyes open, revealing hazel-green irises.

"Jade?" I ask, wondering how much of her is aware and functional.

Osen could have fucked with her memories if he's gaining strength, as I suspect he is.

"Arran?" She blinks even though it isn't bright in here. She startles when she sees Maxum and Calder standing beside the couch, staring at her. "Where am I?"

"Never mind that for now, tell us what happened," Maxum orders.

I notice he's back in human glamour, but he still looks like an intimidating demon without horns.

My protective instincts are in full force. I pull her to my chest.

Encased like a mummy, she can't do anything but allow me to do it.

"Back off," I snarl at Maxum.

"I don't understand. Did you guys kidnap me? What are you going to do to me?" she asks, her fear and confusion ring clearly. Her eyes widen when she sees Calder's bare chest and weapons holster with the swords peeking out over his shoulders.

"Jade, listen to me," I say softly. "You were hurt. We want to know what happened. Let's start there." Fortunately, neither one of my cohorts chimes in that her answers could determine her future.

What will I do? Will I fight to save her? Will I have a chance against both of them while also protecting Jade?

I don't want to hurt them, but I won't let her be harmed again.

"I was working on my book. Then… I thought I heard a knock on my front door." She scrunches up her face, forcing her memory forward.

"And?" Maxum prompts.

She blushes and averts her eyes. "I… I can't."

"Why not?" I ask, gently before Maxum or Calder begins to threaten her.

"I'm pretty sure I'm losing my mind, and Maxum looks like he's going to tear me in half. He already doesn't think much of me."

"No matter how strange, tell us what you think happened," I plead.

Jade bites her lip and squirms. "Can you loosen this blanket? I feel like I'm going to have a panic attack."

I don't want her to realize she's down to her underwear, but I also don't need her panicking… But will she panic because she's only in her underwear?

Forewarning her, I confess, "We found you unconscious. We were worried you had been hurt, so we stripped you down to your underwear to see."

"Why didn't you call an ambulance?" she asks.

"Once we explain, after you explain, you will understand why we didn't."

"Okay." She wiggles again.

I set her down on the couch next to me with her sitting up and help loosen the blankets' stranglehold.

She pulls her arms free.

The guys tense their bodies and watch her closely as if she were about to cast a spell.

I don't think she has enough in her to stand up on her own, let alone use magic.

Jade cradles her face in her palms and tells us her story. "I think there's a ghost possessing me. I know, crazy. I've had dreams that aren't exactly dreams. I knew things I shouldn't have." She peeks through her fingers to see my reaction. "I knew your name was Arran before you told me because I heard it in my vision."

"Go on," I encourage.

"You don't think I'm crazy?" When I shake my head, she looks at Maxum and Calder to gauge their reactions.

"Not about that." Maxum cocks a brow. Is he trying to be playful?

"Keep talking," Calder demands, his arms crossed and his face stern. He's overcompensating because he doubts his position on the witch's guilt.

Jade sighs wearily and continues, "So, this ghost might know all of you. He finally told me his name right before I woke up. Do you know someone named Osen?"

"He was the friend we just lost," I confirm.

"He is?" Jade covers her mouth. "Oh, my god… You mean this *is* real?"

I nod and squeeze her reassuringly. "Continue."

"Well, I heard a knock at my door. When I looked out the peephole, I blacked out. And then the next thing I remember is Osen, um… *talking* to me in what he called a shadowscape."

"Talking?" Maxum says with skepticism. He suspects the incubus did more than talk.

Jade hears his disbelief. "At the start, it was only talk. He said I wasn't powerful enough to protect us from Rob. He said he was an…" She pulls the blanket to her chest, feeling shy about her confession. "That he's an incubus?" She tries to redact everything she's said, "I know, it's a weird story, even for me." The witch looks at all three of us. "So, can you tell me what really happened to me? Why am I here, almost naked, and being interrogated?"

"Flint was watching your house to see if he could catch your stalker ex spying on you," I tell her. "He watched as you invited Rob inside…"

"I did *what*?!" she shouts.

"That's what I said," I agree. "Flint followed Rob and some woman after he left your place. I knocked and knocked, but you didn't answer. Then Maxum showed up. Since I was worried that you weren't answering, we broke in. You were on the ground…" I soften the truth and say, "… dying."

"Uh… what?" Jade goes stone still, then finally, her body trembles.

She's probably going into shock—if not from the subject, from the trauma her body has just been through. "Don't fuck with me," she hisses. "Please."

"We aren't." Maxum crouches down. I believe in an attempt to appear less threatening. But he's fucking massive, and the effort doesn't really help. He's just closer to her now and more imposing. Then again, maybe he wants to get a reaction from her when he asks, "Jade, why would Rob want you dead?"

"Because he must be crazier than I ever imagined?" Her eyes are wild with fear.

I can practically see her mind questioning everything that's happening.

"Were you working with him to attack other supes?" Maxum asks.

"Me… attack?" She looks at me, imploring me to believe her with a desperate expression. "I wasn't working with Rob—at all. Wait, do you mean supes as in supernatural beings? Like an incubus?"

"Yes, supes, as in supernaturals," he confirms.

"I'm *not* losing my mind?" she breathes out, mostly to herself.

Maxum sighs and momentarily looks as though he will reach out and caress her hand. "And you… are a witch."

"That's what Osen calls me. Little witch." Jade waves her hand dismissively. "But I don't have magic. I would know, wouldn't I?"

"You aren't particularly powerful. Or maybe you've suppressed your magic for so long it barely registers," Maxum explains. "But you have a particularly interesting gift—mediumship."

"Spirits of the dead… like your friend," she says, not completely denying her ability.

I take it as a good sign that she will handle the transition from a norm to part of the magical community.

"Yes," I confirm. "Osen has communicated through you, which, as a supernatural being, he shouldn't be able to do."

"Wait…" Jade grips my knee.

My body lights up that she would want to touch me at all. But I remind myself she doesn't know about my deceit yet. She doesn't know I'm a monster.

"Are you suggesting that Rob is some sort of supernatural being?" Her eyes widen, and she looks like she's about to run if we tell her yes.

"Our best guess is that he's a warlock," I answer and clasp my hand over hers, hopefully comforting her.

She stares at our joined hands. "I'm confused. From what I've gathered from Osen and now you, you don't like witches and warlocks. So why do you care if I live or die? Is it only because I can talk to Osen?" She pulls her hand free from mine and tucks them under her arms.

"It's the reason we didn't kill you already," Calder finally chimes in.

Thanks, dickhead.

"So if I can no longer give you access to your friend, you plan on killing me?" Her eyes glaze over as if she's witnessing her future death scene. Maybe she is filling in the blanks of how we'd do it, recalling something from Osen's memories.

"We aren't going to hurt you," I promise.

Jade turns to me, tears welling in her eyes. "This was all a lie." Then she looks up at Maxum. "The whole dating thing was just a ruse to have access to your friend."

"Not for me," I say, but it sounds weak after all we've just told her.

"It makes sense now. You hate witches, meaning I'm your enemy. But you can't kill me, since I have a link to someone you want back. So you'll spare me… until Osen's spirit moves on."

I can almost see her emotionally detaching from this situation. It's a solid and proven defense mechanism.

"I don't hate you," I explain. "But yes, I don't like witches in general."

"We all *hate* witches," Calder grumbles.

"But that's only because witches have hurt us in the past," I say, trying to explain our stance. "Witches and warlocks have declared war on supes... over and over throughout the centuries. Well, the extremists have been the problem."

"You know the rest will fall in line when the battle truly begins." Calder paces the room in agitation.

Maxum is oddly the voice of reason and says, "Witches and warlocks are just as complex as supes. Not all of them will follow the Witch Council or ASO blindly. I have known some witches who have turned against their own covens and fought them when their covenmates' methods have gone too far."

Interesting that he rarely mentions these outlier witches. Why is he doing it now? Perhaps it's for Jade's sake, letting her know this doesn't necessarily have to be us versus her.

"I don't want to hurt anyone." She lifts her head in an act of defiance. "I even helped Osen when I wasn't sure if it was in my best interest. I fed him to give him power."

My monster is jealous as fuck that Osen has been with her. Rationally, I know it was probably to help Osen get stronger, and the act might be what saved Jade's life.

"You only fed him so he could protect you, since you're a weak witch." Calder has lost some of his steam, so it comes out as more of a fact and not quite an insult.

"Yeah, I don't want to die. But I also did it because it felt like the right thing to do to help him solve his murder." She frowns. "And I did it for all of you—because he's your friend. But the gesture is likely lost now, since I'm guessing I'm your prisoner of war."

Calder grunts in agreement.

Maxum narrows his eyes at the phoenix. "We need to keep you here, Jade. But that's as much for your sake as ours. If Rob finds out you survived, he will come after you again."

"Oh! My fur babies!" she gasps. "Did Rob hurt them, too?"

She seems more worried about them than the fact she's our prisoner.

"I didn't think to check on them. But why would he do anything to them?" I ask.

"Rob hates them... for some strange reason."

Probably because he knows they are magical creatures. But I keep that one to myself. This has been enough of a revelation tonight.

"If you plan on keeping me prisoner, please take them to a shelter so they don't die of neglect?" Her sad green eyes undo me.

Apparently, Maxum is affected too. He sighs as if this is sending him over the edge. "I'll check on them." He gets up and goes into the backyard to portal out. I find it telling that he's so kind in easing her into this world.

I'm also happy that she seems to accept most of this without solid proof.

Although, I won't be surprised if she relapses. I've seen it before. Then we will have to show her our true forms to make her understand.

After a moment of her sitting quietly dazed, Maxum calls out that the animals are safe.

"Thank you," she whispers. Her eyelids droop. She sways in her seat and falls sideways over my lap.

"I'm putting her in my room," I announce and carry her into my small space, setting her down on my bed. I brush her long hair from her face and pray she will forgive me when I confess my sins.

HERE WE GO

JADE

"*a*m I losing my fucking mind?" I ask the darkness that surrounds me. I'm back in the shadowscape, as Osen calls it.

"No," Osen says as the room we're in lightens up enough for me to see his shadowform standing in front of me.

I'm in my bedroom, not passed out on Arran's couch.

"You are a witch… as I've been telling you since we first spoke," he reminds me.

"Your kind hates my kind." Feeling utterly depressed about being their enemy, I sit anxiously on the edge of my bed.

My mind registers that I'm naked, and I cross my arms in a futile attempt to cover up.

"No need for that here," Osen says gently, his shadowbody moving closer. "If you are uncomfortable with your nakedness, even after all we experienced together, I can conjure clothes for you."

Osen's right. He's seen all the goods. He's been inside this version of my body—which is very much like my actual body.

"You control all of this?" When he nods, I ask, "Then why do you have me look like this? Is it to make it feel more real because it appears to be my own body?"

I watch for his reaction. I find it's easier to do because he is more solid now. I can see hints of confusion on his face. "I like the way you are made."

"You *like* the way I look?" I try not to be insecure, but after Rob, it has been harder to accept that men want all my curves and imperfections.

His shadowhand strokes my hip and trails up my side. "I enjoy all your softness, your plump ass, and full tits."

"But usually, you're attracted to males, aren't you?" I ask, because that's what it appears to be from his memories.

"I'm attracted to the individual. I believe the closest thing I am is what humans call pansexual or omnisexual nowadays. Yes, typically, I enjoy my males big and brawny, but not necessarily. And I often delight in my females being curvy and soft. Which isn't a common trait for supernatural women."

"Most supe women are thin?" I wonder aloud.

"It's what got me in trouble. Witches are human-born, so they are often thicker. When I was just awakening to my powers, I was attracted to such a witch. She tortured me for a month until I was on death's door. Fortunately, Maxum saved me from that fate. Then years later, I let my guard down and trusted another witch. She tried to end me too."

"Oh, my god, I'm so sorry." I almost reach for him, then realize he might not want my touch.

"Oh, my *Goddess*," he corrects and places his hand in mine. "Those witches are why I hate your kind, but they aren't the only ones who have committed horrible deeds."

"So you believe all witches are your enemy?"

"Maybe not. Being inside you, here in the shadowscape, I merged with your spirit… I see not all witches are cruel."

"*I* changed your mind?" I'm a bit surprised since he's been clearly anti-witch.

"You offered yourself willingly, while also knowing I could possibly do you great harm when I fed."

"I was nervous, but didn't believe you were a bad person."

"Jade," his use of my name is disarming. "I'm afraid you're too trusting."

"And you aren't trusting enough," I add.

"Perhaps." He nods. "But I'm older than you, and I've had more experience with deceit. I've had a dozen people close to me attempt to end me. Rob was just the last of them."

"What did Rob do?" I ask. "I don't remember a thing."

"He knows you're a medium," Osen explains. "He attempted to trigger a mind-control spell that he has in place. He chanted a phrase and then asked what you knew about me and the ASO investigation."

I curse, anger rising up in me. Rob's violated my trust more than I could have ever imagined. "Rob hypnotized me to do his bidding? Like a sleeper agent?"

"Yes. Technically, you were working for my enemy."

I sit in shock, but as I process this, I find it fits with my strange 'dream' experiences, his interest in my dreams, and why he was with me when he didn't seem to like me all that much. "Go on."

"Well, since I had taken over your body, his spell didn't work on me. He realized right away that it wasn't you he was speaking to. He attacked with a spell I've never seen before."

"He tried to… kill me?"

"It was a very close thing. I don't know if he was only trying to exorcise me, kill you, or both." Osen's shadow wraps around me like a hug. "But I was able to keep you bound to your mortal coil. I shared my energy with you…."

"Why?"

"Because I recognized you were a victim, just as I was."

I want to believe him, but part of me is now souring to look for the best in others. Perhaps everyone is only out for themselves. They have played me for a chump.

Arran and Maxum only dated me to get information about Osen.

At least Maxum didn't lead me on and play with my emotions. We had brunch together and nothing more.

When I think about what Arran did with me sexually under the guise of liking me… hurt stirs in my soul.

"You didn't save me for my sake but for your own," I say, and it feels like venom dripping from my mouth.

"Yes. I benefitted, because I'm trapped in your body. But I didn't want you to die. Not when I could help."

"Sure," I say, not wholly believing him. "What about your buddies?" I demand.

"You mean Arran?" Osen sighs. "I'm afraid he really likes you. He would have let me die to save you."

"You're just saying that." I stand up and want to get away from him, but I'm not in control here. Osen is.

He moves in front of me, the shape of his face clear. He slips one arm around my waist, and another moves up to cup my cheek. "I'm not lying, not about my motives, and definitely not about Arran. I sort of wish I were."

"Because you love him?" My heart slightly softens to his plight.

"Yes."

"But he can't want me."

"I'm afraid we both want you. I suspect the others do, too." His lips brush over mine. "*I* want more of you, little witch."

He kisses me. I realize this is the first time. He did almost everything else but this. As if this simple act was sacred to him. It makes sense. This is more than sex. This is intimacy.

A warming wave rushes through me. I sense him, his soul. Osen's telling me the truth. He wants me. He cares, even if he doesn't want to.

"We have this time together," I say, snaking my arms around his waist.

"Yes, but you're about to wake, and it will have to wait." He holds me tightly to his shadowy but firm chest. "Until next time, my sweet, fuckable little witch."

The light of day streams in and makes me curse as if I'm a sun-shy vampire.

"Do vampires exist?" I wonder aloud as I throw my hands up to cover my eyes as the nuclear-level amount of sunlight shouts at me.

"That's a weird waking thought, and yes they do," Arran sounds amused. "Except they aren't what humans have made them up to be. Although they have fangs, love drinking magical blood, and are fast."

I try to sit up and look around, but honestly, my body isn't having it. I'm exhausted.

"Water?" Arran asks, coming to sit on the edge of the bed to inspect me.

"My throat feels like a dehydrated bitch, so yeah," I practically croak, my voice sounding as rough as I feel.

Arran slides his muscular arm behind my upper back and lifts me enough as he places a glass of water to my lips.

My hand automatically clasps over the glass, and I touch his warm fingers. Another lightning bolt of energy hits me with our touch. My heart pounds in response to his proximity. I don't know if his interest in me is real, but my feelings for him definitely are.

I pull back to let him know I've had enough water.

He gently rests my head on the pillow and sets the half-empty glass down.

I study the fairly stark room instead of looking at my sexy-as-fuck-maybe-boyfriend. Things just feel awkward now. I don't know what last night's news means for my future.

Our future.

Do I have a future? Or will one of his buddies kill me because I was born a witch and because Rob used me?

"Where am I?"

"My room, in our safe house." He tucks me in, tapping the blanket edges around my hips. He's nervous too.

I finally look directly at him. "What are you going to do?"

"What do you mean?"

"Are you going to kill me?"

"No. I'm going to keep you safe." He strokes my cheek.

"But why?" I turn my face away. I need to stay focused. "You think I'm your enemy—a witch."

"*You* aren't my enemy. You were being used, from what we can figure out."

"That's what Osen said." I sigh and rub my eyes with both hands. "He told me what happened with Rob. Not that you or your friends will believe me."

"What did Osen say?" Maxum is suddenly in the doorway. Damn, he takes up the entire space.

"He said that Rob was using my ability to talk with spirits without my knowledge and tried to trigger some kind of hypnosis spell. When Rob realized that I had been compromised by having Osen in charge of my body, he attacked and left me to die."

Arran looks at Maxum. "It makes sense—why Rob was so possessive and why we sensed her innocence."

Maxum grunts in agreement. "How are you doing?" he asks me. "Why aren't you running down the street screaming like a maniac about the existence of a magical world?"

"Because I don't like running?" I shrug. "I'm sure my panic attacks will come in waves." I try to sit up, and Arran helps me, placing pillows behind my back to prop me up. "Maybe I'm okay with it because I suspected magic was real with my abuela saying she was a witch and the weird dreams I've had my whole life. I just didn't know it was *this* scary."

Maxum grunts. "You're telling the truth about that."

"Are you a walking lie detector?" I ask.

"I can be." He nods. "But usually, it scrambles the person's brain, so I only do it if I'm desperate or desperately bored."

My eyes widen. I believe him, even with my limited powers of reading people.

Giving Maxum the side-eye, Arran asks, "How much do you remember from last night's conversation?"

"That you're supes. I'm a witch. You hate me."

"We don't hate *you*," Maxum corrects with a sigh, and I'm surprised it's him who does.

"Then why were you mean during brunch?" I ask.

"I thought you might have had something to do with Osen's death." Maxum narrows his eyes and reminds me, "You did spy on us at the bar."

"I said I'm sorry about that." My eyes widen when I think about how he said I wasn't wrong about how I had guessed their personalities. "Wait a damned minute. Was I right? About all your supernatural abilities?" I almost feel giddy that I might have nailed the magical spy thing without having known it.

"Yes. I'm a demon," Maxum confirms.

Arran squirms away uncomfortably.

"What about you?" I ask.

"Let's come back around to that later," he says in an ominous tone.

I pout but then recognize there is a lot to his situation if Osen's dream is to be taken as fact. They mentioned Arran had a terrifying beast that his friends might have to kill if it took control.

Oh...

Arran's beast might kill me after all and not even mean to.

I scoot back from him.

"You need to tell her everything," Maxum says with a firm tone. It's not quite a command, but it doesn't leave room for argument. "You have no excuse now."

I glance back and forth between them. "Tell me what?"

"You're tired." Arran tries to stand up, but Maxum takes his shoulder and presses him back down to sit on the edge of the bed again.

"I'm a shifter." Arran doesn't even look me in the eye.

"That was my guess." I gain a bit more energy with my confirmed projection.

Then it hits me.

"Hold up... are you a *wolf* shifter?" My voice has hit a high pitch. My heart drops to my gut and swirls in confusion.

I loved Beast. But I thought he was just a dog.

"Are you the fucking *dog*?" I cover my mouth and try to remember all the interactions with Beast.

Arran has been eerily still during my enlightenment, which confirms it without his words. "I am."

"You slept in my bed. You ate off my floor. You shit in my yard." I shake my head in disbelief. "I trusted you as both a dog and a human. And you weren't either."

"I'm sorry. Initially, I didn't intend to spy on you inside your home, but you invited me in. I thought at first you knew what I was. Then, I realized you didn't. But I was entrenched at that point and had to know if you were involved in Osen's death."

"You went through my things, didn't you?"

"Yes, but—"

"You pretended to want to date me and protect me from Rob, but that was all a ploy to know all the details about my life."

"It wasn't a ploy." Arran tries to catch my hand, but I pull away. "I didn't want to see you hurt. I fell for you."

"You accuse me of spying, but wow. You guys take it to another level." My eyes burn. "So licking my pussy was just a day at work? A spy's job is never done, huh?"

"Goddess, it's not like that." Arran falls to his knees at the side of the bed and clasps his hands as if praying. "Please believe me. I wanted you the first moment I saw you, but thought you were the enemy. When I sensed you weren't, I was relieved and set out to prove your innocence. I want to protect you."

"I'm supposed to believe all that?" I huff, "What about Osen? Did you use my body to fuck him?"

"What? No!" Arran draws back in horror.

"I remember kissing you. Maybe you did more?"

"You kissed me," he defends himself. "But all I did was talk to Osen."

"So you've known all along that Osen was possessing me?" I hold my forehead. I was barely holding on to my sanity before this conversation. Now I want to crawl away and sleep for a million years.

"I wouldn't have had sex with your body," Arran says.

My first instinct is to be offended, but there's more to his loaded statement.

"What do you mean?" I ask, staring into his golden-amber eyes that radiate pain.

"I wouldn't do it, because I can't." Arran frowns as if this is the hardest thing he's had to say in his life. "I've been cursed by a witch. When my emotions are riding high, I turn into a true beast—not just a wolf. I would hurt you. And I don't want to hurt you."

He's telling the truth because I can see it on his face, and I recall Osen's memory.

"You led me on." I glower at him. "We can't have something between us, anyway,"

"I could only be with Osen after it happened because he can immobilize my entire body. But with you, I was hoping..."

"What?" I demand. "What could you possibly be expecting from me after all this?"

Maxum answers when Arran doesn't, jarring me with the reminder that he's still here watching this whole love life fiasco. "He was hoping you could keep his beast under control."

"It's true," Arran agrees. "Your presence seems to keep him quiet. Calmer."

I don't know if it's his answer or my fatigue from apparently dying, but the room fuzzes out a bit. My head feels light and heavy at the same time.

"She needs to rest." Maxum waves his hand at Arran, encouraging the shifter to leave me the fuck alone.

I'll have to say the demon is winning some points here.

2 8

HEALING

JADE

I've been in and out of consciousness. I wouldn't be so presumptuous to call it sleep. This "rest" has been elusive and in no way restorative.

I haven't even seen my new incubus friend when I've been passed out.

Arran has been here a few times when I open my eyes, looking sorrowful and repentant. I believe he murmurs his apologies even when my eyes are closed.

Twice, I discover Maxum keeping vigil in Arran's room, watching over me. I read the concern in his eyes. And maybe something more, or perhaps I only wish to see that he's as attracted to me as I am to him.

Even Flint shows up, staring at me like I'm a great mystery of the ages.

His gaze is distant as I peek through my lashes at him, studying him. He fascinates me. I want to know more about this quiet, brooding presence. His fingers fiddle with some worn scrap of fabric. I have the sense that it's precious to him.

"Hi," I say, opening my eyes.

"Hello." His unease is visible. "You need something?"

"To talk. Is that okay?" I wince, expecting him to tell me to stuff it. I don't know how this guy feels about me. I am a wicked witch, after all.

"On what topic would you like to converse?" he asks.

"Anything." I want to ask him about his fabric treasure, but I don't want to shut him down. "But I suppose I'd like to talk about Arran, what he did. What do your friends want from me? Are all supernatural beings real? What's it like being a gargoyle? Do you protect places or people from evil? Do you turn to stone? Do you have other kinds of magic?"

"You have a lot of questions," Flint states, a slight upturn of his lips makes me think he's amused by aggressive curiosity. "In which order should I answer them?"

"I don't know." I pick at the blanket, feeling vulnerable. "I suppose I mostly want to know if I should believe Arran's apology and forgive him. But I also want to know more about the supernatural world… the real one, not the crap I make up."

"It sounds as if the stories you invent aren't excrement, but hold value and truth. At least, that's what Maxum and Arran have told me. I haven't read them yet. I don't read fiction." He glances at his fabric and sighs. "Yes, I can turn to stone, but only when I need to safeguard myself from injury. And I have a protective nature. I can't say if I know what it is to be a gargoyle. I just *am* me… and don't know what it's like to be anything else."

"That's what fiction does. It can give you a glimpse into how someone else feels," I say when he pauses.

"Perhaps I should try reading one."

"It doesn't have to be mine. I won't be offended," I add.

He nods and continues, "Maybe you can suggest something for me to begin my literary journey. Maybe not something heavy in a romantic theme?"

"Okay. I can do that." My mind races, compiling a list of books he might enjoy.

"As for Arran, he didn't mean to destroy your trust. He thought you were a threat. But his instinct to be near you made it impossible for him to pull away. He couldn't confess his true nature because you didn't know about your own. It was foolish of him to pursue a relationship with you."

"Because I'm a witch?" I ask, tears welling in my eyes. I believe I stupidly fell in love with Arran, and my heart hurts with the idea he can't be with me because of what I am.

"No, because he is a monster," Flint corrects, his voice soft. "We all are."

"Oh. You think he will hurt me? That you will all hurt me?"

"The odds are not in your favor."

"Are all supes monsters?"

"No. Most are much like humans. Perhaps they are more arrogant, which seems impossible. Supernaturals are often devastatingly beautiful. Obviously, I'm not like most supes."

His face and body are wide, and he epitomizes masculinity to the point of being absurd. "You are extremely handsome."

"This isn't my true form. You wouldn't find it appealing."

"My tastes are broader than most." I offer him a smile, hoping he will show me.

He grumbles, but changes the subject. "Arran cares about you. He didn't mean to damage the relationship you were developing."

"But his beast might accidentally hurt me?"

Flint nods. "None of us want to see you hurt. I don't even think Calder wants that, no matter how he blusters."

"Do you believe me when I say that I didn't hurt Osen? I didn't even know I was a witch. If I helped the witches and warlocks kill your friend, it wasn't my choice."

"I know. You were being used." He frowns.

My fatigue hits me again, and my eyes flutter shut.

"Sleep, sweet witch," he whispers, perhaps not intending for me to hear.

Waking up, I feel like crap, and that's putting it mildly. It seems as though each time I wake up, I feel worse.

My dry throat makes me cough, and it's enough to rouse me to move and seek water. Of course, this is the one time when I open my eyes that no one is here to help me.

With great effort, I get the covers off me and sit on the edge of the bed, summoning the energy to get up.

It takes another few minutes to remember how standing works.

I shuffle to the open doorway, zeroing in on the doorframe as my next life goal.

My hand settles on the frame, and I gasp in a breath, basking in my victory.

My grip slips, and I tumble forward.

At the same moment, someone turns from the hall into Arran's room.

A male voice is cut off mid-word, "Wha—"

My body crashes against what feels like a wall.

Massive arms wrap around my torso, and they freeze.

I look at the literal rock-hard body my face is pressed against—tan-colored marble. I didn't know a gargoyle's flesh was so unyielding.

Flint… the gargoyle version.

"Okay, buddy, you can let go." My arm wanly pats his biceps.

He doesn't move or respond to me.

"Flint?" I call.

Nothing.

I'm worried he's debating the merits of crushing me with his humongous arms. Heck, I think his pinky fingers could crush me all by themselves.

I tilt my head back to look at his face, but it takes some effort with my debilitating exhaustion.

Flint is solid stone.

His eyes are locked onto me but appear to be unseeing. They are no longer filled with their usual quiet inquisitiveness. His face looks as though he is frozen with fright.

Do witches scare this huge guy enough to defend himself like this?

He might scare me more if I didn't get the feeling that he has a gentle soul under all his group's talk of war and revenge.

I try to slip down and out of his hold, but his arms are locked tight enough around my waist that I can't move.

"Fuck," I mutter, my face still pressed against Flint's smooth marble chest.

Is this his true gargoyle form? He appears to be in his human form, but only now, made of carved marble. I was hoping he would have tusks and wings.

Oh, well, another fantasy bubble burst. Unless he has a shifted form since he said I would be turned off by his true form. But I see no other change than his solidity.

Back to the matter at hand… I wonder what could be wrong with him to make him turn. Has someone spelled him?

Can a witch's mere touch do that? Did I hurt him? Accidentally cursed him?

The guys are going to think the worst of me… especially Calder. I hope he doesn't discover us first.

I wiggle to break free, but it's no use. I'm pinned to him. As it is, I can barely take a full breath.

"Arran?" I call to the empty house. I don't know how I know it's empty, but I feel it. "Maxum? Calder?"

I don't know what they could do about this, but maybe they have some anti-statue spell.

Fatigue washes over me again. I tuck my arms into my body, lean my head against the gargoyle's massive chest, and pass out.

. . .

"Jade!" I hear Arran shout from a distance.

I open my eyes and see him peering over Flint's broad shoulder. He's stuck on the other side of the bedroom door that Flint's giant body is blocking entirely.

"Arran?"

"Oh, thank fuck," he sighs. "I thought you might be…"

"Dead?" I finish for him. "No. But this might be my new life now, caught in Flint's hold."

Maxum asks, "What happened?"

"I was going to ask you that," I say. "All I did was get out of bed to get some water, and Flint quickly came through the door. Since I could barely stand, I accidentally fell into him. He grabbed me and froze. I swear I didn't mean to hurt him."

"He's not hurt," Maxum assures me.

"Thank goodness," I breathe out.

"Did he hurt you?" Arran asks.

"No." I look up again at his strange frozen expression. "What's going on? Why did he turn to stone? Did my witchiness do this?"

"Witchiness?" Maxum chuckles, then mutters, "*Womanness* is more like."

"What do we do?" Arran asks Maxum. "We can't get around him even to see how tight of a hold he has on her."

"It's pretty tight," I inform him. "I can't budge."

"Shit." Arran's frustration worries me.

"Is there a spell or something to wake him up?"

"He's not asleep," Maxum grumbles. "He's petrified."

"Forever?" I screech. That's not a great sound.

"Hopefully not," Maxum says with a sigh. "We need to calm him."

"Isn't he a battle-tested warrior? Why would colliding with me in the hallway upset him?"

"He doesn't like to be touched," Arran answers.

"Shit!" I lift my arms away from where they were resting on his. "Can he hear me?"

"Yeah," Maxum says. "He's aware of what's going on in his stone form."

"Flint?" I begin, my voice soft. "I'm sorry I touched you. Please don't be upset with me. I like you, and I didn't mean for this to happen. I will be more careful around you, I swear it. I need you to just soften your stone, and I can stop touching you."

Tears fall from my eyes, because I don't like that my budding friendship with him is on the line. I wanted to get to know him, and now he won't ever want to be around me again.

"I'm so sorry. I keep messing up, making mistakes." I sniff, feeling like a failure. I don't know why, but all my problems tumble out of me. Maybe it's because I'm certain I will die soon. I can feel my life force slowly slipping from my body. Or maybe because I'm so damned exhausted, I can't think straight.

"I didn't even know I was a witch. My abusive, warlock ex-boyfriend only dated me to brainwash me and use me to channel dead people. I caught the attention of the wrong hot guys. I invited a wolf shifter who wanted to kill me into my house. I went on a brunch date with a demon who wants to scramble my brains. I'm possessed by a sex ghost who tolerates me only so he can power up. And I'm pretty sure I'm still dying from Rob's spell. And now? I'm stuck in the arms of a sexy gargoyle who can't stand my touch."

Yeah, I'm leaning into my self-pity.

I'm 'whining'… *whatever*.

People can be sad once in a fucking while. I'm sick of always having to keep my shit together.

Why is it that the only accepted form of emotional expression is snarky anger?

Be tough. Be strong. And be an asshole.

No. Sometimes we just need to grieve. Say how we feel.

Sometimes, we need to call out how fucked life can be.

If we don't acknowledge what's wrong, what makes us depressed, then we rarely make the changes we need to get out of it.

Besides, it's justified for me to have a fucking breakdown after all that's happened. Even the emotionally resilient need a vacation from being strong.

Apparently, my sadness shakes something loose in Flint as I hear a moan that sounds like gravel grinding on itself.

Flint's grip on me loosens until I can slip downward. He still hasn't let up entirely, though. Of course, as I move down, my face drags over his… not six, not eight, but ten-pack abs. I feel a generous package under his pants. I try my best to not be a perv and ignore that, making this as nonsexual as possible.

But the gargoyle does something to my heart. If I thought he'd be into it and had any strength left, I'd enjoy this trip along his body more.

Finally free from his hold, I collapse onto the floor. I don't have the energy to get up.

Flint returns to his flesh form and staggers backward until he slams his body into the hallway wall behind him. His eyes are wide with panic and shame. "I'm sorry, Jade. It's my fault, not yours." He runs off before I can tell him it's okay.

I feel something wet under my hand and see a glass of spilt water that Flint must have been bringing me when I crashed into him.

He was trying to take care of me.

Arran rushes inside and lifts me into his arms. "I got you, sweetness."

This little misadventure took more out of me than I realized. "I don't feel well," I say as I pass out.

My eyes are still closed when I hear the guys talking.

"Jade needs healing," Arran says to Maxum. "The killing hex is still hurting her."

"She won't want it from me," Maxum argues.

I slowly open my eyes. "Why not?" My words come out slurred.

"You would see my true form, and the healing is... sexual in nature," the demon sounds contrite.

"My beast won't like you touching until he's claimed her," Arran whispers to Maxum.

I start to giggle until I'm in full chuckling mode.

"Why is that funny?"

"Because, of course, it's *sexual!*" I believe I've lost my mind. "Why can't anything be simple?" My humor drops like a stone. "Besides, you want me dead. So you wouldn't want to sex magic me up anyway, right?"

"I didn't say that," Maxum says quietly.

My mind spins as I turn to look at him. "What part?"

He squares his broad shoulders. "I don't want you to die. And I would share my magic to heal you."

"But you seem hesitant." Nervousness crawls over me. I wonder what his version of sex magic is. "So I'm guessing you don't want to fuck me."

"It's not that. My true form will scare you." Maxum nods to Arran. "And it will trigger his berserker beast if I have sexual relations with you."

I snicker at the use of 'sexual relations.' I turn to Arran, "Will your beast hurt us if Maxum does his sex magic thing on me?"

"Hold on." Maxum's usually calm exterior cracks. "Are you saying you want to fuck a demon?"

"It's on my bucket list," I joke. Well, I sort of joke... It's totally on my imaginary bucket list. Or it was, when I thought it was fictional.

"Arran?" Maxum looks at his friend. I know he's not asking permission per se, but he doesn't want his beast to hurt us... probably me.

"I... I want to say that I'll be okay." Arran turns to me. "But my beast is riding me right now, since I've messed things up with you."

I take a moment to consider what's really happening. On the one hand, this all feels like I'm caught in some strange fantasy-nightmare. On another, I look at it as if I'm writing one of my paranormal novels. Rules don't apply the same way in a supernatural world. I'm familiar with this concept.

And sure, Arran made mistake after mistake, but I still don't get that icky feeling like Rob gave me.

I believe I've already forgiven Arran after I've thought about all of it and what Flint said.

"Why didn't you tell me before?" I ask, knowing why, but needing it confirmed.

"You didn't know about supes. I thought you'd turn me away. I knew I was over the line with my behavior."

"If I were to forgive you, what would you want from me moving forward? Really want... not just the answer you *think* I want to hear."

Arran gulps. He knows this is his test. It comes down to this. "I want to make you my mate. Love you. Protect you."

Geeze. These supes don't play around. It's let me 'lick your pussy, and then I'm mating you for eternity' in the next breath.

Do I mind? Not really. I write this shit because it turns me on. I've desired to have someone consumed by my existence.

"How can we soothe Arran's berserker *and* have you do what you need to do to heal me?" I ask Maxum.

"I think he's going to need to be inside you when I am."

My body heats with that image. Do I take one in the mouth? One in the ass? I wonder which I would prefer where. And I love all the ideas. I can't choose.

"Oh, wait, what about STDs?" I hold my hands out like they are about to rip my blanket away and fuck me stupid... well, *more* stupid.

"Supes don't carry diseases," Maxum assures me. "You aren't worried about me breeding you?"

Oh, shit. I'm dying inside with his use of the word *breeding*.

I wonder if he has a kink. But I wait as the impulse to giggle passes, and I shake my head. "I'm on birth control."

Maxum looks at his crotch, and then at Arran's growing bulge. "I'm going to get something stronger. Our magic might negate your prevention."

Even though I feel weak as a fragile wilted flower, I apparently died and don't exactly feel double penetrated fresh. "Maybe I can clean up while you get that?"

"You can't even sit up." Arran fidgets, his hands poised to snatch me up.

"Can you help me?" I ask, feeling vulnerable. I've been so independent and isolated. It's a foreign sensation asking for help.

Arran exhales, and his tension falls away. "It would be my honor."

"I'll be back soon, little witch." Maxum nods and heads out of the house.

My shifter smiles sadly. "I'm so sorry. I wish I wasn't cursed. Then I could let you be with Maxum alone."

I hold my arms out to him so he can help me up. When his strong arms lift me and carry me to the bathroom, I confess, "It's okay. I want both of you."

BUCKET LISTED

ARRAN

*W*hen Jade confesses to wanting us both, I almost stumble with her in my arms. Which is not great since we are now on the slip-sliding away bathroom tiles.

I steady myself and try to remain calm. But my beast is waking the fuck up.

What's worse, I don't know how long Maxum will be away.

I need him to keep her safe… just in case my beast loses control. And losing control is on-brand for that part of myself.

"Arran?" Jade calls me softly.

I realize I'm gripping her so tightly that she probably can't breathe. "Sorry."

I loosen my hold and pull the throw blanket away from her naked body—well, almost naked body.

My arm is bracing her against me. Her full breasts are begging to be released from the thin bra she's wearing, and I wonder why she even bothers with wearing the flimsy thing. I want her naked all the time, ready for me to fondle her beautiful tits.

She's strong enough to pull the thin sports bra over her head. I have to resist the urge to lean down and nibble her mounds and suck on her hardening nipples.

Using my free hand, I slide her underwear down her thick thighs.

My eye catches on the only thing she has left on—her golden pendant. She seems to wear it all the time. "What's this?"

"My abuela gave it to me—my grandmother. She said it was a protection pendant." She fiddles with it nervously. "I guess it doesn't really work that great."

"Well, you are still alive, so maybe it does?" I offer.

Jade nods sadly, then glances at my clothed state. "What about you?"

I was ready to go in the shower with my sweatpants on because if I'm naked with her, it will be much harder to resist plunging into her slick heat.

"You are too tempting, and we can't start messing around without Maxum," I warn.

"Because of your beast?"

"I could hurt you."

She nods and assures me, "I'll be a good girl. Promise."

Jade can barely move, so I didn't expect her to be the problem. But the thought sobers me. She's completely at my mercy. Her life is in my hands. I'm alone with the woman I want to make my mate, and I could kill her.

I'm also as hard as Flint in his gargoyle form. And I don't want her to freak out with my eager cock.

I turn on the water to warm it and try to command my dick to deflate.

Slowly pushing my sweats down, I say, "Don't freak out."

"That's not an alarming phrase while revealing a dick for the first time. No, not at all," she says sarcastically.

My cock pops over the waistband.

Jade gasps.

Ugh. I knew she would hate it. I close my eyes and wish I'd been born a warlock instead.

"Holy magic eight-balls." She sucks in a breath. "Do you actually lock inside a woman?" Instead of sounding disgusted, she sounds intrigued about my knot—excited.

"I can. But that's usually done with other wolf shifters."

"Does it stay that size or get bigger?"

"It would swell a bit when I lock in." I blink with surprise. "Do you want that?"

"Uh, I've written about all this fancy peen, but to have the chance to try it out, with a real, live supernatural being? Sign me up."

I frown. "Why do I feel like a glorified boy toy right now?"

"Does that mean you don't want to fuck me with it?" she asks. "Shame."

I smack her ass lightly. "You are a brat."

"If I admit I am, do I get to play with my new toy?"

I smack her ass again, and she moans.

Somehow, my dick hardens even more.

Remembering that I can't fuck her yet, I lift us into the shower, and she squeaks when the water hits her backside.

I lather up my hands with soap and use them to clean her body—slowly and methodically.

When I massage her breasts and slide my fingers over her cunt and asshole, she murmurs how much she loves it.

I can scent her arousal even through the water pouring over her. She's driving me mad with desire and doesn't even realize it. I'm afraid I'm going to be a two-pump chump once I sink into her.

Once she's clean, I lift her out of the shower, set her on the vanity, and dry her off. Her hazel-green eyes watch me with a sly smile. Her gaze wanders over my entire body as I also take in her tantalizing, exposed flesh.

I wrap a dry towel around her and carry her back to my room. I set her down on my bed, sitting up, so she hopefully feels less fragile.

"You're sure you want me?" I ask. It seems like a dream. I pray to the Goddess this fantasy doesn't turn into a nightmare if my beast loses control. Maybe I should have Maxum take me far away and chain me up while he heals her.

"I want you." She gently strokes my cheek. "Are you sure you want me? I don't know if you know, but I'm a criminally ignorant witch." She gives me a sassy grin.

"That's a whole step down from evil witch, so yeah, definitely on my bucket list."

Maxum returns a moment later. He clears his throat and hands Jade a small vial. "It's safe. Safer than human birth control. Effects are immediate."

Thanking him, she swallows the entire bottle with a wince.

"Give us a second?" Maxum asks me.

I don't like it, but his needs come into play here too.

I don't go far, just outside the door. It's as far as my beast will allow. It gives them the illusion of privacy, at least.

30

HORNS AND ALL

MAXUM

"*Y*ou don't have to do this," the witch tells me.

It's true. I don't.

But I want to.

"If I don't do this or find another safe way to help you, you will likely die," I explain. "So I have to."

Do I sound desperate to slide my cock inside her? Because that's all I've been able to think about since I left to get the potion. Fuck, that isn't entirely true. I've wanted her since she told me to fuck off during brunch. I love a feisty woman. So few are that way with me. Either they are begging me to fuck them, or they're scared of the power they feel radiating off me and run far, far away.

Let's just say it's been a while since I found a female I wanted and one who wanted me, too. I don't want to admit it to either Jade or Arran, but I want her around more than for one fuck.

"Is there another way?" she asks.

"Not a guaranteed method, which I am. As for healers? I don't know who to trust. I'm fairly certain someone betrayed Osen within our outer circle. I won't expose you to that risk. Besides, the fewer people who know you are alive, the better. Rob believes you're dead, and I intend to keep it that way."

"I don't want you to do anything you're uncomfortable with." She tugs her towel higher as if that half-inch of skin offends me.

"All I do is shit I'm uncomfortable with," I chuckle darkly. "But I would assume you'd be the one who wouldn't want me since I was an asshole before."

"You thought I was the enemy. I understand that."

With my psychic senses, I pick up that she indeed understands.

"I must be in my true form for this to work." My words come out soft and a bit shy.

"Will you show me who you really are?" Jade adjusts as she leans against the wall, as if to brace herself.

I remove my shirt so she'll see my markings first—ease her into this.

The red lines cover my entire torso and arms.

Her eyes widen as she stares.

I nervously wait for her to respond to my markings. They are sacred to my people, and I don't want her to hate it.

Fuck. Am I falling for her?

"Do they have meaning?" Her hand lifts as if she wants to touch them.

"Sacred markings of my spirit. They appear magically when I have a significant experience. It's written in my flesh."

"That's amazing," she says with awe.

I sit down on the bed and offer my hand. When Jade slips her hand in mine, I place it on my forearm so she knows she can touch me.

She smiles. "You are so warm." Her eyes catch on the broken, jagged lines in the center of my chest. "This shows how you've lost ones you loved."

She gets it—*me*.

I take her finger and run it over one particularly fresh-looking line. "This is Osen's death."

Tears well up in her eyes. "I'm so sorry. I know you meant a lot to each other."

"You've seen some of it?"

"I didn't mean to invade. I didn't see much. However, I saw this isn't your true form. I saw horns in one of the memories, but it was dark."

"Don't be afraid," I say and shift, showing off my deep red skin and curled horns.

This crazy woman, who just discovered the magical world, doesn't look the least bit afraid. She looks entranced by me.

Is it horrible that I'm disappointed that I didn't startle her a little?

Her hungry gaze makes up for it though. She licks her lips as she eyes my horns.

I unfurl my bat-like wings, and she squeals with joy.

She squeals… what the actual fuck?

"Wings!" she claps happily.

Might as well see if she can deal with the rest of it. She's going to see it in a few minutes, anyway.

I yank down my pants and reveal my tail wrapped around my waist and my already throbbing, hard dick.

"A tail!" She bites her lips in anticipation, the crazy witch. "And your cock is…"

Arran bursts back into the room, his skin rippling with a barely contained shift.

"Oh, Arran, come here." She holds her hand out to him, inviting him to be part of this. "How do we help you handle what's going on?"

"If you touch him, I need to be touching you at the same time."

"But you're okay with him touching me?" she asks, because it is an interesting distinction.

"I know I have to share you, but until… *if* I claim you, my beast will be on edge about sharing your affection." Arran looks me in the eye. "If I look like I will hurt her, do what you have to do to stop me. Even if it means ending me."

"Arran!" she cries. "I don't want you to be hurt."

"I'll never forgive myself if I injured you." He presses his forehead to hers. "I believe my beast wants to pleasure you too, so I think we will be okay."

I nod at both of them, and Jade ogles my jutting member again. "You wanted to touch my cock?" I ask.

She nods and looks at both our dicks. "I want to feel both of you."

Her eyes linger on my unusual cock. It's similar to a dragon cock, but with spiky-looking ridges around the head and along the top and bottom of its length.

"Textured for pleasure," I say, stroking myself to show her they aren't sharp.

We each take one of her hands and place it on our cocks at the same moment.

Wisely, she strokes Arran first and lightly squeezes his knot.

He jerks in her hand. "Fuck. You keep playing like that, and I'm going to knot you this fucking second."

She gives Arran a kiss, and he deepens it, claiming her with his intensity. His hand cradles her jaw as he slowly rocks himself into her hand.

Jade turns to me and slowly slides her hand down my length and back again. "Oh. That's different."

Arran growls.

"Be a good boy and suck on my tit," she orders him.

Both our dicks twitch in her hold.

Arran snaps to it. Cupping her breast, he guides her plump nipple into his mouth.

Her hand squeezes me as she's overcome with pleasure.

Tentatively, she strokes me. I have to bite back my moan. I don't want either of them to know how much she affects me. Not yet.

With Arran distracted by his feast, my tail slides up, tickles her thighs, and brushes over the V where her mound disappears between her closed legs.

I need her on her back and open to me.

Besides, she's pushing her limits, and I can feel her energy failing her. I don't want to be fucking her while she's unconscious.

"Open your legs," I order.

She obeys quickly. Both Arran and I slide our hands up her inner thighs, brushing over her apex. Arran presses her backward as he sucks on her other tit.

"I'm going to taste your pussy now," I inform them. I need to make her ready for me.

Arran's barely handling this, but he's keeping the beast on lockdown for the moment. He grunts to acknowledge my announcement.

I kneel between her legs as they hang off the edge of the bed.

Slowly, I spread her thighs farther apart.

My fingers trace over her folds and I familiarize myself with her cunt, finding the bundle of nerves they now call a clit. She bucks when I do.

I lean forward to lick and suck on her nub.

"Oh, damn. Is your tongue forked?" she cries out the question as I use it to stimulate her clit.

"Does that turn you on, little witch?" I say with a smirk. I know it does with how wet she's getting. I flick my tongue in the air at her, and her eyes dilate.

"Fuck, yes." She grabs my horns to pull me in, and I bury my face in her pussy.

I swear I almost spill my seed right then, but that won't help her condition. So I maintain my control and slide two fingers into her, then I add another.

She grinds into my hand.

Goddess, I want her again when she's at full strength. I want her bouncing herself on my cock, my tail in her ass, gripping my horns, and screaming my name.

Pumping my hand into her, I tell them my idea. "I want Arran under you, taking your ass. I will take your pussy as I work my healing."

"My ass?" she pants. "But…"

"We can see if both of us can take your pussy at the same time," I suggest. "Or you can suck him down while I fuck you?"

My hand is instantly drenched in her juices with my dirty talk. My little witch is so responsive.

I wonder if we can share her all the time. Would Calder ever want her, too? Maybe Flint will finally get over his celibacy stint if he sees how she enjoys my true form. And that she can survive a monster fucking.

"What do you want, little witch?" I ask.

"I… uh." Arran pinches her nipple, and she shouts, "I want him to fuck my ass."

"I need your pussy first," Arran snarls, and I move out of the way.

I look for her consent, and she nods as Arran lines himself up. Then he realizes his frenzy. "Jade?"

"Yes, fuck me," she pants.

Arran shoves forward, and she moans with his thick shaft, where his knot pounds against her labia.

"Don't let her come yet, and you'll have to come in her ass," I warn.

"Goddess," she says, picking up on our lingo.

Her eyes glaze over. She's losing her ever-loving mind.

"Arran, on the bed, now," I order.

He glares at me, wanting to finish in her pussy. But he pulls out, lies on his back, and brings her on top of him.

I grab some lube and work it into her ass and over Arran's dick. It's been a while since I've touched him like this, but he moans with pleasure.

"Ready?" I ask.

They both nod. Arran has both hands on her tits, cupping both entire mounds and pinching the large nipples. I'll need a suck on them too.

As soon as I get Arran distracted, I will make it my mission.

I line him up to her back entrance, and he presses inside. Slowly, he slides to his knot, her body welcoming him inside.

I watch the show for a moment, enjoying how she gasps and moans with his steady thrusts. I'm not sure how he's maintaining his composure, but when I look at his hands gripping her breast and one now over her low belly, I see his hands have shifted into fur and claws. The points are dangerously pressing into and dimpling her soft skin.

"Arran?" I question his control.

He looks at me, his eyes glowing amber and his teeth elongated. His mouth and nose have become a snout.

"Arran?" Jade calls him, caressing his monstrous hands. "It's okay. Just be careful with me."

He seems soothed by her words—that she accepts him even as his monster.

My hand rubs over her clit, and I slide my fingers inside again. "You ready, little witch?"

"Yes?" She hears her own nervousness and says with more certainty, "Yes."

I notch my enormous cock at her pussy and slowly press inside.

Arran groans and snarls, equally irritated and turned on by my invasion. I'm not even fully sheathed in her glorious body.

Jade pants as if she's giving birth. Her forehead is beading with sweat. "It feels… so… good. So full." She can do nothing but take what we are giving her. "Keep going," she insists, grabbing onto my waist to encourage me to move deeper.

Her legs drape over Arran's beastly thighs, and his knot teases her back entrance.

I lean forward and suck her unattended nipple into my mouth.

"Hurry, get all the way inside me. I think I'm dying," Jade whines. She isn't taking a bad turn, but I love that she's begging for my cock.

"Whatever you need." I work myself deeper until I'm finally seated. I'm surprised she's taken all I have to give. If she were to become ours, she would be perfect.

I love how her pussy squeezes my dick.

"Look at you, taking our cocks so well," I praise, sliding in and out of her.

Arran begins to work her ass, matching my rhythm.

She smiles, glancing up at me and looking blissed out of her mind.

I use this moment of her attention to give her a show… one I believe she will appreciate, as her monster fucking kink is loud and proud right now.

I pull back, slam into her, and flare my wings out, casting her in shadow, sheltering all three of us from the world.

"Fuck!" she screams and climaxes with the sight. Her pussy clenches my dick so hard I think I might pass out. Her face is lost in the pleasure we're giving her and I've never seen a more beautiful sight.

I begin the chant to heal her, my ancient language droning as I pump into her, extending her pleasure, grinding into her hips, my tail flicking over her clit.

I warn Jade, "Arran's about to come."

I pull the magic he releases with his orgasm into my magic to heal our witch. Her body starts to glow. A pattern of light shines over her.

I'm not sure what this is... a witch's protection warding?

However, it doesn't feel like that. I'll have to investigate later, when I'm not balls-deep inside her cunt.

Fortunately, whatever the glow is, it doesn't stop my healing magic from pouring into her body. I feel her gaining strength. I sense the damage from Rob's hex being repaired.

As I unload my cum deep into her cunt, I finish my sex magic spell and pull my wings tightly around us. I want to be with her again. Without Arran. For hours.

I want to learn everything I can about her body.

I want to teach her things she's only imagined in books.

Her body pulses with the unusual glow, and finally, it fades.

When I catch my breath, I acknowledge there's something *other* about Jade.

She isn't a mere witch.

That might explain her ability to channel and hold Osen's spirit.

And it might mean she is meant for us after all.

31

AFTERCARE

JADE

I'm spread-eagle over the top of Arran's monster form with Maxum curling his massive body over mine. They are both buried deep inside me.

"That was..." I can't finish my sentence as I'm dizzy with euphoria, fatigue, and with the healing magic Maxum just used on me.

Arran's fur tickles my back, and he's huffing, recovering from his orgasm. He's stuffing me full, and I can feel his hot release leaking out of my ass.

Maxum's wings are still wrapped around us, and I don't want to break the moment by moving or saying anything more. While I do feel better health-wise, I'm still exhausted.

I'm also blissed out of my mind. I've never had an experience like that. I'm fairly certain my soul left my body... in a good way this time.

It feels like this is the place I've been seeking my entire life, in the arms of Maxum and Arran. I don't want this moment to end. I want to pretend for a while longer that we aren't enemies and this can somehow work out. To pretend as if I'm one of my own characters, and I can finally have a happy ending too.

The demon dick inside me twitches, and I suck in a breath. Those bumps and ridges do things to me, and I need to experience them again when I'm not at death's door.

I want to take him again, but slowly and with no distractions. I want to use my tongue to explore his cock and everything else. I need Maxum—all of him.

My hand skims his wing's hard ridge, and he bucks into me.

Oh, they're sensitive. Nice. But I should ask before I assume to touch. "Sorry."

Maxum pushes up and off me just enough to look into my eyes. His obsidian orbs have a warm glow to them—magic radiating from him. "You can touch me. I'm just hypersensitive during sexual activities."

His tail flicks over my clit and my pussy clenches. Since Maxum and Arran are still deep inside me, the three of us groan with the sensation.

"Like that," he chuckles.

"Arran? Are you okay?" I ask, turning my head to see him. I have no idea what his berserker beast looks like, but I'm curious.

"Don't look at me." His clawed hand moves to prevent me from seeing him, and he turns his face away. "I'm not fully shifted back yet." His voice doesn't sound quite human.

"I have your huge cock and your cum in my ass, and you won't let me see you?" Realizing this might not be the time for being sassy, I soften my voice. "Arran... I want to know you, all of you." I gently run my finger over the claw on his index finger.

I must have convinced him since Arran warns, "Maxum, get ready to take her away if she screams."

Now, I'm a bit nervous.

When he moves his hand, I see his beast, but he's actually more attractive than I was expecting. His face is mostly wolf-like but with a humanized look to it.

His shoulders are bulkier than his human form and have a thin coat of fur. He still won't look directly at me.

Since my back is on his chest, I can't see more than that. To reassure Arran of how I feel about him, I give his snout a kiss.

His eyes fly wide with shock. "You kissed my beast!"

"Is it mad?" I ask.

Instead of answering, his body shifts back to his human form. Wow. That was weird, but cool. I sink a few inches lower since he's smaller in his normal body.

Arran gives me a searing kiss that conveys all his appreciation that I've accepted his monstrous side.

Maxum hums with interest at this exchange. I turn back to study him.

His demon form is so sexy that I could believe this was a dream. His face is almost the same, with his brow slightly more pronounced. I dare to drag my fingertip over the base of his horn. I peer into his eyes to see if this is okay, but they are closed, and he's smiling in bliss.

"That feels good?" I ask.

"Very much so." He opens his eyes and strokes my cheek. "I sense you're much stronger. But I need to stay inside you for a few more minutes. Is that all right, my little witch?"

He's being so sweet that I want to cry.

I have not one but two males caring for me, and sending me into emotional territory.

I nod so I don't have to risk my voice cracking.

However, Maxum sees beyond my walls which are pretty much windows at this point—and not even double-pane.

He presses his forehead to mine in a gesture of compassion that undoes me.

Tears drip over the sides of my face and land on Arran.

"Sweetheart?" my shifter coos from beneath me. "What's wrong?"

"Nothing. Everything." I inhale and exhale slowly. "You both think of me as the enemy but are still here healing and caring for me. Yet my ex, who told me he loved me, tried to murder me."

"You aren't our enemy," Maxum assures me.

"You are pack," Arran says, his voice deep and authoritative.

Even I recognize the magic in his statement. Goosebumps erupt over my skin as I feel the power wash over me.

I'm one of their people... as far as Arran is concerned. At least, he feels like that at the moment, with the pleasure of release running his brain.

But I've been betrayed and abandoned too many times to trust even a magically imbued claim. My own mother disowned me.

One of my arms goes over my shoulder to cup Arran's strong jawline with my palm. At the same time, I caress Maxum's face with my other hand. "Thank you for saving me."

The demon presses his lips to mine in a tentative kiss, but when I respond to him, his kiss becomes more urgent and consuming.

His hips rock into mine, and the squelching sound from his release makes my pussy throb with need again.

Maxum quickly lifts me off of Arran and cups my ass. When Arran gets up to follow, Maxum warns, "Your beast has been quelled. Let me satisfy mine. *Alone.*"

His textured dick is still inside me, and as he walks, I'm rubbed in all the right ways. I finally let out my groan once we are in another room.

While still holding me to him, he grabs a clean towel and wipes the mess from my backside.

"I'm impressed with your staying power," I say about his cock that hasn't softened one bit.

"You turn me on, little witch." He nuzzles my jaw, and I lean back so he can kiss and lick my neck. His forked tongue feels amazing.

"What's happening now?" I ask, since I'm a virgin to this whole sex magic ritual.

"My own beast needed to have you to himself." Maxum kneads my ass. "I want to fuck you again."

"Oh." I check in with my body, and it feels absolutely on board with this suggestion. It also demands to know why this isn't happening already. If I don't agree quickly, my body is putting in a complaint with the manager.

"Would you like that?" Maxum cants his hips to make me take him deeper again.

"Fuck. Yes, I would." I'm completely supported by his cock and powerful arms around my ass, so I'm able to move my arms freely, exploring him. I stroke over his broad shoulders and then dip behind to see if I can reach where his wings attach to his back.

He curls inward to make it easier to reach around his enormous body.

When I feel and caress the tendons and bones where the wings connect to his back, Maxum bucks hard into me. Apparently, I've found the demon's G-spot.

His tail slides over the back of my thigh, teasing my asshole.

"Are you…"

"Yes, I am." He growls. "I'm going to fuck you with my tail and my cock."

As he slides inside me, where I've been made slick with Arran's cum, I about lose the few marbles I have left. "Are you sure you aren't trying to kill me through pleasure? I'm not objecting, by the way."

"I don't kill what's mine." He licks my nipple, playing with it with his forked tongue.

"Yours?" I ask, breathy from how he's working my body and a bit shocked he would want me.

"Mine." Maxum's voice is rough and possessive. "I can't let you go after this." He thrusts into me. "You're perfect."

I never expected my grumpy, snarky demon to say that. "No. You are."

He claims me with a kiss so passionate that it feels like our souls intertwine.

My hands are at the base of his horns, stroking them.

When he pulls back, he grins wickedly. "Such a good little monster fucker." His fingers lace into my thick hair at the base of my skull, and he fists a handful, tilting my head back until my neck is vulnerably arched and fully exposed. His sharp teeth graze my soft flesh.

I wonder if he'll bite me.

Do I want him to?

"Now that you're mine, all those fantasies you write about? I'm about to make them all come true, little witch." Maxum chuckles, then lifts me up and slams me down onto his cock while he's standing.

I grind against his pubic bone with every downward motion. I'm so fucking impressed with his strength that an orgasm quickly approaches. His tail pumps into me, stirring me higher. When I climax, I cry out at the sensation of his double penetration.

"Maxum!" I take hold of his horns again and ride my bucking bronco.

"Say it again!"

"Maxum!" I shout as I milk his cum from his textured cock.

His wings once again circle around me.

I feel unimaginably protected and cherished, cocooned within his embrace.

My head falls forward against his chest. All the energy I had from the first round has dissipated.

"I got you, little witch," Maxum murmurs, carrying me into the shower.

I fell asleep in the shower and I'm not sure how I ended up back in Arran's bed. I vaguely remember a bit of arguing about where I would sleep when we came out of the bathroom.

Apparently, Arran won. Maybe they are taking turns. Sometimes when I'm half-wake, I feel one or both of them in the bed with me, snuggled up closely.

I sleep and sleep.

It's dark out when I open my eyes, and there's a legit furnace at my back... named Arran.

"You awake?" His hands stroke up and down my side as if they have been itching to do that for hours, but he didn't want to wake me.

"I'm waking up." I rub the gravel from my eyes and turn to face him. I'm not sure if I hoped for the beast. Am I crazy that I find him just as hot? "How long have I been out?"

"A full day." His brows pull down in concern. "Are you hungry?"

"I think so." Then I panic. "Are my fur babies okay?"

"They're fine." He grins like he knows something I don't. "Better than fine."

"Can I see them?"

Arran helps me stand and get dressed in his sweatshirt and shorts. I'm glad for the assistance since I'm still wobbly on my feet.

He holds me to his side as we walk down the hallway.

He pushes a door open to reveal another bedroom and flips on the light so I can see.

Calder curses and covers his eyes.

He's been caught. All my animals are snuggled up with him on his bed. It has to be the most adorable scene I've ever seen.

I squeal with joy and take a couple of steps to pet my guinea pig.

"Thank you, Calder." I smile as he cracks his eyes open, looking chagrined. "You found their food and stuff okay? I'm sorry I didn't think to give you instructions about their care."

"I told him what to do," Trouble, my guinea pig, says proudly.

"What the actual fuck?" I fall back into Arran. "Am I dreaming? Did you hear that too? Did you break my brain through my vagina?"

Arran chuckles.

"You heard me? Well, *finally!*" Trouble shakes his head like I'm dense.

My shifter holds me as I sway with shock. He consoles me. "Calder and I can hear them since we are shifters with the gift to communicate with magical creatures."

"Magical creatures?"

"Well, obviously, not *all* animals can talk," Trouble sasses.

I blink at him. "Obviously?"

Now, even Calder has a smirk. But I think it's because I'm the butt of the joke. "He's been wondering if you were broken," Calder tells me.

"I think I am now," I admit. "You've always been able to talk?"

"You weren't listening. I think your witch hole was blocked."

"My... *what?*"

Calder grumbles, "Well, Maxum and Arran have fully inspected her witch holes now."

Arran smirks. "You're just jealous."

Calder's eyes flare with some sort of emotion, triggering his magic.

I believe he might be jealous, but not about me. Maybe he wants the guys.

"I know you don't like me, so it probably won't mean much to you, but I appreciate you taking care of my friends," I say to Calder as I give my fur babies each a touch.

He grimaces and says nothing. I'll take that as a win. Maybe he will realize I'm not his enemy.

"But seriously, why can I hear them now?" I ask.

"Perhaps it is as simple as accepting that this world exists?" Arran suggests.

"Maybe. I used to have paranormal experiences when I was a kid." I sway on my feet.

"You need to eat, sweetheart." Arran wraps his muscular arms around my waist and practically carries me out of the room and into the kitchen.

"Where is Maxum?" I ask, sitting down at their kitchen nook table.

"Miss his tail already?" Arran teases, fussing in the fridge.

"And his forked tongue," I add.

He grins. "*Fuck*, right?"

"So are you and Maxum…" I make a poking gesture with my two fingers. "Fuck buddies?"

"We used to be—to blow off steam, mostly. We don't mess around anymore, not since I was cursed. As far as our relationship? I don't know if we ever defined it. We're all best friends, care deeply about one another, and since we have trust issues, we've all had our moments together."

"Except for Flint?"

"Yeah, not him." Arran doesn't elaborate, and I don't want to invade the gargoyle's privacy about what happened to make him hate my touch so much. My shifter adds, "Flint doesn't fool around, but he's solid."

"*Solid?*" I roll my eyes and suppress a chuckle. "I see what you did there."

"You'll come to understand just how clever I am," Arran boasts, then he places a beautiful charcuterie board in front of me.

"Will you or the guys mind if I ask questions about being supes? It's just blowing my mind that you are real. But I don't want to get too personal and upset any of you."

"I had my cock in your ass. You can ask me anything now."

"Fair point."

32

DUNGEONS

JADE

I feel much better since Maxum used his girthy, textured healing 'wand' to cure me.

I don't remember Osen visiting me in my dreams after I passed out from what I'll refer to as *Double D-day*.

I worry Osen used too much of his magic to keep me from dying. Can a soul be injured from something like that? Will the guys want me around when I don't have an incubus stowaway?

Is Osen the actual source of my new appeal?

It sort of makes sense they would sense their former lover inside me and become attracted to me by his presence.

Shit. That is far more believable than them wanting me for me—a middle-aged witch.

Oh, well.

I'll just have to enjoy the ride, hoping they don't come to their senses and kill me when Osen leaves my body.

I'm restless. I don't have my computer or phone because the guy's magic in the house would blow up my devices. I can't check my book sales, promotions, or emails. I can't work on my edits for my next release.

Maxum gives me a pen and paper to help take the edge off, but I prefer typing since I can't read my writing when I write too fast.

"You seem agitated, sweetness," Arran says from his spot, snuggling up to me on the couch. It's borderline puppy behavior. And I love it.

"I feel a bit lost and like my life is over." I doodle on the paper instead of writing. They are sketches of shadowy figures with claws.

Maxum comes back through the front door and frowns. "What can we do to make you feel better? Would bouncing on my cock help?"

Arran glares at him. "Not everything is cured with a cock."

"It is with *my* cock." Maxum gives me a wink. "How about a mission then?" he asks. He leans over, captures my chin in his huge hands, and inspects my face. "But I don't know if you have it in you to learn the details and to make the journey."

Last night, Arran told me a bit about the supernatural world. There are three primary realms—Fae, Mortal (where I live), and the Underworld.

I perk up. "I can go on a trip? I want to see the other realms. Can you portal us someplace?"

Maxum shakes his head. "Rob might have spies everywhere."

Giving him a disappointed glare, I huff, "Then where did you intend to go for this *mission*?"

"Calder!" he shouts. "I'm calling for an adventure!"

The grumpasaurus storms out of his room, where he's been hanging out with my magical creatures, aka fur babies. I still haven't asked what kind of supernatural he is, and the guys haven't volunteered. I don't know how touchy the supes are about their other forms, but it seems that Calder wouldn't want me to know since my name is written in an indelible marker on his shit list.

Calder looks at me, then Maxum. "With *her*?" He curls his lip in disgust.

"Yes. You owe me a favor."

The jerk's eyes bulge. "You're calling in your favor—for her—for *this*?"

I don't know what the hell is going on, but it sounds like a big flipping deal. "Don't call in favors for me. Calder doesn't want to be around me."

"He's going to get over it... starting now." Maxum steps up inches away from Calder and glares down at him. Wow, he makes a six-foot-tall man look petite.

What do I look like next to him? A hobbit?

"I don't think she can handle it," Calder snarls.

"My money is on the witch." Arran laughs.

Okay, not sure why he's laughing. This appears like a harrowing task, one in which Calder doesn't think I can keep up.

"Five minutes, and it's go time." Calder surrenders, throws his hands in the air, and retreats to his room.

"What about Flint?" Arran asks Maxum as he hurries to prepare for our misadventure.

"He's due back from his scouting any second." Maxum then informs me. "Flint's never late unless there's trouble."

"Is he okay to be around me?" I ask, feeling confused if I should be changing out of my makeshift pajamas or not. "I haven't seen him since the incident."

"I'm fine," Flint says as he enters the house.

I swear these guys can hear through several walls. I blush, thinking of all the obscene noises I made with Maxum and Arran.

The gargoyle walks up to me and wisely gives himself six feet of personal space so I can't accidentally fling myself at him again.

He lowers his eyes and says, "I apologize for putting my hands on you. I could have hurt you."

"Flint, I know you were only trying to bring me some water. Your touch did not hurt or upset me. I'm only worried that you'll feel awkward around me. I enjoyed talking with you, and I would like to be friends."

"You enjoyed talking to me?" he sounds surprised.

"Of course." I smile. I itch to reach out and hug the massive male, but I stop myself. Why is he so endearing? All I want to do now is cuddle him.

He gives me a shy grin and nods. "Friendship sounds nice."

Gah. He's killing me. Maybe one day I could get him to hug me without freezing up.

"Go get your gear. It's adventure time," Maxum orders.

Arran and Flint rush off to get ready.

"Do I get gear?" I ask.

"Let's see what you are made of first," Calder grumbles as he stomps back into the great room.

He glares at me as he sets a wooden box on their dining table. The table and the box look old and beat up, as if it were from an actual medieval tavern. Maybe they are. With these guys, anything is possible.

"Does she know what she's getting herself into?" Calder asks Maxum.

"Not a clue," Maxum smirks wickedly.

Ruh-roh... I think I'm biting off more than I can chew. "If this is going to be too rough for a recovering witch, I'll manage being bored."

Maxum snatches me by the waist and draws me to his hard body. "One, you shouldn't be *bored* living with four monsters. Especially when two of them are frenemies with benefits." Maxum cocks his brow at me. "Two, I wouldn't push you beyond what I know you can handle. You can do this." He cups his large hand over my cheek in a show of comfort.

Calder announces, "We are going to the village of Caranth to capture the rogue mage."

"Shit, I thought you said I can't be seen?" I ask Maxum.

"We aren't leaving." Arran struts into the room dressed as if he were going to a Renaissance Faire as a knight.

Flint is also dressed in period clothing but with a light cloak, simple leather armor, and a lute.

What is this fuckery?

I look to Calder, and he pulls out a leather-bound book.

"We need you to pick from these races." He hands me a sheet. "Dragonborn, dwarf, elf, gnome, halfling…," he drones on, listing them all. "Then we will discover your strengths and attributes." He explains, "You will roll the dice. You have some items, such as armor and weapons, as a default, but others you can buy if you have money."

Internally, I grin and look at him like a deer caught in a monster's gaze.

"Are you following what I'm saying?" Calder snaps.

"Yeah, I think so… If you're done Monstersplaining me… I have a level 17 Tiefling Bard with a plus-five initiative, leather armor, a light crossbow, and a pair of daggers. Is that good enough for us to start off with?"

"Excuse me?" Calder's eyes widen in disbelief.

Loving the shocked reaction I'm getting from all of them, I continue dramatically, "Orianna believes that freedom and compassion matter more than rules. And she'll never explain her scars."

Calder looks like steam might blow out of his ears. "*You…* play DnD?"

Arran howls with laughter as Maxum chuckles at his shock.

"It's been a decade or so, but yeah." I eye the guys' outfits and their weapons. "And it looks like you guys are *really* into it."

Maxum waves his hand dismissively. "It rarely comes to bloodshed."

"Rarely!" I step back. "I think this game is too rich for my blood. Literally."

"We won't attack you," Maxum coos in my ear and sets his hand on my lower back. "Well, I might with my cock. I'm so hard for you right now. You are too perfect."

I chuckle. "How long have you been playing? And I'm assuming Calder's the dungeon master?"

"He used to be in more ways than one." Maxum swats me on the ass, pushing me toward the table. As I sit down, he pulls me onto his lap. His flesh sword presses against my ass crack. "Fuck," he hisses. "I think this is a bad idea. I'm going to have you riding me right here in a few seconds."

"Let Jade have her own seat. *Please, and thank you,*" Calder growls as he sets up his Dungeon Master supplies.

"What's your character?" I ask Flint.

"Elmell Smoketail, a halfling ranger with a love of music." He points to his legit lute strapped to him.

I think I might die of cuteness. "I love it."

"And you two?" I ask.

Maxum grins playfully. "Neluthel, an Elven rogue, who loves to steal the hearts of his lovers. After he's done with them, of course."

I'll unpack that later...

"I'm a Dragonborn Beastmaster named Gorkilwyrm the Awesome," Arran says shyly.

We play for a few hours, and the guys act out the skirmishes. I see how this helps them let off some steam. However, I find it odd since this is practically their lives. But to each their own.

They gouge some new marks into the table with their swords. And yes, an actual mace gets lodged in the wall at some point.

Calder stretches and pats his belly. "Pizzas?"

We all heartily agree.

The brat asks me, "What does the bard want on her pizza?"

"I don't think I should eat a whole pizza by myself."

"Not up to the challenge?" He shakes his head. "How disappointing."

"I didn't say I couldn't," I laugh. "Challenge accepted. Thin crust though!"

He orders us pizzas from their rotary landline. When they show up at our door, Maxum pays with cash and hands them out to us.

"Is it rude to ask about what supernatural species a person is?" I ask and shove a pizza slice in my pie hole.

"Why do you ask?" Calder watches me.

"I was just curious if you were a dragon."

"Why would you think I was a dragon?" He looks more confused than irritated with me, which is a step up in our dynamic.

"I felt like you were fiery when I first saw you. I imagine dragons can be... standoffish."

"Don't blow dragon-smoke up my ass." He rolls his eyes. "Most dragons are complete dicks."

"There really are dragons?" I bounce with excitement.

"Don't be too happy. I just told you they were jerks." He huffs.

"I can handle jerks—obviously." I give him a pointed look. "So, was I way off base with my guess?"

"Phoenix." His tone is flat.

"Holy crap! A Phoenix! That's so awesome!"

Maxum grumbles. "I'm feeling a touch jealous. Just me?" He looks to Arran.

"Yeah, but he is super rare." The wolf-shifter shrugs.

"You're rare?" I bite my lip so a million questions don't pour out of my face. "I mean, it makes sense. Most legends are probably close to truths, yeah?"

"In my case, yes. I come back to life, and I have a bird form."

He doesn't sound like he wants to talk about it, so I let it drop. "Thank you for sharing. I won't pester you any more about how cool you are."

A strange expression passes over his face. Disappointment, perhaps?

3 3

REMEMBERED

JADE

*T*he day has been lovely, spending time with all four of them.

Then they inform me they need to catch up on their normal routine of patrols for ASO activity.

By the evening, I'm feeling healthier, emotionally and physically, but also tired.

Currently, I'm curled up on the couch with my head on Maxum's lap as he reads and idly strokes my hair. I love that the demon is so well-read. That alone could make me fall for him, never mind all the sexy he has going on otherwise.

As much as I love his affection, I need a proper sleep. "I'm heading to Arran's bed to sleep for the night," I say.

At the same moment, Calder rushes inside the safe house, looking about ready to burst into flames. "There's been another ASO attack. An explosion."

"Where?" Maxum shoots up from his seat.

"The supes' community center," Calder reports.

"Was anyone hurt? The younglings there?" Maxum's red fists are clenched so hard they are almost white.

"It's chaos. People were inside. They need help. Arran and Flint are already there."

Maxum looks at me, and I can see it written on his face clearly. He wants to go help, but he doesn't want to leave me alone either.

"Go," I urge him. "I'll be okay. I'm just going to bed. No one knows about this place, right?"

"She's right," Calder says, but he still looks like I'm about to betray them. Damn, I was hoping we'd made progress today. "Let's go."

Maxum rushes over to me and gives me a passionate kiss. "Stay safe, sweet witch."

He rushes out the door, unfurling his enormous wings as soon as he's outside the front door.

Damn, that's hot.

Calder doesn't immediately follow. Instead, he uses this rare moment alone to threaten me. "If you betray us or hurt one of them through your callous, witchy ways, I *will* end you."

"I don't have *witchy* ways." I glower at him, refusing to let him intimidate me, although he should terrify me. "If anyone gets hurt, it's going to be me. By the way, I'm not an asshole. And I don't betray or hurt people intentionally."

"Watch your step." In a blink of an eye, Calder is out the door and soaring after Maxum.

I slam the door shut and lock it.

It's eerie being left alone in the guys' house. After checking on my pets, and the doors and windows, I curl up in Arran's bed and fall asleep.

I don't know how quickly, but it seems almost immediately that Osen, in his shadowy form, is standing near Arran's dreamscape bed.

Is it wrong that I sort of enjoy his dark shadows? Yet, curiosity pecks at me, wanting him to reveal that part of who he is... or *was*.

But I believe he was drained while constructing imagery in the shadowscape. I note we are in Arran's room now, and I think that's the reason for it. He doesn't have enough power to create anything different than where we actually are in the astral plane.

"So you are claiming my men?" he asks, and I detect a bit of jealousy. Maybe only because he can't touch them anymore.

"I thought you were okay with me having sex with them." I sit up and notice I'm undressed under the covers.

"Sex, yes. But you're stealing them away."

"Are you asking me to stop?"

I don't know what I would do if he said yes. Part of me doesn't expect this whole fling with them to continue. The other part realizes I might not have a choice against an incubus who can take control over my body and mind. I may have to do as he says or find a way to exorcise him.

Regardless, I should probably eject him. I doubt this is healthy.

Being possessed is a generally frowned upon condition.

But at least the sex has been phenomenal.

Osen studies me. Maybe he can read every thought I just had. This is not good.

"I don't think you can stop being with them now," Osen finally answers. "They have claimed you."

"I doubt that, but why would you be upset?" I don't think they've claimed anything but my holes, which I'm perfectly okay with since I've not orgasmed that intensely in my entire life—especially not with a partner. I suspect the sex will only get better since I was half-dead when we fucked.

The guys have kept it casual in their little fuck circle. So I will keep my heart out of the sex—to 'blow off steam' and 'fool around'—as Arran put it.

Osen shrugs. "Does it matter if I am upset? I'm dead."

"Well, I'm sure I'll be moving on as soon as we get you sorted. It's not like Calder appreciates my presence. Flint barely tolerates me." I shake my head and try to not let the uncomfortable burning sensation in my chest take hold. I need to let go of any attachment or feelings of connection I believe I have for them. I stare up at Osen, seeing the outline of the male he used to be. "I'll leave soon enough because I don't want to drive a wedge between the guys. I understand they are family, and I'm the enemy."

"Unfortunately," Osen agrees, and I don't know why that's what tears me up.

Pull it together, Jade.

He continues, ignoring my wave of emotion. He feels me crumbling, of that there's no doubt. "I need you to help me access my last moments."

"How?"

I want to solve this case just as much as he does. One, I'm a fucking curious person. Two, that means he can leave, and I can move on with my life. I'll sell my house and go where no one knows who I am—far away from Rob and the rest of this mess.

"I need to study my death spot." He moves closer, crowding me. "Now."

"Why now?" I try to scoot back, but he presses against my body.

"The guys won't let you go."

"Why not?"

"Rob thinks you are dead. And they intend to keep it that way. Until Rob and his organization are neutralized, I doubt you'll be allowed to leave. But that day might never happen."

"I can't leave… ever?" This sucks.

"I'm certain I learned the ASO's secret right before they killed me. If I can remember what happened before my death, then Maxum and the guys can take them down."

"Okay, let's go solve this."

Fortunately, Maxum and Arran had grabbed a few things from my house earlier today, including my sneakers and some clothes. So at least I won't only be dressed in a guy's flannel shirt and socks for my adventure with Osen.

They also left the Rambler here, so I snatch up the keys from the entry table and steal their car. *Borrow* their car.

I memorized the address and location of Osen's death spot when he gave it to me in the shadowscape. I feel him vaguely in the back of my mind, thrumming with energy.

It's a weird sensation to feel him like this when I'm awake. But he told me that me having sex with the guys has empowered him. He's so much stronger now.

At least he agreed to let me be in control of my own body for this trip. Although he plans to take control briefly when we arrive at our location.

I don't like the idea of that.

But what's a medium supposed to do when there's a murder to solve?

The roads are empty as we get closer to our destination, which isn't completely unusual for this part of town. It's mostly abandoned warehouses. There's not much reason for the city's residents to be here.

Now that I know there's an entire world I never knew existed, I imagine these buildings aren't as abandoned as I had previously assumed.

I feel Osen agrees with my thoughts.

Great. That means he probably has access to all my wandering thoughts.

Again, I get a sense of agreement. Ugh.

When I turn down a dark street, Osen insists I pull over and park. I do. With nervousness pumping adrenaline through my veins, I step out of the car.

I almost stumble because Osen takes that moment to shove my soul aside and take over without warning.

What the fuckity fuck?

However, this time, I'm still conscious of what's happening, but I have no ability to move or speak through my own body. I'm not sure if that's worse. I hate the feeling of being out of control. I'm just his puppet now.

"Remain calm, or I'll put you to sleep," Osen threatens in my mind.

"Some warning would have been nice, asshole."

"Keep quiet. I need to stay alert for danger," he reprimands.

We step forward slowly. He casts our eyes up at the rooftops and down the road. This is the strangest experience I've ever had. And that's saying something since I've just been double-teamed by a werewolf and demon.

Oh, yeah, and I died. There's that.

"Shush," Osen snarls in my mind.

"So I'm not even allowed to think?"

He doesn't answer, and I'm immediately distracted when he pushes his psychic awareness outward. Or maybe it's my power?

"Yours," he answers. *"You need to learn how to use your powers."*

I won't argue about that. This is cool. I can sense the emptiness of the street and the strange echo of magic ahead of me. I realize I've felt magic and power before, but I've always brushed it off as my imagination.

As a child, I perceived so much, and it was all lost because of my controlling mother, who repeatedly told me I sensed nothing.

But she was wrong, and now, I'm weak. I wish my abuela was still alive to teach me. Although she was a bit... intense, too.

"You could try calling on her spirit," Osen suggests. *"But not now."*

"Is this close to where Rob and the witch person went after he attacked me?" I ask.

"Close, only a few blocks." Osen walks down an alleyway and circles a spot, studying the ground.

"There's a dead zone here. Forgive the pun." We don't sense any magic in this spot.

The sound of cars in the distance reminds me we are still on Earth, but for some reason, it feels otherworldly here.

"I agree." Osen rubs our chin, thinking.

He allows his thoughts to drift to the night he died...

I see a moon above and a man in silhouette walking toward us.

"You shouldn't have pushed," the male says. The voice... it sounds so much like Rob, but this is only a memory, and can't be trusted completely. Perhaps it's only my fears in play. "I warned you to walk away."

"You expect me to heed your message from the lips of my dying ally? You truly didn't expect I'd seek justice for what you've done to my kind?" Osen remembers himself asking the mystery man.

"I was hoping you might be smarter than the rest since you have gotten closer than the others to discovering what's truly going on."

"I know the witches are behind the ASO. And it's the Witch Council members."

The man laughs—genuinely amused.

I sense Osen's doubt.

Could he be wrong?

Suddenly, Osen is hit with a blast of energy—magic—from behind. Someone has used the man's distraction to sneak up on him. This energy doesn't feel like anything Osen has experienced before. It's a new magic filled with dark intent.

Osen wonders how there can be new magic.

But he realizes that magic has been dwindling in the realms... and if that's so, then maybe, like most things in the Universe, when one thing dies off, something else slightly different replaces it, filling a void.

Osen's body trembles. Someone is stealing his magic, and his soul feels as if it has detached from his body.

Is this his death?

Osen's spirit floats above the scene.

"I told you he'd come, my liege."

And a woman, who looks very much like me, appears from the shadows. A wicked grin spreads over her face.

What in the Freaky Friday?

"Why are you in my memories, Jade?" Osen snarls.

"I don't know. But that can't be me." I feel the pressure of Osen's anger, as if he's attempting to crush my actual soul. "Wait! Didn't you say Rob hypnotized me?"

"You don't look brainwashed to me now," Osen argues.

He's not wrong. This woman appears to be in *complete* control.

"Why would I come here if I was behind your death?"

"Maybe you didn't think I'd remember?"

I feel my spirit fading. He's draining my life force. "I didn't do this!"

"That woman looks just like you," Osen points out.

"She does, but actually put together—polished. I'm a warmed-over mess most of the time, not even a full hot mess."

"Jade, the game is over. Just tell me why."

"Yeah! If I'm some witch mafia boss, why would Rob kill me yesterday?"

"Because you were compromised by me."

"Maybe it's a glamour like Maxum or Flint wears?"

"Unlikely."

"And I live in a tiny house with magical creatures? And write romance books?"

"That's just some stupid cover story," he says, but sounds less certain.

"This was you!" he growls in my voice out loud.

"Hell, this woman looks more like my crazy grandmother than me!"

Osen stops his stranglehold on my soul. *"What did you say?"*

Now that I take a moment to put a pin in my terror, I realize it's true. *"She looks like my abuela. I swear the women in my family don't age."*

"Witches don't *age like humans."* He shouts, "Fuck!"

3 4

BETRAYED

CALDER

$\mathcal{I}$ don't have much magic outside of my phoenix gift of regeneration and shifting, but I have premonitions, especially concerning death.

It's one reason I was so close to the community center's attack when it happened. My psychic senses were pinging.

In the middle of the cleanup and pulling survivors from the rubble, I have another ping.

Osen's death spot.

I glance over to see Maxum, Arran, and Flint removing debris to get to another victim. They are needed here. All of them are stronger than I am. And I don't want them to get involved if it's nothing.

My mind flashes to an image of the witch.

I'm unhappy that I seem to be mistaken about her innocence. It's getting under my skin.

Her magical creatures adore her as if she were their pet and not the other way around. Magical creatures are usually not wrong about a person's character and are rarely corrupted.

I've been trying to catch them in a lie, but they appear as innocent as they look.

It shouldn't bother me that I might have messed up my chances to spread her thighs and plunder her depths.

I don't want to lust after women—especially witches.

I'm pissed that I want to hear her make those wicked sounds while she chokes on my cock.

Maxum and Arran made her scream so loud with ecstasy that I still hear it ringing in my ears and in my balls.

Maybe she could be the woman to make me forget what happened during my last death.

Sneaking out the door, I take to the sky and soar over the buildings. Osen's death spot is only a mile or so away. So if my instincts are nothing, I'll be back before the guys know I'm missing.

Thankfully, I have enhanced supernatural eyesight, since there aren't many working streetlights in this industrial area anymore, and the moon hasn't risen. The supernaturals who inhabit the supposedly abandoned area like to move in the dark since they don't easily pass as humans, even with glamour. They are far too big or some other inhuman shape. Most have lost the magical power to maintain a glamour at all, even with charms or spells.

As I approach, I see my Rambler parked on the street close to where Osen was killed.

The witch.

Why would she steal our car when no one was home? Why come here? Was I right all along?

I land on the building to observe her as she stands in the dark alley.

She seems strained, her body twitching and bowed as if fighting an invisible force.

Osen?

Has he found some evidence in her mind and come here to confront her?

"This was you!" she shouts, sounding very much like Osen.

Then a second later, Osen screams, "Fuck!"

A man appears at the end of the alley. "Ah, there you are." I'm not sure if he means Jade or if he's speaking to Osen.

The man looks like Rob. I sense he is indeed a warlock.

I want to fly down there and protect Osen, but I also want to see how Jade-Osen reacts to Rob.

"He's still inside you, hm?" Rob throws his hands out.

I expect to see the glow of a warlock's spell, but a shadowy tendril shoots out instead. It looks and feels like Osen's magic.

Osen gasps, realizing the same thing.

Jade's arms fly up in a stop motion, but whatever magic Osen has left is too weak to prevent Rob's assault.

The shadowtendril wraps around her middle and yanks her forward until she's only a few feet from the warlock.

"Don't worry, we'll take care of it," he tells Jade and plunges a shadow into her forehead.

Fuck. Rob's attacking Osen.

I dive off the building's edge to rip Jade away from Rob just as a black sedan pulls up.

I grab the witch around the waist to break her free from his shadows. Then I swing my Katana with my free arm, slicing Rob's chest.

He releases Jade.

His shadow hits me so hard that I fly back into the brick wall.

Somehow, I manage to hold on to the witch.

However, her head cracks against the brick.

I clutch her unconscious body to my chest. I thought I was only saving Osen, but I find I don't want to lose Jade either.

With my last bit of strength, I charge at Rob, my blade poised to end him.

He's smart enough to run.

My head spins as Rob jumps in the car and drives away.

Blood pools around me… my own and hers.

My vision fades to black.

TO BE CONTINUED…

find out if they survive in Charming Her Monsters…

CHARMING HER MONSTERS

BEWITCHING MONSTERS BOOK TWO

YVE VALE

1

MISSING

ARRAN

Obsessive worry pulls my attention away from the chaotic scene I'm in, making me no use to the victims who are relying on me to rescue them.

Yet, I can't help it. I need to get back to *her*. My heart, my love… my future mate, Jade.

I don't know how long I've been moving debris and rescuing innocent supernaturals from the destruction of the community center, but it feels like days. However, perhaps that is only my dread. When I check the old grandfather clock that somehow escaped damage, I see it's been less than an hour since my pack has been here to help.

I hate that so many have been hurt, and the longer we take to find the rest of the victims, the less likely their chances are to survive. Fortunately, reinforcements have arrived, allowing me a moment to take a breath.

Another pang of dread hits me. This time it feels different from the worry over the victims here. I scan the huge, demolished room and the frantic supes here to help.

Maxum has dropped his glamour and is in his huge demon form—red skin, horns, tail, and wings on display. Flint is in his stony, gargoyle body.

Together, we are tossing huge beams and concrete aside as part of the rescue mission. But I don't see our phoenix.

"Where the fuck is Calder?" I call out.

Maxum looks around and then turns back at me with confusion behind his eyes. "I don't sense him nearby. I can't say I have for a while now."

That's not good. The unsettling feeling that's stabbing at my heart takes on a new urgency.

Is he okay?

Then my next thought is… *where is he?*

And … *would he hurt Jade?*

I sure as hell hope he wouldn't. But he's been on edge more than ever since Osen died. I don't think he will ever recover from that loss.

Ironically, it only pisses Calder off more that Osen's spirit has attached itself to Jade. You would think he'd be happy that his former lover wasn't completely out of his life.

My heart pinches with hurt again. As though I'm losing a mate.

"Something's wrong. *Jade.*" My skin ripples. My berserker beast is begging to be released. That's not good. He might attack anyone in sight with his fear. Despite his crazed persona, he likes Jade. Dare I say he loves her—if that cursed part of me could ever love someone.

Could it be that our death-omen-sensitive phoenix felt Jade was in danger and checked it out on his own? It's not out of the realm of possibility, but with his hatred of witches, I doubt he would care.

Unless my pack mate was worried about how Maxum and I would feel if we lost her. Or he might only care about Osen's spirit trapped inside Jade.

I shift into my giant, dire wolf form and rush to the door.

"Wait!" Maxum calls, racing after me. "A portal will be faster."

I keep moving but stop far from the commotion of the community center.

Maxum and Flint follow me.

Behind a shielded corner of a building, so no one can see the location of our safe house, Maxum opens a portal a few houses down from ours.

As I reach our house, I shift back into my human form so I can open the door and charge through. In my hurry, I neglect to test if there's a magical booby trap waiting for us.

Maxum curses behind me. When he sees no spell has been activated, he runs inside and admonishes me, "You need to be more careful! If only for Jade's sake."

He's right that I can't die on her. She'd be pissed. Who knows what kind of power she has? She might catch my soul and punish me for decades for being a bad boyfriend.

"Jade!" I shout and run into my bedroom, where she's slept since she's been hiding out with us. "Calder!"

No answer, and she's not in my room. I shout for her and Calder over and over. I check Maxum's room, the bathroom, then Flint's bedroom, and finally head to Calder's.

"What's all this racket about?" a tiny voice grumbles at me. It's Jade's accidental and unofficial guinea pig familiar, Trouble.

He's giving me a glare for waking him and the rest of Jade's small rescue animals who now have taken up residence in Calder's room.

"Where's Jade? Or Calder?"

"I don't know where Calder is." Trouble yawns. "But I heard Jade talking to the grumpy ghost. She left... maybe two days ago."

"Two *days* ago?" I shake my head at his complete miscalculation. Most animals don't have any concept of human time. I have the same battle with my wolf half.

"Did you overhear where she was going?" I ask.

"Death." He does the guinea pig version of a shrug. My stomach turns, and I almost vomit at the thought of Jade dying.

"Calder's car is gone," Flint reports.

I turn back to Trouble. "Did Calder take Jade somewhere?"

"No. I think she left by herself. She was arguing with the ghostman."

Since Maxum and Flint can't hear them like Calder and I can with our shifter abilities, I tell them what the magical creature said. "He says Jade left on her own to go to Death with Osen. What the fuck is going on?"

"Osen's death spot?" Maxum guesses. "He probably coerced her to go there to investigate."

"Open a portal," I demand.

Maxum glowers at me because he doesn't appreciate being bossed around. Yet, he wants to find Jade just as much as I do, if what I sense about his feelings for her are correct. He opens a portal, and we all step through.

I realize now that I'm naked and hope there are no police officers on the other side. Otherwise, Maxum will have to fuck with someone's brain so I can escape a public nudity charge.

It's late enough at night that no one is around. At least, no one we can see. Supernatural creatures might lurk in the shadows. It's what they do in this neighborhood.

We spot Calder's car parked on the side of the road, not but a dozen yards from the alleyway where Osen was murdered.

The heavy, metallic scent of blood fills the air. I glance over at Maxum, and see by his flared nostrils he smells it too.

"Danger," Flint announces. His sense of smell isn't like ours, but he can pick up danger or if someone needs protection.

Part of me doesn't want to look down the alleyway. I fear that the woman of my dreams is already dead.

She might still be alive and need my help. I have to push forward and see what's going on.

When I brave my fears, I see both Jade and Calder sprawled out lifelessly on the ground. There's so much blood pooling around them. I'm sure they are dead.

Then I notice a glowing bubble over them like a protective shield. A small flower faerie huffs with the effort to keep it going.

"Help!" she shouts at us. But her voice is faint, weak from the strain of casting magic outside of her own realm.

"Are you slowing down time for our friends?" Maxum asks as he runs up to her.

"Yes. My mate and I stumbled upon these poor things being attacked by a strange warlock. We projected images of giant trolls, and he took off."

"Smart," Maxum approves.

"My mate left to get someone to help them."

"A healer?" I ask.

She nods.

I continue, "How much longer can you hold this bubble?"

"Not much longer." She grunts with the effort. "I'm sorry."

"What's your name, warrior?" Flint asks.

"Tavi of Elorith," she says with a raised brow. "You are my first gargoyle. What do they call you?"

"Flint." He grimaces that his kind is so rare she doesn't know any. Besides, most gargoyles aren't likely to associate with the flower faeries. "Tavi, we appreciate you helping our friends, but I sense you are harming yourself to do this. If you need to release the time bubble, you should."

"Flint!" I shout. "Jade might die."

He turns to me and stares deeply into my eyes, which unnerves me. Only Jade dares to do that, since she doesn't understand what a challenge it is to my primal nature. "Arran, we don't know how badly she is hurt. She could recover. And Calder... he will be reborn if he's too far gone."

Maxum places his large hand on my shoulder and squeezes. "No matter how much we want to, we cannot ask the faerie to sacrifice herself for Jade. I recognize Tavi's name and description. She is a leader of her people and a friend to the Fae Queen."

Shit. I can't piss them off. Just as I'm about to give up my pressure on Tavi, a portal opens up.

All three of us react defensively. I shift back into my wolf and the others brace themselves for battle. We can't know yet if the newcomers will be friends or foe.

A woman steps through with a half-shifted phoenix. His wings are out and flaming and he looks ready to defend his partner against us.

I snarl. She is a witch by the smell of her magic.

I can smell the magic of a hellhound on her, too. I back down, confused. What in the world? Why is this witch working with supernaturals?

A male faerie flies through before the portal closes behind them and rushes to help his mate hold the bubble in place.

"Amira?" Maxum asks in disbelief.

"Maxum?" she questions in a similar tone of shock. "It's been ages."

I shift back into my human form and demand. "A witch?" I sneer.

I suppose my prejudice against witches runs deep, and only Jade is acceptable in my eyes. Besides, I was hoping for a mage to heal her. A supe's magic usually works faster.

The witch turns toward me with a glare, but her phoenix jumps in the way, blocking my nakedness.

He grumbles, "Do you mind not waving your dick and all that sexy in my mate's face?"

"Mate? What the fuck is going on?" I say, but they all ignore me.

Maxum takes charge of the situation and informs the newcomers. "Our pack mate, a phoenix, looks to have severe head trauma, maybe more. It's hard to tell. I don't want him to go through a rebirth, but at least he can. We are more worried about the woman. She also looks to be banged up and losing a lot of blood."

"You mean the *witch*?" Amira says with a curled lip of disgust.

Hmm. That's odd… a witch-hating witch?

"Jade's not like that. She didn't even know that she was one, or that magic was real until a few days ago," Maxum explains. "She also has a spirit attached to her."

"Well, that's… different." Amira nods to her mate. "Raithe, when Tavi drops the bubble, can you look after your brethren? I'll do what I can to stabilize the witch."

"Jade," Maxum corrects.

Amira frowns, stares at him for a second, and cocks a brow. "Oh, I'm sorry. I didn't realize you had a bond with her."

What does this witch see with her special sight? Did Maxum and Jade create a mate bond, and I just didn't sense it?

The witch's eyes shoot over to look at me. "Hmm. You, too." Then she smirks at her phoenix. "Things are getting interesting. Let's help this woman recover so she can return to her mates."

I want to argue that Jade hasn't accepted my bond. But my wolf argues it doesn't matter. She is ours, and we will do anything for her.

"Do you have somewhere we can take her so I'm not treating her in the street?" Amira asks.

I finally notice a large bag the woman is carrying.

"Yeah." Maxum walks closer to the bubble. "As soon as she's free, I'll open a portal, and we can go to our place."

My instinct is to not allow this witch into our safe house. But Maxum seems to trust her. Flint isn't protesting, so he must not be getting bad vibes off her either.

"Maxum, you can open the portal. Raithe, you grab the phoenix." Then she looks at me and my beast flashes over my body. Her eyes go wide and then she looks at Flint, "Can you carry her?"

"No." He staggers backward, looking downright panicked. "I can't."

Poor guy. He just can't get over his trauma.

"I should do it," I say. "I can keep my beast at bay for this."

Besides, I need my hands on Jade to feel her once more. I need to pour my love into her, so she knows I'm here. Maybe it will make the tiniest difference to her staying alive.

Goddess, I don't even know if she wants my love. Would it make a difference to her? Could she ever love someone as broken as I am?

Just because she had sex with me doesn't mean she wants forever or even tomorrow. Maybe when she joked about monster fucking being on her bucket list, that's all it was… a fuck.

My wolf howls inside my chest. He doesn't believe that. He tells me she cares about us.

"Okay. Here we go," Amira calls out.

The flower faerie—a creature with more strength and fortitude than I originally would have guessed—sucks in a breath as she releases the time bubble. I will have to track her down and her mate at some point and thank them for their assistance. No matter what the outcome is here tonight. They were brave for risking themselves when it was clear this was a dangerous place to be.

"Thank you," I say quickly, with a nod of gratitude.

I scoop up Jade into my arms.

Her body is cold. That's not a good sign. She doesn't grunt or react to being moved, and my concern for her grows. Her beautiful silver-gray hair is matted with blood. My heart twists in my chest.

"I got you, my love," I whisper in her ear. "Hold on for us, okay?"

Maxum has the portal open, and we are all running through. He's portaled us right into our backyard. Which means he plans for us to abandon this safe house since it's possible someone with the unique ability coupled with enough power could track the magical trail.

I carry Jade inside, following Maxum and Amira as they race ahead.

"On the table," Amira orders me.

I hope Amira's healing skills will work fast enough, and that since witches and warlocks usually have compatible magic, it will be all Jade needs —if not, we are screwed. Unless Maxum has a mage healer he's kept secret from us.

I set Jade down, but don't let go of her completely. I grasp her hand and look her over myself as Amira assesses the damage.

"She's breathing, and there's a weak heartbeat. She has a concussion from what looks like hitting her head on the ground or wall. Maybe both, if the two bumps and gashes are any indication. She's lost a lot of blood." Amira sounds confused. "But there's something else..."

"Her brain waves are all wrong again," Maxum says as he gazes down at Jade with heartbreak in his eyes.

"What does that mean?" I demand.

"I'll patch her up and give her a magical boost for the concussion... but there's something off, but I can't pinpoint it." Amira works, cleaning up the blood, applying salves, and chanting a spell for healing.

I look at Maxum. "What are you saying? Is it Osen messing with her? Is his spirit not attached? What?"

"A supernatural's spirit?" Amira asks curiously. "Not a witch or warlock?"

Maxum admits, "An incubus."

"Well, that might explain what I sense that's so odd about her."

"I don't feel either of their spirits right now. She feels..." Maxum bites his lip, drawing blood. He really doesn't want to tell me. "Arran, maybe we should go outside. And let Amira work."

My head spins. He wants to contain my beast. There's only one reason for that. He thinks Jade is beyond return.

"No!" I howl and my berserker breaks free from my hold.

My claws descend and pierce Jade's hand. What have I done? I've hurt her more.

My berserker releases her and falls back to the floor, scrambling away.

"Arran, come with me," Maxum says calmly. I don't know how he can be so calm with Jade in this condition. Does he not care?

But I can't leave her. I shake my head because I can't speak in my full beast-like form.

"Okay, just stay there and let Amira heal our woman." Maxum stands between me and Amira, protecting the healer.

However, it's unnecessary. Even my crazed beast wouldn't hurt that witch, since her healing ability is the only thing preventing me from losing my mind completely.

2

DISASTER

FLINT

*M*y phoenix friend, Calder, doesn't appear as though he will pull through, but I know he will make it, even if it's through his death. Either this body will heal itself, or he will die and be reborn. My money is on the former. I've seen him go through worse and recover.

The unfamiliar phoenix, Raithe, is working on stabilizing Calder and patching him up. I know he's in expert hands with someone who knows how to treat his own kind.

So instead of worrying about the phoenix, I direct all my concern to Arran, Maxum, and their sweet little witch.

Our wolf shifter is a wreck.

Maxum's putting up a brave face, but the demon was more than charmed by the unusual female. I believe he is falling in love with her.

I also find Jade a genuine delight. Her chaotic, creative mind amuses my overly logical one. It's her pure heart that draws me in, enticing me in a new way I don't fully understand yet. Surprisingly, she actually appears to be interested in being my friend, even though I'm an odd one even among the supernaturals.

If Jade passes away, the realms will be dimmer without her presence.

With the somber mood permeating the house, it feels like her death has already come to be.

In his beast form, Arran is curled into a ball on the floor. I've never seen his berserker side like this.

Maxum paces next to him, watching his old acquaintance Amira work her magic on Jade.

Jade's magical creatures quietly sneak into the great room and watch on as their witch battles with death. They also shoot worried glances in Calder's direction, as they'd started to bond with the phoenix in the last few days.

I wish I could assure everyone that it will be alright. But I don't know it to be true… not for Jade, at least. If she dies, Arran might lose his mind as he loses his heart.

My soul aches for him. He had just found his center and his anchor in her presence. Now this tragedy threatens to take that all away.

I wonder what happened. Why was she in the alleyway? Did Osen force her to go to his death spot? From what the guinea pig said, it sounds like this is the case. But what would be the purpose?

If it weren't for the precarious situation here, I would go investigate the scene myself. But as it is, I need to stay here and help Maxum if Arran's berserker goes wild and tries to harm anyone.

I stand vigil for what feels like an eon. The waiting is torture.

Finally, Amira says, "I've done what I could for her body. The swelling on her brain has subsided. With the wounds healed, she *should* wake up any moment now, but I don't sense that she is."

"Is there anything you can do to bring her spirit back?" I ask. "Don't witches have some ability to call souls?"

"Personally, I don't. But my other mate, a hellhound, might be able to give us some advice." Amira taps her lips, thinking.

I'm shocked that this witch is bonded to not one, but at least two supernaturals. Maybe Jade being with Maxum and Arran won't be such an issue after all. The couple before me seem to have a deep and loving bond.

"Darius might suggest for them to call to her," Raithe says from his place sitting next to Calder on the floor. "Maxum, it sounds like you have mind speak abilities."

"More like mind fuckery." Maxum sighs, waving him off with defeat. "I can pull out memories, scramble brains, or implant false memories, but I don't work with the soul… just the mind."

Amira looks at me.

I shake my head. "I don't see how my limited abilities can help her."

"Perhaps, just try calling her—all of you. Visualize her spirit, her soul, and ask it to come back." Amira waves Raithe over. "Maybe you can use your rebirth magic to assist if we find her?" She looks at the berserker. "Can you shift back to your human form for Jade?"

Arran nods, stands, and forces a shift.

I toss him a blanket from the couch for him to tie around his waist, since Amira's mate doesn't appreciate Arran's naked display.

The amenable phoenix gives me a wink as he passes by. "Thanks. He's too sexy for his own good."

I shrug. I wouldn't really know. I wasn't created to judge or admire sexiness. I only see someone's soul. And no one has called me to have more than a passing interest in exploring more. Well, except two. The first one was four hundred years ago, and now again, with Jade.

I can't say I'm sexually attracted to her, but I want to know her. I'd like to know what she likes to eat. I wish to hear her thoughts on the magical world and discuss the differences in what she dreamed up compared to what is real. I'd like to talk with her about all the things she finds interesting. This makes no sense, because I don't enjoy talking in general.

Yet, with Jade, I want to teach her all about this world that she's just discovered. However, I fear it's too late for me to share my knowledge or to share any moments with her.

"Come around," Amira instructs. "Imagine her in your mind. Place your hand on her body and call her back."

Fear, dread, and longing all smash into my chest. I feel like I'm sinking to the bottom of the ocean.

Touch her? I can't. Can I?

Without hesitation, Arran and Maxum each grab a hand.

Standing by her feet, I stare at her shoes. Slowly and carefully, I reach out to place one finger on the top of her slip-on shoe. That's safe. I can do this.

As soon as I make contact, even with a shoe, my body turns to stone. But that's okay. I'm touching her, and my mind and spirit can still call to her soul.

Fortunately, everyone is so focused on their own meditation they haven't noticed that I've turned to stone. Hopefully, Jade will wake, and her foot will be pulled away from my hand. Then I can return to my normal state with no one taking notice.

I'm glad Jade is unable to see the coward I am right now.

When I froze up before, she pitied me. I can't bear to see the sympathy in her eyes for my pathetic and debilitating anxiety.

Will I ever get over it? Could Jade help me through it?

I believe she could talk me through my fears again. Maybe next time I could be stronger. Maybe one day, without incident, I could brush up against her, hold her hand, or carry her in my arms as I take her on a flight through the clouds.

But first, she needs to return to us. To me. To be my friend, of course.

The image of her sweet smile appears in my mind from when I told her a few facts about being a gargoyle. She's so inquisitive. She's so vibrant that I wonder if she could bring color and joy back to my existence.

"Jade," I call.

I feel the others calling her too. In their hearts, Arran and Maxum are shouting, screaming, and begging her to return.

"Please come back to us," I say in my mind, projecting out into the realms. "We won't be okay without you."

A presence drifts into my perception. There's a weight to it.

How heavy is a soul? And are some heavier than others?

Would Jade be light as a feather like the feeling of joy she spreads? Or would she have more substance and fill up the space the way her smile lights up the room?

I imagine I hear an intake of breath, and Jade mumble, "Dying sucks."

My eyes fly open. Is it real?

Jade is stirring and blinking her eyes as if she can't see properly.

Arran snatches her up, pulling her off the makeshift exam table and into his arms. He clutches her to his chest.

By removing Jade's contact, I'm able to return to my normal state, but I remain stuck still with worry. Watching the scene unfold, I sense danger lingers.

Racing around the table, Maxum presses against her backside, sandwiching her between their enormous bodies.

She doesn't fight it or react, her arms hanging loosely at her sides. That's strange.

"Jade, can you move your arms?" I ask, since I think the others are only focused on the fact that she isn't dead.

With a grunt of effort, she twitches her fingers.

Thank the Goddess.

"What about your feet?" I prompt.

Another exertion, but she's able to shift her legs. I had been worried she had injured her spine. Humans are fragile like that.

"Flint's right. I should look her over before you manhandle her anymore." Amira points to the table for them to return Jade to.

"Who are you?" Jade asks, eyes wide. "What are you?"

"Amira. Another witch," she answers succinctly.

Jade looks at Maxum and Arran. "I thought witches were bad?"

"Not all witches. Amira turned her back on the witches harming supes years ago." Maxum strokes Jade's damp hair back and settles her back onto the table.

Thankfully, Maxum had washed most of the blood out of it earlier when Amira worked on healing.

Her blood shouldn't have bothered me as much as it did. I see blood all the time in battle, but I couldn't handle the sight of *Jade's* blood. It was too much like... before.

Raithe adds, "And she mated with me. I'm a supe."

Jade studies him for a second. "You feel a bit like Calder, but not as smoldery. Are you something like a phoenix?"

"Smoldery?" Raithe chuckles. "Yes, I *am* a phoenix. It's good to have you with us. Your three males were about to lose their minds."

"*My* males?" Jade's eyes widen. She glances at Arran, Maxum, and then at me. "Uh, I... it's not... we aren't..."

"No shame, Jade. Amira has more than one mate," Raithe adds.

Amira swats Raithe away. "She doesn't need your matchmaking just after she returns from death. Can you check on your brethren while I finish up?"

Jade's face blushes with the matchmaking line, and then she almost launches from the table when she sees Calder on the floor, still unconscious. "Oh, my fuck! Calder?"

"Settle." Amira says calmly and holds Jade's shoulders to the table. "You can't do anything for him at the moment. It's more important that I inspect you for any lingering damage."

"But—" Jade points to Calder on the ground, worry and pain clear in her face. "He's hurt."

"We know, but you are too," Arran says, his voice wavering with emotion. "Please, just let Amira look you over so we can feel better."

"Okay." Jade weakly lifts her hand up to touch Arran's cheek. Her arm can barely make the journey, so Arran helps her along by clasping her hand in his and kissing her palm.

"Jade, how does your head feel?" Amira gently touches places over her scalp, focusing on the back of her head.

"Uh, I feel a bit groggy."

"I'm going to check under your shirt and pants now to see if there is any other damage we missed. Okay?"

Jade's gaze catches on my widening eyes.

I quickly turn away to give her privacy, and Raithe follows my lead. We exchange a look and both distract ourselves by checking on Calder.

After assessing Calder's condition, Raithe says, "I think he's going to recover without needing a rebirth."

It's good news, because depending on the nature of the death, it can be a long process. Usually, Calder forgets things about his last life. Sometimes, he mostly remembers the bad. He gets some of his original self back, but not all. He's a bit different after each incarnation.

"Where did you get *this*?" Amira's tone holds fear and a touch of anger.

My spine goes rigid, my instincts wanting to fight. To protect.

I turn to see Amira pointing to the necklace around Jade's neck. Fortunately, Jade's breasts are still covered by her half unbuttoned shirt, so I don't make her uncomfortable.

Why does Amira seem so upset by a necklace?

3

HEIRLOOM

JADE

This witch, Amira, pokes and prods my head for residual damage.

I don't know how long I've been unconscious, but it appears the guys somehow found Calder and me in the alleyway not long after Rob attacked us.

How did Rob find me? And for that matter, how did Calder know I was in that alley? Why did he save me from Rob's clutches?

I thought all four guys had left me alone to help the community center, after it had been attacked with some sort of explosion. Was it all a lie?

Calder appeared to be protecting me… or protecting Osen inside me.

The last thing I remember is Osen's vision of his death. We saw someone who looked like me or perhaps my grandmother, although I thought she'd been dead for nearly thirty years. But the woman apparently killed Osen. Though the more I grasp at the image, the more wrong it feels. *Fake.*

I don't understand how it could be possible for my grandmother to be the one to kill Osen.

Perhaps someone used a glamour to disguise their true face?

I'm also freaked out that Rob grabbed me with shadows, much like Osen's incubus ability.

I believe Calder and I were both knocked unconscious, when Rob tossed us aside. Why did he give up so quickly? Was his magic fading?

When I dip into my mind, I don't feel Osen anymore. I'm worried, but he's slipped into the background before. Maybe that's what's happening now. I hope it's not because Rob snuffed out Osen's soul.

I have ugly and selfish thoughts: Will Arran's and Maxum's feelings for me change if I don't have Osen attached to me anymore? Will they still feel the same? Or subconsciously, was Osen my whole appeal? The incubus ghost probably radiates some strong sexual vibes. His influence would explain my sudden appeal to the local monster population.

Amira announces she wants to check out the rest of me. Arran and Maxum hurry to help. Sweetly, Flint looks embarrassed and turns to give me privacy.

The witch unbuttons a few buttons on my shirt. She sneers and points at my grandmother's pendant. "Where did you get *this*?"

"My grandmother?" I lean away from the witch. My hand instantly clasps the necklace protectively. "Why?"

"I thought they said you didn't know you were a witch? When I accidentally touched it, something pulled at my magic."

"I'm sorry." I put out my hand in a feeble attempt to protect myself.

Arran draws me back to his chest and snarls, picking up on my fear.

"Everyone, calm the fuck down," Maxum snaps.

"You did *not* just tell two witches to *calm down*." Amira glares at him.

Maxum wisely says, "Sorry about that, but we need to keep our heads right now. Arran is about to beast out to protect Jade, and you don't want to deal with his berserker. Let's figure out what secret this pendant holds, because from what I'm picking up from Jade's surface thoughts, she has no clue that it holds any actual power."

Amira's shoulders relax, yet she eyes me like I might start throwing spells.

I can't even *throw hands* right now. Or ever, if I'm being honest. What can I say? I'm a lover, not a fighter. Now, if I could subdue my opponent with ear scratches and belly rubs, then I'd win every fight.

Hmm, I suppose I worked that move with Arran. I just didn't know my new dog was actually the enemy at the time.

Maxum touches the pendant. "I don't feel a pull on my magic. Perhaps it only draws upon witch magic?"

Arran tries and has the same results.

Staring down at the jewelry in question, I explain, "My abuela gave me this pendant. She said it was a protection charm and not to take it off. I've had it for over thirty years. It can't be that bad."

"Don't assume that to be true." Amira studies my face and then the offending piece of metal. "So your abuela is the one with the witching lineage?"

"I guess so." I nod. "She told me when I was little. But my mom didn't let me talk about her much, and I was told she died when I was a child."

"Wait," Maxum stops me. "Why does it sound like you don't believe that anymore?"

I look at Amira and then back to Maxum, unsure what to share with this stranger about Osen's vision. "I'd rather talk to you and Arran in private about that. Let's just focus on the pendant for now?"

"Her being alive might be pertinent," Amira says. "If this thing attempted to drain my magic, it might be slowly siphoning yours."

"Take it off," Maxum says. It's a request more than a demand, but he will insist. I can hear that much in his tone.

The unease that idea creates in me is overwhelming, as if an irrational fear takes hold. My hands hold the chain, but I can't lift the damn thing over my head. And it isn't just because I'm feeling weak right now. "I... can't."

Amira sighs, but pivots her approach. "It looks like a locket. Can you open it? Have you done that before?"

I stare at my heirloom and wonder what secrets it holds. "I've tried before, when I was a kid, but it didn't open."

"You should take it off and see how you feel," Maxum encourages me with a hopeful look.

"But I've never taken it off." I clutch it in my hand and dread stabs my heart.

"That alone worries me." Amira softens her energy. "Someone could be influencing you."

My grandmother's face flashes in my mind. However, it's not from when I was a child, but from Osen's death vision. Are witches the bad guys here? Is it possible I am related to one of the worst? Or was it a glamour like the guys are able to use?

I want to scream in frustration. I don't know if I can talk to the guys about this revelation. If Osen returns, he will tell them I might be a traitor after all, because he thinks it was me or my grandmother who killed him.

Just before Rob's attack, it seemed like he questioned whether that woman was me. Yet, is it any better if it's my relative and my ex-boyfriend who attacked him?

Probably not.

As a show of good faith that I hope wins me some points in the future, I remove the pendant from around my neck. When Amira doesn't appear interested in touching it, I drop it to the table beside me.

We all stare at the damn thing like it might explode.

"How do you feel?" Arran asks, nuzzling into my neck.

"Same?" I shrug.

"You could be so thoroughly drained that you might not notice anything right away. I don't sense much magic radiating from your aura, even now," Amira says thoughtfully. "I would have used my psychometry to read its energy and purpose, but I don't want it to drain my magic, too."

"I can try to open it at least," Maxum offers. "Most curses don't harm me."

I grasp his arm as he reaches for the pendant. "No. I'll try. I don't want you to get hurt. It probably won't harm me."

"You don't know that." Maxum caresses my cheek. "I don't want anything else to happen to you."

Unholy demon cocks. Why does he have to be so sweet?

I snatch up the locket and wedge my fingernail into the crease. It doesn't budge.

"Use the spell, *patefio*," Amira suggests.

I almost object to the idea, but remember, I'm supposed to be a witch.

"*Patefio*," I whisper, still feeling a bit foolish.

The locket loosens. Encouraged, I repeat it and finally the blasted thing opens.

Inside, strange symbols and inscriptions are revealed. After a quick scan and not recognizing anything, I look up at Amira and Maxum for answers.

"Looks like a tracking spell," Amira mutters. "And a siphoning and containment spell on the other half."

"Shit. That must be how Rob found me in the alley!" I shout.

Maxum snarls. "This also means our safe house has been compromised. He could find you here."

"You aren't safe," I say. "Do you have somewhere you can go?"

Arran turns me in his arms, and searches for understanding in my eyes. "Why does it sound like you don't intend to come with us?"

I avert my eyes under his scrutiny and stare back toward Amira. "We should probably have this conversation privately."

Amira takes the hint and wraps up her visit. "Jade and Calder will need to be monitored, especially with Jade's necklace removed. I don't know how her powers and body will react to being free for the first time."

Oh, damn. I didn't think about that complication. What if I explode?

"I'll be able to help her through that." Maxum rubs his hand down my back reassuringly.

"Call on my assistance again… only if you need it." Amira gives Maxum a hug. She whispers something in his ear.

Jealousy and frustration rise up in me. I don't like a beautiful woman touching him. And I don't like secrets, because I know she's keeping something from me. I will have to get him to tell me when we are alone.

Amira's mate, Raithe, nods goodbye as they portal right out of the damn living room.

My jaw almost drops to the floor.

One, I didn't know witches could create portals. And two, it's the first time I've actually witnessed it myself. I was knocked out when traveling through portals before.

Arran doesn't waste a second, turning me again to look at him. "What's going on?"

"And what have you been keeping from us?" Maxum adds. His tone is firm, but he's not angry.

"It's okay, Jade. You are not in danger," Flint says, and I meet his kind eyes. "I would sense it. You can tell us what's wrong and what happened tonight."

With his deep rumbly voice, his words put me at ease, oddly more so than if Arran or Maxum had said it. Perhaps because they both are personally invested in me. But that also means they might be more upset by what I have to say.

Maxum seems to sense how uncomfortable I am. "Let's go sit down on the couches, then we can be near Calder to keep an eye on him."

Arran picks me up, carries me over to a couch, and settles me on his lap. "We'll have to check the rest of you for more damage later. Okay?"

I nod, but I don't know if they will toss me out after everything I confess. "Shouldn't you be relocating right now since I inadvertently compromised your safe house?" I ask.

Maxum shakes his head. "I don't think anyone will attack in the next few minutes while we figure this out."

My mouth is dry, and I cough. Instantly, Flint is there with a glass of water in his hand as if he already knew I would need it.

"Thanks." I take a sip and use the few extra seconds to organize my thoughts. "I'll just start from the beginning."

"That's often a good place." Maxum grins.

"First of all, I didn't know about the pendant tracking me."

"We know," Arran says. "Go on." He nudges me as he strokes down my back.

"Osen insisted I go to his death spot, or he was going to take over my body and do it regardless. While we were there, he had a vision, but I don't know how much is real, or what it means. It's very confusing. Then Rob attacked me, trying to get Osen out of my head. Suddenly, Calder appeared out of nowhere, and I must have hit my head during their scuffle. I don't remember anything until I woke up here."

"Let's go back to what happened in this vision." Maxum puts his hand on my knee and I half worry he will probe my mind and scramble it like he says he can do.

"Well, if Osen's memory was accurate, then it seemed like Rob was there the night of his death." I study all three of their faces, but they don't seem surprised.

"The weird thing—the part that makes little sense—is that someone who looked a lot like me was also in Osen's memory. Although she was put together and Rob seemed to defer to her. At first, Osen thought it was me. However, I thought it looked more like my abuela than it did me. We looked a lot alike. Heck, even my mother looks very much like me, just twenty years older. However, only my grandmother would have had a connection to the witch world since my mom hated the notion of magic."

"But your grandmother is supposed to be dead, right?" Arran asks.

"So you don't think it's me?" My eyes widen in surprise. I'm rarely trusted, even when I do nothing to warrant suspicion. I didn't expect them to accept what I'm saying at face value. They are supposed to be my enemy.

"We don't even know if Osen's memory hasn't been twisted," Arran explains. "When he first possessed you, he was extremely confused by times and dates. That confusion might not have passed entirely."

"We don't know if his soul is intact," Maxum adds. "We also don't know if he has pieced himself together and superimposed your image over his trauma. He *is* living in your imaginative head."

"Oh, yeah. I suppose you're right about that part." I frown when I think about my circumstances. Just like I might work out a troubling plot point, my mind catches on a problem. "I appreciate you not immediately hating me, but I might be connected to Osen's death through my ties to Rob. I'm pretty sure it was actually Rob who attacked me tonight. And that would suggest it was him in Osen's vision."

"Rob does appear guilty of being an accomplice to Osen's death," Maxum agrees.

"Okay. But now, I'm freaking out about the pendant. How is Rob able to use my grandmother's pendant to track me? Did my grandmother want to drain me of my magic? And why?"

"Take a breath." Maxum squeezes my knee reassuringly. "Rob is a warlock, and he's had unfettered access to you, even while you were sleeping. At any point, he could have replicated and switched out your pendant. Or he could have altered your grandmother's pendant to do those things."

"But how did Osen's soul get attached to me?" I ask. "That might suggest I was there when he latched on. What if I am to blame?"

"Or it could mean Rob went to your house afterward, triggered the spell he has on you, and then somehow attached Osen to your mind, hoping to get information through you," Arran argues. "This wasn't the first time you had a spirit linked to you, right?"

"No. Well, I don't think so. But none of them have been as strong willed or aware as Osen is."

The problem is we don't have a clue what's been happening to me.

We might never know. Life isn't often wrapped up in simple answers, revealed to us at the perfect time. No. Sometimes we never know why or how something happens. That being said, I want answers, and I'm determined to get them.

I don't mention that I can't feel Osen anymore. He might still be there and is too weak to reach out after everything that's happened. I don't want to upset the guys if he's only gaining his strength back.

Deep down though, I know the real reason I'm omitting this is the insecure part of me that worries they will abandon me when I'm not useful anymore.

Maybe they are only attracted to me because an incubus is in my aura.

What if all these loving feelings they seem to feel for me are just transference?

"Hey?" Maxum calls me, and catches my chin gently in his huge hand. "Why do you feel so sad suddenly?"

I don't want to confess my insecurities. What if they confirm my fears about what's happening between us?

So I divert his attention. "Is Calder going to be okay?"

"Is he?" a tiny voice says.

Arran points to Maxum to get something off the floor. My demon reaches down and then places Trouble next to me on the couch. My rabbit and hamster join us shortly after.

"He should be fine, hopefully awake soon," Arran tells them.

"Have you been okay?" I ask the other two, "Can you both talk too?"

"Scared for you!" my bunny Sage says.

I pick up the sweet little lop-eared rabbit and snuggle with her. "I'm sorry I scared you, and that I didn't know that you could talk before."

"We know." She licks my fingers and pushes under my chin, her soft fur tickling me. "The metal stopped you."

I point to my neck where my pendant would normally be. "My locket?"

"Yes."

My guinea pig, Trouble, rolls his eyes. "She thinks she *knows* things."

I chuckle at the arrogant tone of the familiar I apparently have. Of all the things for me to think are crazy, my rabbit sensing stuff is not farfetched at all. In fact, that sounds down right normal anymore. I don't poke at Trouble's theory that my blocked 'witch-holes' have been cleared by Maxum's and Arran's dicks.

But honestly, I can't necessarily rule that out. Maybe we need more research in that area to see if their dicks can power up my magic somehow.

Cocks for science. I really should get shirts made for them.

"Sage is probably onto something," I say as I return to the conversation. "But you're right, it was likely also my ignorance about the supernatural world altogether."

Trouble grunts as though validated.

Just as I allow my shoulders to relax and feel the fatigue hit me, something stirs on the floor.

Huge wings blaze with fire, taking up my entire vision.

Calder.

4

FLAMES

CALDER

*M*y life force finally coalesces in my body, and I hear the soft voice of a woman speaking sweetly. For a moment, I'm almost lulled into a false sense of safety with the sound. Then I remember women can't be trusted—especially witches.

Opening my eyes, I see the witch snuggled in Arran's arms, playing fucking innocent and chatting with Trouble, the guinea pig.

My body roars to life, and my anger returns with my last memories. Apparently, I didn't die since I don't feel like I've lost another part of myself.

I lift from the ground and my wings spread out to their full span and catch fire, likely scorching the ceiling.

Flint and Maxum are now in front of me, blocking my path to the witch.

"Move," I snarl at them, not moving my stare from the now frightened witch.

Arran pulls her closer to his chest, readying to race away with her in his arms.

"She's behind Osen's death," I say, firmly. "I heard them fighting at his death spot."

Maxum steps into my line of sight. "Sorry. Old news, buddy. While you were taking your little nap, we got the entire story."

"No." I shake my head. "Osen said it was her that night."

"He remembers someone who *looked* like her," Flint explains. "But his memory could be faulty. Jade said someone there looked a lot like her, but not exactly."

"And you trust her explanation?" I demand. "What does Osen's spirit have to say about this?"

"He hasn't surfaced yet," Arran growls. "Stand down, or my beast is going to tear you apart for threatening Jade."

"You would kill me? Over *her*? A witch?" I shout.

The pain of rejection slices at my soul, along with the thought of the permanent loss of Osen.

"Put your flames out and listen for a moment," Maxum asks of me in his calm, reassuring voice that he laces with his mind-bending influence.

It isn't enough to make me forget my warpath, and it pisses me off that he's using his powers against me—for her sake.

"Stop it, Maxum," Flint says softly. Then he looks at me. "Calder, you have a right to be upset and confused. However, there are few things that have come to light since you were hurt. Jade appears to be innocent. I don't sense danger from her end. We need to keep our heads and leave soon. Someone was tracking Jade without her knowledge. I sense we are all in danger if we stay here much longer."

My fire fades, and I no longer see red. I don't know how Flint is able to calm me. Possibly because he's the most logical of us, and if he's certain, I should take heed.

"We need to go to my last resort safe house," Maxum says, taking a step back when he sees I'm settling.

I don't trust her, and I'm still pissed. I won't believe anything until I hear it from Osen.

But that's the rub, isn't it?

If she has access to Osen's thoughts and personality, then she can lie and mimic him.

How can we trust *anything* that comes out of her mouth?

Maxum palms my shoulder and grins. "I'm happy you have returned to us whole."

He means my rebirth process. I can't say I ever have returned whole, and I don't feel complete now. Without Osen, I feel hollow.

Yet, even when he was around, something was missing. Part of my soul was destroyed when that witch tortured me to death.

"Let's pack our things," Flint suggests, tilting his head toward the hall to our bedrooms.

I follow along, glaring at Jade the entire time.

On my way past her, she says, "I'm happy you are okay. Thank you for saving me." Her eyes are downcast, and she's so quiet and timid.

It's as if she's afraid I will attack. Maybe she *is* afraid of me. Could that mean she isn't as powerful as I assume?

Or maybe she is only grateful that I stopped Rob from attacking her.

But I don't see how she cares if I'm okay.

Besides, her life wasn't the only reason I stopped Rob from diving into Jade's mind. I didn't want Osen's soul harmed, and I wanted answers about what had happened the night of Osen's death.

I grunt as a response to her thanks and follow Flint.

As I leave the room, I hear Maxum and Arran coddling her. They will help her gather stuff from her house before we leave.

It seems like a foolish thing to trust her, yet I get the sense that they actually do.

Even after all that's happened in their past? With her?

She might have a spell over them, since this isn't like them at all.

Trouble and his magical creature mini-pack race after me into my room. I want to tell them to leave me alone, but they are too fucking cute.

"Are you okay?" Trouble asks, the unofficial spokes-*creature* of the bunch.

"I will be." I grab my oversized duffle and start tossing my stuff inside. "What happened when I was knocked out?"

"Jade almost died. The other witch healed her."

"Another witch?" I hiss, shredding the shirt I have in my hands with my rage.

"Yeah, and the other birdman was looking after you."

I sniff the air and scent another phoenix. What the hell?

I had been so focused on Jade that I hadn't been paying attention.

That woman is a distraction, if nothing else, which is just as dangerous as being a conniving witch.

"Then they found a metal thing on her neck so that the warlock can find her and maybe take her power," Trouble continues.

Well, shit. One would think that if Jade was a knowledgeable witch that she wouldn't have allowed a tracker or something to drain her. However, she might just have allowed her power to be drained temporarily so she could *pretend* she was weak—to get everyone to trust her.

"I know you don't like her, but she worried for you," Trouble adds.

I didn't realize that my disdain for Jade had been so evident to the creatures. However, just because she acts concerned doesn't mean she is.

"She tried to jump off the table to help you."

I scoff. "She has no healing ability. She isn't even a real witch, according to her claims."

"She might not know about her powers, and she might be weak," Trouble argues, his feisty spirit coming back into play. "But that doesn't mean she didn't want to help you."

"You want to believe the best about her, but—"

"I've lived with her for a long time," Trouble interrupts me. "Rob knew about her being a witch, but she didn't. I heard him talking to her under a spell, even after she told him never to come back."

"What did they talk about?"

"Rob would ask her questions, but it wasn't really Jade who answered. And she was hurting. Rob is bad and mean."

"I figured out that much," I grumble, throwing the last of my stuff in my bag.

"Don't be mad at Jade anymore. She is a good witch."

I don't promise the little guy anything. There's no use in arguing with him. He loves her. Perhaps he's right. Perhaps she is just a victim of all this, but I don't like any of it. Osen's death is connected to Rob. And Jade's connected to Rob. I really don't like this ex of hers. He almost killed me. I could have lost most of my memories of Osen with that. Would that be a good thing, though? Would it lessen the pain that I feel?

I have to remind myself it's only been a week or so since he died.

I wish I could trust Jade, and that Osen really is coming through her. But does it matter when he will probably fade away soon, and I will lose him all over again?

"Maybe you should help her," Trouble says.

I frown, not wanting to even entertain the idea. "How?"

"Do what the demon and the wolf did. Clear her witch holes."

I cough and then actually laugh at the absurdity of the idea. "I will *not* be touching her... holes."

"Too bad. It seems like it makes her happier," Trouble says with a touch of disappointment. "And the demon and wolf were happier, too."

I say nothing to that.

I don't know if I *want* to be happier. Perhaps I want to wallow in my grief.

5

SAFEHOUSES

JADE

I hate that Calder hates me. From his perspective, I'm the enemy outsider, connected to his beloved Osen.

I've invaded his tribe.

The problem is, until things get resolved with Osen's spirit and his murder mystery, I don't think even Calder will let me out of his sight.

Beyond that? I'm not sure what will happen.

After I thank him for saving me, Calder could light my ass on fire with the glare he gives me.

Arran's muscular arms surround me, and he reassures me that everything will be okay.

I'm not so sure.

Being positive is all well and good, but... life. Well, it isn't always wine and lubed cocks. Or however that saying goes.

It's hard to think clearly with these two hotties pressing close with all their sexy.

Maxum's obsidian gaze locks onto me. "Is there anything else you need to tell us?" He doesn't sound mad, just concerned.

"I didn't realize about the necklace. I would never have put you all in danger." My eyes sting as I acknowledge I'm in trouble, and I don't know what I should do about it. I reach into my mind again to see if I sense Osen, but I feel nothing in response.

"Uh, guys. Hear me out... I should stay behind," I say, focusing on my hands instead of looking at Maxum or Arran.

They suck in a breath to argue, but I hold up my hand for them to stop.

Damn. This is harder to do than I thought. How could they get under my skin so fast?

"Before you argue, I need to confess that I haven't felt Osen since I've woken up. So I can't help you with finding justice for him." I gesture to the pendant left on the table. "And now that you've found the tracker, I can pack up the most important things, skip town, and vanish. I can write from almost anywhere, so I can get lost for a while. I should be safe."

"Safe?" Arran huffs. "Rob and his partner in crime will probably want to abuse your magic again. They will hunt you down. If they have a witch portal maker like Amira, they can follow you into other realms, let alone another part of the country."

"He's right. Until we deal with Rob and probably the entire ASO, you are a target," Maxum says.

"What about Osen? I'm afraid he's gone for good."

Here it comes—they will say don't worry, he'll be back. Then I'll know that's why they want to keep me around.

"Hold on. Do you think that's why I want to keep you safe? For Osen?" Arran asks, hurt rings clear in his voice.

"Uh, partly?" I shrug. A woman can only get rejected so much without expecting the other testicle to drop.

Arran catches my chin and forces me to look at him. "Jade, you are mine. Understand?"

"But I—" I protest, but he shuts me up with a consuming kiss that makes it impossible to think.

When Arran finishes exploding my brain cells with his passion, Maxum captures my attention, his hand cupping my jaw. "You aren't getting rid of me, little witch."

I gasp at the intensity with which these guys are claiming me.

Maxum leans in and licks over my parted lips, then dips in. He growls into my mouth and pulls back. "This will have to wait until I get you somewhere safe. Then I will make sure you understand."

That threat of pleasure rings my clit like a gong. I wish I had more energy to demand he make me understand right now. However, I am still recovering from yet another near-death experience. This is becoming an ugly habit.

Arran stands, lifts me bridal style, and carries me down the hall to his room. He gently places me on his bed and packs his things.

Maxum nods to me from the door. "I'm gathering my stuff. When we are done here, we'll pick up what you need at your place, so think of what you want to bring."

"Okay." My heart flips a few times, dismissing the possibility that they only want me around for access to Osen.

Could whatever is developing between us be real?

The thought is both scary and thrilling. I've always dreamed and obsessed over having someone truly love me. Hell, I write books about it, getting lost in that idea for months at a time. I become each one of my characters, imagining what it must feel like to be so desperately wanted that the men would move mountains or kill any enemy in their way for me.

Now that the potential for that sort of devotion is right in front of me, I'm a bit terrified of how I will fuck it up, and I probably will.

I'm set in my ways. I'm a loner. The relationships in my books are (mostly) in my control. I don't know how to manage an actual relationship with all its ups and downs. Working out healthy compromises and overcoming day-to-day challenges are not my forte. In other words, I can write them well, but suck at real relationships.

Besides, I'm hyper-focused on my career... *usually*. But not lately, since they have been an enormous distraction. Well, and Rob trying to kill me a few times has definitely disrupted my work-life balance.

"I thought I lost you forever," Arran says in a quiet voice as he places the last of his personal items in his luggage.

"I'm sorry to scare you. Osen insisted I go. If I didn't, he would have taken over my body—maybe for good. And I had no way of telling you what was happening."

Arran kneels down at my feet where I'm sitting on his bed. He clasps my hands in his. "I'm not blaming you. I know exactly how obsessive Osen could be. It's what got him killed, and now he's risking your life."

"I still feel like if I were stronger—a better witch—that I could have stopped him."

"I don't plan on letting you out of my sight. But if I have to leave you alone, I will have Maxum or Flint watch over you."

"To babysit me?" I huff.

"To protect you." Arran tucks a loose lock of silver hair behind my ear and tilts my chin to meet his eyes. "At least until you can learn to use your powers and protect yourself. Good news is Maxum can train you."

"Can he teach me *witch* magic?"

"Maxum knows how to do almost everything—it comes with being alive as long as he has been. He gets bored," Arran explains.

The mention of Maxum getting bored hits me harder than it should. How do you keep a relationship fresh when everything in the universe feels stale? I expect love for people who live forever can be complicated. Maybe long-lived supernaturals have to break up before they get too attached? Or do these relationships rarely last because one gets old and the other doesn't?

Or are they like most relationships? Love and lust fade, and life gets in the way of a happily ever after.

It's something to think about while moving forward with these guys— longevity in all senses of the word. When I asked about lifespans, Maxum told me witches can live longer than regular humans, usually around one hundred to hundred and fifty years. It all depends on the strength of their magic.

Arran leans in to pick me up again, but I put out my hands. "I can walk."

Yet, when I try to stand up, I have a hard time getting to my feet.

"Compromise?" He quirks his full, kissable lips and snakes his arm around my waist to help me walk.

I hook my arm over his shoulder so I can stay upright and slowly we make it to the hallway.

"Ready?" Maxum asks.

I look around and don't see Flint, Calder, or my fur babies.

"They went ahead with your familiars," Maxum says when he figures out what I'm looking for. "We'll meet up with them after we get your stuff."

My demon boyfriend chants and waves his hand to open a portal.

I curse with my surprise. "This time, I can feel magic buzzing. I don't think that will ever get old."

"You've never sensed magic like this before now, have you?" Arran asks.

When I shake my head, Maxum growls, "That pendant was holding you back your whole life. Whatever her reasons, your grandmother wanted to keep your power contained."

"Do you think she was the one who put the draining spell on it?"

"Likely." Maxum waves me forward to go through the portal. "We'll never know about the tracker part unless Rob confesses."

"I doubt we'll get him to do anything," I mutter.

Arran and I step closer to the portal, his arm wrapping around my waist. I hold my breath as we move through to the other side. It feels like stepping in and out quickly of a steamy room with a dramatic pressure change, but other than that, I might not think much of the shift from one place to another.

I exhale when I am securely on the other side, standing in the middle of my living room.

Arran chuckles. "Did you just hold your breath?"

"Don't judge. No one gave me any indication of what it might feel like. I'm flippin' brave for just walking through without a thorough explanation of the effects."

He kisses my cheek. "Very brave."

"Don't patronize me," I laugh.

Maxum follows us over and closes the portal. "Actually, your body handled going through a demon portal quite well for someone new to them. It usually takes a while to get used to this sort of travel." Maxum eyes me like I've done something bizarre.

That ability seems odd to me. I get carsick, but I can jump through demon portals with no problem?

I glance around my house, wondering what I'll need.

"Are we going somewhere that has internet access? Or electricity?" I ask, because for all I know, they are taking me to the woods in faerie land.

"Electricity, yes. You should be able to use your cell phone. Just keep it away from me, or I will probably drain it or make it implode."

"Should I take my phone?" I ask. "Rob could have loaded it with a tracker, too."

"Didn't think of that." Maxum frowns.

"But I will need to access the internet. Oh! I have a traveling router. I doubt Rob knew about it."

In my bedroom, Maxum helps me pick out my clothes and neatly places them in my luggage.

When I chuckle about it, he looks at me quizzically.

"It's a bit strange to have a badass demon be so careful with my things," I confess, hoping he doesn't take offense.

"It's a misnomer that we are misbehaving terrors. That's only during sex and in battle. Well, okay, it's true, we are a menace. But I would *never* damage a woman's clothing that wasn't on her body. Then your delicate panties are fair game as I tear them from your luscious body."

A shiver goes up my spine as his obsidian gaze devours me. He must actually like me if he still thinks I look good after the harrowing night I had.

Since Arran is able to go near technology in short, controlled ways, he packs up my laptop and tablet, and places them in a special lead-lined case they brought along for that purpose.

Then he rummages through my kitchen, probably looking for snacks. He better be grabbing snacks.

"Snacks?" Maxum asks as he zips up my suitcase. Then he shouts to the open bedroom door. "Arran, pack up Jade's junk food!" He winks at me. "Got to take care of you."

I catch his hand in mine, use it to stand up, and look him in the eye. "Are you sure you should take me?" I whisper. "I already got Calder hurt."

"Calder got himself hurt." Maxum wraps his arms around me and pulls me against his firm chest. "He ran off without telling us where he was going or why. And Osen forced you to leave the house. This is on them."

"But I—"

"Nope." Maxum places his huge finger over my lips. "Even the stuff Rob did isn't your fault. Or your grandmother. You were innocent, and they took advantage of that." He leans down, kisses, and nips my bottom lip. "But you won't be innocent in *any* way, shape, or form after I get some time alone with you."

My heart beats wildly with his suggestive talk. "Yeah?"

Arran clears his throat as he walks into my bedroom. "Did you get all the toiletries?"

"I can take care of our woman," Maxum says, his eyes never leaving mine. "Let's get you safe, sweetness."

6

HOME

MAXUM

$\mathscr{I}$ open the portal to the fae realm, Elfhame, so that we can shake any tails we might have acquired at Jade's house. I don't want supernatural trackers following us to my home and endangering my people.

My woman.

Correction… *Our woman.*

Arran has a stronger claim on her than I do.

But I don't plan to let Jade slip away, no matter what comes of Amira's warning that there is something odd about Jade's magic.

We'll unravel what's going on, solving the mystery of Osen's murder and Rob's involvement. After that, we'll tackle the mystery of Jade's unknown past and her powers. Then we will live out the rest of her days making love and sharing myself in ways I've never contemplated before.

If I've learned anything in my many years of experience it's that nothing is what it appears at first. Also, I can handle whatever comes at me.

I'm sure the same is true for Jade. She's already proven she can handle what life throws her way—maybe even more than the rest of my pack.

Case in point, Flint and Calder still haven't gotten over their respective traumas. Even Osen was a mental mess before he died.

I'm sure his death has fucked him up even more. Damn, that even sounds weird to me.

My mind drifts to thoughts of Osen. I loved the motherfucker, but he was a pain in the ass too, not always in a good way. Now that he's dead, he's still causing a bloody mess. Leave it to that bastard to piss me off from the afterlife.

Jade gasps, and my attention is brought back to my mate.

Fated mate? Yes, she is mine.

"Is this really…?" Her mouth hangs open in awe. "Faerieland?"

Through her eyes, I see the beauty of the fae realm again. "Elfhame," I correct. "Yes, you are in another realm. However, this isn't your first visit, is it? You've likely astrally traveled to other dimensions in your sleep before, been here in your special dreams."

"Yes, but it's so much more vibrant than in Osen's memories." She smiles brilliantly at both Arran and me. "I suppose it was usually nighttime during his memories, though."

A flower faerie flutters over to us. Their arrival is a response to the call of amnesty that I requested from the fae royalty so we could travel through the fae realm with a witch. Fortunately, during Jade's time of need, I have people in high places who owe me favors.

"Tavi!" I greet her. "Good to see you have recovered."

She smiles shyly and looks over at Jade. "And I am happy your witch is recovering. The Fae Queen and her consorts grant you permission to travel freely. Oh, and Hollis says hello and to stay out of trouble… if that's possible."

I grin at the mention of my former student. He has outdone himself from the scrappy teenager I tutored.

"Please send the Queen and Hollis our regards and our thanks."

"The Queen would also like to extend an invitation to the witch to visit anytime she wishes."

Hmm. That's interesting and a bit odd. But perhaps this is a play to get more witches on the supernatural's side and put an end to the violence. "Much appreciated. However, until we are able to secure my witch friend's safety, we won't be making any rounds of visits."

Arran clears his throat. "Tavi, I want to thank you and your mate for saving Jade. I plan to bring you a gratitude offering in the near future."

"I appreciate the gratitude, but it is unnecessary. May the Goddess light your way." Tavi does a little bow midair and then flies off. However, I doubt she has left. She'll be watching us until we leave her realm. No doubt Hollis' instruction was to make sure that we find our way out peacefully.

I pick up Jade and carry her cradled in my arms.

She squeaks and bats at my chest. "I can walk."

"Barely," I argue. "Besides, I need to do this. You frightened me with your alleyway stunt. And you are much slower than we are," I say with a laugh at her pout.

"Am I too slow?" She rolls her eyes. "It's not my fault that my legs are so much shorter than yours. You are both giants."

"No," Arran says. "But we could introduce you to some actual giants."

"Really?" Jade practically bounces in my arms with excitement. "Wait... are they cool or assholes?"

"Depends on the giant." Arran shrugs. "We'll have to wait to go on an Elfhame tour until things have settled down."

"In the meantime, we can teach you about different species and proper etiquette." I move faster since I want to get to our next portal point. That one is a permanent fixture, so there won't be a trail of my portal magic to follow to my house.

We jump through another portal and to another. Then finally, we trek away from the last one, and I open up one to my house.

The traveling has exhausted Jade, but when she sees the lakeside cabin, her eyes light up. "Please tell me this is where we are staying."

"Because you are done with the portal hopping?" I joke, feeling vulnerable with her seeing the place I call home.

"Well, a little. But no, this place looks exactly like one of my dreamscapes." She's studying her surroundings and appears fascinated by my home.

"Dreamscapes?" I ask as I carry her closer.

"Yeah. It's what I call the places that feel real to me. Like I can go back to them over and over and they don't change or morph into something else like regular dreams do."

"Maybe they weren't dreams at all?" I suggest. "You could have dream magic. It makes sense. You could have traveled here astrally."

"But why would I come here all these years? You think it was like a premonition of sorts?"

Should I tell Jade it is because her soul was seeking mine all these years? That my heart tells me she is my fated mate? My match? That we are destined to be together... No, she isn't ready for that. She doesn't believe it when Arran tells her, and she has a deeper connection with him than me.

No, she's not ready yet. Jade's beliefs and sensibilities are still mired in the human world. Even if she plays with the idea in her books, she doesn't truly believe there are people out there meant for us—who are fated.

Jade wiggles to get me to release her, but I hold on tightly. I'm going to carry her over the threshold into my home, just like the bridal tradition the humans have stolen from supes.

"Oh, Wolfboy? Don't shit in my yard," I poke at Arran.

Jade hides her snicker in my arms.

"Fuck, dude! You aren't ever going to let me live that down, are you?" Arran metaphorically tucks his tail between his legs.

"You took a dump in our mate's back yard. How am I supposed to forget that?" I egg him on.

"I cleaned it up!" Arran whines.

"Throwing it at my head doesn't count," I deadpan.

"He did what?" Jade laughs a bit too hard.

I glower at her, though there isn't much heat behind it.

Then I focus back on our destination. I whisper words of power as we approach, and the wards allow us entry to the property.

When I near the front porch, I use my will to open the door.

Jade squeals with delight, like a child seeing her first magic trick. She makes everything feel new and exciting. I can't wait to delight her for all the years we may have together. She even lets out a playful giggle when I carry her inside.

When I set her down on her unsteady feet and wrap my arms around her waist, she gazes up at me adoringly. My whole body vibrates with happiness. I don't think I've ever experienced this giddy feeling.

She lifts onto her toes, and I lean down to give her a kiss.

Then, like a curious puppy, she bolts away to explore, even though I can see it's taking the last bit of energy she has to even move.

Flint and Calder are already here, as they used a quicker set of portals to travel and had the spell to unlock our place.

I'm about to call out to them when Flint steps into the hallway.

In her excitement, Jade is practically flying at him. She screams, not out of fear of him, but that she will crash into his stone body and upset the lug. Her momentum is such that she will collide, so instead, she purposely falls.

Sliding on the slippery hallway wood flooring, she barely misses Flint's legs.

Her head thuds against the wall and then the floor.

"Jade!" Flint cries out and then almost tries to pick her up. He stops himself at the last second when he realizes what he's about to do.

Arran is there in the next moment, aggressively shoving Flint out of the way, and dropping down to check on Jade.

"I'm fine. Just banged myself up a little." She waves him away, but her eyes are glassy, and she doesn't move to get up.

"You can't afford anymore head trauma," Arran says with the bite of reprimand. "You are quickly killing me, *woman*."

"So dramatic." She laughs it all off. "Flint, I'm sorry for coming at you like a damned baseball player sliding into home. I should have been more careful with my surroundings."

Ugh. I hate that she has been conditioned by jerky ex boyfriends and an unloving mother to take responsibility for everything, even when it isn't her fault.

"Please, don't apologize to me," Flint says with so much sorrow that I feel it pierce my heart. He despises this part of himself, and Jade is only rubbing the old wound lately. "It's my issue. Please, don't hurt yourself to avoid me." He runs outside and takes off, flying over the lake.

"Well, I keep making a mess of things. He won't ever get used to me, will he?" Jade frowns as Arran helps her to her feet.

"He will, but it might take more than a couple of days," I assure her.

But will Flint heal? Could she be the one to help him finally come out of his self-inflicted and literal shell?

"Sweetness, you should get some rest," Arran says. "Today was a lot."

Jade pouts as she glances down the hall. She wants to explore, but that isn't a good idea right now. My cabin is no tiny hovel, it has eight bedrooms and six baths.

I bought it twenty years ago, hoping we all could settle here and give up fighting in the wars. Or at the very least, take a break from the life of revenge. Collectively, we've taken two breaks in total. However, I make use of this retreat and come here alone whenever I need to get away from the noise of city life—which is more often than not.

"Come with me." I take Jade by the waist and help her down the hallway to my enormous room on the first floor.

Jade looks up toward the stairs. "Five bedrooms up there?" she asks. "And three down here?"

I nod at her accurate guess. She *has* been here before in her dreams, further confirming she is mine... *ours?*

"One room is set up as an office of sorts. You can use that as a space for your writing," I offer, hoping she will understand the implications of allocating a piece of this house to claim as her own. "It also has a daybed if you need your... space from our energy. Though I would rather you sleep with me. You and Arran are more than welcome to share my bedroom with me while we are here. The bed could easily fit all of us. Since it's on the first floor, it will be easier for you to move around while you recover. And I have an ensuite bathroom so you won't taunt Flint or Calder with all your delicious naked flesh."

"*Taunt* is a strong and wholly inaccurate word for what I do to them." She brushes me off with a chuckle. "At least when paired with my nakedness. I'm not even trying to be an annoyance! Apparently, I'm just that good at being frustrating."

I push open the door to my huge bedroom. "You frustrate me, but in a good way."

"How so?" She smirks.

"Because you wear way too many clothes and I want to have my dick buried deep inside you at all times."

She shakes her head. "It seems as though we may experience a lot of sunburns and chafing if we played it your way."

I smile at her joke, but my statement wasn't one. I'd love to live inside her. Maybe I can get some sort of harness and I can fill her up while tending to other tasks that I can't avoid.

Hell, my mind now wanders to sexy scenarios just as much as the witch's dirty mind does. We are perfect for each other.

She moves across the room with an awe-filled face. Her hand reaches out to stroke the floor to ceiling tapestries hanging on the walls, then over a jewel-tone damask fabric duvet and pillows that cover the mattress of my four-poster bed. She grins as her fingers trace the gauzy fabric drapes that hang down and over the dark wood of the bed frame.

Overall, the decor creates a sensual space. And it feels as though I've built it all with her in mind. Pride wells up inside me when I see admiration clear in her beautiful eyes.

I rarely allow anyone inside my personal sanctuary. I think this might be the first time Arran has even seen my room.

Jade smiles from ear to ear. "Maxum, it's like you're an omega princess with a pretty nest," she jokes.

"I'll show you who's an omega when I rut you through a heat." I swat her full, plump ass, and she yelps.

"Holy shit!" She pants, worked up. "How do you know about omegaverse?"

"Where do you think humans got the idea?" I waggle my eyebrows.

"Fucking knot me," Jade sputters. Then she hugs me sweetly, clinging to my side. "But seriously, it's so fuckin' gorgeous. I'm not sure what I was expecting, but it's prettier than any place I've seen. It's like a fantasy come true."

"You don't remember my room from your dreamscape?" I ask, sad that she didn't recognize it.

"No. I was never allowed inside the bedrooms, just in the common areas."

Interesting, but it makes sense. Our rooms are sacred to us and each of us has our own form of warding to protect them from outsiders. Even my mate's spirit would need some sort of permission to enter. I feel myself relaxing with the thought.

Jade yawns, but tries to hide her sleepiness as Arran and I set all the luggage down.

Striding over, I give her a kiss on the lips, and then the top of her head. "Get some rest. I'll make sure all is well on the property before I return."

She hums her acknowledgement, then grimaces at her dirty clothes. "I don't want to mess up your beautiful bed."

"Never worry about that, my sweet witch." I wink. "I'm sure we can make you more comfortable." I slowly unbutton her blouse.

Arran comes up from behind. Reaching around, he unfastens and unzips her pants. She kicks off her shoes. The wolf-shifter slides her pants down slowly, skimming her silky skin with his fingertips as he goes.

When I pull the shirt from her shoulders, I'm both aroused and concerned. Aroused by her silky flesh and ample breasts on display. Concerned because she's covered in bruises from her brush with death.

Jade stands before me in only her skimpy underwear, and I admire her strength and resilience, especially for being a witch. They are not built like supes.

Gently, I touch her damaged flesh. "I will heal these with my magic after you rest."

She bites her lower lip, and her voice comes out husky. "Sex magic?"

"Would you like that?" I ask.

"Is it illegal to own six dildos in Texas?" she quips as an answer.

She doesn't know how much I love weird facts, and I chuckle.

"Yes. Yes, it is." I boop her nose like a silly demon and leave her be so I can ensure the safety of my pack and my mate.

7

INTIMACY

ARRAN

*J*ade falls asleep immediately in Maxum's amazing bed. I feel like I need to spruce up my bedroom before she visits it, to make her feel as comfortable and lavished in expensive fabrics as she is in Maxum's space.

I'm lacking as a provider. To be fair, Maxum is far more wealthy than any of us combined—not that he usually flaunts it. He doesn't think much about his wealth at all, from what I can tell.

On top of his ability to lavish her with whatever she dreams up, he can heal her and protect her better than I can.

Besides Maxum being a better provider, I'm also lacking in a whole other way that I don't know how to fix: I might still be a danger to her. Sure, my berserker kept his violence under wraps during sex with her. But Maxum and I kept him reined in the entire time, making sure he didn't get rough. The threat of Maxum ripping him to shreds probably helped to keep him passive, but I can't even make love to her in my human form. I want to be intimate with Jade without my beast. Otherwise, every damned time, I will probably have to invite Maxum to make sure my beast doesn't hurt her.

Will I ever have that? Will I ever be able to lose myself completely in passion with her and in my own body? Or will I always have to hold back?

After a few hours, Jade stirs and stretches. Her mesmerizing hazel eyes instantly find me watching her. "Hey, creeper," she teases, but admires my naked chest and pulls on my shoulder for me to kiss her. "Are you okay?"

"Yeah, why?" Damn, she can see right through me.

"You don't have to lie to me about stuff anymore. Tell me the truth."

Well, that stings more than I expected. She's right, though. The time for lies is done.

"I was just overthinking everything," I confess, then place gentle kisses over her face until she's laughing and pushing me away to catch her breath.

"I should freshen up." She grabs a lock of her matted hair and wrinkles her nose. "This is a fully formed rat's nest. Do you have a hacksaw?"

"That's a little drastic." I guide her to the bathroom and offer, "I'll help with untangling your hair."

I leave her to pee and come back when I hear she is washing her hands. "Sit." I point to a vanity stool, because, of course, bougie Maxum has one. Oh well, I can't fault him for wanting the finer things in life when I know the life he was born into.

Jade smirks, "I didn't know Maxum was such a fancy boy."

I pick up a comb and some oils to untangle Jade's hair and say off-handedly, "I'm sure, with his age, he's been just about everything. Except for being in love, until now."

Jade inspects a lock of her hair, starting at the ends. "Do you mean with me? That's an awfully big assumption."

"Not really, but I suppose it isn't my place to say how anyone else feels."

My witch stares at the mirror and watches my muscles flex as I brush out her hair. I pretend not to notice, but I preen under her attention. I've never cared much about my looks, only that I was strong and honorable.

Now I'm pleased that my woman finds me attractive. Jade even called my wolf handsome. She claims she has no problem with my berserker's looks, but I know she was only trying to make me feel better.

My wolf inside me bounces around, wishing to get some attention, too. He misses Jade from their long days in her home. He demands ear scratches.

I make him wait until I'm done with her hair.

"You are a miracle worker!" Jade swings her long, silver threaded strands.

I grin and then kneel to look her in the eyes. "Beast... my *wolf* misses you. He would like to visit."

Jade strokes my face. "Are you okay with that?"

"Yeah, he's been patient."

"May I ask how this shifter thing works? It sounds like the wolf and the berserker are separate from each other and from you."

I take in a deep breath. This isn't easy to explain, and it sounds baffling to most humans. But I remind myself that Jade writes stuff that isn't far from the truth.

"I suppose it's much like a split personality. Except I'm aware of him, and he is aware of me. His emotions are usually in line with mine. But similar to when you might feel conflicted about something, we can be at odds at times. Usually, that happens because he operates from his instincts and heart. I operate from my mind, humanlike feelings, and sometimes, if I'm lucky, with logic. Then there is the berserker."

"So instead of a dichotomy, you now are a trichotomy," she jokes, trying to ease my tension.

I nod. "Suppose so. We all are impulsive, and that can get us in trouble."

"Like chasing me down from the bar?" Jade smirks.

Thank Goddess she thinks that's funny now.

"Yeah. That's one example. The other is how I got cursed."

Jade covers her mouth. "Sorry. I didn't mean to bring up a sore subject."

"It's okay. I don't want anything hidden between us. And now, this is part of who I am—unfortunately."

"You mentioned it was a witch who did this. Is that why you don't like witches?"

"Partly. Jade, I will understand if you no longer like me once I tell you how I was cursed."

"Well, shit. That's not a great setup to a story." Jade places her hands on mine, calming me instantly. "Just tell me what happened and let me decide what I can handle."

Choking down the emotions bubbling up in me, I begin, "Many years ago, Osen was attacked by a witch named Tanil."

"I remember that name, vaguely." Jade gazes into the distance, lost in the memory she plucked from Osen's soul.

"You might also remember that she had gutted Osen and threw iron in his wound. For a fae-born supernatural being, iron poisoning can be a death sentence. Somehow, he managed to escape. I think she wanted him to be found in the wild, and we couldn't pin his death on her. Using Flint's sense of danger and protection, and Calder's ability to sense death, we were able to locate him and get him the help he needed. We were supposed to wait until Osen recovered, then attack Tanil together."

"But you didn't go along with that plan," she guesses.

"No. I was filled with so much rage for my friend and occasional lover that I raced off when no one was paying attention and attacked her. I tore Tanil apart. I could barely tell she was human by the time I was done."

Jade waits for me to go on, but the tension in her body grows. She probably wants to drop my hands and run away.

"But Tanil wasn't alone. Her coven mates attacked, cursing me with dark magic sealed with Tanil's blood. From then on, whenever I feel potent emotions, my berserker is awakened and takes over."

"Oh."

"Oh?" I squeeze her hands in mine, unsure what to make of her response.

"I mean, I'm so sorry they cursed you like that. But it sounds like there was an ugly cycle of revenge going on. I probably would have gone after Tanil too, if she had hurt one of my people."

"So, you don't think I'm a monster?"

"Technically? Yeah. You are. But *what-the-fuck-ever*. Humans are monsters for much less and for no reason at all." Jade shrugs. "Why did Tanil attack Osen?"

"He believed it was because he broke off their fling."

"Well, trying to kill Osen for a break up seems like a bit much," Jade says flippantly.

I bark out a laugh. "Yeah. A bit much. She knew he was a fickle incubus from the start."

"Anyway, I get why you killed her. She tried to hurt your pack because she was mad she was ghosted." Jade kisses my lips.

"But I murdered someone—a witch," I argue.

"Do you regret it?"

"I wish I had done things differently. Maybe we could have avoided all the violence." I rub my face in frustration. "But we've now come to believe that she was a spy from ASO, and she always intended to kill him. We may never know the truth of it all."

"Then you can't keep beating yourself up about it. Okay?" When I nod, she bounces in her chair. "Can I watch you change into your wolf? Is his name really Beast? Or is that just a joke Maxum made?"

I'm surprised how she drops the subject of my violence so easily.

"My wolf didn't have a name, but he likes it when you call him Beast. He thinks it makes him sound formidable."

Jade palms her face, embarrassed. "Geeze. How dumb was I that I didn't realize a wolf wasn't a dog?"

"To be fair, most wolves don't just trot inside human's homes when invited." I smile with the memory. "And there are some breeds that look a lot like wolves."

"Can I say hi to him now?" Jade asks.

I stand and drop my boxers. My cock being at eye level has Jade licking her lips.

"Next, I want an appointment with your snake." She waggles her eyebrows.

I shake my head but chuckle. Then I sober up with my next thought. "I should tell you, I will only be able to have sex in my berserker form. I won't be able to be with you like that in my human form."

A tear forms in her eyes. The reality of our relationship has set in.

"That upsets you," Jade says, like that fact doesn't affect her.

"Doesn't it upset *you*?" I ask, my brow wrinkles with confusion.

"Only if you don't like it." She frowns, thinking, then asks, "Do you feel all of it? I mean, the werewolf is part of you, right? Do you enjoy the sensations? *You* feel my touch?"

"Well, yeah. But I won't be *me*—in this body. And I can't guarantee your safety with him. I kept him mostly calm before, but he dug his claws into you during sex. We were fortunate that Maxum was able to heal the cuts so easily."

"We'll figure this out." Jade places her cheek in my palm and kisses my wrist. "But now, I need puppy time."

Beast instantly shifts without my permission. One moment, Jade is holding my hand and staring up at me, the next, she has a massive wolf standing in front of her.

He licks her face, chin to forehead in one swipe, and she shouts her shock.

"Beast! Settle down." But she's laughing and rubbing his ears. Hugging him around the neck, she buries her face deep in his fur. "I missed you, sweetie."

He whimpers, conveying he feels the same.

"I'll make sure to spend time with you more often, okay?" she promises.

Beast barks his joy and runs around the room.

"Come here. I don't have the energy yet to chase you." She picks up the brush she had just been using on herself and moves it over my wolf's head and neck.

Without even knowing it's about to happen, my berserker bursts into being, pushing the wolf back into my body.

Jade doesn't even miss a beat as a giant werewolf kneels before her.

"Be good," she warns and continues brushing, but now she's treating my berserker werewolf like a naughty pup.

And… he fucking loves it.

I don't step in and stop it. Not yet. I'm curious what he will do and how he will react, because he doesn't seem crazed with emotion, aggressively possessive, or ready to hurt someone.

He just wants attention.

Love.

So do I.

Since he *is* part of me, I suppose Jade needs to accept him, too. But I feel so exposed while she studies my true werewolf face. She didn't get a good look at me before when we had sex. But now, we are calm, and she strokes my furry body with her brush.

The berserker closes our eyes in bliss as she brushes down over our chest. Methodically, she works the brush over our sides, moving to our waist, but no further.

"I'm going to stand up and brush your back now, okay?" she informs us. Smart—she doesn't want to startle him.

Berserker grunts his approval, and she moves behind him. Her position makes him vulnerable since he cannot see what she might do to him. I'm shocked he allows it.

Then the feeling of trust wells up in our heart. He really trusts her. Loves her. As I do.

However, that doesn't mean he might not accidentally harm her. He is a brute, after all. Am I any better, since I'm an impulsive asshole?

"Your coat is gorgeous. It looks so nice brushed out," Jade says, running her palm over our back, following each stroke of the brush. "Softer than I expected too." When she gets to my lower back, she surprises us and encourages, "Stand up."

Behaving like a tamed beast, Berserker gets to his feet.

Jade kneels and brushes over our ass and down our powerful thighs and calves. She even fusses over our tail. This is the most intimate thing I've ever experienced. My ugliest parts are on full display, and every inch of me is being loved and caressed.

I'm reeling as I feel the love pouring off her. Her acceptance. I've never accepted this part of me. Maybe I've never fully accepted and loved myself in any way—ever. But Jade makes it seem so easy to accept my monster and to love me completely.

Berserker wags his tail. *Wags! His tail!*

I don't even recognize this creature right now.

Jade gasps quietly, likely just as shocked as I am.

I thump her face with our flailing tail. Oh my goddess, how embarrassing.

"Turn around," she asks with a smile in her voice.

We do, gazing down into Jade's adoring hazel-green eyes.

She's on her knees at our clawed feet, looking up at us like we are a god. Her sweet pink mouth is only inches from our hardening cock.

I've never felt so naked or so cherished.

I'm surprised once again when my berserker doesn't grab her face and fuck into her lush mouth. The loving way she looks at us right now, she might let us do that.

But even Berserker knows this moment isn't about fucking.

Jade touches our huge hands and slowly traces the line of my giant razor-sharp claws. "These aren't innately bad, you know. You can use them to protect the ones you love. Just be careful when you get excited with me, and I will be okay."

Maybe there is potential worth in my alternate self. I can protect her.

What would happen if I accepted this part of me? Would it heal this perpetual wound I have?

My berserker nods his understanding of her words. He sees himself as her protector already. Lightly and experimentally, he skims his sharp claw over the back of her hand. He doesn't even leave a mark.

She smiles up at us and continues brushing our thighs and shins. Then she moves up over our crotch, brushing around our cock and balls.

During this sacred moment, she has, only with her actions, told us how much we mean to her.

She moves to stand and Berserker reaches down and helpfully lifts Jade to her feet. He then licks up the side of her face very much like my wolf did minutes ago.

Jade laughs and hugs us, holding *him*.

After a moment of enjoying the affection, Berserker relinquishes control over my body. It's the first time since my curse that he's willingly allowed me to come back. Every other time I have to fight him to win back control and return to my human form.

"Oh!" Jade scare-jumps from my shifting into a human, of all things.

She's so weird. It's my normal appearance that gets her spooked, but I sort of love it.

I'm six inches shorter and less bulky in my human form. And I dare say less furry.

She snuggles her cheek into my bare chest and hums happily.

"Thank you," I whisper. "For accepting them… me."

Jade leans back in my arms to look into my eyes. "Of course. You have accepted me even though I'm your enemy."

"You were never my enemy. My love, you are my savior." I press my lips to hers, luxuriating in her softness.

"Well, that might be taking it a bit far." Jade blushes and tucks her head under my chin.

"It's not. No one has made me feel at peace like I feel right now. You accepting my berserker makes me accept him, too. He doesn't even feel feral at the moment."

"I'm happy I could help a little bit."

"A lot." I squeeze her to me, wishing I could make her part of me too. I suppose when... *if*... I claim her, she will be part of me. "Maybe witches, in general, should have never been my enemy."

"People, no matter what kind, can be amazing or they can be jerks. I don't think it's wise to lump whole groups together and assume we know everything by the behavior of a few."

"If you're finished fixing the world's problems in my bathroom, would you like to come eat the meal we whipped up for you?" Maxum asks with a smirk in the doorway.

"A chef too?" Jade hurries to him, pulling me along by my hand. "A demon of many talents!"

8

MEALS

JADE

Tears had formed in Arran's eyes when he was a berserker. I don't think the monster within him is all beast.

Volatile? Impulsive? Dangerous?

Yes, he is all these things, but also… more. It wants to be accepted. Loved. It isn't just an *it*.

I hope that my affection for the berserker might persuade it to allow Arran to be with me in his human form. Not because I need to have Arran in his non-monster form, but because *Arran* wants to be with me in that way.

Holding both the demon's and werewolf's hand as we enter the kitchen and open dining room, I feel weirdly giddy and happy. Considering everything that's going on, I shouldn't feel this happy. I almost died—again. I'm on the run. My career is likely in jeopardy of taking a nosedive if I can't finish my next book on time.

Yet, it's reassuring to have these two brave males by my side, willing to help me figure out the next completely overwhelming and new phase of my life. It's also more than I expected or hoped for.

I still can't believe what my life has become. First off, I'm a witch. With that, there are realms of existence beyond the one I've always known. There really are magical beings and creatures. I've had sex with three kinds of supernaturals… no, make that four magical people if we include a stupid warlock named Rob.

Might as well add him to the list, as it makes my low 'body count' sound more impressive.

The kitchen and dining area are open to the living room, which has a magnificent stone fireplace. My eye catches a huge framed image I hadn't noticed when I arrived. It looks like a blurry photograph of a werewolf.

"What is… *that*?" I rush over to it. My eyes pop out of my head when I catch sight that all around the larger photograph are framed newspaper clippings.

Each clipping features a blurry, furry *monster*—named to be bigfoot, the Jersey devil, chupacabra, unknown species, etc. Now that I know how the camera distorts a supernatural's image and how Arran looks in his beast form, I recognize the famous and *previously believed to-be-a-hoax* images. "Is this you?" I ask my werewolf lover.

He grimaces and tucks his head down.

Maxum chuckles. "Every time he's been caught by a camera, I like to remind him of his reckless behavior and frame it up for him."

"Maxum!" I admonish, but find myself chuckling too.

"We all have clippings around the house, but Arran is the most famous," he informs me.

Shaking my head in amusement, I turn back toward the kitchen.

Looking shy once again, Flint is back and helping to dish up dinner.

The dining table is set with medieval-style forks with only two pointed prongs and sharp knives.

The plates are thick ceramic and appear extremely retro—like centuries old retro. However, the gas stove is cutting edge and looks like it belongs in a fancy restaurant.

At the head of the table, Maxum pulls a chair out for me next to his, and Arran sits on my other side. Calder storms in and plops down at the far end, clearly stating his objection to my presence with a hard glower.

Flint serves us our plates, being extra cautious around me.

I want to joke that my arms aren't going to flail around and accidentally touch him, but I don't want to draw attention to his discomfort. Besides, I'm slightly klutzy and I might actually bump into him.

My plate has a thick slice of meat that takes up almost the entire surface. It looks mostly like beef, but doesn't quite smell like it. Also on my overly full plate are a variety of unknown vegetables, a chunk of fancy cheese, and a fresh dinner roll. On the table in a big serving bowl is a pile of my snack chips, all mixed together.

My eyes go wide with that last offering and Maxum addresses the weird *dish*. "Flint thought you might want some as an appetizer."

Shaking my head in disbelief, I say, "This is a fuck-ton of food."

"Is that a metric ton?" Maxum asks with a smirk.

I grin at his joke, then slowly look back at my plate. "I appreciate how generous you are with the servings, but I can't eat all this."

"But you have lost weight." Flint leans forward in his seat, with an earnest expression. "You need your strength."

I don't use scales. Not that I've had time to locate and use one lately. But now that he's mentioned it, my pants have been a bit looser. "I've lost weight?"

"Yeah," all four of the males say in unison—with a frown. Even Calder joined in, which blows my mind. Why would he care or comment?

"I need you healthy for what I have planned for you later." Maxum grins wickedly at me. "So, eat what you can."

Healthy? He means curvy. But I can't say I mind them enjoying my curves.

I love my curves more and more the way they adore every inch of me.

Glancing around the table, I see they are all waiting to start—Calder, too.

"What's happening?" I ask. "Do we need to say grace to the Goddess or some supernatural being?"

"You are our guest, so we are waiting for you to take the first bite," Arran explains.

"Oh." Eyeing the meat and veggies again, I ask, half-joking, "Is this unicorn meat? Because it's not beef."

"Unicorn meat is much too gamey," Maxum says. "This is pegasus meat. They are far more common than you would think and quite a nuisance."

"What?" I push the plate away from me. "I don't think eating magical creatures is a good idea. Supes are already pissed off that I was even born."

"I'm just messing with you." Maxum laughs. "It's buffalo. And it was ethically sourced. The buffalo lives out its normal lifespan, with magic to keep its body healthy. And then it passes peacefully in its sleep."

"Are you still screwing with me?" I ask, because who knows with this jokester.

"That's the truth."

I take his word for it, because honestly, that sounds like the most ethical thing you can do if you are going to eat meat. I cut and spear a small piece on my jabby fork and try it.

"It's pretty good," I say, and they all dig into their food. It still has a different taste than the buffalo I've had before, but maybe that's the magic flavoring.

I taste the veggies on the tip of my tongue one at a time and find they taste okay. The seasoning is a bit different from what I'm used to, but I'm adventurous enough.

"So, where are we? Earth?" I ask, since it doesn't have that colorful hyperrealism look that the fae realm has.

"Yes, but I don't want to tell you exactly where, because if someone infiltrates your mind in your dreams, they will know where we are."

"I suppose a lake house is generic enough," I note.

"No landmark features around here for a reason except for a lake. But there are 125,000 lakes in the Continental U.S. alone... if we are even in the States." Maxum winks. "Since you are untrained in blocking, you would be the most likely to reveal our location accidentally."

I don't mention that when I have access to Wi-Fi with my travel router, I'll be able to pinpoint exactly where we are. I don't plan on doing that for exactly the reason Maxum outlined. And thankfully, I've already turned off my GPS location on my devices.

"I don't want to be the weak link," I say.

"Too late," Calder grouches.

"I wouldn't point fingers if I were you," Arran growls. "You botched the whole alleyway incident from beginning to end."

"Stop it," Maxum raises his voice.

I quietly shovel food in my mouth because I still feel guilty for not stopping Osen from demanding I go to that alley. I remind myself I didn't have the tools or magic to stop the incubus.

"Will you really be able to help me block out people like Rob?" I ask Maxum.

He studies me for a second. "Yeah. Your magic is coming in. Soon we will see what kind of power you actually have."

"I'm nervous," I admit openly. "I don't know if I can handle suddenly being powerful at forty."

"You already are powerful," Arran says and strokes my arm. "You're an amazing medium, even when the talisman was draining you, and you have dream magic."

"And you are a fucking grown-ass, professional business woman who has carved her way through a male dominated world," Maxum adds.

"Okay. You're right. I just need to brace myself for whatever happens."

"We'll be here for you," Arran promises.

"Can we lay off the sugary positive affirmations for a few minutes so I can choke down this food?" Calder asks with a sneer on his face.

Having enough of his attitude, I say in a calm but firm voice, "Can you lay off being a dick to me for five minutes? I get you hate witches, and I get you don't trust me because of Rob. But it upset me when you got hurt. One, because the asshole Osen loves you, and two, because I don't hate you."

Calder doesn't respond, which I'm taking as a good sign. Then finally he asks, "You haven't felt Osen again since the alleyway?"

"No. I'm getting worried."

"Why?" he asks firmly, with more than a hint of disbelief. "He's just some cosmic parasite now, if it's really even him at all."

"I've seen a bit of what he's been through—what all of you have been through. Believe it or not, I've grown to care about him. It doesn't matter what you think about me, because I hope he's okay." I offer an olive branch. "If he returns, I'll make sure you get to talk to him."

Calder grunts and focuses back on his plate. I'll take it as a win.

9

ANOTHER ROUND

JADE

*T*he guys encouraged me to eat way more than I had planned. I'm stuffed, and they probably could roll me away from the table.

Fortunately, they don't erase the small amount of dignity I have left by going for that option.

Flint gathers up our empty plates and cleans up with Calder's help.

Maxum takes my hand and walks me back to his bedroom with Arran in tow.

"I know you suggested a night of sexy times, but I'm too full and exhausted for that," I inform him as we step into the beautiful bedroom. "I'm frustrated now."

"I know, little witch," Maxum purrs. "I thought we'd give you a bath and then let you sleep. The sex will have to wait until you can handle what I plan to do to you."

My clit tingles with his sexy threat.

Down, girl.

"Arran, get these pesky clothes off her, and I'll get the bath going," Maxum says and darts into the ensuite bathroom.

My wolf shifter shrugs innocently as he steps closer. "Boss's orders. Nothing I can do, miss."

"Well, if Mr. McBossy said so…" I help Arran along and lift my arms so he can pull my top over my head.

Instead of helping me all the way, he leaves the shirt stuck over my face and arms trapped, and he sucks my exposed nipple into his mouth.

"Arran!" I laugh, hurrying to pull the shirt all the way off. I run toward the bathroom and crash into Maxum's arms.

Arran collides with my backside and presses me between them.

"Mr. Maxum McBossy needs his witch naked by the count of three." Maxum stares at me sternly. "One… Two…"

Behind me, Arran drops to his knees and pants me as he goes. His sharper than normal teeth bite into my ass, and I shout my surprise.

Maxum lifts me, and Arran removes my pants from around my ankles.

The water spout is rapidly filling a gigantic tub that could hold all three of us comfortably.

Maxum's hands stroke up and down my sides, from hips to breasts. "Beautiful."

My eyes drift to the hot water blasting out of the faucet. Wow, he has amazing water pressure here. That's going to feel amazing in the shower.

Focus. I don't want to be sidetracked by future pleasures when I have a current experience happening now.

Fragrant steam wafts off the hot bath water and fills my nose. The floral smell is like nothing I've experienced before. I suspect he added other worldly oils to my bath.

Other *realmly*? Realmly isn't a word, is it? I'll have to look that up. Probably not. It's likely another one of my new words. But I'm exactly like Shakespeare, making up words to fit my wild stories.

I pull on Maxum's tight long sleeve shirt, and he obliges, removing it over his head. No way I was reaching over his six foot five height. These guys are all so tall it makes me feel like a tiny thing.

My fingertips trace Maxum's tattoo-like crimson markings. He's in his human glamour, so it's striking against his lighter skin tone.

"Why don't your markings disappear with your glamour?" I ask.

"Not sure why, but we can't make our life marks disappear. I suppose it could be considered poetic—my life history is always with me."

"I like that answer."

There's a rustle of clothing, and then I feel Arran's naked body and his hard cock pressing up against my back. He moves the mass of my thick hair away from my neck and shoulder and presses sweet, tickling kisses on my skin there.

"I thought you said no sex?" I'm not sure which answer I want.

"I didn't say no sex," Arran purrs and his hand reaches around to cup my breast.

Maxum chuckles, tests the water, then lifts me up and into the deep tub. "Arran, she needs to recover... unfortunately." He sits and sets me down between his powerful legs. His right hand strokes up my inner thigh. "But that doesn't mean we can't tease her."

"Naughty demon!" I smack his hand.

He doesn't stop his exploration, and with his left hand on my left knee, and his tail wrapped around my right leg, he opens me up.

Arran joins us in the water. His hungry gaze locked on my exposed sex.

Arran scoots closer, lathers up his hands, and washes me from my toes, moving up to my hips.

Maxum washes my hair, massaging my scalp with his deft fingers. Oh, wow, I could get used to this sensual spa treatment.

After he rinses the shampoo out, I lean back against Maxum's broad chest and luxuriate in his ministrations as he slides his fingers over my pussy and stimulates me, slowly working me up.

It feels so good that I drift off into a strange half-asleep arousal.

Or I think it's half-asleep.

"Is she snoring?" Maxum asks, with mirth in his voice.

"Dude, she full-on just zonked out during our sexy times," Arran says with a laugh.

I try to wake up, but the jaws of sleep are clamping down on me. I murmur, "Good little monsters are very relaxing."

"Everything you said in that sentence is wrong," Maxum sighs. "We are not little monsters. Morally gray at best. And we shouldn't be relaxing. We should be making you come right now."

"I'm coming, just tomorrow," I mumble.

I'm lifted out of the warm water and the most sensual, huge towel is wrapped around me and I'm in love with it.

"That's a wrap!" I call out like a drunken movie director.

I can feel a deep rumble from Maxum's chest when he lifts me up and carries me out of the bathroom.

I'm tucked into the massive bed. It's so big that I could get lost here for days.

"I'd like to get lost in bed with you for days, too," Maxum says.

"You read my mind?" I ask, snuggling into his chest and feeling Arran tucking in behind me as my big spoon.

"You're saying everything out loud," he informs me. "And I'm a bit jealous of the towel."

"Rain check on the magical dicking?" I ask.

I feel a kiss on the top of my head and drift off, happy to know my two monsters are safely in my bed.

Darkness surrounds me, but I know I'm not awake or in bed next to my guys.

No. I'm lost in a forest.

When I allow my consciousness to reach out to the dark, like Osen inadvertently showed me how to do when he took over my body, I sense I'm in Elfhame.

Not that I'm all that familiar with the fae realm, but I had a good dose of the energetic feel of the place during our cross-realm trek to Maxum's home.

Why am I here?

Of course, my first instinct is to wonder if I'm reliving another one of Osen's memories. I don't have the same sensations as I did when we were connected, though.

I fear, once again, that our incubus is lost. *Ours.* When did I claim him as mine?

Even though he's inhabited my body and brought me immense sexual pleasure, I don't know if I have the right to claim him that way. Or in any way.

"Osen?" I whisper. It's my voice, not his, that cuts through this dark quiet.

So if I'm not in his memory, or anyone's memory, where am I? And why? Maybe I have dream magic as Maxum suggested.

This feels too tangible to be a normal dream.

Eerily, I can hear a woman hum a song—like a lullaby. It echoes around me, from everywhere and nowhere. This song feels familiar.

It sounds a bit like… my abuela?

Now, I'm very confused. If my grandmother was a witch, why is she in the fae realm?

"You shouldn't be here, mija."

"Abuela?" I ask. "Where are we? Are you alive?"

"You are here, because your pendant is gone," she says.

Is this real? Is this now?

"How do you know about the pendant?" I ask, "Why did you suppress my power?"

"I meant to come back and teach you about your power. I didn't get the chance."

"Are you working with Rob? Did you kill Osen?"

"No. Never." I can almost hear her shaking her head. "Your pendant was meant to protect you... hide you... from those who would harm you or use your power."

"What powers?" I wonder if there's more than my mediumship and dream magic. "Why would someone want to harm me? Or use me? Why me?"

"There are always those who crave more power," she answers cryptically. "Those who are filled with hate and bigotry."

"What power?"

"You already know you are unique."

"What? Because I can channel the soul of a supernatural being?"

"Yes, that sort of gift hasn't happened before." She sounds so sad.

"Why can I do it then?" I ask.

"You..." she hesitates, as if she doesn't want to tell me. "You are made differently."

"Are you in the spirit realm watching over me or something? How do you know what I can do?"

She ignores my questions and says, "Now that your full magic has been freed, you need to learn to use it. Quickly, mija. You are in more danger now that they can no longer control you. They won't suffer a witch such as you."

"Why didn't you warn me before? With Rob?" I demand.

"He turned your pendant against me, blocking me," she explains. "Before he corrupted my gift, I had visited."

Conflicting emotions collide inside my chest. "That was really you in my dreams."

"Yes, after I was killed." She warns, "You feel safe with these males, but you aren't meant to be with them."

She was murdered?

Why would she tell me they aren't for me? Her words conflict with the knowledge I have in my soul that they *are* meant to be in my life. It hits me like a lie. Anger rises up in my heart. I wonder now if this is actually the spirit of my grandmother. And if it is, does she care about me? Or is she just mean like my mother?

"Go now. Don't return."

An unknown force shoves me backward and I shout as I fly back into my body. I wake up in bed with hot, heavy limbs weighing me down, pinning me to the bed.

I scramble to break free, not realizing at first it's just my guys snuggling me.

"Jade? What's wrong?" Arran asks. "Is Osen attacking you?"

"What? No." I shake my head. In the darkness, I barely can make out the shapes of them next to me. Why did he instantly think Osen was hurting me? "I just had a weird dream about my grandmother."

Arran's eyes now glow gold, as if gleaming with worry. Maxum's flame with red, and I can actually see their faces with their light.

"Are you sure it was *just* a dream?" Maxum asks, his voice wary, and he appears ready to attack anything that moves.

"It might have been her spirit." I frown, but relax into their hold. "I need to learn how to have more control with this dream magic."

"As soon as you have recovered, I will teach you what I can." Maxum strokes my cheek and gazes into my eyes.

"I wish I could do more to protect you," Arran says.

"It isn't your jobs to do that," I argue. "I need to do it myself."

Both males growl. They don't like that idea, but don't debate my statement either. They know the wisdom in it, even if they're acting out the trope of 'touch her and die vibes.'

Can't say I mind having someone fighting on my team for a change. It helps that they are actual monsters that would have no problem tearing someone apart that was about to hurt me.

My naughty bits tingle with excitement.

"Jade?" Arran sniffs the air. "What are you thinking about, you minx?"

"Just how sexy it is to feel as though you might do almost anything for me," I admit.

"Might? Almost anything?" Maxum cups my chin, his intense gaze dangerous and feral. "You have to know we *would do anything for you*."

I gulp with his intensity. "Not to be a Debbie Downer, but I'm not used to that. My mom essentially disowned me as soon as I was eighteen. And as you know, my ex-boyfriends are the human equivalent of black mold—and that's being generous."

Again, they curl their lips with disgust at the mention of my ex.

"We won't let you forget it," Arran promises. "Even if you no longer wish to be with me intimately, I will always show up for you. I will always protect you."

Well, fuck.

I'm not crying, it's just all the emotion floating in the room that gets in my eyes.

I snuggle back down between the two living heaters and get some more sleep.

10

MUFFINS

JADE

I wake up to the delicious smell of breakfast. Only Arran is with me now, and I give him a soft peck on the lips.

His golden eyes open, and he grins at me like I'm his favorite thing.

"I'm fairly certain Maxum opened up a portal to the land of milk and honey in the kitchen," I joke. "We should get in there before the bounty is all gone." I jump out of bed… Okay, that's a lie. I roll out of bed, then I head to the bathroom for a quick pee and mirror check.

"You're perfect." Arran catches me frowning at the mirror and races forward, throws me over his shoulder like I weigh nothing at all, and takes me to the kitchen. I don't think I'll ever get used to how strong these guys are.

I'm finally allowed on my feet when we get to the dining table. It's overfilled with several serving plates: muffins, scrambled eggs, fruit, home fries, bacon, some things I'm unfamiliar with, and, of course, sausages. Not just the guy kind…

"Whoa." My eyes almost pop from my skull. "You guys eat a lot!"

"Actually, we don't need to eat very much," Maxum says, shaking his head with a smirk.

"Then… why the big spread?" I gesture at the table and sit down.

Standing in the kitchen, Flint, the quiet, nervous looking gargoyle, rubs the back of his neck. His face tints a peach color—his version of a blush, apparently. "When I heard humans need food several times a day, I realized we haven't fed you enough." With a coffee mug in hand, he races over, then slows down as he nears me. "They informed me you like morning bean tea."

"Coffee?" I smell the tale-tell aroma of dark roast. "Yes, thank you."

"Cream and sugar are right there." His thick finger points in front of me.

My heart almost bursts from his adorable attempt to take care of me properly. I truly never expected this level of concern from anyone, but his urge to provide for me is giving me all the warm fuzzies.

The urge to hug-attack the gargoyle is strong, but I keep myself rooted in my seat.

"You should pick up the book, *The Proper Care and Feeding of Your Human*," I say with a straight face.

Flint asks with eyes wide with interest, "Where can I purchase this book?"

"Don't worry, I'll get you a copy." Maxum grins at me, mischievously.

"I appreciate all the thought and effort, but remember, I can only eat small portions at a time." I point to Maxum's plate with a reasonable portion of food. "I usually eat about that much. And honestly, I'm not great about eating three times a day. So please, don't go out of your way just for me."

Calder shuffles into the room, and his eyes widen at the sight of the spread. "Are we not allowed to eat for the rest of the month?" he jokes. He takes a seat, gathering up a huge portion of food. It probably took a lot out of him when he almost died.

I place a bit of everything onto my plate to show Flint that I appreciate his hard work. I take a large bite of a muffin.

The baffling burst of jalapeño causes me to choke.

"Are you okay?" Arran asks and rubs my back as I sip some water.

I feel my face turning red. "I just wasn't expecting a muffin to be… spicy."

"I thought you liked it spicy." Flint glances innocently at Maxum and Arran. "Is this untrue?"

"Oh." I clear my throat and take a sip of water. "I write what they call spicy books, but it has nothing to do with food. I'm sorry about the confusion."

Maxum gives me an evil grin which makes me think he was in on the misunderstanding or wanted to see how it played out. He's such a trickster.

"You don't like it then?" Flint asks, looking completely deflated.

Ah, fuck. "I… they are good. It just was a surprise, since muffins are usually sweet."

"I'll eat your spicy muffin any day." Maxum gives me a wink.

I remember he added a fair amount of hot sauce to his eggs when we went on our brunch date. He places two muffins on his plate and appears victorious.

Rolling my eyes at my sneaky demon, I turn my attention back to Flint. "You are amazing. I appreciate all of this work."

He gives me a shy grin. "If you need anything, I'll make sure you get it. All you have to do is ask."

Calder grumbles under his breath, which sounds a lot like *kiss ass*, but I ignore him as does everyone else in the room.

"Thank you." I turn to look at everyone else. "Are there any plans for the day that I should know about?"

"I'd like to train you to block out psychic invasions soon," Maxum says and takes another bite of his muffin. "But only after you are healed."

I tuck in to my food and then say, "I need to see if I can use the Wi-Fi here, and I need to get some writing done. I'm so far behind on my schedule, but I suppose near-death experiences will put a hamper on timelines."

"I put all your writing stuff in the office," Arran reminds me.

"We are in the human realm," Maxum confirms. "Will you still be able to access the internet with your travel device?"

"Depends if there are any cell towers in the area, but humans have them pretty much everywhere now." I glance out the huge windows at the beautiful lake. "You have a gorgeous place here. Thank you for sharing it with me."

Maxum subtly preens and inclines his head to acknowledge my thanks. "I've been wanting these jerks to spend some time here for a while now, so I suppose our situation has been a good excuse. And now, I get the delightful bonus of having you here."

"Are there other residents living around the lake?" I ask. "I don't see any houses or docks. Do we have to be careful about your true forms here? Or if I shoot off a *premature e-magication*?"

Maxum snorts, then shrugs. "Uh, yeah, no one else lives around this lake."

"How lucky is that!" I take another bite of the spicy muffin and find the taste growing on me.

"Well, I own the entire lake."

I choke again. "What?" I sip some more water.

Then I realize he's been alive for centuries and probably made some smart investments along the way.

"Oh, did you buy this area up when the country was still being formed?"

"Uh, no. It was a couple of decades ago." Maxum turns a brighter shade of red.

"You're… rich?" I brush it off because I don't want him to get the wrong idea. "Or you were rich, *before* you bought this entire area?"

"So now you're a *gold-digging* witch?" Calder sneers.

I level a look at him. "FYI, I thought you were all hot before I knew a single thing about you. Even though you all look like some punk-ass thirst trap models, I would have taken you home for a snack." I snap. "Besides, I don't really care all that much for money, except that *I* make enough to live comfortably so I can keep writing. I'll gladly pay my way while you all help me out." I look at Maxum. "Do you think it will be safe to e-wire transfer you some funds? You have a regular bank account, yeah?"

"Jade, you are not giving me any money. I know you aren't here for a free ride." Maxum looks pissed. He stands up, then glares at Calder. "You need to back the fuck up, or I'll adjust your attitude for you."

"I just—" Calder protests.

"No." Maxum crosses his arms. "Apologize and then drop this bullshit. Jade is innocent, and you know it. She isn't the witch who killed you. She is a victim of other witches, and who knows what else."

What else? I don't like the sound of that.

"I'm sorry that you were upset by my joke," Calder grits out.

It wasn't a joke, but whatever. Also, his apology is blaming me for being upset.

"That's such a weak-ass apology." Arran shakes his head. "Might as well say 'I'm sorry you have feelings.'"

I stifle a chuckle at Arran's comment.

Calder frowns at his half empty plate of food and huffs. "I'm sorry. I'm still not recovered from the attack the other night—both physically and emotionally." He pauses and asks, "Has Osen come back yet?"

"I'm sorry… not yet." To give him some hope, I add, "But he could be still recovering from the attack too."

He hums and doesn't look at me for our entire exchange. It's progress, nonetheless.

After breakfast, I wander into Maxum's office and unpack my gear. I really hope my computers don't melt with all their magic swirling around.

What if I eventually have enough magic to cause problems all on my own? Will I be able to write on my laptop? Or will I have to write longhand and send my work off to someone to type it for me?

Once I have my stuff on the desk, I figure out my travel router, which actually works. No matter how much my curiosity pesters me, I don't check to see where in the world we are. I'm guessing North America, probably the States, since my router works without issue. Beyond that, I don't know, and apparently, it might be dangerous for me to know if someone invades my mind.

I also don't like or comment on any of my public social media posts. If Rob really is watching for signs of me, then I don't want to let him know I survived his attack.

I notice one of my author friends has sent me several direct messages in the last couple of days. I find it odd because she rarely notices when I've locked myself in my writing cave for too long. Somehow, she must sense I'm in trouble. Perhaps she has a bit of psychic intuition. As much as I want to respond, I don't.

Sales are doing okay since my assistant is still promoting, and my ads are running fine. I remind myself it's only been a few days, but part of me is disappointed. I had hoped more people would notice I was missing.

Why am I irked that the world didn't fall apart when I wasn't constantly there? Does that mean I could have taken a day off once in a while before now? Nah, I don't want to believe that.

Opening up my manuscript file, I sigh happily. I finally have climbed over my writer's *wall*, but I've had barely any time to write. Now, I might get the writer's retreat of my dreams, with sexy monster lovers to test out all the sex positions I can think of.

My personal supernatural research and development team is on call.

With that, I'm wondering what kinds of fantasies Maxum wants to make come true for me. I need to write out a lengthy and thorough list of things to try. I had no one I trusted before to do kinky stuff with. Will he chase me through the woods for a primal fuck? Tie me up and edge me to oblivion? Fly me into the sky and fuck me midair?

I open up a notes file and jot down some of these ideas. Never hurts to be prepared.

I'm lost to my imaginings when I feel Arran's presence. I don't even have to turn around to know it's him. Is this a witch's power? Or because we are bonding? I've never had a connection to someone the way I do with him.

"Hey, Arran," I say before I turn.

When I look, he's standing in the doorway. His gaze is locked onto my computer screen as if he eagerly wishes to sneak a peek. The fragrant scent of my favorite herbal tea is wafting from my favorite tea cup.

I squeak with happiness and rush at him. Then blessedly, I remember the scalding hot water, so I stop, place the cup gently down on the desk, and *then* jump him.

He catches me, holding me up by the ass, and my legs wrap around his waist.

"Thank you." I pepper kisses over his gorgeous face. "That was so thoughtful. I was out of my mind and didn't even think to grab it."

"Of course, my sweetness. I know how it's part of your writing ritual."

I think about how he used to watch me as his wolf, unbeknownst to me. "That reminds me—no more peeking! I thought you were a dog that couldn't read. I don't like when people read my stuff before it's done."

Maxum enters the room, his brow cocked and eyeing how I'm plastered to Arran like a baby monkey. "If you are healthy enough to jump on werewolves, then I think I should heal you up and give you your first magic lesson."

"Oh, yes, a magic sexual healing will commence forthwith!"

11

HEALING MAGIC

MAXUM

I hate to break up Arran and Jade's little snugglefest.

Actually, I don't mind one fucking bit.

I want her ass in *my* hands, her legs wrapped around my waist, and her wet center taking my length.

My dick wakes the fuck up with that and wants to say hello to the curvy, unwitting seductress. She has no clue how hot she is.

Thankfully, I'll be balls deep in her pussy in a few minutes, convincing her of her sexiness.

I also have to convince her that my need for her is more than a meaningless fucking. I need alone time with her. Jade is my fated match. I have to know all about her. Because with her modern *human* sensibilities, spending quality time with her will be the only way to make her believe I crave her like no other.

If she were a supernatural being, or raised in any magical community, then she'd already know without question that I'd die for her, even though I don't yet know her like I intend to.

I will discover every ticklish spot on her body, figure out how her wacky mind works, read all her books, learn how to cook her favorite foods, explore her favorite positions and fantasies, understand what makes her laugh, and what brings her comfort.

However, right now, I plan to take care of her body and heal the ugly bruises and cuts that Rob inflicted on her the other night.

Fucking Rob.

I will hunt him down and bring Jade his severed head on a pike.

Is that too much for a mating gift? Not enough?

I'll have to brush up on my courting etiquette.

Ultimately, I blame myself for leaving Jade alone.

I should have expected that *stupid prick of an incubus ghost* Osen would coerce her into sneaking off. What was he thinking, taking an inexperienced witch to a dark alley in a supernatural beings-infested neighborhood where he had died?

What really pisses me off is that he didn't trust one of us enough to escort them there. I would have done it *after* I checked out the entire area and had everyone in our pack there as backup. But like always, Osen does everything in his own reckless way. Damn the consequences.

Look where that got him. He's dead, and now his soul is probably obliterated.

Fuck, and he almost took *my* mate—Arran's mate—away from us.

Jade studies my face as she climbs off Arran's body. "You okay, big guy?"

"Yeah, just remembering how we almost lost you. I'd kill Osen if he weren't already dead."

Sadness and regret flash over her face as she saunters over to me. "I think your wish might have come true."

"Let's see if he's able to return after we have sex. Osen might just need to power up." I smirk evilly. "*Then* I'll rip his soul to shreds."

Jade playfully bats my bicep and winces. "Ow! What is that thing made of? Flippin' steel?"

I flex my naked chest and watch as her face lights up with excitement. "You didn't know that demons were made of carbon steel from the depths of the Earth's core?" I deadpan.

Her mouth drops open briefly and then her eyes narrow. "Don't fuck with me. It's not nice."

"Oh, I plan on fuckin' with you, and I can be as nice or as wicked as you like." I lift her up over my shoulder, and she squeaks. I look at Arran, wondering about how his beast will handle my taking her away like this. "You good?"

"Yeah. I actually am. But I'm going for a run around the lake, so I don't have to hear it... just in case I'm not."

"Aw," Jade whines. "I want to explore the lake, too."

"Another time." I swat her rump, turn, and rush to my bedroom. As we enter, I rip the seam of her leggings, and I slide my fingers over her wet center. "I also have something wet I'd like to explore."

"Maxum!" She wiggles as I keep her trapped to my shoulder. "You ruined my pants!"

"Now, I'm going to ruin your pretty pussy."

"Fuck," she hisses to herself as I circle her clit.

"And these leggings are old and worn out. I'll buy you new clothes so I can tear them all off you." I toss her in the middle of my bed and grab her ankles. "You ready for me, my delicious witch?"

"Uh, getting close," she says with wide eyes as I pull her by the ankles, so her ass lands at the edge of the bed.

With her leggings still on, I descend a claw and use it to slice the hole of her pants a bit more and cut her underwear at the crotch, allowing me free access to her pussy.

I lean down and give her obscenely exposed center a lick. I pull off my pants to reveal my hard cock throbbing with desire.

Jade's eyes widen even more as she takes in the sight of my huge and naturally studded dick. She bites her luscious lip, likely wondering how I taste. Soon, I'll have her suck me and drink me down. But not until I've healed her.

I drop my glamour, revealing my horns, red skin, tail, and enormous wings.

She sucks in a breath. I scent her arousal increase. I love that she loves the real me.

How there is no fear in her eyes is beyond my understanding. She should run away screaming, not into my arms.

But her legs fall open even more while she studies me. "You're gorgeous."

"I'm just a demon. You are gorgeous."

She blushes at my compliment and laughs as if I'm being silly.

"You have no idea what you do to me, do you?" I ask. There is a dangerous edge to my question, and she rightfully shivers.

"Me?" She looks up and down my naked body, seeing the tension I'm holding.

I have to hold back most of my desire so I don't accidentally hurt her. But I want to pound into her for days, consume every drop of her honey, and wring cries of passion from her until she is exhausted and ruined for anyone else.

"Are you going to work your magic on me?" she asks.

"I don't like seeing bruises and cuts on your beautiful body." I tell her. "It reminds me how badly I messed up by leaving you alone with Osen."

"Well, if sexy times with you are what I get out of it, I'm good with that."

"How about I'll give you *more* sex if you stay out of harm's way?" I ask. "Then I can make all your fantasies come true without having to worry."

She grins. "I started a list."

"Do you have any special requests for me?" I ask with a wink. "Any kinks you would like to explore right now?" I snap my sharp teeth and growl.

"*Ohmymightyclit*, Maxum. I think you just made me come. Why do you have to be so fucking amazing? I can't think straight when you look at me like that." She squirms to get the friction between her legs that she craves. "How about dealer's choice? I can show you my list later when I'm not gazing at my fantasy guy come to life."

My chest puffs up a bit with her praise. I can't help it. No one has ever made me feel desired the way she does.

"Shit. Did it sound as if I'm objectifying you for demon sex?" She reaches out to me in apology. "I totally value your brain and great personality, too. You know that, right?"

I chuckle because of the role reversal happening here. "I know, sweet witch. Would it bother you if I told you I only wanted you for your curvy body?"

"Not at all." She smiles shyly. "I like that you like my body. Also, I don't think that's entirely true. You like my weird personality a bit, too."

"You're right. I *love* your weird personality."

Jade gulps at my use of the word love. She's not ready yet for my full affection. That's okay. I knew it would take time for her to accept it.

"Enough talk." I hold open her legs and lean forward, flicking my forked tongue over her center.

She moans as she watches me, her breathing and heart rate increasing.

My large hands massage up her thighs and then slide up to her tits. My claws scrape over the swell of her breasts. As I suck her clit into my mouth, I rip the front of her shirt in half, exposing her flesh.

Jade shouts in surprise, then places her hands over mine as I knead her mounds. She strokes up my huge arms and takes hold of my horns.

Steering me where she wants me, I lave up her sweet honey as she comes undone. I could easily join her, just by witnessing her pleasure. Pleasure that I give her.

She glances down at me, and we make eye contact.

"Come," I command, my growly voice vibrating her sensitive flesh.

"Maxum!" my witch cries as she undulates and surrenders herself to me.

I tear away the rest of her leggings and notch my dick at her opening. My arms wrap around her body, cradling her.

"You ready for me?" I ask.

"Yes, please." She tilts her hips, sliding me into her heat.

Pressing further into her, I groan when I feel how tight her pussy grips me. "Do you know how perfect you are?"

She glances away, trying to play it off.

My hand grasps her throat, just below her jaw, forcing her to look at me. I seat myself completely and grind my hips into hers, causing my soft spikes at my base to stimulate her clit and labia.

As I shallowly grind into her, I tell her, "You might not understand how I can feel so much for you, but you aren't part of the human world anymore. Supes usually listen to their instincts. We know when we have found our mate match. Plus, with my magic, I can feel you and read you on another level. When we were together last time, I tasted your soul."

"You did?" Her eyes are beginning to glow a haunting green. I didn't think witches could do that. "What did I taste like?"

"You taste like a winter's dawn, a summer's night, an inviting hearth, and a whimsical feast for a starving spirit—all rolled up in one. Your soul tastes like magic itself. You taste like coming home."

Jade opens her mouth to reply, but she can't respond. A tear rolls down her cheek. Then her lips crash against mine. She kisses me with the passion of someone finally accepting the love being offered after years of rejection.

I kiss her back with the same intensity and sentiment.

We both have been lonely for so long.

Slowly, I pump my entire length in and out of her slick channel. She moans with the sensual motion, and I swallow down her sweet sounds.

My tail wraps around and fondles her puckered hole.

"Do it," she whispers.

After picking up a bit of her wetness, it slides into her ass. Feeling her next climax coming along, I begin my healing chant.

"Maxum," she whines, the energy gathering around us and weighing us down. She didn't sense it as much before since she was half dead at the time.

I press my forehead to hers to anchor Jade in her body. It works, and her orgasm crashes over her. I unleash my own and follow her over the cliff.

Opening my eyes, I see the strange glowing pattern of light over her body that happened the last time I used the sex magic on her.

I search for identifiable glyphs or symbols, but there's nothing I recognize. However, it doesn't appear to be random lines. There *is* a pattern.

I release my accumulated magic, and her bruises and cuts vanish. I let out a puff of air in relief.

I worried both times I'd used my unique magic, thinking it wouldn't work on a witch. This time I worried since she is no longer being blocked by her pendant that her own magic might reject mine. But it seems her magic welcomes me. It validates my belief we are meant to be.

Jade's eyes are closed, and she appears to have passed out. Her mind is quiet, which is unusual for her. But when I scratch the surface of her being, I sense she is at peace, which is also uncommon for her.

Idly, I wonder what her mind feels like when she's writing.

I don't want to break this contented bliss she has found, though. I would keep my dick hard and deep inside her and my arms braced to keep my full weight off her forever if it meant she was happy.

My witch inhales deeply and grins. Slowly, she opens her eyes and gazes up into my face. With a lazy voice, she says, "Today's pleasure is brought to you by the words: demon dick."

I burst out with a laugh, my cock bucking inside her. With a soft peck on the lips, I roll off, and then I move us to rest properly on the bed. I jump up and get a warm wet cloth and wipe her clean so she can relax comfortably.

"I like this," she says. "Being taken care of. It's weird to experience, but nice."

I snuggle up next to her, pulling my wings back into my form.

"That is so cool." Jade strokes my cheek and then traces her finger around the base of my horns, and I shiver.

"You have something interesting as well. You probably haven't noticed, but when you orgasmed while I was working my sex magic, you glowed. It was a complicated pattern. I couldn't make sense of it."

For whatever reason, she grabs her boobs and looks down at her body in shock. "I did? Why?"

"I don't know why," I say calmly, to ease her concern.

"You've never heard of this?" she rushes to ask. "When you used healing magic on other people, didn't it happen to them?"

I answer truthfully. "I've never used my healing magic on someone before."

"What?" She sits up, her mouth dropping open. "In all your centuries, you've *never* done that? Why did you use it with me?"

"I've never wanted to save someone the way I needed to save you."

"Me? The weirdo romance writer?" She shakes her head. "You need to get out more," she scoffs.

"Don't do that," I urge her, with my voice dropping low, likely scaring her a bit. "Don't belittle yourself."

Nodding, she doesn't argue with me about this. "Do you think my light show could be a bad thing?"

"While I didn't sense evil or ill-intent, it's a mystery I'd like for us to explore. Likely, it's connected to your witch magic. I don't know as much as a witch like Amira could teach you about the various magics you could possess, but I can give you some basic lessons on channeling and controlling your magic. When your power presents, we will know more about what to research."

"I would think you would have plenty more important things to do besides teach me basic witch skills." She quickly adds, "I'm not being down on myself, just the facts. You have the war brewing and supes being killed."

"You realize you are part of my effort to stop all that, right?"

"Oh. If we can unlock what I can do, you might discover who killed Osen, and what Rob was using me for."

I pull her body on top of mine and stare into her questioning eyes. "Don't for one second think that's the main reason I want to train you. My first concern is to keep you safe. The rest, if it materializes, will just be a bonus. Understand?"

"Yeah." She rests her head on my chest and yawns. "I'm exhausted."

"Sorry. Rapid healing can do that." I kiss the top of her head. "Rest now."

12

TAKING FLIGHT

JADE

I'm shocked when I wake up and find Maxum is still snuggled up with me at midday. His outrageously muscular arm is holding me to his side. My head is resting on the rock he calls a pec. Aw, and yes, I do indeed have a bit of drool leaking out on his fine crimson tattooed chest. Apparently, this is my informal claiming procedure.

I've drooled on him, now he's mine.

Hey, we all got to have our signature move. Casually, I lift my head, and rub my hand to remove the evidence.

He does not need to know about this.

Despite my best efforts, Maxum thwarts my crafty plans when he captures my wrist and says in a deep, raspy voice, "I *know* what you've done."

"Uh?" I play innocent. "What do you mean?"

"I have to bite you to claim you. Drooling or licking doesn't work in a cosmic bonding ceremony."

"What? How did you…?" I stir and prop myself up to gaze down at him. Damn, he's a sight. His obsidian eyes remind me of unfathomable depths—the surrender to the oblivion of an orgasm. "An abyss of bliss…" I mumble to myself.

"Is that my new nickname? Seems a tad long," he jokes and wipes the drool from the corner of my mouth with his thumb. How can he make that sexy? Must be a magic demon thing. "But I can make it part of my formal title." He gives me a sweet kiss, and my heart melts.

Arran flings open the door and rushes to greet me. "I was trying so hard, but I couldn't stay away for another minute." He snatches me from Maxum's grasp, and my wolfman clutches me to his chest, inhaling deeply, taking in my scent.

I didn't know it was possible for my heart to further turn to goo, but yeah, it happens.

Flint appears in the open doorway, his back turned to me so he gives me and my nakedness privacy. "I have more food for you." His stone skin around his neck turns a lovely peachy color from his embarrassment. "Don't fret. It is not as much as our last meal."

"You are too sweet," I say. "I'll be right there."

After Flint disappears, and we can hear he's in the kitchen, readying things for our arrival, Maxum whispers in my ear, "It appears our gargoyle might have caught feelings after four hundred years of immunity."

"He's just being nice." I wave Maxum off. "Maybe you don't realize people can be nice without needing to mate."

Maxum shrugs. "True, but he doesn't make *me* meals of his own volition."

My head spins with what he's implying. Is the anti-touch, anti-social, and stoic gargoyle developing feelings for me?

Arran thumbs the crease between my brows. Apparently, I've been frowning. He attempts to reassure me, "It probably doesn't matter much since he won't want to actually act upon them."

Disappointment and sadness rise within me. I kick myself. I should be happy that I have two amazing guys in my bed right now. And if Osen isn't gone, maybe I'd have him, too. I don't need to *catch them all* like this is one of my why choose books or pokémon.

I doubt Flint would be up for sharing my affection even if he could get over the mountain of issues we would have to overcome.

I will just have to be friends with him and ignore my growing attraction— no matter how many spicy muffins he bakes for me.

Fortunately, there is less food this time, and the meal is uneventful, since Calder doesn't show to haze me.

The sun is setting on the lake. It's stunning, and I gasp at the sight of cotton ball clouds of rich peaches and pinks.

Standing from the table, I drift over to the huge picture window and gaze at the beauty. Always being cooped up in my writing cave and getting so caught up in working every single day, I've been missing out on life.

Maxum walks up behind me and wraps his arms around my waist and rests his chin on the top of my head, both of us taking a moment to absorb the beauty.

I suppose it has taken near-death experiences and these caring souls, who the human world considers monsters, to slow me down enough to question the pace of my life.

"How many spectacular sunsets have I missed?" I ask no one in particular.

"I don't know, but maybe the question should be: what are the beautiful moments we have left to share?" Maxum squeezes me. "I know that for the first time in forever, I look forward to finding that out—because of you."

Arran walks over and kisses my cheek. "Me too."

"Would you like to take a flight over the lake?" Maxum asks.

When I sputter instead of answering, he checks in with me. "Are you afraid of heights?"

"Not particularly. But I just didn't think you'd offer."

"I told you… *all* your fantasies."

"Okay, but no sex—*this time*. I'll need to see how scary it is first."

"Oh." Maxum chuckles darkly, leans down, and nibbles on my ear. "What makes you think I would be so damned reckless as to fuck your sweet body amongst the clouds?" He growls for good measure.

My core tingles, and my knees threaten to give out. I grip his brawny forearms and tremble. "Unholy hell, you're gonna make me pass out."

Picking me up like a doll, Maxum rushes through the doors and launches into the air. I can't help it. I scream with excitement and cling to him like a baby ape.

I leave my stomach behind on the veranda, and it takes a moment for me to acclimate to the bobbing up and down from his wing beats. I just try to imagine the pumping motion is sex. That calms me a bit.

The cool evening air whips my hair around my face, and I can barely see. If he had given me any warning, I would have grabbed a hair tie.

"Whoops," he says as he notices my predicament. "I got you." He chants low and in a strange, likely demon, language.

My hair swishes back and twists in a ponytail. "Can you teach me how to do that?" I ask in awe.

He grins and gives me a quick kiss. "Depends if you have an affinity for air."

"I guess we need to figure out what the hell I am soon."

"I wouldn't have guessed you were a hell species, but maybe you are since you light a demon's heart on fire," he jokes. "And yes, we will investigate your magic soon. I feel it building inside you."

"You can feel my magic?"

"Yes. And you will become familiar with sensing magic—your own and others."

As he says this, the glorious sunset catches my attention once again. This is a kind of magic—the beauty of nature and the beauty of experiencing life with Maxum.

He was right that there aren't any landmarks to indicate where we are in the world. There are only trees as far as I can see and rolling, nondescript hills in the distance. This lake could be anywhere, and no one could pluck the location from my mind.

I dare to release one of my death grips on his shirt and stroke his cheek. He makes a strange purring sound, and my center wets with need.

"You sure about not fucking this time around?" he says with a wink.

Goodness! He can sense my arousal even while flying?

"It's tempting."

With my words, Maxum's lips crash onto my mouth, and quickly his tongue tangles with mine. My head spins that I'm in the air with a demon who is consuming any fears I had about flying. When he breaks for a breath, I'm now dizzy from the heights and his wicked kiss.

Maxum turns me so my back is to his chest. He beats his wings fiercely again and we climb higher until we really are in the mist of the clouds. My head is spinning. "Shouldn't we be careful about someone seeing us?"

"No one will see us," he assures me.

His hand slips down and inside my pants and underwear. His thick fingers find my pussy wet and needy. "I think my sweet witch wants to come, doesn't she?"

"Yes," I say, breathy and desperate.

Damn, this demon knows how to work my body like a master. He strums my clit with the perfect pressure. Which, kudos to him, for being able to do that while he's keeping us hovering in the sky.

"Maxum," I moan, praying for release.

His two thick fingers sink into my channel and the heel of his hand grinds against my clit in a rhythm attuned to my body and pleasure. If he were to break up with me, I would mourn the loss of someone who seemed to understand me on every level—physically, sexually, and mentally.

"Come for me, Jade," Maxum commands, and my body that aches for release complies.

I scream out to the surrounding heavens and twist with pleasure as my pussy clamps onto his hand.

"Such a good little witch," he coos, as I pant, attempting to regain my sanity. Then he licks my juices off his fingers and hums with delight.

"Do you know you're too sexy for your own good?" I ask.

"No. But I might be too sexy for your own good." He chuckles, kisses me, then scans the horizon.

I follow his eyeline. With a sweeping gaze, I take in all the area around the lake and realize we are entirely isolated. Which is disconcerting, since that makes me entirely dependent on them to get me out of here. I don't even see a car around his house. Maxum's portals or his wings are my only way to leave.

"Is there a town nearby?" I ask with a tinge of anxiety in my voice. "Anything?"

"Yes." Maxum points to the south. "Ten miles down that road. If, for some reason, you can't rely on one of us to get you out of here, head that way. Mostly humans live there."

I sigh with relief that I have a way to save myself if need be. But it's also unnerving to have someone who can literally read my thoughts and emotions.

We hover, his massive wings beating and keeping us high above the world. Maxum senses my mood shift yet again. "Hey, I won't ever push into your mind and hurt you."

"I don't believe you would, unless you felt it was truly necessary to save someone you care about."

"I care about you," he assures me. "Is there something else bothering you?"

"Are we really safe here? What if the glowing markings are another level of magic that could be used to hunt me down? What if you all get hurt? And we are stuck out here with no one to help you?"

"Take a breath. It sounds like you are trying to work out every possible plot twist for one of your novels."

"Well, I'm not crazy. It could happen."

He shifts his wings slightly, and we glide back toward the house. "Yes, you're right. So many things can go wrong. Or they could go right. But let me worry about the possibilities… for now. You need to recover from all that's happened—all that you've learned about the world. Gather your magic. Write. This is the moment for you to take a break and find some clarity."

His words make sense, but I'm not used to taking a break. "I don't know if I know how to relax. I feel like I'm being lazy if I'm not constantly striving and working toward something."

"That is a problem. Humans are conditioned to be in constant survival mode. Living in a continuous loop of anxiety and stress. It doesn't always need to be do or die. Sometimes, you can take a break from the never-ending spinning wheel."

"Is that something you've learned over your many years?"

"It's something that I've *forgotten* since my early days. I used to know when to remove myself from stressful situations, now I charge into the middle of them. But after meeting you, I've realized I should slow down and enjoy your company."

Warm fuzzies fill my chest. I don't know how I got so lucky.

As a person unaccustomed to good luck, it makes me nervous.

Will all this be taken away from me?

13

DREAMING

JADE

*M*axum and Arran insist I get some rest once I'm back at the house. I insist on writing a bit. I grin wickedly when I think of a prank to pull on Arran. It only takes me a few minutes to set it up.

Finally, when I'm done, I head to our bedroom. Maxum is brushing his teeth when I come in. But Arran is nowhere to be seen.

"Where's Arran?" I ask. "I thought he'd be waiting eagerly for his snuggle time."

"Up to no good. That's all I can tell you." Maxum shrugs.

I smile, since I'm pretty sure I know exactly what he's doing.

Arran bursts through the bedroom door, looking downright frantic. "Cheaper by the Dozen? You need twelve guys?"

"What's this now?" Maxum's interest is piqued and stands at attention.

Oh, boy. This prank may have worked a little too well.

"Jade… she… wrote—" He stops, realizing he's been caught crossing my boundary, but he keeps going, unable to deal with what he's read. "Her female character… she bi-locates to two separate groups of guys and then fucks them all at once! Twelve supernatural guys total in different dimensions! She has to do that because it's the only way she can ever be fully satisfied." Arran falls to his knees. "Jade? Do you really need so many? I don't think my berserker can share you with anyone outside of our pack."

"Wow." Maxum strides up to me, challenging me with a look. "You think you can handle that twelve guys *and* a career?"

Defiantly, I cross my arms. "I have many skills."

"Juggling cocks doesn't seem like one of them." Maxum shrugs. "But what do I know?"

And now I'm wondering if my readers will enjoy a juggling cocks sticker.

"Jade?" Arran holds my hands. "Are we really not enough?"

"You are more than enough." I caress his face and let him off the hook, because I hope he's learned his lesson. "Sweet wolfie, I only wrote that whole thing to prank you. I thought you would see it for the joke it was meant to be. I warned you not to snoop in my manuscripts before I'm done with them. I left it open on my computer to be a brat."

He wraps his arms around my hips and kisses my belly in relief. Next I know, Arran has lifted me up and tossed me in bed. "I need extra snuggles now."

"Not sure if you deserve them. You've been a naughty boy," I tease.

"I promise I won't do *that* again."

They both snuggle with me in bed as I pet Arran to soothe his ruffled hackles. Even though my mind is spinning, once I stop petting him, I instantly fall asleep.

Becoming lucid in a dream, I find myself standing in a hazy and gloomy forest. It's oddly illuminated, much like what Osen called his shadowscape. Apparently, this is another plane of existence where incubi and succubi can interact with their sexual meals. With that thought, I'm reminded that was much of what I was to him, a way to feed his power, even in his death. He'd hinted he might feel more for me. Was it a lie, or was Osen only getting caught up in a heated moment?

I don't know enough about cubi, their personalities, or their abilities. Maybe this is a question for Maxum and Arran. If I have some unusual magical gift with dreams and channeling spirits, then I should know more about this shadowscape realm as I sense they are connected to my power somehow—however loosely.

Thinking he might be here in the shadowscape with me, I reach out with my senses to locate Osen, but I don't feel his energy. I had become familiar with his presence. I felt his passion and protectiveness, which often blurred into anger and resentment.

His energy has a taste and smell to it—tart cherries and wildfires. He was volatile. A fairly classic romanticized psycho, who would burn down the world for the person he loved, and while it's all well and good in a book, I sort of surprised myself that I was into it in my real life.

I don't know if he's still with me, hidden and weakened by the fight with Rob.

If Osen suspects I betrayed him, and he comes back, will he try to kill me?

"Osen?" I call to the dark corners of the room. "Are you there?"

A breeze tickles over my cheek. Is that the incubus? Or just my mind playing tricks on me?

How far could our relationship really go beyond sexcapades in my dreams? I believed things were taking a positive turn for us until we visited his death spot.

I doubt he could return to the living without a body to inhabit. He doesn't have a body left lying around somewhere anymore. Or if he does, it's not viable anymore. I doubt someone would volunteer for him to take over, and I don't want him taking over my body permanently. I'm not a fan of him taking control, even briefly. It's scary, and he makes poor choices.

If it were possible, would he need another incubus body to inhabit? Does he need a body that will align with his powers? Here I go again, imagining all the possible threads. We don't even know if he's still haunting me. First things first.

He might not trust me anymore, which will be bad for me if he returns. Maybe he wouldn't even like me if he hadn't been stuck in my brain.

"Osen?" I call for him again.

Another breeze answers.

Could it be?

My thoughts rush to Calder. Not as I see him when he looks at me, with anger in his eyes, but through Osen's eyes, showing me how he looked at the incubus when he was alive.

Calder's image materializes and moves to stand face to face, hunger in his eyes. I realize I'm taller. Could this be Osen's memory? Is it a leftover from merging with Osen? Or is this memory being pulled from Osen right now?

During our first days together, when his ghost was completely drained, this was how things unfolded. My hopes rise that I will return my guys' friend to them.

The nagging doubt also returns that some, if not all, of their attraction to me is only because of Osen's seductive presence.

No point dwelling on the negative. Enjoy the ride and all that. Nothing is guaranteed. They might talk a big game and perhaps even have the best intentions, but life isn't filled with happily ever afters.

I might have to take the *'happy for now'* for as long as I can.

In this memory, Calder doesn't have the haunted look I have come to know. Perhaps this is from before his last death caused by the witch. My senses tell me I'm correct.

His hand reaches up and strokes the side of my face—*Osen's face*. "Please, hold off your shadows so I can have this moment."

Ah, yes, the incubus shadows will immobilize Calder when he is ready to feed. Does this mean that Calder can never actively participate when they are intimate?

My heart aches from the longing in his eyes… to return a loving touch.

"I'll try," Osen says. "But you know how much I need you."

"More than the others?" Calder is so vulnerable—emotions raw.

It feels wrong to be here, but I can't leave. I've tried.

"You know you are special to me, do you really need me to say it?" Osen asks.

I want to slap the damn fool. Of course, Calder needs it. I can see it written all over his pretty, desperate face.

Osen sighs wearily. "You are the only one who satisfies me." Then his patience is gone, and he slams his mouth against Calder's, claiming him.

The phoenix goes stone still from the paralytic shadows wrapping around him. I'm relieved when I hear Calder's moan of approval.

Osen's hand clenches Calder's jaw. "You are on your knees today." His shadows shove Calder to the ground. "Do you like that? Do you want to suck my cock?"

"Yes, sir, please," he begs.

Well, damn. I feel a rush of power as Osen's shadows feed on Calder's lust.

"Then be a good pet and open your mouth for me."

From my encounters with Osen, I know a cubi's feeding partner can only move their eyes and mouth.

But seeing Calder's hungry eyes stare up at Osen and open his mouth for him, I'm more than turned on by this power dynamic in action. Osen loves being the dom, and Calder is an eager submissive.

I idly wonder if he's only a sub for his incubus. Or is this what turns him on in general? I'm guessing it's the latter and that's why they are a good match.

Osen plunges his cock into Calder's mouth… and holy hell, I can feel all of it. I can never tell the phoenix that I know how it feels to have him suck my cock.

He pumps into Calder's mouth, and his shadows stroke and explore Calder's body.

I swear I think I'm going to orgasm in my sleep. Will Maxum and Arran know how naughty I've been watching this pay-per-view sexy incubus feeding?

When he comes, I think my soul might hiccup right out of my own body.

Osen drops down to kneel in front of his love. He kisses him, tasting his cum on Calder's tongue. "Goddess, I missed you."

The incubus wraps his arms and his shadows around the phoenix, and I feel the love he has for Calder. And weirdly, I sense the love Calder has for him. Then I remember an incubus can feel and feed off powerful emotions too.

Their love overwhelms me. It's all consuming.

Will I ever have love like that? If some part of Osen is still inside me, then my fears might be real. The guys are only attracted to me because of his power.

I wake and stare at the ceiling. I don't like this feeling that I will soon be rejected.

The two living heaters next to me snore softly, but it's too loud for me to go back to sleep. Maxum is pressed too close to my one side and Arran's beast form is practically on top of me. Aw, the berserker really does like me. Weighted blankets have nothing on these guys.

I sort of hate the attention and love it at the same time. I love that they are so affectionate with me, because yeah, who wouldn't love two amazing, hot guys loving on them. They are so attractive, that even the straightest of straight guys would question moving away from their sexy bodies.

But alas, I must pee, and I need to clear my head after the mind fuck I just had.

When I try to extricate myself from the supernatural puzzle pieces, they mutter and groan. I assure them I will be back...

But maybe not this morning... We'll see how it goes.

I open the door to the bedroom and feel a strange sense that someone's watching me. My eyes instantly lock onto the space in front of me.

I am not alone.

14

NEW SENSATIONS

FLINT

I'm startled when I sense the enchanting witch has awoken.

She cracks open the bedroom door and peeks out. Her eyes instantly land on my location, even though it should be impossible for her to see me.

I wonder—not for the first time—what the nature of her power is.

"Hello?" she calls quietly. "Who's there?"

I make myself visible, and she gasps. Her pretty hazel eyes widening in surprise.

"How did you just appear like that?" She frowns, having realized I'm stalking her. "And *what* are you doing out here?"

"I'm making sure no one comes to hurt you." I rub my neck nervously. "Even if it's only to ensure that if Osen is inside you, he doesn't make you do things against your will again."

"Oh, Flint."

With my keen eyesight, I can see her sweet, pale coloring turning a shade of pink.

"You don't have to do that… you need to rest too, don't you?" she asks the last part with confusion, wondering if I do.

"Yes. I need to rest, but not as much as a human. I only came out here to keep an eye out for trouble when I sensed Maxum and Arran drifted off."

She closes the door behind her and joins me in the hall, but keeps her distance. Distance she creates because she knows *I* need it.

I curse myself for my problems. I never wanted to make her uncomfortable or make her hurt herself like she did when she arrived at the house.

"Are you worried that I'm going to bring more trouble?" she asks.

"Not you... not on purpose. I'm worried *for* you," I explain, so she doesn't get the wrong impression. Just because I'm not in her bed doesn't mean that I'm in Calder's camp.

"You didn't know that Trouble is my middle name?" Jade sighs and frowns.

I have failed her. "I didn't. Is this why you named your familiar Trouble? Please, forgive my ignorance. I will learn what I can to better protect you."

She folds over with mirth and almost reaches out for my arm to stabilize herself before quickly pulling back. Once again, I regret my condition.

"Oh, sweetie. I don't expect you to know anything about me. And I'm sorry. I was just messing around. I thought you would have heard that joke before."

I've been far too serious for too long. Maxum tries to jest with me. So I take a page from his book. "Well... I thought your parents may have had a premonition and knew your nature."

"You have been around for centuries, right?" She smiles and somehow I don't feel like she is mocking my ignorance. "Wait a minute! You are messing around with me! You knew my parents didn't name me Trouble from a premonition!" She is wheezing with laughter.

It makes my heart thump wildly that I've made her joyful.

When she settles a bit, I answer, "Yes, I have been around for four hundred and twenty three years. However, I'm not usually attuned to the current lingo or... jokes." I hang my head in frustration. The knowledge that I have missed things because I haven't been more adaptable in my long years or engaged in banter with the pack more often weighs heavily in my mind.

"Hey, I didn't mean to make fun of you. I only tease the people I like." Jade bites her lip and then asks, "Were you really that worried about me?"

"I am worried. Osen shouldn't have forced you into the alley, and I'm frustrated with myself that I didn't sense the danger you were in. You almost died."

"Do you always sense danger?"

She knows so little of our world. Maxum and Arran need to correct that. I suppose she is asking me now, so I should impart whatever wisdom and knowledge that I can.

"I do. It isn't a foolproof detection system—obviously. However, I can usually sense when an innocent is about to be harmed."

Her lip protrudes in what I assume is a pout. "Maybe I'm not all that innocent. What if I did something wrong, and I just don't remember?"

I step closer and then realize that might intimidate her because of our size differences, especially in close quarters, so I take a half step back. "Do you believe that?"

"I don't remember what happened when Rob hypnotized me with a spell. So, what else could I have done?"

"If he used you, then you would still be innocent." A silence settles between us, and I nod toward the kitchen. "Were you on your way to seek sustenance?"

"Yeah. A *snack*," she says with emphasis, subtly reminding me of the current vernacular. "I've been diagnosed with a medical condition."

My whole body goes on alert so I can help her with whatever ails her.

With a heavy sigh, she grabs a bag of chips out of the huge walk-in pantry. "I have insom-*nom-nom*-nia," she says as she munches on the crispy processed potatoes. Her eyes twinkle. It's not a metaphor, they truly light up like she is more than just a witch.

I grin at her jesting with me and because I'm delighted by her unusual magic. "I recognize that *is* a joke."

"I can't seem to help it." Jade worries her lip, thinking. Then she slides onto a stool at the kitchen bar, taking another bite of chips.

"You need something more nourishing than that." I nod to the bag and am tempted to pull the garbage food from her hands. But that's something Maxum or Calder might do, and I'm not that rude. "Your magic needs whole, clean ingredients to thrive. And you especially need good food since you are building your magic inside you to its full potential, possibly for the first time."

She drops the handful of chips back into the bag and sets it down. "I suppose you're right. I've been meaning to eat healthier for a long time now. It's just…"

Something inside me suddenly realizes *why* she's been holding back in taking proper care of herself. It's a feeling I'm all too familiar with.

I lean forward, daring to get closer. Even though there's an entire kitchen island between us, it feels like I'm pressed up against her body. Another feeling stirs within me… lower. I swallow nervously since I haven't felt *that way* in four hundred years.

Once I'm clearheaded enough to speak again, I say, "You are worthy of everything good."

Jade shivers ever so slightly.

"Are you cold?"

She must be. The tiny scraps of clothing she has on for sleeping can't keep her warm enough. Human witches are sensitive to heat and cold.

I rush over to the couch in the adjoining living room and grab a small blanket.

Turning around, I regain my composure as I cautiously approach her. Her eyes are wide, studying me. She's trying to hide a smile. Is she happy that I've thought of her? But my heart grows heavy—why does she feel like she has to hide any response?

"I have made you uncomfortable," I say, setting the blanket down over the barstool next to hers.

She shakes her head. "What makes you say that?"

"You were hiding a smile. You don't feel you can express your emotions around me."

"I was worried I might make *you* uncomfortable." She places the blanket over her lap and seems to be lost in thought. "Okay. I think I should try something."

I am intrigued. "What is that?"

"I'm going to be completely honest with you."

Alarm sets in. "What? You haven't been honest before now?"

Her eyes widen. "Oh, shoot. No. That didn't sound right. Okay. I mean… I will say exactly what is going on in my mind, but you have to try and be okay with whatever I say."

"Yes, we can try this." I'm nervous. I haven't been truly nervous in so very long.

"Just now. When you thought I was cold, I was really shivering because of your voice."

"The sound of my voice repulses you?" My already heavy heart feels like it has stopped beating. "I don't know how to change it."

"No." She smiles reassuringly. "I like your voice… a lot. Maybe too much. When your voice dropped lower and with such intensity, it gave me good shivers. But I know you don't really like females, so I didn't want to smile when you were trying to be so nice and take care of me with the blanket. I didn't want you to think that I was expecting *something* from you."

"Oh." I think about what she has said. "I see, but I don't dislike females. I enjoy your company."

"So, is it just touching females that bothers you then?" she asks, her hands fiddle nervously with her blanket.

I want to tell her the story. For the first time in my life, I wish to share with someone who might understand. However, she might fear me afterward.

"Yes. I…" I'm at a loss for what to say. "I will tell you my story one day." I turn and begin to pull out ingredients from the pantry. "But for now, I wish to feed you. I want to see your magic grow. Then you won't be as vulnerable to attacks."

"Can I help?" she asks.

When I glance over, she looks ready to spring from her seat.

"No." Seeing her deflate a bit, I offer a compromise. "Maybe you can wash these fruits?"

"I can chop them up too." She hops off the stool, bounces around the island, and grins at me expectantly.

"I'm not giving you a knife," I inform her.

Jade blows out air in protest. "Uh, I'm not a child." She braces her fists on her hips. "I can wield a *blade*!" she announces dramatically, and grabs a knife out of the block.

Giving in to her demands, I warn, "I won't forgive you if you cut your pretty typing fingers."

"Awwww! You think my fingers are pretty?" Excitedly, she grabs her chest where her heart is and almost stabs herself with the action.

This woman!

"Give me the knife." I hold out my hand. "You almost killed yourself already."

"Nope!" She challenges me. "You can't take it from me."

I chuckle darkly at her assumption. Jade thinks that I won't because I can't touch her. She is a menace just as Maxum teases.

I reach out, my hand turning to stone as I wrap it around the sharp blade and tighten my grip.

Staring into her startled green eyes the entire time, I slowly pull the knife from her grasp, leaving her unharmed.

After an alarming moment when she moves closer, then she staggers backward. "Holy shirtballs, that was flippin' hot!" Then she sucks in a breath and bites her lips, like they are what made her say such a forward compliment.

I'm pleased by her praise. I never thought I'd feel that way. What is this witch doing to me?

Jade appears anxious, waiting for my response to her suggestive comment.

"You are enjoying the discovery of the supernatural world, aren't you?" I ask and turn to hide my smirk.

I've observed that she is easily amused by what she thought of as fantasy just days ago.

Jade exhales, realizing I'm not upset. "I suppose. Do you think I'm foolish or simpleminded because I'm excited?" she asks and turns on the faucet to wash the fruit.

I spin to capture her attention. "Never. I find it... entertaining. I learned most of what I know so long ago that now it feels like the world was never new."

"What's it like to live as long as you have?" she asks.

"Hmm." I contemplate my answer. No one has asked me this before. Honestly, no one has really cared to ask me deep questions about my thoughts about life.

Am I not a deep person? Or do they assume that my mind is filled with rocks? I suppose I don't dissuade them from that assumption.

After a moment, I explain, "Longevity isn't as exciting as it seems from someone as young as you are."

She snickers at that. "I'm not that young."

"I guess not in human terms." I continue, "At a certain point, you learn to navigate the world and how to live day to day as an independent person from your family. The assumptions I had about the world have shifted over time. Well, more accurately, how I exist in relation to the world has changed. Beyond that, I just have to keep up with the human world. After my first few decades, my personality did not change much. Is it pathetic that I have had little growth in all that time?"

"I'm sure you have had growth in all your years. But maybe it was so subtle that you didn't notice it happening." She glances up from the sink and shrugs. "There are two types of growth: gradual and catastrophic."

"I've had catastrophic events," I say with sadness and regret.

"Does it have to do with the touch thing?" she asks.

"Yes."

Her eyes lock with mine, and I want to confess everything. I crave to replace the horrific image of my worst experience with the pleasure of seeing Jade's face.

Craving. Such an interesting and new sensation.

I crave more of Jade.

What would it be like if I could allow myself to touch her?

Could I really change after all this time? I feel unchangeable, like an actual stone right now. But I remind myself that stone can be reshaped… usually by humans.

What if…?

A shout from upstairs grabs our attention, and we race toward the stairs. I move faster, even with my heft and size. Although Jade is faster than I thought she'd be for a human witch.

The shout is Calder's. I hear continued cursing and things being tossed about in his room.

What is happening? Is he being attacked? I don't like Jade running into a possibly dangerous situation with me, but I don't know how to stop her other than yelling at her to stay put. I can't bring myself to be a bossy alpha like the other males can be.

I hear the door downstairs to Maxum's room being thrown open. Good, we'll have backup. Maxum can hold Jade back from whatever is happening with Calder.

I fling his door open, even though it's sealed with magic, and I'm tossed backward by his magical ward. Fortunately, I don't collide with Jade, who is right behind me.

Calder charges through the door and into the hallway. His eyes are wild with anguish. He's so out of his mind that I don't think he even sees Jade. He's about to plow into her and knock her down the stairs.

I react without thinking and grab her arm, pushing her against the wall with my body, protecting her from Calder if he should attack or just knock her down.

He launches off the landing, releasing his fiery wings and then darts out the back door and takes flight toward the lake.

My body reacts to Jade's body pressed to mine, but not in the way I expect.

I'm hard… mostly below the waist. My hands are locked into place over her upper arms. Though I am only partially frozen, I feel incapable of moving away. I'm not sure I want to.

"Oh no, Flint?" Jade asks, worry and affection fill her hazel eyes. "Are you okay?"

"I… I don't know," I answer truthfully.

Maxum calls me. I glance downstairs.

When Maxum sees Jade is unharmed, he says to Arran, "I'll go see what's going on with him. You got this?"

Maxum launches after Calder when Arran shouts for him to go.

Arran comes up the stairs and sees me unmoving and pinning Jade to the wall. "Shit. Not again."

"Uh, no, it's different." Jade looks back up at me. "How are you able to move your head or talk? I thought…"

"I suppose you must have changed something inside of me," I whisper.

She shivers once again.

This time, I know it's because she enjoys the sound of my voice.

15

CRACKING STONE

JADE

"*I* suppose you must have changed something inside of me."

Flint's gravelly voice vibrates right down to my clit. Not fair. I'm trying to be a good girl and not the horny horn dogger who grinds against his boulder.

His massive, hard body presses me to the wall, and I can't say I mind all that much, especially when he doesn't look bothered by the touch. The concern over what is upsetting Calder fades into the background as I stare into the gargoyle's light gray eyes.

Flint's giant bat-like wings deployed when he was protecting me from Calder's outburst. I take a moment to admire them in their solid state before locking gazes with him again.

The shy guy seems just as surprised as me about his half frozen state. At least he can speak to me. And if the protrusion poking my stomach is any indication, his body is very interested in what's going on. Or maybe that's just his normal resting state.

Good Goddess.

My vision fades while I imagine what he might be packing and if he might wish to unleash it on me one day.

If any of them pull on my romantic heartstrings, it's this guy. I want to wine and dine him. Show him affection. Yet, I worry that his heart would literally crack if he suffered another heartbreak. I couldn't do that to him. Not that I'd ever hurt him intentionally. But what-ifs float and clog my logic-monster brain.

The most significant what-if circles around what secrets we will uncover about me and my past. Sure, Arran and Maxum would be upset if I turned out to be the true monster, but I didn't pursue them. They pursued me. And I can't chase Flint when I don't know what will happen in the future.

At the moment, I need to free myself from his hold before I lose my resolve and make a fool of myself.

When I wiggle, his hands feel solid and like stone.

"Are you *half... stone*?" Arran asks in shock, peeking under Flint's wing. Then he looks at Flint's grip on my arm. "Are you okay?" he asks me.

"Yeah." I look toward the room and wonder about my fur babies. "Can you check on my little guys?"

Arran's eyes widen even more. "Of course!" My wolfie rushes toward the room and I hear him curse. "The hamster is missing."

"Maybe that's what upset Calder?" I suggest. "He seemed to be really into the little ones."

I hear Arran inhale. Then he's stripping off his sweatpants as he says to me, "I'll sniff them out." He shifts into his wolf and races down the hallway of bedrooms, shakes his head and then rushes downstairs.

"It will be okay," Flint assures me. "They'll find them."

With all my worry, I briefly forgot I'm stuck with my half concrete gargoyle. "I should have had them with me," I say, tears in my eyes.

"It's only been a day or so. They would have disrupted your healing, and you need to gain your strength and get some rest." Flint frowns. "From what I heard from Calder's room, he was constantly talking to them."

"I suppose they were probably pent up, unable to talk to me all these years."

Flint picks up on my guilt and frustration. "Don't blame yourself. You didn't know about the supe world. Everyone else before had failed you. Your mother, grandmother, warlock boyfriend. Maybe others you don't even realize."

My head spins with that realization. How many other people are 'in the know' and let me skip along through life with my ignorance?

I dare to look into Flint's stunning eyes again. They have been so full of sorrow and sadness, but now when I look, I see something else.

"I guess you are getting used to me?" I cock an eyebrow, wondering what's going on with my usually taciturn acquaintance.

"Yes, I... I'd like to get over my fear of touching. I don't want to be like this anymore."

I swallow down my own nerves, secretly wishing it's because he wants to do more than just touch me. "Why not?"

"I don't want to make you uncomfortable. This is the second time I've trapped you. It's dangerous. What if I need to act and I'm frozen?"

"I suspect if you really had to protect me, that something would make you act."

"Well, possibly. However, I wouldn't mind giving you a hug... you know.... for friendship. I sensed a few times you were open to doing that with me."

I don't say how I'd like to do more than just hug. Horizontal, naked hugging maybe. I'd hug the hell out of him and make him see stars if he'd let me. But I, too, would love a plain ole hug.

"I wish my arms weren't pinned down, or I'd give you a friendship hug now for making sure I didn't take a deadly tumble down the stairs."

"I panicked. I doubt Calder would have let you get hurt."

"We don't know that." I turn my head up to get his attention and make him see my truth. "I don't mind being here with you, even like this. I don't know what has caused this condition, but I want you to know that I trust you."

"Maybe you shouldn't."

"Did you hurt someone on purpose? A woman?" I ask, my voice soft. The question is out of my mouth before I have a chance to think it through. This is a problem for someone like me who isn't used to working with a filter. I usually try to allow all my wild thoughts their due so I don't censor what comes out. That's what the editing process is for. But in life, there's no delete button.

I hope I didn't strike a nerve with my invasive question.

He tenses, but then shakes his head. "Not on purpose. It was an accident."

"Maybe it will help to talk about it."

"You may be correct. Trying to avoid it all these centuries hasn't seemed to help."

"Ignoring trauma usually delays healing. I would know."

"I suppose you have had your fair share of trauma... in just the last few days." Flint regards me thoughtfully. "You find it helps to speak of your pain?"

"I do. I don't think it helps to dwell and go over it constantly because then it can become your only story. We all can fall victim to being a victim. I have done it too. Reliving the trauma repetitively can solidify it as our main

315

narrative. But talking about it, and hopefully understanding why it happened or how the experience changed us, I think that can be therapeutic. It allows the space to heal."

"I thought not talking about it would make it go away. But it did the opposite. I've relived the tragedy over and over, allowing it to shape everything in my life."

His thumb moves, stroking my biceps ever so slowly and softly. I don't draw his attention to it. I want him to get his words out. Give him space to lance the wound that has festered for hundreds of years. I don't expect it will be easy for him.

"She was the first person I killed." Flint glances away, unable to look me in the eye anymore. Likely thinking I'll judge him.

"She was also the first human I saw. I was young, only eighteen years old. Marie was so pretty and sweet. She'd sing while I'd watch her gather wild fruits and berries, never knowing I was there since I used my gargoyle camouflage. One day, I decided to be bold and speak to her. For the first time, I used my glamour and appeared to her as a human. She was taken aback by my size, but otherwise was friendly to me. I told her a lie, that I was traveling through her area and would only be around for a short while."

He takes a deep breath and gains more courage when I nod for him to continue. "Marie invited me back to eat with her family behind the castle walls. I accepted because I was curious to see how the humans lived. I expected it to differ greatly from living in Elfhame and the rocky cliffs where my people are from."

I'm itching to know more about his people, but I file away the million questions I have for a more appropriate time.

"I met her mother and father. They were kind and friendly to me. However, no one knew what I was. Marie invited me up to the top of her liege's castle. It wasn't as fine as the ones in Elfhame, but the tower she took me to was high enough. As we climbed the stairs, I sensed magic, but it didn't feel like fae, so I ignored it."

I bite my lip. I fear what he's about to tell me next. And my guilt swells again.

"There was a witch in the tower, and she immediately sensed I was not human. She cast a revealing spell to force my glamour to drop. I was young and untested so I didn't react quickly enough to stop her. When Marie caught sight of my gargoyle form, she stepped backward. I reached out for her, but she was scared of my appearance, and she slapped my hands away. I failed to grab her. She fell…"

Flint's voice chokes up, and he doesn't continue.

"In her surprise, she fell down the stairs and died?"

He nods, his body shakes with his held back tears.

"My sweet gargoyle, that wasn't your fault." I place my hands on his forearms, the only thing I can reach with his tight hold on my biceps.

At my words, and touch, his floodgates are released. His body softens and almost his entire weight pushes me against the wall. His hands let my arms go, and he slides them around my waist in a hug, lifting my feet off the floor.

I return his embrace, feeling as if I'm holding him together, even if my arms don't reach all the way around him.

I'm not even sure if he knows he's doing it when he presses his forehead to mine. Not wanting to break the spell of the moment, I don't tell him he is almost crushing me, and take in shallow breaths instead.

His eyes pop open, and they seem brighter—glowing. He also appears a bit shocked by what's happening, being able to touch me without freezing up.

He pulls back enough for me to breathe again, but my feet are still dangling off the floor.

"I..." He loosens his tight grip around my waist. "Did I hurt you?"

Thankfully, he doesn't drop me out of instinct. "I'm okay. How are you?"

"I'm touching you," he says with awe, and looks down to see our hips are pressed together. "Oh, I'm sorry."

He moves to pull away.

I don't easily let him go. "This is all okay. Unless you'd rather not be touching me." He stops moving.

"But our lower halves are...," he whispers.

"Does that make you feel bad?" I ask. "Or good?"

"Good, but..." His skin flushes that beautiful peach color, and I can't help but wonder how far down it goes.

"What is it? You can tell me." I realize he might not know he can ask for what he needs. "If embracing me makes you feel weird, we can stop hugging whenever you want."

"It's not that... not exactly. It's just... you don't know the real me yet. My true appearance. How ugly I really am."

"I feel like I know you in many ways already. As far as your looks are concerned, I doubt I will find your appearance unappealing. Do you want to show me? Would that make you feel better about being near me? If I know the real you?"

"Uh, I think it would, but maybe not..."

"Hey, I get it. This is already a lot," I say gently as I stroke his sides affectionately. I want to lean forward and kiss him or stroke his cheek, but it feels like too much for his first experience. "Sweetheart, I never want to make you feel bad."

"You… you called me sweetheart."

"Is that okay?"

His smile lights up my entire being. "Yes. May I call you a name of endearment too?"

I giggle. I almost roll my eyes at myself for the silly sound I make, but he's so flipping sweet. "Of course you can. You can even try out different names until you find something you like."

"Thank you for being you, beautiful soul." He sets me down on my feet and takes a hesitant step back.

I'm flustered because I miss his solid body against mine. Even in its supposed soft form, it's almost as hard as stone. And if I'm not mistaken, he was getting harder below the belt.

"May I hold your hand?" he asks shyly.

"Anytime you'd like." I slide my tiny hand within his massive one, and I shiver with the thought of his hands holding me in other places.

"Are you done with the mating dance yet?" my obnoxious guinea pig familiar says with his tiny hands on his hips. His beady little eyes glare at me.

"We weren't mating," I gruff.

Flint turns a brighter shade of peach.

"Did you have something to say? Or are you just acting out your name?" I ask my little furry brat. I recall how, even though I never knew he was a magical creature, I occasionally sensed his snarkiness.

He scurries from the room and tells me, "Shut the door and come with me."

"He wants me to follow him and close this door," I translate for my gargoyle.

"Sounds like a bossy little thing," Flint mutters and does as the furry boss says.

"Wait until he demands treats," I joke.

"*Treats! Where?*" After his outburst of excitement, Trouble huffs when he realizes I'm treatless. "Damn you, witch. That was mean. Unless you are hiding something…"

"You'll get some treats if you just get on with whatever you want to tell us and stop being sassy."

Trouble sniffs indignantly and continues, "I think… I think Floofer is a spy."

"Floofs? The hamster is a spy?" An icky feeling of betrayal washes over my body.

"Goddess dammit," Flint growls.

I try to remember but can't recall everything from the other day. "Does Floofer talk?"

"A little. I didn't think he could understand much," Trouble explains. "He seems... to have simple thoughts, like Sage. But now, I'm not so sure."

"Is that why Calder ran out of here in a panic?" I ask.

"Tonight, Floofer opened the ward on the bedroom door with his mind. I saw a shimmer around him. He felt odd. By the time the birdman listened to me, Floofer was gone. I don't know if he also suspects Floofer of being a spy. I didn't have time to say anything."

"If he isn't a magical creature, what could Floof be?" I ask.

"*Where* could he be?" Flint scans the hallway and growls low, rumbling my body with the vibration.

Holy clitatory.

Flint doesn't even know how sexy he is. So protective, and I wonder what four hundred years of repression would be like unleashed in the bedroom. My body heats and thrums with anticipation.

Why is it *more* sexy when he has no clue what he does to me?

16

FLOOFING

CALDER

Staying in this house with the witch here is pure torture. I might as well be in prison. I'd probably be happier if I was locked up.

To hear her sucking Maxum's and Arran's souls out of their cocks is maddening. My entire existence is at war. My dick loves the sounds, but my mind revolts.

Even if she is innocent of Osen's death or all the other stuff that we've uncovered, she is still a witch.

To add to my suspicions, Osen hasn't shown up after the alleyway. Is she suppressing his spirit, so she isn't found out?

Ugh. The more I watch her, the more I realize it's likely she's just an ignorant witch. However, even an ignorant witch can cause a lot of problems.

I've been taking care of her magical creatures. Their warden of sorts, although they don't realize it. Sure, they all say Jade didn't know what she was, but there's something off. I just can't place my finger on what is wrong.

I can't shut Trouble up—incessantly talking, that one. And the rabbit, Sage, doesn't seem to be a schemer. Simple yet wise, much like her namesake. But that's animals for you. They carry their own kind of wisdom. Maybe superior in some ways.

And Floofer... *for all that is sacred.*

Could Jade have picked a more ridiculous name? I don't think he would have chosen that moniker, had he been given a choice. But what do I know? He barely speaks. I've only pulled out one-word answers from the hamster. Maybe he is a bit touched. Not all magical creatures are blessed with intelligence.

Hell, not all supernaturals or humans have been blessed with smarts, either.

That's what nags at me, I suppose. Jade is smart—smarter than she acts sometimes. She spaces out and often looks lost when I've been around, but then she can allegedly write books, making up entire worlds and magical systems all on her own. Yet she also appears to be perceptive and insightful. So I think the ditsy spacey shtick isn't real.

I suppose both could be true. She can lack focus *and* be extremely hyper focused other times.

I just… have never met someone like her.

To be fair, I don't get to know many people. At least, not since I died at the hands of that cruel witch. I'm not friendly or social anymore. Why should I be? The world is just out to rob me of any joy I have.

Losing Osen is just one example of that. In my last incarnation, I couldn't even enjoy his touch anymore. Now that he's dead, I will never have an opportunity to get over my pain, or help him get over his.

I've been tossing and turning in bed, trying to not eavesdrop on Jade and Flint in the kitchen. Except her voice is like a siren's call, and Flint's voice rumbles like an earthquake's incoming wave, ready to decimate the landscape.

Drawn to their conversation, because of course, I must know everything that damned witch does. I get up and crack the door to better hear them.

Sounds like Flint is falling under her spell, too. He's yearning to bond with her in any way his broken spirit can. Why is it so easy for my pack to reveal their hearts and souls to this blasted woman? What am I not seeing?

Could I be jealous that she doesn't appear to want to catch me in her devious net? Or will I be her last conquest since I'm holding out and being a proper asshole to her?

Frustrated, I throw myself on the bed again and cover my head with my pillow. Not that it helps to block out the world. I chant a spell Maxum taught me to soothe my turbulent, broken soul.

"Birdman!" Trouble shouts, breaking my attention on my chant and the ugly train of thought I'm still riding.

"What is it?" I snap and spin to glare at him. He knows I hate it when he calls me that.

"Floofer is gone! He just ran out."

"What the fuck?" I feared something like this would happen. I hated to keep them cooped up in their cages. This is what I get for trusting them to stay in my room.

Another fear rises... one that I kept pushing down. What if the creatures aren't what they appeared to be?

I need to find him and discover what he is up to. I don't have the amazing sense of smell that Arran does. But my eyesight will do, even at night or before dawn, as it is now.

I glance down the hall and see all the doors are closed. So Floof must have gone down the stairs. Am I that obsessed with the witch that I allowed something to slip past me like this?

I am. I did.

Fuck!

I race toward the stairs and almost collide with Jade. Fortunately, Flint is quick with his reflexes and snatches her out of the way.

I'd stop and explain, but I fear I've fucked up. I can't look her in the eye and confess I lost her pet. Or worse, that I may have allowed a spy amongst us.

Either way, I'm pissed at myself.

Off the living room, I see the patio door slightly ajar. I'm out that door before it registers that Flint touched Jade.

I hear Arran and Maxum rushing out of their bedroom and figure they can handle whatever mess I made with the gargoyle and the witch.

My eyes frantically search the shadows. I'm completely screwed. A hamster could literally be under a leaf and I wouldn't see it.

Maxum joins me outside, flapping his huge wings as we both hover over the yard behind the house. "What the fuck is going on?" He rubs the sleep from his eyes and glances around.

I land, but continue to scan my surroundings. "Floofer is gone."

He touches down next to me. "What the hell is a floofer?" he asks, completely baffled.

"The hamster." I growl. I hate that he never took the time to get to know the creatures. "You should have investigated them!"

"You told me they were just magical creatures," Maxum says with confusion.

"I thought they were. Maybe instead of sticking your dick in the witch, you should have been probing their minds."

Maxum tenses, realizing this is more than a missing pet. "Explain yourself.

What do you think is going on?" His eyes dart about, trying to catch sight of our potential infiltrator.

"Something felt off. It's possible he was a spy."

"Then you should have *asked* me to investigate."

I sigh. He's not wrong. "I should have. And this is just a guess. However, disappearing like this isn't a good sign."

Maxum glowers at the dark forest that surrounds the lake, and we walk toward it. "He's going to have a hard time getting outside of my wards."

"Unless he's a shifter and a mage. If he's powerful and skilled, he could break through."

"But why would a mage be spying on us?" he asks, confusion filling his face.

"On *Jade*," I correct him.

Maxum lets loose a string of inventive curses. After a moment, he gazes again into the darkness. But this time, I feel the swell of magic gather around him.

I try to shut down, quieting my wild and crazed thoughts so he can focus without me broadcasting all my messy ideas and worries.

The demon shakes his head and frowns. "Whoever… whatever Floofer is, I can't sense their thoughts. So either they are truly a dimwitted hamster or they are powerful enough to block me completely."

Dammit. I was hoping he could sense the hamster.

"If they are that powerful, why are they wasting their time masquerading as a hamster for a witch who isn't even at her full power?" he asks.

So many accusatory answers pop up in my mind, instead I focus on what we know for sure. "If she is ignorant of her power, then maybe someone wants to keep it that way. If she didn't know about the pendant's intentions, its presence would suggest someone wanted her magic weak. Or the hamster could be someone, other than Rob, who hoped to use her ability."

"None of the possibilities are good." He turns his attention fully on me and studies my face. "You really don't believe she's innocent?"

I must tread carefully here. He's bonding with her and I will be the enemy if I continue my stance that all witches are guilty simply by their existence.

"I don't know what to believe anymore." I shrug and as I say it, I know it's my truth. "Nothing about her has a clean cut explanation."

"Nothing in *life* has a clean cut explanation," Maxum retorts.

"Fair enough." I grimace and push on. "She represents everything that has ruined me. And then, on top of it, she's tangled up in Osen's death, whether or not she's innocent of any crime."

"You don't believe that she hurt him, do you?"

"No, not on purpose. But she might be a weapon that someone controls. Then she…" I can't even finish my sentence.

"She captured Osen's soul. I know that must be very upsetting… for you, especially." Maxum pats me on the shoulder.

I allow the touch because he means well.

"You aren't freaked out by that?" I ask with more than a bit of irritation.

"Yeah. But only because something like her has never existed before. At least that we know about."

"Don't you wonder how a witch can capture a supernatural soul?"

"That's why I plan to train her to reveal her magic. There's something different about her, and we all need to know what that is. Jade needs to know, too."

"She really has no clue?" I rub my hair and pace. I don't want to hear his answer.

"I haven't probed her mind deep enough to crack her marbles, but yeah, from what I've picked up, she doesn't have a clue. I can also tell she isn't trying to block me. She doesn't even know how to put up mental walls."

"Well, if she is as innocent as you believe she is, then you should train her. I have a bad feeling all of this is going to get worse before it's over."

"Let's just hope we are on the winning end of it when it's all done." Maxum sighs and gazes back at the house.

Even as dense as I am, I feel his longing for her as tangible as an ache in his bones. He wants to claim her, but he knows he can't—not yet. Maybe not even after we deal with Jade's situation.

With my keen eyesight, I turn back toward the house and see Jade and Flint staring out after us and holding hands.

Holding hands!

This woman has more natural magic than all of us combined.

17

INTERROGATION

MAXUM

*B*y the time I've circled my land and its boundaries several times over, in a fruitless attempt to locate the runaway hamster, the morning sun has quickly become noon.

When I enter the house, Arran is in his wolf form, curled up in the hallway outside Jade's makeshift office. The door is shut, and he looks about ready to whine.

If I weren't feeling the same distance created by the simple act, I might tease him. As it is, I want to grumble as well. She's likely making up for her lost writing days and the quote "never ending amount of promo stuff" she told us she had to do to keep her books selling.

Even if she doesn't accept my bond, I'd make sure she'd never have to worry about making money with her books. I've been around long enough to know writing is her passion so if I were to help her with the money aspect, it would be to hire people to help her with the advertisement so she could focus on writing and engaging with readers in a more pleasurable way.

Maybe she would take my money if I offered it in that context, as an investment? Then, if she is freed up from her constant striving, I might be rewarded with more quality time with her.

"Shift and tell me what's been going on here," I demand of Arran.

The wolf lets out a huff of air and drops his head back down on his huge paws. His golden eyes glance at the door, worry and vigilance in equal measure pour out of him.

"Fine. Keep your eye on the room, but we should move down a bit and keep our voices low so she isn't disturbed," I suggest.

Arran stands and shifts, walking down the hallway without letting his eyes leave the door. "I gave up the search, since I needed to be here, protecting Jade. But when I returned, she said she needed her space to work. She doesn't want me spying and reading her stuff anymore."

I grunt, indifferent to his need to read her books before she's ready to share. I have a whole set of books I grabbed from the stack at her house so I could read what turns this woman on. I'll share my stash with him when the time is right.

"Anything else going on?" I prompt, nodding toward the rest of the house.

"Calder has been searching through the house just in case Floofer doubled back."

"Smart."

"Oh," Arran lowers his voice and gets excited. "Flint touched Jade. He spontaneously grabbed her so she wouldn't fall down the stairs. After that, he was able to somewhat un-stone himself—for the most part. When I circled back to the house to make sure we didn't leave Jade open to attack in our frantic state, they were actually holding hands without him freezing up."

"He freed himself from his hangup?"

I didn't believe that the gargoyle would ever even *attempt* to break his self-inflicted curse. Jade really is something else. I grin, realizing she is becoming more entrenched in our pack. If only Calder would let his walls fall down, we could be a proper pack with a loving heart in the center.

Osen liked to believe he was the nexus of the group, holding us all together, but he was just as much of a divider as any sort of unifier. He was too obsessed with revenge, war, and sex to be a true center. If he's no longer inside Jade, I'd be okay with that. I worry he would only corrupt her and coerce her to risk her life for answers again.

I want answers too, but we need to be smart. His sneaking around almost cost my mate her life. If he's still with her, I'm going to demand he make a promise on his soul to include us in any plans. Or I will find a way to drive him out of Jade for good.

I hope the male I love is still whole enough to remember how amazing we once were when we acted as a team. Could being around Jade's energy balance him? I fucking hope so. He isn't so bad when he isn't obsessed.

We all need Jade. Osen would see it too, if he just took a moment. I dare say she is someone he would fall madly in love with as well. Too bad he's dead. Yet, it doesn't sound like that stopped him from enjoying her sexually in the shadowscape.

Once Calder lets go of his righteous anger, then he will be able to heal... likely with her love.

"I'm going to investigate the creatures and see what they have to say about all this," I tell Arran as I squeeze his shoulder. "Keep up your protection detail. We don't know if we are safe here now."

He places his warm hand over mine and smiles. Although his grin has melancholy behind it. Without needing to probe his mind, I sense he is a tornado of emotion—his love for Jade, his worry about her safety, their future, and how we will share the love of our woman.

He's also worried that we have drifted too far from each other since his curse. What he doesn't realize is that it feels too good to have my companion back, and I won't let him slip from my grasp so easily next time. Besides, even his beast seems to have been tamed by Jade.

I head upstairs to deal with our possible spy situation. I growl, first at myself, then at Calder for not suspecting something could be off with the "fur babies" before now.

In my defense, they didn't radiate anything but magical creature vibes and brain waves. But if I'm to keep my mate safe, I need to do better.

I knock on the phoenix's door. "It's me."

"Come in," Calder bites out. He isn't happy. Well, join the damned fucking club.

I slip in and shut the door behind me.

The magical creatures sit huddled together on Calder's bed. Wide eyed watching their interrogator pace the room, they look adorable and nervous.

"How long ago did Floofers join your group?" he asks.

Trouble answers, sounding irritated.

Calder interprets for me, "He said maybe fifty years ago? You know how animals are with time, but it's probably been a while." The phoenix rolls his eyes and sighs, falling onto a wooden desk chair with exhaustion.

"May I?" I wave my hand toward the little tufts of fur.

"You won't explode their brains?" he asks.

The guinea pig squeaks and runs under Calder's pillow.

"I won't," I assure him, then add, "... probably."

"Be careful. If they are innocent, I won't forgive myself." Calder rubs his eyes and then decides he can't watch and covers his face with both hands and tilts his head down, using his elbows to prop himself up.

He likes to pretend he's such a hardass, but he's softer than all of us.

327

That's exactly his problem. He knows he will melt into goo when Jade finally wins him over.

I wave to the guinea pig since he seems to be the most human-minded. "Come here. I won't hurt you. It might feel uncomfortable, like someone petting you too hard. The more you fight me, the more it will hurt. I know you are brave, and I know you want to help Jade, so allow me to get some answers, and I will give you all the treats you can handle."

Trouble rushes toward me with the mention of Jade, and even faster with the mention of treats.

"Ready?"

Trouble squeaks, and Calder confirms it. "He's ready. He says he won't fight it. He has nothing to hide except that..." Calder chuckles softly. "Except that he peed on the carpet when Jade warned him not to."

"Don't worry. I won't share that with Jade," I promise.

The shivering mass of fur settles and closes his eyes, awaiting my mental probe.

Despite their small size, a magical creature's energy is sometimes bigger than the average human. I wonder if it's because their magic is just naturally bigger or because humans don't really connect with the world around them. I think it may be the latter. Human's natural magic has become diluted in the last several decades as technology has replaced thinking or being with nature. However, I've noticed that engaging their minds is beneficial for them.

Nevertheless, all the magic in a creature as small as this one has been concentrated. His brain is tiny. So I must be gentle, or I will accidentally squash it.

I decide instead of diving in, rooting around, and potentially causing damage, I should ask questions to bring the right thoughts to the surface. Then I will only need to skim his thoughts like I do with most people, without consequence.

"Remember back to when Floofer first joined you," I instruct.

The image of Rob pops up, and I also sense irritation toward him. The guinea pig isn't a fan of the warlock.

This is a good start.

"Did Rob bring Floofers to Jade?" I ask.

I get the impression that Rob first showed up in Jade's life and then Jade found Floofer immediately afterward, outside of her home. Rob acted as if he didn't like the magical creatures, but he almost completely ignored Floofer compared to the other animals.

"Did Rob ever take Floofer away from the rest of you?"

I don't see an instance of that in Trouble's memories, but that's inconclusive. If Rob could put a spell on Jade, he could have done something to the creatures as well.

"Did you ever witness Rob asking Jade questions when she was possessed by a ghost?"

In Trouble's mind, I hear the muffled sounds of Rob asking about names and locations of people. Jade's voice sounds odd, just like it did when Osen spoke through her.

I need to know if Jade was there *during* the murders. Maybe that's why Osen thought he saw her there at his death in the alleyway. Either he saw her in the weeks when he was investigating, or she was actually there against her will during his murder.

"Did Rob ever take Jade out of the house just *before* a spirit possessed her?"

Trouble doesn't think she was. He shows me a memory of her snuggling up to Sage and then a spirit rushed toward her, through the pendant, and into her body.

Shit. The pendant had been used as a focal point, just as I suspected.

It's also interesting that the guinea pig can see ghosts. Though I had heard that even regular animals, especially cats, often can perceive spirits.

"Is the last ghost still with her? The grumpy one?" I ask about Osen, and Calder comes to attention, waiting for any response.

I get the impression that something lingers around her, but Trouble has sensed nothing definitive since the alleyway.

"Well?" Calder asks Trouble directly.

The guinea pig chirps out a response, and Calder deflates.

"He might just need a power up," I try to console him. "Despite your claims, we haven't been relentlessly fucking Jade, so if Osen's still in her, he hasn't had many meals yet."

"I just can't get over all of it," Calder half-ass apologizes.

"You *can*, but you aren't allowing yourself to let go." I sigh, because I don't enjoy lecturing him, but he's not snapping out of his poor attitude. It's been years since he last died and came back. He's more twisted up than ever before. "Jade isn't anything like the witch who killed you."

"I know. But..."

"No. No buts. I'm not saying you have to be lovers or even best friends. I'm just saying give her a damn break. You are so focused on your anger, we might never get our answers if you aren't helping us find them. The pain of losing Osen made you miss out on a great opportunity to talk to him again. Hopefully, if we get him back, you don't let that opportunity slip through your fingers again. And you might be missing something else important if you keep this up."

"I..." he starts to defend himself and then stops. After a moment, he concedes, "You're right. I'm kicking myself that I didn't talk to Osen more when he was alive. And that I didn't pursue closure when he was in Jade."

"Promise me you won't make that mistake again?"

He nods, but doesn't seal the promise with his words. I just hope he doesn't fuck up his chances anymore than he has.

18

BOUNDARIES

JADE

*A*fter all the early morning strangeness with Floofer and the intense breakthrough with Flint, I attempt to write.

Keyword: Attempt.

I get a few words on the page, but mostly it's just notes, ideas, and snippets of dialogue that I will have to expand and enhance for it to make any sense.

I can't focus with all that's happened recently, my mind is a chaotic mess. It was bad enough when I was just dealing with a jerky boyfriend and our breakup.

But everything going on in my life is so far beyond simple problems that I might as well be in another realm... which now, I suppose, I have been to.

What is my life?

It is no small thing to discover that your entire world is a lie. Or more accurately, completely misrepresented. What was up is now down. Monsters and supernaturals are real. My abuela really was a witch, not just loco, like my mother would have me believe. I have two (possibly more) lovers who are supernatural beings. Oh, and one of my fur babies might have been spying on me for the past few years.

I shudder, thinking how I petted him and held him to my breast when he might have been some mage in disguise. Ugh.

I hope the jerk hated every second of it. Otherwise, I want to be sick.

Ultimately, I'm just pissed off about how ignorant I was to literally everything happening in my life.

Every once in a while, I hear Arran whine softly outside the office door. His wolf, and-or beast, and-or the human part can't handle this closed door.

I can't say I'm a fan of it either, but I need to maintain healthy boundaries. As an introvert, I'm so used to being alone that this constant touching and attention feels scary and overwhelming. I'm collapsing in on myself with all the energy it takes for me to be around all these new people. I need time to gather myself.

After a slew of author administrative duties, I give up trying to force the words and curl up on the daybed. Weirdly, I can actually feel Arran outside in the hallway and Maxum upstairs. My magic must be coming to me. If I strain, I can even feel Flint in his room... pacing?

I suppose he's had his world rocked as much as I have. I hope our upheavals turn out to be good things in the long run.

I don't feel Calder though, and I wonder if that has to do with the fact I have no emotional bonds with him. I search inside myself and a shadow seems to brush up against me. Is it Osen? I hope he comes back in full form and is happy to be with me.

There's a soft knock on the door, and I sit up. "Come in."

Maxum opens the door, glances at the computer, and then thinks better of coming all the way inside. He stops, but Arran brushes past him to sit next to me on the futon. Apparently, shifters like Arran with little bonus magic rarely mess up computers.

"I couldn't find Floofer," Maxum tells me. "However, I successfully read Trouble's mind without hurting him. I believe Floofer was a spy, and was likely working with Rob."

"You're sure Trouble wasn't hurt?" I ask.

"Yeah. He's demanding extra treats for eternity for his bravery, from what Calder translated for me."

"Sounds like he's fine," I say, then move onto the other news. "What do we do about Floof? Do you think he is still hiding around the house?"

"I didn't pick up that he has crossed my wards or dismantled them, but if he's a highly proficient mage or witch, there's a slim chance that I might not know." Maxum pauses and then says what was likely on his mind this whole time. "I was thinking I should check in with my various contacts and see what they found out about Rob or his associates since I last asked."

"You are leaving?" My heart doesn't like the sound of that.

"Just for the day. I will be back before nightfall."

I jump up and run to hug him. "Promise?"

"Worried about me?" he says with amusement.

"Uh, yeah, of course. Should you be going alone?" I ask.

"I'm going too." Arran hugs me from behind, and I hear in my mind what sounds like a whimper.

I'm not worried about being left alone with Flint. It helps that he doesn't freeze up completely anymore, but I don't know about the phoenix. "You think Calder won't just let me be dragged off if it comes down to it?"

"He didn't last time." Maxum sighs and brushes the wild silver hair from my face. "He's promised to protect you, and I think he's beginning to regret his pissy attitude. Besides, Flint will be here too."

"Okay." I go up on my tiptoes and Maxum leans down to give me a kiss. Once satisfied, I turn and tangle tongues with my sweet Arran.

I'm completely worked up by the time we are done with our goodbyes, and regret they will be gone the entire day. Geeze. Can I pick a lane? First, I need my space, and now I'm all needy. A classic case of wanting what I can't have.

"Calder is also willing to teach you how to shield your mind," Maxum adds.

"He knows how to do that?" I ask, skeptical since Maxum had made it sound like he was the only one qualified before.

"Yes, he's capable of teaching you the basics, and I can test you when I get back."

I harrumph, because I'd rather not play with the grumpy antagonist.

"I'm sure he just needs to get to know you a bit more, and he will melt in your hands, just like Flint is," Maxum assures me.

"Calder's so damned stubborn," Arran huffs.

"But Calder means a lot to you both," I say. "So he must have some redeeming qualities he has yet to bestow upon me, other than being sexy looking."

"He has a big heart… when he allows himself to care." Maxum kisses my forehead. "I dare say he will fall hard for you once he gets out of his own way."

"Wait, a sec." I ask in surprise, "Do you want me to hook up with him?"

"Do you want to?" Arran asks.

"So you both are okay if I'm with your whole pack?" I ask.

"Only if you are going to be happy with that arrangement," Maxum says.

"Exactly," Arran agrees. "I believe your heart is big enough to love all of us."

"Okay, well, let's just see if he can say hello to me without a snarl. We'll go from there."

19

BUILDING BRIDGES

JADE

*M*axum and Arran leave for their investigations, going the direction we had arrived at the house.

After a sigh and wistfully longing to join them, I climb the stairs to see if Calder indeed intends to teach me a damn thing.

I just hope he doesn't either attack me verbally or physically. Although, I highly doubt even with his crazed anger toward witches that he would actually hurt me.

Just as I'm about to knock on the door, I glance down the hallway and wonder if Flint might help me with shielding my mind. Although, it seems unlikely since I'm sure Maxum would have told me to work with the gargoyle instead if he was an option.

Calder's door flies open before I have a chance to knock. He gives me a quick once over and asks flatly, "Why are you lingering out here?"

Do I tell him I've been working up the nerve to talk with him? Or would that only feed his ego?

"I was debating whether this was a good idea." Yeah. Honesty. That could work. "If you don't want to help me with my shields, then I can buzz off."

"I didn't say I wouldn't help," he grumps and steps aside as an invitation to come into his room.

"You're okay with me in your space?" I ask, a bit taken aback.

"Your spy already invaded my room. I don't see how it's sacred anymore."

I flush pink with the reminder that I had a spy with me for the last few years. "If I would have known… Well, I don't know what to say. Just that a week ago, I didn't even know it was possible for a hamster to be anything more than just a cute ball of floof."

Calder grunts and waves me in. "I know."

"You believe me now?" I ask as I take a tentative step inside his room.

It's nicer than the one at the temporary safe house. But I suppose that makes sense. Maxum intended for this place to be a proper home for them.

Calder's space is filled with burnished wood and beautifully intricate wrought metal—not iron, but another metal I've never seen before. I assume this metal is fae-born friendly since I know iron had hurt Osen.

His room is a mix of deep reds and rust orange—exactly as I might expect a fire being's color choice to be.

I realize I'd like to see Arran's personal room, and Flint's if he'd let me. What would Osen's room reveal that I don't know yet? Perhaps it might draw him forward if there is anything personal he might attune to.

But the most precious thing to Osen that's here might be Calder himself.

Trouble and Sage gaze up at me from a thick shag rug.

I titter over them and squat down to give them a pet. "Hey, are you both doing okay?"

"Birdman gives good ear rubs!" Sage announces.

I peek up at the phoenix, who blushes slightly and turns away quickly, busying himself with something on his desk.

"I bet he does," I agree. "How are you doing, Trouble?"

"I'm mad."

"Oh?" I worry he will say that I've been ignoring him. I haven't meant to, but when I think about it, truly, not much time has passed since my life was turned upside down. Knowing how wild it's been, I relax a bit. Besides, Calder has been keeping an eye on them, and it sounds like he might be a better caretaker than I've ever been.

But Trouble isn't mad at me when I hear him say, "Floofer was lying to us."

"It sounds like that's the case. Did he ever do anything to hurt you?" I ask.

"Uh, no. I don't think so. Not when we were awake."

I sigh with relief, and I hear Calder echo me. He really has a soft spot for the little ones. I just wish he wouldn't be so hard on me because I'm a witch. I never asked to be born this way or have the power to channel spirits.

Well, I suppose it's time to bite the bullet and have him help me. I give each of the fur babies their favorite petting. Sage likes her ears rubbed and Trouble likes a rump scratch.

"You sure you want to help me?" I ask the phoenix. "Maybe I should wait until Maxum gets back."

"Sit down." Calder points to his wooden desk chair. He perches on the side of his bed and stares at me.

I feel pressure at my temples. "What are you doing?"

"You felt that?" He nods and tilts his head. With his movement, I can see the bird part of him clearly.

"Like fingers pressing on the sides of my head," I tell him.

"I'm not a proficient mind reader like Maxum, but I've been known to get into some weaker minds."

"What did you see?" I ask. Because I hope he didn't see how I admire how he looks in his tight black t-shirt and gray sweatpants.

"Nothing," he says, like it's obvious. "Your mind isn't weak."

"Oh, I thought since Rob could hypnotize me and spirits can invade my mind that I would be considered weak."

Calder leans forward, his elbows propped on his lap. "From what we understand, Rob put a spell on you, likely when you were asleep. That's different from being hypnotized. Essentially, he assaulted you when you trusted him, and he took your choices away. As far as the spirits go, mediumship is a power, not a weakness. You can call on souls and even channel their magic."

"You make it sound like I'm in control of the spirits, but Osen controlled me."

"Only because your magic was weakened by the pendant. Osen is particularly gifted at manipulating things in any dimension—in the shadowscape's astral realm or physically."

"You don't believe I am lying anymore?" I ask.

"I don't know what to think. But yeah, the more I see of you, the more I suspect you don't have a fucking clue."

"Thanks?" I lean back in the chair and frown. "You're right. I don't have a clue. It's like this isn't even my life anymore. Everything I thought I knew about the world and myself was wrong. I believed Rob and I had a typical bad relationship. He was a bit of a narcissistic douche and then straight abusive when I broke up with him."

Calder perks up. "You broke up with him?"

"Yeah. I was tired of him being a jerk. Nothing about the relationship was good. Nothing. So I ended it. All of a sudden, he seemed to care about me. Or rather, that he didn't have free access to me. He even broke into my house a couple of times."

"More than a couple," Trouble adds. "Sometimes, you didn't wake up."

"Shit." I rub my face, and I feel the burn behind my eyes. But I don't want to cry over Rob—and definitely not in front of Calder.

"What did he do when he broke in?" Calder growls.

I'm surprised by how protective he sounds. "The times I woke up, he demanded I take him back. He would try to… kiss me. I had never been sexually attracted to him and definitely didn't want him touching me after we broke up. When he realized forcing himself on me wasn't going to work, he… hit me. I stumbled into the kitchen and pulled a knife on him, and I was able to call the cops. Then I bought a gun. That stopped him from coming back… or so I thought."

Both Calder and I look at Trouble.

He shakes his head. "Rob came over a few times after that and incanted his spell while you were sleeping, and he asked spirits to talk through you."

I curse and feel hot tears rolling down my cheeks.

Calder's voice is soft as he asks Trouble, "Then what happened?"

"Rob would ask questions about names and places and then he would leave," Trouble says.

"Just using me. That's all I ever was to him—a tool."

Suddenly, Calder is on his knees in front of me and pulls me into a hug.

Startled, I don't know what to make of this new version of the phoenix who is willing to comfort me. For a moment, I'm stiff, but then I give in to the affection and rest my head on his shoulder and wrap my arms around his torso.

"You are not just a tool. Don't allow Rob to make you feel small," he whispers over my hair.

I don't know what to say to that. Calder has hated me since before I was probably born.

"But I'm a witch… and I don't even know the first thing about being one." I suck in my tears and add, "I don't even have my magic."

Calder breathes in deeply and then pulls back to look me in the eye. "Your magic is coming in now. I suspect you will be at full power soon."

"I will?" I glance down at my hands and wonder how magic works in reality. I need a change of subject. "Does magic get depleted when a magical person uses it? And if it does, does it have to be refilled like recharging batteries?"

"If you use too much at once, you can become drained. Some beings drain faster than others, depending on the magic they have and how much control they have over it. And some take a long time to draw the energy, depending on what their source is."

"Oh, you mean like how Osen draws from sexual energy?"

Sadness flashes over Calder's face. He glances at where his hands still rest on my knees. He appears a bit bewildered by his actions.

"I didn't mean to upset you," I say. "Oh, and I should tell you I thought I felt him. But his energy must be low after Rob's attack. I'd give him what he needs to regain his strength, but I don't know how to do that. Before, he just showed up and you know… did stuff… in the shadowscape."

"You really didn't mind being intimate with him?" Calder removes his touch, sits back on his heels, and studies me.

I pick at my fingers for a moment. I don't know what to say. He was in love with Osen, and it feels like I'm the other woman.

"Hey?" Calder places his hand back on my knee. "We weren't exclusive, even when he was alive. It's okay if you enjoyed being with him. But if you didn't want it, I'd like to know that too. I would be angry if he forced himself on you."

"Even if I'm a witch?" I ask. I can't believe he's being so kind to me. It's like a switch has been flipped. When I think about it, it's often the tough guys who are so damned sensitive that they put up walls upon walls.

Maybe he cares too deeply and can't afford to allow anyone inside.

"I can't keep blaming all witches for what a few have done to my pack and me. I can see it in your eyes. You could never be that cruel."

I'm stunned by his words, and I feel a weight being lifted that I didn't realize I was carrying. As if I was taking on all the sins of my kind and now I'm able to drop that to only carry my own sins.

"Did he force you to do anything you didn't want to do?" Calder asks again.

"Not sexually. I enjoyed that part. But he coerced me to go to the alleyway. He said he would take my body from me and go anyway if I didn't."

Calder breathes out. "He's a stubborn asshole, isn't he?"

"From what I've experienced, yeah." I bite my lip.

Will he ask about what I've seen in Osen's thoughts?

Just with that worry, my mind flashes back to the scene in the hotel. I remember myself as Osen, with an aching, hard erection. I can actually feel the sensation of sliding into Calder's tight ass. My skin heats, and my clit perks up, wondering if she's going to get some play time.

He cocks a brow, reading me like a neon sign. "You saw me in his memories, didn't you?"

"Uh, yeah. A little." I hurry to explain, "But I didn't mean to see *that*. I just sort of fell into the memories. At the time, I didn't think they were real. I thought they were fantasies."

"And seeing two men together is a fantasy for you?"

"I mean, it's not like an obsession or anything. But two beautiful men, expressing their desire, what's not to like?"

"Do you put yourself in the middle of these men you fantasize about?"

"Well, not always, because it isn't even about that. And sure, sometimes, I imagine being included. I suppose I write romance because I haven't had much love in my life. I haven't had the epic story where someone falls for me so hard that they would do anything for me."

"Except now you have," he says poignantly.

"Maybe," I whisper.

"Maybe?"

I sigh. I might as well tell Calder, as he will confirm my concern. Then I can deal with the painful truth. "I'm going to let you in on something I'm worried about. My theory is that Arran and Maxum are attracted to Osen's energy inside me. Their affection is not really about me, per se."

Calder stares at me for a long minute. Perhaps he's wondering what I've done to encourage their affections. Or he senses that I'm correct. "Sorry. Nope. Maxum and Arran were never gaga over Osen the way they are with you. Flint is definitely into you all on his own. And I haven't sensed Osen's energy radiating out of you in a way that would attract them to you."

"But guys rarely want me... not like how deeply they are hinting at."

"You have a magnetism all your own. It just needed the right people to attract."

"How can you say that? It isn't like you know what's going on with the other guys. It's not like you feel an attraction for me."

Calder drops his gaze, and he tenses. "Even when I was against having you around, I thought you were... attractive."

"Is that why you hated me even more?"

"Hate is a strong word."

"Repulsed? Sickened?" I offer.

Calder chuckles, shakes his head, and makes eye contact again. "Let's go with irritated."

"Okay. I know I can be irritating. It's what my ex-boyfriends call me."

"Witch, you had some terrible taste in males."

"Apparently. Let's see if supernatural guys are any better."

20

TRAINING

JADE

*a*fter Calder instructs me to stand in the middle of his room, he tells me to close my eyes. "Imagine your aura has a bubble around it. Then another one around your body, then another layer around your mind."

I crack open my eyes and look at him, "You sure this is how I shield myself? Imagining bubbles?"

Calder gives me a long-suffering sigh. "Magic is all about intention. I thought you would know this from all your supernatural books you supposedly write."

"I do write those books, but I guess I thought it was all made up bullshit."

"How do you think things get made up? From what is real… or the other way around. You get my point. Form follows thought and thought follows form."

"So the whole 'as above, so below' theory?"

"Exactly." He nods at me. "Now, close your eyes and focus."

I do as he says, because it's hard to focus when I'm barraged by his handsomeness. I hate to say I'm flustered by the intense presence of this hot guy, but yeah… I am.

"Envision those bubbles. Make them as solid and as real in your mind as you can. Imagine that your enemy cannot get beyond your boundaries, no matter how hard they try."

I focus on creating these bubble boundaries, and finally, they feel like they have solidified.

"Good," he praises. "Now hold on to that feeling, no matter what you feel."

I smile at his approval. Then I feel energy moving closer, pushing on my boundaries. I push back with my mind.

"Boo," he whispers.

I jump. My eyes pop open at the sound of Calder so close to me. When I see he's in my space, less than a foot away from my face, I yelp, "What are you doing?"

"Testing you." He smirks.

I sort of want to test him by leaning in a few inches and pressing my lips to his to see what he might do. But I'm being a good girl today. Or trying my fucking best to be. No promises.

I don't pull back or cower. I lean in ever so slightly. His ice-blue eyes widen just a fraction.

"So you testing me includes getting this close?" I glance down at his full, lush lips to make him nervous.

He swallows, fully realizing his mistake. I can almost hear his mind shouting, "Abort mission!"

"I, uh, yes, I have to test you with distractions," he says, regaining a bit of his composure.

"Rub her ears!" Sage suggests. "And she might lick you!"

Calder turns bright pink. Whoops. He's lost the upper hand again.

I have to hold back my laughter. I'm sure Sage doesn't realize how sexual that sounds... right? Oh, my goodness, she *is* a bunny. Maybe she does mean it sexually.

I lock eyes with the phoenix and tuck my hair behind my ear as a not-so-subtle taunt. "Well?" I hint about my petting.

"Well... what?" He pulls back an inch and glances at my ear.

"Did I keep my mind bubble in place, or did your distraction work?" I ask in an innocent voice.

"Oh." He concentrates briefly. He's lost the thread about why he is so close to me. Hmm. Interesting... maybe he's more attracted to me than I originally thought. "Yeah, you were able to keep your shields up. Very good."

"So what do I get as a reward?" I tilt my head, dragging my gaze down his body to egg on his frustration and ire.

"Reward?" he echoes.

I swear he's more of a parrot than a phoenix at the moment.

"My treat. For being a good girl?"

Calder narrows his eyes, finally seeing my suggestive talk for the teasing it is. "Hmm." He steps closer, looking every bit the menacing grump he can be.

I instinctively step back. The back of my legs hit the desk behind me.

He presses closer, his body aligning with mine. He leans over, and I arch backward. His hands land on the desk. His huge arms bracket me in, pinning me in place. "Is this you being good? Because it feels like you are being naughty."

"I suppose it depends on your definition?" My eyes flicker up to meet his flaming blue gaze, noting his teeth are now biting his full lower lip.

"I suppose it depends on the context," he replies. "What do you feel you deserve for a treat?"

Okay. Tables have officially been turned.

I'm flustered, and my pussy is throbbing with his body pressed against mine. I swallow down my nervous sexual energy. I must regain my senses, or he won't let me live this down.

He leans in farther, his lips about to graze mine. "What would you like me to rub?"

Be strong. So many retorts pass through my mind. I want to tell him I'd like to watch him rub his own cock, but he is just waiting for me to break like this.

I hold my shields strong, or so I hope.

What does he wish to gain from this suggestive scenario?

Does he want to prove I'm a weak-willed slut? Or that he has the power to distract me? Or is he attracted to me too?

Or is he really just trying to test my mental fortitude and figures this is the best way to test me? Because he isn't wrong.

The only other thing he could do that might distract me more is to physically attack me.

I focus on his mind. If I'm coming into my magic, would I be able to read his mind? Is he so focused on my walls that he might fail to reinforce his own?

Without knowing the first thing about what I'm doing, I go with my intuition and reach out with my intention, much like Osen did the night he took over my body in the alleyway.

My energy tickles over his temples. I pick up the vague impression that I intrigue Calder.

As I scramble to probe deeper to understand what he wants, Calder straightens and pulls away.

"Was that you?" he asks, touching his forehead nervously.

"Maybe?" I grimace, a bit concerned he might not have liked that. Will my spur-of-the-moment action fuel his distrust of me?

"How did you do that?" he asks.

"I don't know how I did it. I just wanted to mess with you a bit for trying to antagonize me." Shuffling sideways, I move closer to the door. I might need a quick getaway.

His eyes narrow. "What did you see?"

"Nothing much. It felt like I intrigued you... like you were probably wondering when I was going to break." I offer as a way for him to save face. I'm sure he doesn't want to admit he might be interested. And I want to keep this newfound peace.

"Intrigued?" He saunters back into my space, now pressing me against the door. "Yes, I'm intrigued by you."

"Oh?" Behind my back, I place my hand on the door handle.

"You should know I have a ward over the door. It will zap you if you try to leave."

"Are you trapping me here?" I ask, trying to keep the nervousness out of my voice.

"Your lesson isn't over."

"It isn't?" I gaze up into his intense eyes and wonder what he has planned for me. "What else is there?"

"Protection—what to do if someone gets beyond your shields."

"What do I do?"

"Try reading me again," he dares.

Dammit. I'm not going to let him intimidate me.

My mental intention pushes out again, quicker this time, but I try to keep my own walls up.

In his mind, I see flashes of me—having rough sex with Maxum, Arran, and Osen.

Oh wow. These are all fantasies he's had of me.

A shock like a burning live wire hits me right between the eyes—Calder's defensive measure.

My body slams against the door, and I shout, "Fuck!"

Then I'm thrown forward into Calder. We tumble to the floor. I barely have the wits to pick myself up off Calder's body. The phoenix looks as stunned as I do about our new position.

"Jade!" Flint rushes inside the room and cries out when a magical veil lights up in the doorway as he enters. The big guy looks frantic, as if he might pick me up by the waist. But he quickly changes tactics and holds out a single hand to me.

As I reach out to take Flint's hand for support, I inadvertently straddle Calder. I find he's packing some heat from our recent smoldering exchange.

Can this moment get any more awkward?

"What are you doing?" Calder growls at Flint.

"You hurt Jade!" Impatient with how fast I'm removing myself from Calder, Flint easily lifts me off the phoenix and sets me behind him.

Still surprised by his ability to touch me and how he didn't seem to be affected at all, I stand stunned while the two argue.

"I was training her." Calder scrambles up to his feet and glares up at the taller gargoyle.

"She cried out." Flint takes a menacing step toward Calder.

"Hey, Flint." I step to the side to get both of their attention. "I'm okay. He was training me."

He doesn't look at me. Instead, he glares at the phoenix. "What. Did. You. Do?"

"I zapped her senses when she tried to enter my mind. It's not damaging. She needs to know what's possible so she can protect herself."

"You did it so you could inflict pain," Flint snarls.

Wow. This protective side of Flint is turning me on.

Calder dares to look away from Flint. He asks me, sounding put out, "Are you alright?"

"I think so. It stung, but I suppose I learned my lesson not to go poking around in your mind." I mutter, "I won't do that again."

"See, it's fine," Calder says to Flint, taking a step back. "I get you are protective of… innocents, but Jade needs to learn how to shield herself. She also had an early lesson in someone defending their shields. Not all of us have your innate ability."

"You have an innate ability?" I ask, hoping to steer this confrontation into a more friendly chat.

"My mind is sealed off from others." The big guy turns and his pale gray eyes gaze into mine. "Except for the one who I would have a bond with."

"Like a bonded mate? Or could it be one of your pack?"

"With a mate match." He frowns slightly and heads to the door. "Come, both of you. Time to eat. We need to keep your strength up."

I look at Calder with an *are you okay* expression.

He shrugs it off and gestures for me to go first.

"Don't forget my treats!" Trouble shouts at us as Calder attempts to shut his broken door.

"If you stay in here and behave, I'll bring you something extra good," Calder bargains.

"Fine," Trouble grumbles.

When Calder turns to follow me down the stairs, I'm standing there watching him with adoration. "Thank you," I say softly.

"For what?"

"For taking such good care of them."

He sighs wearily and walks toward me and herds me toward the stairs. "But I messed up too. I shouldn't have been so obsessed with your guilt or innocence and been more attentive to what was right under my nose. It's understandable for you not to know about Floofer, since you didn't know about magic. But there's no excuse for me. I was just blinded by my pain and anger."

"You had just lost Osen, then I showed up. It's totally understandable why you didn't like me. And I was a witch on top of it. I don't even like witches now."

As we join him in the kitchen, Flint watches me as he readies the plates for us to eat. "You don't have to dislike your own kind. Maxum's old acquaintance, Amira, was a testament to a witch doing good. She didn't have to come to help you and Calder."

"I wish I would have been awake to talk to her phoenix mate," Calder says with sorrow in his voice.

"You don't get to meet many of your kind?" I ask.

"No, we are a *dying* species—pun intended." He states it so plainly, I have to take a moment to get beyond my sadness for his kind.

I cover my mouth when I realize the double meaning. "Please don't. Wordplay is foreplay to me."

Calder chuckles and shakes his head. "Be good, witch."

When I look at Flint, his mouth is hanging open slightly, confused by our light flirting.

I get back on track. "So you don't know another phoenix?"

"No." Calder dishes out some fruit and cheese and sits down.

It sounds like that is a loaded subject, so I let it drop. "You didn't get any bad vibes from Amira?" I ask Flint.

"No. She wasn't particularly fond of other witches. However, she was still open to helping you. We may have to take her up on that offer at some point, even if it's just to find another witch to help you with your magic. Maxum's knowledge is limited, and I have a feeling if you are going to remain in our company that you will need to learn to properly control your magic and defend yourself."

With a fork, I poke at the food Flint hands me. "I'm so far behind in my abilities. If I didn't have that pendant draining me, I might have been alerted to my witchiness before now, instead of just thinking I had strange dreams."

"Speaking of the pendant," Calder says. "Trouble says he saw the spirits pulled through it and into you."

"What does that mean? Am I really a medium then?"

"Yes, you couldn't do that if it weren't your affinity," Flint assures me. "But I think it could have been used as a focal, a beacon, if you will."

"Is that why I can't bring Osen back? Do I need to go back and get the necklace to channel him into me?"

"No," both Calder and Flint bark.

"Okay! I'm just brainstorming here."

"I believe you have the natural affinity of mediumship, but just like anyone with an inclination toward a talent, you must practice it," Calder explains. "Like someone might be a natural at music, but that doesn't mean that person can sit down at a piano for the first time and play Beethoven. You have to learn how to use your natural gift. At least the basics."

"Okay. That makes sense. But how do I learn? Do any of you know how to channel spirits?"

"That's a human witch thing." Calder frowns and leans back in his chair. "Fae-born mages don't work with souls or spirits. The closest thing would be someone like Osen."

I grouch, "But he's the one we can't talk to. Is there someone else? Maybe Amira knows of a trustworthy witch with the ability?"

"I don't know. Maybe Amira herself knows enough about the basics to get us started," Calder ponders. "When Maxum returns tonight, we will ask him."

I nod, but when he says this I am hit with a bad feeling. Will Maxum be returning?

21

INFORMANTS

ARRAN

*M*y wolf and berserker do not enjoy leaving our mate behind. Neither do I. They are snarling and growling inside of me. It feels as though their claws are shredding my insides, but I know it's the separation causing it. Perhaps the anguish wouldn't be so overwhelming if we were properly bonded, and she wasn't in danger.

I'm actually surprised that Maxum would leave Jade with only Calder and Flint to protect her.

He must feel that getting this information is more important. I remind myself that this little field trip of his is only meant to last the day. Hopefully, the hamster spy doesn't take this moment to attack. However, I'm soothed by the idea that Floofer hasn't attacked Jade, even with multiple opportunities over the years with her, and at both the safe and lake houses.

The odds Floofer would go after her now are slim to none. Calder and Flint are not to be trifled with and are a deterrent all on their own. And Jade... well, she's a wild card. With her magic coming in, she might be a formidable force. Without training to control her new magic, she could be unpredictable and deadly if threatened.

As we portal to our hometown, we walk down the sidewalk through a quiet part of the industrial area. I've never met his hacker friends, but I know Maxum trusts them more than most. High praise for humans.

"I was thinking—" I begin.

Maxum cuts me off. "That's a dangerous thing."

"*Ha ha*," I grumble. "I'd expect you'd like me to be more thoughtful instead of just reacting."

"Just messing with you." Maxum pats me on the shoulder. "I suppose I'm anxious about leaving Jade behind. I want her by our side at all times."

"I know what you mean." After taking a moment to get my beasts under control, I say, "I was wondering why Floofer would take off now. He could have stayed hidden under our noses, but he didn't."

"Yeah, you're right. We have been so preoccupied with Jade, he could have stayed where he was. Even Calder was mostly oblivious to anything wrong." He comes to a stop and turns to me. "So, what do you think made him run now?"

"Maybe he wanted to get away from Jade *because* she is coming into her power. What if he knows what sort of magic the pendant was blocking? What if he's afraid?"

"Could be that." Maxum nods. "It could also be that someone out there, who Floofer answers to, would want to know Jade's pendant is gone."

We stare at each other for a moment, wondering what power our witch holds in her luscious body. Then Maxum huffs and returns to his long strides toward what looks to be an abandoned building.

He knocks on a large metal door. A minute later, I hear light footsteps down a metal staircase.

The door swings open, and a petite human woman stands with her hands on her hips, looking fierce and a bit miffed. She has the side of her head shaved and the rest of her straight shoulder-length hair has been dyed a rainbow of colors.

"Mal, still losing fart fights with a unicorn, I see," Maxum jokes, pointing to her unusual hair.

She cocks a pierced brow at him, breaks the stern glare, and snorts out a laugh. "Yep. Maybe if you taught me some of your *Elven* fighting moves, I'd have a chance."

"Wrong again." He chuckles, then explains to me, "She's trying to guess what sort of supe I am. She's not particularly good at this game of hers."

I'm amused that she hasn't figured out he's a demon. I thought his obsidian black eyes and the red tattoos that sometimes peek out of his shirt at his neck and wrists would be a blatant clue.

"Bet I can guess this guy's deal," Mal challenges, eyeing me.

"Are we actually wagering?" Maxum asks. "If so… when you lose, I get to pick your next hairstyle."

"I don't think it's worth it." Mal smirks. "Unless I get to pick out yours."

"Deal." Maxum waves his hand over at me. "Make your guess."

I'm about to bust up that this woman has made a deal with a devil.

Mal steps closer and studies my eyes. Likely, she is wondering what my amber-colored eyes could mean.

My appearance is similar to most wolf shifters—tall, muscular, dark hair, unusually pale blue or golden brown eyes, with warm-toned skin. While I'm not considered particularly beautiful in the supernatural world, I am appealing to humans. However, the only human's attraction that has ever mattered is Jade's.

She might guess just from my standard looks, but who knows how many interactions this woman has with the supernatural world and all their species and halflings.

"A demon," she guesses with a shrug.

Maxum looks downright offended, and I burst out into laughter.

"Dammit," Mal hisses and waves us inside. As she locks the door behind us and asks, "So how bad is my new hairstyle going to be?"

"Mohawk, so shave the other side, but keep the length and color. I want to see it straight up and in stiff spikes."

"Well, I planned on shaving the other side, anyway." Mal chuckles and climbs the stairs ahead of us.

Maxum gives me a wink behind her back. He knew she planned on doing that. "Hmm, maybe I'll change my mind. Shave it all off? But carve 'I lost' into the stubble?"

"Hilarious." Then she stops and spins to look at him, almost eye to eye, even though she is a few steps higher. "You wouldn't make me do that, would you?"

Maxum shrugs. "I get bored."

The door opens up to a stereotypical warehouse apartment. It's spacious and sparsely decorated. There's a living room area and a huge computer station outpost. I don't know that much about computer technology, but I know enough to get by. There are stacks of hard drives and laptops. A wall of screens tower over a massively long desk. Half of the screens are turned off, but I see a few are displaying the security feed from around the building.

The others have Rob's face and what looks like files on him.

After a nod, Maxum greets his other friend, "Dwayne, hope you are well." He then ushers me over to the couches far from the computers. We sit down and make ourselves comfortable.

"Yeah," Dwayne says. "We purchased some mage spells for protection with your donation. Thanks. Seems like it wasn't a terrible investment, considering the community center bombing and the attack at the fae portal."

Both Maxum and I sit straight up and perch on the edge of our seats.

"I knew about the bombing. We helped clean up the mess." Maxum's hands grip his knees, and I'm afraid he's going to crush his own bones. "Do they know who attacked the portal?"

"From what we hear, no witnesses." Mal answers, "The two fae guards stationed there were killed."

"Any leads?" I ask.

"None that we have heard about." Dwayne frowns and pulls up a report. "It happened only a few hours after the bombing. Maybe some random asshole was taking advantage of the distraction."

Maxum and I lock eyes, both wondering if someone was chasing us.

What if the assailants were able to track us somehow? Is Jade in more danger than we realized?

"Or it wasn't connected at all." Maxum stands up and paces in front of me. "We'll circle back to this. Dwayne, I see you have Robert Holden on your screens. Anything become of your search?"

"Yes. But I doubt you'll like any of it." Dwayne clicks and clacks on his keyboards. "Robert Holden is an alias, as we suspected before. From his photo, I was able to determine his real name is Robert, but Robert Blackwell."

"Blackwell. As in the infamous witching family?" Maxum stops pacing and rubs his chin.

"He's not one of the favored lines, but yeah. But he seems to be the family grunt worker. He gets the jobs no one wants from what our sources confirm."

"Did you tell anyone why you were asking after him?" I demand.

"Of course not," Mal snaps. "We are professionals."

"Sorry." Sighing, I pinch the bridge of my nose. "I'm just stressed." I look down and see my claws are out. Running my tongue over my canines, I can feel that I'm on the verge of a shift, but I realize, this time, it didn't hit me the same. Usually, it feels like a wall of painful twisting when my berserker is ready to burst from my skin. Perhaps my slow acceptance of him is helping me ease the shift.

I'm not sure if not noticing a shift is a good thing. I will have to be more aware of myself than before.

"You okay?" Maxum stands in front of me, blocking Dwayne's and Mal's view.

"Yeah. Just the thought of Rob is enough to rile me." I watch as my claws retract and I take a deep breath.

Maxum turns and continues with the reports. "What else did you dig up?"

"He is not all that popular from what we could suss out. He's had a few known acquaintances over the years. Mainly it has been Galiana Collins, an older witch and coven leader and from what we figured out, an activist for witch superiority. I'm sure you already suspect her to be one of ASO's top members. Likely one of their leaders."

Galiana looks much like I remember from when I've spied on her before. She appears to be around forty, but is truly closer to ninety. About the same height as Jade, slimmer build, and only a few streaks of gray to show any signs of her age. She isn't ugly, but she's definitely not my type because of the truly evil glint in her eye. She reminds me too much of Talin, the witch I killed to earn my curse. I heard once they were distantly related, fifth cousins or something. If they were related, I must be more careful around her. Witches are usually protective about 'family' no matter how distant. I didn't see all the faces of the witches who had cursed me, but I wouldn't be surprised if Galiana was one of them.

Maxum grunts a response about Galiana being Rob's associate. "Yeah. One of my people saw her with Rob recently. Who else?"

"A warlock reported having a rare transmogrification affinity, named Sloan Winter." He pulls up a picture of an unassuming guy with mousy brown hair and pale skin. "But he hasn't been seen much the last couple of years. So I don't know much about him or if he's still in contact with Rob."

Maxum gives me a quick, knowing glance. *Floofer.*

"And who is that?" I point to the last image on the screens. It's a woman who looks more than a bit like Jade.

"Jadeana Jones." I don't know much about her. "Rob was seen with her on a few occasions."

"Jadeana Jones?" I repeat softly, still fixated on my mate's face on the computer screen. That isn't her author pseudonym or the name on her driver's license.

"Anything you can tell us about her?" Maxum asks, his tone devoid of emotion.

"You know witches are secretive as fuck. Fortunately, we know a few who aren't particularly happy about the never-ending war between supes and human-born magicals. From what we were told, Rob's been a person of interest for a while. So they knew about his dealings. They had looked into his mistress, but couldn't find much on her. What we do know is Jadeana is sixty years old from a driver's license I finally found when she lived in another state. Records now show she lives in town at 42 Brighton Road. No record of employment. Couldn't find much else on her, actually. It's like someone put a spell on all her records so they would disappear or get mixed up. I've seen results like this before—usually it's a supe or a witch hiding their identities. But other than Rob, I couldn't find any connection to the magical world."

42 Brighton Road? That's Jade's place. It must be her.

"Any more about Jadeana?" I ask.

"Sorry. I didn't know I needed to dig too deep into her. She didn't seem to be of any consequence." Dwayne types on his computer and begins a search. He sits back in his swiveling office chair and spins to look at us. "Patricia is the mother's name on what appears to be her birth certificate. A father wasn't listed. I don't see any other record of the mother, Patricia—not even a death certificate. That's odd by itself." He narrows his eyes at the screen. "The year on Jadeana's birth certificate is also smudged on the form. Like I said, weird."

Maxum and I walk out of the hackers' building in a bit of a daze. Once clear of the building, we both glance around to see if there is anyone in the area.

I say, "What do you—"

Maxum cuts me off. "Not here. Too many eyes and ears in this realm."

We duck into a dark alcove of a building, and he opens a portal to Elfhame. After he shuts out Earth behind us, he does a quick mental scan of the area for active minds and I give the air a sniff.

Once satisfied we are alone in the meadow, Maxum begins in a hushed voice, "We know nothing yet. So we must keep our worries about Jade's truthfulness to a minimum."

"I can't believe she would lie to us like that."

Maxum growls. "I never picked up that level of deceit."

"What if Rob did more to her mind than we realized? What if he tricked her into believing a false persona?" I ask, my voice rising with the fear my mate has been twisted so thoroughly she doesn't even know who she is.

Maxum sighs. "Fuck, I hope not. But there is another, more feasible possibility."

"What's that?"

"The information they found about Jadeana is wrong."

I blow out a huff of air, feeling a bit of relief just from the thought. "You're right. Most of what Dwayne said was rumors, and he noted how records were missing. Her grandmother may have put a spell on them."

"We must wait to freak out until we get Jade's version of the facts," Maxum says, then grinds his teeth. "But if she wasn't honest about her age, then what else did she lie about?"

I don't want to believe she lied to me. Because her being my mate match *isn't* a lie. I feel that in my bones. But if I'm matched to a liar, I don't know what I'll do. I've fallen for her. My wolf and berserker have already bonded to her.

No matter the truth or the reasons—we don't want to lose the one person who has made us feel whole again.

I suspect Maxum feels similarly.

He's right. Until we talk to Jade, we can't dwell on this information. There must be an explanation. Hopefully, a simple one.

22

TESTED

FLINT

*J*ade has cracked my mantle, and I'm experiencing a tectonic shift.

I don't think I've ever felt this way. My usually cold insides are churning lava. I feel like a volcano about to erupt. Parts of my body I believed to be long defunct are now awakening. My crotch aches from only listening to Jade's voice.

Closely, I watch her eating the meal that I made her. I observe, as she builds a foundation for a relationship with Calder. I'm not jealous. Not that I ever expected to be a jealous male. Her worry lines around her eyes are easing with his acceptance of her being in our lives, and they are beginning to talk to each other.

I overreacted when I heard her cry out when I was in the hallway, listening in on them. I didn't mean to spy, but I worried that Calder's hostility toward witches would cause him to take it out on Jade. And I will not stand for that behavior anymore. His pain allowed him some leeway, but he can't keep spitting his angry fire at others.

"Flint?" Jade looks at me as if she had been calling me more than once and perhaps she did. "You okay?"

"Just thinking." I smile, hoping I'm doing it right. I'm so out of practice with human expressions and nuances.

"Do you feel like sharing?" she asks gently.

"I shouldn't have interrupted your lesson. I just don't enjoy hearing you being hurt."

"Uh, yeah, Jade..." Calder appears shy and unsure of himself. "I could have warned you, and I feel badly that I didn't."

"I appreciate the sentiment, but you both can stop treating me with kid gloves. I need to know all of this, and I'm sure there will be a few bumps and bruises as I learn about my powers. I'm a grown-ass woman, and I'll let you know when I've had too much."

"I wasn't trying to make you feel less than the powerful witch you surely will become," I hurry to apologize. "I just... I feel protective of you. If that makes you uncomfortable, I will stay away."

Jade grabs my hand, and I freeze... At least, my hand is unmovable stone. Apparently, I'm not completely beyond my psychological block.

Her eyes widen, and then an almost imperceptible frown pulls at her beautiful lips. "I don't want you to go anywhere. I like that you are protective of me, but I'm asking for you to realize I might get hurt as I learn."

"I don't like it."

Jade strokes my hand. "I know, my giant sweetie."

She returns to finishing her meal, and Calder and I do the same.

He gives me a helpless grin when Jade isn't looking, and I return it. She has cracked open his chest too. Soon, she will have all our hearts at her mercy.

"What's next in my training?" Jade asks, then smirks. "Or are you just planning to zap my brain over and over?"

"Your magic seems to be coming in," I say. "You may want to meditate and become familiar with how it feels inside you."

"It feels a bit like I'm high on sugar or adrenaline. Or I shocked myself with an electrical outlet. My whole body sort of feels like it's buzzing." Jade holds out her hands and stares at them. "Is that how your magic feels?"

"We don't have a lot of active magic like you will have," Calder explains. "I have some magical ability, but it has mostly to do with mental shields, my rebirth process, sensing impending death, and... nevermind." His cheeks turn pink, and he picks at his food.

Jade glances over at me. She's curious, but doesn't push the obviously flustered phoenix. I believe I know what he avoided mentioning, and I don't blame him for omitting it. However, I find it interesting that he came so close to disclosing his intimate secret.

I divert attention to myself. "As you witnessed the other day, I can camouflage my presence, essentially becoming invisible."

"Hold up. Did you ever do that inside my house? I had felt like someone was watching me. But I suppose that feeling could have been from Floofer..."

"I didn't watch you from inside your house. But I stood guard outside of your home the day Rob came by and almost killed you." I remember the first time she truly caught my interest. "You kept looking in my direction when you would peek out of the window. I thought you might have been able to see me."

"I felt you. Were you over on the side of the blue house with the pink oleander bush?"

"I was." Though my delight quickly falters as I remember the rest of what happened. "I wasn't able to protect you. I believed you had let Rob in on your own volition. I should have known better."

"From what you told me, Osen let Rob into my house without a fight. Besides, you didn't know me then. You barely do now, so I don't blame you."

I don't like the reminder that I barely know Jade. I believe I know the most important part—how she makes me feel. She is also caring, forgiving, smart, funny, and thoughtful. There's no doubt in me she is a good person.

Now that I'm coming to know her, I see how beautiful she is on the outside, but her inner beauty is what's awakened my attraction.

I must finally show her my true gargoyle form so I will know if she can endure to even hold my hand again. I dare not hope for her to ever kiss me or to mate.

If all she wishes to give me is an occasional hug. I will have to be okay with her decision. I don't believe I can live without her in my life in some way —however that may be. Her comfort and happiness comes before all else. Even before my makeshift pack, but I feel in my bones she *is* my pack, so fortunately, there is no conflict.

Perhaps with her human sensibilities, she might never understand the depth at which I will love and adore her. I have perceived that she doesn't quite comprehend how deeply Maxum and Arran feel already. Their feelings and commitment to her will only solidify and grow.

"May I ask what else you can do?" Jade eyes me. "You mentioned sensing the danger of an innocent. And I know you can turn to stone. But can you explain how that is possible?"

My heart dances in my chest that she is interested in what I am. "Our people are said to have first come from huge magical stones. Fae mages found us over a thousand years ago and carved our forms from the blocks. They claimed they could sense there were souls ready to be born from the earth. They just removed the excess material to reveal who we were. The first of us were even larger than I am, and the elves taught the first of us to come alive, to move and then to fight and protect. They taught us to shape our magic, and we were able to mimic the softness of humanoid flesh. Over time, we became more Elven-like in our natures. Or what you might say... we became more humanlike. We began to eat food and have emotions. It was then that our own people began carving the rest of us into existence. I am one of the last born from the living stones, made by my own people."

"Holy shit," Jade says, her mouth hanging open. "You were really made from stone? You are like... walking, talking magic." Her pretty hazel-green eyes twinkle again. I want to understand what that means, but I don't think she knows she is doing it or what it could mean.

I grin at her awe. I really expected her to be turned off by my origins, but she surprises me at every turn.

"My origins aren't that extraordinary. Technically, we all come from the earth." I downplay my uniqueness. I don't want to be so different that she might not see a future with me.

"No. Don't dismiss how cool you are." Jade leans back and smiles widely. "I mean, yeah, humans being born out of a woman's body is the miracle of life. Blah, blah, blah. Or being hatched from an egg is amazing too. All great stuff. But to be brought into consciousness from being carved out of stone and given a form? Whoa. My mind is blown."

I tuck my head down and hide my huge smile. She sees me as special, not odd. But what did I expect from such a loving woman? Why did I fear she would shun me?

My fears have controlled how I live. No more.

"Hey," Jade calls me softly. When I look up and make eye contact, she says, "Please, don't hide your smiles from me. They make my heart glow."

"They do?" I ask, surprised she could see such a thing.

"It's a metaphor, but it makes my heart feel warm and joyful to see you happy."

I nod, then glance over at Calder, but he isn't looking at me. No. His sights are locked on Jade. His face is soft, and he appears to be longing for what this wonderful woman has given me... acceptance. I suppose I should show her my true form soon. I have to know how to proceed with her. Because I am falling hard and fast, and I don't want to hope for something that will never be.

After a long silence while we finish our plates of food, Jade finally breaks the quiet. "A thought occurred to me... before the guys left, I was able to sense Arran and Maxum outside my office door. Do you think I could sense others?"

Both Calder and I ask at the same time, "You didn't feel me?"

Jade nervously takes a sip of water before she answers. "I hope I didn't just make a supernaturally sized faux pas." Her gaze snaps to Calder, since he would be the most likely to throw a fit for her spying on us.

"No," Calder says. "Your magic is coming in and you have no control. Although, I'm surprised by your natural ability to wield it. Typically, you would have learned how to manage your magic as it developed over time and fully bloomed at adulthood. Spying on people is definitely frowned upon. However, getting a vague impression of where someone is located is done often and as long as it isn't more invasive, then it's acceptable."

Jade lets out a breath in relief. "Flint, I had a vague impression of you in your room. But Calder, I didn't pick up your energy."

Calder seems oddly tense that Jade didn't sense him. He is so confusing. Maybe he wants the witch after all. I offer an explanation. "If I were to guess, it's because you have deeper connections with Maxum and Arran. You and I had just had an emotional conversation, so we had bonded on some level. But until your training with Calder, you both hadn't talked or been around each other much."

"True." Jade gazes out the window toward the lake. "I was around Floofer for a couple of years. Do you think I could pick up on Floofer's location? Should I even try?"

"He might not sense you reaching for him." Calder scratches his chin and frowns. "I don't want you risking yourself reaching out. However, you seem to have a natural talent for that and maybe if you can track him down, we can capture him."

My protectiveness rises within me. "I don't relish the idea of calling on the unknown with only the two of us to protect Jade."

"He's out there, so he could attack any second. I'd rather be proactive." Calder huffs. "We don't even know if she can do it."

"I think it's worth the risk," Jade says. "Calder's right. He could be lurking right now, ready to strike when we go to sleep."

Goddess, give me strength.

"Then I won't sleep." I stand abruptly and snatch up our empty plates.

Jade flinches ever so slightly, but I notice. What have I done? I'm proving that I'm the monster I fear I am.

I drop to my knees and the plates fall to the floor. "Forgive me. I didn't mean to scare you."

Her soft hand cups my chin, and I completely turn to solid stone. When I freeze, regressing in my progress, tears roll down her cheeks.

"Oh, sweetheart." She keeps her hand on my skin, and her warmth seeps into me. I am greedy about absorbing anything and everything she will bless me with. I would lick up her tears for an eternity until she was finally happy again.

"I wasn't scared of you," she explains. "I have had a lot of unpleasant experiences, and I suppose my body just reacts to certain stimuli. We aren't much different that way. My triggers are someone's frustration combined with movements toward me. It's okay. We're okay." She drops her hand, likely hoping I will return to my 'fluid' state.

It works, and when I can move again, I miss her touch desperately. In a fit of emotion, I stand, pull her to my chest, and hug her.

Since I'm so tall, her feet are dangling.

"May I hug you with my legs?" she asks. Her cheeks bloom with color.

"Yes," I whisper.

"Flint," Calder says. "I'll clean up here. Why don't you go spend some quiet time with Jade... If you are cool with that, Jade?"

She doesn't break eye contact with me. "Yes. I would like that, if you want to, Flint."

23

REVEALED

JADE

*M*y sweet, sweet gargoyle.

I do not know how to help him heal except to show him support and understanding whenever and however I can.

Flint nods. "Yes. Calder, thank you for cleaning up."

"No problem." Calder waves us away. "Now go before I change my mind."

I'm not sure where this new and improved version of Calder came from, but I like him. I just wasn't expecting the phoenix to be a bit of a matchmaker by essentially telling us to go off and fool around.

Flint shows no signs of letting me down, so I wrap my legs around his hips.

Oh hellstone, our private bits press against each other with only our pants separating us. He practically impales me with his grappling hook. Yeah, I'm sure it probably isn't that, but damn if it doesn't feel huge.

I'm so flipping curious that I'm tempted to accidentally pants him if he doesn't show me what he's working with soon. Perhaps I can ask him to show me his equipment for "research purposes." Would that make it better or worse?

Nah, I'll get there the old-fashioned way, through hard work in seduction. Because it is hard work for me. It doesn't matter that I write this stuff. I have zero game in real life. Okay, zero might be hyperbole, but I'm not naturally gifted.

Thankfully, Flint won't know that I have no game since he probably doesn't even realize there is a game to be had.

Flint lets out a groan when I wiggle a bit to adjust myself when he carries me toward the stairs.

"You can hold me by my ass or thighs if it's easier." It also would be easier on my back since he's carrying most of my weight in a bear hug.

"Oh." Flint moves one giant hand down, cupping my full ass, and then the other. "Is that okay?"

"Yes," I whisper, wrapping my arms around his neck. My body is alight with tingles. I don't know how far this will go with my innocent guy, but I'd be happy with snuggles. I'd be even happier with a make-out session. *Fuck.* He's probably never kissed someone before.

Now I'm sweating, I'm so nervous. This is an enormous responsibility.

Sweet grandmother moon... When he climbs the stairs, my pussy rubs back and forth and side to side, and I'm about to come just like this.

Deep, calming breaths, Jade.

Flint carries me into his room, down the hall from Calder's.

I'm not sure what I was expecting his room to look like, but just as with Maxum, Flint surprises me.

The glass balcony doors open up over the unending forest, allowing in enough sunlight for me to see without having to turn on a light.

He's filled the generous sized room with soft velour and chenille fabric comforter, pillows, and curtains. The colors are all in muted gem tones. A huge fluffy rug is on the floor. In contrast to the softness, there are rocks, crystals, and stones displayed everywhere.

I gasp. "It's beautiful!"

"You really think so?" Flint sounds so vulnerable.

These guys are breaking my little witchy heart. They are all so amazing and such a catch, and none of them really feels like they are.

I suppose they'd say the same about me.

They are so gorgeous, strong, and sensitive. I've only known them a short time, but I could make a list of wonderful attributes that could go on a mile long.

Separate from the rest of his collection, a plain rock sits on his desk. It looks to be the size of the regular gravel from my yard. "What's this one?"

"Uh." He blushes again. "It's from when I kept an eye on your house, watching over you."

Holy hell. My heart melts to heat my core. Has he liked me from the beginning?

I'm unsure what happens from here, but I want Flint to take the lead. I don't want to pressure him into something he's not comfortable with.

He glances at the bed, finally breaking his intense gaze that's lasted from the dining room to here.

I smile. "Whatever you want to do." I nod at the floor. "I'm happy to sit on the floor and just talk. Or we can snuggle on the bed. Or sit on the balcony and stare out into the forest. Or if you have the strength to hold me up like this for hours, which it seems, most impressively, that you do, we can do that."

"I'd like to do the snuggle thing. How does that work?"

I grin, feeling lighter just with the innocence of my guy. "We have a few common options. We could spoon or you could lie on your back and I tuck to your side."

"Spoon?"

"That would be both on our sides. Think of it as one of us sitting on the other's lap but lying down. You can drape an arm around the other person's waist."

"Is there one where I am on my back and you are on my front?"

Geezus, man. My body heats instantly from that visual. That kind of snuggling can escalate quickly.

"Is that how you want to... snuggle?" I worry for a moment that he doesn't know the difference between a snuggle and sex. Is he asking for sex?

Either way, I'm in, so I will adapt to his cues.

"Yes."

Flint walks over to the bed, and I move my legs to let them dangle. He lays back and shifts to the center of his king bed, taking me with him. I swear these huge, powerful guys make me feel so petite and dainty.

For good or bad, my legs fall off the sides of his hips and since he didn't pull me up his chest, I'm pressed to his pronounced bulge.

I rest my cheek on his upper chest and allow my body to relax.

His massive hands are still gripping my ass. I wonder if that's their new future home. But slowly his right hand moves upward, caressing my lower back and up, until his fingers are tangled with my hair.

"So soft," he breathes out, playing with my long wavy locks. "I've been wishing to touch your silver hair since I saw you."

"You like it?" I ask, because I've debated for a while if I should dye it, chop it off, or both.

"It's the most beautiful hair I've ever seen."

Not what I was expecting, but I love the compliment.

"May I touch your hair?" I ask, because I'm not sure if it will be hard as stone or soft. It's a few shades darker than his travertine colored skin, thick, and may well be as hard as a helmet for all I know.

"It isn't as nice as yours." I hear a pout in his voice.

I lift my head, bracing my arms under my chin, and look him in the eye. "I would like to explore you as you explore me, if that's okay."

He nods, and I touch the incredibly and oddly firm but soft short hair. "It's like nothing I've ever felt before."

"I'm sorry."

"Are you kidding me? I love it! You are precious to me. Understand that, please. If I'm mesmerized or excited by your uniqueness, take it as the praise and for the compliment it is meant to be."

"You are such a blessing, Jade." He squeezes me tightly to his chest.

"Flint, you are too." I say, "You are a completely unexpected treasure, and I'm so happy that we are here together right now. Understand, my delicious, spicy muffin?"

He grins at the reminder of his unusual baking choice.

I love being with him like this, just being. But I'm also itching to kiss him. My hands want to explore his flesh and see if it brings him joy.

"What does my skin feel like to you?" I ask.

"Wonderfully soft and warm. Why do you ask?"

"People go through life usually assuming everyone feels like they do. Or sees the same way they do. But that isn't true. Some people can't feel certain emotions or they feel them more intensely. Or someone might not see colors the same, or at all. And with supernatural and witches being real, that likely expands the parameters of what's possible. One thing that I try to do as an author or a reader is to get into the headspace of another person—to know how someone might be made differently than me. And my goal is to love and embrace that uniqueness. You truly are made differently from me, and I want to know more."

"So you can learn to love... my uniqueness?" When I nod, his huge hand that was cupping my ass moves up and under my shirt, skimming my lower back.

His touch is so light that it tickles.

"You're so gentle with me," I say.

"My strength and size are used to crush our enemies. I've had to learn to be careful with my actions so I don't break things."

"I trust you. And if you hurt me… too much, then I will let you know."

"Too much?" Confusion fills his face. "You need to tell me if I hurt you at all."

"Uh, yeah. About that." I bite my lip, and his eyes dart to my mouth. "Sometimes when people are enjoying each other intimately, a bit of pain can feel good."

He sits up, and I'm fully straddling him now. His arm is around my waist and the other is still tangled in my hair and massaging the nap of my neck. "You'd want that with me?"

"When and if you were ever wanting that with me."

"But…" He glances down at where I'm riding on his bulge. "What if you can't be with me like that?"

I swallow hard. I have no idea what he's working with. I know it feels big, but I shouldn't be making promises I can't keep. He very well could be too big for me to take without perforating my vagina or rearranging my organs.

"There are many ways for people to bring each other pleasure. If there are challenges, we can find a solution."

"I don't know how I am so lucky to have met someone like you," he says with reverence.

I'd like to say he was lucky if he had to wait four hundred years for me. But I feel just as lucky to be in his arms.

His eyes drop to my lips and in my mind I hear a faraway voice say, *"I want to kiss you."*

"I hear something… in my head," I say, reaching for the owner of the voice.

"Osen?" he asks.

My first instinct was to think it's Osen, but it sounds like Flint's voice.

"I don't think so," I answer without confidence.

"What did the voice say?"

"I want to kiss you," I repeat the words.

Abruptly, Flint crushes me to his chest in a possessive embrace.

"What's happening?" I wheeze out.

"Sorry…" He pulls back. "It's just I was thinking I wanted to… and… you *heard* me."

"But isn't it only your mate match that can hear your thoughts?"

"Yes. But don't fret. Being someone's match doesn't mean you must mate with me. If you don't wish to have a bond, you can reject—"

I interrupt him. "Slow down. No one is rejecting anything. Let's just see how this all goes, yeah? If anything, I'm worried that I'm not a good fit for you. Perhaps you would be the one to reject me."

"Why would you ever think that?"

"I'm a witch, remember? And we don't know what's going on with me or my magic. We don't know how Rob might have messed with me. What if it's permanent and what if I'm damaged? What if I'm a danger to you? You mean too much to me to hurt in any way."

Flint announces, "I am kissing you now."

That shuts me the fuck up. Flint's taking the lead, and I don't mind one bit. His massive hands cradle my head gently.

He waits a beat for me to protest, and when I don't, he leans in with no further hesitation.

Slightly cooler, his lips are smooth yet firm as they press to mine. Both our eyes open, studying each other's responses.

I explore his mouth with mine, kissing his bottom lip and his top. He's a quick study and does the same with me. When I suspect he's ready, I let my tongue dart out and skim over his seam. He gasps and touches his tongue to mine.

It's all too much for him suddenly. He pulls back, but then presses his forehead to mine, staring into my eyes and breathing heavily as if he's running a marathon.

Something below grows more pronounced.

Holy bell towers. This guy is packing.

"I need to show you who I am. It's only fair, as you are my match. You should know before we proceed further with our courting."

"Courting?" I blush. "You make it sound so formal."

"I want to do what is right by you." He strokes my cheek and then lifts me off his lap like I'm nothing but a tiny thing and sets me down on the bed. "I should inform you I won't be able to give you children."

"I'm sorry if you had wanted them. But if I had wanted kids, I would have had them by now. I only need you, not children."

"And you need Maxum and Arran? Maybe even Calder? Or Osen, if he returns?" he asks. He doesn't sound jealous, but curious.

"Would that bother you if I were to share my affection?" I ask, because we should deal with this now if it will be an issue for him. I don't see breaking things off with Maxum and Arran, not willingly anyway.

"I don't mind. It's not uncommon among supernaturals to have multiple partners."

"Okay, good. I will do my best to be a good girlfriend," I promise.

"I shouldn't delay further." He stands, his face is devoid of everything except sadness. He believes I will reject him because of his appearance.

Slowly, he pulls over his head the tight-fitting, thin sweater he enjoys wearing.

His beautiful flesh is sculpted beyond my expectations. The unusual tone and coloring only adds to his unique beauty. So far, other than on his head, he hasn't any body hair to speak of.

He pauses as his thick fingers find the waistband of his pants. The fabric at his crotch is stretched from what he's hiding.

He shuts his eyes tightly to block out my reaction. Poor sweetie. My heart aches for him. I don't know what he hides or what his true form is, but I know the fear of rejection.

Rob used to make me feel ugly with his degrading words. It's only with Arran's and Maxum's affection and appreciation for my body that has me starting to feel confident in my skin again.

No matter what's unveiled, I won't hurt Flint like that.

The pants fall down around his ankles.

I sit stock-still, stunned. Between two powerful thighs, not one but two generous hard cocks jut out toward me.

He's a doubleheader.

Whomever carved him had naughty things in mind. And I appreciate their skill. He's definitely large, but not to where I couldn't take him with a bit of stretching involved. The possibilities are fascinating.

"I'm sorry. I know I am not made right."

I snap out of my admiration, realizing that I haven't said a damned thing. I scramble off the bed and grab his hands. He finally opens his eyes and gazes down at me with fear.

"You are perfect."

"But I have two cocks. Males should only have one. They are too big for you, aren't they?"

"With the right preparation, they will fit. And well, if you were open to the idea, you could use both of them at the same time with me, satisfying me in ways other males can't."

"At the same time?" His eyes glaze over. "You mean one in your vagina and one in your anus?"

I nod, because I don't know yet if he's disturbed or intrigued.

Then, in my mind, I see him visualizing pumping into me. His cocks harden further.

"Yes, I like this idea." Flint takes a step backward. "But now, for my original form."

His huge wings unfurl from his back, and I squeak happily.

"You like my wings?"

"Very much," I say.

"Then if you accept me, I will not hide them from you anymore." Flint turns serious again and a sparkling shimmer washes over him, revealing an even taller form. He's thicker in his chest and hips, too. His wings have grown with his size, scraping the ceiling.

The biggest difference is in his larger face, head, and horns. His brows and cheekbones are more prominent. His smaller fangs have now become larger lower tusks, like an orc in my romance novels would have. He definitely would not be mistaken for a human.

"You are gorgeous," I say in awe.

"What? No. You lie." He turns his head, refusing to look at me. "This is the face and body that made Marie terrified and fall down the stairs. This version of me kills people."

I reach up and have to stand on my tiptoes to reach his cheek. "I don't know what was going on in her mind. But likely, she never knew someone as marvelous as you existed. Being surprised isn't the same as repulsion. Besides, I find you sexy."

"Sexy?" He whips his gaze back to me and studies my eyes. "Truly? You would want to still be intimate with me now that you have seen what I am?"

"Yes. Very much so." I want to run my hands over his body and bring him pleasure. "May I touch you?"

"Feel free to explore me… anywhere. Everywhere."

Frisky gargoyle. I like it.

I run my hands over his stone skin on his chest. Delightfully, I discover he feels like smooth marble, but yielding at the same time.

He watches with interest as I drop my hand over his thick, muscular torso. Not wanting to out myself as the perv that I am, I don't immediately grab onto his dual joysticks. I have to approach this tactfully. Warm him up to my touch first.

I run my hand over his bulky arm and step around his huge wings, grazing my hand over his batlike feature. The bones are solid and thicker than I expected, but his wings feel almost like thick leather. I'm surprised he could fly given how big he is.

He shivers when I place my hands on his back where his wings grow from his body. Maxum seemed to appreciate my touch there too, and Flint groans happily with my caress. I trail my fingers down, letting my nails lightly scratch his back until I reach his perky ass. I try to cup his bum, but my hands are too small to take the whole thing.

I walk back around, keeping contact with him the whole time. He stands so still for me he might as well be frozen into stone.

My hands slide over his waist and move toward his groin.

My fingers can barely circle around his first hard cock. Gently, I test his rigidity, and find he has just enough flexibility to make it easy on me.

Flint's huge hand takes hold of mine. I stop moving immediately, worried I've crossed a boundary he wasn't ready to cross. His firm grip doesn't allow me to release his cock, and I don't know what to do now.

24

BONDING

FLINT

*J*ade gazes up at me like I'm actually someone she finds attractive.

I only recognize the look because it's how Arran and Maxum look at her and how she looks at them.

How could she see me as anything other than a hideous monster?

Her soft warm hands on me are so much more than I ever dreamed possible. I collected all these soft pillows and fabrics to approximate the touch of someone who may have affection for me, but they are so far from being like the real thing that I'd laugh at myself right now if it weren't so sad.

Her reverent touch makes me question my belief that this is all for my benefit. Her eyes follow her hands, over my chest, stomach, and my sensitive wings.

When her hands finally circle my first cock, the moment overwhelms me.

I grab her hand. Thankfully, not too hard.

Her beautiful eyes widen, and she appears as frozen as I can become.

"I thought... I'm sorry," she whispers.

"It's just a lot of sensations," I breathe out. "I'm trying to stay calm while a frantic need almost takes over me."

"If it's too much, I can stop."

"No," I blurt. "I like it. But I am having urges."

She smiles, and there is a glimmer of mischief behind it. "What kind of urges?"

"Ones I've never had before. I wish to rip your clothes from your body and dive into you. But I'm afraid I'll be too rough, and I'll hurt you. I don't know how to please you and prepare you, as you mentioned earlier."

I hate that I am so inexperienced. I'm failing her again.

From the look on her face, she hears my thoughts. "I'm going to do that complete honesty thing again. So... sure, I like a guy who knows how to please me. But it's also a fantasy of mine to be with a guy who I can show what I like. That I will be his first experience."

"You actually desire a... virgin?"

"You were a quick study with the kissing. I'm sure you will be with everything else." Jade shrugs. "And you don't have any bad habits to break."

"So, then it's a good thing? It makes you, as you say, *turned on*?" Relief washes over me when she nods.

"Would you like me to show you my body now?" She blushes. "To see if you will be attracted to me, too?"

"I don't see how I couldn't like your body. It's connected to you—to your soul."

Tears well in her eyes. Through our developing bond, I finally sense her. She isn't upset with me, but overwhelmed by my acceptance of her.

Jade pulls off her t-shirt, revealing a silky bra. I'm thankful for the bit of modern knowledge I have and know what to call some things.

Her full breasts are pleasing to my eyes. I can see her nipples are hard. From Maxum's jokes, I know that is often a sign someone is sexually excited or they could be cold. Given the context, I suspect she is becoming excited.

When she drops her pants, she takes her underwear with them. Then she reaches back and unties her bra. The fabric falls to the floor, and I gaze upon her naked flesh.

"You are beautiful. Like a masterpiece painting by the artists of old. Full hips and breasts. Soft and inviting."

Her hand covers her waist. "I'm soft alright."

"And absolutely perfect because of it." I step closer, wishing to touch her —needing to touch her. "May I?" I reach out.

She takes my hand and places it over her left breast. I feel the wild thumping of her heart. "I need your hands on me, please."

I restrain myself from grabbing everywhere and feeling her all at once. I have seen mating dances before between people. There is a time and place for being frantic. Besides, I'm huge and overly strong, and this is my first time exploring a woman. I also want it to last for more than a few moments.

I allow my hand to slide down and cup her breast. She takes my other hand and places it over the exposed one. I feel the lovely weight of them in my hands and bounce them slightly. Then I run my thumb over her tight, pert nipples and she sucks in a breath.

"I like my nipples pinched or sucked as I'm about to climax," she tutors me.

I'm pleased she feels comfortable telling me this, and I log the information with top priority in my brain.

I walk around, admiring her backside. My hand grazes the full ass I had been naughtily cupping earlier. It's just as plump and perfect as I was hoping.

"May I see… between your legs?" I ask, my voice low.

Jade shivers and nods.

I lift her and place her on her back onto the bed. "I know females often like to be licked, and I want to taste you." My huge hands spread her thighs wide.

Her skin is darker there, has folds, and it's glistening.

"My pussy is wet to prepare it for your cock. You can touch me there."

I use one finger to slide over her silky slit, and I instantly want my cock inside it. "It's so soft!"

"Move your finger up to the top. You will feel a bud of flesh." She bucks when I find it. For a moment, I worry I have pushed too hard. "That's it. I like that. That's my clit, and it likes to be touched, or licked and sucked."

I run my finger down and find her entrance. She tilts her hip and the tip of my finger slides into her. Slowly, I sink my thick digit all the way in and my woman groans, wiggling her hips.

"Yes," she whispers.

I pull out and slide in again, feeling inside her.

"You can add another finger to make me ready for you," she instructs.

"You want my cock this time?"

"If you'd like to give it to me."

I add the second finger, and she winces, whimpers, and then finally moans.

Instead of towering over her, I kneel and drag my cheek down her inner thigh. Removing my fingers, I find I cannot wait any longer before I taste my mate. Because that's who she is.

She is mine now. I will not let her go.

My long tongue snakes out and slithers up her center.

"Oh, Flint," my goddess whispers my name, and I'm an addict.

I need more. "Yes, say my name."

She glances down her body at my face, going in for another taste. My long, thick tongue first teases her hole and then swirls around her clit. "Flint, I'm going to come if you keep doing that."

"Then come on my tongue so I may taste your pleasure and memorize it."

"Damn, just like I thought. You're a fucking natural," she praises me.

I bury my face in her pussy, my tusks rubbing her outer folds, and suck on her bud. As I slip my finger back into her channel, she cries out.

Then she tenses. Her body bucks and trembles. Her vagina clenches around my finger and I'm rewarded with another dose of her slick hitting my tongue.

Jade is panting heavy breaths and reaching for my horns. "I want your cock inside me." When she finally gains purchase of my horns, she pulls me to move over her body.

I grip the bedding on either side of her head and pray to the Goddess that I don't hurt my love. "Maybe I should be on the bottom so you can control things? I'm afraid I will crush you, too."

"I trust you, but we can do that."

I roll over and lay nervously in the middle of my bed that suddenly doesn't look very big anymore, with my full gargoyle size sprawled out on it.

"Hmm, with your size..." She looks at my wings. "Do you think you would feel comfortable propped up slightly by the headboard? Like, almost sitting?"

I scoot up the bed and move pillows under my low back.

My cocks are standing straight up, craving to sink into her.

"Perfect." Her wide, expressive eyes lock onto my oddity, and she licks her lips. "I want to taste you, too."

"You do?" I don't know if I'll be able to handle her soft, warm, and talented mouth on my sex. I was nearly undone by her kisses and her touch drives me to insanity. Her taste is like the nectar of the goddess. I was worried about sinking into her sweet pussy, but now I worry I will lose control with her mouth. "Oh... okay."

I feel her magic brushing up against my heart and mind, making sure I'm actually okay.

Satisfied that I'm only nervous, she crawls over and gently strokes both cocks with her hand. "How does that feel?"

"Good. Incredible. Unbelievable." As I watch her caress my cocks, a bit of liquid leaks out of my tips. "I've never had that before."

"Uh, Flint..." she pauses. "Have you never had an orgasm before?"

"No." My skin heats with embarrassment.

Jade stares at my cocks for a moment. "You've never played with yourself?"

"I haven't had a sexual urge until you," I admit.

"Holy shit. I did this to you?" she whispers, then looks at me. "Okay. I should tell you what to expect. It might be overwhelming. It will probably feel like losing control. You sort of have to surrender to it. I've even blacked out before. Or seen stars. I don't know how it will feel for you, but I'm here for you. And please feel comfortable telling me how it feels. I get turned on with sexual talk. This is a safe space. At any point, if you want to stop, we can do that too."

"*You* are my safe space."

"I believe you're mine." She smiles. "I'm going to lick and suck on you now, and I won't mind hearing how good I make you feel, even if it's only sounds."

Her tiny tongue swipes up between my two cocks and flickers between the two heads.

"Goddess," I gasp.

"Oh, fuck, you taste so damned delicious." She licks and sucks on my head, trying to get more of my fluid. "Like rock candy!"

Then she slides my first cock into her mouth, gripping the base, while stroking the second with her hand. I grab the sheets in a vain attempt to hang onto my control.

She pumps her mouth on me and then swallows me down until I feel the head hit the back of her throat and down. She swallows, and I cry out.

Is this an orgasm?

No. The impending wave recedes as I resist the urge to buck into her mouth and down her throat again.

She sucks on my second cock and gives it the same treatment.

"I don't know how much longer I can hold off if you want me inside your pussy," I warn her.

Her mouth pops off my cock, and she crawls up my body, giving me sweet kisses over my chest as she goes. When her sex is spread over my groin, she pauses and looks deep into my eyes. "Are you sure you want me as your first?"

"You are it for me. There will be no other," I tell her.

She kisses me without warning, and I taste the sweetness of my cocks' fluids on her tongue. It isn't as satisfying to me as her nectar. She pulls back and asks, "Does one of your cocks have more sensation than the other?"

"I don't think so."

"I can focus on one or the other in my pussy, but I'm willing to take one in my ass if you'd like that."

"At the same time?" I nod vigorously. "Yes, I want that. I want all of you."

"Okay, first I'm going to sink down your second cock to get it wet. And then I will attempt to take them in both holes. But I will have to go slow to stretch."

I nod and brace for the sensation of entering my lover.

She notches my second cock with her hand and squats down onto me, lovingly gazing into my eyes the entire time.

Her slick warmth envelops me. I moan as she slowly works herself down my shaft in waves.

Finally, she is seated as far as she can take me. She's sweating and panting.

I feel guilty that she's working so hard to please me, but her cute whimpers as my first cock rubs against her clit makes me realize she is pleased too.

She grinds her hips into mine, finding pleasure with one cock rubbing the outside and the other inside her.

"That feels so good, my goddess," I groan. My voice sounds nothing like what I am used to. I sound desperate and crazed and entranced.

"I could come again just like this," she says in small gasps.

"Then come on my cock," I say, my voice hoarse with need. The cosmos is pressing into me, and at any moment, I will burst apart in response. But I must wait until I know she is fulfilled.

"Flint, oh, Flint," she says, closing her eyes and thrashing on top of me. She is losing herself in the bliss I've given her.

Her channel grips me like a vise. Finally, I allow myself to hold on to her hips. But it isn't enough. I need to touch more of her. My hands move up, cupping her gorgeous, lush breasts. I give each nipple a squeeze as she mentioned she enjoys, and her orgasm hits another level.

Oh, I could do this for an eternity, keeping her riding this wave over and over.

Blinking her eyes, she looks dazed as if she's lost. She takes a few centering breaths and asks, "Ready?"

My second dick is coated with her slick. She lifts off it and notches herself with my first dick.

"I might need your help here." Her already flushed cheeks turn a brighter pink. "Can you guide your second cock into my ass?"

Instead of answering her, I have a creative thought that I hope she will enjoy. I move my hand over her full ass, then finger her wet pussy around where my cock is aching to dive into. She moans happily.

Satisfied I have enough wetness, I slide my thick finger into her asshole and she gasps and pushes up my body a bit. I curl my head down to sample her breasts with my mouth. With my free hand, I bring her nipple to my lips and suck, all the while preparing her ass for my cock with my thick fingers.

Jade looks down at the sight of her tit in my mouth. "I have to say your tusks dimpling my breast is probably one of the hottest things I've ever seen."

I suck and then graze my teeth over her sensitive flesh, and she is squirming again.

"I'm ready. Please, I need to be filled up by you," she begs.

I guide her hips back down, helping to take the work out of it for her. Her hungry pussy seems to be a magnet for my cock. And I place the head of my second cock in her back hole. Easing down, she gradually takes all of me.

Something in my mind snaps.

I pull back and buck up into her, fucking her from below.

"Yes," she chants over and over as I make her ride my cocks.

No longer satisfied being underneath, I spin both of us, still inside her. She's below me, as I pump into her… She appears so tiny like this. I don't know if her shocked look is good or bad.

I feel like a beast ravaging her as I thrust my weight and huge double cocks into her.

Her hair is spread out like a fan behind her like a halo.

Images of Jade broken in the alleyway, and then of Marie, flicker in my mind.

But I am a beast. A monster. I don't deserve this affection—this pleasure. I failed in the past. I failed to keep Jade safe. She almost died because of me. I wasn't powerful enough to sense the danger or magical enough to heal her wounds.

What if I'm damaging my mate now? My love?

No. I can't go there now.

I completely freeze into stone, mid-thrust.

"Flint?" Jade cries out. "What happened? What should I do?"

She wiggles to get away from me, but I've now trapped her on my cocks. The way I'm holding her shoulders so I could get leverage, brokers no room for her to escape me.

"I'm so sorry," Jade apologizes. "I pushed you too fast."

I want to tell her she isn't to blame. This is all because of me and my hangups.

"I don't know what to do." She reaches up and strokes my frozen face.

I need to move past this, but how? Perhaps if I kept going, I'd break free. I remember it was my fear of failure… of losing her. That I'm too much of a brute.

I remember our fledgling mental connection and try to communicate. *"Keep going."*

"You want me to keep going?" she asks, confused. When she senses my agreement, she says, "You are afraid of hurting me?"

I send her a mental agreement.

"Okay," she says and cants her hips to take me deeper and then tilts away. Fucking herself on me. "Goddess, this is weirdly hot, but I want you to unfreeze at some point. Because you haven't hurt me yet. I believe in you."

After several more thrusts, I feel myself returning to my fluid state. Her words have worked their magic over me.

She believes in me.

I should believe in myself too... after all these years.

"That's it, my love, come back to me," she coos.

My love? Does she feel for me what I feel for her?

My hips regain their motion, matching her rhythm.

A strange tingling at the base of my spine grows and grows, and my thrusts increase in intensity. And then it feels as though the entire universe has broken apart and reassembled just for my pleasure.

My mouth crashes down on Jade's and she greedily licks into my mouth, consuming and transmuting all my doubts and fears.

My body freezes with a tension I've never had before. But I'm not stone, I'm living magic at this moment.

I am free, and I am anchored only to her. My mate.

Pulsing fluid gushes into her, and she cries out with surprise, then pleasure.

"I love you," I yell as I spill into her, and she milks me until I'm dry.

My head collapses on the pillow by her head, and I fight to regain my composure.

Thankfully, I didn't crush her. I had braced myself with my elbows, but the effort is too much now. I am spent.

Rolling over onto my back, I feel my softening cocks slide out of her. She grunts and moans when I plaster her on top of my chest.

We lay there for several minutes, until she says, "That was... amazing sounds too shallow. Life changing?"

"Life changing is an excellent choice," I say as I rub circles over her soft back.

She squirms up my body and gives me a peck on the mouth between my tusks. "I should probably clean up." She worries her lip, as if she has more on her mind, then says, "I... I don't know how it happened so fast, and I'm sort of freaking out about it, but I love you too."

I never expected her to return my feelings so quickly, either. And although it would have saddened me, I would have understood if she never had felt the same.

If someone told me a week ago that I'd be in bed with my mate making love, I would have thought them insane.

However, here we are, blissful in each other's arms.

If I didn't wish to spend every moment with her for the rest of her life, I could finally die happy. As it is, I must wait to die happily years and years from now.

25

RETURNED

JADE

I've fallen, and I can't get up. No, I don't *want* to fall out of love.

I'm in a bit of daze after my experience with Flint. He's still in his full gargoyle form, and I'm teetering on top of his enormous chest with his massive arms keeping me in place.

After my confession of love, he remembers I need to clean up. He shifts to his smaller, more human-like form and pulls his wings into his back. I pout a bit at this, but I understand he's too big to move around easily if he remains in his true form.

Besides, I don't think he's used to showing that side of himself. I'm filled with pride that I was the one he felt he could be vulnerable with and the one he trusted to be himself and connect with.

Of course, the sweet gargoyle doesn't let my feet touch the floor. He carries me to the spacious bathroom off his bedroom. The walk-in shower is thankfully large enough for both of us. Flint steps in, turns on the water, and sets me down, blocking the stream until it warms up. Then he cleans us both. I do my best to wash him and maybe thoroughly hand clean his cocks.

He's quiet the entire time, meticulously touching every inch of my body to the point he's kneeling down and stroking the bottom of my feet.

"Flint! It tickles!" I try to dance away.

Instead of letting me go, he grabs my body, pressing me to him and leisurely licking between my legs with his long tongue to clean up his release.

I *might* be able to come again, but honestly, I'm exhausted. I don't even know if he wants to ramp me up again, but the sensations are wonderful, so I relax and enjoy his attention. He seems content just to be touching... and licking me. I have a brief flash of a fantasy that I wake in the mornings with him between my thighs, licking me as my very own orgasmic alarm clock.

"If I stay in the water any longer, I'll turn into a prune," I joke.

He pauses mid-lick and stares up at me in shock. Then he grins when he gets my meaning.

"That workout has me craving a snack," I say as my stomach grumbles.

"Alright, I suppose I should feed you... actual food." He chuckles and the deep, resonant sound delights me. "Do you get it? Because you tried to eat my cocks."

I giggle with him because he's so sweet and innocent that he doesn't even know that it's an old joke. "You are catching onto my humor quickly," I praise, because he is. None of the sexy stuff came naturally to him before me, apparently. I'm still coming to terms that I'm someone's only flame, especially when it's someone as wonderful and thoughtful as Flint is.

And it appears he's an extreme case of a demisexual—that he's only sexually turned on by someone he truly likes.

I'm honored and humbled that I'm this special person to him. Out of all the people he's met in four hundred years, I'm the one he wants.

We are still making googly love eyes at each other when Flint carries me downstairs. It seems I might never have to walk again. I glance out the windows and see that it's almost dark out. I begin to worry since Maxum and Arran should have been home by now.

Sitting on the floor of the kitchen, Calder gives us a strange look when we arrive. Trouble and Sage are keeping him company and literally eating out of his hand. Sage is adorably munching on a carrot stem, and Trouble is blissed out of his mind with his banana slice.

"So, you two have officially mated?" Calder asks, his tone lacks any of his usual indignation. If anything, he sounds depressed.

"Officially?" I ask. *Did we? Are we?* I know nothing about real supernatural bonding, but I thought Maxum and Arran needed to bite me.

"Yes," Flint answers confidently.

Shiitake mushrooms. Did I just accidentally mate Flint for eternity? I don't regret being with him, but I hope we haven't rushed this.

"I am courting Jade, and our bond will soon solidify," he continues. "She has heard my thoughts, and I have heard hers."

Nervously, I fidget and hope to shield my nerves from Flint.

Calder glances over at me and reads me clearly with just a look.

Bless his soul, Calder doesn't draw attention to my fretting, but diverts it to another subject. "We should talk about Floofer."

"No." Flint sets me on the countertop and pulls out a variety of cheeses and freshly baked bread from the fridge and pantry.

"You don't even know what I'm about to say," Calder huffs.

"I'd like to hear him out," I announce. Flint needs to understand he can't make my decisions. Not that I'd expect him to. I know he's just trying to protect me.

He captures my hands and kisses my knuckles. "You're correct. I just don't want to put you in harm's way unnecessarily."

"I know, sweetheart. But harm's way is already my road."

"Truer words and all that," an unfamiliar voice says from the back patio door.

"Fuck!" Calder shoots to his feet and places himself between me and the intruder.

When I spin around from my perch on the countertop, I see not one, but three intruders. The first is a mousey looking male who I sense is Floofer in his human form.

Of course, one of them is Rob, and the other one is a woman. I'm guessing she's a witch.

Flint shifts back to his larger gargoyle form in anticipation of an attack.

"I hear you lost your trinket." Rob strolls inside, swinging a locket on a gold chain from his finger, as if he were attempting to hypnotize me. I can see from here that it isn't the same one my grandmother gave me.

"You didn't get me jewelry when we were together, so I don't think it's appropriate for me to accept any now," I sass.

"Oh, yes, I hear you are creating a little coven of supernaturals. But now, you are coming with me."

"Hmm, I don't think we're the right fit for each other," I say, like this isn't a standoff. "Trying to kill me was kind of a red flag that I can't quite ignore. Plus, you're a douche on top of being an abusive jerk, an idiot, and a lousy lay."

"You're the idiot who stayed here when you must have known I would be coming for you," he counters. "And did I really ever try to kill *you*? Or did I only try to rid you of the psychic parasite? You should be thanking me for that."

I think about what I know about his attacks. Rob might have *accidentally* gone too far when trying to exorcize Osen both times. Maybe he hadn't meant to kill me. Not that he gets points for that. He still did all the other horrible things, and he's been using me for years to interrogate ghosts.

"So what's the play here? Why do you want me so badly?" I demand.

"You haven't figured it out yet? I suppose you have been too busy fucking monster cock to learn a damn thing."

Out of the corner of my eye, I see Flint opening the drawer that contains random weapons.

To distract from his movement, I shout, "Hey, jerk! No slut shaming. And it's only been a couple of days since I found out about all this shit."

The other man and the woman move into position, likely readying to attack.

The witch looks at me with pure hatred in her eyes. I start to worry if looks can kill, because I'd be dead soon with the way she glowers at me. What the hell did I do to her?

I shore up my mental shields because I sense magic gathering around Rob and his associates.

"Calder." Flint states, "Remember Rome."

What is that? Some secret code?

Keeping his eyes on our unwanted guests, Calder jerks his head in acknowledgment.

Then I recall what Calder said about intention. The magic has been bubbling inside me all day. The bonding I had with Flint actually seems to have settled the turbulence, and I wonder if I am able to defend myself with my magic. But I have no idea how to wield magic or what I can do other than channel spirits. What if I accidentally unleash some deadly power and hurt Flint, Calder, and my fur babies?

Combat magic is not an option then. But I do need to create protective bubbles, since I'm worried Rob will activate his spell on me, and I will lose myself and become his zombie to do his bidding.

I glance at the dark sky, and again I worry about why Maxum and Arran aren't back yet. Did something happen to them? Are they about to walk in unsuspectingly and get hurt?

Focus, Jade. I can't afford to spiral now.

Rob looks at Calder and Flint. "If you stand down, you don't have to get hurt. Just give us Jade and we'll leave."

"Right." Calder sneers, "You're just going to leave peacefully and let us be."

"You hate witches, so what do you care?" Rob looks him up and down with disgust on his face. "All of your group hate our kind. So, give her back."

"Nah. I think I'll keep her just to piss you off," Calder taunts.

"Wrong answer, pigeon," Rob mocks.

Then all hell breaks loose.

The witch shoots an energy ball at Flint, but fortunately, he doesn't seem fazed.

Formerly known as Floofer, throws actual daggers at Calder. They look like they are made from iron. He curses as he bats them away faster than any human could.

Rob murmurs a chant, and I feel a wave of pressure roll over my body. He collapses the first level of protection, my auric bubble.

He chants in some strange language even louder when his first attempt to reach inside my mind fails.

The pressure builds until I fear he will pop my energetic shield around my body.

"Calder, now!" Flint shouts as he leaps into the air and, with his expansive wings, lands in front of the phoenix, blocking our attackers.

Thank goodness for high ceilings in the open great room.

Calder snatches me up and races down the hallway.

I want to protest that we can't leave Flint behind, but I can barely fight for my consciousness.

I'm losing the psychic battle with Rob.

What? You mean a five-minute training session doesn't make me a super-witch with unlimited powers? All the books and movie montages have lied?

However, I'm proud that I am able to fight off Rob at all. I just don't know how long I can hold out.

"It's okay. I got you," Calder whispers.

My mental shields are crumbling as Calder places his hand on a door I hadn't seen before near Maxum's room. He mumbles a chant, and the door opens. It shuts behind us, and we are in total darkness. I can't see a damned thing, I only know we are moving down stairs from the jostling.

He must figure out that I'm scared because his wings catch fire, not huge flames, but a low burn and enough for me to see.

My last shield is crumbling to Rob's will. I grip Calder tighter.

The last thing I register is that we are running down an underground tunnel that's cool and damp. And we keep going deeper.

26

BUNKER

CALDER

$\mathcal{I}$ should have known Floofer was going to return… with fucking Rob. We don't seem to get any breaks.

With Jade in my arms, I race down to our bunker, nicknamed by Maxum as *Rome* after their ancient catacombs. I sense she is losing her psychic battle. She's fighting the spell Rob tried to activate to make her a puppet for his use, and his spells are eating at her fledgling defenses.

I shiver, thinking about what he has done to her in the past. I know all too well how devastating it is to lose one's power to another.

For Jade, this means he's forced spirits into her body… into her mind. It's a disgusting violation that raises the hackles of my protective nature.

"Hang on," I encourage her, even if she might not hear me. "Keep fighting."

I risk looking down at her while I race down the steps. She winces with pain. It is no simple thing to fight a spell at all, but one that already has its roots in you. It's near impossible.

I hate leaving Flint behind, but if anyone can fight them off by himself, it's Flint or Maxum. They are both naturally resistant to witch and warlock spells —most of them, anyway. I also know he wouldn't survive emotionally if they took Jade.

Hopefully, Maxum and Arran show up any second to help.

I try to pull on our pack connection, even if it isn't a formal, magically bonded one. Often in a pinch, such as the time in the alleyway, the others can sense when something is wrong with one of us.

The ground rumbles under my feet. Debris shakes loose from above me, raining down over Jade and me.

Picking up my pace, I worry that the battle above ground might bring the tunnel down upon our heads. We'll be safer in the reinforced bunker. We just have to reach it.

Another earth rumbling magical blast makes the tunnel quake. Behind us, I hear a collapse. A plume of dust wraps around us as I reach the bunker door, and I quickly chant our pack's spell to unlock it and rush inside the panic room.

When I see what sits in the center of the room, I jolt to a stop with surprise, bile rising in my throat. I can't process what I see, not yet. I have to keep my shit together. Ignoring the disturbing sight for now, I slam the door shut behind me and seal it with a warding spell.

I set Jade down on one of the large cots we have in here. She doesn't seem to register anything around her. She makes small noises as she fights her internal war.

Maintaining my focus on her, I keep my back to the horrid sight in the center of the room. I kneel beside her and hold her hand, wishing I had more magic to help her repel the spell that's working to take her over.

Suddenly, she goes limp, and I fear she has finally lost her battle.

"Jade?" I call, actually hoping to hear a sassy retort from the witch.

"How may I be of service, master?" she says, her voice is flat and void of emotion.

Fuck! I launch to my feet and pace back and forth beside her cot. I don't enjoy seeing her like this.

Quickly, I realize that this might be a unique opportunity. She believes I am her master. Perhaps she will be in a state to answer questions she doesn't have access to otherwise.

I sit down on the edge of her cot. With one of my rarely used talents, vocal mimicry, I ask, in Rob's voice, "Do you have a spirit with you now?"

"He won't come forward."

"Is it Osen?"

"Yes, he's hurt and hiding."

My chest aches with the thought of Osen still hurting. I thought in death he could rest, but apparently that blessing is not for him.

Time to get answers—for all of us.

"Do you remember the other times you've helped me?"

"Yes," she answers succinctly.

"Were you there when Osen died?"

"No."

Okay… one-word answers aren't getting me very far. I must use open-ended questions from now on. I've never been good at this sort of thing. I'm not the interrogator. This is the sort of job that Maxum or Osen used to do.

There's another rumble from above. I take heart that it likely means Flint is still alive and fighting.

"Do you know how spirits come to you?" I ask the spellbound Jade.

"You send the spirits to me so you can speak to them."

Damn, I hate pretending to be that asshole, Rob. "What happens after I talk to them?"

"After you finish asking questions, you take them from me. You absorb their power… their magic."

This explains why Rob has become powerful in unusual ways. He's stealing magical souls.

"What sort of beings have you hosted?"

As if listing a boring grocery list, Jade says, "Witches, warlocks, fae born, shifters, demons—"

"Okay," I cut her off. It's what I suspected. Osen wasn't a fluke. For some reason, Jade can channel the spirits of supernaturals, which should be impossible. Or maybe it's as Maxum says and we just never knew about someone like her before.

"When you are *not* under this spell, you don't remember doing this?"

"You told me to forget. Do you want me to remember now?" Jade asks with a hint of confusion. I'll give her credit. Her mind and reasoning processes are strong enough to be able to formulate a deduction even while under a spell.

"Yes, I want you to remember everything that's ever happened to you after this conversation," I answer, hoping I can snap her out of this state soon.

Something occurs to me. If Osen is still with her and hiding, maybe I can call him forth. "Osen? It's me, Calder. I need to talk to you."

Jade intakes in a sharp breath. Her eyes, that had been closed this entire time, pop open. They are the swirling shadows of black irises of an incubus… *Osen.*

I doubt our witch can fake something like this.

Our witch? Ugh. I think I'm definitely maybe falling for her charms.

"Osen?"

"Calder? What's going on?"

I'm not sure how much he needs to be reminded of. Does he remember his death? Jade? Anything?

"What is the last thing you remember?" I ask instead.

He frowns as he struggles to collect his thoughts and perhaps his very spiritual essence. "I... I was in a witch's body." He lifts Jade's arm and looks at it. "I suppose I still am linked to her. Jade, is it? And then... we went to the alley where I died. We both saw her there during my murder, but... we realized that person might not be her. Then Rob attacked and drained me. It felt like he was ripping me to pieces, trying to separate my magic from my soul. How am I still here?"

"I pulled you... well, Jade, out of his grasp. Then Rob took off, leaving all three of us in the alley to die."

He struggles to sit up and grasps at me in desperation. "Oh, no. I didn't know you'd died again. How bad was the regeneration? Dammit. I didn't know it would spiral out of control like that," Osen says, actually sounding remorseful for his actions, which is a rare thing.

"Fortunately, I was able to recover without a death."

"Thank Goddess." He breathes in deeply and relaxes his grip on my arm. But then he leans forward as if to kiss me.

"Osen. No." I pull away. I know he forgets what his touch does to me. I can't experience that right now, not when I'm on the verge of losing my mind. We haven't had that since my last rebirth. Besides, I'm afraid he might get carried away. "Your powers... I can't... Also, it doesn't feel right to kiss with her body. She didn't give you permission."

"Fine." He sighs, as if I'm being difficult. But I won't use someone's body against their will—even my enemy's. "Sometimes, I forget how things are."

"That isn't your fault."

"Wait. We snuck out when you all were gone," he reasons. "So, how did you know Jade and I were in the alley?"

"My phoenix power. I sensed her potential death moment."

Osen nods and then realizes the next issue. "But how did Rob find us?"

"Apparently, Jade's pendant had a tracking spell. It was also slowly draining her power to keep her weak and malleable."

The earth shakes again, and Osen glances at the ceiling. "What is that? And why are we in Maxum's lake house in the bunker?"

"Uh, longish story. The guys rescued Jade and me. We all retreated to Maxum's lake house, but we accidentally brought a spy disguised as a magical creature with us. The spy escaped, then returned with Rob and another witch. They attacked. Rob triggered Jade's spell, and I got her out of there before she could be taken."

"You?" Osen shakes their head. "I thought you didn't like the witch. You hate all witches."

"She's not so bad. And the guys are sort of falling in love with her. I won't be blamed for losing her."

He narrows his eyes at me, detecting my deflection of my own feelings about the witch. "I'll let that excuse slide… for now." Osen rubs their temples, likely feeling the residual pain of Jade's fight against the spell. "So the three of them are up there fighting while you hide away down here?"

I grit my teeth. I don't like his implication that I'm hiding. "It's only Flint up there. Unless Maxum and Arran have returned by now."

"The witch seems to be regaining her wits... Her soul is fighting to push me aside and surface," my incubus grunts out as if he is fighting her return.

"Osen?" Weakly, Jade's voice sounds like herself.

"It's me, *witch*," Osen says back to her out loud.

"So, I'm just the witch again, huh?" she asks, sounding hurt.

Their gaze travels back to me. It's Osen, watching for my reaction.

"Is there a reason for you to no longer call Jade by her name?" I ask, wearily.

"I… I don't like being this way. Trapped. Weak," Osen admits.

"I don't think any of us are happy with you being dead," I say. "But I'm done blaming Jade for this situation."

A tiny, shy smile graces her face. "Thank you." She looks around, taking in the room. Luckily, I'm still shielding her from the horror that's right behind me. "Are we in a bunker?"

"Yeah. We're locked in a panic room of sorts," I say.

"Talk about a forced proximity trope," she mutters.

The witch makes no sense to me half of the time. "What?"

Another earthly boom rattles the bunker.

Jade's green eyes shine through the shadow of Osen's presence. "Where's Flint?"

"He's still dealing with our invaders."

"We need to help him! If anything happens…" She can't continue as her voice chokes up with emotion, already grieving for the gargoyle.

"If anyone can survive a witch attack, it's Flint," Osen calms her.

"But we know that there's something more going on with Rob. He seemed to have incubus shadows. What if they use a freezing spell on him, like in your memory?"

"He's tougher than he appears and resilient to most magics," I assure her. "I wouldn't have risked leaving him otherwise. Besides, they all would be upset if I let something happen to you."

Reluctantly, she nods and doesn't argue.

"Uh," I begin, then pause, rubbing the back of my neck nervously. "Osen, I need to take advantage of this opportunity to talk to you. I regret not doing so before."

"Um…" Jade hesitates, then finally seems to make up her mind. "If you guys want to… like touch or kiss, I'd be okay with that. Calder, not that I'd presume that you would want to… because… it's me in here too. But I'll try to give you some space."

"You would do that for Osen?" I ask, shocked by her generosity. It's no small thing she offers.

"For Osen, but for you as well." Jade worries her bottom lip, and my gaze catches on her lush mouth.

Earlier, during our training session, I'd been tempted to kiss her. But now, it's confusing. I don't want to mix up my feelings for Osen with what might happen with Jade on its own.

"Thank you for the offer, Jade," Osen says, using her name once again. "But Calder and I no longer had that sort of dynamic when I was alive."

"Oh, sorry." She pulls away.

I see her spirit retreat, feeling foolish for offering.

"Hey, Jade." I reach out and grasp her hand. "I appreciate it."

All three of us seem to be startled by my gesture. Sure, I've touched her before. But it was in the context of rescuing her from Rob both times. Oh, and I suppose she fell on top of me when Flint knocked her down. Then I hugged her when she was upset, but this is a kind touch that I don't often offer to anyone.

"I'm going to try not to pay attention now, and you can talk freely. And the offer still stands for any affection you need to show each other." Jade closes her eyes, and when they open again, it's clear Osen is back in control.

27

VOYEUR

JADE

*N*ow I feel a bit like a creep for offering my body for their reunion. At least Calder didn't seem to take offense.

Osen, however, seemed strangely opposed to the idea. I'm trying not to dip my consciousness into his. I don't want to go back into any of his memories. Now that I know they are memories and not some crazy dream I came up with, it doesn't feel right to see them anymore. My gut tells me it has to do with his powers, and that perhaps things weren't great between them when Osen died.

Except, even though I'm trying to block out what's happening, I can still hear and see Calder.

"I, uh, I want to say I'm sorry for how I pulled away after my last resurrection," Calder begins. His icy blue eyes seem to melt when he looks at Osen. Part of me craves for him to look at me this way. But I'm being greedy.

"It's understandable," Osen says, my voice coming out deeper and with a hint of an accent to match how he sounds in my mind. "You were paralyzed then. I'm sure my magic reminded you too much of that torture."

"It did. But I should have gotten over it," Calder argues and rubs his eyes with the heel of his hands. "Why didn't I just push past the memory?"

"You might have, if we had more time," Osen's voice holds so much sorrow. "But I messed that all up. I failed you. I failed us. I'm so sorry, my love."

Emotions overcoming him, Calder clasps our face and kisses my lips... kisses Osen. Years of repressed passion and love pour into us.

Calder peppers kisses over my cheeks and forehead. "I missed you so fucking much."

My heart pounds, and my sex tingles. Osen's turned on. To be fair, I am too.

Then I feel Osen's shock. He didn't expect to be turned on and have his lover still able to move. He believed his incubus feeding shadows would paralyze Calder like they had always done when he was alive.

Was that why he was hesitant to touch Calder when I offered?

I mentally nudge Osen to respond instead of him remaining in shock.

He catches Calder's frenzied mouth with his, and they kiss. Their tongues tangle and they hold each other so tightly I can't help but to feel like a third wheel. And damn if these guys don't know how to kiss.

When they gasp for air, Osen speaks to me, *"I never got to kiss him like this. So freely."*

"Never? Because of your powers?"

"Yes." A wave of gratitude hits me square in the chest. *"Thank you, Jade. But I need to pull away before I'm tempted to take over your body and do more than kiss."*

I don't know what to say to that. Part of me wants to be generous and offer myself for them to connect more. The other part doesn't want to be a passenger in my own body. While I'm debating what to do, Calder comes to his senses.

"We should slow down." He presses his forehead to mine, closing his eyes, likely imagining that it's just Osen with him now.

"I love you," Osen says. "I didn't say it all these years, and I should have shouted it every day."

Calder sucks in a breath. "I love you too. It breaks my heart that I've lost you."

"I'm not gone completely yet," Osen reminds him.

"But how long until you move on from this plane?" Calder asks.

"I don't know, but it doesn't feel like I'm going anywhere for a while." Osen looks down at my hands, turning them over and studying our shared body. "I would have thought I would have been exorcized when Rob attacked Jade. I think it might be her who must cut some sort of tether to let me go."

He's probably right, but I don't like knowing I have that kind of power over someone's soul—holding onto it.

I try to remember how I released the spirits in the past, but the returning memories are fuzzy. It's there, just out of reach. Calder's suggestion, when he pretended to be Rob, seems to have opened the door. Perhaps, over time, I'll be able to remember all that happened under Rob's spell.

Osen's emotions are crashing into him again, and he embraces Calder in a tight hug. Calder melts into me and strokes my back lovingly. The love that these two have for each other resonates in my own heart. I just wish I could fix the broken pieces.

But right now, all I can offer is this... this strange moment, deep underground, wondering how many more moments we have left.

Something different tugs on my heart, and it isn't the scene we're playing out here.

"I think it may be Flint. Or even Maxum or Arran," Osen tells me mentally, reading my thoughts.

My concern for my guys puts me in a spin. They should have been here by now. At least Flint should have come for me if he won. I want to reach out using our developing mental link, but I don't want to be a distraction if he's still fighting. But what if he didn't win the battle?

"Jade, don't," Osen says softly.

"I'm sorry. My brain is being too loud for you to enjoy this moment," I convey inside my mind.

"That's not what I meant. And I'm not complaining... I wouldn't have this moment if it weren't for you."

In the shadowscape, Osen appears standing in front of me. He's in his shadowy form as usual, and I'm barely able to see what he might have looked like when he was alive.

"What are you doing here with me? You should spend this time with Calder," I say, with a bit of reprimand.

In our private moment in my mind, he caresses my face and hugs me. *"Until we know what's happened, we can't worry. But our guys are tough."*

"Our guys... You don't mind me being with them anymore?" Previously, he had expressed a hint of envy.

Osen sighs heavily. *"I'm a jealous, possessive prick. Not sure if you picked that up before."*

"There might have been a few crimson flags waving around," I tease.

"Ah well, I see in your mind that you finally broke Flint open like a geode, revealing a sparkling center. I was never able to do that. And Arran? He's accepting his beast, which is healing his pain. Maxum never wanted me for more than my friendship and an occasional fuck." Osen tilts his head and stares into my soul.

His shadowy appearance takes form. He's still not completely whole, but I can see his eyes are dark gray, not just shadows. And of course, he's as handsome as I expected, with a fit, but not overly muscled, build.

I gasp. *"I can see you."*

"With your bonding with Flint, and the moment with Calder, I have enough power briefly to show you myself, before I will need to rest and restore my magic again."

"Why show me yourself now?" I ask.

"You gave me a moment with Calder that I hadn't had before. Ironically, it took you to be my open heart so I could be present with my love. Thank you for helping to heal his wounds, too."

"I'm not really doing anything." I shake my head.

"You are being you. Genuine, and that's enough." Osen corrects himself, *"No, that's* exactly *what my pack needs. What I need. So… thank you."* He leans down and presses a sweet kiss to my lips.

"I have to go for now," Osen says and fades away from the shadowscape.

I open my eyes and find I'm still embracing Calder. "Uh, Osen had to rest. It's just me. Sorry." I pull away from the embrace.

However, Calder doesn't let me go. He tightens his grip.

"Thank you, Jade," he whispers over the side of my neck.

Goosebumps rush down my flesh.

When he releases me and leans back, he traces a thumb over my cheekbone. "I'm sorry I was so unpleasant before."

"It's not a big—" I begin, but he cuts me off by placing his thumb over my mouth.

His eyes stare at my lips, and his hand on me. "No. Don't be dismissive of your amazing patience with my behavior."

His thumb traces my bottom lip lightly. I feel he's debating if he should kiss me. If it were only up to me, I'd lean forward and take the lead, but it isn't.

It sounds as if his choices were taken from him during his last death, and I won't pressure or force him into anything. Especially not with me, a witch.

Calder blinks a few times, shaking himself out of whatever lustful thoughts he might have been having. He stands up and walks over to the center of the bunker.

He had been blocking something from my view this entire time. I stand, unsteady on my feet and walk over to the glass and metal casket-sized box.

"What the fuck is this?" I hiss. "Is that… *him?*"

2 8

STUCK

MAXUM

My other contacts don't give me much more information than Mal and Dwayne did.

Arran is restless, and I don't blame him. His bond with Jade is incomplete, and he won't be settled until they formalize the mating process. *If* they formalize it.

First, we need her to explain her name, and why she lied about her age.

Once again, I remind myself that information might not be accurate.

"It's getting late. We should go back." Arran glares at the evening sky like it's his enemy.

"I have one more person I'd like to visit and then we can return." A string is plucked at the back of my mind as soon as I say this. Someone has crossed my wards. "Fuck."

"What?" Arran grabs my shirt collar and growls in my face. "Is it Jade?"

"My ward alarm was triggered." My eyes lock on the place I had planned to portal out, and I race toward it.

Arran is on my heels and in his full werewolf berserker mode by the time we get across the street and into an alley. Thank fuck no human is around to see him. We don't need to be reported for revealing our supe natures to the mortal realm. He's been caught too many times already, and the authorities will punish him if it happens again.

We rush through the portal and stare at the lake house. It was reckless to portal directly to my home, but time is of the essence when my sanctuary is potentially threatened. Besides, my home has already been compromised by the enemy.

There's an actual magical skirmish happening on my front lawn. The area is about an acre of mostly open space, dotted with large ponderosa pines. If I'm correct, by the look of the damage, this battle began at the back of the house, or perhaps inside.

Flint is limping but throwing a boulder at someone who looks very much like the bastard Rob. Blasts of magic hit Flint's back, and he staggers from the impact. When I look at where the blast originated, it's just as Mal and Dwayne said. Sloan and Galiana are indeed Rob's companions.

"Where's Jade?" I mutter. "Or Calder?"

Arran's berserker shakes his head, telling me he doesn't see them either.

I don't appreciate trespassers... especially witches and warlocks threatening my pack and my mate.

"Let's take these assholes down," I snarl.

Arran's berserker charges right at Rob.

Bummer, I was going to call dibs. Oh well, if he has issues, I'll tag in.

Sloan. This is the dickhead who snuck into my fucking sanctuary—who tricked Jade into staying in her home. Spied on her. On us.

Yeah. I could definitely satisfy my bloodlust with his death.

I reach out with my gift to read him, then I plan to scramble his brains. Ah, Mr. Fucking Floofer has great mental shields. It will take time for my magic to smash them down, but I will make it happen. Then I'll see what's inside and scramble his memories and personality so damned much that he believes he actually is a hamster, after all.

I storm over to Sloan's hiding spot behind a tree trunk.

Righteous anger rises in me—mostly at myself for believing I could leave Jade today with Floof-Sloan escaped and still missing. He likely had been watching and knew this would be a suitable moment to attack.

Perhaps to snatch up Jade?

Sloan spins, finally realizing that I'm almost on top of him. His eyes widen and the magical blast he intended to lob at Arran hits me square in the chest, burning my shirt.

It stings a bit. He's either weakening due to all the magic he's thrown around or he's not that powerful to begin with. Probably both. And sure, most spells bounce off of me, but that doesn't mean it can't be painful when they do.

I swat the flames out on my shirt, then grasp his head. He squeals like a rodent. That's a little too on the nose.

Tightening my hold on his head, my magic works double time to crack his shield. The witch, Galiana, hits me from behind with a blasting spell. Wow! I would have thought she'd have more punch, but maybe she has been exhausted already.

It makes me believe the witches' claim that supernaturals aren't the only ones suffering horribly from the disappearing magic in the realms. Perhaps witches are being hit even harder than we are and won't admit how bad it is.

Perhaps the excuse that they believe that supes are depleting magic by just our existence does have a more desperate origin. Weaker witches are likely to be hit harder than those with more innate power.

It makes me wonder if they expect Jade to have more power than they do, and if they wish to harness and manipulate her magic for themselves.

Not on my watch.

My vengeance for them having dared to invade my home gets the better of my control, and I hear the telltale sound of cracking a skull. I refocus and realize that I haven't killed Sloan... yet. However, he goes into shock and drops his shields.

Well, that worked out nicely.

Fortunately, Galiana is busy assisting Rob against Arran and Flint, so I now have a moment to probe into Sloan's mind and rummage through it for information before he dies.

Unfortunately, it's a freaking mess in his pathetic mind. He's pretty upset about dying and all the pain. *Boohoo.*

Maybe he shouldn't have messed with a demon or his witch.

When I search for his memories of Jade, I see flashes of her. He watched on as Rob interrogated the ghosts they had placed inside her.

Sloan would shift and sneak out of the room when the guinea pig and rabbit were asleep and go through Jade's computer. He'd send emails of information that she had accidentally channeled from Rob's victims and written into her books, notes, or journals. I also see he would watch Jade sleep and ask the spirits questions when Rob wasn't around.

She truly had no clue what was happening to her or who was spying on her right under her nose.

I dig for Sloan's connection to Rob. From there, they met during a secret Anti-Supernaturals Organization meeting. They had conspired to become major players in the movement. Galiana was already one of their leaders, but Rob has been slithering his way up to the top by being her lackey. Then several faces of the ASO members flicker through my mind, and I make a point of memorizing them.

I see the trio plotting to target Jade. I also get a vague impression Galiana believed there's something unusual about our witch. Something... *other*. Galiana first wanted to destroy Jade because of whatever she is, but then realized they could use Jade for her abilities before they finally eliminated her.

Why is Galiana so intent on destroying Jade? What is different about Jade from any other witch?

I try to press for more, but Sloan's heartbeat falters and I feel his soul slip away. I wish I had gotten more out of him, but he was a minor player even among the three of them. He was expendable enough to live at Jade's home during the last couple of years. Honestly, he was only a grunt. The real power player is Galiana.

When I turn back to the ongoing fight, Flint and Arran are cornering the witch and warlock against the side of the house.

Galiana sees that I'm free to turn my ire on her, and that they are officially outnumbered. She chants and throws out her hands. A portal opens up, and they both race through, escaping our wrath.

Flint collapses onto the ground and grunts in pain. The warlocks and witch did more damage than I would expect to the magically resistant gargoyle.

Arran is in terrible shape too. Half his berserker's fur is burnt off. Hopefully, a shift into his human form will heal most of the major damage.

I'm fucking losing my mind with worry, since I don't sense them in the house or the nearby forest. "Where's Jade and Calder?" I ask, trying to not lose my wits.

"Rome," Flint says.

"The bunker?" My eyes widen. "Fuck!"

"Rob activated his spell on Jade," Flint explains. "It wasn't safe for her to be around the warlock."

He couldn't have known not to send Calder down there, so I remind myself not to be upset with him. It makes sense on a strategic level to have the phoenix take her there. But Calder might freak out with the sight of Osen's body and take it out on Jade.

"Arran, can you shift?" I ask, because I assume he's going to want to go down there with me. I need him to heal up and be in his more logical human form to help Jade and Calder.

He howls in agony as he shifts. Painful burns have healed a bit, but his usually gorgeous naked body looks fucking rough, and I wish I could do something to help him. But I can't even offer him a salve before we find Jade. He wouldn't accept it even if I did.

"Flint, can you walk?"

"For Jade? Yes." He struggles to find his feet, and I give him a hand. Not that I can mind-read the gargoyle, but I sense something has changed about him.

"I can't reach her mind," he says.

"What? Why would you be able to—" He must have realized she is his mate match, and they have bonded on some level.

The same realization must have occurred to Arran as he asks, "Did you… were you… with Jade?"

"Um, yeah," Flint blushes his bright peach.

"Goddess." Arran is shocked, but not upset. "I'm happy for you."

"I'm happy for all of us," Flint says. "But first we need to ensure our mate is alright."

"True." I pull Flint's massive arm over my shoulder and help him walk through the front door and to the bunker's access door. After chanting to disable the first warded spell, I continue to help Flint down the wide stairwell. "I should tell you… Osen's body is down there."

"What?" Flint is downright frantic. He now knows what he's accidentally done to Calder. "Why did you keep his body instead of securing him in the ice caves until we could arrange a funeral?"

"I… I don't know. Well, you'll see. Something odd is going on."

"We aren't supposed to keep secrets. Look what it did for Osen," Arran reprimands.

"I know." Then I stop moving with the sight just ahead. "Dammit."

The tunnel has collapsed. My heart beats wildly, imagining Calder and Jade never even making it down to the room. What if this crushed them? What if they are underneath all this rubble?

Flint urges me forward, and I panic because I had added extra wards to the bunker to not allow portaling in and out of it. I remind myself that might also be why we can't sense Calder and Jade.

Calder would have a nightmare of a time if he died under the weight of the rocks. If we couldn't dig him out, he would keep dying over and over until his magic was exhausted. Then he would finally experience his last death.

Part of him wants to go. I know this. He hasn't been the same since he came back from his past rebirth. But I will not let him leave us so easily. And I will not allow him to suffer an ongoing death like that.

If they are under this mountainous weight of debris, I also need to get Jade's broken body out.

I won't be the same if she is lost.

Arran appears strangely unaffected. Has he finally shut down emotionally?

"I don't think she's under all that. My wolf says he still feels she's alive."

The pessimist in me, who has seen centuries more devastation than the wolf shifter, doesn't argue that maybe she isn't dead *yet*, but she may still be dying.

At the blockage, Flint falls to his knees since his injured leg barely works and tosses huge pieces of rock behind us.

"Wait, we don't know if they are under this." I grab the current small boulder from his hands and set it down. "We should check the bunker first. I should be able to portal just outside of the room, if it's clear on the other side."

We move back. I open a portal and sigh with relief when I see the bunker door. First challenge down. Now, to see if they made it safely inside. Then to see what condition they both are in.

I leave the portal open, since we may have to retrace our steps if our people aren't in here.

Chanting my unlocking spell, I crack open the door and hear Calder cursing.

Not good.

The door slams back shut, and I try to push it open again.

"Maxum?" Calder asks and then releases his hold after peeking around the door and seeing my face.

Flint and Arran storm inside after me. We all stand in shock at the sight.

Jade is lit up like a candle, her aura so bright she looks to be on fire. Her eyes appear unseeing, although they are cast toward Osen's glass casket. As if seeing him this way has triggered her, but she is no longer herself.

"Jade?" Arran calls, stepping closer.

"Don't," Calder warns.

"Why not?" Arran snaps.

"Because you'll get zapped," Calder says, rubbing his hand. "Her magic finally manifested when she saw Osen. Not sure what the fuck sort of magic this is."

I can't make horns or tails of the kind she has either.

Flint limps closer to Jade. I'm not sure what the hell he's doing. He's in no condition to take any more damage.

"She needs an anchor to draw her out of this. I feel her mind swirling," Flint says.

When I let myself skim her mind, I sense it, too. "Do you have a suggestion?"

"Don't come near the witch," Jade says.

"Osen?" I ask.

He whips her head to stare at me. His shadows are in her eyes. The shadowtendrils undulate, reaching for the glass. His spirit wants to return home.

"How did you return?" I ask.

"Her magic can feed my soul... my magic. With her, I can take my revenge... for this." He points to his body on display. Then he steps toward the door.

At first we allow him to maneuver by us, because he might lash out. It could hurt Jade. But then I realize he might hurt Jade more if he gets away.

"No." I step in his way.

Osen narrows their eyes.

It surprises me when Calder jumps in front of him. For a moment, I wonder what he plans on doing? Will he aid in Osen's revenge or stop him?

"You aren't going anywhere with Jade," Calder growls.

"But with her power and my ability, we could kill them all," Osen argues.

"No. Give control back to Jade right now." Calder fires up his wings, displaying how serious he is.

"But she doesn't know what to do with it." Osen takes a step closer, challenging.

"You got yourself killed. You can't risk her like this. She is too important to her mates."

"To you?" Osen asks Calder, sounding concerned for the first time.

"Yes, even to me," Calder admits. "I don't know if I want to pursue something or not, but I want her alive. *Your pack* wants her alive and healthy. And with you in charge, that doesn't seem likely."

The power emanating off Jade lessens. Osen reaches out and kisses Calder. I don't like him using Jade this way, but maybe if he does this, he'll leave her be.

The magic sputters out, and Jade passes out in Calder's arms. The gentle way he looks at her and holds her, I realize Jade not only captured Flint's heart today, but something has shifted between the phoenix and our witch.

"We can't stay here," Arran says as he collects Jade from Calder. He winces as her body presses against him, agitating his burns.

"You're right. This place is compromised now," I say and hold out my arms for Arran to hand over Jade. "Let's collect our things and get out of here before Rob returns."

"But where will we go?" Flint asks. "This was the last place we had left."

"There's one place… it might solve all our problems… if they let us stay. Finding out what sort of witch Jade is, how to use her power, and a place to hide off the map."

29

ALL WRONG

ARRAN

After we get back up the tunnel to the house, I shift back and forth again to help the healing process along and do a quick sweep of the house to make sure no one is lurking.

I throw on a t-shirt and sweatpants and pack up Jade's things from the office, knowing she wouldn't want to leave them behind.

I really love our home here, and I wish we could have stayed longer. But with our lifestyle, I've never been able to set down roots for long. With the ASO and the witch attacks escalating and the missing supes, we haven't felt settled for a long while.

My wolf and berserker whine within my chest as we all wish to hold Jade, but Maxum has her resting unconscious on the bed in his room as he packs up Jade's clothes and his own.

When I enter the bedroom, he's finished up, zipping up his duffle and staring at our witch. I observe him, wondering what's going on in his mind.

Tossing my clothes and toiletries in my bag, I ask, "You picking something up?"

"She's in there. Strong. Stronger than before." He finally looks at me. "Her magic makes no sense. It doesn't feel like anything I've felt before."

"Is it bad for her?" I ask. "Maybe we shouldn't have been so quick to have Jade ditch her pendant."

"I don't think the magic is hurting her. But it feels all wrong."

"Could it be because her magic had been blocked for so long?" I ask, wandering over and caressing her cheek with my fingers.

"Arran?" she murmurs.

"Yes, my sweet love?" I say, hoping to coax something from her. Maybe my words will wake her. Sitting down on the bed beside her, I wait and hope for a response.

"I feel weird," she says, opening her eyes and blinking at the light.

She sighs in relief when she sees both me and Maxum. "You're alive. I was so worried when you didn't show up when you said you would." She holds my hand and reaches out for Maxum to do the same.

Instead of coming closer, he apologizes, "It took longer than I had expected, but we returned as soon as I sensed a problem here."

"Are you hurt?" I ask, because I haven't had the chance to do a thorough inspection of her body. Although, I assumed Calder would have told us of any injury she sustained during the attack and their retreat.

"I'm okay… I think." Jade sits up and sees the bags. "Are we leaving?" Her bottom lip poofs out in a pout.

"Yeah, as soon as Calder finishes packing upstairs."

"Where's Flint?" It hits her that she hasn't seen or heard mention of the gargoyle. She moves to launch off the bed to track him down. "Is he okay?"

Maxum catches her as she runs for the door. "He's banged up, but he will recover."

She hugs Maxum now that he's in her grasp, but he seems resistant. Sensing something is off, she pulls on Maxum's hold around her waist. "What's wrong? Let me see him."

"In a minute, we need to clear something up first," he says with all the seriousness he can muster.

"Why does it sound like I'm in trouble?" Her energy recoils.

She withdraws her hands from Maxum and holds them protectively over her chest. He releases her and gestures to the desk seat.

I want to snarl at Maxum for even questioning her, but I also know why he must.

"We heard some rumors, and we need the truth."

"Okay." Jade glances over at me, wondering what fresh hell is coming now.

"What is your name?" Maxum asks.

"Which one?"

Maxum blinks. "How many do you have?"

"I have my author name, my birth certificate name, and my new name."

"Then who is Jadeana Jones? Who is Patricia? And how old are you?"

"Jadeana Jones is my mother. Patricia is my grandmother. And I'm forty... Well, next month I will be. Why? How old do you think I am?"

I look at Maxum, then back at Jade. "You took your mother's name?"

"She named me after her for some bizarre reason. Obviously, she didn't know at my birth that she would later disown me. Anyway, she often goes by her middle name, Ruth. I still liked Jade and legally changed my name to the shortened version. Then for my author name, you've seen my book covers so you know it's Juniper Jade."

"I'm confused. Why would my informants think you were your mother and she was dating Rob?" Maxum's voice still holds a shred of suspicion.

"Well, years ago, when I first leased my house, I hadn't changed my name yet. Maybe that's where they got my name and got us mixed up?"

"And you aren't sixty?"

"I would say that's ridiculous, but now that I know witches age better than humans... No. My mom is sixty. However, I'm sort of used to having mixups all the time. I suppose people rarely expect women to pass down their names. We'd often have problems with paperwork and such because we had the same name and look a lot alike. Apparently, my grandmother's genes are dominant, because we could all be mistaken for each other. Although, from a picture I found on the internet, my mom mostly looks her age."

"My guess is that your grandmother put an obscuring spell on your records to hide you." Maxum sweeps Jade up in an unexpected hug, and she squeals as he picks her up and crushes her to his chest. He says with complete relief, "I figured it had to be something stupid like this. Thank Goddess."

"Yeah, stupid seems to follow me around."

Calder peeks his head into the room. "We're ready when you are."

"Need Flint, now!" she orders Maxum, pointing to the door.

He obeys and carries her out to the living room where Flint is sprawled out on the couch. Already, because of his supernatural nature, he's healing, but he looks beat up. His skin is more marbled with discoloration than normal.

Jade scrambles out of Maxum's arms and rushes to Flint, hugging him fiercely when she reaches him. His massive arm circles around her waist and gingerly pulls her closer.

"I'm so sorry! I wish I could have helped fight so you wouldn't have gotten hurt."

"Your magic is still coming in, my love." Flint strokes his large hand up and down her back as she holds him. "We don't even know what you can do with it once it does."

Jade lifts her head off his broad chest and stares lovingly into his eyes. "The magic feels so strange. Maxum thinks there might be something wrong with me."

Maxum corrects, "I didn't say anything is wrong with *you*, but there is something different about your magic."

"Hey?" Flint cups her cheek gently. "You are perfect. Being different isn't wrong."

Jade kisses Flint, and he returns it, claiming her mouth like a pro.

My brain still takes a minute to process this new version of the gargoyle who can touch... and who can touch *our mate*. Fortunately, my alpha nature, my wolf, and my berserker all accept Flint into our mating pack.

Electricity arcs off Jade's body and into Flint's chest.

Well, that's fucking new.

I have a feeling our witch will continue to be full of surprises.

Flint gasps, but quickly looks as though his injuries are mending.

"Did I...?" Jade strokes down his body where his flesh had been damaged and is now healed.

"See," Flints says with a wide grin. "I told you. Perfect."

"Perfect or not," Calder says with a bit of irritation. "We need to get the fuck out of here before someone returns. None of us are ready to handle another fight right now."

"Birdman is right," Maxum teases, using Trouble's name for him.

"Shit!" Jade glances around. "Did anyone check on the little ones?"

It's then we hear scratching coming from the kitchen.

"Oh, yeah." Calder mumbles. "I put them in the cupboard for their safety." He points to the kitchen island. "I was waiting to get them out until we were ready to leave, just in case we were attacked again."

Jade rushes to the kitchen and Calder guides her to the correct cupboard. He stands closer than I'd expect him to. He's warming to her.

"Is it safe *now*?" Trouble grumps.

Opening the cupboard, Jade picks up Trouble and Calder gets the bunny, Sage. Our witch and phoenix face each other, smiling, and take turns petting the fur balls. Several times, I notice their hands touching. Hmm.

Something dramatic has shifted in Calder.

Both our affection-phobic pack members don't seem to mind Jade's touch anymore. Perhaps they even crave it. Speaking of which, I crave her touch, too. But that will have to wait until we are safe.

"Let's go!" I bark.

Everyone snaps their gaze at me. I suppose that came out more aggressive than necessary, but I'm suddenly feeling a sense of urgency to get us somewhere safe.

"Yes, Mr. Bossy Sweatpants," Jade teases, but quickly puts Trouble and Sage in their travel carrier.

Maxum picks up his bag and tosses it onto his shoulder as he heads out to the front. The doors begin to seal and lock around the house... not that we will be able to return any time soon. Well, not until we kill Rob, Galiana, and anyone else who knows its location.

Jade can walk without issue, but I still want to hold her in my arms. I need to confirm she is okay—that she's alive.

If I wasn't carrying all Jade's stuff and my own, I'd be holding her, but I'll bide my time and make use of it later—wherever Maxum is taking us.

I just hope for our sake, it's somewhere we can rest for a damned second, breathe, and figure out what sort of witch our beautiful mate is.

30

HELL

JADE

I understand why Maxum needed to ask me about the rumors. I'd probably have one of my characters do the exact same thing. To be fair, my situation is a bit wonky, growing wonkier all the time.

Is wonkier a word? Well, it is now. Even with everything that's happened, I still have the Shakespearean flare.

"Ready?" Maxum says as he pauses, surveying what is left of his huge front yard.

The damage around the lake house makes me stagger a bit, imagining Flint fighting on his own for so long. He's lucky Maxum and Arran returned when they did.

"Jade?" Osen calls me in my head.

"What?" I'm not feeling overly warm toward him since he almost ran off with my body. Again.

"I fucked up."

"No shit," I snip.

"I don't mean to be so insane. I mean… I was always a bit of a hothead. It's one reason I understood Arran so well. But since I died… I'm not okay. I'm broken. I don't mean that metaphorically. Something is missing in me. It makes me do dumb shit without thinking it through."

I sigh as I watch Maxum create his portal. I know this is hard for Osen to admit his weakness. From what I hear, he didn't do that in his life—ever. To admit it now, when he is so vulnerable and reliant on me, must be killing him. Well, not exactly, since he's already dead. But it's dang hard, I'm sure. He's struggling to deal with what's happened to him.

"I get it," I say, softening to the incubus' plight. *"Are you okay after seeing your body?"*

"Not really. Why the fuck did it look like it's preserved?"

"I don't know. Can Maxum perform magic like that?"

"Not that I know about. But why would he do that?" Osen asks, completely confused. *"Our traditions would have him burn or bury my body, not keep it frozen in time."*

"I can ask him," I offer.

"Not now. Let's all get settled first. Otherwise, they might fight if they don't like his answer."

"Okay. That's smart, to be patient." Then I say what I need to get off my chest, *"Speaking of patience... All of us want revenge for your death and will help you find it. So how about you stop stealing my body and trying to run off?"*

"I'll try. I promise."

"Do. Or do not. There is no try," I sass.

"You are seriously quoting science-fiction to me?" he asks. *"I thought you were strictly into fantasy-paranormal romance."*

"My horizons are broader than that, thank you very much."

"Jade?" Maxum calls.

"Huh?" I snap out of my mental conversation with Osen to see all four guys are staring at me. "I'm coming!"

"Not yet, you aren't." Maxum winks and holds out his hand for me, pulling me through to our next destination.

Okay, not quite our final destination.

Maxum uses the same tactic to lose any potential tracker as we did when we traveled to the lake house. We crisscross through the realms and countries. Flint, Arran, and Maxum take turns giving me piggy back rides when my short, human legs have a hard time with the terrain.

Maxum asks me to come to him just before he opens a new portal. I'm losing count. Maybe our fifth? "Stick close to me."

I don't like the urgency or concern in his normally even-keeled demeanor. When I peek through the magical doorway, I see darkness, barren land, and orange flames in the distance. The vibes aren't exactly welcoming.

"What the fuck?" I whisper.

We step through, and Maxum informs me, "It's the second ring of hell."

"You take me to all the best places." I joke. But then I feel bad. It's his origins, after all. "Sorry."

"Don't be. I hate it." He strokes his hand down my back and for a moment I wonder if he's making the gesture to soothe himself too. He watches the rest of the guys join us and simultaneously keeps an eye out for danger. "Sure, it isn't what humans believe it is, but it's usually an unregulated, lawless place. And its inhabitants are often out for themselves. It's dangerous for anyone, but especially so for anyone not from here."

There's a smoky aroma in the air, but it's not the inviting scent that Maxum naturally has.

"Let's go," Maxum says as he rushes toward what looks like a cavern.

Not to be a 'fraidy cat, but I'm nervous.

Then I realize. I'm literally in hell. I don't think many paranormal authors can claim that and mean it. Although, we often feel like we are when we run up against deadlines.

The atmosphere feels heavier, thicker. My breathing is labored as we tromp across the rough and barren landscape.

"Where are we exactly? Are we under the Earth like some humans believe?"

"No. It's in another dimension layered over Earth's plane, just as the fae realm is. And just like the fae realm, there is energetic overlap, where the mortal realm and hell bleed into each other. That overlap is destroying a lot of hell, just as it has with Elfhame."

"Humans are destroying the other realms?"

"Not to mention their own," Calder adds.

"So it's not wrong when some fairytales say the fairies are dying off?"

"Where do you think those stories come from?" Maxum frowns. "The truth."

"And there are a lot of supernatural beings who have contributed to the mortal literary world," Calder explains. "Books even stolen from other realms and distorted to fit human sensibilities."

"I've known some famous supernaturally inspired authors in my day," Maxum grins at my excited face. "Also, I helped invent rock n' roll... at least the human version."

"Fuuuck," I say, but I sort of always wondered about the arts being otherworldly inspired. I can't wait to learn about all the things he's done in his life.

And this guy… this demon… this fine ass male, who has experienced more things than I can imagine (which is saying a lot), wants *me*?

As I hurry to keep up with his long strides, Maxum pulls me closer to his warm body and gives me a kiss on the top of my head. "You don't give yourself enough credit."

I snap my gaze up to him. "You read my mind too easily. I didn't even feel it."

"This is my power source. My magic is stronger here."

I think about his compliment. I suppose I'm more interesting now that I'm a witch.

"You aren't special to me because of your magical side. That's a dime a dozen in my life."

"Okay, so why?"

"Even when faced with adversity and abuse you have suffered, you are yourself. To still be genuine and kind after a hard life is a rare thing."

"Many people are nice. I'm not unusual in that."

"No. Kind and nice are two different things. Being *nice* is doing things because they are expected in your society's norms. It isn't necessarily genuine or good-hearted. Being kind sometimes doesn't even mean being nice. Kindness comes from the heart. It's thinking of someone's needs and suffering, then doing what is best for them to grow."

"I get what you are saying. Like someone might not be sickly sweet about it, but they will save someone's life or help them in an important way."

Maxum tilts his head toward the other guys and says in a low voice, "Your kindness, understanding, and compassion have healed them."

He gives me a grumpy look when he hears my brain, wanting to argue that I haven't done *that* much.

"Okay, fine. I'll play along. But I haven't helped you."

"Jade, you have. In my long life, I have never had love, with the exception of my affection for these guys. Honestly, I've never cared if I died. Then you showed up, and for the first time in six hundred years, I have something to live for. Someone to love."

I feel my face heating with emotion.

Or perhaps it's more than that, because Maxum snatches me up and breaks out in a full run for our destination. Bouncing in his arms, I glance over his shoulder and see a huge dog-like creature racing toward us. I swear the thing is as big as a mule.

Its eyes are flaming with orange fire. The cracks in his dark gray skin reveal lava circulating underneath.

A hellhound?

The rest of our group races to keep up with us. The demon dog is hot on their heels. Genuine fear reflects in my guys' eyes.

Maxum chants, opening a portal ahead of us.

Mid-stride, Arran shifts to his berserker form.

Calder is the slowest of us. He's carrying the fur babies, slowing him down further.

The hellhound snaps his massive jaws at him.

Calder unfurls his wings, but beating them only slows him further.

I know this won't end well. My power swirls inside my body and, with an instinctive gesture, I throw my hand out to stop the hellhound from harming my phoenix. A bolt of lightning shoots from my fingertips and crashes into the hellhound's snout.

Its head hits the ground with the force of my assault, and it flips over, letting out a painful howl.

A portal opens up in front of us to what appears to be a dark forest, and we race through.

Maxum snaps it shut and grips me to his chest. "You okay?"

"Yeah?"

"What the hell was that?" he asks.

"She threw a damned lightning bolt like a mage!" Calder's eyes are round, and I'm not sure if he's scared or excited.

"Is that bad?" I ask.

"Having a huge aura and getting zapped in the bunker was one thing. That could easily have been a regular yet powerful witch's magic, reacting instinctively," Calder explains.

Maxum continues, "But the way the magic came out of you now was more like a mage. You didn't need to use a spoken spell to create it."

"I need a spell?"

"Witches usually need a verbal incantation to focus their intent," Flint elaborates. "You are too new to magic and untrained to throw a spell like that."

Calder rushes up and hugs me, surprising the *hell* out of me. Wow, any phrase with the word hell in it will have a lot more weight after my last field trip.

"Thank you for saving me," he whispers.

"Who dares to trespass?" a deep, growly voice echoes from the surrounding forest. Then the fiery eyes of a hellhound appear.

"Oh, fuck, it followed us," I say and feel my energy swirling and waiting to be unleashed again.

With a quick squeeze of my shoulder, Maxum silently pleads for me to bring my anxiety down a notch. Then my demon holds his arms up in a show of surrender. "It's Maxum, a friend of Amira. I seek asylum and a witch's protection."

"Dammit," the hellhound grumbles. "I thought I was going to get to eat you."

The huge demon dog glowers at all of us. I get the impression he's psychically reading us. He flicks his head at me. "What the fuck is she?"

"She's the reason we are here," Maxum says.

The hellhound sniffs the air. "Mostly a witch, but why do I pick up an incubus and something else?"

"Long story, but she won't harm you."

"This is the same witch Amira and Raithe aided?" the hound asks, with a curled lip.

"She is," Maxum confirms.

"Very well, come with me," the hound gives me a suspicious glare.

Nothing like a warm welcome.

SANCTUARY

JADE

*V*ery much like Maxum's lake house, Amira's place seems to be in the middle of nowhere. As we follow the giant hellhound, I get a strong urge to turn away, avoid this place, and forget it exists. I wonder why. Is it not safe?

Osen perks up in my mind. *"That's a witch ward. Well, it's their first line of defense. If they can make you go around and ignore their existence, then they don't have to bother with people wandering onto their property. I'm impressed you identified the intent, since the point is for you not to notice."*

I hate to admit I preen a bit with Osen's praise, but I quickly dismiss what I did. *"Could it be that I only noticed because I'm following someone and going against the spell?"*

"Hey, sweet witch. Don't downplay your accomplishments. I bet the guys only feel anxiety. They might have put it together by now since they know what to expect, but you don't have their years of experience."

I let the subject drop. *"Why did Maxum phrase it like that—we seek asylum and a witch's protection?"*

"Because it's an ancient custom, before the witch-supe wars. We used to be able to come to each other and seek refuge."

"That sucks that we can't get along anymore."

"I suspect Amira is getting along quite nicely with her supes."

I chuckle at that, but I admit I'm curious how the trio are able to overcome their differences. *"After we were attacked, I met Raithe, and he seemed nice enough. A bit more amenable than this hellhound,"* I say.

"Hellhounds are nothing to be trifled with. You saw the one in hell. This one is much older, and has become more human-like with his sheer will to evolve, probably to be a suitable mate for his witch."

"Evolve—?" I'm too busy concentrating on my conversation with Osen, and I trip on a root.

Flint catches me so I don't tumble onto my face.

"Great. She doesn't even know how to walk," the hellhound grumbles.

"Leave her be," Flint growls. "She has a spirit distracting her."

My gaze swings to take in my gargoyle. I'm shocked that he figured out what was distracting me, because to be honest, it could have easily been Maxum's tight ass swaying in front of me. "How did you know?"

"I hear your mind, remember?" He blushes. "I wasn't meaning to eavesdrop."

"Why don't I hear you anymore?" I ask, frowning at my inability to use our mate connection.

"Well, my mind isn't as busy as yours. It's quieter. And I've been shielding, so you wouldn't be overwhelmed by your magic coming in, as well as Osen's return."

My heart melts a bit with his thoughtfulness.

"Thank you, but please don't hide completely. It felt like something was missing," I tell him.

He grins shyly. "You missed me?"

The hellhound looks over his shoulder and eyes Flint. "Looks like this witch is collecting herself a coven."

"I'm Jade, by the way. You don't have to keep speaking about me as if I'm not here."

"Until you prove you aren't an issue, I'll behave how I see fit, witch." He stops abruptly at a clearing and glowers at us. "If I discover any of you are a danger to my family, I won't hesitate to eliminate the threat. Understood?"

We all agree. He isn't fucking around. But I don't really blame him. I'd probably say the same thing in his shoes to protect my guys.

"I think they've been fairly warned, you can stand down," Amira says as she steps out from nothing. "So, demon, your witch seeks asylum?"

"I know you usually only protect supernaturals or humans anymore, but we are being attacked by witches and warlocks," Maxum explains. "And

Jade's power is coming in, and we could use your help to guide her in how to use it."

Amira looks me up and down. "Her power has come in, but it's erratic and unusual." After a thoughtful pause, she sighs. "Fine. You may stay here under my protection while we sort out her magic and figure out a new place for you to go."

It's always fun to be talked about like I'm not even a person. But I keep my mouth shut. My instinct says she's testing me.

Osen chimes in, *"Witches and warlocks are known for their quick tempers — especially those with a tendency to turn dark. Amira is trying to push your buttons to see what you'll do. If you are prone to snapping. If you'll turn evil."*

"Thank you for taking us in," I say with as much genuine gratitude as I can squeeze into the sentiment. Because even if they're attempting to taunt me, they are also doing us a huge favor. They are risking their safe place to take in a known risk.

I can handle some bullying, if I would even call it that. This is nothing compared to what I've experienced in my life. I was brutally bullied in school. Even my mother abused me after her mother died. This is barely on my radar. Hell, even Calder was a bigger pain in the ass than they are being, and I'm already over his attitude.

Amira turns and vanishes in front of us. Then the hellhound does too.

Maxum turns and winks at me. "Let's disappear." He holds out his hand, and I take it, but keep hold of my gargoyle's, too.

We step forward and a large cabin, a barn, and small cottage now sit in the middle of the clearing.

"Wow, was that illusion made with Amira's power?" I glance up at my demon. "Do you think I will be able to do that? I mean, I'd love to pull a disappearing act when I don't want to chat someone up."

"Someday. *Maybe.*" Maxum squeezes my hand when I frown with disappointment. So much for insta-magic.

When we reach the large log cabin, Amira points to a smaller outbuilding —a bungalow about fifty long strides away. "You will all have to stay in the guest house." She glances at all the guys and takes in their size. "It will be a tight fit, but it's all I have to offer you for accommodations. It has the basics, and it was where we stayed while building our home. Let one of us know if you need anything, since I suspect you left your former safe house in a bit of a hurry. We'll have dinner in a few hours."

"Thank you. As long as my pack is safe. That's all that matters." Maxum bows to Amira.

We follow him over to set our stuff down and get a look at our new hideout.

"Witch?" Amira calls, as we walk away. "Tomorrow, come see me."

"Will do." I salute casually. *Oof.* What was that? I don't salute, but perhaps it's because I expect she will be part drill sergeant and part witch.

Maxum looks as though he's holding back a chuckle.

Arran looks like he might consume me right on the lawn.

With a determined stride, Calder rushes ahead to check out our small cabin.

Flint scans the surroundings, likely assessing the threat level. With my attention on him, he says, "I have to ensure your safety, my mate."

Will I ever get used to the guys calling me their *mate*? The thrill of finally being desired to that level may never wear off. It makes my heart pound harder and my skin heats up.

Calder comes back out of the cabin and actually blushes. "All clear. But uh, Amira wasn't joking about tight quarters."

We all walk in and notice the space is mostly open, with an enclosed bathroom. The bedroom, if you could call it a room, has a partition wall to separate it from a living area and kitchenette. There's only one large bed. We might all be able to fit on it, but it will be a dog pile. Thankfully, there's a long couch, so Calder has that as an option. I doubt he wants to share a bed with me even if he was overwhelmed with emotion and wanted to kiss me, we are still getting over our differences.

It could have been a friendship kiss... okay, maybe it wasn't *that* innocent. But it doesn't mean he wants me for more than a sweet moment of thanks for allowing him to speak to his dead lover.

"I think he might have wanted to kiss you for more than just a thank you," Osen whispers in my mind.

"Perhaps, but I'm not going to dwell on it. I have bigger issues to deal with, like survival. Learning about my magic. Smiting our enemies," I tell him.

"I'm all for that, especially the last one," he says happily.

"I figured. And remember, I want to get revenge for you. For all of us. So don't get a wild hair and stick it up my bum."

"I'd love to put something else up your bum."

I bark out a laugh, and everyone turns to look at me. "Sorry, Osen's being a brat."

"The more things change, the more they stay the same," Calder jokes with a playful grin.

Damn, I wish he'd smile more. He's always devastatingly handsome, but even more so now. My panties have caught on fire.

. . .

We quickly tidy up the place and put our limited items away.

We are all covered in dust and sweat. However, being the gentle-monsters they are, they tell me to go first. I pout a bit since I've gotten used to them washing with me.

As soon as I close the bathroom door and strip down, I hear the muffled debate between Maxum, Arran, and Flint about who will get to join me.

I grin like a fool that they all want to be in here with me. No matter who it is, I'll be happy.

I turn the faucet knob to warm up the water before stepping in. My back to the door, I hear someone enter. Immediately and without question, I know it's my demon.

"Maxum, how did you win the fight?" I ask.

"Sneaky witch, how did you know it was me?" He wraps his hulking arms around my waist and lifts me into the shower tub stall.

I squeal as the cold water shocks me, but my devil just laughs.

Osen seems to fade into the background, allowing me some alone time with my demon.

Maxum gently wipes the wet hair from my face and gives me a passionate kiss. "You can't scare me like that again."

"What did I do now?" I ask with sincere confusion.

"I was so worried when Rob attacked," Maxum growls. "Again." He squirts some of my liquid soap into his hand, and uses his hands to wash my chest.

Of course, he starts with the boobs. But fuck, I love it. However, it's very distracting.

"You know I don't blame you for the attacks," I try to console him, figuring out he blames himself. "And unfortunately, I doubt that's the last we will see of that jerk."

"I'm not really blaming you either, but..." He leans down to give me a good scrub between my legs.

"You aren't used to not having control," I finish for him.

"Yeah. I'm not used to it. But recently, my life has been chaotic. With Osen's death, falling for you, and then the attacks, I'm about to lose my mind," he says.

"I know how I could make you lose your mind in a good way." I use some of the soap to make his cock and balls slippery and stroke him, making him moan.

Wanting to take this further, I rinse off the soap on his cock. Kneeling down in the tub, I take a moment to look back up at my demon's face, staring into his obsidian eyes that reflect the flames of my desire.

He grips my hair and holds me in place, not allowing me to move forward and take him into my mouth. "You want to suck my cock, sweet witch?"

"Please," I beg. I can tell how much that pleases him as his cock jerks, trying to reach my lips all on its own.

I stick my tongue out and open wide.

He moves my head forward, shoving his huge, ridged cock into my eager mouth.

Using my tongue, I play with the soft spikes along the base, as he pumps into me, reaching my throat.

"Good little monster fucker." He pulls out and asks, "You want to swallow me down?"

"Yes, I want to taste you."

He squeezes the base of his dick and pre-cum leaks out. "Here, taste me."

I swipe the tip of my tongue, and his warm, spicy taste explodes in my mouth. Overcome with need, I grab the backs of his thighs and plunge down onto his cock, slurping and sucking like a madwoman.

"Rub your clit," he orders.

I do as he says and moan with the arousal that rushes through me. I'm on the edge.

"Goddess, Jade." His grip on my hair tightens, and he grabs the shower curtain as if that could support him. "I'm coming," he warns.

His hot and spicy cum fills my mouth and throat. It's too much. But I do my best to take all of him. With a strum of my fingers, I bring myself off. It's not a brain-numbing orgasm, but I doubt this is the end of our fun. He lifts me immediately and plunges his cock into me without warning.

"Fuck!" I shout, more out of surprise. It barely twinges with pain, and I'm quickly given over to pleasure.

"I will claim you, my sweet witch," he says, and my heart races twice as fast. "But when it's the right time." He pins me against the tile and slowly pumps into me.

"What if I'm ready now?" I ask.

"It's not the right time. Besides, not in a bathroom. I want it to be... as perfect as it can be."

"I love you," I say, then kiss the ever-loving hell out of him while he brings me closer to my bliss.

"I love you." He whispers over my lips, "You've ruined me... in the best way."

32

HUNT

ARRAN

I know hiding out at Amira's is for the best, but I wish we were back at our lake house. There's no space to move in this tiny cabin. We aren't little creatures. Well, the magical creatures are, but they are running around without a care.

I envy them.

My skin itches to claim my mate. Instead, I've had to listen to Maxum giving her pleasure just mere feet away.

Flint stares at the door, longingly. And Calder surprises me by doing the same. He even casually grinds the heel of his hand against the erection contained in his tight pants.

I can't stand it anymore when I hear her shout out with her orgasm. I crash through the door. She's dripping wet and bent over the vanity with Maxum taking her from behind. His hand is wrapped around her hair, pulling her head up and making her arch her back. In the reflection of the mirror, her eyes lock with mine.

Maxum has dropped his glamour. His horns are out and his skin is deep red. With a loud smack to her ass, he orders her, "Look at me when I come inside you."

"Oh, fuck," she hisses, turned on by his demands.

He finishes inside her, crying out her name.

When he's done, he glances over his shoulder, grins wickedly, and pulls out. His hand knotted in her silver hair, holds her in place with her ass in the air and on display.

"Clean her up," Maxum orders me.

I fall to my knees and lap at her swollen and abused pussy, cleaning out Maxum's spicy cum.

"Arran!" Jade shouts and squirms. "Holy hell." Her body is on the verge of another orgasm. I can feel it.

I also now sense Flint standing in the open doorway, watching.

"Do you wish to join us, gargoyle?" Maxum asks with a bit of mirth. He loves this new side of our reserved pack member. "Maybe have Jade suck your cock?"

"I do, but this is Arran's moment. So I will refrain and just enjoy our mate's sounds of pleasure."

I'm thankful for Flint's judgment, because I don't know if my berserker could hold back if he touched Jade. He's barely holding out from coming forward and taking control. He's putting up with Maxum's hand on Jade's lower back only because he's allowing us to clean her out.

I'm pretty sure my berserker is going to insist on licking out their cum whenever he can, to remove their scents. His small protest that we have to share our mate.

My nails turn to claws as I get excited by this thought, the tips dimpling her plump ass.

But my naughty witch loves that feeling of danger, and she immediately comes on my tongue.

I want to dive into her pussy and knot her, but I must wait. It will be a sweet torture. But I have a surprise brewing in my mind—one that I believe she will enjoy and will scratch one of her fantasies off her list.

So instead of satisfying my urges, I pant and lean back against the open door, still on my knees.

"Did you like the wolf tasting you?" Flint asks. "And the demon fucking you?"

Stars and stones. Even I'm turned on by his gravelly voice, dirty talking after all these years.

His two thick fingers slide down her ass and dip into her honeypot, stretching her. "Are you sated, my witch?"

"Flint," she whines. I can hear in her voice she is spent. "Why do you have to be so fucking sexy? But…"

"I know, sweet mate," he soothes. "You are tired. But just know, I'm going to take you again, and soon. I will claim you completely. I will lay claim to your body, your mind, and your soul."

"Bloody hell," Calder whispers from the main room. His cock is out, and he's stroking himself. As soon as we lock eyes, daring me to call him out, he comes.

Witnessing this break in his armor makes me happy.

We *will* have a pack with Jade as our nexus. We will all finally be whole.

Jade doesn't see Calder's release or when he races out of the cabin to clean himself up in private. But by the knowing look Maxum gives me, I'm sure he sensed our phoenix's pleasure.

Damn, I can't wait until Jade experiences Calder in the bedroom... or wherever they decide to fuck. I'm excited to see how it will blow her mind with what he can do. Goddess, I hope for his sake he finally overcomes his intimacy hang-up.

After a quick rinse, Maxum dries off Jade and carries her into the bedroom area to get her ready for our dinner with Amira and her mates.

Flint rinses off, then I do.

With a downward cast of his eyes, Calder returns and also takes a quick shower.

We hear a dinner bell ringing from the main house and head over.

Our entire pack is nervous. Though, I suppose we are also curious to see how a witch gets along with her supernatural mates.

The phoenix, Raithe, is standing outside his front door and gives us a friendly wave as we approach.

"I hope Darius didn't scare you too much," he says with a smirk, indicating he knows he did. "I'd say he's a big softy, but that'd be a lie... Well, to anyone else but Amira and me. So if you need anything, I recommend asking me for it."

"Thank you." Jade smiles. "We really appreciate you helping us out. I apologize that we have to impose at all."

"Don't worry your pretty little heart over it." Raithe waves her off, then his eyes settle on Calder. "Hello, brother-cousin."

"Are you related?" Jade asks with a gasp.

Raithe is the first to correct her. "Not in the way you think, but all phoenixes are related in some way. It's tradition for us to acknowledge we are family, since there are so few of us in existence."

"Hello, brother-cousin." Calder dips his head in respect. "I look forward to getting to know you during our stay."

"As do I." Raithe grins welcomingly at Calder and a lot of the tension I had about being here fades. Perhaps between Jade's compassion and now a connection to his people, Calder might heal.

When we sit down at a large dining table, it's clear there aren't usually more than three seats. Someone has brought in huge wood stumps and brought over another table to extend the existing one, making room for us all.

Flint bows as Amira comes in. "Thank you for accommodating us."

I guide Jade to the seat next to where I intend to sit. I would like for her to use my lap as a chair, but I don't want to make her uncomfortable in another witch's home.

We make formal introductions after all the food is put out to share. It isn't a huge feast, but it will do. We did come by unannounced. None of us would ever think to complain. Besides, if we are still hungry later, we actually brought some of our non-perishable provisions from the lake house.

Maxum and Calder offer to help hunt for wild game in the area. And that perks up my wolf and beast.

"How safe are these woods?" I ask. "And how far does your magical influence extend?"

"We have one hundred acres. The line goes up to the ridge and to the top of it. Then along the creek, to beyond the meadow, the way you entered," Darius explains. "Why? Do you need to let your wolf free?"

"I do," I admit as I dish some offerings onto my plate. "And I was concerned for Jade's safety if she were to wander the property."

"You both will be safe within our boundaries. If someone were to trespass, I will know immediately," Amira assures us.

Good. I smile, thinking of what I have planned.

For the night, we barely fit on the large bed. Calder opts to use the couch as I had thought he might. He's not ready yet, and I understand.

Flint sleeps on Jade's one side, Maxum on her other. My need to be near her has me between Maxum's and Jade's lower halves. I'm holding her legs, burying my face in the seam of her thighs, and breathing in her fragrance.

After they are all asleep I decide I need to find the perfect spot for what I have in mind.

I make it just outside the front door when I hear rustling behind me. Jade.

I spin and pin her to the outside of the building and capture her mouth with mine.

She sucks in a breath of surprise, but quickly melts into my arms. When I break away, she asks, "Are you okay?"

"I'm fine, my sweet witch." I grab her ass with both hands and pull her hips into mine. She can feel my growing member wishing to claim her. Only a thin, long t-shirt she borrowed from Maxum and tiny panties separate me from my dream woman.

"Then what are you doing out here so late?" She glances down at my nakedness. "Are you going to shift?"

"Yes, I was going to hunt for something. But now, I think I'll hunt you." Nipping at her bottom lip, I scent her perfume blooming with the arousing thought.

"Me?" Her hazel-green eyes widen and glow with excitement.

Her magic is coming in, and it doesn't quite feel like any witch's magic I've felt before. But perhaps she is something different. She's able to channel supernatural beings after all.

I grin wickedly when I see she's wearing her slip-on shoes. "How does that sound? Would you like me to chase you, catch you, and fuck you into the ground like the naughty, delicious witch you are?"

"I don't approve of running as a rule, but I'm willing to make an exception in this case. Sign me the fuck up."

I chuckle and inhale her natural perfume along her neck. Then I rub my cheek against hers, marking her with my scent. I step back, letting her see my bare form.

She licks her lips in anticipation.

"You better run, because I'm going to devour you once my berserker catches you."

"Holy hell," she curses and runs for the trees, her plump ass jiggling perfectly.

My wolf and berserker want to launch forth from my body and give chase now, but I force them to be patient. We need to give her something of a lead or it will be over too soon.

I sniff the air and pick up the harmless creatures of the surrounding forest. I approximate where the river is, which Jade is heading toward now. We hate letting her out of our sight, so I shift into my wolf form to heighten my senses, and trot after her.

It saddens me knowing that my sexual time with Jade will always be with my berserker. He's the one in control when I'm feeling too much. And I'm so deep in my emotions when I'm with Jade that I don't see how I, in my human form, will ever be the one to make love to her. Thankfully, I'm present and conscious when he's in control… even more so in the last few days, since Jade helped me accept that cursed side of myself. I no longer believe he will hurt her.

My wolf scents Jade's excitement, and my berserker bursts forward, no longer content to wait. He was patient when we licked her sweet pussy in the bathroom earlier, but he's done waiting.

Honestly, we're all done. We want her. We want to claim her as ours.

I howl at the moon, knowing it will happen tonight.

She. Is. Ours.

33

CAUGHT

JADE

*O*ne of my most reckless fantasies is coming true. I just hope it turns out okay. Arran had warned me that his berserker is exactly that: he's out of control. And I've agreed to be hunted by the most dangerous hunter out there.

I don't think the berserker wants to hurt me, but he's huge, much bigger than Arran's usual form. Standing over six foot six, he's pure muscle, claws, and teeth. They created the berserker as a curse to represent how beastly and out-of-control Arran can be. He was created to keep him separate from his humanity and lash out at the ones he loves.

Except the berserker has shown me kindness and care. Perhaps it's because I'm a witch? Am I breaking the curse? Or is Arran's acceptance helping him integrate this wild side?

As I race through the forest half naked, the adage to be careful what you wish for buzzes in my mind. The berserker might forget his affection for me in the middle of a hunt—an act that will only feed his primal nature.

Fuck, what have I done? Have I put too much trust in them?

I push harder to run, but I'm already winded. Okay. Seriously, I need to do more cardio. I make a resolution that I will start tomorrow if I survive tonight. Sitting at a desk for hours on end has done little for my endurance. Besides,

I'm pretty sure I'm going to need a lot of endurance to keep up with my guys in bed or running with them in a forest.

A bone chilling howl cuts through the night air. *Crap.* If I didn't know that was Arran, I would have pissed myself.

I'm reminded that even though my guys are sweet to me, they are apex predators guided by their primal natures.

Fear courses through me now. My adrenaline answers the call and races through my bloodstream, making my legs move faster than they have ever moved before.

A presence brushes against my mind—a spirit. It's probably Osen, but I don't have the time or energy to deal with him now. This is Arran's experience. I shut down the intruder with a magical shield, partitioning my mind.

I'll deal with it later.

I don't even hear his footfalls, it's his breathing that gives him away.

Daring a glance over my shoulder, I see it is, in fact, Arran's massive and dangerous berserker form chasing after me.

His hard, swollen cock bounces menacingly with each stride. His knot is engorged and ready to lock inside me. I shiver at the sight.

What will it be like to experience it for real? Will it hurt? Will it make my body spasm over and over in bliss like the romance books suggest?

His claws swipe out and shred the back of my oversized sleep shirt. With another swipe, he tears the rest of the ruined shirt from my body. All I am left with now are my shoes and panties.

Like the klutz I am, I trip over a rock and fall on my side, knocking the air out of my lungs. The frantic excitement takes over my rational brain, and I scramble to get up.

My effort only makes me present my ass to my werewolf like a dang omega in heat. I might as well have served my pussy up on a platter.

Arran's beast slices off my underwear and grabs my hips with his huge hands. He lifts my ass up and licks my throbbing pussy. His licks quickly turn to frenzied nipping and laving at my sex.

It has me moaning and whimpering into the damp leaves on the ground.

After he gets his fill of my taste, he drops me back to my knees and plunges his thick cock inside me all the way up to the hilt of his knot.

This is taking doggie style to a whole other level.

Thank goodness I've been stretched out recently. Otherwise, his sudden intrusion would have hurt a lot more than just the sting that quickly turns to pleasure.

His claws dig into my tender flesh without breaking it. My werewolf pulls back and slams home again, mindlessly seeking his bliss.

This will be an untamed fucking.

Part of me is more than a bit nervous. He might forget I'm a fragile, human woman, so I move to get away again.

His massive, furry body leans over and presses against my back. He growls a warning in my ear.

I glance over my shoulder and see his golden eyes, wild and glowing with unbridled lust.

One paw-like hand takes hold of my entire full breast, which is an accomplishment in itself.

The beast ruts into me again, hard and fierce.

He pinches my nipple with his sharp claws, sending a fire to my clit. Somehow I know that it is Arran. He's breaking through and adding a bit of his own intention.

Knowing my Arran is here with me alongside his beast makes this whole experience more fulfilling and powerful. My arousal slicks my passage for his intense thrusts.

"Fuck," I shout, while the knot hits against my outer pussy, sending me straight toward a climax cliff.

His large balls bounce off my clit, and I'm launched into a gripping orgasm. Stars flash behind my eyes, and the world falls away. All the struggles and worries vanish. Nothing exists except us.

My pussy clenches around his dick.

The werewolf roars, spilling into me and filling me up.

But it doesn't end there. While I'm still coming, he shoves his knot into my channel.

I cry out with the stretch. He ruts into me with shallow and yet vigorous thrusts.

My orgasm is prolonged, and I shout and curl my toes from my uncontrolled release.

Arran's voice comes through in his full beast form, which I thought was impossible. "You are mine. My mate."

I crave for him to claim me with his bite, just as his essence is with my insides. "Yes, yours. Make me yours."

His razor-sharp teeth pierce the juncture of my neck and shoulder, claiming me.

Our bond immediately snaps into place.

Wholly.

Completely.

We are one.

My body glows with sigils and strange writing, just as Maxum described before. The unidentifiable magical symbols over my body dissolve like they are evaporating into the ether.

Have they vanished for good? Or is this how they always appear and disappear? I wish Maxum was here to see this.

"Oh, Jade..." a woman says in my mind. She sounds completely mortified and distraught. *"What have you done?"*

I shake my head to clear my confusion. "Abuela?"

"You made the same mistake I made."

Mistake? What mistake did my grandmother make?

TO BE CONTINUED...

Find out now what happens next in Enchanting Her Monsters.

ENCHANTING HER MONSTERS

BEWITCHING MONSTERS BOOK THREE

YVE VALE

1

INTERRUPTED

JADE

*a*fter being chased into the forest surrounding Amira's home, I'm covered in dirt, marked with scratches from branches and werewolf claws.

Through his dangerous teeth, Arran pulls me closer. "You are mine. My mate."

I crave for Arran to claim me with his bite. "Yes, make me yours."

There's no hesitation on his part. His razor-sharp canines pierce the juncture of my neck and shoulder.

The threads of a mating bond immediately snap into place, linking our souls.

Wholly. Completely. We are one.

The feeling is like nothing I've experienced. It's as though I've discovered a lost piece of myself I didn't know was missing—like I've come home.

Then my body glows with sigils and strange writing, just as Maxum described before. The unidentifiable magical symbols over my body dissolve like they're evaporating into the ether. Have they vanished for good? Or is this how they always appear and disappear?

"*Oh, Jade...*" a woman says in my mind. She sounds completely mortified and distraught. "*What have you done?*"

I shake my head to clear my confusion. "Abuela?" I call out to the dark woods.

"You made the same mistake I made."

Mistake? What mistake did my grandmother make?

After hearing my grandmother's disembodied voice, I instinctively push the spirit away. I don't want to hear more. Not now.

Arran's grip around my waist tightens, if that's possible, and he growls at the surrounding darkness.

Since it's only a spirit who spoke to me, I know he doesn't understand what the threat might be. I'm sure he's feeling over-protective and vulnerable because we just sealed our mate bond. He's still locked inside me, so if we were attacked, this could get awkward fast.

Given my current circumstances, I don't want a conversation with my dearly departed grandmother right now. Although her ominous words about making the same mistake she did echoes in my head.

Did she mate a wolf shifter? Is my grandfather a supe?

Oh, my goddess. My grandma is watching me get busy with my mate…

That's it. I'm calling this experience a new level of embarrassment for me. If I didn't finally have someone—correction, *someones*—to live for, then I might just die from mortification. As it is, I must live and endure this. My guys had better appreciate this gesture.

I'm not embarrassed by sex. I mean, I write this stuff for a living.

Well, the steamy romance part, not the 'grandma watching them bump uglies with a legit monster with special equipment' part.

Yeah. I'm burning with flushed skin in more ways than one.

Arran just rocked my body, then my soul. I feel our spirits intertwining. It's the magical equivalent of a marriage, but a heck of a lot more permanent.

It hits me again. We are mated.

I was so caught up in the moment that I begged him for his bite.

When I check in with my emotions, I don't regret it. I only regret my grandmother's ghost for an audience. Now, if Maxim, Flint, or both of them, were here watching, that would be hot.

Arran's berserker gives the darkness another snarl for good measure before he licks the fresh wound on my neck, tending to his mating bite. I feel it sealing closed as he administers the aftercare.

My other, more permanent ghost, Osen, slides forward in my mind, but I don't want to deal with him either, so I throw up a mental wall and demand, *"Is this a life or death conversation?"*

"Uh, no," he mutters.

"Then fuck off… for now, okay?"

Thankfully, he fades into the background again.

Forgetting my ghostly audience for now, I turn my attention to the person who should have it.

My berserker is slowly grinding into me, giving me his entire release so his knot will subside.

I glance over my shoulder and watch as the berserker version shifts into his human form.

"Jade!" he shouts.

"Arran!"

He fists my hair and guides my mouth over my shoulder to meet his lips. He claims me all over again. Our tongues tangle, and his shallow thrusts become more urgent.

Breaking the kiss, he nuzzles the spot where my neck and my shoulder meet—where he bit me. "Goddess, Jade. I never thought…" His voice cracks with emotion. "We're really… Is this real? Are you mine?"

"Yes, my sweet Arran, my wolfy, my Serky."

He chuckles lightly. "Serky… for berserker?"

"He deserves a name, too."

"I suppose he does. Thank you, my sweet witch." His duller human teeth scrape over my flesh. "For the first time in my life I feel blessed." Deft fingers slide down my soft stomach and then find my sensitive bundle of nerves like a heat-seeking missile.

I cry out with pleasure as he works my body.

"My perfect love," he mumbles over and over. "I will never stop claiming you, Jade."

My body quivers with his words and his ministrations. The bliss he's driving me toward barrels at me.

I shatter into the universe. Stars go supernova. I'm blasted to the far ends of time, then I'm reassembled around Arran's perfect instrument of mass pleasure. I coalesce as someone who has their person.

I arch into Arran's powerful body as he shouts through his release.

He collapses against my back, breathing hard.

Fortunately, his arm braces me against him, while the other props us up from the forest floor. He leans back on his heels and slips free.

Arran turns me on his lap and cups my face with his other hand.

"Sorry," he laughs, "I made a mess of you. You're covered in dirt."

"Worth it." I smile wide, and I'm sure I look dreamy eyed. "Mud wrestling at its finest."

"I don't want to return to the others, but I know you need your rest after all you've been through lately."

"I understand your possessiveness, but I doubt I'll get much rest out here."

Arran doesn't let go of me. Instead, he lifts me in his arms and carries me back.

I silently call out again to see if the ghost is still lingering. *"Abuela, was that really you?"*

I hear a long-suffering sigh. Great. Now I know it's my grandmother. Other than Osen, who would sigh at me like that?

"Mija, I warned you not to become attached to these males."

I answer her in my mind so I don't upset Arran. *"Uh, well, damage done and all that. I don't want you ruining this for me."*

I hear a feminine grunt of disapproval, and I feel her presence slip away.

My heart aches. I wish I could have talked to her more, but this isn't the moment.

We quickly see our cabin ahead of us.

I bark out a laugh. "Geez. It felt like forever when you were chasing me."

When we get close, I give Arran another kiss and study his eyes. "Do I need to be careful about touching the guys until the bond settles?"

"You'll know if I can't handle it, but I think we should be okay. My wild side sees them as pack."

I sigh with relief.

Coming into my magic for the first time in my life must be enhancing my eyesight, because I can clearly see Flint, Maxum, and Calder standing outside, watching us return.

First, I wonder if something's wrong. Then, I worry I've frightened them.

As soon as I'm close enough to not shout, I ask, "What's wrong?"

Maxum chuffs and smirks at me like I'm a naughty child. "You just played a dangerous game of roulette. Thank the Fates, you won."

"Serky wouldn't have hurt me." I squeeze Arran and gaze adoringly at him.

Calder throws his hands up in exasperation. "You didn't know that for certain. A primal chase with a werewolf is dangerous, at best." It appears he's concerned for me, not just for the body attached to his ghost love.

Flint rushes forward and wraps a warm blanket over me. "It's too cold for you to be out here."

My eyes snap back to Calder. I don't believe he's seen me naked before and perhaps never wished to. Although he might have accidentally caught a glimpse when Maxum had Arran lick me clean. I thought Calder had been in the cabin when that happened, but when it was over, he wasn't around.

I reach out to give Maxum and Flint a soft touch. "I'm sorry if we worried you."

Maxum quirks an eyebrow. "You're living for more than just yourself now. You have us. So, keep that in mind, stunt devil."

"You should have seen me run!" I say proudly.

"Sweet witch, I did." Maxum shakes his head. "I loved watching your juicy bottom bounce and jiggle, but you weren't as fast as you think you were."

"I was scared," Flint says. "Please let us know when you plan to do something spontaneous again."

I suppress a laugh at his comment. He's so protective, and I don't wish to squash his need to be the protector he was created to be. "I will plan all my reckless behavior from now on."

"Good." Flint pulls a twig from my hair. "I've realized that my danger-compass is broken around you. It's very unsettling."

"Oh, shit," I say, and think about it. It really is broken—he hasn't felt his spidey tingles when I'm in danger. "Why is that happening?"

"Could be your magic?" He shrugs.

"Or the wards your grandmother placed on you, scrambling his senses like it does with your legal documents to hide you from the world," Maxum suggests.

"Or his heart is always on alert, worrying about you." Calder throws out like a bomb. But as he says it, I feel the truth of it.

"Calder might be right on that." Flint frowns. "Not reassuring."

"But my sweetheart, it's so romantic," I point out.

"I will have to find a new baseline so I can protect you."

"Speaking of your grandmother, uh, why did you call out to her during our mating?" Arran asks.

Maxum goes on alert and demands details with a growl. "What happened?"

"I felt her pushing on my senses when I was playing out my primal chase fantasy, and I put up my wall," I explain. "But when Arran bit me, I lit up with symbols like Maxum said he's seen on me. Then they sort of dissipated into the air. Almost like they dissolved in the wind. Is that how it happened before?" I ask Maxum.

"No. They lit up and then faded back *into* your skin."

"Oh. Hmm. That's weird." I don't know if this is a positive twist, but there's not much I can do about it now. "Then my grandmother's voice popped into my head and said, 'You made the same mistake I made.'"

"What the hell does that mean?" Calder hisses. "Are you part supe?"

2

AFTERCARE

JADE

"*A*re you a supe?" Arran and Flint echo Calder's question.

"I don't know. I didn't ask her, I was in the middle of mating so I told her to bugger off." I bite my lip, wondering what I am. "Do you think that might be why you all are attracted to me? Because I'm not really a witch?"

"You're a witch," Maxum says with certainty. "However, it appears you might have something extra. But just so you know, that's not why we like you."

"But—" I argue.

"No. Stop trying to find reasons we don't just like you for you," Maxum says with his bossy tone.

"Okay…" I rub a hand over my face, feeling self-conscious. "I'm not usually this insecure, but—"

"Rob made you feel worthless," Calder interrupts with no malice. Damn, this guy is hitting the bullseye with all his comments tonight.

"Yeah. You're right." Magically suppressed and conscious memories trickle back. "He did say horrible things to me about my body and personality, especially toward the end. I now remember when he had me under his hypnosis spell to channel spirits, that also he used that time to degrade me. He tried to make me feel like I was unlovable. Probably so he could control me."

"But it didn't work, not completely," Calder reminds me with a sympathetic smile. It surprises me that he's saying such supportive words. He isn't exactly my biggest fan. "You broke up with him. That takes strength when you're being manipulated and beaten down on all levels."

Maxum cups my face with his large hand. "He's correct. You're strong. Stronger than they know how to control. I believe those witches and warlocks are afraid of you."

"Of me? Why?" I ask.

"I don't know, but we'll find out. Together." Maxum's gaze turns to my hair, his fingers comb through the strands. "Your hair... it's silver."

I roll my eyes. "Yeah, I have gray hair."

"No. *Silver*. Like an elf might have," Arran agrees and then stares into my widening eyes. "And your irises... they're glowing green."

I need to see this.

"Jade green," Flint adds. "Like the beautiful, powerful stone."

"They are no longer hazel." Maxum touches my hair reverently again. "Silver. That spell broke whatever was hiding your more obvious fae traits."

"We'll figure it out, but first we should bring our sweet witch inside. It's cold out here," Flint says and picks me up, clutching me to his chest. He braces the back of my neck with his large hand and it feels like polished marble. His thumb skims the bottom of my jaw, and he whispers in my ear, "Are you sure you're alright?"

I give my protective gargoyle a kiss on the lips. "I'm fine, sweetheart. I'm sore between the legs from the knotting, and I have some minor scrapes from tree branches and Serky's claws, but nothing serious."

Flint gently places me on the bed and makes me lie back. He pulls the blanket off me and inspects my body for the injuries. His smooth, thick fingers trace over my collarbone, over my breasts and stomach, to my thighs. I'm covered in drying mud and debris from when Arran's berserker claimed me and fucked me into the ground.

Flint pulls another twig from my hair.

Without asking, he spreads me wide for Arran and Maxum to inspect my abused pussy, running a thick finger over my center. "The werewolf made a mess of you."

Holy Geezelbub. Does this gargoyle know how hot he is?

Calder hangs back behind the partition in the living area and sits on the couch out there. He wants no part in this. Not yet. Maybe not ever. No. He only longs for the trapped ghost inside me, his former beloved, Osen. I shouldn't be greedy, but I want him to be with me, too.

"Eyes on me… Stay with us, my mate," Flint says as he strokes my thighs. I'm beginning to wonder if he's been reading my books for spicy inspiration. But I realize he's sensed with our budding mate bond my wandering thoughts about Calder.

Our gazes lock, and I'm drawn into his pale gray eyes.

"All in good time," he whispers, reading my mind.

"Arran, your tongue might soothe her cuts now that you're bonded," Maxum suggests.

Arran snarls at Maxum, nudging both males out of his way. "I planned on taking care of my mate. Thank you very fucking much. I came back here to do just that." My wolf shifter picks me up and carries me into the tiny bathroom in our hideaway cabin.

I'm thankful Amira took us in and offered us this haven, but I miss Maxum's beautiful lake house and his spacious luxury showers.

Arran turns on the water to warm it up and presses his forehead to mine. "Goddess, I can barely stand not touching you. I was ready to rip Flint apart for carrying you inside."

I clasp his cheeks. "Will you have a hard time, then? Me being with them?"

"I think it's only since the claiming bond is still settling. As soon as it solidifies, I should be fine." He looks me in the eye and strokes my cheek. "Don't worry. I won't keep you from your other loves."

I smile sadly. I'm happy to hear this, but also worried about how he feels about the arrangement. "Are you sure you're okay with sharing me?"

"As Arran, yes. I mean, would I prefer to keep you all to myself? Fuck, yes, I would. But I see how you are with them, especially what you did for Flint." He whispers, his lips brushing over the shell of my ear, "And how you have already healed something in Calder."

I frown, worried about how Calder will handle things now that I have officially bonded with Arran and I'm forming a bond with Flint and Maxum. They are his people, his pack. Then I came along and turned his world upside down. Although I suppose his world was already screwed up when Osen died just before I stumbled into the picture.

My thoughts are brought back to my new mate when Arran licks over his mating bite.

Holy macaroons. The sensation travels like a lightning bolt directly to my clit. I shiver and press into his firm, naked body.

"I'd love to rut you again, but I'm worried that you won't be able to take me so soon. You aren't a wolf shifter. You weren't made for taking knots."

"Does it bother you that I'm not a shifter?"

"Not at all. Actually, I'm a bit surprised how well you took my knot and how rough... Serky was." He gives me another seductive kiss that makes me tremble with arousal. "But if you have supe blood, perhaps that's why it feels so natural for you to be with us."

"What if I'm some sort of freak supe-witch hybrid?"

"Then I will love and protect you just as much." He shrugs playfully. "And apparently, we love freaky."

I release a heavy breath, feeling less stressed about my mysterious background. "How did I get so lucky?"

"I'm the lucky one. I stalked you and tricked you into believing I was a dog. I never thought you would forgive that lie."

"I don't blame you for protecting your pack. You didn't know if you could trust a witch taking sneaky pics of you."

"I'm glad you were a bit of a perv and horrible at being sneaky." Arran chuckles and lifts me into the shower now that the water is warm.

He runs his fingers over my neck, prompting me to ask, "Do I need to bite you now to complete the mate bond? Or is that not how it works in the real magical world?"

The corners of his lips pull down ever so slightly. "You can try to bite me, but I doubt it will do anything more for our bond because you aren't a shifter."

It doesn't matter that he says it's not a big deal. I wish I could offer him what his kind can—the way I sense he *wants* it to be.

Arran lifts my chin with his finger and makes me look into his eyes. "I love you, Jade. *You're* all I need."

"Okay." I hate that I'm so worried, but they are all so special to me, and I don't want to disappoint them.

Osen's voice breaks through my barrier I've learned to create to block him out. *"Just be you, and you won't disappoint them. They picked you because you're perfect the way you are. You don't need to change or be more. You just need to remember the confident version of yourself before Rob hurt you,"* Osen speaks in my mind, then pauses. *"We will help you get there."*

I take a deep breath. I used to be more confident before Rob the Worm infiltrated my mind.

"You want to help me?" I ask.

"As best I can... considering what I am."

"You feel stronger," I say, trying to change the subject. His kind offer makes

me want to leak water from my eyes (as Flint might say), and I don't want to get emotional over something he's said since I'm still irritated with him.

"Your mating powered me up. But we can talk more later. I'll let you have your time with Arran now." He pauses and I feel the tension inside me brewing. *"We must talk about the situation with your grandmother."*

"Okay." I send him a mental wave goodnight to let him know I appreciate his support and care.

"Talking with Osen?" Arran asks.

"Uh, sorry."

"It's okay. I could see that you were somewhere else."

"It's weird to have your former friend and lover inside me, isn't it?"

"It's all weird, but it's what it means to be with you." Arran leaves a trail of kisses from my shoulder, up my neck to my mouth. Then he claims me with a fierce kiss. "For now, I'm going to hoard your attention, because to do otherwise might kill me." Arran licks over the bite again, and I moan with need. "I need to be inside you again… soon."

3

FAMILY BINDS

CALDER

*T*hankfully, after Jade showered off her mating dance dirt, the guys initiated nothing more with her.

I'm not jealous. Okay, maybe a bit. I wish I could enjoy someone's touch again. Now that Flint has overcome his aversion, it's given me some hope, but he was never broken like I am. He didn't lose a huge part of himself because he died a horrific death.

I will never be the same. Though, perhaps I don't have to be completely healed to endure being close to someone again?

Remembering the moment with Osen, while he was inside Jade's body, I mull over how I was able to share a kiss with my old love.

That's something, isn't it?

But if I had to listen to my entire pack fucking that sweet witch while basically in the same room? *And* I couldn't join in? Nope, that's a whole new torture.

I might be over the possible evil witch thing with her, but that doesn't mean I'm ready to pursue something with Jade. Besides, I don't expect that she would be into me. Not after what an ass I've been.

I wouldn't want her to think I liked her just because Osen possessed her, either. For some wild reason she confessed to me she worried about that with the other guys, and it struck me hard in my gut. If I'm honest, I don't want to make that mistake with her if it really is Osen's energy that attracts me to her. It wouldn't be fair to any of us.

In the morning, I wake to discover Jade's magical creatures sleeping on me—Sage, the rabbit, and Trouble, the guinea pig. I'm scratching the bunny behind the ears when Jade shuffles into the main room and finds me snuggling with the little ones. Her sexy curves are barely contained in her skimpy sleep shorts and tank top. Not that I'm looking.

When she sees her creatures with me, her eyes soften and the corners of her mouth lift in a small smile. She takes a step toward me, but then thinks better of it and asks, "Can I pet them too?"

"They're your familiars, so yeah," I say in hushed tones, not wanting to wake the other guys. I flick my chin for her to come over.

"Uh, I didn't want to encroach on your space." Jade kneels down beside my makeshift bed on the couch and strokes Trouble's soft fur.

We share a quiet moment where it feels like the terrors of the realms aren't pressing in on us. I watch her gentle fingers gliding down the guinea pig's fluffy coat and find myself enchanted by her delicate hands. Loving hands. She isn't at all like the witches that have hurt my pack and me.

Jade hasn't looked at me since she kneeled down to pet her animals. She bites her lip then says, "I'm sorry."

"About what?" I ask, skimming my finger over the rabbit's incredibly soft ears.

"You're stuck here like *this*. It must be uncomfortable."

"The couch isn't too bad," I say. I know what she really means, but I want to avoid the topic. What can I say about it anyway?

"No, about having to share this small space with me. It was probably bad enough when I was invading your pack's huge lake house. You had your beautiful room to avoid me." She swallows down the emotion bubbling up. "And now, you're forced..."

"Hush," I admonish her with a tender yet firm voice. "We're good. Okay? You're pack now. Arran officially claimed you. Flint and Maxum are already bonding with you. Osen is..." I choke up a bit despite myself. "You're literally carrying his soul inside you. Don't worry about me. If I need a break, I can take a walk."

Her hypnotizing green eyes finally meet my gaze and I swear there's a glow behind them, like a supernatural being might have. I wonder what she might actually be besides a witch.

The bunny wakes up and licks my hand. Then she says happily to Jade, "You lick birdman now. He likes it."

Jade's eyes go wide, and she covers her face in embarrassment. "Sage, he doesn't want me licking or petting him. *Please* stop saying stuff like that."

Even my face heats, feeling self-conscious. I swear this rabbit fancies herself a matchmaker.

Of course, Trouble pipes right in. "I think Birdman might like it more than he says."

Jade frowns at both of them and gets to her feet, stepping back. "No more of this talk. You will *not* pressure us anymore about me touching him. He's only comfortable with you guys. It's not nice."

"Sorry," Sage and Trouble say.

Jade looks at me, worry written on her face. "I'm sorry about all that."

"Not your fault." I sit up and set both creatures down on the floor so I can get breakfast ready when I hear the others rolling out of the huge bed they've all shared inside the small cabin.

I sense that they've been awake since Jade got up and approached me. I suppose they didn't want to make her think they're going to hover over her as much as they want to.

Flint enters the room and nods at me. We set things out on the counter and table for us to eat as Arran and Maxum join us.

Dressed in only sweatpants, Arran sits down at the kitchen table and pulls Jade into his lap. She squeaks as he does, and a blush creeps into her cheeks.

This woman confuses the hell out of me. We watched her come back filthy and naked from the woods last night after a werewolf knotted and claimed her, and *now* she's embarrassed sitting on his lap?

Maxum and Flint give her glances filled with longing, their hands clenching as if they are resisting the need to snatch her up and into their own laps.

I'm jealous for my own reasons. I wish I could get over my touch aversion and be comfortable, like Arran is with his mate.

I had always wanted a mate, but do I want that anymore?

With a heavy sigh, I place a couple of chocolate muffins on the table and some fruit for us to eat.

Arran grabs a muffin and lifts it to his mouth.

Just as he's about to take a bite, Jade screams, "No!" Then she smacks it right out of his hands and to the floor.

We all stare at her in shock.

"What the hell?" Arran asks, more in confusion than anger.

"It's chocolate!" she says, pulling away from him a bit.

"So?" He shakes his head, puzzled by her behavior.

"It could kill you," she explains, like he's daft.

Then Maxum lets out a booming laugh.

Her eyes dart to him with a snarl. "What's so flippin' funny about killing my mate?"

Dang, she's fierce. It's hotter than it should be.

"He's not a damned dog, little witch." Maxum wheezes with laughter. "It doesn't poison him."

"Oh, whoops." She turns bright red again and sinks down into herself, burying her face in Arran's chest. "My bad."

Arran chuckles and strokes along her back. "I appreciate the sentiment, but please never try to choc-block a werewolf," he jokes and kisses her temple.

"Arran has a sweet fang, but he won't admit it," I add, and I'm rewarded with Jade's laughter.

Flint picks up the damaged muffin, pulls off the crushed side that impacted the ground, and eats the rest.

Jade offers Arran her muffin as an apology. After a bit of fuss, he accepts, then feeds her a few bites when she finishes eating the sliced apples and peanut butter Flint gave her.

She licks Arran's fingertips clean of crumbs, and I imagine her licking something else... Dang, I need to get my shit together. Maybe I should go buy a tent and rough it outside of this cabin.

"Amira wants me to meet with her soon." Jade appears apprehensive at the idea.

"Hopefully, she will be able to help you control your new magic and understand how you connect with spirits," Flint says, taking Jade's finished plate from her to clean.

"I hope so too," Maxum agrees. "And I'd like to chat with Darius about our home realm. Find out what's been going on lately in hell." He smiles at Jade. "I'll walk you over to the main house."

"I'm going to do a sweep of the area," Flint says and hurries out the door. He doesn't like new places or situations, and he's on edge, being at the mercy of another witch's protection. No doubt he's worried about Jade being attacked again.

Jade pouts while she watches him run off. The big oaf didn't even give her a hug or kiss goodbye. He's going to need some pointers on how to be in a relationship with a mostly human woman.

I see the angst clearly written on Arran's face. He doesn't appreciate the idea of being separated from Jade so soon after their mate bond. Goddess, I have no idea why he bonded with her with all that's going on.

He should have waited until Jade's ex wasn't a problem anymore.

Maxum pulls out a sheet of paper with a sketch on it and places it in front of Jade.

"What's this?" she asks, studying the page filled with sigils and glyphs.

"These are the markings I saw on your body. I thought we could show Amira to see what she recognizes."

Jade's eyes widen in shock. "Do you have an eidetic memory?"

"Mostly… for the things that interest me." He smirks. "And you interest me."

I roll my eyes but lean over to check out the designs. "Strange. They almost look like fae sigils, but not quite. Are you sure you got them right?"

The demon gives me a pissy glare. "I got it fucking right, bird brain. That's why they confused me. But I had hoped it was some sort of secret witch thing and maybe Amira would tell Jade about them."

Maxum leads Jade away toward the main house and Arran huffs out a breath just like his wolf might.

"Get a grip, buddy," I tease and finish cleaning up our morning meal. "She's going across the field, not to another realm."

"It's the bond. For a little while, every time she leaves the room, I'm going to be a pathetic mess." Arran sets his golden gaze on me, and I know he's wondering where I stand with this development. "Well?"

"Well, what?" I ask, just to drag it out. I don't want to answer him.

"Dude, really?" Arran shakes his head. "Out with it. Tell me I'm a dumbass for claiming Jade."

"You're a dumbass?" I say with zero conviction and as a question.

"So you're cool with us?" Arran cocks his head like a confused dog.

"I'm not pissed at her anymore, but I think your timing is a bit screwed up."

He runs a hand through his thick, cropped brown hair and frowns. "I know. I don't want to admit it to Jade, but her grandmother's disapproval is worrying me."

Sighing, I focus on him and empathize. Relationship stuff can suck ass, but when a disembodied voice offers him an ominous statement during the most vulnerable and fulfilling moment of his life—claiming his mate—it had to have rocked his world.

"We don't even know if it really *is* her grandmother," I say with a shrug.

"And… uh, I am happy for you. It's no small thing to have a bond with someone you feel you have a mate match with."

He nods, but still looks a bit off-center. "I'm going for a run."

"I'm going to track down the other phoenix here."

Arran strips down, shifts into his regular wolf form, and races off to the woods. He's chasing his personal demons. With the image of his terrifying monster form in my mind, I still can't believe he didn't hurt Jade during their mating. She really did tame his berserker werewolf.

I fuss a bit in the house, delaying my talk with Raithe. As I open the door, I find him standing outside, ready to knock.

"Hey," he says with a wide grin.

Raithe is so much more easygoing than I am. I wonder how many times he's died and regenerated. I doubt if any of them could be as bad as my last rebirth. He wouldn't be so smiley if he went through the torture I did.

"Hey." I try to relax my shoulders and appear calm, but being around another phoenix stirs up a lot of emotions for me. Loss, anger, longing, and jealousy. "I was coming to see you."

"Good to hear. I didn't want to push myself on you if you weren't up for company." Raithe glances behind himself and then suggests, "Would you like to take a walk or maybe stretch our wings?"

I consider my emotions right now. "Uh, walking is probably best." I shut the cabin door behind me and step out into the sun. We are on the earth plane, I can sense that much, but nothing beyond that. However, I haven't been trying too hard to pin it down. If someone were to mind probe me, then I don't want to give up our secret location. And I really don't want to bring down the witches and warlocks upon Raithe and his mates.

"I know the cabin is cramped, but I hope you're able to make it work. When Darius and I shared it with Amira, it was tight. I can't imagine adding two more large males to the coven and staying in there."

"We aren't a coven," I correct him. "Well, *I'm* not one of Jade's mates."

Raithe's eyebrows rise with disbelief. "Oh? I could have sworn I sensed something between you. Sorry."

"Uh, yeah… it's complicated." I rub the back of my neck and feel my heart racing. How much do I tell him? Maybe I should tell him everything and get an outsider's perspective. I'm all turned around and twisted up.

Raithe nods and walks toward the woods. "I understand complicated. I hadn't expected to be with a witch… or a woman, for that matter. I'm usually attracted to males. But then Amira came along and captured my heart *and* my balls." He laughs, shaking his head, likely remembering falling for his mate.

"I'm bi with a leaning toward males. But I don't think I can be intimate ever again," I confess.

His gaze darts down to my crotch, probably wondering if I've lost my *dangly bits* as Jade would say and why they didn't come back in a regeneration.

"No. Not *that*. My last death fucked up my head pretty badly."

"Sorry to hear that, brother." He reaches out to pat my shoulder and thinks better of it, dropping his hand to his side.

I don't tell him it's okay, because it's not. A stranger's touch makes me want to scream. Sure, I allow my pack to occasionally buddy-pat me, but even that doesn't bring me any comfort.

Oddly, Jade's touch during our mental shield training didn't seem to bother me. I wonder if Osen being inside her was the reason. Then I remember I didn't enjoy Osen's touch since my last incarnation.

There's something different about her. But I still don't know if it's wise to pursue it when so much is unknown about her origins and who she may be.

I can't risk it.

"So… you left a big piece of yourself behind last time?" Raithe asks.

"Yeah. You know how it is. We always lose memories or some bits with each death. After the last one, I wish I didn't come back."

"Fuck," Raithe hisses. "My flames feel your pain."

We start on a path in the woods that appears well traveled. The forest swallows up the morning light, but my eyes quickly adjust to the darkness.

"Have you ever had a death like that?" I ask.

He nods slowly.

Goddess, it feels strange talking about this with another phoenix. My father is long gone, his magic was snuffed out when I was just a fledgling. I didn't get much guidance from him since he was taken when I was so young. My heavy heart feels as though it's been lifted as I realize I finally have another phoenix to help me.

But quickly, my anger swells inside again at what the witch who killed me did to me. Memories of her torture fill my mind.

Then what's been eating me up since that death finally comes out as I shout, "I can't shift!"

After a long silence, where I see his concern on his face, Raithe asks, "At all?"

I can't believe I admitted that to him. I've never even told my pack.

I want to punch Raithe for the sad look of pity on his face.

I want to scream.

I want to fucking shift!

447

Turning my gaze away so I don't have to look at his pity, I admit, "I can only manifest my wings and fire."

"I understand now that your last death wasn't an ordinary one. But if you have your wings and fire, your phoenix is still inside you."

I fall to my knees, emotion overcoming me, covering my face with my hands in shame. "But I'm broken. It's like a piece of my soul is missing, not just my memories."

Raithe kneels next to me and says quietly, "My last death was the worst yet." He sighs heavily. "Without going into a long ass story, I'll say I only survived it emotionally because of Amira. Because I finally gave in and trusted her, she saved my soul on so many levels. And I'll never be able to pay her back."

Scraping together my dignity, I get to my feet, considering his words, and we continue down the forest path.

"So you truly don't have a problem with Amira being a witch?" I ask with no small amount of skepticism, but my voice comes out as small and weak—it matches how I feel.

Raithe stops abruptly and looks at me. "She has essentially given up being a witch, and chose Darius and me as mates. If it weren't for her, we'd be dead or still being tortured. She has done more for supernaturals than most supes, so no, I don't have a problem with her." He levels his gaze at me, and I feel the weight of his focus like a threat. "Jade is in your pack, whether you like it or not. So you better figure out how to drop your prejudice or leave them."

My feathers are ruffled, but the asshole isn't wrong. "I'm trying. It isn't easy."

"Maybe, but it's not as hard as you're probably making it." Raithe turns and continues back on our walk. "What everyone seems to forget is that we are all individuals. We are more than our species, or magic, or lineage, or sexuality, or whatever the fuck there is to see on the surface. More importantly, we are the choices we make every damned day."

I think about his words. Who have I been if I only considered my choices?

I don't like the answer.

And Jade? She has only been kind, accepting, and giving.

I just hope I can repair any damage I might have caused and develop a friendship with her.

Because no matter my hang-ups, she's in my pack now.

4

TRAINING

JADE

"I'm nervous about talking with Amira," I admit to Maxum as we walk up to the main house.

"How so?" His voice is calm and filled with authority, like a hot professor might sound in one of my novels.

"Uh, well, she's a witch. And probably a powerful witch to be able to protect and ward her vast amount of land. Besides, she doesn't seem to be overly fond of other witches. I feel like a burden."

Maxum stops and turns me to face him. I look up into his dark obsidian eyes and sigh. My gaze travels over his crimson skin and horns, admiring what a handsome demon he is. Not that I've met other demons, but it doesn't matter.

He's my demon. And he's gorgeous.

His hand cups my cheek. "Amira has an ugly past with other witches, just as our pack has. She doesn't like being a witch. So don't take it personally. Learn whatever she can teach you, and we'll figure out the rest together."

"Thank you." I lean into his palm. "It means a lot that you're helping me."

His expression turns fierce. "How else should I act? You're my mate match. Even if you rejected me, I would help you in any way I can. I would die for you."

My insides melt into goo, and my eyes widen. "You really think we are meant to be? What about my abuela's warning when I mated with Arran?"

"We don't know what that was about. And honestly, I don't care." Maxum steps closer until I'm flush with his body. He pulls me up by my ass, and I wrap my legs around his hips. "*You. Are. Mine.* And no one can tell me otherwise, except for you."

His lips crash down on mine, and by the time he's done reminding me I belong with him, I'm panting and grinding on his growing bulge.

"Understand, little witch?" he growls.

"Yes," I breathe out. Damn, he just erased my worries with a mind melting kiss.

We hear someone clearing their throat, and snap our eyes over to the porch of the main house.

"You going to hump on my lawn all day?" Darius asks with his gruff, gravelly voice.

Darius and Amira are standing side by side. Amira looks slightly amused, and Darius appears his standard irritated. I haven't seen him with another emotional setting yet.

He must have one, right? I mean, Amira loves him, he can't be one dimensional. Perhaps he doesn't let anyone but Amira and Raithe see another side.

Reluctantly, Maxum allows me back down to my feet and gives me a peck on the forehead before swatting my ass as I walk toward Amira.

I throw a dirty look over my shoulder. He's being a brat in front of them. "You'll pay for that," I threaten.

"I've already paid dearly for my time with you," Maxum says with a laugh.

I turn around and try to hide my hurt about that statement. I cost him two of his safe houses, one of which was his special secret home he had hoped to have for his pack. Guilt doesn't even cover it when I think of what he's lost since I came into his life. Hell, one could even say Osen's death is on me. Rob might not have killed him if I couldn't channel his spirit. And now, we are on the run because Rob and Galiana are hunting me.

Huge arms wrap around my waist and Maxum hugs me to his chest. He leans down and whispers in my ear. "Sweetheart, no. Stop this. I was talking about my heart. You own it now. Don't blame yourself for the houses. They mean nothing compared to your safety."

I lean back into his arms and look up into his handsome face. "Thank you."

He gives me another kiss and Darius grumbles. "Can we bring the public displays of affection down to a fucking minimum?"

With a blush on my cheeks, I pull away and hurry toward Amira so I don't get lost in Maxum again.

"Morning," I say to the witch, and we watch Maxum and Darius wander off together around the house.

"Never mind Darius. He likes to give people a hard time," Amira says.

"I understand why he would want me to leave. I'm a witch invading your territory, and possibly bringing trouble with me," I add, feeling bad about the whole thing. I didn't ask for my magic and all this drama. I only like drama in my books, thank you very much. If I could have all the yummy monster love and not be chased around by an asshole ex who wants to magically fuck with my head, then I'd be a happy little witch.

"Most witches and warlocks are a problem." Amira ushers me inside her home. "If they would drop their prejudice and work with the supernaturals, we might be able to figure out what to do about the loss of magic."

"Do you think that's why they are after me?" I ask.

She studies my face and then her eyes lose focus and I suspect she is reading my magic and aura. "Maybe. You have an unusual magic." Then she motions for me to sit down on a meditation cushion near the large picture window overlooking the rolling forested hills on her property. She takes up the seat in front of me.

"Can you figure out what I am?" The desperation in my voice is clear.

It truly is disconcerting to become the FMC in my story and receive weird powers.

Will I answer the call to adventure?

Well, I suppose I answered the call to monster cock adventures. That hasn't killed me yet, so I'm on a roll.

"Can you tell me what you know about your lineage? Your gifts?" she asks.

I swallow down my nerves and give her the quick summary. "As I mentioned before, my grandmother told me she was a witch. She implied I would have powers as well. She was odd, so I thought she was playing pretend with me. My mother didn't seem to have any magic powers, and she didn't like my abuela saying things like that to me. When I was a kid, I saw what I thought was my wild imagination—auras, monstrous forms under someone's face, and sometimes energy swirling around me. Then it all disappeared after my grandmother gave me that necklace when I was around ten years old. I was told she died not long after that visit. The only thing that didn't fade was my strange dreams. It felt like I was experiencing other people's dreams. It turns out I might have been channeling spirits this whole time. And my ex took advantage of this ability."

"Yes, your mates mentioned you can channel the spirits of supernaturals," she says thoughtfully. "I've never heard of that ability. It might be why the Anti-Supernatural Organization wants you."

"Yeah, I have the spirit of my guys' former pack member permanently tied to me now. But I don't know how to control this gift, and we were hoping you could help me figure it out."

"I know some things about channeling, but I'm far from an expert." Amira frowns. "I'll share what I know."

"I also believe I have heard my grandmother's spirit a few times now." I bite my lip, feeling nervous to admit what happened. "Uh, when Arran claimed me last night, she said that I made the same mistake she did."

Amira's eyebrows rise in question. "So, you're wondering if your grandmother had a supernatural mate and if you have supe blood..." She nods to herself and says, "That would make sense. Usually, only humans and supernaturals can mate and create offspring. If you have a witch-supe combination in your lineage, that might explain your unique ability. Did you ask her what she meant?"

"She sort of interrupted us during the mating, so I told her to go away," I admit with a blush.

"Oh, well, yes." Amira barely suppresses a laugh. "Do you have a process to connect with the spirits? Maybe you should try to ask her about it now."

"I don't have a process. It's one reason we came here—so you could teach me," I admit. "Do you have any suggestions on how to call on spirits?"

"Being a witch, I'd suggest meditation and some sort of focal object."

"I had my grandmother's pendant until we realized my ex used it to shove spirits into my body so he could question his victims after he murdered them." My hand automatically touches the now empty spot at my throat. "But we left it behind because of the tracking spell."

Amira watches my gesture and frowns. "I would offer you a focal object for a replacement, but I don't think you need that—not if supe magic enhances your power."

"It's so strange to think I lived almost forty years with no clue that these other realms existed and that I might have magic."

"Unfortunately, magic isn't as wonderful as some humans might imagine." Amira studies her hands as if she is contemplating her power. "I did some terrible things because of magic and my struggle for power—for control. I hope you never have to do something you'll regret."

I swallow that comment down with all that it contains. I can tell by the haunted look in her eyes that she's seen some shit. Maxum told me she is older than she appears. I idly wonder how long I will have with my guys if we can survive Rob and Galiana.

"I'll teach you some meditations to help access your magic," Amira says and then guides me through some visualizations.

They are nothing profound, but I expect they will help me focus and center my thoughts.

I've used exercises like this before, especially when I first started writing professionally. But over the years, it only takes me sitting down at my computer with my tea to trigger my brain to enter the proper wavelength to write and create.

I realize as I allow my mind to wander that it seems channeling or using magic will probably be similar to my writing process.

I will have to create a mindset or mental space—a trigger—that I can use to access my gifts.

Osen's spirit vibrates gently, letting me know I'm on the right track with this idea.

At the end of the meditation, I open my eyes and find Amira staring at me.

"Is something wrong?" I ask when she appears a bit disturbed.

"No. I've been using this time to study your magic. It truly is odd. I've never sensed anything quite like it, but it also feels familiar."

I hum to acknowledge her statement, but I don't know what to say. "I don't need to try now, but I was also wondering if you would know how to release a spirit from my hold. Eventually, I expect Osen will want to move on. Or I might have another spirit try to attach to me."

"I did some research already in this area. Darius is a high-level hellhound. He said that there are many ways to separate a possessing spirit from a host. One is a complex ceremony mostly used by normal humans, since they rarely have magic. You're a witch, so there is a spell I have written out for you. However, it may not work since Osen is not a normal human or witch soul. Darius says for the demons and hellhounds dealing with supernatural souls, they use their intent to handle souls. Often seeing a severing in their mind's eye."

"So… just imagine it?" I ask.

"Yes, but with *intent*, with your will and magic."

"Oh!" I remember the sketch Maxum made. "I have something we wanted you to look at." I pull the paper out and hand it over. "We're hoping you can give us an idea of what this is."

Amira studies it for a while before her eyes snap up to mine. "Where did you get this?" her voice is almost accusatory, *threatening*. "Where did you see these symbols?"

Instead of answering, I ask, "Why? Is there something wrong?"

"Answer me."

I can't refuse her, but I rationalize it won't hurt me to tell her. She already knows too much. "They were magically embedded in my body. But they're gone now. They disappeared after I bonded to Arran."

"Hmm." She narrows her gaze at me. "Who was your grandmother?"

"Patricia Jones."

Amira tilts her head and her eyes widen as if something's clicked into place. "No, not Jones, it's Rosethorne," she states confidently and chuckles without humor. "I thought you looked vaguely familiar. I should have recognized you right away, but it's been a long time since I've seen her face."

"You knew my grandmother?"

"Not well, but yes." Amira looks back down at the paper but does not really focus on it. "Patricia disappeared around forty years ago, from what I understand." Her gaze snaps up to meet mine to gauge my reaction. "She was a member of the ASO."

"How do you know?" I ask, feeling like an ass that my grandmother was part of the witch-warlock organization whose goal is to destroy supernaturals.

Amira must see my disappointment. "I worked with her a few times. She was a powerful lust witch… not that she didn't have other talents."

"Lust witch?"

"They mostly used her as a *spy*."

Spy likely means she was used as a seductress that slept with targets to obtain intel.

"Does that mean I'm a lust witch too?" I gasp when I realize I'm probably attracting the guys with my powers. Is it why I write steamy romance?

"Powers are often passed down, but I don't sense that lust magic is what is strongest inside you." Her eyes seem to lose focus as she gazes at me, like a scryer would over a crystal ball. "No, there's other magic in you that's more prominent, and it doesn't feel like witch magic. That's why these unusual sigils and your grandmother's warning about making mistakes concerns me."

"So you think I'm part fae?"

"Yes, and perhaps something else. As odd as it would be, I suspect you could have some demon in your family tree." She hands the paper back to me. "If I had my guess, your grandmother was mixed up in a lot of trouble in all the realms. She had someone from the hell realm working with her, if this mishmash of concealment and containment sigils are any indication. It appears to be long forgotten arcane spell work from all three realms, blended to form its own unique casting. Only the creator of this masterpiece *or* the person it was cast upon would have been able to break it."

"But then, what was the necklace for if I had this binding on me?" I ask.

"A necklace can be torn away. Besides, I believe the pendant's purpose might have been more to syphon any magic that leaked out of you, if the sigils weren't maintained over the years."

"So my grandmother meant to lock away my magic forever?" Sadness fills me as I conclude my abuela kept part of what I am from me. I've been living a half-life because of her.

"Don't assume the worst," Amira consoles me. "She might have believed she would come back and train you in your powers when you were ready."

My heartache and betrayal must be written on my face.

With everything that's happened, my entire being is suddenly exhausted. "I appreciate your help, but I think I need to rest now."

"Of course. Your magic is coming in. It will take time to adjust in your body. And if it's as unusual as I sense, then it might be even more challenging to manage at first."

Amira hands me a slip of parchment paper with the exorcism spell written in Latin on it and I walk toward her front door in a daze.

5

TEAM SPIRITS

JADE

I thank Amira for her time and information about my grandmother, my sigils, and the meditation techniques. Then I wander back toward our cabin so I can take a nap.

In my mind, I sense Osen push forward to catch my attention.

"Yes?" I ask with a bit of irritation. I still haven't completely let go that Osen has highjacked my body twice.

"I don't sense your grandmother right now," Osen reports.

"And you sensed her before?"

"Uh, yeah, that's why I was bothering you when you were mating with Arran. She was trying to stop you from doing that."

"Did you get any idea why?" I ask, curious to what he picked up from her.

"She didn't wish to interact with me. However, I did get a few flickering images from her. I swear I saw Galiana. I believe she knows that witch. It makes sense since they both were in ASO together."

I absorb that information, but until I talk to my grandmother, I won't have any answers. *"If you pick up her presence again, can you let me know?"*

"Of course, sweet witch."

I roll my eyes at his kiss ass nickname. He knows he fucked up, but I need him to sweat it out a bit more before I forgive him… again.

"*Amira isn't wrong about you having strange magic. Now that it has been unlocked, it feels like fae-born to me. The electric bolts you can innately summon aren't a witch's ability. At least not without training and a spell. And the soul magic you demonstrate with me is more akin to some types of demons or a hellhound.*"

"Could that mean that I have demon blood? Is that why Maxum thinks I might be a mate match?"

"*Maybe. But until we get answers about your lineage from your grandmother or elsewhere, we won't know for sure what you might be.*"

"Which means it will be probably harder for me to learn to control my powers until I know," I say aloud.

"*Not necessarily.*"

"What do you mean?"

I sense Osen is delighted and proud that I'm interested in what he has to say, and that he can help me.

"*We are all built to control the magic within us,*" Osen explains. "*Some might need more guidance than others. Some are more inclined to abuse their power. But ultimately, we have an instinct to use it. Just like how birds fly and snakes bite, we innately access that part of ourselves if nothing is blocking our way.*"

"Like how my grandmother's pendant blocked me."

"*Yes, but now, you'll likely find your powers come to the surface with little thought.*"

"That seems dangerous."

"*It can be. That's why magic schools and tutors are mandated to teach supes control. But you have us to help you. You have me.*"

His offer to help would mean more if he hadn't betrayed my trust. "I remember you tried to steal my body to use that power."

"*Not my finest hour.*" Osen sighs. "*I promise I won't make that mistake again. I'm feeling more like my old self. More complete. More in control over my reactions.*"

"Why would that be?"

"*Maybe your mating bond fed my incubus magic. Or it could be our connection. Your unleashed magic is healing me and strengthening my soul.*"

"I'm happy you're feeling better," I say and mean it.

"*I won't go rogue again. I realize how my stupid, impulsive decisions have hurt my pack, most significantly Calder and you.*"

Entering our empty cabin, I shuffle to the enormous bed and flop down. My mind wanders over all the things I should be doing now for my author career. I have promotions to run. Books to write and edit.

"Do you think I can set up my computer stuff and check my accounts?" I ask Osen.

"*I think there might be too much interference with Amira's cloaking magic.*

Besides, it's probably best to ask Maxum to portal you somewhere else far from here, just in case Rob can track you somehow."

Not being a computer expert, I don't know how likely that is. But I've seen spy movies that suggest if Rob has someone skilled in hacking, they might be able to ping my location. "You're right," I say with defeat in my heart. Things may never be normal for me again.

"Rest now, Jade. We can get all that figured out when you wake up."

As I close my eyes and drift off, Osen's presence shifts from just a disembodied voice in my head to a fully formed male in my dreams. He's standing in front of me in what he calls the shadowscape—where an incubus' magic resides.

He hasn't bothered to render imagery of the surrounding setting. We stare at each other amidst the darkness. There's only enough light to see each other. I study his handsome face since it's the first time he's appeared in a highly detailed human form. Before, I've only seen him as a shadow person, each time with increasing detail.

He's also completely naked and my eyes dip down to appreciate his toned and well-equipped body. But it's his intense gray eyes that draw my attention. His shoulder-length, wavy brown hair frames his masculine face in a casual, yet stylish, way.

Seeing him how he was in life assures me that Osen never had an issue feeding his magic with sexual partners.

He's fucking gorgeous.

Even his dead body was beautiful, since it hadn't decayed at all. The only thing that took away from his allure was the obvious lack of life in his body as it rested in a glass coffin.

Too bad that true love's kiss couldn't wake his sleeping beauty.

But then part of me wonders if anyone tried. Calder probably didn't attempt that with his aversion to touch.

"Your mind is somewhere else." Osen smirks. "I thought seeing me naked like this would at least amuse you."

"My mind has more than one track," I tease. "Horny isn't the only setting I have."

It's strange that he can't just read everything going on inside my mind. But I'm grateful for that now. My chaotic, wandering author's mind would likely baffle him.

"We need to ask Maxum about your body—why it looks so well

preserved," I say with a frown of concentration. This has been low-key bugging me since the bunker when I saw his body in person.

"Yes, I hope now that things have settled, we can unravel that mystery," Osen agrees, then opens his arms.

I don't fall into his embrace even though his gorgeous naked form is acting like a magnet to my nether regions. "What if I'm a lust witch? You heard that, right? Isn't that what you thought I was when we first talked?"

"I was worried that you were seducing my pack, yes."

My heart squeezes with fear. "What if it's not really me—"

"Shush." Osen's face becomes fierce. He steps closer and places a thumb on my lips. "If you even have that ability, it isn't why they like you. I should know. You aren't the only one who has dealt with this bullshit."

That thought shuts me up. He's an incubus. I imagine that's a far more powerful influence over others than a lust witch.

I move my trapped lips to talk. He slowly drags his thumb away as he stares at my mouth with interest.

I resist the urge to bite my lip and force myself to remain focused. "In your life, you've worried about whether your intimate partners actually cared for you, too."

"Constantly." His jaw flutters with the emotions raging inside him. "*Always.*"

"How did you deal with it?" I ask.

"I didn't. It's only now I realize that Calder really cared for me."

"*Cares,*" I remind him firmly. "He *loves* you."

"I didn't trust it when I was alive. Not completely."

"Do you want to talk to him again?" I offer.

"I might take you up on that soon, but that's not what I want at the moment." He opens his arms again, inviting me into his embrace.

I hesitate, since I'm not sure how to proceed with this enigma. Osen is wrapped up inside me in a way no one else has ever been. If we pursue something deeper, the chances of it ending horribly are an enormous risk. The consequences could be devastating if he were to take over my body again in spite or in a rage over a fight we had. I hate to say I've been a victim of that too many times to not consider it a real possibility.

He can deliver an incredible sexual experience, but I'm not ready to engage with him that way again. Not yet.

"What are you expecting from me?" I ask.

"In general or right now?" He smirks and part of me wants to kiss that damned look off his pretty face.

"Now."

"I wish to do something I never tried before." He shrugs, but I sense it's a bigger deal than he's playing it up as.

"What's that?"

"Cuddles." He lowers his smoky gray eyes and drops his arms. "With your power released, I sense you're able to resist my incubus paralysis. So you would be the first person I could really do that with."

"You mean you freeze everyone else up when you're intimate? Even with snuggles?" I ask. I'm still shocked this is a default thing for the incubus.

"Well, I've only known high-born demons to resist my power. Maxum can. Until you came along, he wasn't a cuddler. And yeah, my incubus power feeds on emotion. My mother was a succubus and didn't care for children." Osen glances up to see my reaction. "It feels nice when the guys hold you. I wanted to try."

My heart turns to mush.

"Dammit. I'm too soft for my own good." I curse and pull him into a hug.

The next thing I know, I'm on a bed with him. He curls into me, placing his head on my chest. His muscular arms wrap around my waist.

I stroke my fingers through his long silky locks, and he hums with contentment.

"Goddess, this feels good." He murmurs over the swell of my breast. "I wish I could have done this when I was alive."

"I'm sorry you didn't get this experience." I kiss the top of his head. "Just ask if you want to do it again."

"Every night?" he practically begs. "We can meet when you fall asleep and hold each other and talk."

"I'd like that."

Eventually, I fall into a deeper sleep and dream of my guys holding me... even Calder.

6

OH, HELL

MAXUM

$\mathcal{E}$ ven for a hellhound, Darius is a grump. Sure, I can be a surly pain in the ass, but I also know how to have a laugh. Obviously, he's irritated by my pack invading his sanctuary, but I suspect this is his usual personality. It's likely why Amira didn't think to ever introduce us before. Not that I've interacted with the witch in a few decades.

I completely understand why he doesn't want us here.

Raithe probably doesn't either, but he seems to be the peacemaker of the bunch.

I can't say I would be happy either if their coven had knocked on my door, potentially bringing trouble to my pack.

"If my affection for my mate bothers you, I'll tone it down," I offer. It's the least I can do as a thank you. And some people are more riled by displays of affection.

Darius grunts and continues to lead me toward his hothouse. "If you think she's your mate," he says without judgment, "then why haven't you claimed her? It's not like our kind to wait. I sensed the wolf did so last night."

"Don't bring up what our kind normally does," I warn. "We both aren't like most of them. We don't just take without permission."

He nods, then he arches a brow. "Seems like she gave you permission from the way she was about to rut you on my damn lawn."

"Yeah, well. It's been a wild ride. She didn't know about the other worlds just days ago. She's… not what I expected. Not that I ever thought I'd find my match." I don't know why I'm rambling nervously. It's unlike me.

"You didn't expect her to be your mate match because she's a witch or because she's Ms. Klutzy Sunshine?"

I chuckle at his name for her. "Both. But even though she isn't what I imagined, somehow the way she fits with me and my pack makes sense."

"Hmm." Darius opens the door to the small structure and some of the heat escapes.

We both sigh contently at the searing temperature that only hell-born are comfortable with. Our shoulders relax, and we sink onto the wooden benches.

"There's something off about your little mate," Darius says, breaking the silence.

Protective instincts rise inside me, expecting I will have to defend my witch's honor. "Explain," I demand as a cold threat.

"Don't get your tail in a knot." Darius waves me off. He's more relaxed now and maybe that's why he feels like he can say whatever he likes about my love. "She's not just a simple witch. My nose can pick up that."

"We suspect she might have fae blood. Or something supernatural."

"Maybe… but doesn't she seem like she has a bit from home?" he asks.

With his suggestion, I recall how she passes through my demon portals with no side effects. That rarely happens to non-hell beings. The rest of my pack doesn't react anymore because they've gotten used to it in the countless times they've used one. It didn't even phase her the first time. She also didn't seem affected by being in the hell realm on our way to Amira's. Curious.

"I don't have your acute sense of smell for our kind," I say. "But yes, there's evidence to suggest she has some hell-born blood in her."

We sink into silence again, and I ponder my connection with Jade. If she has demon blood, that will make the idea of being fated mates more reasonable. Not that I needed validation for how I feel about her.

My conviction to wait to claim her until Rob and Galiana are removed as a threat wavers. I don't know if it will be better or worse if I bond with her immediately.

No. I *should* wait. She's still coming into her magic. She accidentally mated with Arran during this delicate time. I don't want to mess with her balance further.

She needs to get control over her energy before I add a bond to it.

Although everything screams at me to claim her. To sink my sharp teeth into her flesh and feel the connection snap into place, linking us forever. Then I'll claim her pussy, marking her with my cum.

I'll declare to all and the fires of hell that she is mine.

"You realize if you mate bond with her and she has demon blood, you will probably send a ripple to the hell realm and the high lords will be alerted to her."

Ice pours through my veins at this devastating reminder.

Demon females are rare and the high-born lords may come to kill me so they can claim her for the hell realm, even if she is only part. She could end up as a caged, broodmare since she could potentially carry a demon child.

"Fuck!" I bellow.

"We don't know for certain if she has a drop of demon blood in her." Darius attempts to console me. "And maybe Amira can create some sort of protection spell to mask your female."

That eases a bit of my worry. Amira might not like to use her destructive magic anymore, but at least she still makes an exception for her superior protection, healing, and cloaking abilities.

"I also know you aren't the simple demon you claim to be." Darius gives me a knowing look and I snarl. He holds up his hands and assures me, "Don't worry, I won't be outing you to anyone."

I should have known a high-level hellhound would sniff out my secret. Not even my pack knows.

Why do I have a bad feeling that they will soon find out who I really am?

7

MEMORIES

OSEN

*T*his sweet witch is breaking my shadowheart.

Jade's soft touch—physically and emotionally—has me on my metaphorical knees. Even though she has fallen into a deeper level of sleep beyond the shadowscape where I can interact with her, she is still somehow manifesting here with me. She's snuggled into my arms with her head tucked under my chin.

The shadowscape is an extremely convincing representation of real life. An incubus or succubus can create our surroundings and lure in our next target and feed, making our food source believe they are somewhere safe or terrifying, depending on our fickle moods. We can mimic almost anything, but it falls short in many ways. Mainly, that it *isn't* really living. I can't freely interact with my pack, and I can't help make the realms a better place for those I care about.

And Jade? I can't truly enjoy her the way I want to. Every time I bring her here, I feel like I've trapped her or forced her to be with me.

In a way, I have. Though not on purpose. My soul being stuck inside her body and mind isn't either of our faults. But I feel more like a leech than I ever did in life.

When she spoke about releasing my spirit earlier, I panicked. I shouldn't. I *should* just accept that my reckless actions finally caught up to me in that alleyway.

But now that I've found her and I realize how much Calder feels for me, I don't want to move on from this life. I want to find a way to live—with them.

Jade hasn't said it, but I sense she would allow me to remain with her forever, as long as I behave myself.

I'm tempted to go along with that, but for my sanity I need to materialize in a tangible way or let go somehow and move on beyond the veil.

I don't want to move on though. I want to become a real member of this pack again. More than I was before.

I want Calder. I want to help heal him as I should have done before. Like Jade is doing now.

I can see it. He's changing. I'd love to claim it was about me. That my death shook him up enough to come out of his unhappy existence. Except that would be a lie.

Jade is our savior—for the entire pack.

I stroke her soft cheek and wonder how accurate my illusionary shadowscape is.

Closing my eyes to this imaginary place, I focus on Jade's energy and how she truly feels intertwined in me. In some ways, this bond we have is more intimate than what the others have. Not that I deserve it. Not yet.

I sink into the darkness and fall deeper into the place where Jade dreams.

I open my eyes to find myself inside her dreamscape.

A shiver goes through me when I realize where I am.

The wretched alleyway where I died.

I'm standing next to her. Jade has taken my spot, reliving what I remembered from that night and what we saw together right before Rob attacked us.

"Jade?" I ask as Rob's cloaked figure appears at the end of the alleyway.

She tears her gaze away from his ominous presence and looks at me in confusion. "Osen? Why are you outside of me?"

"You're dreaming, and I'm along for the ride."

"Oh, lucid dreaming. I do that." She bites her lip, looking a bit confused, and glances between us. "I'm just not used to seeing your memories with you beside me."

"Same for me." It's strange. I've been her ghost since I first died and possessed her. But I'm more aware now. More myself.

Jade takes a nervous step back, glancing around for an escape. "We should go to a different memory now," she says with a shaky voice.

I capture her arms and make her focus on me. "I don't relish the idea of reliving my death moment, but I wonder if maybe we should both witness this again with an analytical lens. Maybe catch something we didn't last time. A clue."

"Yeah, okay." She nods vigorously, regaining the courage I know she possesses. "It's just that when we were both in this alley... everything fell apart. I almost lost you, and I almost died."

"I know now that you aren't my enemy." I brush back a lock of her hair and caress her cheek. "We are remembering in your mind, okay?"

Her lucidity returns, and she turns to face Rob again.

I snatch her hand in mine, and we create a united front to experience this horrible moment together.

She squeezes my hand in solidarity. "I know this will be hard for you. Just remember, I'm on your side. I will fight to avenge your death," she promises.

"Thank you, sweet witch. But now, I only want to focus on answers."

We both turn our attention to the warlock Rob walking toward us, silhouetted by the light of the moon.

"You shouldn't have pushed," Rob says. "I warned you to walk away."

"You expect me to heed your message from the lips of my dying ally? You truly didn't expect that I'd seek justice for what you've done to my kind?" I counter.

"I thought you might be smarter than the rest since you're the only one who's gotten close to discovering what's truly going on."

"I know the Witch Council members are behind the ASO."

The man laughs—genuinely amused.

Suddenly, I'm hit with a blast of magic from behind, along with a chant.

This energy doesn't feel like anything I have experienced before. It's a new magic filled with dark intent.

My body trembles on the ground. Someone is stealing my magic, and my soul is detaching from my body.

"I told you he'd come," Rob says with an evil smirk.

Then someone who looked very much like Jade appears from the shadows.

I die.

Both Jade and I float above the scene. It's an unnerving sight to see my dead body on the ground. Thankfully, Jade is floating beside me and not splayed out below.

I freaked out last time when I saw her appear, but now I'm much more rational and intend to find out the rest of this situation.

Astral Jade glances over at me, and I reach out to pull her closer. Her nervous energy about my reaction settles.

Rob leans over my body and chants a strange spell. Dark shadows escape my body and Rob absorbs them. He's grunting and whimpering as he's stealing my magic.

The witch's face shifts, revealing it's actually Galiana, not Jade or her grandmother. Darkness swirls around her, too. They both have incubus magic.

But how?

"Send his soul to the abomination and get answers about what he knows," Galiana orders. *"Leave the body here for his kind to discover."*

"Can I kill the bitch after this one?" Rob asks, looking eager.

"No," Galiana snaps. "Jade's mine to destroy. And she will be useful for a bit longer."

Rob chants something new under his breath, but I don't recognize the language. It's not Latin or the other common magical languages. It sounds like an odd mixture of demon, Elven, and something else.

Then both Jade and I clutch onto each other's spirit forms, flying through the city to her house, and we fall into Jade's sleeping body in her home. We are back in the early morning when I first possessed her.

I hear Jade speak as a spirit to me. "This is the morning before I saw the guys at the bar. I woke up feeling strange, worrying maybe Rob broke in again to harass me."

Jade's body jerks to sitting, and she glances around her room. She's filled with fear.

She gets up and grabs her gun, checking around her house before relaxing after finding herself alone.

"I'm sorry you had to live like that. Afraid your ex was going to hurt you. And now to discover he actually was hurting you."

"I'm not the only woman in the world dealing with an abusive and manipulative man," she says, sounding both angry and sad.

"Still. It makes me feel horrible for any damage I've caused being an incubus. But if I'm sticking around longer, I will do my best to not harm you anymore. If I do it without realizing, please tell me so I can be better."

I sense her agreeing to my request.

We observe as the front door flies open, and Rob rushes in already chanting a spell.

Jade drops to the floor.

He hovers over her. "Osen? Incubus?"

I let out a wheeze through Jade's lungs. Being freshly dead ghost, I am unable to do much more.

"Good. You're in there," Rob says. "I'll be back in a few days to have a chat." He sneers at Jade's body and then reluctantly tosses her on the couch. Likely, he wants Jade to come out of the spell like she only fell asleep, so she doesn't wake up on the floor and become suspicious.

After a chant, he closes the door behind him. Jade is none the wiser.

She shifts on the couch and mutters, "Weird. I must be more tired than I thought."

The memory fades, and we are left standing in the shadowscape once again.

"I was so off that day. I forgot to eat. I couldn't write worth a damn." Jade recalls from this memory. "Now I know why."

I wish I could comfort her, like she deserves, but I feel like I will fall short in every way. I don't really know how to comfort.

I've never done something like that before. I've only offered a sexual release for my partners. I wasn't the one people went to hoping to ease their worries or to be their pillar of strength.

Maxum was our strength and courage. Flint was our rock bed foundation, never wavering. Arran was often our confidant and comfort before he was cursed. Calder was our passion and spirit until he was damaged in his last life.

And now, Jade is our heart. She brings compassion and understanding. She brings the group together in a way I never did.

Moving forward, what can I offer? Even if I could return whole and in my body, I don't see what I could contribute.

I know one thing. I won't do anything to hurt her. Never again. If it comes down to it, I will sacrifice myself to ensure her wellbeing and her happiness with our pack.

"Osen?" Jade calls me. "Are you okay?"

"I will be," I answer, and then ask, "Will you do everything you can to help Calder?"

I sense her unease, and she asks with an uncertain tone, "What are you saying? Are you moving on?"

"No. Not yet. However, when I go, I want to ensure that you'll be there for him."

"Of course," she hesitates. "But you're still here. Maybe you could help too. I'm out of my depth with him."

Wondering how to respond to her worried expression and reaction, I ask myself, *What would Jade do?*

Then I pull her into an embrace. "Whatever you need. Whatever Calder needs, or the pack needs, I will do my best to deliver."

8

REVEALS

JADE

$\mathcal{I}$ refuse to wake up from this delicious dream. An eager tongue is skillfully licking my center, and both of my nipples are being sucked.

Pressure builds in my core, but an orgasm is just out of reach.

I wonder if this is one of those dreams where I wake up to find myself incredibly horny and have to bring out Ole Faithful to vibe me to completion.

Then I remember I have three guys who'd likely be *up* to help a wanton woman out.

The soft, insistent swipes of a tongue remind me of Flint.

And the two hot mouths on my breasts make me think of Maxum and Arran. Both guys run so warm.

I imagine it's their hot hands wandering over my skin.

This dream feels so realistic that I wonder if it's Osen making this fantasy come to life in the shadowscape.

Without opening my eyes, I reach down to work my clit, but find an entire head between my legs.

My eyes pop open with surprise, and I see all three of my guys tending to me.

"Oh!" I gasp.

The noon sun filtering in through the window lights up Flint's fully gargoyle form with his broad shoulders, horns, tusks, large wings, and heavy brow. The sight alone almost undoes me.

Maxum has his wings out for good measure, and I just want to grab one of his horns and yank him back to sucking my breast.

Arran almost seems out of place in his human form. But if Serky comes out to play, I'm worried no one else will get a chance to be with me.

Maxum uses my shocked, opened mouth to kiss me dizzy, delving inside with his forked tongue and exciting me more. Then he pulls back and whispers over my lips, "You mentioned you wanted to be woken up like this. And Flint told us you gave him permission to touch you whenever he wanted to."

I gape at them all. "Yes... but..." I shudder with pleasure when Flint goes back to sucking my clit. "Okay... yes, yes, yes, I did say that. Why am I fighting this?"

Arran chuckles. "Don't know, but if you want us to stop, we will."

"Please, keep going," I beg, trembling. "I want you, and I need a release." Then I catch Arran's glowing golden eyes, seeing Serky is just under the surface. "You're okay with them touching me like this?"

Arran bumps my nose with his. A shifter's gesture of affection. "I'm keeping Serky in check. He seems to be happy enough to see you pleasured even if it isn't him doing it."

Flint pauses his ministrations to look up at me with his otherworldly, light gray eyes. "Maybe one day we can wake you up with our cocks inside you?"

"Yes, please, and thank you." I smile mischievously and my body undulates to show them how much I crave them.

"You and I need to complete our bond, my little mate." Flint says and slowly slides two thick fingers into me. "When would you want to do that?"

His eyes shine with his eagerness, but it doesn't feel right to bond with an audience.

I wink at him. "How about we talk about the details tonight?"

Flint smiles and pumps his thick digits into my pussy at a faster pace. "Yes, I can wait for the perfect time to have you all to myself. Now, come on my tongue so Maxum can have his turn."

"Holy fuck, Flint." My cunt clenches around his fingers. "I almost came just with your naughty talk."

"I'm about to as well." Arran chuckles and nuzzles into my neck.

"Make our woman scream your name," Maxum orders Flint. Then he fists my hair and claims my mouth again.

My once-shy gargoyle feasts on my pussy as he adds yet another thick finger inside me. I'm stretched so wide the thought of it ramps up my excitement.

Arran uses his partial shifting ability to elongate his teeth and his wolf's sharp canines pinch my hardened nipples.

I squeak and thrash, losing control. I'm flailing, feeling too much.

"That's it," Maxum breathes. "Come for us, our love."

I fall off that cliff and soar with bliss. Each clench of my pussy around Flint's hand feels like a flutter of imaginary wings that takes me higher.

Then I slip back into my body with a silly grin plastered on my face.

Flint licks his lips, tasting my juices. "If you'd let me, I'd live between your soft, pillowy thighs."

I might have taken offense for calling my legs *pillowy*, but that was when I was with Rob. My hard-bodied gargoyle thoroughly adores softness. He craves my soft, squishy body.

I reach out to him. He answers my summons, leans over my flushed body, and gives me a possessive kiss before moving aside.

Maxum strokes his hands over my knees and then spreads my legs wide. "Ready for my monster cock, little mate?"

My demon rubs his unusual member over my slick center. He slides inside of me, and I feel every one of his soft spikes that run along the top and bottom of his cock and around its base. It only takes a few strokes until he's fully sheathed. His textured cock stimulates my clit and outer lips when he grinds his hips into me.

I'm gifted with a unique sensation deep in my pussy as he hits the spot that makes my toes curl.

Flint's hand grasps my breast, and he flicks his tongue over its peak.

At my other side, Arran's hand shifts into his werewolf's claws and the tips dimple my flesh. "I love your body. Pliant and thick, so we can grip onto you and hold on as we fuck you."

"It's perfection," Flint murmurs as he sucks and nips. His tusks scrape along my sensitive skin.

Maxum moans. "I love watching them monster-handle you."

I flick my gaze back to Maxum as he spreads out his giant wings that take up the entire width of the bedroom.

He pounds into me, getting more excited with my moans.

I'm launched toward an orgasm and my body spasms.

"I want to make you mine," Maxum grits out through his sharp, clenched teeth.

"I want you. I want *all* of you!" I shout. Right now, I really, really need them. I need them as my bonded mates.

All of them.

There's a tug at the very core of who and what I am.

I sense the others' energy... their souls. I don't mean to, but I'm pulling them to me. Yanking their souls, their spirits reaching for me as well.

Even Osen glows in my inner eye.

Despite the unusual sensations, my orgasm hits me like cannon fire, making me shake and buck.

Maxum spasms with his climax, gripping me like he might fall off the edge of the world.

Maxum crashes onto me as if someone's shoved him. Fortunately, he's able to brace himself with his arms. He appears dazed.

I hear a thump and a curse from the main room.

Calder must have been lurking there, listening to our lovemaking.

I pulled on his soul so hard he fell.

Am I hurting them?

I feel it when their souls are released from my strange hold.

"What was the hell was that?" Calder hisses from the other room.

Maxum's broad shoulders press into me.

Grasping his upper arms, I encourage him to move back so I can see his face.

He shifts away slowly, and I glance over at both Arran and Flint, both look a bit bewildered and confused.

Did I hurt them? What have I done?

Panic wells inside me. I worry, but wonder if this could be a mate thing? It happened when I wanted them.

"*I'd like to know what that was too,*" Osen says in my mind.

"Get in line," I mutter.

"*If there is a queue for your affection, I'll gladly buy tickets for that train,*" he retorts in a frisky tone.

I roll my eyes. But his joke relaxes me, just as he intended.

Flint recovers first and cups my cheek. "Are you alright, my mate?"

"I think so." I cover his hand with mine. Well, what I can cover, given his hand is so much larger than mine.

Still on top of me, Maxum braces himself on his elbows to relieve most of his weight from crushing me. "It felt like you tried to pull my soul out through my dick."

I wince. "Sorry. I didn't mean to."

"I'm not complaining." Maxum slides backward, but only enough so his hips are between my ankles.

"What was..." A disheveled Calder appears in the doorway and doesn't finish his sentence when he sees me between my three guys. His striking blue eyes hungrily take in my naked, recently fucked body.

I'm splayed out and exposed. I have an urge to cover myself, so I move to pull my knees together.

Calder growls.

Okay. Apparently, he doesn't like that.

"I thought you didn't want—"

"It doesn't matter what I want. I *can't*." His hand drops to cover the tent in his pants, then he hurries away to the outer door.

I lurch to go after him, but all three guys place a hand on me to stop me.

"Calder, wait!"

He's already opened the door, but I hear him pause and sigh heavily. "I just need a moment. I won't go far."

"Okay," I whisper and settle back on the bed. When I hear the door shut behind him, I ask, "Is he going to be alright?"

"I expect Calder is overwhelmed with a lot of emotions he's finally having to deal with," Maxum says with a frown. "Let him work some of them out." He kisses my inner thigh. "He'll come to you when he's ready to talk about how he feels."

"I wish I could do something so he didn't hurt so much," I say.

Arran kisses my neck. "He has to meet you at least halfway… like I did. You helped me just by being you and accepting me with all my broken pieces."

"You're not broken," I protest.

"Not anymore." He grins widely, then kisses the hell out of me.

"Arran's correct," Flint says. "Your very presence seems to be enough to heal. And Calder has the worst past of us all."

"But he's not what I'm interested in right now." Maxum gazes at me, his obsidian eyes glowing with a fire I've not seen before. "We need to know how you almost took our souls right out of our bodies."

"I didn't mean to!" I gasp, sitting up and leaning against the headboard. "Did I hurt you?" I grab a pillow and hug it to my chest.

The guys all grumble when I cover myself.

Maxum realizes playtime is over and slips his pants back on. "It felt odd but didn't hurt. I don't think you were trying to kill us."

"It felt more like a bonding to me." Flint stands at the side of the bed, revealing he never took off his pants.

Maybe he's still shy about his special equipment. I'll have to ask him about what his comfort levels are in group situations, so no one pushes him.

"Would that be something a lust witch can do?" I ask. "Or a... demon?"

All three guys stare at me in shock, quickly understanding what I'm implying.

Maxum goes unnaturally still. "So, you know?" he asks cautiously.

His guarded behavior unnerves me. I debate for a moment what to say, but I'd rather be honest than skirt around this. If he has a problem with what I am, then we should get to the bottom of it now.

"Uh..." I realize we know nothing for certain. I will need to contact my abuela to know exactly what I am and what happened. I clear my throat and clutch the pillow to my nakedness. "Amira suspects that I might have a bit of demon blood because of the sigils we discovered embedded in me. She also knew my grandmother and said she was a lust witch. That might mean I have some of that sort of magic."

Maxum reads the worry on my face and quickly races to embrace me, pinning the pillow between us. "Oh, shit. I'm sorry if you thought I'd be upset. I was worried about you. That the news would unsettle you. I've suspected the demon part. I sense a little lust witch energy around you. Just a touch, but in all the right ways." He pulls back and winks at me. Then he caresses my face and kisses me. "Whatever blood you might have, I know *who* you are... my loving mate."

I throw my arms around his waist and bury my face in his chest. "Thank you. But I probably should find out about my family's past. It's so odd that I never even considered it before."

"Not odd at all," Arran says. "The spell your grandmother put on you masked your presence to authorities, and I believe it probably made you uninterested, so you wouldn't go digging, either."

My stomach turns thinking how much I've been manipulated and controlled by magic my whole life—mostly because of my grandmother. If she hadn't put a spell on me, then Rob might not have been able to use me. Or it would have been harder for him to do so. If she only had stuck around or found some fairy godmother to come along and teach me if she was no longer around, then I could have had my power all this time. But no, I was hobbled and forgotten for decades.

Anger stirs in my heart. Even if her intentions were good, she harmed me.

And now, I'm blindly trying to discover my way and survive.

At least I have my guys. I reach out my hands to both Arran and Flint. For a moment, I fear they won't take the plea to be close to them. But within seconds, I find that concern is only my programmed bullshit raising its ugly head again.

With help from my guys, I hope to rid myself of the insecurity my mother and my ex created in me. My memories of Rob telling me under the spell over and over a hundred times that I was unlovable, echo in my head.

Tears fall, my mates grasp onto me, blocking out the negative thoughts until they are only a faint whisper.

9

MIC DROP

JADE

$\mathcal{I}$ feel much better after our snuggle session, like I can conquer anything.

I highly recommend monster snuggles. At least *my* monsters. I can't speak for other monster scenarios. But embracing my demon has been a very therapeutic exercise.

"I need to find Calder," I say after we get dressed.

"I'm not sure that's a good idea," Arran hums. "He likes his alone time to cool down and center."

Osen's energy comes forward, and he asks, *"May I speak to them for a moment?"*

I give him the okay.

His spirit takes over my body. This time it's different from before. I sense I could claim it back with little effort. Is it because I'm stronger magically? Or is Osen not trying to be as controlling?

"Both, sweet witch," Osen says in my mind.

Then he addresses the room. The guys all freeze when they see the shift in my presence. Arran told me before that my eyes change from my green eyes to dark shadows of an incubus.

"Osen?" Arran moves to block the exit. He must think Osen is ready to force me to run off again.

"Yes, it's me. And don't worry. I asked for permission. Jade is aware of everything that's happening right now."

Arran, Flint, and Maxum lose some of their tension.

"I know I've fucked up. Partly because I'm a reactionary asshat. Partly because my spirit was damaged, and I couldn't think straight. I'm stronger now. Clearer."

"You aren't going to take off again?" Maxum crosses his arms.

"Not unless Jade wants it. She is also stronger. I don't think I could just take over anymore, even if I wanted to try. But I don't."

"Did you have a message for us?" Flint tilts his head, studying us. He doesn't like Osen possessing and talking through me—not at all. I don't blame him.

Osen turns and smiles at Flint. "Always to the point. I never admired that enough about you when I was alive." He sighs and looks at all of them. "Yeah, there are a few things. I'd like to talk with Calder. But I also was feeling cooped up and isolated. Jade's been a gracious host, but it isn't the same as having a body of my own. Speaking of which, I'd like to understand why my corpse hasn't appeared to decay. We need to investigate what Galiana did to me when she killed me."

"So it was her?" Maxum asks.

"Yeah. Jade and I had a memory of it. They seem to have cast a spell to pull out my magic and absorb it. Then they yanked out my soul and sent it to Jade."

"That isn't a normal death. Perhaps that's why your body is hanging in a sort of stasis?" Maxum guesses.

Osen paces the room, something I sense he used to do when he was alive. "We know magic can be stolen, but this is a new method... it's a different magic. It was as if they had used a supernatural being's magic, but as a witch. That isn't possible, is it?"

"Just because we haven't seen someone successfully use it before doesn't mean it's impossible." Arran motions to me. "Jade shouldn't have both sorts of magic, but she does."

Osen stalls our pacing, and our mouth falls open with the revelation. "It felt a lot like her magic. I didn't realize before because her power was suppressed."

"*Perhaps they used the pendant to siphon my magic and wield it?*" I suggest.

"Oh, shit." Osen falls heavily into a chair. "Jade's necklace was a two-way conduit. Sending souls to her and channeling her magic for Galiana and Rob to use."

"Thank goddess we got rid of the cursed thing." Arran looks about ready to shift and go seek vengeance for me.

My protective gargoyle frowns. *"That's* why they are after our mate. They've lost their power source."

"Which means they won't give up easily," Maxum adds.

"Osen, did you remember anything else important?" Flint asks. "Like why you were in the alleyway that night?"

"I was on to them. I dug up some secret. Sounds like they killed my source," Osen recounts. "Or they just lured me in to steal my shadows. Now that Jade and I are stronger, we might be able to see more from my last days."

Flint grunts and then nods toward the door. "Go. Talk with Calder if you must, so I can have my mate back."

Osen hangs our head in shame. "Sorry. It must be upsetting to see her like this."

"Mostly because you have hurt her," Flint interrupts, glaring at Osen.

Dang. I don't enjoy being on the other end of that anger. Thank goodness it isn't directed at me.

"I promise that's over." Osen raises my hands in surrender. "But if you need to, you can keep an eye on me while I talk with Calder. Just give me some space. Okay?"

"Fine." Flint ushers us to the door. With a gentle hand, he stops us as we get to the threshold. "Jade?"

My consciousness moves forward so I can take the reins. "It's okay, sweetie. I'm right here."

His eyes soften as he gazes at me. "I'll be watching."

I sense Osen wilt with Flint's distrust of him, unhappy he damaged his relationship with his pack.

"Prove to us you can be better," I mentally say to my ghost.

Flint lets us go, and I don't have to look to sense him flying over our heads, watching as we walk across the yard. Through our own special telepathic link, which sounds weaker than it has before, he tells me, *"Calder is by the creek."*

Osen leads us in that direction, but he sits down to watch the water instead of chasing down his phoenix.

"Letting him come to us in his own time?" I ask.

"Yeah. I don't know if it will work being in your body, but that's how we used to connect. I would have to wait for him to come to me. Especially since his last death."

"Are you okay?"

"As much as a dead guy can be," he chuckles, but I can sense his joke is forced.

He's not alright.

"It's okay not to be okay," I let him know.

"Same goes for you. This can't be easy, dealing with all of us. Your life turned upside down."

"No. But it's weirdly easier than I thought it might be. The biggest hurt has been that my life was a lie. My abuela squashed my magic. She was an ASO spy, and who knows what other awful things she did. I need answers from her. I want to know what I am."

Just as I say this, I fall back against the boulder we are sitting on. I feel Osen being forcibly shoved deeper in my body and another presence appears in my mind.

Abuela.

"What are you doing?" we both demand at the same time.

"No." I throw my hand up for her to hear me. "You don't get to demand things from me until you give me some damned, long overdue answers."

Her mouth purses with irritation, but then she slowly nods. "I suppose you deserve some… after everything."

"Let's start with why you mentioned the mistake you made when I bonded with Arran. Am I part supe?"

"Yes." She glances down at her hands, avoiding my eyes. "I've kept far too much from you. But know this: I never meant to harm you. I thought…" Her voice cracks. "I thought I was protecting you."

"From Galiana?"

"Yes, and others." My grandmother straightens her shoulders. "I'll start at the beginning. I was a powerful lust witch. Galiana told me that supernatural beings had killed my parents. Right away, she recruited me into the ASO, using my hatred so she could manipulate my magic. I worked various jobs for Galiana and the anti-supe cause. During that time, I conceived Jadeana Ruth with a mortal male who I met for a one-night stand."

"Wait, if my mother was half mortal and half witch… where does my supe blood come from?"

"Ruth isn't your mother… I am."

I stagger back, and my world spins.

"Ruth is your older sister by almost twenty years. We put a spell on her mind to make her believe she was your mother. Although the spell faded quickly once I died."

Thinking back on the time of my grandmother… my *mother's* death. Ruth had suddenly shifted in her personality. Not for the better. She was angrier than she had ever been and was harder on me. I had chalked it up to the loss of her mother. It was, but not in the way I had thought.

"So, *you're* my biological mother?" I shake my head and frown. "Why did you do that to us? To Ruth?"

"For your protection, I could hide you with a normal human like Ruth, since she didn't inherit my witch magic. I put a spell in place to mask your presence to those searching for you. If I didn't, Galiana would have killed you as a baby."

"Why didn't you just tell Ruth or me the truth?" I ask.

"I was going to do that when you came of age. But I was murdered before I could—tortured to death by Galiana in her attempt to get information on you and your whereabouts. Unfortunately, a couple of decades later, she found you anyway."

My heart sinks. She died to protect me. "I... I didn't know."

"How could you know, mija?" Her voice softens. "I wanted to teach you about your powers when they developed when you came of age. When you were born, I had hoped I could kill Galiana right away and we could be a true family. But it wasn't meant to be."

"And my father?"

"He was my target on an ASO job. I had to seduce a special individual, learn his secrets, and then eventually kill him. He was highly unusual, as he was a product of a demon and Elven mating. Both lines were from powerful, high-born blood. He was a double spy for the two realms. Brilliant and talented."

"And I was an accidental pregnancy from that job? A fucking mistake?"

"No." She smiles wistfully, her gaze far off, remembering. "As I got to know him, I soon discovered he was immune to my lust witch magic. We fell in love anyway—*true* love. Lust witches never get to experience actual love. So you can imagine how overjoyed I was to find him. But our circumstances made it so we had to hide our relationship. I fed Galiana lies. And he told me the truth of my family's murders—that Galiana was behind them all and used it to turn me against supernaturals."

"What the hell is wrong with her?" I blurt out.

"Broken. Angry. And power hungry. Power is all that's ever mattered to her."

"What happened between you and my father?" I ask.

"When I found out I was pregnant with you, we knew Galiana would want to kill you just for the fact you were of mixed blood. He helped me create the binding and concealment spell that was embedded in your body. We brainwashed your magicless adult sister since she would be the perfect hiding place for you. Then I had to disappear and only visit when I believed it to be safe and to reenforce the spell work."

"No wonder Ruth hated me—hated you."

"I don't blame her." My mother frowns, and I sense she isn't as callous as I've imagined. "I'm sorry I couldn't be there for you growing up... or now. I wish I could train you, but it's taking all I have to communicate for this long."

"What about my father? Is he still alive?"

"I never saw him again. He had to go into hiding too, so Galiana couldn't kill him. And to protect your existence."

"He might still be alive?" I ask, wondering if I want to find him or let it be.

"It's possible."

I refocus on what's happening now. "It doesn't appear Galiana's goal is to kill me anymore."

"No. She's found another use for you—your unique powers. But if she gets you back in her clutches and you don't prove useful or under her control, she will end you."

I'd rather die than allow Galiana to harm other people, and especially not my mates, with my power. "You don't want me with my mates, but they are protecting me. So what *are* you suggesting I do?"

"Go back into hiding... but not with them. They will attract attention. They are easier to track. They will compromise you."

How dare she screw with my life and then expect me to give up the only people I trust and who actually care for me?

"No. I'm not making the same mistake you made. I'm keeping my loved ones near me. Look at what you sacrificed. It was all for fucking nothing." Tears threaten to pour from me. "You ruined my life. You lied to me. How can I trust a fucking thing you say? I can't talk to you anymore. Unless you can give me information that can *really* help me right now, then I don't want your—"

"Jadeana!" my mother snaps. "You need to..."

Her voice fades, reality pressing in on me. Someone shakes me to bring me out of my trance.

"Jade?" Calder calls me, panicked.

I blink against the bright light of the sky and raise my hand to shield my eyes. But no, when I look, it isn't the sky, but Calder's wings alight with a blazing fire. He's kneeling over me and appears frantic.

Osen pushes forward when he sees his lover. "Calder," he says with my voice sounding rough and concerned.

Calder sees it's Osen in charge of my body and not me. He leaps back to his feet in surprise and snarls at us. "What have you done?"

"Me?" Osen says in shock. "You woke us."

"Us?" Calder shakes his head in confusion, then glowers. "If you took Jade's body against her will, I won't forgive you this time."

"I didn't!" Osen shouts.

I take control and ask, "What's wrong?"

"You were passed out and non-responsive," Calder says, indignant but less upset. His flaming wings die down.

I grimace. "I was talking to my grandmother... uh, mother."

"Huh? Your mother's dead now, too?"

"No, well, yes. But my grandmother is really my mother. Turns out the woman who raised me was my older sister."

Calder sits down next to me and studies my eyes. I can sense they are my normal green and not Osen's gray. "You're okay? Osen didn't take advantage of you?"

"It's very sweet of you to worry, but I'm okay. And Osen has my permission to talk to you." I reach out to pat Calder's arm to comfort and thank him. Just before I make contact, I remember his touch aversion and pull back.

He catches my hand and holds it, giving it a little squeeze.

My eyes widen as I stare at our clasped hands. "Actually, Osen wanted to talk to you. We came out here for that. My mother showed up to drop some crazy secrets on my ass." I look up into his pale blue eyes. "You have my permission to do whatever you need to do together. Just no leaving Amira's property."

His thumb traces over mine. "I won't put you in danger." Then he grins. "I appreciate the offer, but I won't take advantage of your generosity."

I shrug. "It's not like it's a hardship kissing you." I didn't mean to say that. My mouth clamps shut, and I blush. "I, uh... I didn't mean I'd be..."

"Jade, stop." He chuckles. "I get it. You don't have to be so cautious around me. I know you aren't like the witch who hurt me."

"I wish I could undo what she did." I feel my eyes sting with emotion, hating that he was so damaged by my kind... or half of what I am.

Hell, I'm going to have to adjust to the idea of being more than a witch, and so soon after I wrapped my head around being a witch.

Osen presses forward, and I give Calder a little finger wave goodbye. He seems to understand and returns the silly gesture.

10

THE TALK

CALDER

*M*y heart aches when Jade's spirit fades to the background.

I bite back a curse. I wouldn't mind more time alone to get to know her now that I'm not hung up on her witch heritage.

Maybe part of me doesn't want to deal with Osen either. He's never been particularly talkative, so I know he has something significant to say if he's pushed to come forward.

I brace myself for what's coming as I watch the eerie change from Jade to Osen. Her face takes on an entirely different expression, one I've never seen her make. It's almost as if she's a shifter.

Her inquisitive and kind green eyes become the swirling smoky gray of an incubus.

"Calder." Osen frowns when I stare at him without emotion or response.

"Osen," I finally say.

"Why are you upset with me?" he asks.

I suppose he has a right to understand, but I'm still trying to understand what's got me riled. "It feels wrong for you to be inside her like this."

"You'd rather have me gone forever?" he asks, with a pained strain to his voice.

I sigh heavily and look at him. "No. It's just confusing."

"Tell me about it." He rubs his face like he used to, over his eyes and then over his non-existent beard. "Jade and I are getting along. We hope to discover more about what happened to me… to her."

"I'm glad you aren't fighting her anymore."

"I'm glad to see you're accepting her as well." He gives me a knowing look when I raise my brows. "I've been paying attention. More than she probably has."

"Don't—" I warn. I don't want him to push me into anything. I need to set this pace. *If* I set a pace.

He smirks playfully. "I wanted to tell you I'm falling for Jade."

Their body jerks as if Jade was surprised by this information enough to animate her shock.

"And how is that my business?" I bite my lip. I figured he was becoming infatuated. How could he not? She is his entire world—literally. And she has mind blowing sex with our pack. Jade is an incubus' dream girl.

"It's your business because I still love you, and you're part of our pack. I'm still here, watching. I see how Jade is healing us. I was hoping I could take her lead. Help you like I should have done the last time you died. I was scared and too caught up in myself to help heal what that witch did to you."

"You couldn't have helped," I argue. But is that true?

"Maybe, maybe not. But I know now why I didn't try. I felt rejected when you no longer wanted my touch. Selfishly, I made it about me… that I wasn't good enough. Wasn't lovable enough. I believed *you* should have fought your trauma to be with me again." He curses himself. "But I should have done more to fight for you. *With* you."

"*You*… were insecure?" I say in disbelief.

"Are you kidding? Behind all my swagger, I'm a fraud. Sure, I can make someone orgasm just by a snap of my fingers, but that doesn't equate to real love. Or being worthy of love. A fucking vibrator can do the same thing I can."

"Not quite." I chuckle. "But I get your point. Although it was a wonderful bonus how you could make me feel sexually, I didn't love you and want to be with you for your incubus magic."

"Why did you love me?" he asks, sounding more vulnerable than I've ever heard.

"Yeah, there was the physical aspect, but there was also the laughter. The loyalty. I loved how your mind worked, your passion for life, and your protectiveness." My voice comes out strong and with conviction, but I can't look at Jade while I talk. It feels like it would betray my feelings for Osen by gazing at her beauty when I did. And my budding feelings for her might get mixed up in all the emotions I have for him.

"I feel the same," he whispers, modulating his voice lower, likely picking up my reservations about talking through Jade. "I love you."

"I love you too." I gaze at the creek, watching the water cascade over the smooth rocks. "But I don't know what you want from me right now."

"I want you to be happy—whatever that looks like," Osen says earnestly.

Daring to look at them, I demand, "What? You want me to fuck Jade and pretend it's you? Because it's not you. Not really."

"Then maybe you should give in to your feelings for her. See if you can touch and be touched again."

My eyes flare with irritation. "Stay out of my relationship with her!"

"Fine. But I know for a fucking fact that she would let you take her right now if it would heal you."

"I don't need to be a thing of pity!" I jump up and clench my fists at my side.

"Neither of us thinks that." Osen jumps to his feet to match me. "She wants you, you idiot!"

I shake my head, confused. "No. That can't be true. I was an asshole. She's only getting mixed up because of you being inside her."

"Believe what you want." Osen gives me a dismissive wave.

"Osen!" Jade shouts, cutting through to take over her body again. Her face instantly softens, and she says quietly, "Calder, I like you. And I care about you. But I won't ever pressure you into anything."

"What are you saying?" I take a step closer. Is it hope bubbling in my heart? Could she really see me as someone she might desire?

"I want to be there for you in any way you'd want me to be," she says.

I charge forward. I need to set her straight. She *can't* want me. I grab her by her wrists and pull them behind her back. I clasp them together in one of my hands, pinning her so she can't move—or touch me.

My other hand grasps her jaw, forcing her to look at me.

She gasps that I'm suddenly towering over her—manhandling her. Her eyes are wide with shock.

"Is this what you want?" I demand, searching her face, taking in her beauty and her strength.

Even though I'm sure she wants to, she hasn't tried to pull away and run. Maybe she understands how dangerous that is to do with a predator.

"All I can offer is to tie you down so you can't touch me," I confess with an edge to my voice that bleeds with my pain. "Then I'd take your body. I'd be rough. Maybe violent. Uncaring if you enjoyed it. I can't say you'd walk away uninjured."

"Is that how you want it to be with me? Painful?" she asks with all the calmness in the world. "Do you want to make me pay for what happened to you?"

I jerk my head back and blink. How can she be so calm? "I don't want to hurt you. Not really. But I'm broken, so I might." My thumb brushes down over her pulse that is thumping wildly.

"I get it. You don't want me to touch you. You need to be in control." She licks her lips. Is the subtle act from nerves or interest? "But do you even want to be with *me*?"

"My cock has woken up for the first time in years. My hands itch to reach out for you. My heart aches to truly feel again." I skim my nose over hers. My lips are so close I might die from holding back. "Because of you."

"Me?" Her green eyes seem to glow electric. "If I let you tie me down so you're in control, would you want to see what happens?"

"I can't... but goddess, yes. One day, I want to get beyond this." I bury my face in her silky silver hair, inhaling her sweet, addictive scent. "You'd do that?"

"It's on my bucket list. Osen did something similar in the shadowscape, and I enjoyed it. And if you need to feel safe, I'm willing."

"We'd need someone there, so I don't go too far."

"Maxum," she offers. "Flint and Arran will be overly protective and possessive."

"Are you sure?" I ask, pulling back to watch her expression. "And what about Osen's power?"

"It hasn't been triggered when I'm with the others." Jade blushes. "And... I'm sorry for earlier. I didn't mean to tug on your soul when I climaxed."

"Why did that happen?"

She drops her gaze and chews her lip for a moment. "I, uh, wanted you. I didn't mean to upset you and make you run off."

"I ran off because I wanted to come into your bed and offer my soul to you."

Jade sucks in a breath. I'd be lying if my ego didn't inflate along with my cock at the look in her eyes.

Something primal takes over and, still clasping her hands behind her, I pick her up and crash us against a huge sycamore tree.

"Keep your hands there!" I growl as my hand fists the hair at her nape and the other is at her throat.

She whimpers deliciously, her pupils blowing wide with lust.

My mouth slams down on hers, consuming her like she is the air I need to survive. Tasting her like no other being can, I brush against her soul. She is my key to regaining my life.

She *is* life. Personified.

I don't know what she is exactly, but it feels like she could heal me just by being close.

Our tongues tangle, and I want to be inside her any way I can. If I could crawl inside her, I would. I will have to make do with my tongue, fingers, cock. And when we make love, I'll give her my magic—a magic I thought was long dead.

I grind my body against hers. She's being such a good witch, keeping her hands to herself. Part of me wants her to give in and run her hands over my skin. But I'm unsure if I can truly handle it if she does.

I suck on her tongue, pulling it into my mouth. She goes willingly.

Then I'm ripped away from her warmth, being thrown clear by twenty feet or more.

The ground shakes as heavy footsteps draw closer to where I've landed. "I won't let you hurt her!" Flint snarls in my face.

"I wasn't!" I hold up my arms, waiting for a brain bashing blow that will probably kill me.

"Flint! No!" Jade cries, jumping on to his shoulders to get his attention. "He wasn't hurting me. I liked it."

"Calder threw you into the tree. He threatened you, telling you to keep your hands to yourself! He held your head and was forcing himself on you!" Flint kneels and easily moves Jade around to his front. "He…"

"Sweetheart," she coos as she cups his massive, angry face that should terrify her. "It might have appeared he was rough, but I won't even have a bruise."

"You promise?" Flint softens and strokes her face gently, as if she were a delicate flower that will be destroyed if he looks at her the wrong way. The expression she wears shows she loves his tenderness. "If I had handled you the way he did, I could kill you."

He's right… Am I a brute? Do I even deserve to work through my issues? What if I can never have a sweet exchange like this? What if I remain broken?

"Flint," I call. "*If* Jade and I do anything again, I'll have Maxum watch to make sure I don't hurt her. Okay?"

He turns a glower at me, then he must see the sincerity in my eyes. "Fine. But she is pack. She is my mate. Our mate. If you fuck this up, I will deliver to you your final death."

For the first time in years, I don't welcome a threat like that. I have a reason to hope. I have a reason to live.

"Understood."

11

FLESH AND STONE

JADE

*M*y mind is still whirling from my kiss with Calder when Flint pins me to his chest and says to the phoenix, "I'm taking my mate to cement our bond. Tell the others I won't be back until morning."

"Oomph," I breathe out as we launch into the sky. His massive wings flap effortlessly, and I envy his ability to escape so easily.

His thick fingers lace into my hair and feel my scalp, likely checking for injury since he thinks Calder pulled my hair. "Are you sure you're alright? You can tell me the truth now."

"I told you the truth. Calder was excitable. Yes, he was pinning me to the tree, but I enjoyed his kiss. Remember when I told you I don't mind it a bit rough sometimes? Calder needs to get to where he can be gentle. Until that day comes, I'll make sure he understands my limits. He didn't really hurt me anyway, although it was surprising he even kissed me."

"I didn't think he liked intimacy with women, especially witches," Flint says as he banks right and soars toward a hill that might be classified as a mountain in some flatter terrains.

"I suppose I'm the exception?" I grin at myself.

My gargoyle picks up on my delight. "You want him even though he is damaged?"

"He didn't hurt me. Maybe he isn't as damaged as he thinks. He definitely needs boundaries so he can feel safe, though."

"You need to feel safe too. But enough of the phoenix," Flint says succinctly.

Yes. Our bond. With each wing beat, I feel his hardening cocks rubbing against my center. "Is that Mount *Shafta* in your pants? Do I need to get my hiking gear?"

Flint gives me a lopsided smirk. "Don't worry, I'll fly you to my peak."

I love that he's picking up my humor more.

Then his face falls back into his stoic gargoyle mode. "Jade, if we don't complete our bond soon, I fear it might slip away. I can barely hear your thoughts anymore."

"Our bond can fade?" Fear shoots pain right through my heart. "How?"

"We initiated, but I haven't been able to commune with you since then. Not with the attacks and travel and the others getting in my way."

His endearing possessiveness makes my pulse flutter. Though I don't like to hear he feels I've neglected him.

"Flint, you should have told me. With this whole arrangement, you'll have to be forthcoming if you need my attention. I'll try my best, but I wasn't very good at having one boyfriend, let alone several mates."

"Oh, I..." He stutters on his next thought. "I'm new to this as well. You just seem so naturally gifted at relationships and feelings. But you're correct. I shouldn't expect you will always know what I'm feeling or need."

"I can't assume you'll know either, even if we have telepathy. We need to be clear with each other." I squeeze him tightly around his waist with my thighs while I take a moment to admire the view he's given me of the surrounding wilderness. "I'll have to do better. I'm sorry."

"Do not feel bad. Any other week and any other situation, I could wait for my alone time. But bonding is special and time sensitive for gargoyles and their mates."

Flint dives right at the hill, and I screech a bit when he only slows down a fraction before a hard, jarring landing. "Sorry." He rubs his huge hands down my back to calm me. "I've should have warned you. Gargoyles aren't known for their graceful landings. I'll have to work on that too if I plan to carry you around more."

Keeping hold of me in his arms, he walks over to a mouth of a cave.

With a little giggle, I have a flashback to the monster story I was trying to write about my characters, Goliath and Nora, right before I met the guys.

Oddly enough, when we enter, it looks eerily like my scene from my unfinished book. Except my sweet gargoyle has soft blankets laid out neatly in the center and several unlit candles in a circle around the perimeter of the cave.

"When did you do this?" I ask as he places me down on the pallet of blankets.

"I scouted the location when we first arrived. And I've been modifying the structure to make it bigger and smoother inside, so it will please you." He returns to the opening and places a thatched handmade door in front of the opening.

"What!" I gasp as the cave is cast in darkness. "You carved this cave?"

"Yes, I asked the mountain to shift for us."

"Holy boulders! That's fucking amazing." I shake my head in disbelief and watch while Flint uses a long match to light the candles in the space.

"I suppose I forgot to mention my ability to connect with stone. It's easier when the land holds magic. I believe the witch Amira has helped keep this land alive in that way."

Flint finishes with the candle lighting that gives our hideaway a romantic vibe. "I thought you would be more comfortable if you could see during our communing."

"Communing?" I ask. "Is that what a bond is called for gargoyles?"

"The process is done through communing, but the bond is known as a merge." His thick fingers slide under my shirt and skim over my waist, leaving goosebumps in their wake. "Are you cold?"

"No. Excited," I admit. "Nervous."

"Are you nervous about bonding with me? Do you not want to?" He leans down and his beautiful pale gray eyes search my face for the truth. "I will not force a bond on you if you're uncertain."

I snatch his horns in my hands and pull him to me, kissing the heck out of him. He moans and meets my passion with his.

"I want you. I'm nervous because I don't want to mess up," I explain. "And I guess I'm worried part of the reason our bond is fading is because of my bonding with Arran, or what I am now that my magic-containment spell has been undone."

"Arran's bond shouldn't affect our bond." He strokes his thumb over my cheek. "I will guide you through the process so you can't mess it up. Or do you worry that being a witch will make our bonding impossible?"

"Apparently, I'm half witch, a quarter Elven, and a quarter demon."

His thick brows rise. "Demon?"

"Oh, no!" I shake with anxiety. "Is that going to ruin things?"

"It doesn't ruin things." To ease my fears, he pulls me to his broad, hard chest. "Only surprising that you have such an unheard-of combination." He shucks his pants and kneels on the blankets in front of me. "My sweet love, will you be my mate?"

He's so large in his full gargoyle form that he's now my height when he's on his knees.

I wrap my arms around his neck. "Yes, I want that very much."

Slowly, he lifts my shirt over my head. His hands slide down my arms and over my bra covered breasts. I help unlatch it at the back. He drags the shoulder straps forward and intently watches the show as my full breasts are revealed.

"I'm very lucky that my mate is so beautiful," he murmurs as he dips his head to suck each nipple. His large tusks brush over my sensitive skin, and my pussy becomes slick with need.

He slides my pants down along with my underwear, and I help him by stepping out of them when they get to my ankles, kicking off my shoes as I do.

His hands move up to cup my ass. "So soft." Then one hand slides to my front and dips between my thighs. "Open for me?"

I move my feet apart and give him better access.

He slides a finger through my wetness and rumbles with happiness that I'm already needy. He bends lower, lifts my left thigh, bracing me from behind. His long tongue snakes out to fondle my clit.

I suck in a breath. With his solid hold, I can tilt my hips and grind into his face. "Flint," I whisper on a moan.

"Come on my face, sweet mate," he purrs, and it's better than any vibrator I've procured in my many years of flying solo. "You will come again on my cocks as we commune."

He takes me right to the edge, then I'm falling, clenching on nothing, but imagining his thick length inside me. I'm still panting and whimpering as he pulls back and shucks his pants.

With a grace I don't expect from such a huge male, he sits back cross-legged. His large wings are unfurled at his sides, taking up the width of the cave.

He offers his arms for me to fall into. His hard, thick cocks are standing at attention and begging for relief.

I step over either side of his thighs and prepare to sink down onto him. But before I can near his cocks, he captures me by my waist and hovers me over them.

"With this body, I merge with you, my fated heartstone, my center. I will protect you from harm. I will be the bedrock to bring you stability. I will devote my life to bringing you joy. I offer you all that I am. My body, my soul, my love."

Tears flow from my eyes as I hear his sincerity and devotion. I take a moment to absorb his vows. Then I panic because I didn't know I had to prepare for a ceremony.

"That was so beautiful. Do I repeat it? Or am I supposed to make up my own?" I ask, feeling silly and unsure.

"Whatever you say will be perfect."

"With this body, I merge with you, my fated heartstone. I will also protect you from harm. I will be the softness you crave. I will devote my life to bringing you joy. I offer you all that I am. My body, my soul, and my unconditional love."

Still bracing me, Flint's huge hand cups the back of my head and pulls me forward for a loving kiss. Gawd. My heart is always melting around this giant sweetheart.

The apex of my thighs presses against his ten-pack abs. I don't mind if I do as I grind along his sculpted washboard on the way down to my impalement. The friction is delicious.

He uses one arm to hold me in place while he lines up his second cock with my vagina. The one that juts out closest to his stomach glides over my drenched clit. I groan with relief at the contact.

Inch by thick inch, Flint slowly guides me down his shaft that's hard as stone, filling me up until I'm panting again.

He lifts and sinks me down on his massive cock a few times before I'm fully seated. I shift and grind against his second cock and feel myself heading toward the orgasm I've been waiting for.

Large wings close around us until we are fully encased. Candlelight filters in through the space at the bottom of his webbed wings and the floor.

"I feel like a butterfly in a chrysalis," I say in awe, running my fingertips over his wing.

He groans with the intimate touch that apparently is an erogenous zone. "We are like them in many ways. We will leave the safety of my wings changed forever."

I swallow down the strange emotions this idea stirs in me. I don't know how many more transformations I can handle. I've gone from lonely author to psychic medium to witch to wolf-mate to part-fae to part-demon, and now to a heartstone mate to a gargoyle.

Or is it I'm only revealing more and more of my true being, and I haven't changed at all?

"I need to come inside you," he whispers, then rocks me on his cock.

I sway with him to create the most friction. The cock outside of me gives me the perfect sensation over my clit.

His hand slides down around my ass, helping to lift me up and down his dick. He moves his hand lower and stimulates my rosebud, taunting me with his fingertip.

With his size, he has to crane down to kiss me.

I claim his mouth with my tongue, licking into him and making him moan with need.

"Goddess, I love you." His free hand grazes over my breasts, kneading them. Then, as if cherishing me, he smooths his palm over my heart and sternum before going back to pulling on my hardened nipples.

"I love you too." I don't know how it happened in such a short time, but it did. I look forward to feeling that grow with time as we deepen our relationship.

With the perfect amount of stimulation on my clit and breasts and the rhythmic stretch of my pussy around him, I'm close to coming.

"I'm about to…"

"I know, Heartstone. Milk my cum now."

"Fuck, Flint," I curse with his naughty talk as I feel the tingle up my spine and my cunt contracting around his cock. My body spasms, and I'm floating in bliss.

Flint floods me with his release, and his top cock splashes cum over my chest.

Then, as I focus back on him, I watch as he turns to stone.

What the fuck?

"Flint! Are you okay?" I ask.

"I'm okay," he answers inside my mind. *"I should have mentioned this. I'm locking my essence inside you."*

I feel his cock swell at the base, much like a shifter's knot.

"We now must commune via our telepathic link to solidify our bond."

I have no idea what communing might mean to a gargoyle during this ritual. My pussy is still clenching and fluttering over his cock. Shouldn't that be enough?

"Commune?"

"I will share with you my emotions and thoughts. We might be able to share images too."

I take a deep breath and press my forehead to his broad brow.

"I'll go first," he says and then a flood of images and emotions hits me like a semi-truck.

I'd fall back on my ass in shock if it weren't for me being locked in his embrace and cocooned in his wings.

After a moment, the dizziness passes.

"Oh no. I was too excited when I shared." I sense he feels like he's messed up.

"It's okay, sweetie, just give me a moment to process that download." I stroke his sides and he seems to relax, although it's only a feeling since his body is currently stone.

I sift through what is four hundred years of longing. Pain, both physical and emotional. Loneliness. I know that even though he had a pack, he always felt like the odd one out. He didn't participate in their sexual explorations and bonding. He'd risk his life for them without hesitation, but otherwise, he was distant.

He had no one to share his emotional side until I came along and shook his heart. He began to fall in love with me the moment our eyes inadvertently locked when he was invisible and guarding my home. He felt seen when I sensed him beyond the mask. I brought back his curiosity and joy at just being alive.

I blink and feel tears dropping off my cheeks.

"Did it hurt?" he asks.

"No, not like that. I just feel badly that you were lonely for so long." I sniff and wipe away the tears off my face. *"I'm more than honored I helped awaken something in you. Your happiness. It feels like a big responsibility."*

"I don't expect you to do anything but be yourself. I am responsible for my happiness. Although you're the one who inspired me to live again. And I will love you no matter what you do."

I sense I'm meant to share my feelings now. What do I share? How do I do it?

In my mind, I think about my gargoyle and all the sweet moments, our late night chats, and snuggling. I love his sincerity, earnestness, and his nurturing nature. With his solid strength of character and loyalty to his pack, I feel myself healing. His absolute acceptance of me that embraces me by just being in his presence. The unconditional love he offers is a cure to all the assholes who rejected me before him. His virtuous and brave nature stirs in me a desire to be the best version of myself. I treasure his immense trust in me, and I vow to never betray it. I think about how he had made me feel like the most beautiful creature alive when we first made love. He makes me feel that way every time he's looked at me since.

I take all that and visualize offering it to him through our telepathic link.

He mentally gasps when it enters his consciousness.

"Goddess, I can feel your feelings for me," he says in awe. *"You really do love and accept me."*

And now I'm fucking crying again. Damn the big sweetie.

"I do," I confirm.

A powerful pulse of my love radiates out from my body and meets his. Our bond swirls like a tangible thing between us, glowing and tying together in an intricate pattern. My body lurches to meet his, my soft flesh molding to his hard muscles.

Then there's a strange ache in every one of my bones. It's almost painful. I whimper, wondering if something has gone wrong.

Has his gargoyle magic rejected me?

I want to ask what's happening, but I'm overwhelmed, and I sense he is, too.

The pain increases until finally it breaks just as Flint returns to his non-stone form.

We both gasp and grasp onto each other. Asking at the same moment, "Are you alright?"

Something feels off. I grab his sides, and I'm able to grip more than I could before, like his skin is softer—more flexible.

More human.

"Flint!" I cry. "I think I made you weaker!"

"No. Softer," he whispers. "What I've always dreamed of."

"It's a good thing?"

"Yes." His huge hands palm along my ribs. "You... your bones... I sense they took my stone nature. They are stronger—less likely to break or weaken."

"I'm... unbreakable?"

"Close enough."

"I'm Wolverine," I say with utter delight. "I'm an X-*woman*."

He shakes his head in confusion. "No. I didn't make you into an animal shifter. And you're still a woman, just reinforced with *stone*."

I suppress a giggle because I keep forgetting like most of these guys. He doesn't have a clue about most pop culture.

"Wolverine is a character in comic books who has bones plated with the strongest metal."

"Oh, then yes. You're like this Wolverine." He strokes my cheek and then cups my jaw. "Are you alright that I changed you? I didn't know that could happen. When gargoyles mate, they share part of their stone, but I didn't think it would work like that for us. I thought it would only be a sharing of the hearts and minds."

"I don't mind. But I'm worried that you will be more prone to injury with softer skin." I run my hand over his massive arms. "I don't want you to get hurt because of me."

"I heal fast, and I'm still hard."

I wiggle on his engorged cock. "Yeah, you are."

He blushes peach. I notice it's a deeper shade, as if he is more human because of me. "I *am* hard, and I want to make you come on my cocks again."

As an answer, I lean forward and kiss him while grinding into his massive knot inside me.

1 2

TRIPPING

JADE

*T*he following morning, I'm close to limping. Flint catches me as I exit the cave and we fly back. Fortunately, he lands softer this time.

He sets me down but doesn't lose contact with me as we enter the small cabin, as though he can't stand to be even an inch away from my skin.

Maxum and Arran observe us with avid interest.

"We bonded," Flint announces proudly, puffing out his already enormous chest.

"I can see that." Maxum smirks and waves a hand over his face. "She has that just-bonded glow."

He's playing it cool and lighthearted, but I sense he's a bit envious. I wonder what's holding him back. Perhaps he isn't ready emotionally. I get that. I'm not sure if I'm emotionally ready for all this.

Arran gives me a serious look. "But how do you feel? Something's different."

"During the bonding, I got an upgrade on my armor package," I joke.

"Huh?" Arran tilts his head.

"You can fuck me as hard as you like. I won't break."

From behind, Flint quickly covers my mouth with his huge hand. "Heartstone, don't make that a challenge. You still might break."

I lick his palm, and he jerks his hand away in surprise.

He then cups my chin and makes me tilt my head back until I'm looking up at him. *"If you want to lick something, I have other appendages for that,"* he says via our mind link.

I chuckle and lean into him and feel his appendages poking into my back. "I'll take a rain check. I'm pretty tired and sore."

I glance around when I feel what's missing. "Where's Calder?"

"Haven't seen him since he ran off yesterday." Arran shrugs.

"He didn't let you know I was bonding with Flint?" I ask.

"Didn't need to," Maxum answers. "I saw Flint take you in the cave and figured as much."

Panic rises in me. "But where is he? You aren't worried that he's been missing since yesterday?"

"Should we be worried?" Arran asks, standing at attention now that he sees my concern.

"Uh, yeah! Guys, you know as well as I do, he hasn't been okay for a while. Osen's death was hard on him. I thought you were supposed to be a pack." I shake my head and turn around to race out the door to find him.

"He's a big boy," Osen chimes in.

"No, he's someone who's hurting," I argue aloud so all of them can hear. "And there are evil murderous assholes on the loose!"

I storm outside and crash into the broad chest of a phoenix. I hit him with such force that we both go down to the ground. He makes sure that he takes the brunt of the fall and cradles me in his arms with me laying on top of him.

Once I realize it's him, I lift my arms up and try to roll off like a fucking worm.

But he doesn't let me go. "Crap. You hit me like a tank."

"It's my upgrade. Sorry!" Not only am I reenforced with stone, I'm faster and more powerful. Dang, I could hurt someone. "I hulked out."

Calder captures my face and has me look at him. Concern flashes in his eyes. "Jade, why are you upset?"

I'm basically planking off his body, trying not to touch him. I don't know how much longer I can minimize my contact. Besides, it feels awkward as hell. I'm pretty sure it looks stupid, too. I never thought of myself as the klutzy heroine, but dammit if the guys don't bring that out in me. Although I'm impressing myself with my record-breaking plank time.

"I heard you didn't come back after we talked," I tell him. "I was worried."

I'm surprised he hasn't thrown me off. Instead, he sits up, holding me to his chest. My legs automatically fall to the sides of his hips.

"You didn't have to worry."

Keeping my arms tight to my sides, I lean back, but that only makes my sensitive pussy rub against his groin. I ignore that heated sensation and say, "Of course I'm going to worry."

His warm hands are on my upper arms. Are they there to help me balance or keep me in his lap? I'm not used to this touchy-feely side of him.

"I was keeping an eye out for you, guarding the cave while you had your bonding time with Flint."

"You were?" My mouth hangs open in surprise.

His eyes drop to my lips, and I nervously close my mouth.

"I knew you'd both be vulnerable and preoccupied." He finally lets go of my arms and rubs the back of his neck. "I tried to give you your space."

From his blush, I figure he heard my cries of pleasure. But he's been around that before. Maybe it's different since it was a bonding ceremony.

In one fluid motion, Calder stands and easily sets me on my feet in front of him.

I'll never get over how strong these guys are by handling me like I'm a feather.

Turning, I see the shocked and strange expressions on the guys' faces.

Osen chuckles in my head. *This is going to be interesting to see how this all unfolds.*

"They aren't jealous, are they?" I ask.

"Not really. But we were never great at sharing, even if most of us shared our bodies at various times. We were never intimate at the same time."

"Oh, so I'm a wild card?"

"And I love everything about that."

Calder's warm hands drop away from my waist. Instantly, I miss the connection. If the tiny sigh that escapes his lips is any indication, he misses it, too.

Arran clears his throat and waves us in. "Let's feed our woman breakfast."

Flint snatches me up before the others can and carries me inside and sets me on his lap. Then he feeds me the sliced fruit Arran places in front of me.

Arran cocks a brow and Flint shrugs. "What? You did it after your mating. Seems like a nice tradition."

I lock eyes with Maxum, and he smiles at me. But I sense an uneasiness behind his carefree gaze. I wonder if it's about me or that we haven't taken that step yet in our relationship. That's something to talk about next time we're alone. When I glance around the room, I wonder if I will ever be alone again.

I don't mind being by myself, but I hated being lonely, which happened often even when I had a boyfriend.

With these guys and the bonds, I won't be lonely again. Though I will have to carve out some time soon to be alone with my thoughts so I can finish my book.

I suspect Maxum would say I don't need to worry about making money. But my career isn't only about that, not really. I want to write. I love to write. However, I could do without dealing with ads and all the promotional stuff.

Will I write again?

If I only cared about making money, it isn't an easy career. There are a thousand other jobs I could have chosen instead. It isn't easy for authors to rip our hearts open, expose all our insecurities, agonize over every word choice and plot point. We bleed our deepest thoughts and fears into a book. Then we must sit back and watch as reviews come in. Hopefully, sales too.

Some reviewers aren't just unkind, they are brutal. I wonder sometimes if they realize there's a human being on the other side.

Fortunately, I developed a thick skin. And not every book is meant for every reader. Instead I focus on the lovely people who reach out to me and tell me how much they enjoy my stories. That gives me the fuel I need to keep at it—knowing we all can escape together into a world that once only existed in my mind.

Then I wonder…

Do these stories only exist in an author's mind?

Or have we been channeling another reality?

Because now I'm living in one of these alternate universes.

I get dizzy with the idea that the stories we make up all have a truth to them. We could stumble into any of them at any time. If it's true what scientists say about the multiverse, perhaps all these worlds we write about actually exist.

"Heartstone?" Flint calls me out of my haze of thoughts. "Do you need to rest?"

As he says it, I feel the fatigue hit me since we were up the entire night bonding.

I nod, and he lifts me from his lap and carries me into the bedroom.

He places me in the center of the huge bed and crawls onto one side, pulling the covers over us.

Calder appears at the doorway, looking tired and lonely.

If he kept a lookout the whole night, I understand why he was.

"There's enough room." I scoot into Flint some more. "I'll do my best to keep my hands to myself."

He gives me a half smile, and after a moment of hesitation, he joins us, but on top of the covers.

Maxum peeks in and tosses the blanket that Calder has been using from the couch at him.

Calder thanks him and lies on his back, appearing uneasy.

"I'm going to turn away from you, but just so I can make you more comfortable." I say to Calder and then nuzzle into Flint's chest.

I wake hours later with a warm palm on my hip over the blanket and someone's face buried in the hair at the back of my neck. It slowly dawns on me it isn't Arran or Maxum, but Calder snuggled up to me.

Opening my eyes, I see Flint watching him. There doesn't seem to be anger or jealousy, just curiosity.

Using our mental bond, I ask my gargoyle. *"Have you been watching him the whole time?"*

"Yes."

"Does Calder touching me upset you?"

"No. I now understand what happened yesterday. I also see you're good for him. I sense he's tired of being broken... to the point he welcomed my threat of death if he hurt you. It makes my heart weep for him. Especially since I know how wonderful it is to feel healed and loved by you."

My eyes sting with tears, thinking about how they have lived just getting by. Flint and Arran now have happiness, and I helped open that door for them. Calder and Osen are still hurting. I know it's not my job to heal them, but I want to do what I can.

Thankfully, it seems Maxum has only been lonely. Unless there's something else hidden in his heart. Could that be why he hesitates in bonding with me?

I hear Calder suck in a breath when he wakes, realizing where he is. Yet, he doesn't move away like I expect. No, he pushes his nose deeper against my scalp, inhales my scent, and hums.

"What do I smell like?" I ask quietly, letting him know I'm awake.

He jerks ever so slightly. "Uh... you smell like hope."

"Is hope a musky scent, or does it have more of a flowery note?" Maxum asks from the doorway.

I glance over and see him casually leaning against the door frame with his muscular arms crossed over his chest.

Has he been watching Calder the whole time, too?

It makes me nervous that both Maxum and Flint were so worried they couldn't let him sleep next to me without monitoring.

"Shut up, asshole," Calder grumbles at Maxum, but when I look over my shoulder to gauge his mood, he has a relaxed expression. His eyes are soft and hooded as he returns my gaze. He rolls out of the bed and rubs the back of his head, ruffling his auburn locks into more disarray. "Taking a shower."

Maxum smirks and waggles his eyebrows.

Calder punches Maxum's arm on the way out.

When the bathroom door closes, my demon crawls up next to me and whispers in my ear. "He's going to abuse himself in the shower while thinking of you."

I smack Maxum on the shoulder. "Don't tease him."

"What?" Maxum grins wider. "It's good for his mental health."

"Harassing him is good for his mental health?" I roll my eyes.

"Yeah, because it's how we used to be. Before." Maxum strokes the hair away from my face and smiles. "I'm taking this all as a good sign."

"We shouldn't push too hard," Flint adds.

"I agree with Maxum. I'm encouraged by his new energy today," Osen says in my mind.

As I relax back into Flint's embrace, I feel a psychic urge to leave the safety of Amira's sanctuary. I've been compelled to do things before, and my intuition hasn't led me astray yet.

Will the guys refuse to let go so they can keep me safe?

13

FUNISHMENT

JADE

I fill everyone in on what happened with my grandmother-mother and who I really am.

With the confirmation that I'm part demon and fae, Maxum says, "If you wish, I can reach out to a few demons I'm still in contact with and see if we can find your father." Something in his demeanor tells me he doesn't think this is a good idea.

"No. Not yet," I decline his offer that feels too dangerous to pursue. "We would only bring him into this mess *if* we found him."

"He might be able to help," Arran suggests.

"I doubt it." The bitter pang of abandonment hits me hard in the chest. "If he wanted to find me, I'm sure he could have found a way around his own spell. After all, Galiana got to me. Besides, I don't want to waste energy if he's not even alive."

Maxum grimaces as if he's upset by my negativity, but ultimately agrees. "And we might be also drawing unwanted attention if we put feelers out."

His energy seems to fold in on itself.

I need to get Maxum alone so we can talk about us and how he feels. I don't think asking him around everyone else around is a good idea.

Although I'm always stuck with an audience for my most private moments. Osen is around for everything since he's conscious and aware, probably even when I'm not.

That brings up a good question. *"Osen, are you paying attention, even when I'm asleep?"*

"Yes. If anything were to go wrong when you were sleeping, I'd wake you. And if I couldn't wake you, I'd get you to safety and wait for you to come around."

I'm relieved and reassured that someone is always looking out for me. Then I chuckle to myself—Osen is the ultimate stalker.

I glance at Calder and force myself to hold his gaze. I vocalize the strange urge I've had. "I need to go to your death spot."

"What?" He jumps up, and his eyes go wide. "Why?"

"Because I feel guided to do that. Drawn there." I soften my voice and check in with him. "Do you think you can handle going back?"

"I… I don't know. Maybe." He runs his hands through his hair and pulls on the strands. "Do you think it will help me?"

"I don't know. But when I've had feelings like this, they usually lead to something big."

"Okay," Calder mumbles and paces. Then he regains his nerve and straightens his shoulders. "Yeah, let's do this."

"Hold the fuck up. Not so fast." Maxum puts his hands up as if we're bolting out the door already. "You aren't going anywhere right now."

I don't like being told what I can do. It feels too much like Rob controlling me again. And my finding out how my mother and father manipulated and controlled me… And with Maxum's strange energy since he found out I'm a demon… I'm not in the mood for this bossiness.

"I'll do what I need to do," I snap.

"You *need* to explore your powers a bit more before we run off into the world." Maxum clenches his jaw in irritation. "If Galiana or Rob show up, I won't have you completely unprepared."

Dammit, he's right about the threats I face. But I'm still going to push for this since I don't want to become someone's puppet again.

"You can't just order me around. My gut tells me going there is a part of how I figure out how to use the magic I have."

Maxum strides over to where I'm perched on Flint's lap. He cradles my chin and leans down, staring into my eyes just inches away. "I'm not rushing to leave our safe haven if we don't have to. As much as I want Calder to be healed, I won't risk your well-being, running off half-cocked."

I nod with a smirk, feeling extra spicy. I cross my arms and sass, "Come on, I've recently been *fully* cocked. So stop arguing with me and get on board. *We are going.*"

"No."

My hackles rise. "I will do whatever the fuck I want."

Maxum narrows his obsidian eyes, fire burning in their depths. With a calculated, even tone that sends chills up my body, keeping his eyes zeroed in on me, he says, "Flint, your mate needs a bit of punishment to remind her who the leader of this pack is."

My gargoyle holds me tighter. "What kind of punishment?"

"A spanking." Maxum grins wickedly. "She wants to act like a brat, then I'll meet that accordingly."

Why does his fiery gaze send a thrill down my spine? I've forgotten what I was arguing about.

Flint must sense my interest because he releases his hold. "Then we should all watch," he says with a glint in his eye.

Maxum breaks my gaze to eye him appreciatively for a moment. "I'm loving this new side of you, brother."

I pout at Flint since he's offered me up. But I'm blushing, thinking about how I love the new dynamic too. "You're just making up an excuse to punish me."

"That's not it," Maxum breathes in deeply and adds, "well, not exactly."

My demon sits down on one of the dining chairs and pats his knee. I feel the bond thread between us flare back to life. He enjoys me challenging him, but I sense his worry too.

Sure, I've written and read plenty of scenes like this, but I never had more than a sloppy swat on the ass during sex. I never had a lover I trusted or wanted to play with before now. My heart is pounding more than I expect.

Glancing around the room, I see Arran leaning forward, his corded forearms braced on his thighs. By the smirk on his handsome face, he is highly interested in this display. Even Calder has heat simmering in his eyes. Although his head is lowered and he's looking through his eyelashes as if he shouldn't really be watching.

When my gaze lands on him, he nods to the door. "I can leave."

"You don't have to." I walk over to my crimson demon. Before I surrender to my funishment, I say, "Unless you aren't comfortable."

Calder shakes his head and the auburn locks fall forward and over his brow, giving him a roguish appearance.

I take the last step to Maxum. He's looking deadly serious now as I stand between his muscular thighs.

"You think this is going to be a sweet, little punishment, don't you?"

I swallow and take a half step back.

He snatches me by the waist and has me face down over his lap before I can blink.

"It's gonna hurt, little witch."

"I'm not just a witch anymore!" I huff. "And I didn't do anything wrong yet!"

"Oh, I heard your admission of insubordination." He pulls down my pajama bottoms along with my underwear, exposing me to the room.

His hand comes down swiftly over my right cheek.

"Ow!" I jerk and instinct has me squirming to get away.

His thumb sweeps over my ass. "Oh, yes, I knew you'd mark beautifully." He rubs the sensitive sting out and says, "Do you know why you're being punished?"

"Cuz you're a meanie," I answer.

Smack! Dang it, that really smarts.

"Try again," he orders.

"Because you're a grumpy demon?"

"No." *Smack!* "You're willing to risk yourself for some intuition. I'm not just your potential mate, more importantly, I'm your pack leader now. You accepted that by bonding with my pack members. And *none* of us can run off without thinking through our actions. Look where that recklessness got Osen? Killed."

"But I want to help... Do something." I'm frustrated now. "I won't be controlled. Not anymore."

His hand soothes me up and down my back. "I understand. And your voice is important and valued as much as the rest of us. And you *will* help, but when the time is right. When we all agree. When we are prepared." Maxum's voice is cracking with pain. "Do you know what I would do if I lost you? If *we* lost you?"

I didn't think asking to go to Calder's death spot was completely impulsive and ridiculous, but was it? I refocus to answer his question, "Uh... you'd be upset."

"No." *Smack!* "We'd be devastated. Without you, we would die."

"I..." Tears are gathering in my eyes, partly from the sting of his swats and partly thinking about how they would suffer without me. Then another level of pain slams into my heart. "No one really cared about me before."

Not even the woman who raised me really cared. My mother—or rather, my older sister—never showed me much affection or concern. And now, looking back with my new knowledge, when the spell was lifted, she resented and despised me. When I left home at eighteen, that was it, there was no more contact.

Maxum must sense my shift in emotions. Instead of giving me another swat, he curls over my body and hugs me. "That changes now. You have me. Flint. Arran."

"*Me,*" Osen whispers in my head.

Calder clears his throat and says, "And me."

My head whips up to look him in the eye. What I see surprises me—adoration. How did he change his feelings toward me so quickly? I guess after I stopped being his enemy, his hate shifted into something else.

Maxum sits back, and his hand caresses my ass. "Did you learn your lesson?" He asks.

"Yes."

"Then I'm going to make you come now."

Relief overwhelms me and I almost come with his promise. "Yes, please," I say, still gazing into Calder's eyes.

Smack!

I whimper with the burn.

Maxum's fingers slide down over my crack to my exposed pussy. His fingers sink into my folds, then inside me. "So wet for us. And so perfect since you're healing like a supe now."

With his observation, I realize the soreness I should feel from Flint's cocks and our bonding ceremony is non-existent. Well, this solves a significant problem that having a harem would cause.

Magically resilient pussy... check.

"*Just have to remember to stay hydrated,*" Osen chimes in with amusement.

"*Then that's your job,*" I quip back. "*Water boy.*"

I hear his chuckle.

Calder kneels in front of me. I brace my forearms on Maxum's thigh to look him in the eye.

His gaze drops for a moment to my cleavage. My tits are about to fall out of my shirt. Then he searches my face for a moment. "I crave to capture and swallow all your whimpers and moans." He brushes away a stray lock of hair and tucks it behind my ear. "But I don't feel I've earned the right."

"You saved my life twice now. Once in the alleyway and then hiding me from Rob in the bunker. But if you're with me, you should know it isn't about owing you favors or earning my affection. I want you to touch me... kiss me..." Should I say it? "I want more when you're ready."

"And I want more with you... when I'm ready." Calder then glances at Flint, Arran, and Maxum to judge their reactions. He must see something in their eyes that gives him the encouragement to lean forward and claim my mouth.

His kiss consumes any worries I might have. Calder is passion and fire, pent up need just like my other mates and desperate to channel into someone.

Fuck yeah, I'll be that for them.

Maxum's long, thick fingers sink into my cunt, and I clench around them.

There's some movement in the room, and then I feel a tongue fondling my clit, working around Maxum's hand. I'd know that talented tongue anywhere —Arran.

"Why do you taste like rock candy?" I hear him whisper when he pulls back.

I'm about to break my kiss with Calder to answer, but right next to my ear a deep voice of my gargoyle says, "That would be my cum." Then he frees my tit, squeezing and rolling my nipple.

"Goddess damn." Arran frantically laps at my inner thighs and pussy.

I groan happily into Calder's mouth.

"That's it, baby," Calder whispers over my lips. "Let me hear your pleasure. And I told you Arran had a sweet fang. He won't ever leave your pussy alone after Flint cums inside you."

A shiver runs down my spine and my pussy flutters around Arran's probing tongue that has replaced Maxum's fingers.

Maxum reaches around and works my clit, and I detonate.

My body spasms and arches against Maxum's lap. I cry out in bliss into Calder's hungry mouth. Arran's clawed hands clamp down on my ass as he licks up my release.

I tremble for a few minutes before I collapse like a wet noodle over Maxum's strong thighs.

"See! Birdman likes licking faces!" my bunny Sage yells out in triumph.

"She's not wrong," Calder says with a blush and a wink.

My demon lifts me up and carries me the short distance to the bed, setting me down in the center. "You need more rest."

I yawn and feel the hazy contentment and exhaustion hit me again.

I hear Flint, Arran, and Calder whispering out in the main room, but I don't pay it much mind. I'd pay more attention, but I don't think they'd give Calder a hard time about kissing me and joining in.

Arran slips into the bed next to me, fully back in his human form. He smiles that megawatt smile that could ignite panties. Pulling me to him, he kisses me sweetly.

Flint curls up against my back.

"Everything okay?" I tilt my head toward the main living area.

"Yeah. Calder was just checking in with us." He skims his thumb over my cheek. "And I was demanding some snuggle time. I missed you last night."

"We're going to have to set up a schedule." I chuckle when everyone grunts a yes.

"I'll get on that, my sweet witch," Maxum says and pats my foot before heading out of the cabin with Calder.

Flint tucks a blanket over us.

In the safety of my two mates' embrace, I instantly fall asleep.

1 4

BONKERS

ARRAN

I feel guilty for wanting to abduct my mate and hide us away like
Flint did. Though the others would track Jade down to demand
their time with her. And she'd be pissed too. We wouldn't really be alone
since Osen is still haunting her. So there's that.

Oh, well. That plan is out.

But I will put my foot down after our matings are completed. We can't just
run off unexpectedly like Flint did with her—hoarding her all night.

My berserker was going nuts.

Okay. It was me. I was going bonkers, but he was pissed too.

Taking her without warning set Maxum and me on edge. We don't want to
make Jade feel like she is some sort of captive, so we won't make a big deal in
front of her.

However, the guys need to know we can't do that to each other. Unless it's
life or death, we can't run off. No matter how much we want to.

It's another reason Maxum gave her a spanking... to remind us we can't
just take off.

I'm not sleeping as Jade naps, even though I should, since I didn't get
much rest last night. No, I'm watching her. The movements of her eyelids
suggest she's dreaming. Her breathing is even and shallow. I memorize every

freckle and line on her face. I notice how different her hair is from the day I met her. Instead of the look of graying hair, it's now a consistent silver and almost glows. Fae hair concealed by the spell that I broke when I mated her.

My mate. She's my gorgeous, amazing, loving mate. I wonder how I got so lucky after my shit show of a life. Then I remember I have the harrowing responsibility to ensure her safety. She's the target of the most dangerous witch we have ever come across.

Galiana knows Jade's family secrets, and likely knows more about Jade's powers. She killed Osen and who knows how many more supes. Plus, this evil witch has a way to use Jade's magic to drain and kill us.

Eliminating Galiana seems impossible. The only hope I feel is in the possibility that she's gone rogue and the rest of the ASO witches don't know about Jade's abilities. That means she's separating herself from her main support, and we can take advantage of the vulnerability that comes with that.

If Galiana hasn't had access to Jade's unique magic for a while, then it might be fading. Soon she will be the same as any other witch. Witches are normally easier to kill than a supe since they don't have the accelerated healing ability that we have. She's a powerful witch, but she's still killable.

Still asleep, Jade groans and wiggles her body closer to me. She tucks her face into my chest, and I kiss the top of her head.

Flint's gaze finds mine now that Jade isn't blocking our view of each other. I think he's frowning. It's hard to tell with a gargoyle. His face always has a stern expression, unless he's admiring our mate. He nods to me, finding the camaraderie in this moment alone with her.

I return the gesture.

Then, with a sigh filled with longing and fear, his fingers delicately comb through her soft hair. It's strange to see the awkwardly bulky male, so careful and attentive with her. He's come a long way out of his shell. It's a shell he's used to hide himself, even from us.

I realize now how much more there is to him that as a pack we all ignored or didn't even suspect. But Jade knew. She drew it out of him. Just like she drew the positive out of me.

Because of her love and encouragement, I'm finally feeling sane again after all these years. I've accepted my berserker and made peace with him. My wolf is calm after feeling angry that his nature was mutilated into a rabid monster.

Wrapping my arm around Jade's waist, I hold her closer, and she hums happily in her sleep.

Or at least, I think she's asleep... until she says, "Good puppy." Then she lets out a sleepy giggle.

I palm her lower back, but say nothing, hoping she rests longer. It's been a few hours since we had the little spanking scene, and I want to make sure she's ready for what Maxum has planned next.

I wish it was more sex. But he wants to see if we can figure out her magic before we leave Amira's sanctuary and rightfully so. He wants to please her and agree to her plan, but he needs assurances.

Since she feels a magical pull, we know we must take her to Calder's last death spot soon, but we won't do it completely ignorant of her abilities.

"Is it wrong that I want to stay snuggled up with you two?" Jade asks.

"I'd say I'd prefer it." I kiss her forehead.

She tilts her head back and peeks up at my face. "I wish I had more than two sides so I could snuggle all of you at once."

"We'd like our one-on-one time too though," Flint says and strokes his hand down her arm.

Jade hooks her ankle behind her and over Flint's leg. "I need to give you all enough love."

"Things will settle down soon," I assure her.

"Once we annihilate our enemies," Flint adds with a gravelly growl.

"You always say the sweetest things." Jade looks over her shoulder at Flint and grins.

Then her face falters, and behind her beautiful green eyes, I see the wheels spinning in her mind. Through our mate bond, I feel her sadness and sense her anger.

"You're angry," I say, hoping to get her to talk about it.

"I talk a big game in my books. Killing characters off with the only concern being if it serves the plot." She rolls her lips inward and bites them, thinking. "But real life is different. There were times I thought I'd have to shoot Rob if he broke in and attacked me again. I worried that if I killed him, taking a life would mess me up, even if it was his. But now, after what Rob and Galiana did. They killed Osen and used me. She tortured and killed my mother and mother's parents. Those assholes need to go."

"Yeah, killing in theory, killing in cold blood, and killing in war are all different. But this is war," I say. "It's either us or them."

"And you didn't ask for this," Flint reminds her. "The only thing you did was dare to exist and refuse to be used any longer."

She nods vigorously, as if she's shaking her fears away. "We have to be careful. I don't think I could stand to lose any of you. Like Maxum said, it would destroy me. Especially since you're all trying to protect me."

"Whatever happens, you can't feel guilty." Flint captures her chin and guides her face to look at him. "Understand?"

Jade doesn't answer. She won't lie to him and to promise this would be untrue.

"Would it make you feel less guilty in all of this to know we would fight Galiana and Rob, no matter what?" I ask. "They killed our packmate. And before that, they were killing our kind. We've been hunting them for years."

"Yeah, okay." She acquiesces, but still doesn't promise a thing.

Flint glances up at me, asking for my help.

I give my head a shake. *Not now*, I tell him with my look. If it comes to pass, we deal with the fallout then.

We can't live in constant worry over what may be.

I'm learning that lesson by allowing myself to open my heart and love my mate. Yes, many things could go wrong, but what if everything goes right?

15

CAPTURING SPIRITS

JADE

$\mathcal{A}$fter my nap, Arran joins me in taking a long shower. He dotes on me, shampooing and conditioning my hair and scrubbing my back. He doesn't fool around... much. He must worry that if he gets too frisky, then Serky will break through and take over. Or perhaps he's just trying to be a caring mate and not make everything about sex.

I could see how that could easily happen with a pack like this. I'd enjoy the hell out of it, but I need more. Deep conversations, laughter, and being there for each other in any way that we're needed.

Arran shuts off the shower, and we towel ourselves dry before slipping on some workout clothes.

In the living area, Flint has a glass of water and fruit and nuts waiting. "Eat. You'll need your strength."

As I finish the snack, I ask, "What do they have for me today?"

"Maxum has asked Darius to help," Flint informs me as he gazes out the window. "If you have some demon soul magic, then he's the one to identify it and guide you."

I walk up next to him and stare out the kitchen window, watching Maxum and Calder chat with Darius in the clearing between our cabin and the main house.

The hellhound is still a bit scary to me, which makes me chuckle. *That's what I'm afraid of?* But my bunch of monsters are no biggie. Perhaps because I feel the connection between us. I have no sense of Darius. I doubt he'd try to hurt me, not while Amira's blessing of sanctuary holds.

Though I can't say he'd spare me another thought either way if we were to meet as strangers on the street. If anything, he might kill me just for sniffing out my witch blood.

"You're not wrong," Osen agrees. *"He only has kindness in his heart for his mate and mate brother. He tolerates Maxum because he likely reminds him of the positive aspects of their homelands."*

Squaring my shoulders, I head out to join them, with Flint and Arran following behind me. Raithe and Amira come out of the main house to meet us.

"The gang's all here," Raithe announces happily, with a playful clap of his hands.

This phoenix is a sunshine to Darius' grump, although I don't think they're an item as well. And I suppose Amira's disposition lands somewhere in the middle. I make a note to write something like this in the future... if there is a future. *If* I ever have time to write again.

Le sigh.

I hope I find a way back to my passion for writing smut. I mean, I have all these guys to test out all the things. It seems selfish to not share my research.

But first, kick some magical ass.

"Maxum tells me you tugged on their souls," Darius says, narrowing his fiery eyes at me. That isn't a metaphor. He has flames blazing right out of his eye sockets. I've seen Maxum and Calder with what looks like fire behind their eyes, but this is full on roasting my marshmallows level fire.

Damn if this dude doesn't make me shiver with nerves. What if he doesn't like my answer?

I don't think he would try anything with my guys all around.

Swallowing my anxiety, I answer with a small voice, "It was an accident. I was in a moment of pleasure, and I wanted them closer."

Darius grunts, sniffs, and tilts his head, studying me. "I can smell it more now. Demon blood. High born." He flicks his gaze at Maxum and says, "She'd be too good for you if she weren't a mutt."

"Hey!" I snap.

"I wasn't trying to offend you." Darius waves me off.

"I don't care what you say about me, but I won't have you putting Maxum down."

Maxum pulls me to his side and kisses the top of my head. "Thank you for defending my honor, just remember you're talking to a fancy pants fire puppy."

Darius chuckles or at least that's what I think he's doing. It's hard to tell.

"If you pulled their souls, then you have a magic similar to mine. I can take a soul out of a body and then release it beyond the veil. You may be able to do something like this. Or perhaps what you did earlier was actually siphoning their life force."

My face and arms go numb. I stand stock still, panicking.

Is that the magic that Galiana and Rob were stealing from me and used to kill Osen? Did I almost murder my mates?

"Can you tell if I hurt my pack?" I ask, terrified to hear the answer.

"I don't sense any damage."

Relief fills me. I need to be fucking careful until I know what I'm doing. Maybe I should lay off getting laid. I could rip the soul out of my partner with a big O.

I'm a cumming black widow.

I hug my arms over my chest.

Maxum rubs my shoulders with his huge palm, and he comforts me. "It will be okay. This is why we are out here... to figure it out."

"But how do we *figure it out* without hurting someone?" I demand, snapping out of my paralysis.

"I'm here," Darius reminds me. "I can help you return a soul to its body if you start to pull it out."

"But what if I'm siphoning their life force?" I throw my arms in the air, ready to walk away and never use my magic again.

"I will see that and immediately alert you to stop." Darius steps closer. His hellhound nature is right on the surface. His skin is dark gray like charcoal with cracks that reveal lava like fire underneath his fur. His flaming eyes narrow in on me.

I gulp, but somehow stand my ground.

"All you need to do is do what you did before, and I will identify your ability. You need to know, so you then can use it properly. And I'd like to go about the rest of the day."

I wonder what the rest of his day might look like, but I'm pretty sure it has something to do with his mate. I get it. I'd enjoy being with my mates, too.

"Okay. I'll try."

I shake out my shoulders, and Darius steps back to give me space again.

"Target me." Maxum turns me to face him.

"Why you?" I ask.

"Because I'm more akin to Darius."

I hear an omission in his tone. He doesn't want me to yank on one of my bonded mates, or further injure Calder. That only makes me more nervous since he expects shit to go wrong. I tilt my head back and stare at the blue sky, trying my best to keep my wits about me. This is no time to lose it.

Recalling how I felt when I tugged on their souls, I focus on bringing Maxum closer, needing him. Wanting him to be part of me.

Energy swells around me, and I give him a tug.

Maxum lurches forward.

Darius barks, "Release him!"

I let go of the thought and energy. I fall backward, expecting to land hard on my ass. But Flint has me around my waist and keeps me upright.

"Well?" I demand.

"You're a soul sucker."

I choke out a laugh. "Well, I've been called a lot of horrible things, and that actually *is* one of them," I joke. I have to make light of this, otherwise I might collapse into tears. I don't want this kind of power. I could hurt my guys.

"It's not a bad thing. I have this magic," Darius explains.

"She's worried about hurting us," Flint says, likely reading my mind through our bond.

"Now you know what it is. You can control it." Darius shakes his head, confused. "I don't see what the problem is."

This guy has the emotional intelligence of a brick.

"Remember, she's new to magic," Amira says. "Not all of us want the responsibility over life and death." There's a heaviness to her words. She's had to make that decision in the past and regrets it.

"Hmm." Darius eyes me. "Doesn't matter if you like it. That's what it is."

I huff at his dismissive behavior. But what do I expect? "Fine. Tell me what I can do to make sure I don't hurt an innocent."

"I don't recommend calling their souls to you," he states simply.

"No shit." I grump.

Darius sighs wearily. "If your magic activates, and when you feel the tug, release your hold. Or if you want someone to die, pull harder and rip them from their mortal coil. With a thought, send them through the veil."

From what I'm gathering, supernatural magic is mostly innate. Instinct guides them. He makes it sound so easy.

Human born witchcraft often sounds more involved with spells or focal objects.

"What about my fae side?" I ask.

"From your magic display when we were in hell, it seems you're an electric mage," Maxum says. "Most fae-born mages come from Elven and human matings."

"And that's where a lot of the supernaturals come from, such as vampires and shifters," Arran adds.

"*And the incubi and succubi, among other species,*" Osen chimes in.

My head swirls, thinking about my lineage. I thought I was a plain ole human, but nope. I have DNA that comes from three different realms.

Who were my father's parents? Are they alive even though they may be centuries old?

There's so much I don't know. Sure, I've briefly traveled through the fae and demon realms, but what are their towns like? The people? I only have a limited picture from what my guys have told me and from Osen's memories. Yet his memories weren't much for daily living and seeing the cities and populations.

Will I ever be free to visit and travel to these places? Will I ever meet my father or perhaps distant relatives?

"What is the extent of your electric magic?" Amira asks, breaking my mind's wanderings.

"Uh." I look at my hands. "I threw a ball of energy at a hellhound that was chasing us and about to bite Calder."

"With no spell or training?" she probes.

"No. I just wanted to protect him, and boom—lightning fingers."

"With that affinity, you may have the ability to drain the power from a mortal's building," Raithe says appreciatively.

"Or restart a heart," Arran adds. "If an electric mage is strong enough, they could affect the weather."

Flint steps closer and strokes his thumb over my cheek. When our eyes meet, I know he's sensing my chaotic thoughts and worries. "Heartstone, can you call upon that gift now?"

"All I can do is try," I say with a shrug. "What should I target?"

"I recommend holding your hands out in front of you about a foot apart and try to form a ball between your palms," Amira offers. "But if you have to throw the energy, then aim for the lightning rod over the hothouse." She points to a small building near the tree line.

Maxum and Flint both step back to give me space. And Arran moves out of my path to the rod.

I ground my feet shoulder's width apart and hold my hands in front of me.

Electricity. Where to start? Is it as simple to summon as throwing a switch in a house? Or do I have to feel my people are being threatened to call upon it?

I concentrate on the space between my palms. I imagine a ball of energy glowing blue and white, since that's what magic looked like when I threw it to protect Calder.

My hands begin to itch. Encouraged, I focus harder, thinking about zapping the fuck out of Rob. Then Galiana.

A flash of light explodes from my hands.

A chorus of curses surrounds me.

I blink to see properly again and fortunately my accelerated healing repairs my eyes quickly. "Is everyone okay?" I ask with a wince.

Glancing around, I see nods and find everyone blinking as I am.

"Needless to say, you'll need to work on that," Darius grumbles. He turns and saunters away, throwing an offer over his shoulder. "If you have more soul questions, I'll answer them after you get a handle on your fae magic."

I'd growl at him if I thought it'd do any good. But he's probably right. I need to figure my shit out.

Why isn't it as easy as in books? Why can't I just wave my hands around and be the biggest badass magic wielder around?

I need a montage!

Then the words that I'm a *'good-for-nothing loser'* ring in my head, in my sister-mother's voice and in Rob's.

Why can't I instantly disregard all my emotional abuse and trauma from my entire existence? Why can't I get over my insecurities? And why can't I accept the kind words from strange, sexy monsters when they tell me I'm amazing?

Okay, I'm handling that last one better than I thought. But I have enough life experience to know my emotional hang-ups will rear their ugly heads occasionally.

I've been alive long enough to know I'll have days when I'm feeling vulnerable. Because the scars and effects of abuse don't just completely vanish because the source of the pain is gone. Even when the new people in my life are wonderful.

But I know with my guys at my side, any trauma will be easier to move past and conquer.

16

ELECTRIC FIRES

JADE

"*I can help you learn to control your electric powers,*" Osen offers. "*Calder could help too since he has fire affinity that I assume would be similar.*"

"I'd like to work on this without the pressure of an audience," I announce. As the crowd disperses, I hurry over to Calder. "Would you help me?"

He looks over my shoulder at the other guys, then back at me in confusion. "You want me?"

"If you want me to find someone else, I get it." I wave my hand, erasing the request. "Osen said your experience with fire magic might be helpful."

Calder uses his fingers to comb back his auburn hair, and I watch his arm muscles flex with the simple movement.

"Uh, I..." he pauses and waits for everyone to leave the area.

I wait patiently for him to tell me what he needs to get off his chest. Either he wants to help, or he doesn't. I will not force him.

"It's just... I haven't been able to work with fire magic since my last death."

"Oh." I cover my mouth, feeling regret for bringing it up. "I wouldn't have asked. I didn't know..."

"I don't think Osen or the guys have figured it out yet." He nods behind him, where his now hidden wings would be. "My wings light up. I guess they didn't think much about it."

"Is your magic gone forever?" I ask, then grimace. I probably shouldn't ask that sort of thing. "Sorry, ignore me."

Calder fiddles with his fingers. "No. It's okay. You can ask me anything. Weirdly, I don't feel defensive talking about it with you. I suppose I thought the guys would think less of me."

"How could they? You're a freaking amazing phoenix!" I say with enthusiasm.

His mouth turns up at the corners, and he lets a gorgeous smile out on his handsome face. "Thanks. This is what I mean. You're so new to all this, you're excited by the little things."

"You're definitely not little." I chuckle when I hear the innuendo. "But yeah, I try to be excited by life—even the mundane—which you, being a mythological creature, are not. Take the compliment, brat."

He smirks at my sass. "I suppose I can guide you through some things to get you going. I don't currently need magic to talk about it."

"And maybe you just have the yips."

Calder jerks his head in confusion. "Yips?"

"It's a human sports thing. Usually, it's thought of as a state of nervous tension affecting an athlete, making them freeze or spasm. They get all up in their heads and have performance anxiety."

He glances down at his crotch.

"It sounds like you went through a horrible experience. I'd be surprised if you didn't have some blocks from something like that."

He stares at me for a long time. I wonder if he's pissed and is trying to compose himself.

"I suppose it might be that. I lose part of myself when I die, and the last one was a particularly traumatic death."

I want to hug him and tell him it's all going to be alright. Fortunately, I remember myself before I leap at him and encroach on his boundaries.

Calder surveys the area and flicks his chin toward the hothouse. "Let's get away from prying eyes and go where it's a bit more private. You don't need the extra pressure to cause the yipping."

I grin to myself as we walk to our destination, loving how he's making sure I feel comfortable.

When we're in what looks like a more private location, I stop and stare at the small building.

Calder's powerful presence slides up behind me. It's closer than I expect him to be. I feel the heat from his beautiful body.

His hands cup my shoulders, and he leans down to whisper over the shell of my ear, "You can do this."

Goddess, how I want to press back into his muscular chest and feel his arms wrap around me. At this point, I'd settle for a friendly hug, just so he can get over his aversion to touch.

I wonder why I have such a draw to them, including Calder, other than the obvious. I've seen a lot of gorgeous guys in my life, but none has made me ache with the need to make them mine.

"You're still denying this? They're your fated mate matches," Osen says wistfully.

"I suppose I thought it only happens in books." Then I ask him in my mind. *"But what about what you had with him?"*

"Yes, I believe Calder and I were a mate match, but it seems you're matched with the entire pack."

"Well, that's not heavy or anything." I had thought maybe the gravitational pull between us might have been a bit of Osen's influence. But what if it isn't?

"First thing to do is to relax." Calder brings me back to the moment. "I watched you earlier and your instincts are good. You rooted your feet in the earth with the intention of grounding yourself. I would suggest that before you call upon your power that you visualize what your goal is." He points over my shoulder at the weathervane, staying close. "Do you want to throw a ball? Or a lightning bolt? What does it look like in your head?"

"Yeah, okay. I understand." I suck in a breath and shake out my hands. Instead of holding my palms facing each other like Amira prompted, I lift them up toward the building's lightning rod. Then I call on my magic. I'm paying more attention since I don't feel like I'm performing for a crowd.

The magic doesn't flow until I think about how I could use it to protect my pack from Galiana and Rob. It must be triggered by the need to keep them safe.

Energy seems to gather from inside me and then draws from outside of my body.

"Very good," Calder encourages. "I can feel it. Keep going."

Excited that I'm a flipping mage and I'm doing this, I open myself even more to the magic.

My hair is rising on my arms and head.

Maybe too much? *Shit.*

I throw the energy like I did in hell, and it streaks out of me like Zeus' bolt, fully formed.

It crashes against the lightning rod and obliterates it.

Metal explodes out.

Calder grabs me, spinning. He protectively expands and curls his wings to shield us. I can feel his feathers slide across my arms.

Glowing scrap metal lands all around us, sizzling in the grass.

Calder jerks as though he's been hit with debris.

Then I realize his wings are on fire. I expect them to burn me, so I recoil. But other than heat, I don't feel like I'm being hurt.

"Calder! Are you okay?" I ask.

"Fine," he grunts and yanks his wings away from me. "*Fuck*, Jade, did I burn you?"

I touch my arms and hair, then I turn for him and pat my sides. "I don't think so."

"How?" He keeps inspecting me for damage. "I swore my wings touched you, didn't they?"

"Maybe?"

He looks disturbed by that revelation.

"What the fuck?" Darius barks as he charges out of his house, staring at the scattered lightning rod pieces smoldering in his yard. "Woman, you owe me a new rod!"

Protectively, Calder moves in front of me and growls, "Back off, hellhound."

I peek around the phoenix to see that we've gathered a crowd again.

Amira waves her hand and mumbles a chant and the flames on the grass are snuffed. "You told her she could use it as a target."

"I didn't think she had *that* much juice." Darius shakes his head, studying the damage. "You better use that power to fight our enemies."

"I will."

He gives me a once over. "Not bad." With an approving grin, he spins and disappears back into the house as he takes Amira's hand in his.

My jaw drops in shock. I didn't know he could smile.

Calder turns and gazes into my eyes. He smooths back my hair as the guys approach to check on me. "She wasn't burned by my flame," he says. "Does that mean…"

"We don't know what it means. Your flames probably didn't touch her," Maxum cuts him off and grunts. He glares at me, probably reading the look in my eyes. "Witch, I'm not going to test to see if you're flame proof."

"It could be a small test… and you can heal me, right?" I offer. I should know this for any potential battles, shouldn't I?

"Absolutely not!" Maxum slashes his hand through the air. "I will not hurt you!" He waves his fist at the others. "And none of you fucking try it!" He storms off before anyone can argue with him.

This feels like more than just seeing if I will get a tiny burn.

I want to ask what it could be, but I understand if something is bothering Maxum, I have to talk to him about it alone.

Calder clears his throat to draw my attention away from Maxum's retreating backside. "Jade? Are you sure I didn't hurt you?"

I check myself again, but don't even see singe marks on my clothing. "I'm good."

"Guys?" Calder looks to Arran and Flint. "Can we have a minute?"

My mates give me a quick kiss to reassure themselves I'm okay before they leave me alone with the phoenix.

I stare up at him, curious to hear what he has to say. He appears nervous and sad while he studies my face, like he's trying to remember what he wanted to say.

When he doesn't speak for at least a minute, I say, "If you're worried about me, I'm okay. I'm fully aware I might get hurt playing with my magic. This isn't your fault."

"Well, it is. I was supposed to be teaching you control."

"And that doesn't happen the first try." I shrug, then tilt my head, attempting to read him. "What's really upsetting you?"

Calder drops to his knees in front of me, staring up at me with a pained expression. Surprisingly, he takes hold of my hands. I will myself to remain calm. Whatever this is, I need to let him process it.

"I'm so sorry," he pleads.

I can't stand to see him so torn up, so I drop to my knees to meet him where he is. "I don't understand."

"I've been such an ass—"

"You haven't been lately," I interrupt. "And I know why you were before."

"But I'm so fucking broken."

"I'm not asking anything from you." As I say the words, they feel like acid on my tongue and the pain of rejection stings my eyes. I want him more than I should.

"I curse the Fates," he mutters and turns his head away. "But maybe this isn't that..."

"Huh?" I lean over to catch his attention. I don't understand his erratic emotions. "Can you explain?"

"It might be nothing. Or perhaps my flames aren't the same since my death. But *if* my fire touched you and left you completely unscathed, it means we could be mates."

"Told you," Osen whispers in my mind.

"Not now," I scold, then refocus on Calder. I'm unsure of what to say to

make him feel better. I struggle with every response I come up with, since I don't want to make his suffering worse. "I'm sorry."

That snaps him out of his torment. "Why are you sorry?" he asks softly.

"I'm sorry it upsets you this much that you might be matched to me."

His brow furrows. "It has nothing to do with it being you. Not like that. I wish I wasn't broken, and I could be a mate you deserve. You're everything I'd want in a woman."

I smile gently. "I will accept whatever affectionate companionship you're willing to offer. Even if it's only friendship." I glance down at our clasped hands. "If this is as far as you can take things with me, I understand."

Calder's glacial blue eyes pierce my soul and flame with heat. He lets go of my hand and grasps the back of my head and pulls me in for a bruising kiss.

I surrender to his passion and find I'm swept up in it. I return his kiss, swiping my tongue over his lush lips, and he draws it in to suck.

We are in a frenzy until we finally gasp for air.

He rests his forehead on mine and sighs. "Fucking hell."

"Good fucking hell?" I ask, biting my lip and gazing at his handsome face.

"Fantastic." He nuzzles my nose. "Jade, I don't know how this is going to work. But I will try to manage my damage. I'll do what I should have done for my other mate and failed."

I know he's speaking about Osen. My heart aches for them. I wish I could just write some better ending for them.

Then I wonder…

Maybe I can.

17

THE PAST

MAXUM

I feel Jade's presence before I hear or see her. I fear our souls are already intertwining, even without a bonding mark.

She approaches cautiously, unconcerned about the woods or what creatures might hide in the brush.

No. She's nervous about me.

That upsets me more than I would have guessed. Only weeks ago I might have reveled in giving her a fright, but I don't wish her to flinch away from me in fear again.

I'm sitting at the edge of Amira's boundary, and it gives me a view of the neighboring valley.

Jade picks through the brush and leaf debris as she comes slowly closer. When she's fifty feet to my right, she calls out in question, "Maxum?"

"Come." I wave her over.

She still appears skittish. "I understand if you need some alone time. We're a bit on top of each other in that cabin."

"And some of us are on top of *you* quite a bit," I joke.

My flirty smile eases some of the tension in her shoulders, which eases my heart. When she gets within arm's reach, I can't resist and pull her into my lap.

Jade lands with a surprised yelp.

I curl my body around her as we both face the view. My chin rests on the top of her head and my arms snake over her waist, caging her to my body.

She squirms a bit.

"Don't," I hiss.

"Am I hurting you?" she asks with alarm.

"No, but if you wiggle your sweet ass over my cock anymore, I might explode all over your back."

She chuckles, then sighs. "I thought I might be crushing you with my weight."

"Never. You're perfect."

We sit in a comfortable silence after that. My hand slips under her shirt, and I stroke my thumb over her soft belly.

Finally, she breaks the quiet. "Out of this bunch, I think you're the most like me."

"A psycho demon?" I ask with a smirk.

She shakes her head, and I pin her with my chin to make her squirm again.

"You aren't *that* psycho," she argues. "Besides, if I lived eight hundred years dealing with dumb douchebags, I'd probably be even more murderous than you."

"Yes, well then, I'm quite restrained when you think about it that way."

"And you're usually coming from a place of love, protecting your pack."

"I could see you protecting, killing for them as well," I say, knowing her electric magic seems to awaken with the need to keep her pack safe.

"For *all* of you," she counters with emphasis, squeezing my arm.

I sigh, thinking of the people I've failed to keep alive—most recently, Osen. "Maybe, but I'm not always good at protecting."

There's another lull in the conversation, and she breaks it again. "So, what happened back there?"

Here it is. I knew she'd call me on it.

I could just try to ignore her question, and she'd probably let me slide. She's good at giving us space to work things out. She's being a fucking saint with Osen's and Calder's baggage.

"I don't want to see you hurt," I say. It's the truth... just not all of it.

"Yeah, but in the scheme of things, it was about testing for a minor burn. I could easily get hurt worse in my kitchen." She tilts her head back on my shoulder and looks up into my eyes, her jade irises shining with magic. "It feels like there's more to it than that."

I grunt, but don't elaborate. Kissing her temple, I try to sort out my thoughts and emotions. "If you need to do any tests, then do them."

"I was going to anyway."

With my demon sense, I feel her need to set her boundaries with us. I can't blame her. We are possessive and protective more than she even realizes yet. I regret the spanking even though I know she enjoyed it. I want her to have a voice in our pack. To be free. I only fear that if we leave the safety of Amira's sanctuary that she will be stolen from us. Then she wouldn't have any freedom if taken by Galiana or the demon lords, if she survives at all.

"I also want to go to Calder's death spot. And before you ask, I don't know why exactly."

"Fine," I yield. I promised myself centuries ago that I'd never be a controlling mate if I were lucky enough to have one. "A quick trip should go unnoticed. And I doubt they'd think to look for you there."

Her soft fingers trace over my hands, as if memorizing my flesh. "Is the reason you got upset about the fire the same reason you don't want to mate bond with me?"

"I never said I didn't want to mate bond."

"Is it because I have a haunted koochie?" she teases, trying to lighten the mood. I know she's driven by the same call I am to claim each other.

I chuckle softly. "The ghost vagina is not an issue." I pause, unsure what to say.

"Yeah, I know. You said you weren't ready yet. But—"

I lift Jade up and spin her so she sits facing me. "I will mate with you when it's the right time and if you still want me, once the dust settles."

"Why wouldn't I want you?" Her brow furrows, and she looks fucking fierce, like she's going to fight me.

I love it. Too much. And that's the problem. I'm a danger to her. And now with her lineage revealed, I'm the last demon she should bond with. They may take her just to spite me, and I can't protect her the way she will need me to.

I press my forehead to hers, my lips brushing over her mouth as I confess, "I want to possess you just as much as Osen is in your mind, or Flint's stone is in your bones, or Arran's bite etches your flesh. I want my mark burned into your skin like a brand that can never be removed. I want your love to reveal itself in my markings, branding me and announcing I'm bonded to the most beautiful soul I know."

She's panting by the time I'm done, and she claims my mouth. Her tongue sears my next protest into smoke. Our kiss is hard and almost violent, and it's *exactly* what I need from her. Any tentativeness she had before is long gone. I wouldn't be surprised if I walked away with her mark burned into my flesh by the time we are finished here.

Her nails dig into my shoulders, feeling sharper than ever. In response, my hands grip her hips so tightly that I'm sure I'll leave bruises.

Fuck. This is what I am worried about. Now that I know she's part demon, I'm positive she'll trigger me into a rut. I can't guarantee her safety. Some fully demon females don't survive the mating process. I thought I could keep myself in control when she was a witch, but now?

Now unbound magic stirs in her veins. Her blood sings for mine, and I will answer with a brutal mating.

And if the demon lords sense her presence, they will come for her.

I break the kiss and guide her face to my heaving chest.

"Maxum?" she asks, sounding out of breath and confused. "Are you okay?"

"No." I should pull her off my lap and step away. I should run away, but I can't bring myself to do that. "I can't be intimate with you anymore."

"Why not?"

"The spanking? I was on the edge of losing my control. I shouldn't have done that." I sigh. "Or kiss you now."

"You never seemed to have a problem before. And I can handle it."

"Your magic... your demonness was bound—masked—before. I don't think I can resist the wild nature of a demon mating."

"Oh." Jade pulls back to look me in the eye.

I don't meet her gaze until she catches my chin and makes me look. Stars, how many times have I done that to her? How the roles have reversed.

"Do demons go into a sort of frenzied rut?" she asks.

"Yeah. I don't think your body could deal with what might happen. You're only a quarter demon. Maybe if you were half demon or more fae..." I run my hand down my face in frustration. "You're still vulnerable. You're only just coming into your magic."

"Okay." She coos, sadness lacing her words, "It's okay."

I dart my eyes back to her, searching for her meaning. Has she already given up on us? Do I want her to fight for me? Should I be that selfish?

"Stop it," she says firmly. "I can see your thoughts spinning. I don't need your mind-reading power to glean that. I'm saying it's okay. We can wait until you're sure. This only makes me want to test my resilience more. If I'm able to take flames, magic, and hits, then I'll be able to handle you."

"We don't know that."

"Then we find out what I can handle." She clasps the sides of my face and stares right into my soul. "I'm not giving up on you."

She's so understanding it cracks my black heart. I haven't even told her the main reason I can't claim her. Not yet. Maybe never.

I've never felt the need to cry more than I do now. If only I were capable, she would know how deeply I feel for her.

But I can do something else...

"I love you more than you'll know," I whisper the phrase, like the sacred words they are.

"And I love you."

18

MISSING PIECES

JADE

*T*here's more to Maxum's resistance, but I don't push him to explain. When he's ready to tell me the full story, he will.

A demon mating rut might be intense, but I'm sure there are ways to ensure my safety. Maybe we could chain him up… that would be hot.

But only if he's ready to make that commitment.

It's strange to have him wavering now. He was so confident about us until we found out about my demon nature.

Perhaps this has something to do with his aversion to the hell realm. Do I now remind him of what he left behind? What he escaped?

He holds my hand as we stroll back to the cabin. At least he hasn't completely retreated from me. I won't pressure him to be with me. He has to want this. Want us. If he's having second thoughts, I have to find a way to be okay with his decision. I hope if he doesn't want me, he will be my friend, because I don't want to lose him completely.

We're quiet, and I use the time to assess how my mate bonds feel with Arran and Flint. Separated like this, even if it's not more than a quarter mile away, I can feel the cord pulling thin.

I wonder what it feels like when mates travel to different locations. Does it pain them to be apart? I suppose I'll likely find out if we ever get to move on to a normal life.

I chuckle to myself.

"What's funny?" Maxum asks with a curious expression.

"I was thinking about my life in the future and realized I won't ever be normal again."

"You will find normalcy within this new reality," he assures me.

"I guess so." I nod noncommittally. "It might take a while since there's so much I don't understand about supes and demons and whatever else I don't have a clue about."

"We will help you navigate it." Maxum squeezes my hand. "You aren't alone anymore."

That simple promise hits me in the chest like a punch. I stumble with the emotions that come with it. He won't abandon me.

I'm not alone.

"Fuck," I mutter and grasp at my heart.

"Are you alright?" Maxum rushes to stand before me, holding my upper arms, fearing I might fall.

My eyes sting, and my throat closes up. "I never fully realized how alone I've felt all these years... my whole life, really. But now, it's all changed." I gaze up into his smoldering obsidian eyes. "I have you, and a pack to watch out for me."

Maxum presses a kiss to my forehead. "We are pack. We will care for you with every ounce of our being."

I collapse into his embrace and soak up his warmth.

We return to the cabin several minutes later. Flint and Arran collide with me bodily and I oomph out a breath.

What a weird, wonderful feeling to be missed.

For the next few days, I spend time with my guys, talking, kissing, snuggling, and magic training. At night, Osen and I spend my dreamtime talking, playing, and getting to know each other.

The guys take turns helping me channel my electric magic. I'm not perfect at it, but I can conjure a ball of energy to toss, and I've gotten pretty good at actually hitting a target.

Once Maxum is satisfied I can do that to protect myself, he agrees to take me to Calder's death spot.

Of course, the entire pack is going since no one wants to leave my side.

Amira guides us out to beyond her magical boundary. As we pass it, I turn to see the cabins disappear.

"I plan to be back at sunset," Maxum informs her.

"One of us will be here to cross you back over the wards," Amira says. She looks at me. "Good luck."

She must sense the strange weight I feel in my soul. The need to go to Calder's spot has grown over the last few days.

Then the witch vanishes before our very eyes, back in the protections she has placed.

"So cool," I whisper in awe. I'd love to protect my guys like this.

Although he's been brave about returning to the place of his nightmares, I turn to see Calder as pale as I've ever seen him. "Are you sure you can handle going back?"

"Yeah. It's just not the most appealing thing to do." He then nods to Maxum.

Our demon takes the hint and leads us away from the magical border, and when he feels it's safe, he opens a portal. We run through a few different portals before we end up with one that opens to the back of a run-down industrial building. From the lack of cars midday, I'd say we're in a sketchy, desolate area.

Calder's breathing becomes uneven.

Knowing he will probably deny me, I offer my hand anyway.

Staring at it, he frowns and shakes his head. "I'm not sure that's a good idea. If I lose my shit, I don't want to hurt you."

"Okay. But if you want it, I'm here."

"Thanks." Calder pulls himself together and leads us inside after breaking a thick chain around the doors handles like they were made of paper.

I always forget how strong these guys are.

Before I can step inside after Maxum, Arran pulls me into his arms. "Not yet. Let them check for traps first."

Flint follows Maxum inside and Calder stands near us, scanning the surrounding area for threats.

After a few minutes, they come back. "Looks clear, and no one's inside, but stay alert," Maxum warns.

"I can help," Osen says in my mind.

"Okay. Let me know if you pick up on anything."

I've noticed he's become stronger lately. As my magic grows, so does his energy in my body. He sounds more rational and determined to help. But he's also been quiet when we are around the others.

I worry about him and how hard it must be to be like this—living, but not.

I'm wondering if I should offer him freer rein with my body. Allow him to speak to the others whenever he wants.

I had been so worried about him taking off without my permission again that I've been hesitant, but he's trying his best not to be intrusive.

I no longer fear for my wellbeing.

I worry his mental health might suffer without an outlet. Who knows how long he'll be with me?

But now is not that time.

I follow Calder and Maxum through the messy, dusty ruins of the abandoned factory. Arran and Flint protect my back. Even though the place is creepy, and death seems to linger in the air, I feel surprisingly safe with my monsters.

There's trash strewn around, evidence of this place being used by the homeless, but it feels like it hasn't been used in a long time. I wonder if anyone has been inside since Calder experienced his last death.

I'm careful not to touch a thing. Can a supernatural being get tetanus? Probably not. From what the guys tell me, most supes are immune to human illnesses. Guess that's why I never even had a common cold before.

We can still be susceptible to magical ailments and poisons, so I make sure not to brush up against something or step into a trap. Fortunately, Maxum can sense stuff like that and is resistant to most witch curses.

That's mostly what they are looking for. The witch that killed Calder might have left a boobie trap behind in case his friends came to help.

I don't know what I'm searching for by coming here. Maybe a clue to the ASO's plans. Or perhaps some part of my subconscious hopes to heal Calder.

As we approach a corner of the large room, my skin tightens and goosebumps.

Calder stops his slow walk, and I see his fists clench at his sides.

Everyone else goes on alert and freezes, waiting for what Calder might do next.

I can't see his face from my angle, but I know he's glowering at the place he was tortured to death. There's a simple twin sized cast iron bed frame with no mattress on its support beams. Broken chains hang from the corners onto the floor.

Old blood stains the floor underneath and spreads out several feet.

Fuck. This is Calder's blood, and I want to cry out for the pain and injustice he suffered.

He's drawing in heavy, ragged breaths, his shoulders straining against his shirt. I expect his wings to spring free and light on fire, but they don't. I suspect he's too overwhelmed to do a damned thing.

"Open up your senses," Osen prompts.

Taking his suggestion to heart, I open my psychic sixth sense as Osen taught me the first time we were on a field trip in the alleyway—at *his* death spot.

Another wave of death hits me hard. When I quiet the sensations, I see something I wasn't expecting. Shadows moving in my vision. Not in the physical realm, but the astral or spiritual level. But these aren't the shadows that an incubus commands.

There is a strange light flickering within each amorphous shade.

Shades…

Are these specters—echoes of some poor lost soul?

My gaze darts to Calder.

Are these fragments of his essence?

19

FALLING

CALDER

I'm unsure what I expect to find here. The memories of that witch flood my mind. How she tortured me. What she did.

While she demanded secrets about my pack and the supes I work with as she carved into my chest with a knife. She slowly pinned my wings. She sawed them off. Finally, she hacked off my malehood, letting me bleed to death.

It's no surprise I couldn't get it up for sex after I was reborn.

During the regeneration, my body was made whole again, but parts of my soul were missing. I lost my desire for friendship and love. I lost my phoenix form. At least my wings had returned.

I no longer had sexual desires. At least not until Jade showed up. She has stirred my needs both physically and emotionally.

I stare at the bed and chains, and I can almost feel the iron burning into my flesh. They were enough to keep my naked body in agonizing pain during my time here. Preventing me from healing properly. The witch thought she had exhausted my magic enough for me to never to be reborn again.

Luckily or unluckily, depending on how one looks at it, when I died, I exploded. I scattered into an ash so small and fine. The witch didn't see my remains as she escaped.

She left, thinking her job was done. But slowly over the course of a day, my ashes pulled back together, and I burst forth from a fire of rebirth.

I don't know how long I've been standing here staring at the evidence of my vicious torture, but Jade sidles up cautiously beside me.

Her gorgeous green eyes glow with magic. She isn't even looking at me, but staring up at nothing, like she's watching butterflies flutter in the air.

What does she see I cannot?

Finally, her gaze falls on to me. "Can you feel what's here?" she asks in a quiet voice.

"What?" I ask in a hoarse whisper, even if I don't mean to.

"I believe... its soul fragments." She waits for my response, but I'm so stunned, I can't react. "They feel like you."

I turn back to search the air above us but see nothing.

Jade holds out her arms, palms up, as if calling someone into an embrace.

She closes her eyes, and I feel that same odd tugging sensation she did when she climaxed the other day. Except it's not as strong.

After a few moments, she gasps and jerks backward.

Out of instinct, I catch her before she goes down to the floor and pull her to my chest.

Jade opens her eyes, which are now glowing like a freaking spotlight.

She rises to her toes and parts her mouth. Her hands grip my shoulders and guide me down to her lips.

I kiss her, but it's nothing like I expect. Instead of her tongue snaking inside my mouth, it's energy. Or maybe it's magic.

No... it's *me*.

My soul fragments fall into me. They ping and bounce into my body like a pinball machine.

I grab at Jade, then some part of me fears I might hurt her, so I push away, falling to the dirty floor and onto my back. My body spasms, and I erupt in flames.

Jade gasps, scrambling toward me on her hands and knees.

Arran snatches her up in his strong arms and carries her several yards away.

My eyes lock with hers, filled with fear.

My entire being feels like it's being ripped apart and jammed back together. It hurts worse than anything I've felt before—even in my last death. It feels like my last death on replay and amplified.

There's a blood-curdling scream.

It's me. I'm screaming. Tears leak from my eyes, and they evaporate with the heat of my flames.

Am I dying? It feels like I'm dying again.

My bones ache and snap. It's a familiar feeling that I never thought I'd feel again.

I launch into the air, wings spread, talons out, my beak snaps at the pain.

As Arran goes slack in shock, Jade stumbles out of his arms.

"Calder!" she cries, taking a step closer as she stares up at me in wonder.

I'm overcome with emotions that I haven't been able to deal with yet.

I dive toward her…

2 0

BURNING UP

JADE

*H*oly firebirds. Calder is a magnificent, giant flaming phoenix. His bird form's wingspan is at least twenty feet. I feel the heat on my exposed skin as he flaps his wings, hovering over our heads by thirty feet. His flames scorch the high ceiling just above him.

He glances around, as if looking for a way to escape through a window. Except the windows are all too small for him to clear, even if he broke through the panes.

"He appears out of his senses," Osen says.

Fearful he'll fly off and lose himself, I stumble forward and out of Arran's muscular arms. "Calder!" I plead for him to come down and return to us.

His piercing blue eyes watch me as if I'm prey. I can't say it's the same Calder I know behind these eyes. Even Arran's berserker still has more of him than this creature has of the man I've come to know. I sense Osen agrees with me.

The phoenix dives straight at me.

Shit. Is he attacking?

Flint is on top of me in an instant, moving faster than a gargoyle should be able to move with their bulky mass. I'm pinned to the floor. He curls around me the best he can with his body and wings, covering and protecting me from Calder.

He turns to stone just as I feel Calder crash into Flint's back.

Flames swirl around us.

I bury my face into Flint's stone chest in an attempt to avoid being cooked alive.

Blazing heat brushes over my back, but I don't feel the searing pain of being injured. More like standing in rays of a summer sun too long.

Shouts and sounds of scuffling feet surround me. I dare to peek beyond the safety of Flint's massive arms.

Calder is unconscious on the floor next to me in his human form. His flames are gone, yet his wings remain, but they're contorted in a mangled way.

My heart pinches. Are they broken?

Maxum and Arran are standing over him, their chests heaving with exertion.

Arran's face glints with sweat. His shirt is torn to shreds, and his skin is burned.

"Fuck!" I scream, as if I'm wounded. He must be blocking the pain from traveling through in our bond. "Flint, turn back! I need to get to Arran."

My gargoyle's stone form softens, and he falls a bit more into me before catching himself and pushing up onto his knees.

With my back flat on the concrete floor, I move to roll up and get to Arran and Calder. Flint grasps my shoulders to stop me.

Frantically, I turn back to him, fearing that I've missed something else. Is Flint okay?

My eyes search him as his hands grope to check me for my injuries.

"You're not burned," Flint says in shock.

"Are you alright?" I ask.

He gives me a quick nod. "He can't melt my stone."

I hold out my hands in a silent request for him to help me to my feet. He does without protest now that he's certain I'm okay.

I run to Arran, but quickly realize I could hurt him if I hug him like I want to. I'm still carried on my momentum, and Maxum catches me by my waist and pulls me to his chest. Flipping me around to face him, I see his shirt has been burned off... and his pants. My eyes search for damage.

He shakes his head in answer. "Demons are hard to burn. Not that phoenix fire doesn't sting like a motherfucker."

I spin in his grasp, almost clawing my way to get to my sweet wolf, Arran.

He holds his arms up to stop me. "Give me a little while to heal, my mate. I should probably shift a few times to speed up the healing."

I'm in shock that he didn't berserker out for this. But maybe he did, and now he turned back to his human form before I could check on him.

My gaze drops to an unconscious Calder. His chest doesn't seem to move with a breath. "Guys? Is he...?" I can't say the words.

Osen's ghost inside me stills, waiting for an answer.

Maxum drops into a crouch and feels his neck. "Alive. His body is behaving like he's in a regeneration. It slows down to nothing until he's ready to reanimate."

Flint moves so he's on the other side of Calder's body. Then he glances up at me. "What happened to him, Heartstone?"

"I think I put the missing pieces of his soul back inside."

"Stars, you can do that?" Arran asks with awe and concern.

I shrug. "I sort of did it on instinct."

Arran removes his fire-damaged clothes and shifts into his wolf. My heart breaks at the missing fur from his burns. Tears fall from my eyes, and I bury my face in Maxum's hard chest.

"I'm so sorry," I cry. "I didn't know he'd do this. Hurt you."

Turning back, Arran's muscular, naked body presses against my side. "Baby, don't blame yourself. This isn't the first time the bird burned me. I'll be okay in a bit."

I turn to look into his beautiful glowing amber eyes and find he's telling me the truth. He's more worried about me.

Arran strokes a hand softly over my hair. "Besides, you helped fix him."

"Although he might be more broken until his soul's returned pieces come to terms with what happened." Maxum frowns. "He could be a mess for a while."

I just shoved unhealed, traumatized pieces back into the guy without thinking it through. What if I fucked up any progress he's made?

Flint gently picks up Calder's body. "Let's get him back somewhere safe, where another phoenix can help him through this."

Maxum glances down at his naked body and says, "We'll have to make a few jumps before we can return. Hopefully, he'll stay knocked out until we get back."

Thankfully, Calder remains unconscious for the entire journey to Amira's. We also stop by one of their old abandoned safe houses to grab clothes for Maxum and Arran.

Oddly enough, though my clothes and skin should have burned, I don't have any damage.

To my surprise, Arran is almost completely healed, too.

It's Raithe who meets us just outside the concealment ward of his coven's property. His eyes immediately snap to his fellow phoenix when we arrive.

"What happened?" He runs forward, looking Calder over. "Did he die?"

"No," Maxum answers. "Let's step over into a secure area before we get into it, if you don't mind."

"Yes, of course." Raithe rushes back to the boundary and waves us through, inviting us all into the safety of Amira's magic.

Now that I'm more aware of my magic, I can feel her power wrap around me like a warm blanket.

Raithe doesn't press for more information as we head straight for our tiny cabin. Amira and Darius must have sensed something off because they appear quickly as we come to the large clearing between the two main buildings.

Amira inspects us all quickly, then her gaze falls back on Calder cradled in Flint's arms. "Were you attacked?" Her voice is firm. I assume she's ensuring we didn't bring more trouble.

Maxum shakes his head. "Apparently, Jade has the ability to return soul fragments to their bodies."

"Interesting," Darius drawls, giving me a once over. "Few can work with such a delicate skill."

"I don't know how delicate it was since he freaked out immediately afterward."

"Fractured souls have a tendency of panicking and reacting on primal instinct," he explains. "You'll need to monitor him when he finally wakes up."

"You can use my regeneration space. It won't burn down." Raithe nods toward a hill with a metal hatch. "It's as fireproof as I could manage."

Without question, Flint carries him over and Raithe helps him inside.

I bite my lip, wondering what I should do. I want to be with Calder, ease him through this process, but I worry he won't find my presence comforting. He might hate me. He might never forgive me.

Fuckinggoddessdammit.

"Maxum and Flint will tend to him," Arran whispers over the shell of my ear as his arms wrap around my waist. "Come, you need some rest."

I resist and take a step toward the underground shelter.

Arran growls and snatches me up in his arms, bridal style. I fight him, shifting in his hold, but I'm unwilling to hurt him to break free, so I'm left with few options against his strength.

"Please. He's going to hate me." I plead. "He'll think I've abandoned him."

I won't be able to live in this pack if he hates me. He will make all our lives miserable. I'd be guilty of ruining their family. I've already mated with Arran and Flint... What have I done? Rushing into mating when things are so chaotic?

This isn't like me. Do I even know *myself* anymore?

Dammit. I'm having an out-of-body experience. It's as if I can see my mind and body and some other rational part of me is helplessly watching on as I'm spiraling. I can't stop. Because things *are* fucked up. And I'm the reason.

Maxum appears suddenly in my field of vision, and Arran abruptly jerks to a stop.

My demon grasps my jaw and forces me to look him in the eye.

I'm instantly back in my body and alert. I almost recoil at his fierce glower. I know he's a force to be reckoned with, but I don't back down from meeting his gaze because in my gut I know he won't hurt me.

Not on purpose.

But the way he's peering into my damned soul rattles me.

"We will get through this. *Together*." He waits for me to acknowledge what he's said, but I only stare up into his beautifully heated eyes. "Don't do anything reckless. You belong here with us, and that means with Calder too. He just needs to wake up, settle down, and remember what's happened."

Maxum sears his words of promise into my flesh with a passionate kiss. When he's done, he storms off toward the cellar.

21

LEVELED UP

JADE

"*H*e's not wrong," Arran says, gazing down at me as he walks toward the tiny cabin. "I could feel your emotions reeling through our bond. Bastard just beat me to helping you settle. My only consolation is that I get to snuggle you while he's busy."

Arran sets me down on the edge of our bed and strips off his clothes before he lifts off my shirt. Before long, we are both naked, and I'm studying the remaining pink scars of Calder's fire. My finger tentatively skims along his shoulder when he leans over to place a sweet, chaste kiss on my lips.

"I'll be completely healed by tomorrow. No need to fret." He tucks a loose strand of my silver hair behind my ear.

"But Calder won't be okay. I messed up." I sigh and rub my face. "I did what so many FMCs do—something impulsive and screw it all up."

Arran doesn't let me brood. He has me by my thick thighs and lifts me up in his arms, wrapping my legs around his waist. My pussy lands squarely over the length of his hardening cock.

My werewolf drags his luscious lips down my neck until he licks at his mating mark at the juncture with my shoulder. I moan, his attention to it sending a wave of lava straight down between my legs.

His cock grinds into me, his length slipping through my silky wetness. "Then what happens in your books?"

I loll my head back and surrender to my alpha. I grin up at the ceiling, realizing what he's done. "They somehow work it all out."

"Exactly. It's just like life. Shit happens, and we work it out." Arran moves forward and places me in the center of the bed. He gives me a brain melting kiss, stroking his tongue over mine and then pulls back. His eyes travel down my body, admiring all I have to offer.

Under his gaze, I feel like a goddess. Like all my feminine curves and softness are a blessing to celebrate.

Another pang of guilt for Calder hits me. "Maybe we shouldn't..."

"I'd argue that we should. Even Calder would say that life goes on and we have to hold on to the precious moments because we don't know when it all will be taken away from us. There's nothing we can do until he wakes up."

I suppose he's right. Calder is safe and recovering. Our lives are dangerous. This might be the last time I have Arran in my arms.

His glowing golden eyes slide down my body to my exposed pussy. My thighs are spread wide around his hips, and he growls low and hungry. "I'm going to eat you, diving my long monster tongue into your cunt. Then I'm going to fuck you until you come around my knot. Understand?"

I nod and bite my lip. His berserker is right under the surface. But even in the likely event Serky ends up being the one knotting me, I know Arran is right there too.

Arran dips his head down and licks over my nipple, and it hardens under his attention. With his other hand, he pinches and rolls my other nipple to a peak.

He licks and sucks, moving lower and lower down my stomach as he nips at my flesh. "So fucking perfect."

My hips rise and tilt to meet his tongue as he lazily brushes it over my clit.

Arran lifts and holds my thighs apart and hums as he gazes at my wet and needy sex. "It's eager for my knot, isn't it? So wet for us. You must have some shifter blood to make you slick like this."

"Please. I need you... your knot, too."

Light flashes in his golden eyes. He dives for my center and feasts like a man possessed. Which I suppose he is. Two fingers slip inside my clenching channel, and he pumps slowly. With a hard suck on my clit, I come undone and scream out his name.

He crawls up my body, and I feel the heavy weight of his cock rest against my throbbing pussy.

I wonder if this is when the man disappears, and I'm face to face with his werewolf. I now know Serky wouldn't really hurt me, but he's a monster and I expect a few scrapes. Yet, Arran craves to have full control of his body when we are in the throes of passion.

"I love you, my moon mate," he whispers over my lips and then ravages me with a kiss before I can return the sentiment.

I taste the tang of my release on his tongue and tilt my hips to meet his.

Without breaking eye contact, he pulls back and braces himself on his elbows. Then he sinks in slowly, enjoying the entire journey, inch by inch. "Fuck. I don't think there's a better feeling in the world than being inside you and gazing into your eyes."

He pushes all the way to his bulging knot. I lift my hand and brush away his mess of wavy brown hair, more out of the need to touch him, to make sure he's real. I don't want to wake up and find this whole thing with my guys was all just a fever dream.

Arran hums and closes his eyes in bliss for a moment, sliding in and out of me.

Then his eyes open, and they are bright with magic. He smiles, displaying Serky's sharp canines. His skin ripples, and I discover fur has erupted at his shoulders and chest. Arran is part Serky, and it's like they are sharing this experience.

He begins to pound into me, grinding his knot against my clit with every thrust.

I'm riding closer and closer to a climax.

"Come for us, mate," Arran purrs in a deep, monstrous voice.

It's all I need to fall off the precipice. I cry out and spasm around his cock. He uses the moment to force his flared base into my cunt and lock inside me.

I come again on the tail of the first. "Love. You!" I shout. My toes curl, and I grind against his deliciously muscular body.

"Mine!" he growls, dragging his teeth over his mate mark, ratcheting me higher.

Overcome, wild with my need for him, I shout, "Mine!"

I bite at his shoulder, getting a mouthful of fur.

But surprisingly, my teeth sink into his flesh. I taste the metallic flavor of blood, but also magic. Something snaps into place.

He jerks like… well, like someone bit him.

"Mate!" He pumps into me frantically, as much as he can, while still locked inside me.

Then I realize what's happened. As deep as Flint's bond, I've completed the mate bond like a proper shifter. Is this possible because the containment spell is truly broken now?

I don't care how as long as I can give this to my wolf-mate.

I'm winning this mate thing! At least with Arran.

After an hour of Arran luxuriating as he lazily pumps his knot into me with a fucking grin as big as I've ever seen, he finally slips free and pouts. "I wanted to stay inside you forever."

"I know, baby, but I gotta pee." I move to roll out of bed, but he snatches me up in his arms and carries me to the bathroom, setting my naked ass down on the toilet.

"Out." I wave him away.

"No." He crosses his arms. "If I can lick that spot, then I can watch you while you pee."

I huff. "Okay then, and you wanted me to watch you while you were taking a dump in my yard as a dog?"

His ears turn pink from embarrassment. "No, but…"

I can't hold it any longer, and I piss anyway.

He smiles smugly, like he's won the argument. "See? No big deal."

Rolling my eyes, I wipe and flush. As I lean over the sink, I see Arran gingerly touching the mark on his shoulder.

"You did it. We're fully bonded," he says in awe. He glances down at my ass, his hands land on my hips. "I need to be back inside you. Now." His cock comes to life and rests over my ass crack.

"My poor pussy is sore. Give a vajayjay a minute after all that knotting business."

"I can make your ass sore."

I spin and playfully swat away his hand. "I'm serious about needing a break. And I'm hungry." Right on cue, my stomach grumbles.

"Fuck, I'm sorry!" Arran's eyes widen as he panics, scrambling out of the room and to the tiny kitchen. "I need to feed you. I'm such a bad mate!"

I hurry over and soothe him. I can see his instincts are riding him hard. "You're doing a great job. Okay?"

He shakes his head and grabs a leftover bowl of pasta salad from the fridge. He pulls me to him by my waist with his other hand and sets me down on his lap.

"Food. Now." He rips open the container and lifts a forkful to my lips.

I grin at this caretaker's behavior and gladly accept. I'm getting used to being taken care of.

"I can't believe it. We're fully mated," he whispers, as if he doesn't want to wake from a dream either. He licks and nuzzles my neck where he bit me.

"Maybe I have shifter blood," I say with a glow in my heart. And I do the same for him, tending to the bite I gave him.

"Seems like the wolfboy likes licking, too." Trouble's voice squeaks out.

"Yes. Good mates," Sage agrees, bouncing beside him in their corner. "They will make a hundred million pups."

I palm my face. "Sage! I definitely won't be making a bunch of pups. I'm not a bunny."

"We can hope!" she says excitedly.

"Don't you dare start with that," I warn. "No more from you about licking or breeding."

"But that's all we have to entertain us," Trouble whines.

Arran nuzzles my neck. "We could get them some toys to play with."

"And treats!" Trouble grumbles. "You and Birdman haven't delivered what you promised."

"My wolf agrees we need more treats soon," Arran says with a straight face.

I hold back a snicker. "Then we need to go on a shopping trip soon."

2 2

FUSION

FLINT

I thought my Heartstone was going to die by the flames of my pack brother, but she walked away unscathed. None of us have talked about what this means.

Ultimately, it's Calder who will have to decide if he wants to walk away from his misery, move past his painful death, and accept the bond with Jade.

Maxum and Raithe stare at Calder's unconscious form then we all give each other a worried look.

My heart goes out to our phoenix. I hope he can fuse his pieces back together and become stronger for it.

Stronger for her.

Through my mate bond, I sense Arran is easing our mate's stress with his attention. She's finding pleasure with him. I'm not angry or jealous, though I wish I could be there with her.

Maybe I should assist him. It's not like I can offer Calder words of wisdom like Maxum or Raithe can. I'm not eloquent like they are.

Besides, they are strong enough to subdue him if need be.

But before I can ask to be excused and leave, I feel Arran's presence through my connection with Jade.

What? How?

They've somehow deepened their mate bonds. I sense Jade's and Arran's joy, and realize I should give them some time to be alone and revel in their full bond.

It's the least I can do since I had an entire night with my Heartstone, making love to her. By the end, she had no doubt of my utter devotion to her.

She is my center.

Without her, I would lose my mind.

I stare at Calder, wondering if he will heal and find the peace and comfort to soothe his broken heart.

Finally, Calder stirs, still out of his mind. He mumbles unintelligible words until one rings out clearly, over and over. "Jade."

I cannot say if it's because he wants her there or because he's having a nightmare. I glance over at Maxum to see if he can understand with his mind reading abilities.

His lips are pressed into a flat line. That doesn't give me much to go on. I've never been great at reading expressions, especially the subtle ones. It's why I love my Heartstone so much. Jade doesn't make me guess because she is so open with her emotions. She doesn't seem to understand how precious that is to someone like me or in the supernatural world.

All supes seem to mask their genuine needs and feelings. I hear humans and witches are much the same. I often wondered why, until over the centuries, I witnessed many times how a person can turn that knowledge against another. Then that injured person turns wary and guarded.

It breaks me to think Rob could have done that to our Jade, but she is strong. Stronger than she realizes for still being able to be vulnerable with us.

"Do you feel that?" Raithe asks.

"The room has grown warmer," I answer. "That's all."

Raithe pulls his gaze away from Calder, and it lands on me, then Maxum. "I believe, on top of everything else, that he's entering a mating fever."

I can deduce what that means from context, but I need to know more, "What does that mean for them?"

"If he doesn't consummate his mating bond with her, he may die..." Raithe pauses and frowns deeply. "With how weak he is, it could be the final one."

Maxum jumps to his feet and hits his horns on the low ceiling. "Are you sure?"

"You must pick up from his mind that he's craving Jade." Raithe eyes Maxum, waiting for confirmation.

"Yeah." He rubs his hand down his face. "I just thought... he's been that way for a while now."

"But his fire... it touched her? Tasted her?" Raithe asks. "It should have consumed her?"

"Yes," I say. "I tried to block his attack, but I don't think it was an attack per se."

"It was a call to be close to her," Raithe says. "I had something less dramatic, but similar when I met Amira."

"But he was out of his mind because he just had his soul fragments returned to him." Maxum sits back down, his shoulders slumped. "We thought..."

"He's out of his mind because of the tortured soul pieces, but he's also out of his mind because he's been denying his mate," Raithe explains.

"I should let Jade know how he is," Maxum announces. "Warn her what to expect."

Raithe explains how the phoenix bonds work and says, "Go. Both of you. I can keep an eye on him." He nods to the hatch's stairs.

Maxum and I are quiet on the short walk over to the cabin.

Before we enter, I hold out my hand to make him stop. "Whatever happens, whatever Jade decides, I cannot allow her to be harmed. I don't want Calder to suffer or die, but I *will not* let Jade die."

Maxum turns, facing me head on. "I love that grumpy bastard, but I will kill him myself if he hurts her. She is our heart now and her death means we'd all die."

I give him a curt nod and a grunt of agreement.

Maxum opens the door for us to see Jade naked and snuggled into Arran's lap at the table. He's feeding her chocolate, and she's licking it off his clawed fingers.

My cocks come to life and press uncomfortably against my pants. I hold my hands in front of my groin and enter, quickly sitting down at the table on the other side so no one notices. I'm not ready for their jokes about my body, and now isn't the time.

Maxum plasters on a playful grin to ease Jade's anxiety spike after seeing us return. I sense through our bond she worries something bad has happened to Calder.

"Is he okay?" she asks.

"He's still asleep," Maxum answers vaguely and then he notices the teeth marks on Arran's shoulder. "What have you been up to?"

"We're fully bonded," Arran says proudly.

Maxum whips his gaze to Jade. "But how?"

"Probably because I'm a mutt." She shrugs and winks at Arran.

Maxum kneels in front of her, taking her hand in his and daring to irritate the wolf with his new mate, but Arran doesn't react. The completed bond must soothe his territorial nature.

"You, my dear anomaly, are a designer breed." Maxum kisses the tops of her knuckles and Jade giggles.

Maxum sits down next to them and sighs heavily. His good cheer fades like the drop of a mask.

The blood drains from Jade's face, as she knows bad news is coming. "What's wrong?"

"I want to preface this with you promising me you will take time to think about what I have to tell you before rushing off to be the heroine."

"*Okaaay?*" Jade says, drawing it out as a question. She glances at me for some clue as to what's going on.

I don't shut down our bond, but I don't feed her any information.

Out of all of us, Maxum is the best to deliver news. His stone-cold killer instincts allow him to be rational when he needs to be, and over his eight hundred years, he has developed the ability to communicate.

During my long life, I've shied away from talking and connecting.

Connecting is something that I only want to do now, exploring it with my Heartstone.

Maxum leans forward and presses his lips flat. "I was hoping it wouldn't come to this. At least not so quickly. It's his place to tell you, but he's stubborn and messed up from his past."

"Is he not going to live?" she whispers.

"It doesn't look good."

"Because of what I did?" Tears fall down her face. "Because of the soul fragments?"

Dammit. Maybe Maxum *isn't* the right person to tell her.

"No," I say firmly, just below a shout, so she listens. I correct my volume, but I still am forceful when I finish, feeling angry at the birdbrain male. "Because he's rejecting his fated mate."

Her hand goes to her chest and she guesses, "Osen?"

"You," all three of us say together. Even Osen's voice chimes in through her mouth.

"I can't be his *fated*, can I? He was only starting to get past despising me because I'm a witch. He was fine before we left." The words fall from her lips like a chaotic storm. Her eyes are wide and frantic. "He said he didn't think he could be a mate. And I can't make someone accept me. He barely can touch me. How is this even happening?"

I'd find her rambling endearing if it weren't that she was so stricken with sadness. She wants to help him.

Goddess, she is a blessing—one that none of us truly deserves.

"His phoenix flame touched you, tasted you." Maxum takes her hand in his and rubs his thumb over her palm, calming her. "After that, it was all over. Raithe said Calder is now suffering from a mating fever on top of his soul mending."

Jade swallows down her nerves. With our connection, I can feel her fear and confusion. She doesn't understand how to fix this and is desperate to find a way.

"I can't just mate him without his permission. He doesn't want my touch. Any touch! And after the raw, tortured parts of his soul have just been returned, the likelihood he would want me around is less than it was before."

"I'm not suggesting you take him by force," Maxum agrees. "We will have to wake him and see how he responds to the fever. I needed you to know all the facts so you can decide about what's right for you. It wouldn't be fair to go into this situation blind."

"If he rejects the bond, could he die?"

"Chances are good that he might, especially if you say yes and he doesn't." Maxum then adds, "Only a few species react in such a dramatic way to rejecting a mate bond, so I don't think you would suffer from that fate. At least he won't take you with him and harm you and your other mates."

"What if he says yes, but I reject him?"

"His odds are better in that scenario, but not great." Maxum studies her face. "If there was no pressure, would you want him?"

Jade bites her lower lip. "I like him quite a lot, even when he was being a bit of a jerk. I haven't given myself much space to consider it since he can't handle me touching him, and he didn't seem very interested in me until just the last few days."

"My Moonmate," Arran breaks his silence. "You must think about it now. Just in case he asks that of you."

She nods, but then looks to Arran and then to me. "What about you guys? How do you feel about it?"

"If I'm being honest," I admit. "Nervous. Because I feel Arran through our bond. I suspect he feels me too now."

Arran grunts his affirmation. "When Jade bit me and I calmed down, I sensed your presence."

"Oh, wow." Jade looks at me again. "So you don't want Calder in our mutual bonds?"

"I don't mean it like that," I correct her assumption. "But I worry that because he is so broken, his energy will harm you."

"Aren't you worried about yourself?" she asks.

Holy stones below, she is so considerate—almost to a fault.

Feeling my face pull into a frown, I say, "I could shoulder it for my brother, but Calder and I have a history and loyalties whereas you do not owe him anything."

"I may not owe him anything," Jade says firmly. "And I might not have a history with him. But I want him to have a future with me… us… if he wants it, too."

Arran nuzzles into her neck and inhales. "You're too caring, my moon."

23

CALDER, TAKE ME AWAY

JADE

*H*e's eerily quiet, but I sense Osen panicking inside my head.

Who am I kidding? I'm panicking too.

The guys laid out the whole Calder might die thing so matter-of-factly, there was no other choice but for me to help him.

I understand they didn't want to force me into mating with him.

I just hope he accepts me so he'll live, maybe even one day find happiness with our bond.

Then I think about what Flint said…

What if Calder harms us because of his fractured soul?

I can't think like that. If Flint and Arran can shoulder his pain, so can I. Calder saved me from Rob and Galiana. I don't believe it was only for Osen's sake.

He likes me. He is attracted to me, even though he fights it because of his trauma and aversion to touch.

I think about how Calder kisses me. His lips sizzled when he swallowed down the orgasm the others gave me over Maxum's lap. I think about how his eyes light up when he looks at me.

He's pack. And *I'm* pack. We take care of each other. That deep compulsion to make sure my mates are alive and well resonates in my bones.

Literally, since Flint has gifted me his stone to make me stronger. Unbreakable.

I won't be unbreakable if Calder or the others die. Or if I lose Osen.

Damn, how things change. A few weeks ago, I was lonely and aching for someone to share my love. I wanted to finally live out my fantasies—not just the paranormal ones—and find my soul mate and true love. I wanted someone who would do anything for me, and I would do the same for them. Just like the romance books.

I didn't want my heart to only exist in fiction anymore.

And here they are. Bigger than life and better than I could have imagined.

I won't let Calder just give up without fighting for him. Our story was just getting started.

I hope we're almost to the point where the book usually ends and the characters are finally happy. I want to experience when all the big bad antagonists have been conquered, but in real life, and we can enjoy lazy days in bed, and travel the world, or in our case, realms.

We just have to eliminate Galiana and Rob, and we'll be free to live our *Happy Ever After*.

Hell, I'd be good with having a *Happy For Now* for the first time in my life.

"Jade?" Arran nuzzles my mating mark.

"Yeah?" I blink and return my attention to the room.

Around the kitchen table, Maxum, Arran, and Flint are all staring at me like I'm about to lose it. Whoops, I guess I spaced out for a while there. I stir in Arran's lap and suddenly feel claustrophobic.

Thankfully, I don't have a panic attack because he doesn't resist when I slip out of his hold.

"I need some time alone." I glance down at my naked body and don't feel the urge to throw clothes on. "I'm going to take a bath."

"Of course," Maxum says, then rushes into the bathroom.

I follow him inside. I'm about to grumble and throw him out when I see he's wiping down the bath tub of any dirt and grime to make it clean for me.

It strikes me as one of the nicest, most thoughtful gestures someone has ever done for me. Screw saving my life. It's the little things, like making sure I'm cared for, that make me all misty eyed and glowing heart.

I realize I *am* crying by the time he's done cleaning and running the hot water for me.

"Oh, sweet woman, why are you crying?" Maxum asks as he scoops me up in his huge, muscular arms.

I've never felt so safe and cherished as I do in these guy's embrace.

A sob rips from some deep primal place in my soul and hits Maxum in his broad shoulders.

His warm hand strokes up and down my spine, comforting me. "It's okay. We'll get through this."

I nod, but don't answer. I sure fucking hope so.

But life isn't like books. People rarely get their happy ending.

When I'm all cried out, and the tub is almost full, Maxum dips his tail in the water to test the temperature and then lifts to place me inside. He holds my elbows to keep me steady until I've sunk down completely.

I sigh as the lovely warm water surrounds me.

"You still want to be alone?" he asks, bending down to study my eyes.

"Just for a bit." As he moves to leave, I grab his forearm to stop him. "Thank you."

He takes my hand and kisses my palm. "Anything for you, my love."

When he shuts the door behind him, I realize he's slowing down our courting. Is it for Calder's sake? For the fresh bond with Flint and Arran? Or is there something else?

I don't believe he's worried about hurting me during a rut. That's not the complete story.

I sense Flint and Arran through our bonds. They're worried about me. I'm worried about me too, but mostly about them.

The three of them slip out of the cabin, I imagine, so they won't disturb me with their conversation.

I lean my head back and give myself a damned minute to relax.

It then hits me. I have two mates, maybe a third soon, then another.

I'd pinch myself to see if I'm dreaming up this entire life. I know the test is bullshit. The only proper test is trying to read, and I've written while in this new reality.

Which reminds me... I need to finish my book.

But it seems so unimportant now. Between almost dying several times, my new mates, and the revelations about my origins, what does a preorder deadline mean in the grand scheme of things? Not much.

I don't want to disappoint my readers, but if they knew what was really going on, they'd likely understand. And then they'd want detail accounts of the sex.

"Jade?" Osen whispers. *"I know this is probably a bad time, but I don't have anyone else to really talk to."*

I'm not even mad that he's bothering my quiet time. It speaks volumes that I really do care about this incubus ghost.

"I'm sorry about Calder," I say.

"Why are you sorry?"

"Hurting him with his soul fragments. Being his mate."

"I've known you're his mate for a while now. And the soul fragments returning are probably for the best once he settles."

"I hope so." I sigh and skim my hand over the water. "When I returned his soul to him, I had a fleeting thought. I wondered if I healed him, then you and Calder could finally be together."

"Through you? With your body?" he asks.

"No. Not like that."

"What do you mean?" He sounds interested.

Does he sense what I'm about to suggest? Has he wondered the same thing? He's smart. I doubt it would take him long to figure it out.

"Osen," I hesitate. "I'm scared to even suggest it. Calder might not be okay. And that means you might not end up okay, either."

"Jade," he presses with just my name.

"If your soul is with me and I can put souls back in their bodies..."

"You mean... do you really think that's possible? But what about my magic?"

"I thought about that too. If Galiana and Rob used me to steal it from you, that means I could steal it back. If you didn't have enough when you were put back together, that is."

"I don't believe I would. Supes don't last long without their magic. That's what killed me. It being ripped out of me."

"Then we need to go after them, see if we can steal it back," I say, worried that I won't be able to pull all this off.

"No." Osen sounds like a fierce leader right then. "I won't risk you like that. Not for me. I made my mistakes. I won't make another to fix it."

This version of Osen is a far cry from the one I knew that forced me to go to his death spot in the alleyway. He truly cares about me.

"Don't you dare mention it to the others," he warns. "I won't be the reason they lose you. I will find a way beyond the veil before you can risk it. Do you understand? I will use that unbinding chant Amira gave you."

"How?"

"I memorized it when you glanced at it."

"Fuck."

"Yeah, fuck. You're too precious to lose over an asshole like me. Think of our pack."

That's what stops me from arguing further. "Okay. But if we find a way that will work, hear me out."

"I doubt it, but fine. First, we need to get Calder on his feet."

Fortunately, Osen allows me the rest of my bath time to feel like I'm alone and stays quiet.

I sense he's thinking about what I've proposed. Maybe he's wondering if there's a way to make my plan work that won't risk everyone else.

I push those thoughts away. There are too many variables. And my mind can go off forever trying to anticipate all the variables and possible solutions until I'm exhausted. But I don't know enough yet to make it a reality. I don't know what I can do. I don't know how to do it, or even if I actually have that ability. And I don't know enough about how this universe and magic work.

I need to be prepared if we encounter Rob and Galiana. It seems likely that Galiana will hunt me down. She wants her weapon back.

A shiver races through me with that realization.

I'm a weapon.

Then a thrill zips up my spine.

Yeah, I *am* a fucking weapon.

If I can get a handle on my magic, Galiana and Rob will be afraid of me.

They *should* be afraid. They hurt me. They've hurt my pack. My family. They're a threat, and I will do what I have to do to protect my guys.

When the bath water turns cold, I slip out and dry off with the fluffy towel Maxum left behind.

I stand at the vanity, staring at the reflection in the mirror. Cliché, I know. But I rarely ever looked at myself. Now, I see someone else, except what I see in me seems oddly familiar. It's as if I've been waiting forty years to unmask this version of myself that's lurked just under the surface. Under a spell.

I comb my fingers through my wet hair, noting how different it looks now. It's an ethereal silver that a fashionista influencer would kill to have. I lean in and study my eyes. No longer hazel, they shine, literally shine, a soft jade color.

My skin subtly glows too, but I could pass for a human if I needed to. Besides, most people don't really *look* at others. Everyone's too busy, distracted with their own thoughts or glancing at their phones to notice my minor oddities.

I flex my hands, thinking about my enhanced bones. With a thought, my fingertips crackle with magic electricity.

Wild.

I leave the sanctuary of the bathroom and find the cabin empty. On the bed, someone has set out a red slip dress with a skimpy pair of red silk panties.

I know it was Maxum who picked these out.

He's fulfilling his promise to replace all my destroyed clothes.

I slide on the pretty dress and find it fits perfectly. My nipples are hard and their outlines are clearly visible, but whatever. Time for these girls to be showcased a bit. And I'm certain that Amira's guys have zero interest me and likely wouldn't spare me a glance if I walked around naked. Not that I want their attention. I have enough with my own hulky males.

Instead of calling out to my mates with my bond, I go out to find them, slipping on my leather clogs as I leave the tiny house.

Maxum and Arran are standing by Raithe's bunker and talking in low voices. Using my bond with Arran, I reach out and pick up how worried he is.

They catch sight of me immediately, smiling and waving me over.

I can feel the heat of their gaze as I saunter toward them. Damn, I've never felt sexy in my life and now, with my mates, I feel like a goddess.

"Gorgeous," Maxum murmurs and slides his hand down my side to rest on my hip.

Arran does the same on my other side. I'm pinned between these devastatingly beautiful males, and I forget how to breathe.

How can they affect me like this?

My wolfboy kisses his mating bite mark and asks, "Feeling better?"

"A bit more grounded." I flick my chin toward the cellar door. "How's Calder?"

"He seems to be waking," Arran answers and steps back. "You want to see him?"

My nerves coil up tight and I worry I'm overstepping. "Is that a good idea?"

"Your presence might soothe his mating fever," Maxum suggests. "He'll need a clear head so he can mend his soul."

Squaring my shoulders, I gather my strength. "Let me see him."

24

FEVERED DREAMS

CALDER

I wish I'd just die already.

I don't care if it's my last death.

I hope it is.

The witch drags iron chains over my exposed chest, burning a trail over my flesh. The toxic iron of the bed sears into my back and legs. I hear the sickening sound of my blood dripping to the floor from my multitude of wounds she's inflicted. When I look over to the side, I can see the stain of my life marking the concrete.

"Tell me what I want to know and this can all be over," the witch falsely coos.

I doubt she will give me a release of death, even if I were to spill the secrets of my fellow supes. If I tell her what I know, she will keep me as a plaything.

No. I'll have to anger her and get her to kill me so I can burn to ash.

I've already been tortured for weeks. My mind spirals with only moments of lucidity, as my fae blood allows my body to heal. My self-healing magic is almost exhausted now. Every time I regain my wits and realize my plight, I wish to fall back into madness again, so I don't have to consciously feel the pain she doles out.

My pack, my love Osen, and my allies haven't found me. I'm giving up on a rescue ever happening since this witch is clever and has warded our location too well.

Can I *make* myself die?

Just when I'm about to try, I hear a commotion. My vision is blurred, but I sense my packmates are near.

My phoenix instincts sense impending death.

Please let it be mine. Not my pack.

"In here!" Osen shouts.

The witch hovering near me, curses and begins a chant.

Other witches pour inside the building, battling my pack. Magic is flying across the warehouse, crashing and exploding.

Shadows swirl over the fray… Osen's incubus magic.

The witch screeches the last of her strange chant, in a language I've never heard before. She raises up her dagger and slams it down into my chest.

I hear something shatter.

But it isn't glass, it feels like my soul.

Before I can think about it, I'm consumed by my own flames.

The next thing I know, I'm hovering in the corner of the warehouse while the ash gathers and my body is remade. Osen and the others stand by in silent vigil. The witches and warlocks who fought them are piled in a heap, but I don't see the one who tortured me.

I don't understand why I'm seeing things this way, from above, out of my body. This has never happened before. When I see my body suck in a breath, I panic. I should be in there now.

Who is in my place? *What* is in my place?

After my body has completed its regeneration, the *thing* pretending to be me leaves me behind. With my friends and my lover.

I rush to follow, but I slam against some invisible barrier.

I've been trapped.

I don't know how many days, years, decades that have passed. I've gone insane waiting for my body to return.

Like a whisper, I feel it. A call. A gentle caress over my spirit.

Then I watch as an angel walks in with the thing that kidnapped my body.

She can't be an actual angel. The Seraphim race is rumored to be long extinct. But she appears like one to my senses. Glowing brightly with perfect features and containing a powerful magic.

The angel looks up and *sees* me. Maxum, Arran, and Flint are with her, but they don't see me. Not even the being inside my body. I'm worried when Osen isn't among them. What happened to him? I don't want to entertain the thought that he's no longer alive, but that's the only thing that makes sense. He would be here.

Pushing that aside for now, I test my theory that she is aware of me by swirling around the warehouse. She watches my acrobatics in awe.

I'm tugged in her direction, and I go willingly. I don't know why I trust her, but I do. Besides, what do I have to lose?

I slide into her body and sense I'm not the only extra soul in here. Before I make sense of it, I'm moving again. It's like someone pulling a plug in a sink, and I'm sucked into my body.

Finally reunited.

"Calder?" a woman's voice draws me back to consciousness.

I fight to greet her, to answer her call, but my body doesn't respond to my wishes. I sense I'm in my phoenix form, which means I'm on fire.

Am I hurting this angel who has returned me to my rightful place?

That thought frightens me.

Why do I feel like I know her?

I don't know her name. Do I?

Jade.

I've been stuck in that warehouse for years, but I've also lived a life with my pack. I lost Osen. My heart contracts and spasms with the grief.

But I've not lost him completely. He still lives on inside her—my angel.

The urge to claim her love is overwhelming. Then all goes black.

Images flip through my mind—of her, my mate. Then I see flickers of the time between my torturous death and now.

I pry open my eyes. I'm no longer in the warehouse.

"Jade?" my voice cracks, hoping she isn't gone. That she isn't an enchanting hallucination.

"I'm here," she whispers.

My eyes dart across the small space to see her beautiful, expressive face lit by the glow of my skin that simmers with flame.

Maxum and Flint are here as well, standing like giant guards at her side. Their gaze is wary and protective, as if they expect me to lunge at her. Hurt her.

"Are you okay?" she asks. "Do you remember what happened?"

The answer formulates as memories merge in my mind.

My soul was fractured, left to rot. But now my phoenix form is back. *I'm whole.*

"Yeah. The warehouse. You put me back together." I wipe my brow and frown at the sweat I find on my forearm. "Why is it so uncomfortable in here?" I glance around at the strange room. "Did something else happen? Where are we?"

"We're in Raithe's regeneration cellar," Jade says, then glances at Maxum as if she's questioning if she should say more.

"Please, just tell me." I sigh, rubbing my face and scooting back to the wall to lean against it. "I'm horribly fatigued, and I don't have patience for anyone skirting around the truth." I stare into her eyes, like she's the only one I'm willing to hear it from. "Am I dying the final death?"

She bites her plump, crimson lip. "It depends."

Blood drains from my face. I don't know if it's from the dread or from how much I want to suck her lip into my mouth. Probably both.

"Your flames." She pauses, then goes on. "You dove at me when you were in full phoenix mode."

"Goddess!" My whole body goes on alert and my eyes search her for injury. "Did I hurt you?" Not seeing anything obvious, I quickly look at Maxum and Flint, wondering why they let me live if I did. Or maybe they've already killed me a few times to get it out of their system and I don't remember.

"You didn't hurt me. But that's part of the problem. Your fire engulfed me, and I didn't burn."

"And... that confirms... you are..." The pieces all fall into place. My feverish skin, my urge to worship her body, and her worried expression. I have mating fever. "No. This can't be happening." I yank my hair. I already knew it, didn't I? I *did* touch her with my fire during the first day of training. From the beginning, even when I thought she killed Osen, I felt the pull to mate just as much as my brothers did.

"I didn't mean to hurt you," she murmurs, her voice full of regret and heartbreak. "Or put your life in danger because of a bond you don't really want."

"What?" I gasp, realizing she's taking the blame. "No. I'm sorry that you feel burdened by my trauma."

"But you might die now... because I came into your life." Tears fall from her glowing green eyes.

"I'm the broken one." I scoot closer, craving to reach out, but I fear the emotions swirling inside. "It's you who shouldn't even consider bringing me into your heart and into your bonds."

She stills, eyes wide. "You're pack. And I want to be with you."

"No. I won't have you pressured into a mating bond with me." I shake my head vigorously and scramble backward until my back slams against the wall.

My heart screams in agony. It wants her more than it wants blood in my veins.

Then the broken, angry pieces stir in my mind. Confusion.

"Your soul is trying to reconcile these last years," Maxum explains, like I can't feel that slamming sensation in my thoughts, trying to jam everything together. "And Raithe said that the mating fever might be eased by being close to each other. Skin to skin, if possible. But if you use touch to defer the fever, and *then* you decide against mating, it will probably mean your death. No touching and furthering the bond, and you still have a chance to recover if you reject her."

My hands itch with the need to caress her soft skin. "I'm terrified I'll hurt you."

"And I worry I might trigger your trauma," she says.

"We can stay. Watch over you both," Maxum offers.

Jade fiddles with her thumbs nervously. "You could tie my hands behind my back so you'd know I couldn't touch you. Hurt you."

It pains me to hear her suggest that.

It unsettles me how my body reacts hungrily to such a thing. I want her tied down and writhing for my cock. I want my hands and mouth exploring her soft skin, making her wet. Maybe she would enjoy that, too. She's been open to other things.

Maxum cocks an eyebrow, likely sensing my interest.

I glance around at the horribly wretched environment. A cellar? For my twin flame? I want to argue and demand better, but I don't want to burn down Amira's buildings. The bed I'm sitting on seems to be a flame-retardant bed pallet.

There is one quick way out of this—reject her and face the consequences. Every cell in my body revolts at the idea. I want her. But I shouldn't drag her and the pack down with me.

I'm fucking weak, because when I gaze into her eyes, shining with affection, I want it. I want to wake up with that face on the pillow next to me. I want to give her the realms. I want to be a better male for her.

"Okay." I scoot over and look at Maxum for his assistance.

Jade stands from her makeshift chair on a barrel and I finally take in her curvy body under a short, red silk dress. My cock aches even more with her beauty.

Her hands fall to catch the hem. "On or off?"

I bite my lip so hard I taste blood. "On… for now." I don't have the willpower to hold back and defer the mating if I see her tits and her round ass.

She turns for Maxum to tie her wrists behind her back. It does things to me I've never truly explored before.

I'm sexually submissive by nature. I loved when Osen would dominate my body. And with his incubus magic, he *completely* dominated me.

But that evaporated with what felt like a nuclear meltdown after what the witch did to me. Tied down, I was helpless to all her torture. And she was creative and utterly vicious, abusing me, then cutting off my malehood. Blood everywhere.

I shake that ugly memory away. I don't want it to cloud our moment. My flame offering herself to me, trusting me.

Jade is *not* that witch. She is the opposite.

Flint and Maxum assist and guide Jade to lie down next to me. On her side, she stares at me, a look of longing in her eyes.

"Are you comfortable?" I slip down so we are face to face.

"As much as I can be." She smiles weakly, sounding vulnerable.

Slowly, I reach out to tuck a lock of her beautiful silver hair behind her ear. My hand slips down to her cheek. I trace my fingers over her jawline, her brow, exploring and memorizing every feature.

Already some of my mating fever seems to dissipate. But I know I'm a goner now. If I reject her, I'm dead. And if I reject her, I'll want to die. Permanently.

"Hi," she says sweetly.

"Hi," I say with a smile. Leaning forward, I skim my lips over hers.

She sucks in air and her eyes glow brighter.

Encouraged by my response and hers, I move my hand down her arms, then the dip of her waist, over the swell of her wide hips. I drag the hem of her slip dress up her hip as my hand returns, revealing her fuck-me lace panties. I want to burn them away and slide my fingers over her seam. Dip inside her wet heat and make her cry out in pleasure. I want to give her the bliss the others do.

Fuck, even Osen has given her pleasure and he's dead.

Dead, but not gone.

I retreat a bit at the thought of him, as he's likely watching this whole thing through her eyes.

I clamp my eyes shut and hear Jade's voice change to signal Osen's control. "It's okay. I'm here, my love. She's our center. The center I could never be. She is the loving heart we all needed. We both knew we craved more. We were just waiting for her."

"But you…" I feel my eyes sting with sorrow. "You aren't really here."

"Not like I used to be, but I'm here. Let's love this beautiful mate as if we weren't broken. Because that is the very least she deserves."

When I crack open my eyes, I see the charcoal swirl of Osen's magic, but also the shine of Jade's.

They are both here… *loving* me.

We are all together.

My mouth crashes into hers… *theirs*. They return my passion, our tongues tangling. My hand grips her hip and draws her against me. My erect cock pokes into her stomach and I grind into her to feel some relief.

I pull her thigh so her leg curls around me. My hand slides up to cup her full breast. I squeeze and roll her nipples through the thin, silky fabric, and she lets out the cutest needy whimper.

She loves this.

I pull down the top of her dress enough to reveal her nipple. I draw it into my mouth and she moans, canting her hips into me.

"I want to taste you," I whisper over her wet flesh. "I've never gone down on a woman before."

"Whatever you need from me," she breathes out. "But don't do anything you don't want to do."

"Oh, I want to." I grin and kiss her again, stroking her tongue with mine. This action is all hers. She's so soft, so gentle. Nothing like Osen's demanding kisses.

Making my way down her body, I press my lips to the silk dress, feeling the heat of her body through the fabric. I kneel between her legs. Both of my hands skim up her thighs, pushing the material until I reach her hips.

Her panty covered pussy beckons me, and I hook my fingers over the elastic straps and draw them down slowly. Once they are off, I toss the pair to Flint, then turn back to admire my mate's cunt.

I lean over, adjusting my hard cock in my pants. I don't plan on fucking her today. I need to take this slowly. I'm still afraid of myself. But I do plan to make her come several times.

Taking her by the knees, I pull her legs open so I can feast on my woman.

I lick up the inside of her soft, thick thighs. Glancing up at her face, her pupils have blown wide with arousal. There's only a tiny ring of green.

"You enjoy being pleasured while your other mates watch on, don't you, my flame?"

Her eyes dart to Flint and Maxum. "Yes, but I like the one-on-one time just as much."

I hum my approval. As much as this is turning me on having them watch, when I can get a grip over myself, I want some personal time with her, too. Eventually, I hope to be able to have her freely run her hands over me.

Seeing her surrender to me, with her hands tied behind her back, is making my cock ache for her.

I get close and inhale her scent. Lilacs and blackberries and fire. My fingers slide through her wetness, and I use it to lubricate her clit and lips.

Then I swipe my tongue through her slick, my eyes fall closed to remember this moment.

"How does she taste, brother?" Flint asks, and his low, gravelly voice makes our mate shiver.

"She tastes like the thrill of an electric storm. Like the warmth of the hearth during a blizzard. She tastes like fate incarnate."

Jade gasps and stares down at me as I give her another long lap with my tongue over her clit. Her eyes roll back in bliss. I haven't even used my gift on her yet and she's already this turned on by my attention.

I explore her entirely. Kissing, licking, and sucking to find what makes her toes curl. To discover what makes her groan and moan with an impending climax.

I sink my fingers into her soaked cunt and pump into her, finding a spot that makes her lift her hips off the bed, and I suck her clit. She comes undone and shouts my name. My heart rejoices that I can give her this.

She's panting, completely limp in my arms. I crawl up her body and snuggle against her side. I study her face as she turns to study mine.

"Don't you want to come?" she asks, a flash of confusion on her face.

"If I pull my dick out, I will mate you right now," I admit. "I'd like to take the process slowly."

She nods and tries to suppress a frown, but a bit of it slips past her hold, tugging at the corners of her lush mouth.

"Maybe we can just talk for a while?" I ask.

Her eyes light up with the suggestion. "Would it bother you if my hands were untied?"

She must be slightly uncomfortable, and it will only get worse as the hours pass.

I sit up, with a smirk I roll her over on her stomach, then get a magnificent view of her plump ass. I swing my leg over her and straddle her upper thighs, essentially pinning her down. Her ass is like a gravitational force for my hands and eyes. I grab each globe and squeeze.

She moans into the mattress and wiggles her tied wrists.

I spread her ass cheeks and thumb over her puckered hole. "I'm going to fuck you here. And both you and Osen will feel me claim your submission."

"*Fuuuck*," Osen and Jade hiss together—a strange dual tonality to her voice.

My thumb teases her tight hole, and she squirms, but not away, toward me.

"But not now, sweetheart. You'll have to wait for that until after I feel your sweet pussy wrapped around me, milking my cock."

She groans in need and disappointment, and it makes me chuckle. I swear I haven't laughed in years, since my last death.

Not until this crazy angel saved me... *us*.

I untie her hands and gently massage the red indentations.

How can something make me fucking hard and break my heart all at the same time?

I suppose when I've *hopefully* recovered from my PTSD enough to allow her to freely touch me, then it will be only for play to tie her up and make her come.

My hand pats her hip, and she rolls over onto her back. She stares up at me, waiting like a good girl for my next request, hands tucked at her sides.

With a tug on her dress and a look, I ask if I can remove it. She slowly raises her arms, and I slide the garment off and find my body is hovering over her naked glory.

Capturing her wrists above her head, I pin them in place. "Keep them there."

"Yes, sir," she says with a playful smirk.

"You *are* perfect for us, aren't you?" I grin at the blush that rises on her cheeks. She is still coming to terms with how much we want her. She has to erase all of the venom Rob programmed into her mind while she was both under a spell and their day-to-day life.

Fucker. I hope I'm the one to kill that bastard.

I was tortured, but so was Jade.

Instead of wallowing in the injustice, she's doing what she can to help me. So if I can rid the world of the assholes who hurt her, I'll give her the security to know her enemies have been vanquished.

I shake off my dark thoughts of death. Torture. I'm spiraling, my mind falling back to that warehouse where I lost myself.

I take in a deep breath, locking eyes with Jade, and center myself.

Then, letting my gaze wander, I admire her full breasts, licking my lips.

"I crave to bite and suck this sensitive flesh into my mouth."

Her back arches, inviting me to do just that.

She's begging for me to break my promise to wait. And I can't blame her one bit because everything inside me is screaming to claim this wonderful woman and make her mine—body and soul.

25

THE LITTLE DEATH

JADE

*M*y fears fade when I see the way Calder looks at me. *Passion. Affection.* Perhaps he won't be irreparably damaged now that I've returned his soul fragments.

Sure, I expect he'll likely have a long road to a full recovery. But he's able to push his anger and pain aside to be with me. And Osen.

Maxum and Flint are standing quietly in the corner. If it weren't for my connections to them, I would swear they weren't in the room with us. I appreciate how they're giving Calder enough space to figure this out and letting me know I'm safe in case he loses his mind.

Our incubus ghost hasn't said much to me, but he's enjoying every second and every caress as much as I am.

"He never got to touch me like this," Osen finally confesses in my mind as Calder hovers over my body and pauses to eat me up with a look. *"My incubus power took over too fast and immobilized him. He always riled me instantly. A blessing and a curse."*

An idea occurs to me, and I ask Calder, "How does a phoenix claim a mate?"

His gaze snaps up to mine. He considers me for a moment, then answers, "We… uh, during the mating, our talons pierce our mate's flesh. Then, when we experience the little death that is a full body orgasm, I share my flame with you. My essence."

"So, with me being your potential mate, could you still have sex without mating me? Or could that happen without you meaning to?"

He cocks a brow. "It would be hard to resist claiming you, but yes, I believe I could deny the compulsion."

"Not that I'm asking you not to," I hurry to add. "You just mentioned you didn't want to yet."

"You really can't live without my cock inside you now?" Calder says with a smirk of pride.

I smile wistfully, wishing I could caress him. He must sense my need and leans down, kissing me, then rubs his cheek over mine. The light stubble of his beard only makes me want him more.

When he lifts back up, I find my words. "I want to feel you inside me. And Osen wants it too. Would you make love to... *us*?"

His eyes widen, and he swallows hard. His ice-blue eyes search my face as he thinks about my offer. "Jade, I don't want to dishonor you. Or what Osen and I had."

"I don't think of it like that, but do you?" I ask.

"I think I'm in love with you." He rests his forehead on mine and clenches his eyes shut hard, like he's expecting me to shove him away. "*And* I still love him, too."

"Hey," I call softly. "Look at me." When he does, I go on, "I love Flint, Maxum, and Arran. And I pretty sure I'm in love with a certain bratty ghost too."

Calder smiles, but then it fades.

"And I love you too," I add. When his blue eyes blaze with affection, I say, "I want us to have this, but only if you want it. Osen is part of me now, so you might as well embrace this situation as much as I am. I don't want to shut him out and pretend he isn't here when we're together."

"Okay, yes." His luscious mouth claims my lips and tongue, and I'm panting when he breaks away. His eyes flicker up to my unrestrained hands, appearing nervous.

"Tie me down," I say firmly so he won't second guess my request.

He bites his lip and grabs a long strip of fabric. Like a pro, he wraps one end around my wrists above my head, then he ties the other end to the frame of the pallet under the mattress. His finger grazes my binds.

"Comfortable?" When I nod, he says nervously, "If it gets to be too much or if I'm hurting you. Or the binds are hurting you—"

"I'll say yellow for slow down and red for stop," I interrupt. "And if you're fucking my mouth, then I'll mentally reach out to Flint."

"Stars, you *are* made for us," Calder whispers and stares at my mouth. "I want to feel your sweet lips wrapped around my cock."

I open wide and stick out my tongue, flattening it.

All three males groan, and even Osen does in my mind.

I remind him. *"I want you to be here with us. Maybe teach me a thing or two about sucking cock."*

Calder stands and shucks his pants. His cock is beautiful and looks painfully hard, already leaking pre-cum. With a firm hand, he gives himself a few casual strokes while gazing at my body. "Open those legs. Show me that pretty pussy I'm going to ruin."

I spread my legs, and he kneels next to me and takes a bit of his pre-cum to rub over my clit. My hips jerk with the sensation.

"Maybe I should take your ass now, so I can finally fuck Osen like I've always wanted to."

"Yes, fuck our ass," Osen says.

It feels like Osen and I have become one being now. Sharing this body for our pleasure, and for Calder's pleasure and healing.

Calder sees the swirling charcoal and green glow of our eyes. Hell, I can see the glow cast on his face.

The kiss he gives us is heartbreakingly sweet and somehow filthy all at once.

He pulls back and cups the back of our head and lifts. "First, I need you to suck my cock."

"Yes, sir," we say.

Calder guides the thick and weeping head of his cock to our lips. We use our tongue to flick out and lick the pre-cum from the tip and probe the slit.

"Shit, I don't think I'm going to last a minute." Calder moves away and drags in a ragged breath. "It's been a long time since I've been touched."

We open our mouth, inviting him back. He moves faster now, slipping his cock down into our mouth, and we swirl our tongue around his shaft.

He presses farther in, and it feels like he's going down to our throat. When he reaches it, he blocks our airflow and holds for just a second before pulling back.

Testing my gag reflex? Or testing his control? I'm not sure.

He pumps forward again, claiming our throat. We swallow around his tip, and he groans happily.

"You enjoy sucking cock, our monster fucker?" He smiles down at us, adoringly. "Yeah, I'm talking to both of you."

We hum our response and rub our tongue against his shaft.

"Fuck, I'm definitely not gonna last," he says, pulling out of our mouth.

He sits back on his heels, appearing as if he's in a daze. His eyes are locked onto our bound wrists, expressionless.

We know he's back in that torture chamber.

"Love, come back to us," we whisper. "You're here. *Safe.*"

Our words crash into him, and he blinks hard, flinching. He then stares at us for a beat too long. Did he snap?

Calder shakes his head, flicking away the nightmare memories.

His hand slips into ours, holding them with a gentle touch. He places sweet kisses over our face. "You're so beautiful. Your hair is like an ethereal halo, marking you for the angel you are."

"Are angels real?"

"They used to be. No one has seen one in a long while." He bites our lip. "But my pack is mated to one."

He refocuses and moves down our body and slides his thick fingers into our cunt. "So wet for me." He pumps his digits inside our channel and curls against our g-spot. Pulling out, he uses the slick to wet the head of his cock and down around his shaft.

"I need to have your pussy. I've been dreaming about it since you first had Maxum and Arran at the safe house." Calder positions himself between our legs and grips his dick to run it through our folds.

We shiver with need, feeling empty inside. "Please, fuck us."

Instead, he takes one of our breasts in hand and rolls our nipple, then sucks and bites. We cry out, the pain delicious.

We thrash, our hips bucking to meet Calder's cock, begging for relief.

Then he slowly slides into our pussy, working his length inside with shallow pumps of his hips. He cradles our head, and we look up into his beautiful blue eyes and see the love that radiates like a blazing sun.

It's almost too much to look at directly. Like we might melt into nothing under the heat of his gaze.

We force ourselves to meet his eyes and fall deeper in love with him.

He seats himself fully inside, hips grinding against each other and whispers over our lips, "Thank you. Thank you both for loving me."

He doesn't give us a chance to respond before his mouth is on ours, tongue thrusting past our lips and his hips pounding into our sex. His hand moves down, strumming our clit and bringing us closer to an orgasm.

"Come for me," he demands.

And we do. Our body shudders and pulses with the pleasure he gives us. We cry out and find ourselves lost for a moment.

"Holy shit." He pulls out, breathing hard, but he hasn't come yet.

Then we feel slippery lube at our back door. His thick fingers slide past the tight ring, and he hums while diving deeper, scissoring. "That's it, baby. Nice and ready."

"Please," we whine.

"Please what?" he taunts.

"Need your cock." A whimper escapes as the sting easily gives way to pleasure. We rock in time with his probing.

"Since you asked so nicely, I'll give you what you want." He keeps us facing him, and lines up his lubed dick, ping-ponging his attention between watching our face and as he sinks into our ass.

Calder gets to the hilt and groans, "Jade... Osen... feels so good."

He takes care with us, making sure our body can handle him. Satisfied by our moans that we're alright, he pumps with vigor. His face contorts, and he grunts, mumbling words of love and adoration.

It feels right that it's the three of us together in this moment.

And it's beautiful for both Osen and me to see our phoenix come undone in this way. He's a work of art. His skin is on fire as he gets closer to his climax. But the flames don't burn, they only tickle and stimulate us.

We pull against the binds, wishing to grab onto him and anchoring ourselves as we spin out of control. He was right to tie us up.

Our orgasm rushes toward us like a freight train. We're sure when it hits us, we'll be obliterated.

Calder remembers our clit and pinches it hard as he shouts his own release. "Come with me!"

The pleasure shoots down our spine and crackles like electric magic.

I'm unsure why, but Osen and I seem to break apart inside my mind back into two beings. For some reason, he's giving me space.

Then an consuming urge takes over.

My soul reaches out and grasps onto my phoenix's soul.

My essence seeks to be bonded with my fated.

I sense Calder cannot deny his need any longer either.

His fingers become sharp talons, piercing my shoulder blades, the similar spot where Calder's wings erupt from his back.

His fire, like lava, flows into me.

I'm melting and reformed all in one moment.

The love that radiates from our combined emotions overwhelms me.

I shout with the unexpected pain of his talons, but it quickly shifts to overwhelming pleasure that seems to echo into eternity.

My bliss magnifies as I feel his bliss as my own. I even sense how my body clamps down and caresses his length. How my skin feels under his fingertips. The climax shooting up and down his spine. The release of years of pent-up tension. The warm embrace of his love.

I see the cosmos open in front of me.

I feel the fabric of life woven into my body.

I sense the many lives my phoenix has lived.

And finally, after what feels like an hour-long climax, I black out.

26

BORN AGAIN VIRGINS

JADE

I swear all I do is blink, and I'm untied. Osen has stepped back from the profound unification of our souls and is allowing us space to process this whole wild ride.

Calder has his muscular arm over mine, holding my wrists together in front of me, as he becomes my big spoon.

I jerk and freeze, assessing what's happening. Why did Calder untie me? Why are we canoodling like this? With only a tug of my hand from his hold, I would be free to touch him.

"Are you okay?" Calder nuzzles at the back of my neck.

"We… I thought… you didn't want to mate," I stutter to get out.

"I felt the pull, your soul… I couldn't deny you. You wanted that, right? Oh no, you didn't, did you?" His voice is full of worry.

"I did. I felt the call to bond too. My spirit reached for yours." I turn my body to look over my shoulder at him, so close I can see the swirling of blue flames in his eyes.

"I never expected to feel the completeness of a matebond. It's more profound than finding my fractured soul."

"I'm untied. What if I accidentally touch you?"

"I'm okay with holding you like this." Then a moment of uncertainty must come to him, and he asks, "How do you feel? Are you alright?"

"Yeah…" I check in with my body and sense Osen purring happily in the back of my mind. "That was intense, but in a good way."

"No kidding. It felt like I was a virgin again."

"But with mad hot skills." I chuckle, then tease, "In each life, aren't you a born-again virgin?"

He laughs easily. "I suppose so. Theoretically."

"Osen loved experiencing you being in control for the first time with him," I tell him.

Calder traces my fingers and lets out a long sigh. "I enjoyed being in control more than I expected. But one day, I hope I can handle you both dominating me."

My mind is swept away, envisioning that very thing. Calder on his knees with a collar. While I'm dressed only in a black leather corset and heels, my fingers clenched in his hair as I direct him between my legs to feast on my pussy.

Calder chuckles, bringing me back to now. "You did that steamy author dream sex sequence thing again, didn't you?"

I giggle and wiggle back into his firm chest. "Guilty. How did you know?"

"Probably the lusty haze over your eyes and the bit of drool here." He skims his thumb over my lips.

"Well, you're great writing inspiration." A strange, desperate longing hits me in the chest.

"Why are you sad? Did I do something wrong?" he asks, sensing the turn in my mood through our new bond.

"No. With everything… I haven't been able to write in a while. I miss it." I glance down at my fingers. "And now, with my magic free, I don't even know if I'll be able to use a computer to type anymore."

"There are a few spells and meditations you can use to make it easier. Or you could make Arran be your secretary and dictate to him. He can handle computers if he doesn't get too excited."

"I'll be writing smut…" I laugh, but it sounds tired and resigned. "He's going to be excited."

"We'll figure something out," Calder assures me and gives me a squeeze.

Because my writing career is on hold for the foreseeable future since people are hunting me, I change the subject, "How are you feeling?"

Calder kisses the back of my head. "I'm good as I can be. I think the bond is helping me stay grounded. And the fragments are working to line up with what my body has been up to since the split. I feel like I should be more fucked up, but it's also a relief for those lost pieces. For me too."

"How so?"

"I know why I didn't feel whole all these years—why I was missing my phoenix."

"It gives everything you felt context."

"I don't feel like I'm insane anymore," Calder explains. "Phoenixes never quite return the same, but it's usually some memory loss, loss of connections. Or, in some extreme cases, we can have significant personality shifts. But the last one felt bigger, more destructive than any other death before it."

"Why did it happen differently?"

"The witch used a curse on me right before I died. She fractured me on purpose."

"Fucking bitch," I growl. "If she isn't dead, I'm killing her."

He stills in surprise of my wrath. "I didn't think you were a vengeful sort."

"I suspect most people can be when you fuck with their mate."

Calder's hand guides my chin, so I'm looking over my shoulder at him again. "You don't mind being my mate? My twin flame?"

"No." I blink back the tears connected to the vulnerability we are both feeling. "How do you feel about it?"

"Like I'm the luckiest male, besides your other mates, obviously. But also like I don't deserve someone as kind and beautiful as you are."

"I can start acting like a bitch, if it helps you." I smile playfully.

"Even your bitchy mode is far too kind to me."

"And I'm not *that* beautiful." I roll my eyes. "Besides, you're hot as fuck. You could just walk straight up to a random supermodel and hump their leg and they'd be cool with it."

"Arran's the leg humping dog, remember?" Calder jokes. Then he rolls me over onto my back, props himself on an elbow, and stares down at me. "And you need to release the bullshit Rob programmed into your brain."

I gulp at his intensity and nod. "I'm trying. Unfortunately, society offers the same bullshit programming for curvy women over twenty. And before you all came along, I didn't exude magnetic sex appeal. So I never felt all that attractive. The magical vagina is a new development."

He chuckles at my joke, then turns serious. "Your soul knew it had five mates out there and likely kept that magnetic appeal on lock down, waiting for you to find us. And now you're our gravitational force. Our center. Our nexus. You're the most gorgeous being. Even when I was being a bratty dick and resisting, I could see your beauty. I felt drawn to you. And honestly, it killed me to push you away. I didn't want to do that anymore."

Calder takes my hand in his, feeling the weight of it, like one might test the balance of a weapon. Then he lifts it to his face, placing in on his cheek.

He sighs, a painful moan that I'm not sure how to interpret. When he opens his eyes, the blue flames of his love burn brightly.

I don't move, allowing him to get used to my touch.

A tear falls from his eye and lands on my cheek, melding with the salty tears I didn't know I was shedding.

"You're safe with me," I say. "I love you."

"I know, and I love you. I won't let anyone hurt you ever again. Not even me."

27

PHANTOM MENACING

JADE

*a*fter Flint helps to clean me up, Calder and I snuggle in bed. His mating fever abates with our bond. He's clear-headed again. He confesses to me what he can stomach to tell me about the torture he suffered. How she violated and mutilated him. It makes my stomach turn, picturing him abused like that.

I'd say I wouldn't wish that on anyone, but it would be a lie. I wish that witch would feel the same pain she inflicted on him. I want her to experience how she ruined him all these years.

However, I suspect she's messed up because someone hurt her, but that doesn't give her a free pass to be a torturer.

"I'm sorry. I shouldn't have burdened you with all that," Calder says, turning his face away from me.

"No. It isn't a burden. I'm here for you, just like you have been there for me. Even when you didn't like me or trust me, you listened when I told you about Rob's abuse. I didn't feel so alone when you understood how much he had hurt me."

Calder's hand lightly strokes my cheek. "I hate that when you were under the spell that I asked you to remember it all."

"Are you kidding me? That was a brilliant idea. Now I understand why I felt the way I did. I was brainwashed." I search Calder's face, trying to read him. "Are you unhappy that I gave you back your soul pieces?"

"Of course not." He presses a kiss to my lips. "It will take some time for my soul to integrate. If I didn't have it back, I don't know what kind of a mate I would be for you."

Calder sits up and moves the pillows to the wall at the head of the mattress. Then he rests his back and opens his arms, inviting me.

I get to my knees and knee walk toward him.

My gargoyle moves closer, worried.

Calder nods to Flint. "Stay close."

"She enjoys this sexual position. Bouncing on top," Flint says and gives me a slanted smile when I blush.

"*Flint!* I didn't take you as a kiss and tell type." I pout, then laugh.

"I'm not planning on fucking… right now, but thanks for the tip, big guy." Calder catches me by my waist and easily lifts me onto his lap, my knees landing on either side of his hips.

Damn, these guys are fucking strong.

His cock perks up with my vagina's proximity.

I feel awkward, unsure where to put my hands, so I rest them on my thighs until I understand what's going on. I know he's trying to get over his nightmare experience, but I worry he's pushing himself too hard, too fast.

Calder's finger catches under my chin and lifts my face so I'm looking into his eyes. They no longer look as haunted as they did when we first met. "I want you to touch me, my flame. Explore my body. I need to get used to it. And I crave your touch. It's driving me insane."

Taking my hands in his, he places them on the sides of his face.

I don't move, waiting to see his reaction. Instead of fear, I see hope and affection in his expression.

"If it gets to be too much, tell me," I say, moving my fingers to trace over his fantastic cheekbones and his chiseled jaw.

His unshaven beard is softer than I expect. I've kissed him, but I was so overcome with desire that I didn't notice how unusually soft his whiskers are. I feather my fingertips over his strong brow, and he closes his eyes in bliss. I run my thumb over his plump lower lip, and he pokes his tongue out to lick the tip.

I move my hands down over his neck. He snaps his eyes open and shivers when I stroke my hand over his throat. He tenses, and I worry I've triggered him.

An image flashes in my mind. Osen's hand wrapped tightly around Calder's neck during sex.

Osen speaks to me, *"Maybe one day we can play again like that, but not now. Not yet."*

I explore Calder's collarbones, his huge deltoids, and down over his pecs. My hands practically thump over his washboard abs.

I skim my hands up his arms, admiring his corded forearms and his defined triceps and biceps.

Looking for the next place, I ask, "How do you feel about me touching your back?"

He holds my wrists, leans forward, and slides my arms around him. I stroke up and down his spine and touch the place where his wings usually emerge. In response, he groans with pleasure. His arms wrap around my waist, and he pulls me flush against his chest. I fall into his embrace, my face nuzzling into his shoulder and neck, and he hums happily.

It becomes clear that he isn't likely to have an episode and hurt me. When he realizes this, Flint leaves to make us some food.

Maxum stays to monitor us. He sits in the corner, watching over me like my personal guardian demon.

I giggle at that thought.

"Jade." Maxum narrows his eyes at me, likely sensing I was making a joke at his expense. "What did you just think?"

"Who needs angels when I have a demon to keep me safe?" I blow him a kiss and the sweet and sappy demon reaches out and catches it. Then he wickedly tucks it in his pants, then stares down wide eyed, like it's working some blowjob magic.

Calder and I bark out a laugh.

I'm still cautious and don't initiate touch. Calder's been holding my hands since our touching session and snuggling with me.

Hope fills my heart that we might get past this. If not, I will still love him the way he needs.

The cellar hatch opens, and Arran and Flint are carrying plates stacked with sandwiches.

"Guys, we don't have to eat in here," Calder grumbles. He looks at me with a frown. "It's bad enough Jade has to be down in a dark hole at all because of me."

"Yet you got down my holes anyway," I say and waggle my eyebrows suggestively.

Every one of my guys groans at my joke, even Osen.

"What?" I wave them off. "You all are joke snobs."

"I'm new to jokes and even I know that one was bad," Flint teases.

"Heathens!" I announce. "Want to get barbaric?"

"Not until you eat." Arran places a plate in my lap as I sit at the edge of the mattress. He lifts my chin gently and gazes into my eyes. "Missed you."

I grasp his wrist, moving his hand so I can snuggle into his palm.

After a quick glance to judge Calder's mood, Arran dips down and gives me a soft yet dizzying kiss.

He walks around the bed and then shouts, arching his back and his body ripples with a shift. I'm freaking out. It appears something's attacking him.

"What's wrong?" I frantically ask my werewolf.

Arran grabs his crotch and doubles over. When he glances up at us, it's not pain but embarrassment written on his face. "I just came in my fucking pants!" he hisses in surprise.

"I believe that was my ectoplasm," Osen says through me. "Ecto-jism, if you will, that was floating in the room from having sex."

Arran scans the space, warily. "Your incubus ghost cum is hovering around like mines in the air, waiting to explode our cocks?"

Maxum swiftly rushes around the room with a wicked grin. When he doesn't cum, he says with a laugh, "Dammit, Osen. Can you jerk out another one?"

"*Haha*," Arran grumbles and uses some napkins to clean up his mess, but it's already soaked into his pants.

Flint shrugs and sits down on the ground next to me. His shoulder presses against my leg like a puppy needing his attention fix.

After the spontaneous ejaculation, we quiet down and eat, enjoying each other's company.

It's wonderfully pleasant except something's niggling at me. The situation is far from where it needs to be. We still must rid the realms of Rob and Galiana so we can stop hiding and find a proper place to live.

And Osen. I want him here, sitting next to me, in his own body.

As amazing as it was to experience a new way with him riding along inside me. I want him physically inside my body with his real cock. I want him to have a relationship with Calder, independent of me. The way they both deserve.

"Guys, I was thinking…" I hesitate, stalling as I try to figure out how to suggest it.

"*No. Don't,*" Osen warns, sensing where my mind has gone.

"I have to, Osen," I argue aloud so the others can hear me. "If they shoot down the idea, then fine."

Calder shifts, turning on his perch next to me. "Tell us."

I focus on Calder as I explain. He'll give me the most honest feedback. "With what happened at the warehouse, I think there's a chance, maybe a slim one, to bring Osen back."

"Jade, doesn't it give you pause that fucking *reckless* Osen doesn't want to do it?" Maxum growls.

I look over and find my demon fuming. "Just because he's skittish now after he died doesn't mean it's a bad idea."

"Do you even hear yourself?" Maxum jumps to his feet, coming close to ramming his horns into the low ceiling. "No. We would need his magic back. That means putting you in Rob's path so you can attempt to snatch it from him. You don't even know if you can do that. Souls are one thing. Magic is different."

"But we're pretty sure he used my siphoned magic to take both," I argue.

"He might have, but he would have used a spell to manipulate it to do that." Calder makes a stupidly smart point.

I want to scream. Why didn't my grandmother—dammit, *mother*—leave me with someone who knew what I was and how to train me?

If she did, I wouldn't be starting my new career as a fucking magical freak at forty.

"Then maybe we need to see if I can steal magic," I say with a shrug. "Then if we just happen to wander across Rob, I can rip it from his body."

"Fuck." Maxum drags his hand over his face. "Fine. I can see you aren't going to back down. And we should know what a little monster you've turned out to be."

"We can hunt down some ASO witches and warlocks," Flint proposes. "And beat them to the edge of death, then they can't hurt our precious mate. She could test her powers on them."

"Aw, always thinking of me." I kiss his horn that's only a few inches from my face.

He smiles at me, looking pleased.

We finish up our meal, and Calder insists we return to the tiny cabin.

I don't argue. I could use another shower since the washcloths Flint used to clean me up after Calder fucked me could only do so much.

While we get ready to sleep, Calder gives me a kiss and hug. I soak up the affection and try to radiate it back out to him as much as I can. "I'm going to sleep on the couch since I'm not quite ready for a dog pile on the bed."

"You're welcome when you're ready."

"Hey!" Trouble grumbles at Calder. "I thought this was my bed now."

"You take up a tiny bit of this entire couch!" Calder argues. "I'll put you outside if you want your space."

"No need to get dramatic," Trouble squeaks.

"Yay! Cuddles!" Sage cheers as Calder sets them on his chest.

Seeing them snuggled up makes my heart glow, and I crawl into the middle of bed and what I expect to be another sweltering night of body heat.

Once we get settled in a new permanent home, I'll need Maxum to fork out the big bucks on an industrial sized air-conditioner so I won't suffer a heat stroke at night with them.

As soon as I'm horizontal, the heavy weight of massive arms and legs falls over me. My mind envisions I'm in a horror movie, being pulled down into a dark pit and slowly suffocated. It's not far off, but fortunately, it's like a warm, fuzzy version.

It's as if I'm drugged with happy endorphins, and I fall into a smothering oblivion with a smile on my face.

28

STRANGER DANGER

MAXUM

*I*n the early morning, I find Jade in the yard between the two cabins, sitting in a meditation pose with Amira.

I wait patiently for their training session to be over, knowing Jade needs to work on her focus. It isn't horrible, but she allows her mind to wander if she's triggered with a new shiny thought or a problem to solve.

For her writing career, it works perfectly. In a magical battle to the death, not so much.

When Jade and Amira blink back to their surroundings, I give them both a nod. "Thank you for your help, Amira." Then I turn to Jade. "Darius is going to meet us in a bit, but I'd like a word alone with you first."

"Okay. Thank you for making me the magic containment talisman." Jade smiles widely at our host.

Amira slightly bows her goodbye and walks back to the main house.

"Ugh." Jade grumbles and hops to her feet. "That sounds a lot like *we need to talk* talk."

I know from reading romance books, that's the breakup talk. A bit of trepidation fills her eyes and her shoulders curl in slightly.

"No, darling. But you might not like it."

The statement has her shoulders straightening and her eyes narrowing.

"Might as well get on with it then, instead of me imagining all kinds of random stuff."

To the point it is then. "Osen was correct to discourage you from the dangerous path of resurrecting him," I say firmly. "It's one thing to channel Calder's fragments, and quite another to hunt down our enemies and use your untested powers. We don't even know the spell they used to rip the magic out of him."

"Actually, we do." She crosses her arms, looking triumphant. "Osen heard it when they used it on him."

I thought he was against this plan! I guess he might change his mind now if he hopes it will work.

I swallow hard. "His memory was while he was dying. He might not have caught the whole thing or accurately."

Osen's charcoal eyes appear, and his deeper voice cuts through. "I see and hear your concern. I have it too. I won't let her do this if it risks her life."

"It *will* risk her fucking life!" I shout. "Not *if!*"

"Okay. Maybe it's better to say if it's too much of a risk." He shakes his head. "Jade's already argued for this, and she has a point. As long as those assholes are alive, she isn't safe. No one is safe. We should go after them."

"No." I throw my hands in the air in frustration. "She needs to work on her powers. *If* we get caught, she can fight back."

"Amira won't let us stay here forever. And you know as well as I do that eventually we *will* get caught if we leave. If we wait for our enemies to find us first, then they'll have the upper hand."

Dammit, why does he have to make sense?

Osen continues. "I'm not saying we go today or even this week. We need to test this spell and her magic. We all need to be ready to go on the offensive as soon as possible."

"Tracking down *any* witch or warlock is fucking dangerous right now," I huff.

"Don't you want your mate to be free of a parasitic ghost?" Osen snaps.

"Shush up, you aren't a parasite," Jade interrupts, sounding irritated, like she's had this conversation a million times.

I shrug, because he's not wrong about being a psychic leech.

Jade rushes to me. "I have to try to help him."

I catch her by the shoulders, and she gasps. I stare down into her glowing green eyes. "I know. But, my love, everything in me is warring against this idea. I wish I could burn the realms and keep you safe and properly fucked and sated."

"For fuck's sake, can you keep it in your pants for five seconds?" Darius snarls from behind me.

When I turn to scowl at him, I see a glimmer of mischief in his eyes.

He's a prick, but he also knows the need our kind has for our mates and is busting my balls about it. I doubt he waited long to mate with Amira once he found her.

I'm surprised I haven't given in and claimed her soul, but I know how dangerous that might be. I can't have us running from both witches and demons.

"Let's get on with it." Darius grunts and eyes Jade with a glower that would make a lesser being crumble.

Not her. She's studying him right back, like she's making notes for her next book. I'm almost jealous. I want to be her next main character. Though she could just as easily make him an irrelevant side character, so I relax.

With Darius's special hellhound sight, he evaluates her magic, her life force, her demon energy signature. "Good news is that even after her magic has bloomed, she won't come off as a demon right away unless they dig, so that's a fucking miracle."

"If she doesn't put up any wards, what *will* people sense?" I ask.

"I don't know what people will sense. But a hellhound will leave her alone. Unless she throws demon magic around and catches their attention."

Jade shivers. "And what happens if I do that?"

"They'll drag you down to hell."

He's about to explain the gruesome aspects of demon culture, so I stop him short. "Yep, let's avoid that!" I say almost cheerfully.

Jade cocks a brow at me, but doesn't press for answers. When I skim her mind, she thinks that I'm just sensitive about my ancestral roots. That isn't the half of it.

Thank fuck, Osen keeps his trap closed. I doubt he wants to worry her either.

"You have Amira's talisman?" Darius prompts.

Jade pulls the metal charm from her pocket and dangles it from the chain.

"It needs to be in contact with your skin to work," Darius explains. "Put it on, and I'll take another gander at you."

Jade slips the necklace on, and I feel her magic mute. Amira said she could make another more powerful one if this one didn't work, but it would take longer for her to create.

"I assume most supes or witches wouldn't give you a second glance with this in place," Darius says with a shrug.

"Agreed." I cross my chest and a growl escapes me when I realize Jade is set to leave Amira's wards.

"Cool!" Jade says happily. "Can we please go to the grocery store and maybe a coffeehouse? Oh, and I'd like to get some more clothes. Can we bring my computer so I can see if this talisman will allow me to use it for writing?"

Darius looks over at me as Jade rambles on. "I'm glad Amira's the quiet type."

Jade stops talking and pouts. She opens her mouth, likely about to insult his grumpy behavior, but I stop her with my comment.

"Jade is perfect for us, so I suppose it all works out as it should."

Her pretty eyes light up, and she crashes into my body in an all-consuming hug.

Fuck. I love this woman.

Of course, absolutely no one wanted to be left behind as we left for civilization. If you can even call most human cities civilized.

The plan is to wear our glamours and split up, blending in and keeping an eye on each other.

One beautiful woman with four intimidating males will draw unwanted attention. Hell, just one of us with her will probably get noticed. And the witches have eyes everywhere. We'll have to watch for fucking tattling familiars too.

Luckily, I'm paired with Jade since I have the innate portal magic. Not that Calder can't make one too, but it takes him a lot longer and drains his reserves. Seconds can mean the difference in life or death.

Jade is still fuming that she didn't inherit demon portal magic. She could probably learn the complex skill like Amira has, but again, it's magically draining for those without the gift.

Osen could create one in his own body, but he needs his incubus magic for it to work. He just doesn't have enough magic other than to seduce our mate in the shadowscape.

I've often wondered if the shadowscape was the final resting place for incubi souls. But with what we've learned about Osen's death, it seems like that theory is bunk.

We only got to visit a rundown haunted warehouse when we left Amira's sanctuary before. This time, Jade bubbles with excitement as we make the trek beyond the borders.

I don't like that we're leaving again so soon, but we're all going a bit stir crazy. We're used to fighting and hunting. Hiding is not in our natures.

After I create the first of many portals, I take Jade's hand. She swings our arms between us like we are human spawn on a school field trip.

"Don't use magic in front of humans if you can avoid it."

"Because the Supes Council will be mad I outed them?" she asks.

"Because we don't need the attention. You're unregistered, which is how we want it. If the magic world knew what you could do..." I trail off not wanting to say it.

"I'd be the new lab rat."

I grunt in agreement. "Don't talk to anyone," I remind her.

"Stranger danger, got it, sir." She salutes me and laughs at me when I roll my eyes. I appreciate she can be so lighthearted with all that's happened, but sometimes I worry she believes this is all some wild hallucination.

She's too brave for her own good.

Jade accepted five monsters into her heart and into her bed like it isn't a fucking big deal. She's pushing her limits to make sure we all get our individual happily ever afters. It makes me love her even more than I do. But damn if it doesn't irritate me that we aren't focusing on Jade's well-being. Although she's already argued that making sure the pack is happy also benefits her.

Thank goddess she has more than human and witch blood to keep her alive. Now that it's free inside her, the demon blood alone might offer some protection from most magical attacks. Jade's fae blood is already helping to speed up her healing. She needs that healing just to recover from all the sex she'll have with four and, possibly soon, five mates.

I portal us through several places before we arrive at our destination in the human realm—a coffeehouse that allows computer use.

I give Jade some cash to buy whatever she likes, and I order a black coffee to drink as I wait outside.

With her mocha and pastry in hand, she finds a seat where I can easily watch her from the sidewalk. She sets up her computer and tests out her magic containment talisman. I do my best to not look like a stalker, but my eyes can't help but snag on her every time I do a sweep of my surroundings.

She's so gorgeous, even in plain, baggy clothes and no makeup, my heart aches to be near her. I want to sit next to her and listen to her silly (and usually dirty) jokes as she giggles at herself. I want her to confess all her thoughts and dreams and share all my secrets.

I snap out of my daydream and scan the area again, finding the other guys just as transfixed as they watch her.

Jade blissfully is unaware of our possessive longing as she types away on her computer. Good. This will ease her anxiety about her future since she can continue her writing after we vanquish Galiana and Rob.

I allow myself to indulge in her fantasy, where we steal back Osen's power, kill them off, and then return Osen to our pack. Then Jade can claim each of us as mates.

I have no doubt he would be a better, more considerate member than he ever was before.

After a half hour goes by, Jade packs up her laptop computer into the lead-lined case to protect it from magic.

She gives me a wide smile as she sashays toward the cafe's main door.

Then all hell breaks loose.

29

DRAWING THE DARKNESS

JADE

I smile to myself when I feel the gaze of all four of my guys on me as I sit in the cafe window, using my computer to check on my accounts and sales.

No surprise that my sales have slumped a bit, but not as bad as it could be since I'm not around to promote them. I resist the urge to pop onto social media and see what the latest situation in the book world is.

I take the last bite of my pastry and mouth-gasm from the treat. We've been living off some bland meals lately and I'm looking forward to stocking up on some groceries today.

I check my emails and find a few from fellow authors who noticed my absence. My virtual assistant, who creates graphics and promotes book releases, has inquired about the book I was supposed to release in a couple of weeks.

I'm definitely missing that deadline. I can't reach out to her right now, though because it could give away my location if someone is watching our interactions.

Damn, I swear there are nine flipping million emails in my inbox. I need to unsubscribe to the businesses that blast me every single day. It didn't feel that overwhelming before since I checked my email several times a day in my old, regular non-magical life.

My blood runs ice cold when I see a newer message from Rob. Sent right after his failed attempt to cast his hypnosis spell and abduct me from Maxum's lake house.

My cursor hovers over the email, debating if I should open the email with the subject:

RE: THIS IS YOUR LAST CHANCE TO CHOOSE ME OR...

Like we had a real relationship, and he's giving me some ultimatum.
I doubt he will know if I read his email, so I click on it.

"YOU'VE HAD YOUR FUN, BUT YOU KNOW YOU BELONG TO ME. COME BACK BEFORE IT'S TOO LATE. YOU WOULDN'T WANT TO SEE HOW MUCH IT COSTS YOUR LOVERS IF YOU REMAIN WITH THEM."

I'll give it to the bastard. He didn't technically threaten them, but he did.

I turn off the computer and pack my crap up. Fuck him and his click bait. Taking a deep breath, I shrug off his threat. He wants to get me riled up, and I can't let him win yet again.

Remembering how he hurt me on so many levels, I force myself to take another deep breath to calm down.

I give Maxum a wide, unbothered smile as I saunter toward the door to join him.

A shout comes from behind me. Which is odd. There aren't kids in the cafe and it's been fairly quiet this whole time.

I spin to see what's going on and find a strange glow coming from the restroom hallway. A man flies from the corridor and slides along the tile floor.

Then someone else emerges—the attacker—and he's storming straight for me.

Fucking Rob.

Survival instincts kick in and I whirl around to run from my predator.

Maxum tugs on the glass door handles, which only warp from the force of his pull. The glass glimmers with magic, likely some sort of force field to keep my guys out.

Magic that feels like a giant fist slams me in the back and I fall on my face, knocking the wind out of me. I lay prone on the floor when something wraps around my ankles and yanks me, dragging me quickly toward Rob.

He begins to chant his spell to hypnotize me.

I throw up my mental shields to prevent him from controlling my mind.

Once I'm at his feet, I come to an abrupt stop.

Rob takes a handful of my hair, roughly lifting me up by it.

I scream from the pain in my scalp and try to hold on to his hand so it won't pull so much.

Once the shock subsides, I twist in his hold and swing my heavy computer case at his gut.

Rob grunts with the impact as I hear his ribs crack. I shove at his chest to break away and run.

Unfortunately, he hasn't let go of my hair. He swings his fist at me, aiming for my face.

Dumb move. Hitting someone in the head isn't easy on the knuckles. Maybe he thinks I'll have a glass jaw.

Guess again, sucker.

His hand collides with my cheekbone, and he screams as his hand shatters —my newly enhanced stone bones saving the day.

Just as Rob releases me to baby his broken hand, glass shoots across the coffee shop in an explosion. Thankfully, the few customers and employees inside have already sought shelter behind the counter.

Rob's eyes widen when he sees Maxum and Flint charging up behind me like they are going to kick his ass.

For a moment, I worry about Arran and Calder, but Osen assures me, *"They will have held back to surround anyone trying to flank you."*

Using my bond, I sense Arran is alive, and he's freaking out. But it doesn't seem he's in danger.

Maxum rushes ahead of me, grabs Rob by the collar, and opens a portal below Flint, Rob, himself, and me.

We fall through the floor and a scream catches in my throat.

Rob screeches as we free fall.

I glance down and see we're a thousand feet in the sky, falling fast.

Flint swoops under me. A gust of air leaves my lungs as I land in his arms and his wings completely unfurl to slow our descent. I glance back at the portal above us and see a dark feathered mass fly through.

Calder.

I panic. Where is Arran? Did they leave him behind?

The portal snaps shut.

Calder is diving toward us, tucking in his wings. When he gets close enough, I can see Arran in his arms. Relief washes over me.

Full demon version Maxum soars next to us with his wings out. He still has a solid grip on Rob's collar, whose head wobbles, his eyes closed.

I wonder if my ex is dead, but he jerks back to consciousness only to scream like a baby and pass out again.

"It's clear now that the only way this wimpy piece of crap could make you fall for him is to put a spell on you," Maxum shouts over the wind.

"I'm going to rip his body to shreds for violating you like that," Flint growls.

"Get in line," Maxum growls back.

Is it wrong I'm getting warm, tingling feelings?

It's easy for me to forget when they are so sweet to me, but this display of pure murderous rage keenly reminds me again that my guys are dangerous monsters. Thank goddess, they're on my side.

Calder and Arran catch up to us and Maxum nods to where he plans to land.

Maxum drops Rob to the ground about ten feet up and my ex grunts as he rolls to a stop.

Flint lands but doesn't let me out of his arms.

A half-shifted Arran jumps from Calder's hold before the phoenix lands and rushes over. Werewolf ripples over his skin. He still has on his sweatpants, but his shirt has been torn to shreds. His clawed hands clasp my face as he checks me for injury. "He bruised you," he snarls.

"He's done much worse than that to me," I say almost flippantly. I don't mention the missing chunk of hair from when he just yanked on it.

"If we weren't going to kill him before, he's definitely going to die painfully now," Calder grits out with barely restrained fury as he steps to where Rob has collapsed, opposite Maxum.

They both stare at the jerk warlock with a fiery glow in their eyes, their fists clenching at their sides, waiting for him to wake up.

I shift to get out of Flint's hold, but he grips me tighter.

"Sweetheart, this is my chance to use my power," I say, giving his firm chest a soothing rub. "I have to see if I can get Osen's magic back before you all kill him."

Reluctantly, Flint loosens his hold, and I slide down to my feet. I drop my computer case, because yeah, I held onto that mofo. I wasn't going to let this dickhead make me lose my stories.

Flint and Arran flank me as we all stare at the bane of my existence. Well, one of them. It sounds like Galiana might be the one who has ruined my life and everyone I care about.

But with Rob, it's personal. This asshole took advantage of my good nature, my body, my mind, and my powers. He invaded my home and made me feel like crap. He wanted me to feel worthless so he could do any horrible thing to me and I'd beg for another scrap of his attention.

But Calder is right. I was strong enough to push him away. I broke up with him, even when he had the power of his magic over me. In a way, that makes me a badass.

"*You ready?*" Osen asks me.

"*Not really. You?*" I feel the heavy weight of this moment on my shoulders.

"*I'm excited and terrified,*" he admits.

I nod, feeling the same. I take a moment to center myself. The last few minutes have been bonkers, and my guys' aggressive energy is distracting.

I go inward so I can unleash my power.

After the feeling of calm washes over me, I open my eyes and focus my magic on Rob. I reach out with my psychic senses and feel energy writhing under his skin.

"I feel shadows," I announce. "I'm pretty sure it's Osen's incubus magic."

"It is," Osen confirms, moving forward inside our body to work with me, guiding me with the extraction spell.

"*What if I mess this up?*" I express to Osen in my mind. "*I don't want to rush this and ruin your chances.*"

"*No matter what, I don't want him to have my power,*" Osen says. "*If we cannot bring me back, we'll deal with that later. I'd never blame you.*"

Reassured by his words, all of my magic wells inside of me—fae, demon, and witch. I sense these parts make this ability possible. Like I'm the magical equivalent of a perfect cocktail that looks innocent but knocks you on your ass.

I reach out with my mind and dive into Rob's chest, feeling the angry lashing of Osen's shadowtendrils. Osen whispers the spell that I must recite.

I struggle with concentrating on both the words and the action, as I'm still new to wielding magic.

When the chant is done, there's a release of some sort. It's subtle, but there. I gently tug on Osen's shadows, his power, and it slowly leaks out of Rob.

It's working! Excitement fills me.

It also wakes Rob, and he cries out as he witnesses the shadows being taken back.

He chants to regain his hold on Osen's magic, but Maxum kicks him in the teeth, shutting him up.

Rob sways and falls on to his back again. "Bitch," he mutters.

Flint charges forward and places his foot over Rob's mouth, pinning his head down and applying more than a little pressure.

Rob squirms and flails.

"I wouldn't recommend insulting our mate," Flint growls, and the ground shakes with his anger.

I remember to focus on my task, coaxing and drawing out Osen's shadow magic.

It slinks across the ground and winds up my legs, finally sliding down my throat.

I panic as I sense the shadows taking over.

I can't move.

My mind goes blank, and I sink into darkness.

30

UNGHOSTED

ARRAN

*T*he moment Jade inhales the shadows, she drops like a lead weight.

I snatch her up into my arms to keep her from hitting the ground.

When her eyes open, it's all Osen. No trace of Jade's glowing green eyes.

"Where is she?" I demand.

"Still here. Just overwhelmed by my magic because it's united with me again," Osen answers, finding their feet and standing.

I don't let go. It doesn't feel like Osen is unaffected, either.

"We should go, get my body," Osen says. "See if this works."

I snarl, hating that I can't see my mate when I look at her face. "Always thinking about yourself, huh?"

"No!" he snaps. "I'm worried that Jade won't be able to handle my energy for much longer!"

"Enough!" Maxum shouts over us, drawing our attention. He looks over at Rob, clearly debating if we kill him quickly now or slowly later. "Let's go. We can bring this piece of garbage along for the ride. We'll take care of Jade and Osen, then we'll claim our pound of flesh."

We tie up Rob's hands and gag him as a precaution.

Maxum has us jump through a few portals before we end up in the partially collapsed tunnel under the lake house. We stand outside the bunker door as the final portal closes behind us. Maxum presses his palm to the door and unlocks the safe room. When the door swings open, all our eyes fall upon Osen's body inside the glass coffin set in the center of the room.

"You preserved his body?" Rob mumbles behind his gag in disbelief.

Calder shoves him forward and ties him to a cot frame.

No one bothers to answer Rob's question, but it wasn't us that did the preserving. Something about Osen's unnatural death froze his body in time.

Now we'll just have to see if he can be brought back to us in his full glory.

Jade needs to expel Osen's magic, whether it's to resurrect or to just release it into the cosmos. Rob shouldn't have it. Not that it would have been a problem for long, because that asswipe is going to experience a slow and painful death if we can control ourselves enough to make it slow.

I've been helping Jade and Osen make it through our journey here. Her body is rejecting the magic as if she's ill.

"Jade?" I call to her, holding her close, searching her face for a sign she'll be okay.

A faint pulse of green shines through from behind the shadowy gray of Osen's magic.

"She's here, just fighting to stay with us," Osen grits out.

Maxum and Flint remove the top of the coffin.

Calder looks ready to lose his freaking wits. I thought I'd be the mess with being a berserker and all, but no, it's the phoenix.

Tears stream down his cheeks. "Let's go, come on."

He has two mates on the line. In one fell swoop, he could lose both if this goes sideways.

Not that it means a fucking thing. If we lose Jade, then Flint, Maxum, and I will have lost our fated mate. Because that's what we are to her and she to us.

There's no coming back from that loss.

My beasts howl inside of me, and I'm having a hard time containing them. If this goes wrong, I won't contain them any longer. I will retreat so far back in my mind that I'll be completely feral. No one will be safe.

I don't expect much less from the others. Flint would likely turn to stone one last time and return to the earth, releasing his soul back to the cosmos.

Maxum will... I don't even know what he will do, but nothing good will come of it.

Calder will probably end himself with the final flame.

Osen? I suspect he won't forgive himself for allowing Jade to sacrifice herself. If he survived, he'd go insane. And if he died, he'd likely become a vengeful wraith.

I shake myself out of my dark thoughts.

Jade was born to do this. This *is* her power. It's what makes her a valuable weapon. If a hack like Rob can steal and wield her ability, then, even untrained, Jade should be able to figure this out.

And we're here. Not that I'm much help. What do I know about souls or controlling death? Nothing.

"Help us get closer," Osen asks.

With my arm around Jade's waist, I bring them closer to the coffin.

"Fuck, this is weird," Osen hisses.

"No shit," I grumble.

"I feel a tug," Osen gasps. "It's like my soul and magic *want* to return to my body."

"That's good, right?" I ask, excited to hear something might go our way.

"Jade?" Osen calls. "Come on, sweet witch, you gotta help an incubus out."

There's a long pause, and everyone holds their breath.

Well, except Rob. He's just scowling.

"I have to do all the work?" Jade mutters, sounding tired. "What's the point of having a harem then?"

"It's a polycule, sweetie." Osen smirks.

"No. I definitely signed up for a reverse harem with a MM side quest."

With their levity, my chest releases some of its anxiety. She can't be that bad off if she's joking around. Well, knowing Jade, that's probably untrue. Her last words will probably be something to make us laugh.

It's one reason I love her so much already. She's brave, sexy, and quick-witted.

"Hey," Osen says and glances at all of us. "I just want to say something in case this doesn't work out."

"Don't!" Calder throws his hands up. "Don't think like that."

"I won't risk not telling you all how I feel." Osen turns to Flint. "You're the rock bed that keeps us all sane. I'm sorry I didn't appreciate that enough when I was alive. And I have no doubt you will be the most incredible mate to our girl."

"I will do my best with that honor." Flint bows his head. "And may you live to see that happen."

"Arran, you have been the best pack mate. And seeing you heal with Jade has been a blessing in this situation."

I nod, biting my lip so hard it bleeds. "I love you. Try not to leave us again."

"Maxum, *dude*," Osen chuckles. "It isn't like you don't know how much I treasure our friendship since you can read my mind."

"I know, asshole," Maxum says with a playful smirk. "Now get the fuck back into your own body so I can have some alone time with my woman."

Osen shakes Jade's head with a wide grin. Then he turns to the phoenix. "Calder, I love you so much, it aches in my very soul." As Osen says this, Calder rushes forward and gives him a bruising kiss.

"Same." Calder presses his forehead to Osen-Jade and then drops away.

Osen doesn't offer Jade words, or perhaps he does through their mental connection and wishes to keep it private. Likely, since he usually isn't one for public declarations of affection.

"Focus," he guides her. "See in your mind what you want to make happen. Feel my soul and magic gather into your grasp and then coax it back into my body. This is your birthright. You can do this."

Jade closes her eyes. Through our bond, I sense she's calling upon her strange magic. Her skin begins to glow and when she opens her eyes to gaze at Osen's body, they shine like stars. Almost too bright to look at.

She opens her mouth and a bizarre combination of light and shadow flow from her lips. The shadows I recognize... Osen's incubus magic. The light must be his soul.

The cloud of energy slides into Osen's nostrils.

Jade falls backward when the transfer is complete.

I catch her, holding her close to my chest. Her eyes are half closed, and she's spent. Wielding magic this powerful, especially for new magic users, can be taxing.

I cup her head to my chest and expectantly watch Osen's body. I was hoping for a gasp of air or a wiggling finger. But nothing.

"It didn't work?" Calder asks, sounding heartbroken.

"Give it a minute," Maxum whispers. "He was dead for a while. I suspect the body will need to heal and reconnect to his spirit."

We wait and wait.

I don't know if it's been a minute or an hour. It feels like days as we wait for our friend, former lover, and pack mate to wake.

But he remains frustratingly still.

"Anything?" Calder asks as he leans over the casket, his hands fisting in agitation.

"I don't sense brain waves. I thought by now..." Maxum drops into a crouch and hangs his head, giving up.

"Jade?" Flint calls and strokes her hair. "Heartstone? Do you feel him? Or is he truly gone now?"

Jade blinks and rouses to the room, her eyes falling onto Osen's inert body. "He's in there. Feels stuck." She struggles to talk.

"Fuck!" Calder slams his fist into the wall. "We need to release him!"

"I could try taking him back inside me," Jade suggests.

"No," we all say in unison.

"He was hurting you." Maxum stands again and walks over to stroke her cheek. "His magic and soul together were too much for you to contain. I'm afraid he might take over and you'd cease to exist."

"We don't know that would happen," she argues, but I hear her concern that it could.

"He wouldn't mean to," I explain. "But incubus and succubus naturally drain other people's magic. That's how they feed. His magic would feast on yours."

"I believe that's what happened when you brought his magic inside you," Maxum adds.

"But it didn't hurt Rob," she argues.

She has a point there.

"Why is that?" I ask Maxum, because he's the most knowledgeable amongst us.

"Look at him, he isn't alright. His witch magic is drained. This whole time we've been down here, he hasn't even tried to attack us," Maxum points out. "He used Osen's shadows to attack Jade at the cafe. Besides, he didn't have Osen's soul also inside him. Only his magic. He used that to suck the magic out of others. We know from recent events that stolen magic has a short shelf life."

"Why?" Jade asks. "Is it because Rob's body isn't set up to naturally regenerate the magic energy?"

"Yes, exactly." Maxum smiles. "For example, a vampire needs blood from a magic user to replenish. Someone who steals a vampire's magic only has what was in that vampire at the time. The thief can't drink blood and extract what they need to keep the magic thriving."

"But if Osen's magic *and* soul were inside me, it would be different?"

"I believe if he has both, he *could* replenish, even in another person's body." Maxum nods. "Incubi are different. They are adaptable... existing in another plane as well as this one. He would overtake you."

"So then what?" Jade demands. "I'm not giving up on him so easily."

"I never expected you would." Maxum offers her a sad smile. "But we are *not* losing you for his sake. And he wouldn't want to hurt you again. He brought this fate onto himself by acting alone and outside of our pack."

I don't like victim blaming, but Maxum isn't wrong. Osen might have lived if he had kept us in the loop and had us as backup.

"Move out of my way." Jade waves Maxum aside.

I growl and grip her tighter.

She turns to face me, her face full of determination and irritation that I've prevented her from her objective.

"Let me see him. Now," she orders.

31

IT'S ALIVE

JADE

"Let me see him. Now," I snarl.

I'm not sure why I'm so pissed. I had been dreaming and hoping that Osen would join us in our life together, but now, he seems entirely lost to us.

I didn't even get to say goodbye.

Arran releases his hold, but still has a hand on my back to keep me stable as I shuffle to the coffin. I'm not okay. Maxum wasn't lying about Osen draining me. I used up a lot of magic just to get Osen's shadows out of Rob and into his rightful body.

From what Calder has told me during our lessons, I will get stronger with my magic as I use it. Like a muscle. But there is a maximum capacity for every individual in what they can take on. I'm just beginning my training, so I have only so much strength.

I gaze at Osen's handsome face, wishing I had a chance to kiss him in this life. To feel his strong hands hold my body. To feel him make love to me in this reality.

Is this really the end of what we have?

I'm fucking mad. I carried this guy around and was doing everything I could to make this right. But in the end, what I could offer was fleeting.

Calder will be heartbroken. Truly mourning his lover and mate.

I will have lost a potential mate and partner. Someone I was growing too fond of. Someone who I was spending my nights with during the sleeping hours. Talking and making love in his shadowscape world.

Tears stain my face. I've been so lost in grief that I didn't even realize I'm crying.

I wipe my tears from Osen's bare arm and find a current of something.

Him. His magic. His soul. But sluggish. He isn't stuck as I thought. He needs something to stir his life force.

An image of an old movie pops into my mind.

"Do you know one of the first science fiction books was written by a woman?" I ask.

"Mary Shelley," Maxum says confidently.

I eye him. "Knew her too, didn't you?"

Maxum shrugs. "Met her in passing."

This guy… acting like that isn't a big flipping whoop.

"We're talking about that later." I refocus back on the thread. "Frankenstein's monster was based on an idea at the time, bio-electric Galvanism."

"Don't they use a gigantic bolt of lightning in the movies?" Arran asks.

I hold up my hand, electricity sparks off my fingers. I reach down over with both hands, palms flat on Osen's broad chest, and send a bolt of electricity into him.

His body arcs and shakes. It looks more like I'm hitting him with a defibrillator than magic, but that's exactly what I'm hoping to do. Restart his heart.

I remember in medical dramas, they sometimes have to try a few times.

I stop the flow of electricity. "Maybe someone can breathe life into his lungs?" I look at Calder. Life-giving air from a phoenix seems fitting.

He rushes over and pinches Osen's nose, and blows a deep, intentional breath. He releases him, and I shock Osen's chest again.

Then we do it again.

His body arcs and rattles.

Then a gasp. An intake of air.

It's the most wonderful sound. I release my magic, and Osen flops back flat against the bottom of the coffin.

His eyes barely open. He takes in another ragged breath.

"Water!" Flint calls.

Maxum throws him a bottle from their stockpile down here. Flint splashes some over Osen's closed eyes and then tips the container to Osen's lips while Calder lifts his head.

They only wet his lips, then when Osen seems to be aware, they allow a few drops, then a mouthful into Osen. Finally, Osen swallows down the water.

His limbs don't seem to be working, but I'm hopeful about his ability to drink.

Osen blinks a few times, then gazes up to Calder's face, who's still hovering. He smiles, then turns his head toward me. Our eyes lock, and I feel the weight of the connection between us.

We have something few people, if any, have experienced. His hands lift slowly from his sides. One for Calder and one grasping for me.

"Thank you," he croaks out, his throat still horribly dry and his vocal cords unused.

"We have a modern-day Prometheus amongst us," Maxum says as he comes up behind me, kissing the top of my head. "Good job, my little demon."

I just fucking brought someone back to life. Dead for weeks, then not dead. I *did* just steal fire from the gods.

I hope they aren't going to be pissed.

But then the room swirls. I fall back into Arran. "I over-magicked."

Arran scoops me up into his arms, bridal style, and I let the world fade away.

"Rest, sweet mate."

When I awaken, I see we aren't in the bunker anymore. I don't know where we are. It's dark, but I can make out that I'm in a bedroom. I've been stripped down to my panties and bra. And a thin blanket has been thrown over me.

Osen is asleep beside me. The moonlight filtering through a window reveals Calder's silhouette sitting on a chair near our bed. He's watching us like some dark protector, flames burning low in his eyes.

"What's wrong?" I ask.

Calder rushes to the side on the bed's edge near my hip. His warm hand grazes down my cheek, over my hair, and settles over my heart. "Nothing. Everything."

"That doesn't help to clear things up," I say with a hopeful smirk.

"I want to be here with you both, but I also want to have my turn ripping Rob to shreds."

"I'm surprised he isn't dead already."

"I'm sure he wishes he was. The guys have shown him no mercy."

"Why aren't you helping them?" I ask.

"I found the sight of torture... triggering," he explains, and I nod in understanding.

Osen hasn't stirred with our conversation, and I worry. "How is he? What happened after I passed out?"

"He rallied enough to sit up and wiggle his toes. So that's good." Calder frowns. "We gave him a shower and some food. He passed out not long after. He still needs more time to heal. Unfortunately, I don't have healing magic beyond regenerating myself. And Maxum believes his sex magic only works on his true mate."

Hmm. He didn't mention that to me. I suppose he hadn't wanted to scare me before when he used it.

Then I remember. "Hold up. I healed Flint after we were attacked at the lake house. Maybe I can help now."

"We'll have to see if that will work, but should wait until you recover more." Calder narrows his eyes. "You're completely spent. And we still don't know what replenishes your magic. Other than time and rest."

Being a late-blooming freak has more drawbacks than I expected. I will have to figure out the replenishing thing soon. But since I'm not quite a proper witch, fae, or demon, I may never know.

"Why wouldn't my healing work on Osen?" I frown, studying Osen's profile in the low light.

"You had initiated a mating bond with Flint when you healed him. Some demon and fae have a healing ability... but only with their mates."

"Oh." I bite my lip. "And I haven't mate bonded with Osen."

Calder rubs the back of his neck, thinking. "But we don't know if you healing Flint was that or not. It will be worth a try when you're replenished, my flame."

I grin at his mating nickname. With my depleted magic and overall fatigue, I feel more like a little flickering candle, and not a roaring bonfire.

Curling up against Osen's side, I place my hand over his heart. A heart that wasn't beating yesterday.

His shallow breathing instantly becomes deeper.

I try to recall how it felt when I healed Flint. The need to take away his pain and suffering was overwhelming. All-consuming.

While I concentrate on Osen, I stir those same feelings. It seems ridiculous that we'd get this far, so close to having it all, for it to fail now.

He deserved better than dying alone in a dirty alleyway. He died fighting to protect his pack, his people, and innocent fae children from being killed by a fanatical group of witches and warlocks.

"Come on, Osen. I need you here. Calder needs you. I want to know what those lips feel like on mine. I want to be with you, all of you. Don't you fucking dare slip away now."

The pain of losing him before I even have him stings my eyes. Love thrums in my heart. A wave, a pulse of magic so pure radiates out of me and into his chest.

His body twitches, like he's waking up from the deepest sleep of his entire life.

"Sweet witch," Osen murmurs. "You're not getting rid of me anytime soon."

I exhale with relief. Joy springs inside my heart.

"Besides, I need to claim you and Calder, my mates. And I plan to show your pretty pussy a good time."

I bark out a laugh. "Because, of course, that's what a naughty incubus would have at the top of his to-do list."

"I'm not apologizing for my sexual desires. It *is* how we power up. But I've been aching to connect with you since the beginning. Instead, I had to sit back, watching all these other punks give you pleasure in the real world." He chuckles, then he rolls over to stare into my eyes. His charcoal eyes swirl with need. "But truly, I just want to make love to you without my damned powers."

"Powers or no powers, I want you too. I'll be here when you're ready." I pour more of my healing into his body because I can tell he's still suffering.

"I sense your reserves are low. You should stop giving me your magic."

I frown. I want him to be completely healed, but I remember touch and sex power him up, and I can do that. So I pull back my magic and sweep my hand over his chest.

"Do you think this healing means we're mate bonding already?" he asks, stroking my hand with his fingertips.

"We were bonded in a way. So maybe?" I shrug. "I'll have to try healing with someone who isn't a potential mate."

He hums thoughtfully. "Is it wrong that I don't want these beautiful hands on anyone but our pack?"

I roll my eyes. "I didn't say I was giving out hand jobs."

"Unfortunate, since that might help me right now," he says with a wink.

"How can I give you a hand job if your magic takes over and paralyzes me?"

"Oh, my shadows can keep your hand moving."

"That just sounds like fancy masturbation," I tease.

Calder laughs, and it draws our attention.

"Will you join us?" Osen asks, his voice cracking with vulnerability.

Calder gives me a sweet kiss. Then he goes around to Osen's other side and crawls into bed. His hand reaches over, stroking my arm, then he places his hand over mine that rests on Osen's chest.

Osen keeps his hands at his sides, not wanting to trigger Calder's PTSD.

Calder presses his forehead to Osen's temple and sighs. "I still can't believe you're back. I fear I will wake up from this dream and lose you all over again."

Suddenly, I feel like I'm invading their space. They deserve to have a moment for themselves.

I pull my hand free and roll over to get out of bed.

Hands are on me in an instant, dragging me backward over and between Osen and Calder's body. "Where do you think you're going?" Osen growls playfully.

"I was giving you a moment to reconnect."

"Why do you assume we'd want to do that alone?" Calder asks.

"Because I'm not so self-centered as to believe I should infiltrate the relationship that you have together."

"Too bad, because you're in it." Osen crashes his unyielding mouth over mine. He commands my entire being with a kiss. I know he isn't using his shadows, but it feels as if he's binding me to him, gripping my body and soul, drawing me to him. I'm being possessively dragged into his world. Claimed.

Now he possesses me from the outside, reaching in.

Osen breaks the kiss. Still cradling my face in his hands, he turns to claim Calder's lips. I have an intimate, front row ticket to the most passionate kiss I've ever witnessed before.

I don't feel left out. No, I feel my heart beating in time with theirs, sharing this moment of reconnection.

Calder then turns to me and gives me a consuming kiss like I'm the fuel to his flame. Our tongues stroke along each other, and it feels like the moment before an explosion.

Osen groans with delight.

My body is taut with need, and I rub my legs together to ease the searing burn of lust.

Osen slides his hand over my thigh and presses at the seam where they meet, running his fingers back up to my apex, grazing my sensitive lips through my underwear. "Fuck," he hisses. "I can feel how wet you are for us. Your panties are soaked."

"I need to check for myself," Calder says with a wicked grin. He runs his fingers down my stomach and over my mound. "Such a needy pussy. Maybe we should give it some relief?"

"Yes please," I beg.

Calder's fingers shift to talons, and he shreds my underwear with a few swipes. I gasp as it falls away in tatters. He cuts my bra where it joins between my breasts and the fabric slides to my sides, revealing my already hardening, aching nipples.

Calder and Osen each grasp one of my knees and they pull me open, my pussy exposed and glistening. Osen slides his fingers over my sensitive flesh.

I moan with how delicious it feels, and I don't think he's even using any incubus magic on me yet.

Calder joins in. Their fingers work in tandem, brushing over my clit and inner thighs, and teasing over my entrance.

Both lean down, laving and nipping at my tits as they plunge their fingers into my pussy. I cry out with the sudden invasion and then tilt my hips, inviting them to continue. To give me more.

They play thumb war over my clit and they're ramping me toward an orgasm.

Then, right as I'm about to crest and fall off that cliff, they both pull their fingers free. Locking his heated gaze onto me, Calder sucks on his fingers and hums.

"I need to taste you," Osen growls into my neck. "From the source." He slides down the bed and plunges his face into my wet heat. His tongue delves deep inside, then he laps at my clit before inserting his fingers once again.

Calder squeezes my breasts, pinching my nipples so perfectly it's like he's been trained his whole life in how I enjoy it.

Osen whispers over my lower lips, "Come all over my face, sweet monster." Then he feasts on my pussy like a man possessed. Well, as no longer a ghost possessing me.

Calder claims my mouth as I whimper and moan.

I fist Osen's long hair, and he groans with pleasure. I had a feeling he'd like it a bit rough and passionate.

His fingers curve, rubbing along that sensitive spot inside me, and my toes curl in response. Then I'm shouting at the heavens with my release. I float through the cosmos, pleased that I've finally found my loves.

I'm quaking in their hold when I return to my body.

"Wait!" I gasp, realizing something that feels off.

I was able to move. Calder was moving, too.

"Why aren't you using your shadows? Why am I not paralyzed? Is your incubus magic not working?"

Osen smiles and his entire face lights up like the sun when the clouds finally part. "My magic is being fed, but not with intention."

I glance at Calder, remembering the frustration that Osen's magic always took over and Calder was immobilized during sexual encounters. "I thought if you were sexually excited, it just happened." Then that rejected part of me rears its head. It's one thing for him to sex me up when I was his only source, and he was only in my mind. But in real life, it appears the spark just isn't strong enough. "Oh, you aren't enjoying this very much?"

Feeling ridiculous, I try to close my legs and wiggle away, but Osen is solidly between them, his face hovering over my crotch.

"Stop," Osen growls, holding my legs open and my thighs against his shoulders. "Remember, I figured my incubus paralysis magic wouldn't work on you in the real world because of your demon magic. Believe me, I'm very much enjoying this and am fighting my release with all I have."

Still not one hundred percent believing him, I ask, "But what about Calder?"

"Your bond, our bond, when I was inside you, has given him immunity, too."

"Oh!" I smile excitedly. "So you can be together in any way you like now?"

"I believe so," Osen says, kissing my inner thigh, making goosebumps race along my flesh. "Thank you for that."

"Will you be able to use your shadow magic on us at all?" I ask. I sort of wanted to play with that sometimes.

Two shadowtendrils shoot out of his body and wrap around my wrists, pinning me down. It's just like extensions of his body, but I can still wiggle and squirm.

I grin, wanting to give in to this some more, but I also feel I have a responsibility to give Osen and Calder a moment to figure out what all this means for them.

I tilt my head. "Are the other guys here?" When they nod, I say. "I think I'm going to get something to eat and give you both a moment alone."

The shadows slip away. "What? You sure?" Osen crinkles his forehead in confusion. "We want you. Here with us. Between us."

"I want you both too. But I want you both to figure out how I fit in with what you have. You need to discuss your boundaries with me, with each other. I'm not going to assume that because we have bonds, it means a free for all. When you've decided how I fit with this, I will be here for you both in whatever way you decide."

"You don't have to leave for us to talk about this," Calder argues.

I kiss both on the lips and sigh. "Yeah, I do. I won't pressure you. And I don't want you to regret anything with me."

Osen captures the back of my head, pulling me to look into his gorgeous, haunting gray eyes. "How could I ever regret being with you?"

"You're not the only one in this room," I remind him and pull away, leaving them to work out how their new lives together will be.

32

IT'S NOT ME, IT'S YOU

JADE

*W*alking out of the bedroom, I find myself in a cozy, small, unfamiliar house made of stone and mud, like an ancient building with old-world plaster.

Magic seems to flow around my body, caressing me, and I suspect we are in the fae realm.

The strong metallic scent of blood fills my senses. When did I get a detective nose like that? I suppose being a supe comes with its perks. Although I don't know if smelling blood is a perk.

I hear the thud of someone being punched. When I come to the end of the hallway, I discover Maxum, Flint, and Arran towering over Rob who's been strapped to a chair.

With all that's happened with Osen's return to the living, I'd almost forgotten about that asshole. I'm glad I put on Calder's shirt before I left the bedroom. Not that Rob hasn't seen all my merchandise, but I'd rather not have his eyes on me again, especially like that. Besides, I'm sure my possessive monsters would throw a fit.

Maxum swings his head around to eye me entering the room. His wild gaze travels up and down my body, lingering on my exposed legs.

He blocks Rob's line of sight to me. Not that Rob is even aware of his surroundings.

Maxum grabs a long robe and wraps it around my shoulders. Where the hell did he materialize that from? "I don't want you here for this. Though if you insist, we don't want him seeing your body."

I snicker to myself. Apparently, even showing my legs is too much for them to bear.

Maxum steps out of the way as I tie the robe at my waist and move closer.

The torture session is set up in the kitchen area. Tiled floors will make it easier to clean up the mess. My eyes scan Rob for his various injuries. His clothes are in scraps, dangling off him. He's missing chunks of skin on his legs and arms. One eye is swollen shut, and a couple of fingers have been cut off. His flesh is marbled with fresh bruises and lined with cuts and claw marks.

His head hangs listlessly to the side, unconscious.

I study the damage already done, and I don't feel one ounce of sympathy for him. In fact, I hope he suffers a bit more for all the damage he's caused. The pacifist in me is not reporting for duty, not for him. He hurt me for years, more than I ever knew. He had a shifter warlock masquerading as my pet. He used me, shoving ghosts into my mind and interrogating them through me. Abused me while I was under his spell, convincing me I was worthless and unlovable. Then he stole my magic to create dark spells to kill Osen and who knows how many others.

Arran's hands have shifted into his werewolf claws and his canines are poking out from his mostly human face. Serky is fighting to make an appearance and slaughter my ex.

On the surface, Flint appears calm, but through our bond his rage seeps through. I know he's trying to protect me, but he needn't worry about that. My rage is brewing to a pitch-black cup of revenge the longer I'm in this room.

I remember how Rob couldn't just let me go when I broke up with him and moved on and started dating Arran. Instead, he almost killed me in my home when trying to exorcise Osen. When I ran, he hunted me down in the alleyway, intending to expel Osen again and hurting Calder. Then he came for me at the lake house to abduct me, almost killing Flint.

There will be no mercy for Rob and no letting him go. He won't stop. It's us or him. He doesn't deserve a chance. He wouldn't give me one.

"Have you got anything out of this douche canoe?" I ask, my voice deadly cold.

"A few glimpses," Maxum answers, glaring at Rob. "He has strong mental walls. I'll give him that."

"We're trying to break them down," Flint informs me. "If Maxum pushes too hard, it will melt Rob's brain."

"We might only get one answer if I do that," Maxum adds, resting his hands on his hips.

Arran snarls at Rob, and I pick up that my wolf shifter is perfectly on board with melting my ex's brain.

I drag over a chair, place it about ten feet in front of Rob, and sit down, waiting for the show to resume.

"This will not be pretty, Heartstone," Flint warns.

"I understand."

We wait until Rob is just coming around. From behind, Maxum brackets Rob's head between his hands, his eyes gaze off to the middle distance as he dives into Rob's memories.

"If he wakes, ask him questions," Maxum instructs, hands still in place, but his lip is curled in disgust at having to touch the bastard.

Rob blinks his eyes open and lifts his head. His eyes land on me instantly, and he glowers. "I recognized you were trash as soon as I met you."

Flint and Arran growl, but I hold up my hand for them to stop.

"I knew you were about as useful as a cup of piss in a shitstorm, but you used magic to make me put up with your flaccid... *personality*. Besides, I wasn't the one pursuing the whole fucked up relationship now, was I? So what does that make you?"

"You think you're better than me? You're a mutt, an abomination."

"It's sure funny how worthless you claim I am, but you needed me for your little world domination scheme."

"Useless other than as a weapon."

"Weapons are often more important than those who wield them. You think Galiana will be upset when you're dead? No, she'll probably be relieved that a problem has been taken off her hands... well, other than losing Osen's magic. You're nothing but a pathetic pawn to her. A replaceable one at that."

"Shut your whore mouth," Rob spits out.

He gets a solid punch to the gut for that outburst from Flint.

I sense Rob is so filled with rage and focused on arguing with me that his walls are dropping, so I question him, hoping to make him think about the things we'd like to know.

"Do you believe Galiana was going to keep you around after she had me in her clutches?"

"She's figured out how to claim your powers permanently. Then she'll throw your dead body out with the garbage."

"And then what?" I demand. "She kills off all the supes? What's the point of this madness?"

"They're stealing our magic, so we're going to end them before they end us."

"We aren't stealing magic, you fool," Flint growls.

"We both know that isn't true. You think we didn't hear about what happened in the fae realm? We know that was just the beginning of the fae's plot to control all the magic in the realms. So we found a way for us to do it too."

"Stealing Jade's ability." Flint glances over at me.

"Fight fire with fire." Rob looks smug for someone with one foot dangling in the grave.

"How many others know about me?" I ask, worrying that I might never get to rest.

Rob bites his lip and refuses to speak, but I can tell by Maxum's raised eyebrow he's got an answer.

Then the question that has been burning in the back of my mind rises to the surface. "How did you and Galiana find me? I thought I was hidden by the pendant."

"You're so stupid." Rob laughs. "And so was your traitorous mother."

His insults bounce right off me. Why should he rile me with his hateful words? His actions prove he's only worth the time to make sure he's dead soon.

It irritates me that he knew my true origins before I did.

Great job, abuela. Ugh. It was so hard to get that she wasn't my grandmother at all. And although she was my biological mother, she wasn't really my mom. Even my sister didn't do a great job being a mom.

I sometimes wonder how I can be a kind and loving person when I didn't have a good example. Can't say I feel very loving right now.

"It's in your nature, your soul, to be loving," Flint says through our mental link, reading my thoughts like a book. *"Sometimes it isn't nurture that makes us who we end up being."*

"Well, I want blood now," I say aloud for Arran and Maxum to hear. "It pisses me off what this bastard and Galiana did to me. And they hurt you guys."

"It's your revolting, violent fae and demon blood that make you a savage," Rob says.

I laugh heartily at that. "I wasn't a savage until you fucked with me. You prove witches and warlocks can easily be revolting and violent. Savage." I bite back a burst of fury from the injustices I've endured. "Do you think forcing a spell on me to be your girlfriend was anything less than sexual assault? And you call these guys monsters?"

"Believe me, I didn't enjoy being with you other than laughing about how I'd stolen your power."

I stand up, my limit reached with his bullshit. It stings even if I don't want it to. I wish I had thick enough skin that the thought of him touching me didn't make me want to scrub my flesh from my bones. "I'm done here. In case there's any doubt, you were so vile that I dumped your ass even while under your dark magic spell."

Rob opens his mouth with a rebuttal.

"We can kill him now," Maxum announces.

Rob's flustered, red face pales instantly. "You need me," he pleads to stall his fate.

"I *never* needed you," I snarl in his face.

Maxum grips Rob's head, and Rob screams.

"Keep your psychic guard up to block his ghost," Flint warns.

Rob's eyes bulge with pain and turn glassy as the life drains from his body. For a moment, I'm tempted to destroy his soul, but I don't feel like it's my place to go that far. I sense karma will come for him in the afterlife.

I see a gray wisp slip into the astral plane and beyond.

Finally, I'm free of him, but I know there's at least one more person we need to eliminate before we can relax.

"Are you okay?" Calder comes up behind me from the bedroom, his hand landing gently on my lower back.

Osen is right beside us, glaring at the warlock who stole everything from him.

"Not yet. But I'll be better when we take out Galiana." My jaw is set with my determination. Then I soften as I look at Osen. "You?"

He nods. "We can talk later." He presses a kiss on my temple.

"Jade's right," Maxum says as he washes Rob's blood off his hands in the kitchen sink. "We need to cut off the head of the snake."

"Did you get any intel?" Osen asks as he walks up to Rob's corpse and shoves his chair over, so the body crashes to the floor with a wet thump.

"A bit." Maxum frowns, drying his hands on a dainty tea towel. "The good news is that it doesn't appear that Galiana trusted many people with her plan to use Jade's magic. There is one other witch I saw briefly flash in Rob's mind. Not even Floofers knew all that was going on with you, just the mediumship, not the unique powers."

"But how did they even find Jade in the first place?" Arran demands, his werewolf quelled, relaxing with the death of the warlock.

"When you asked him about that, I saw your books," Maxum says to me. "Do you know why that might be?"

I shake my head, but I think about his question. How could my books lead them to me?

"Even before I met Rob, I had weird dreams. So I was probably seeing a ghost's memories. Maybe I wrote about something that happened in real life? But even then, I'd be shocked if witches are reading smut by an indie author. Besides, it isn't like I just wrote verbatim what happened in my dreams. Or... I don't think I did."

"We can't rule that out completely." Maxum gives me a grin and a wink. "It's a great excuse to take the time to read your books like I've been meaning to."

It's so weird it makes me jittery to think of him reading my work. Maybe because it's a whole different kind of vulnerability. Authors pour their souls into their worlds, often giving up a normal life. And for those keen enough to read between the lines, they can see past the words and right inside an author's being—their wounds, healed and unhealed.

I worry Maxum won't like my writing... that he won't like the parts that are me.

"Time to take out the trash." Osen bends to drag Rob's body out of the house.

"No," Calder snaps, catching his arm. "Go. Rest. We can deal with this."

Osen grumbles, but takes my fingers in his and gently guides me back to the bedroom. "You could use some rest too, sweet monster."

33

TOGETHER SEPARATELY

JADE

I'm in a bit of a daze as Osen leads me back to the bedroom.

Watching Rob die was a mind-fuck. I think that's the first time I watched a human's life force leave their body. The effect was eerie, but oddly, I don't feel upset by it.

Now, an animal dying, especially a pet, would have me ripping my hair out and tears flowing until I was gasping for breath. Perhaps it's because an animal is pure, whereas Rob was corrupt.

A weight in my heart has been lifted. He was a threat to me and my guys, and to the supe population at large. I will no longer have to fear him breaking into my home and hurting me.

Osen leads me over to the bed, but stops me before I crawl in. I realize just how tall he really is as he towers over me. He's not as broad or as tall as Maxum or Flint, but definitely six-three with an athletic build. His long, brown hair drapes over the tops of his shoulders with a soft wave. His hypnotic gray eyes are light right now and not the dark charcoal of when he's feeding.

His fingertips trace the planes of my face as he studies me like I study him.

"It's strange to see you like this. In real life." He places a feathery kiss on my forehead. "You're more beautiful than you believe you are in your mind."

"And you look a whole lot better alive," I say with a smirk.

Osen's hands skim down my neck, and he slowly pulls the robe down and off my shoulders and unties the belt, letting it fall to the floor. He pulls the shirt over my head. Then his hands slide over my breasts, admiring me, then around my waist. He draws me close, dropping his head down to give me a soul searing kiss.

"I don't have the words to communicate how much I appreciate what you did for me. Being so kind to me when I was possessing you, then risking yourself to bring me back from the dead." He twists a lock of my silver hair around a finger. "And now, to be able to touch you and Calder... to love you both the way you deserve... it's beyond any fantasy I could have had about how this would turn out."

I'm blushing at his words. I suppose I've never been great with compliments. "I'm happy you're here with your pack." I pause, and then ask what I've been curious about. "Did you and Calder talk about what you both want moving forward?"

"We did." Osen steps toward me, further encroaching on my space.

I back up a bit. It's intimidating, having his commanding presence here in real life. My legs hit the edge of the bed, and my ass lands on the soft mattress behind me.

I look up, my gaze hungrily traveling up his bare muscular chest to his handsome face. I'm keenly aware that my mouth is almost level with the bulge in his pants.

His fingers comb through my hair and massage the back of my head as he gazes down at me adoringly.

I swallow as the silence continues. "And?"

"Do you really believe we wouldn't want you in any way you'd let us have you?" he asks.

I place my hands on his narrow hips and say, "That's not exactly what I was wondering."

"I think it is." Osen drops his pants, and his erect cock appears in 3D, not far from my face as I take in his thickness. "Calder and I don't want boundaries between us. Between all three of us. We'd like to continue our individual relationships, *and* we'd like to have a relationship that is all three of us being intimate together."

"I like the sound of that, but I'm worried. You already have an established relationship that I might intrude upon when I don't mean to."

"It isn't just about Calder and me together. We both will want alone time with you, too." His fingers tickle under my chin, and I smile. "We will need to make it clear if we need alone time with a certain person, such as a date or sex. And if there's no designated parameters, then the third person is free to join in."

"So if I stumble in on you fucking, I can just grab a dick and play?"

Osen growls with need. "That sounds amazingly hot. I might have to find ways to get *caught* by either of you."

My stomach gurgles, and I chuckle. "With the whole Rob torture display, I forgot to eat."

"I have something for you to eat." He waves his cock in front of my face.

"Uh, no offense." I smirk. "But I need more than a protein shake." Although I'd love to indulge in this, my shoulders slump. I'm feeling the fatigue again from all the magic that has been pushed through me. I wouldn't be able to actively participate in sex right now. I doubt I even have it in me to orgasm at all.

The bedroom door swings open, and Flint bustles in with a food tray filled with all sorts of treats. He fully ignores the naked sexual energy of Osen towering over me. "In bed, both of you," he orders, then places the tray over my lap when I comply. "Eat." He folds his arms and stands there like a warden about to force feed us. "Osen, I remember you enjoyed almond butter and fig jam sandwiches." He points to the plate with two sandwiches stacked on it.

"Thanks, brother." Osen smiles widely and moans when he bites into it.

I eat some crackers and cheese, washing it down with some apple juice. Osen shares a bite of his sandwich with me, and I can tell by Flint's surprised expression it isn't a normal thing for the incubus to do.

"Why do you look shocked?" I ask Flint through our special mental link.

"Incubi don't share food from their plates unless it's with a mate. I didn't realize his feelings for you were so profound. Even with Calder, he never shared before."

"So it seems I was meant to be with all of you."

"Fated, my Heartstone. I suppose I'm still surprised my entire pack is blessed with such a perfect mate."

Not long after Osen and I finish our meal, Maxum, Arran, and Calder strut into the bedroom. The space isn't tiny, but it feels like that now with all the massive, muscly males crammed inside.

"Is he gone?" I ask, staring at my four beautiful guys standing in a line.

Arran rushes over and nuzzles into my cheek. "All gone. We've cleaned the house and our bodies of his slimy presence."

I wrap my arms around Arran's neck and breathe in his freshly showered scent of lightning storms and sage. "Where are we?"

"It's a property of an old friend," Maxum says. "He offered it to me as a safe house in return for a favor I did for his mate. It's good in a pinch, but we shouldn't stay here long."

"Why?"

"We're in the fae realm. There are too many nosey creatures that might sense your unusual magic since you're no longer contained."

I pat at my neck, realizing the concealment talisman is gone. It must have been lost in the fight with Rob at the cafe.

Then panic takes over. "What about my computer?"

"Right here, Heartstone." Flint points to the corner of the room. "I made sure to grab it."

"Thank you." My pulse returns to a normal pace.

I shift to get out of bed, and Maxum charges over, blocking me in. "What are you doing?"

"I thought we had to go because of my weirdo magic."

His large crimson hand palms my jaw, and he inspects my face and aura. "You're much more drained than you're letting on. Rest some more."

I throw out my lower lip in a pout. "I'm fine. I won't draw more attention than necessary if I can help it."

"Flint and I will create a few measures to dissuade anyone from coming too close." Maxum brushes his thumb over my still pouting lip. "In the meantime, you actually need sleep, no slumber party chats or playing hide the shadowcock with the incubus."

"Dude, don't shadowcock block me," Osen jokes and gives his friend a lopsided grin.

"Fine. I'll rest," I concede.

Maxum helps me slide on underwear and a large t-shirt that smells like Arran's.

Thankfully, the bed is enormous, and we have enough room for Calder and Arran to join Osen and me for a nap.

Because that's all it's going to be... a short, little nap.

34

FEED ME, MI AMOR

OSEN

I hold my sweet savior and future mate, and she reluctantly falls asleep telling me, "Just a little, tiny nap."

But it isn't a little nap. Jade falls so deep, so fast that I can't even snag her subconscious to bring her into my shadowscape with me.

My magic is slowly replenishing with the intimate moments we've had since I was been brought back to life, but it's not quite enough to fill my magical pockets. I'm barely hanging on to my sanity and my life. I don't want to push Jade or Calder, and I definitely don't want to make them feel like they are only a meal to me.

It hasn't been easy. I suppose I've failed and pushed some already.

Instead of falling asleep and resting with her like I should, I study Jade's gorgeous face, and my heart swells with the gratitude I feel for her.

She didn't need to forgive me after I took advantage of her trust. Yet she helped me come back and made sure my relationship with Calder was going to survive.

I wouldn't have faulted her if she had turned her back on me or blatantly hoarded Calder for herself.

It's an incubi gift to sense the emotions of others, since we feed off powerful emotions, too. With my special sight, I can see this woman glows with magic but also from the massive amount of love in her soul.

I've never been one to feed from emotion, preferring the spicy flavors of sex.

Except now, my death seems to have changed me, and I'm just as willing to feast on experiencing the love that pours from this woman into our pack.

I want to claim her. I want to make her cry out my name as I make her come over and over on my cock. I *am* an incubus after all. The shadowsex we had in her mind was wonderful, but it isn't the same as feeling the warmth of her skin and the subtle, involuntary reactions of her body. I want to smell the fragrance of our combined releases. I want to taste the desire of her body on my tongue and in my soul.

I want her. Completely.

The guys have accused me of being obsessive, and they aren't wrong.

And Jade is my new obsession.

I'll have to remember to share. Just not today.

As soon as she wakes, I'm going to fuck her into oblivion. When I'm done, she won't remember her own name.

Consent… I must remember to get consent.

I haven't told her yet, but I need to. My shadows are already bonding with her. She is mine. If she were to reject that bond, I'd be torn into pieces and set adrift in the darkness.

I cannot live in darkness anymore. No, I need my lightbringer for my shadow. And she can truly be my shadowmate. I know a trace of my magic still resides inside her. I didn't mean to leave it behind, but I don't think it's an accident. Maybe some part of her wanted to keep me with her.

I hope that's it.

Jade snores softly, and I chuckle like it's the cutest thing in the world. I suppose it's precious because of what it means. She trusts me—enough to have me inside her body and to be vulnerable with me. That's a big fucking deal. I don't even think my pack ever trusted me completely.

Calder didn't.

If he did, then he would have come to me when he was broken.

He trusted Jade more than me, even when he didn't know her to be anything other than a witch—a witch who might have killed me, no less.

Fuck. What *does* that say about me?

Guilt swims in my mind as I remember how I behaved before my death. I was secretive, stubborn, hotheaded, and reckless. I deserved to be the one cursed as a berserker more than Arran did, which is saying something.

I have to do better. For Jade. For Calder. For all of them. Earn their unwavering trust again.

I must fall asleep for a while. When I open my eyes again, the only light in the room is from the moon leaking in through the window.

Jade shifts against my body, electrifying me in a way that should be illegal. She groans when she wakes herself up. Her half-lidded eyes blink slowly, trying to remember where she is. "Osen?"

I squeeze her to my chest and kiss her forehead. "Here, my sunshine."

She grins sleepily and nuzzles into me. "What the hell is on my legs?" she says in a wary tone.

I glance down and see Arran in his wolf form, curled up and pinning down her feet with his huge body.

"Beast," I laugh. Then I see Maxum on her other side.

A hand slides over my hip, and I instantly recognize Calder's touch.

"Where's Flint?" Jade asks with a worried tone.

"Patrolling the area to make sure no one sneaks up on the house," Maxum grunts, and grinds his hips into Jade's ass.

"Who's going to guard my ass against your sneak attack?" she jokes.

"The only one with the authority to do so… *you*." He kisses her shoulder. "But go back to sleep for now. I promise I won't invade."

"I'm awake now." Jade sighs, rubbing the sleep from her eyes. "I'm overheated with the living wolf blanket."

Arran's wolf whimpers, but Jade sits up and gives his ears a good rub and coos over him like he's an innocent puppy and not the apex predator he is.

Beast is eating it up, thumping his tail against the bed, rattling all of us with the beat. I sense Arran isn't immune to her sweet talk, either.

"I'll get up with Jade," I offer.

Calder moves out of the way, and I drag Jade out from under a bratty wolf who refuses to lift off her legs.

I help her to her feet, and she says with a bit of amusement, "I've lost feeling."

"You can't lay on her like that," I reprimand.

The wolf covers his snout with his paws in shame. Fuck, even I know that's adorable.

"It's okay, sweetie," Jade says to him in a baby voice.

I lift her into my arms, and she squeaks at the unexpected action.

"I won't have you fall down on my watch." I carry her out of the bedroom and set her down on the long couch in the living area. I sit beside her and lift her legs into my lap and massage her feet. After a minute, I ask, "Better?"

She sits silently, staring at me with a strange look on her face.

"What? Something wrong?"

"No. It's just weird having you here. Really here." She quickly adds, "Not in a bad way."

I'm irritated by that comment, and I'm not sure why. Though when I think about it, I realize she's correct. It *is* weird.

I pinch my lips together, feeling awkward for the first time in my entire existence.

"What is it?" she asks. "Did I upset you?"

"I... I don't know how to be *me* anymore." I turn my face away, trying to hide my inadequacies.

"Hey?" Jade leans forward and with a gentle finger, she guides me to look at her. "You can talk to me. No judgment."

"I'm a selfish asshole most of the time. I fed off Calder and others only when it served me. And now..." I choke up and stop talking.

"What's different now?" she prompts in a soft voice.

"I don't want to be just a magical sex leech." I rub my eyes and feel the sting of tears. What the fuck? I don't cry. Shit. This must be the influence from dying and being trapped in someone who's actually in touch with their emotions.

When I don't go on, Jade says, "From what I've seen, you weren't *'just'* anything. Your pack meant more to you than a meal ticket. And they loved you too. You were a complex person with a full range of traits, both good and bad. Just like everyone else."

I sigh long and hard. "Jade, you don't realize that I'm the monster other monsters fear. I can destroy a person, get past any locks, and dive into any mind and bend them to my will. I have consumed people whole, leaving them an empty husk. I can rip the dirtiest secret from someone's thoughts or drive them to madness. I am *the* monster. And I'd understand if you broke the bond building between us now that I'm explaining this all to you." I look into her eyes, trying to implore her to grasp the truth in my words. "At my core... I'm just a monster who uses people for sex and magic."

"Are you though?" She frowns like she knows something I don't. "Tell me this, are your powers working?"

"Yes," I answer warily.

"Then why haven't you fed off me yet? Or Calder?" she asks. "If you were a mindless sex-machine monster, then you would have pressured me into sexual feeding or you could have *forced* us, as you say, but you haven't done that."

"Yeah, but..."

"No more buts. I need to hear what *you* want to be in this new life of yours. And don't tell me what you *think* I want to hear." She sits back and waits for me to answer.

I take a long moment to consider truly what I hope for. "I'd like to finally participate in life. During my death, I got a taste of how removed I really was. I had time to reflect on how I always pushed my pack away. But now, I want to be a proper mate to you and Calder. Sure, I was loyal to the pack, but I didn't participate. Engage. I mean... did I really know Flint at all? Not really. I want to truly know them. Be there for them." I shake my head, feeling like the asshole I am. "I'd like to be someone you come to for comfort and love. And I'd like it in return."

"And sex?"

"I mean, I'm not going to turn down sex with you and Calder," I confess. "But I don't want that to be the only connection between us."

"It isn't," she says, like it's a fact. Perhaps she's right. "We are connected through a freaking crazy bond of our souls and our experiences. We have spent hours in the shadowscape just talking."

I pull her into my lap and kiss her like she is my very soul that I need to merge with. Not for a feeding but because she's my mate.

"It's okay to ask for what you need in a relationship," she says, soothing me with soft strokes of her fingers over my brow and jaw. "Are you hungry?"

I growl with need. "Yes." My mouth crashes over hers, and I murmur as I claim her, pulling her to me. "I'm hungry for your body, but I also hunger for your love. I want to devour you so I can keep you safe inside me. I want to give you the worlds and share all the beauty in them with you." My lips brush over hers. "I love you, Jade."

"I love you too."

I pull her underneath me on the couch and cage her in with my body. I could use my shadows to pin her down, but I want her hands on me. Having her as a partner is a revelation. Only Maxum could thwart my paralytic power with his demon energy, not that we were physical very often. And now, Jade can give me that blessing and, by extension, give me Calder in a new way.

"How do you want me, sweet witch?" I ask, nipping at her lips.

"How do you want me?" she counters. "You know I can take pretty much anything you offer. Although I don't think I can deal with being whipped with a cane."

I chuckle darkly. "I might want to spank your plump ass, but I'll never want to chance leaving a permanent scar on you. Besides, I doubt this house is equipped with a full arsenal of toys."

My hand slips down between us and under her waistband.

Jade grips my biceps and squirms as my fingers find her wet center gliding over her clit. I press forward and sink two thick fingers into her cunt.

She lets out a tiny gasp, trying to be quiet for the others.

"Make as much noise as you need to," I growl. "I want them to know how much you enjoy me fucking you."

"Yes, sir," she says with a smirk.

My shadows slide around her throat, and her eyes widen. I hold her with enough tension for her to feel it, but not so much that she can't breathe.

My lips claim hers and our tongues stroke against each other. My fingers pump into her wet heat with an obscene squelch of how needy she is for me.

I lift up her shirt. Two more shadowtendrils slide under, winding around her breasts, squeezing in time with my thrusts. She undulates into my hand, taking as much as I'm giving and more.

Curling my fingers and circling her clit with my thumb, I bring her to a climax. Her body shudders and she moans, clenching around my fingers. "More. I need to feel your cock inside me."

"As you wish," I pull back, tearing her underwear from her body.

She pulls her shirt over her head, revealing her full delicious breasts, while I yank off my sweatpants.

My shadows seep out of my body, reaching for her, needing her.

She purrs with delight when she studies my muscular body and monstrous incubus tentacles in the moonlight. "You're beautiful," she says with awe.

I blush at her praise. I don't think I've ever had anyone say that about me before. Certainly never about my paralyzing shadows ready to pounce, claiming a victim.

Is she a victim?

I wasn't lying. I am the true monster in the pack. Yes, the others have killed and maimed, but they're also honest about it. I've manipulated and bullied. Even Maxum, with all his demon nature, wouldn't have blatantly used people the way I have. He just kills them by ripping them to shreds or scrambling their brains. But never for fun, always with a purpose.

When I was killed and shoved into Jade's mind, I changed. Perhaps it had a lot to do with being separated from my magic and my body.

I don't want to be the monster I once was.

Can I learn to be giving and compassionate? I was able to when I was inside Jade. Can I do the same at her side?

"Um… should I call you handsome instead?" Jade asks, biting her lip and watching me with a vulnerable expression.

She is bare to me in every way. I spent all this time getting to know her. After talking and dreaming together every night, I know her better than the others do. She might even know me better than all of them put together, too.

Fear crawls up my spine and constricts my airway.

Will I fuck this up?

"Call me anything you'd like," I say with a lopsided grin, pushing past my insecurities. If I plan to make this work, I need to be honest. It's what Jade values above almost everything else. "Goddess, I don't deserve you."

"Because you've done bad things?" she asks, reading me like a damned book.

"Am I that predictable?"

"I know you, Osen. And yeah, you're playing hard into the '*Am I Redeemable?*' trope right now," she says with a wicked grin.

I cross my arms over my chest, and her eyes eat up the sight of my muscles. It makes my dick ache with pride and the need to satisfy her.

"Poking fun at the recently dead guy, huh?" I tease back, but with an edge so she can sense I'm not completely joking.

"You can poke me." She points to her vagina. "Right here is a good spot. Or here." She indicates her mouth and licking her lips. "Dealer's choice."

I bark out a laugh. Because yeah, she's antagonizing a monster incubus into having sex with her. It's ridiculous.

Without warning, I descend on her. My hands wrap around her thick thighs as I wrench them wider for me so I can dive into her wet pussy. My shadows capture her hands and hold her down. I kiss the living hell out of her.

I pull back and see her eyes are wild with lust. "Is this what you want? Me to fuck you like a madman? To lose my mind?"

"Yes!" She heaves her chest up to rub against my torso. "Fuck me like you need to."

I slam into her channel, and she sucks in a breath. Her cunt flutters around my length, adjusting to my thickness. I slide out slowly to the tip, then thrust back into her. And again.

Her eyes roll back into her head with each thrust as I grind against her clit.

She murmurs my name over and over, thrashing her head back and forth while I work her into a manic state, edging her with my calculated rhythm.

My magic feeds on her sexual excitement. My shadows torment her with a mix of gentle and gripping touches, sipping her pleasure like a fine vintage.

"Please, Osen," she cries, panting beneath me.

My mate is a beautiful mess, writhing and sweaty with need.

"Please *what*?" I ask, biting her lip and then sucking the pain away.

"Please, let me come."

I release her hands, and they are instantly on my body, searching and exploring every hard plane of my flexing chest and arms as I pound into her. Nails dig into my back, carving her will into me.

My own desire unleashes inside me. I lose all restraint and fuck her with abandon. The couch rocks into the wall with each of my thrusts. It's as if I'm trying to crawl back inside her body through her pussy. I want to be one with her again.

"Jade..." I grit out as her body clenches around my cock, milking me.

As I spill inside her, I gaze into her glowing green eyes and discover a bliss I've never experienced in all my years. I feel truly, unconditionally loved.

My shadows soak up all the pleasure, the desire, the love we've created together. The energy around it is unmatched... like it's a work of art.

I absorb all her affection and feed that dark place in my heart that has been closed off for far too long.

My shadows intertwine with her soul's brilliant light. We bond. Light and dark. Yin and yang. The other side of the same coin.

She is my perfect shadowmate.

We are the two in one.

I just hope I haven't cursed her by being linked to me.

35

GROUP DYNAMICS

JADE

*B*eing with Osen in real life is… intense.

I can't say if it's the merging of what felt like our essence, or if it's doing things that have only taken place in my mind, but the energy between us feels different. Binding.

His eyes swirl with dark gray clouds as he hovers above me. He hums and gives me sweet little pecks over my face, admiring me and cooing sweet *somethings*. Because they aren't sweet nothings. No. Nothing he does is nothing.

Especially when it comes to affection. In all my visions of him, he'd never shown this warm intimacy. But I had only seen him with guys. Maybe it's different because I'm a woman.

He lifts off me and sits back on his heels as he admires his cum leaking out of me. His fingers push it back inside.

"*Fuuuuck me,*" someone hisses in the room.

We both snap our gazes over to see Calder with his cock out, stroking himself and watching us. His eyes are filled with desire and angst. He wants to be smack dab in the middle of this.

"You enjoy seeing our mate well-fucked?" Osen asks as he sinks his fingers into my pussy, pressing his release back inside me.

"With all five of us, it's going to be her constant state of being," Calder says with a cocky grin.

"Looks like you could use some love too," I say, beckoning him closer with hooded eyes and a curling finger.

"Come here. Both of you. On your knees," Calder orders.

Osen and I share a surprised look because dom-Calder is fifty shades of hot.

"Wait," he says with a wicked grin. "First, lick that cream from her pussy and bring it over here and use it when you suck my cock."

I spread my legs wider, and Osen takes his sweet time, licking up his cum from my center. Then he knee-walks over to Calder. I follow right after, eager to see this play out and show them my love.

Calder presses the tip of his cock to Osen's lips. "Paint my dick with your releases."

Osen slides Calder deep inside his mouth and when he pulls back, Calder is slick with our essence.

Calder turns for me to take him in my mouth.

I taste the mixture of our salty, tangy sex and groan with the pure debauchery.

"Jade, up," our phoenix orders.

I stand, and Calder claims my lips and dives in, savoring all of us. He grabs the back of Osen's head and guides him to continue sucking his cock and taking him right to the root.

"Osen, you better feed off me, too. Understand?" Calder says with a commanding tone that sends shivers down my spine.

Osen swallows Calder into his throat like the pro he is and hums his agreement. His whole body swirls with shadows as his power is ignited by our lust.

Calder kisses me, running his hand down my body and squeezing my tits. Then he smacks my ass before coating his fingers in my slick and plunging them inside me.

I whimper against his mouth, and he consumes the sound.

"Goddess, yes." He grunts. "I almost came when I was watching you together. But this is so much better."

I notice Osen's shadows aren't binding Calder. He's careful not to trigger his PTSD and keeps his touch light. And so do I. My hands are on his chest and bicep as he works up to his release.

"Fuck!" Calder shouts, thrusting into Osen's face. After his ridiculously long climax subsides (thank you incubus power), he pulls Osen to his feet and pants with such joy. "I love you both so much." And then we all three collide in a sloppy kiss.

As the sun rises, Flint returns from his patrolling and Maxum takes to the sky for his shift.

Flint smiles at me with my head in Calder's lap and my feet in Osen's as we relax on the couch. Calder's fingers comb through my hair. Osen skims his hand up and down my legs.

"You all look cozy," Flint says before dropping to his knees in front of the couch and giving me a gentle yet passionate kiss. "Hungry?" he asks as his finger traces along my neck to my cleavage.

"For food? Yeah." I give him a wink. "I don't have the energy to help, though."

"No need, Heartstone." Flint stands and walks over to the open kitchen. "We should be careful not to tire you so much that you can't even stand."

"I can probably stand, but I'd walk funny," I say with a chuckle.

Osen smacks my naked ass and growls with approval when it jiggles in reverberation. When I glance at his face, he snaps his jaws like he's going to bite it.

Arran enters the room and pops Osen on the back of the head. "Biting her ass is *my* job, shadowcock."

"I can bite her too," Osen pouts.

Arran growls and lies on top of me, crushing all three of us. "Missed you," he whispers over my lips as Osen and Calder try to extricate themselves from the couch.

Osen uses his shadows to lift both of us and then sets us down gently after he and Calder get to their feet.

Then Osen wraps his shadow tightly around Arran's throat, leans down, and says over the shell of Arran's ear, "You hit me again, and I'll hold you down and fuck that pretty ass of yours."

"Promises, promises." Arran winks at me. "Jade might like that too much."

Osen barks out a laugh and smirks. "Yeah, I can sense her arousal around that thought. But I'd rather have her or Calder now. No offense, puppy."

Arran launches off me and at Osen. They tussle for a moment, getting out some pent-up energy. They break apart, splayed flat on the floor with wide grins on their faces.

Looks like some good ole fashioned Greek nude wrestling.

"I missed you, dickhead," Arran pants out.

"Same." Osen gets to his feet and gives Arran a hand up.

Flint is filling the dining table full of fruits and pancakes. I roll up to a sitting position and barely have time to stand before Arran has me in his clutches and sits down, placing me in his lap. It's weirdly natural to be naked in front of them like this. And with Arran's shifter body radiating more heat than a normal person, I'm mostly warm in the slightly chilly house.

Arran grins with pride to be the one feeding me, but the others offer me bites from their plates as we eat.

With a bit of food in me, I find I'm regaining my energy.

Then I wonder what rejuvenates my magic. I feel some part of me charging up with the feeling coming through my bonds. Can love power me?

I muse aloud, "I don't have just one kind of magic in me, but three. Does that mean I have to use three different methods to charge each one?"

"Well, rest, time, and food will recharge almost all supes and witches." Osen explains. "But it's slow going and doesn't help if you're in a war zone."

"Witches usually charge by the nature of their magic," Arran adds. "For example, green witches need to be outdoors or gardening. Your witch heritage is from a lust witch, so you would be like an incubus—feeding off sexual energy and desire."

"Hmm. Do you think that's why I gravitated to writing smut?" I ask.

"Probably," Osen agrees. "We should ask Maxum or Darius what might fuel your demon side."

"And the electric mage stuff?" I ask.

"Lightning storms are the fastest, natural way," Arran answers. "My old Shadowcraft Academy professor said that electric mages can also use power outlets from the human realm in a pinch, but that can be dangerous."

"But any friction or spark of energy will do to some extent," Osen adds. "Like churning water or a spark of fire. Winds. Even the sun. Hell, maybe even fucking. It's one of the more versatile powers. Some of the more powerful mages have been able to pull magic from the ethers to recharge."

"Cool." I study my hands and wonder what kind of power I can channel.

"Speaking of which... How are you doing since you've recharged your magic?" Arran asks Osen.

"Surprisingly good." Osen flexes his hands. "Almost as good as before."

"I'm feeling strong enough to travel." I slide off Arran's lap and stretch. "We can head back to Amira's place now."

"First, we need to finish our errands and grab some more supplies," Flint reminds me as he comes up behind me and wraps his arms around my waist, holding me close. He's so solid that it feels like I have the strength of an entire mountain at my fingertips.

I glance down at my body and remember my clothes were torn in my fight with Rob, and then further destroyed by my passionate lovers. "Uh, I'll need clothing for a public appearance."

"Oh, yeah. Maxum grabbed some clothes for you from the lake house before we left." Arran guides me down the hallway, pulling me away from Flint. "I'll help you shower and dress you."

"*I'm* capable of doing these things." But I grin happily after my half-hearted protest, because doing them with Arran sounds much more fun than alone.

"Hmm." Arran rubs his chin thoughtfully, but with a mischievous gleam in his eyes. "Not sure if you've recovered yet. I should be there to supervise."

He herds me into the bathroom like a border collie. I can't stop laughing at his antics. I love this silly side of my werewolf. And I sense he loves the idea of playing and having me alone for a moment.

This brings up an issue that I've only had to deal with as a *Why Choose* author, but now I must juggle in my real life. How to make sure I give so many men my attention.

I worry again that I'm going to fail at this. I could barely handle one guy, even if he didn't really want to be around me much.

"Hey, sweet mate." Arran brackets me in with his muscular arms against the sink vanity. He presses his forehead to mine. "Don't fret."

"Do you know how I'm feeling?" I ask, meeting his golden gaze.

"Yeah. Mate bond and all that."

I avert my eyes, feeling crappy. "I should tune in more to our bond. Also protecting you from my emotions. It's like I'm on a rollercoaster lately."

He places a finger over my lips and gives me a sad smile. "Don't hide your emotions from me. It's my role as a mate to be there through all of it."

"I'm messing up this mate thing."

"My moon, I only have you to focus on. You have five bastards with all our chaos and baggage. I'm happy you've been able to block out our possessive, violent minds over the last couple of days, especially as we dealt with Rob."

"But I didn't mean to!" My head drops to his broad shoulder.

"Sweetheart, we are all charged up with emotions and with our mate bonds clicking into place. Once we settle into them, we'll find our rhythm. Osen just returned from the dead. Calder just got the pieces of his soul back. Of course, you're going to be there for them. I suspect you'll give a big chunk of your energy to Maxum when you finally solidify things between you two. It's the nature of this dynamic."

"Logically, I know you're right." I say, and he puffs out his muscular chest. "But please let me know when you need me," I plead.

"Wolf shifters are very touch oriented. Even a brush of your hand or a snuggle will ease a lot of my tension. And when I need more, I'll just chase your plump ass down and fuck you in the woods."

I burst out in laughter. "Deal."

"And the same goes for you." He snags my gaze and holds me hostage with his golden eyes. "Come to me with anything you need. To talk, to snuggle, to fuck. Whatever it is."

Through my bonds, I sense Flint's love enveloping me, echoing Arran's sentiment. I idly wonder how it will feel when all the bonds are fully formed. Will I be overwhelmed? Or will it become as natural as breathing?

Arran turns on the shower to let it warm up, which is instantly.

"Wow. Fae plumbing is great!"

He guides me into the shower stall. "This one has a few great spells on it."

Arran proceeds to make me properly filthy and then ensures I have all my bits clean before we get back out.

36

COMEUPPANCE

JADE

*a*fter my shower, Arran and I discover Maxum pacing in the bedroom.

My handsome demon watches silently while I get dressed in leggings and a long sweater. He's uneasy.

I pull on an expensive pair of new boots that I definitely didn't buy, so they must be something Maxum purchased before we fled the lake house. "Thank you for grabbing some clothes for me."

Maxum grunts, obviously distracted.

"What's up?" I ask, stepping closer to grab his attention.

"I had time to think while being on watch." He pauses his pacing to hover over me like the towering possessive male he is. "I don't like that Rob found you so quickly. I'm worried about Galiana tracking you down. She will try to use you. Or if you no longer serve her plans, kill you. She's far more powerful than he was, and she has stolen cubi power, too. Maybe most of her witches don't know what exactly she's doing, but they *are* willing to die for the anti-supernatural cause."

I rest my hands on his forearms and stare into his obsidian eyes. They flame with anger, and for the first time since I've known him, I see genuine fear behind them.

Fear for me.

"After eight hundred years of being alive, you should know that worrying doesn't help," I tell him.

"This is the first time I actually give a fuck about what happens in my life. If we lose you…" He swallows down his strangled voice and can't continue.

"Maybe we should go on the offensive and hunt her," I suggest.

"No," Maxum and Arran growl in unison.

Dang, why do I love a protective male so much? Maybe because I don't want to be the only one fighting for my survival. It's the first time someone has cared like this in my life's history. Not even a few months ago, I would have scoffed at the idea of trusting someone enough to help me, but these guys have convinced me that sometimes we can have faith in someone other than ourselves. I not only have one guy to lean on after all the years of pain and loneliness, but five. Maybe because of this, I feel invincible. I want to end this shit so I can be happy with them.

"As smokin' hot as that growly moment was, I still think we should consider taking action and gain the upper hand instead of being at her mercy."

"Okay," Calder's voice chimes from the doorway, with Osen and Flint standing right behind him. "But hypothetically, how do we entrap her? Because we need a plan, not a prayer. Look at what happened to Osen because he went full gangbusters without thinking it through."

"Hey!" Osen protests, then frowns, rubbing his mouth. "Alright, fine. I deserved that."

After a brainstorming session, we pack up our things and leave via a demon portal. We travel through a few places before we end up near the edge of a quaint New England town. I can see the State Park not far in the distance. When we scoped it out earlier, we found it empty of tourists, a blessing if our crazy plan works.

"We stick together," Maxum orders, leveling his gaze at me.

"What?" I grumble. "When have I wandered off?" I rub his huge arm. "I'm going to stay real close to my big, meanie demon so he can keep me safe."

He growls and yanks me to his side protectively. "Fucking right you are, sweet monster."

I chuckle, but nod. "I'm not dumb. All this kicking ass stuff is way above my pay grade."

"That isn't necessarily true. You're powerful," Osen argues. "But as Calder pointed out, there's safety in numbers. And it's likely the witches will have them on their side."

In their glamour to make them look like your run-of-the-mill insanely hot guys, they crowd around me like fierce bodyguards. We get a few strange looks from people, likely wondering if I'm some celebrity with my entourage of supermodel bodyguards.

Alas, I'm only known in the spicy romance world, and apparently now I'm making a splash in witchy society, too. *Yay, me.*

We make our way through the streets, hoping to attract the attention of any local or tourist witches. Do witches go on road trips? Witch retreats? Do they have coven support group meetings with donuts and old coffee? Do they gather around the water cauldron and exchange gossip? Whispering, *"Did you see Martha try to substitute the eye of newt for gecko? Goddess bless her heart."*

Okay, plot bunnies are now officially loose. I want to write an office witch romance. Should it be enemies to lovers or billionaire boss? Both?

I need to refocus...

Maxum tells us there are rumors that indicate there are a few witches and warlocks from the ASO living in this area.

When our parading doesn't seem to get a reaction, we move to Plan B.

Without my containment necklace, I can't risk handling my computer. So the task lands on Arran's shoulders since his magic rarely affects electronics, and he has some familiarity with them.

Besides, he's familiar with my actual computer—the sneaky spy. I idly wonder if he did a deep dive into my search history. Geeze, I hope not. A smut author's browsing history is not for the faint of heart. Graphic sexual images, weapons, poisons, bondage, torture, how to kill someone with almost anything I can think of, and ways to dispose of a body are only a few of the nefarious topics. It suggests the makings of a very bad person.

At the park, I talk him through setting up my travel router and logging onto my computer.

All my guys are standing in a circle facing outward to keep watch for an attack.

Fortunately, we've already set up this place with magical booby-traps and other surprises.

With my enhanced vision, it isn't too hard to see over his shoulder from a few yards away. "Check my email. Rob sent me a message. When I opened it, not long after, he showed up."

Arran snarls when he opens and reads the email. "What? You *never* belonged to him! I wish that bastard wasn't dead, just so I could kill him all over again."

"Samsies, babe, samsies," I quip. "Any other emails?"

"Uh, nothing that looks odd."

My computer chimes with a notification from my social media account.

"Click on the messenger icon. And tell me who just messaged me."

"I see a bunch of unread messages from what looks like a few other authors," he answers. "And just now, it's someone named Minerva Marvin. It's a request to video chat."

"Odd. We've never done that before." I pace behind Arran, wondering what this means. "Decline the invite."

"She's asking what's wrong... why she hasn't seen you online. She's worried."

"Reply to her via text," I dictate to him.

> Jade: A lot has been going on lately. Turns out my ex is a psycho.

> Minerva: Are you safe?

> Jade: Yeah. Just had to leave town.

> Minerva: Where are you?

Warning flags are flapping wildly in my mind. But we are fishing to see if we can catch a witch. Maybe Minerva is one, or maybe she's just an innocent, yet naughty, paranormal author.

Telling her where I am is a test and a trap.

> Jade: I'm in a little town on the East Coast.

> Minerva: Oh, I know.

Suddenly, we're surrounded by witches and warlocks. None of us move, everyone waiting for the other to throw the first magical strike.

A pretty witch saunters forward a few steps, and an alluring energy floats off her and curls around us. I almost snarl. It feels like she's trying to sway my guys to her will.

"Hello, Jade."

"That's the fucking witch that tortured me!" Calder cries out.

Flint holds him by the arm, keeping the violence at bay. For another few moments at least.

My blood electrifies with his claim. I'll kill her for what she's done, but first, I want answers of my own.

"Minerva?" I ask. I've only ever seen her author logo online, but never her face. Many spicy romance authors don't show their faces, so I had no reason to think there was something odd.

"Yes, that's me."

"I don't understand… we've known each other for years."

"We have, because I was the one who discovered you." She smirks and cocks her hip out. Another wave of magic swirls out. She's pure sex embodied, and she shoping to attract my mates' attention and enchant them.

"How did you discover me?" I demand.

"You're such an ignorant bitch. Your mother did you no favors, leaving you in the dark. How fortunate for us." Minerva shakes her head with a self-righteous sneer. "It was your books, dumb dumb. You wrote about things that were too accurate. About actual events. When we hunted down the author, we found you, a witch who had no idea that she was channeling the dead. Not just any dead though… supernaturals. With details that no one else should know about our crimes."

I think back and realize Minerva had reached out to me as a fellow author just a week before Rob showed up in my life.

"So you sent Rob and the hamster to spy and manipulate me," I surmise.

"It was going so well for our cause until you got rowdy and took up with this lot." Her gaze slithers all over my guys, appraising them. "But I have to say, for supes, they are pretty hot. I can't exactly fault an ignorant lust witch from sampling these tasty snacks. I'm sure they fuck like monsters, too." She eyes Arran like she's tempted. "Especially this one. My coven gave him exactly what he deserved with the curse, but I'd love to tie him down and unleash the berserker." Then she spots Calder and licks her lips. "And how could I forget how easily I *fractured* this tasty morsel?"

Anger flares inside me. How dare she minimize what I have with them and what she put Arran and Calder through? "They aren't fucking snacks, you piece of shit."

"My my. Someone is feeling protective over their lust meals." Minerva doesn't seem to sense my bonds, or she dismisses them as nothing. She takes another step closer.

I feel her power wash over me, but I suspect my lust witch blood allows me to resist her.

Her voice turns steely and cold. "Galiana is waiting for you. Let's not keep her waiting any longer, shall we?"

She lifts her hand, and her people rush forward to capture us.

Electricity cracks in my hands, but I hide the magic since I don't want to use it while my enemies are watching. These witches don't seem to know about my unique heritage and powers. Maxum has warned me that the more others know, the more dangerous it is for me.

My guys surround me, fighting in a protective circle.

I watch helplessly as our magical booby-traps are destroyed by a few witches.

Osen's shadows shoot out and knock people to the ground several feet away. I know from my visions of his ability that he's not even close to recovering his full power.

Calder is throwing balls of fire with his flaming hands, but his attacks bounce off some sort of witch-shields.

In full gargoyle form, Flint's huge wings are taking an onslaught of magical blasts to protect me. Through our bond, I sense he's weakening.

Arran slices his massive claws at our attackers, dodging and weaving. But he takes more hits than he dishes out.

Maxum takes a bastard down with his mind magic. The warlock drops dead, crumpling at our feet after his brain turns to mush.

There are far more people on their side than ours, and I'm afraid we might not win if I don't join in the fray.

Dare I expose my electric mage ability?

Calder transforms into his full phoenix form and circles around us, keeping the witches at bay as best he can. He dives low to burn them with his fire, but most of his prey have strong magical shields protecting them.

A blast of magic hits him dead on, and he screeches with rage. He's blocking our mate bond connection to protect me, so I can only hope it's that he's pissed and not hurt, but his movements aren't as smooth as before.

I'm at a loss for what to do to help. My witch powers are passive and seem to be a low-level lust power and mediumship. Not helpful in my current situation. Unless I can somehow seduce ghosts into attacking our enemies. Which doesn't seem very practical, even if I could accomplish the feat.

For now, I'm crouched low to the ground like a coward or damsel in distress. I don't like either label. Maxum's warning echoes in my mind that I can't let anyone know what I can do. Only as a last resort. Yanking souls from bodies with this many witnesses who could escape isn't advisable either.

The ground vibrates under my feet, and I hear a chant droning from a group of witches not actively engaged in the battle.

I quickly glance at Arran and Flint, but I don't see them noticing it. Though I'm uncertain, since my eyeballs are rattling in my head.

"Fuck!" Maxum shouts.

Spinning to see what's happened, he stares at the ground below his feet that's shuddering. "*Nooooooo!*" He turns to see that I'm also affected.

He dives for me. As his body collides with mine, I feel the ground below us give way. Our drop ends quickly, and his huge body crushes me as we land.

The wind is knocked out of me. I suck in a breath before I can crack my eyes open. When I do, I see we're in a large, dark, concrete room with no windows. It appears to be empty. No people, no furniture, nothing.

Maxum pushes off me and curses a string of expletives that must come from the bowels of hell and fills me with dread. He slams his body against an invisible wall.

I glance down to understand where the little light in the room is coming from and find there's a glowing red circle with sigils surrounding us. I smell blood in the stale air.

"What *is* this?" I ask, but in my heart, I already know.

Maxum throws his body repeatedly against the invisible barrier that lines up with the outer circle, ignoring me completely.

"Maxum!" I cry, to get him to stop. I can tell he's only hurting himself, not making progress. "What is this?"

"A demon trap!" he snarls and slices at the air again, but his claws skid along the trap's boundary.

"Where are we?" My heart crumbles as I worry about my other mates. "What about the guys? We need to get back to them!"

He spins, eyes wide and feral, and I shiver with his madness. "Do you still feel your bonds?"

My attention drops into my heart, and I can sense the tethers linking my soul to theirs. "Yeah."

"Then they're alive for now." Pointing at the place he was attempting to break through, he then demands, "See if this trap holds you!"

I scramble to my feet. No one is down here, and if this trap doesn't hold me, then I can help us escape. I rush to the edge and smash against what feels like an electric fence. With a yelp, I'm thrown backward and crash into Maxum.

"Dammit!" He catches me as I fall and holds me while my dazed wits come back online. My vision is spinning, and I wonder how he could have bashed against the barrier like he did.

As he presses me close to his massive body, I realize we are both completely naked. "Where the fuck did our clothes go?"

"Part of the demon summoning process. It strips a demon of all possessions, so the summoner is protected from retribution." He snarls, "I'm going to *retribute* their ass."

"But how did they do it?" I shake my head. "Why didn't they do this before?"

Maxum slowly calms his breathing, and some sanity returns to his gaze. He considers my question. "There are only two ways to summon a demon like this. One is to know a demon's true name. Only a few of my family know my secret and it's solely in case of emergencies. Two is to have the demon's blood and a line of sight to cast the ritual. The second option is dangerous for the summoner, since a demon could catch and kill them before it's done."

"I heard witches chanting... that must have been it."

"And they must have found our blood at one of the battles we fought," he grumbles.

"But why target both of us?"

"I assume she was targeting me, and you were just pulled along for the ride. They were likely worried if they captured you that I might track you through our matebond."

"But we haven't mate bonded yet."

"They don't know that. And they wouldn't believe a demon would have waited this long to claim you."

"Uh, Maxum?" I hesitate because it feels wrong to confront him now, but I don't know if I'll ever get an answer. Things aren't looking good for our longevity. "Why haven't you bonded with me? If you don't want to, I'll try to understand, but I feel like I did something to upset you."

"What? No." He clasps my face to make me look into his flaming obsidian eyes. "It's not that I don't want to."

"Tell me what it is, then. This might be our last chance to clear the air."

He sags to the hard floor and sits cross-legged. Then he invites me to sit, cradled in his embrace. I'd rather have his body as a seat than the cold concrete, so I slip down into his arms and find comfort in his warmth, sitting sideways so I can look up into his beautiful crimson face.

"I'm afraid for you."

"Because of rutting me? I don't believe you'd fuck me enough to kill me."

Maxum studies my face for a long time, deciding what he should confess. Then, with a sigh, he begins. "No. It's about the demon lords. There are so few females. If I mate you, the lords in hell might be alerted to your demon nature. If they come for you, they will kill our pack, use you for power plays, and attempt to breed you."

"Well, shit," I whisper. "Force me to make babies?"

"They'd likely first try to make you amenable to the process, so you weren't overly stressed and unable to impregnate. High-powered demons might try to stake a claim, or they might share you until someone's seed took hold."

"But you're so loving with me. How could they…"

"Most demons aren't as empathetic as I am. I think the decline in female numbers has made the males even more aggressive. Historically, demons often shared a female mate. But the problem has only gotten worse. And it's difficult to find a female outside of our realm who can procreate with us. They are valuable, but a commodity, a possession. It's likely the main reason your mother kept you and herself a secret. If either of you had been discovered, it could have meant you would've been taken to the demon realm until you were of age to take mates."

"Shit on a hellstick," I mutter, barely able to process what he just said. "So, when you found out about my demon blood, you felt you had to pull back in case they found me because of our mating."

"I couldn't be the reason they found you. I'm not… *popular* in the demon realm," Maxum admits with a heavy breath. "Most of them would have no problem killing me and taking you. Mate matches are so rare that most demons don't even believe in them. They wouldn't respect what we have. They wouldn't understand, or care, that you'd be devastated by losing your bonded mate matches."

"Not that it matters what demons might do to you," a cold, threatening voice of a woman cuts through our conversation and echoes around the large, chilly space. "Your fate is mine to deliver."

37

IT'S A TRAP!

JADE

Galiana slowly steps into the glow of the demon trap and looks like the villain she is as she glares down her nose at us.

Maxum clasps me to his chest while I sit in his lap. He angles away from the witch, hoping to protect me.

"Relax, demon," Galiana says with a dismissive tone. "I'm not going to kill her… yet."

Good to know that it's still on the table.

"Maybe I don't have to kill you at all." She shrugs like it's no big whoop either way.

"Explain," I snarl, wishing I could rip her head from her shoulders and dance as her still-pumping arteries rain blood on me like a fountain. Oh my. That was a bit dark. My demon blood might be kicking in.

"If you give me your power willingly. All of it. Then I won't kill you. And I won't kill your little harem."

I roll my eyes because I wasn't born yesterday.

Maxum captures my chin and speaks directly to me. "There *is* a slim chance your body *might* survive without magic. But she won't spare mercy on our pack."

"I figured."

Galiana slowly paces around our demon circle. "Minerva is going to have so much fun during her reunion with the phoenix."

Maxum and I launch at her in unison, snarling, and we're blasted backward for our efforts by the trap.

She tsks us as though we are poorly behaved children. "I'll let you sit with your options for a bit, and if you deny me, I'll allow Minerva her entertainment. I might join her and rip apart the other males. It'll be a party."

My heart pounds so frantically, I expect it to leap out of my chest and die. The thought of these two witches hurting my mates is too much for me. My breaths come in fast and shallow. The room spins.

Maxum gathers me up in his arms and rubs his warm hand up and down my back. "Slow, deep breaths," he guides me gently. He cups my hands over my mouth to curtail my hyperventilation.

"I'll be back in a few hours for your answer." Galiana smirks evilly. "Be smart. Make this easier on yourself and hand over your power to me." She saunters off and a loud, metal clang signals she has shut the door on us in here.

After several minutes, my breathing slows to a regular pace and my mind whirls with questions that tumble out of me. "I don't understand. Why does she need me to hand over my power?"

Maxum jerks his head in confusion. "That is odd. I was so pissed about us being trapped, I didn't question that."

"Do you think she captured the others?" I ask, fearing he will confirm it.

"As much as I don't want them hurt and killed. You can't decide based on saving them. If she's captured them, then she isn't letting them go, no matter how you negotiate."

I check in with my mate bonds, and I sense they are alive, but not okay. "I feel them, but they're emotionally distraught."

"Of course, they're distraught. Their mate has been taken from them." Maxum kisses my temple in a bid to relax me. "But their distress isn't an indicator of *their* captivity."

Bile rises in my throat, and I hold back the urge to retch. I don't know how to get out of here or how to help them. I just hope they're safe now.

Time for answers…

"How do we break out of a demon trap?" I ask.

"*We* don't." Maxum grumbles. "It has to be broken from the outside."

"Like anyone? Or does it have to be the person who cast it?"

"Anyone who has a touch of magic," Maxum sighs. "But we are warded inside. And I don't expect Galiana to drop it until you agree to comply."

"She must need my cooperation to take my power. That's probably why they didn't just take it before when Rob was dating me."

"Makes sense. From what the magical community understands, it's that *stolen* power fades. But perhaps Galiana found a workaround to keep hold of a willing donation."

"Coerced, not willing," I growl. "She's threatening you."

Maxum allows a smirk to fill his face. "It's sexy when you get protective of us."

I nuzzle into his shoulder. "It might kill me to watch any of you get hurt, especially because of me."

"I don't think she's a witch of her word. I expect she'll kill us as soon as she has what she wants from you."

I bite my lip and curse my luck. We're screwed. This might be our death.

"Why aren't you popular in the hell realm?" I ask, an idea forming in my head... likely a very stupid one.

Maxum blinks at that non sequitur. "Uh, well, I'm a disappointment in their eyes. I don't fit in there. I ran off to help weaker or underprivileged supes and demons. Let's just say that philanthropy and community assistance aren't a priority among demons. Most believe that I'm a traitor."

"Oh." I frown, not because of what he said, but that I hoped he'd have more supporters in hell.

"What are you thinking, my sweet monster?" he asks.

"You mentioned demons might sense if we bond. So what if we did, and they showed up and broke us out of the trap? If we stay here, we're both dead. But maybe we have a shot to survive with your people."

"*Survive,* yeah. But you might not want to survive a life with them as your masters." Maxum caresses my cheek and shakes his head, likely thinking of the worst possible scenario.

"We could escape the demons," I say with hope in my heart, and give him a kiss.

He returns my kiss, deepening it until we're panting with need. We've both been holding back our desire for each other, and it feels like something snaps.

"Fuck it. I don't want to go to my death without claiming you as mine," Maxum growls.

"Yeah, fuck it." I laugh wildly. "Why should we stop living our lives just because we are trapped in a demon circle in an underground witch stronghold who is hell bent on my demise?"

Maxum chuckles against my throat as he kisses down my body. "My teeth ache to claim you, but this is not the romantic setting I was hoping for."

"Hey?" I grasp his horns and make him look me in the eye just as his mouth gets to the swell of my breast. "It will be perfect because it's with you."

Maxum bites down on my tit and growls. "No. You are."

He snaps his gaze up to my eyes, and his are wild with need.

Oh, my spicy ovaries.

I've unleashed his true inner demon.

Maxum's claws scrape down my flesh, leaving thin lines behind, but never deep enough to bleed. Not yet, anyway. It's a good thing that I don't have any clothes, because they would have been torn to shreds.

His mouth is everywhere. In a frenzy of passion, he bites me with his sharp teeth and licks the sting away with his forked tongue. Like he's searching for the best place to mark me. He only avoids where Arran's mate bite silver scar glows against my skin and where Calder's talons mark my shoulder blades.

"Jade. I need you," he murmurs over my flesh.

"I'm yours."

It's all the encouragement he needs.

He stands, lifting me as he does. His arms hook under my knees, spreading me wide. Placing his hands around my waist, he lifts me so my pussy is level with his face. He swipes his tongue over my center and then plunges inside.

I grab hold of his horns out of pure instinct, but his bruising grip on me ensures I won't fall.

His tail fondles and prods my entrance. Then it slides alongside his tongue, filling me, stretching me. Something begins to vibrate inside me, and I cry out as my pussy clamps down on him.

I'm seeing stars and swaying as he moves me back down his body, then his cock slides into me.

Maxum powers up into my wet heat in one hard thrust.

I grip onto his neck and cry out as he fills me, hitting all my places to drive me wild. His thrusts are frenzied, and I sense he's on the verge of the rut he warned me about before.

His hand fists in my hair and he pulls my head backward, making me arch my body. He descends on my breasts, biting and sucking.

He's barely holding together his sanity.

"Take all of me," he growls.

His tail wraps around my waist, then slips down to stimulate my clit, then slides inside my channel alongside his cock, making me whimper with the stretch.

He bounces me on his cock and tail with his powerful body, grunting and swearing promises. His massive wings expand, crashing against the demon circle boundary. He's so consumed with claiming me that the electric zap of the magic doesn't seem to faze him. Or perhaps it's only adding to his experience.

My skin buzzes and sparks wherever we make contact. My own magical electricity is dancing with the current flowing through him.

"Fuck yes. Mine! All mine!" he chants as he pistons up into me with a fierce expression, like this is exquisite torture.

I'm thankful for my reinforced bones, because I'm sure he could easily shatter my hipbone with his intensity. My enhanced healing is going to help with the bruising and scrapes, too.

I love every possessive snarl and harsh grasp of my flesh.

"Jade," he breathes out, and I know he's close.

This desperate sound, his need for me, catapults me toward my own release.

"Come with me," he shouts.

And I do. My pussy squeezes, milking his thick cock of his cum.

He sinks his sharp fangs into my neck, opposite to Arran's mark.

I cry out with the enhanced pleasure the link brings.

His forked tongue swirls over the flesh, still pinched between his teeth.

I whimper and moan as his energy ties us together and my soul sings.

Tangled up in each other, we listen as our breathing evens out and our heartbeats return to normal. Such a strange quiet after all the frantic bonding, but I luxuriate in the sensation of his skin on mine.

Maxum releases his bite with a gasp.

We both glance down at his muscular chest. Over his heart, his dark crimson markings shift, creating an intricate knot with six threads.

"My mate," Maxum says in awe. "Look."

Over my heart, my chest now glows with the same symbol, just the size of a quarter, then sets into the same color as Maxum's mark.

The meaning of six is not lost on me.

We are truly a pack, through their bonds with me.

38

LOST AND FOUND

JADE

*A*s we catch our breath, still tangled up in Maxum's embrace, a male appears through a portal outside our demon trap. The doorway snaps shut behind him, and his intense gaze lands on me.

A shiver goes down my spine. We've been found. Hopefully, this crazy plan doesn't backfire.

His long, silver hair falls around his broad shoulders. He's strikingly handsome, built, and tall, yet I'm not drawn to him like I am to my guys. Nonetheless, there's an unusual pull to him I don't quite understand. He doesn't look like a demon, but he definitely isn't human. He's likely in a glamour like my guys often wear in public, hiding a supernatural's otherworldly features.

Maxum quickly scans the room to see if anyone else has popped in, and then he stands us up and tucks me behind him protectively.

"Mine," the male whispers, ignoring Maxum completely and staring unblinkingly at me.

"No, mine. *My mate*," Maxum challenges with a low growl.

"Yes, of course." The newcomer waves him off, dismissively. "Jadeana? Is it really you?"

My eyes almost pop out of my head when he says my given name. I glance up at Maxum and find him jerking back in surprise and he pulls me tighter to him.

The male finally focuses on Maxum, and his brows knit in confusion. "Maxumus Drakona?"

Maxum doesn't answer to the name, but asks cautiously, "Do I know you?"

Footsteps echo from outside the room. Someone's coming.

"We don't have time for this," the male says and shucks his coat. "We need to get you both out of here and somewhere safe before other demons arrive or the witches discover me here." He eyes Maxum. "Do not attack me when I bring down this trap."

Maxum peeks down at me. Then he turns his gaze back on our presumed rescuer. "Swear you won't bring her to harm."

"It appears I've already inadvertently done her harm, but I swear on my firstborn's life, I'm here to save your mate from a horrible fate."

I don't like the sound of that. But something tells me to trust him. "Maxum, this is our chance."

"I won't attack unless you put her in harm's way," Maxum promises.

The male's hand glows, and he slaps his palm down on the circle on the floor. A wave of energy flares out, breaking the circle. He throws me his jacket so I can cover up my nakedness. As I do, he opens a portal.

We step out of the circle, but Maxum hesitates when the male waves us to the unknown destination.

The metal door flies open and slams against the concrete wall. Galiana shrieks when she sees us escaping. A shadow tendril flies out like a whip.

Before it can hit us, an electric bolt shoots out to block it. Another crashes into Galiana, sending her to the floor.

It takes me a half a second to realize it's not my magic that did that. It's this mystery guy.

"Go!" the male orders and grabs my hand, dragging Maxum and me into the portal.

The doorway closes before Galiana can follow.

I glance around. By the magic in the air and the unique colors of the foliage, I deduce we're in a remote location within the fae realm.

"Come. We need to throw off any tracking."

Maxum snarls. "I know the drill."

We run a quarter mile, then pop through into a closed clothing store in a strip mall. The new guy grabs a couple pairs of sweatpants and two t-shirts off some racks and tosses them at Maxum and me.

Maxum doesn't protest, and we quickly put them on. I see a fixture with some flip-flops. Not the best gear, but I tuck my feet into them to protect myself from whatever running we have left to do.

The male tosses some cash on the sales counter and shrugs when we give him a questioning look. "Karma is a bitch. Don't want to test her right now."

"Who *are* you?" I ask.

"Don't you know already?" His face is strained, like he's in pain. "Sense it?"

"Are you... my father?"

He nods slowly.

"Are you Erwald Krathion?" Maxum steps closer, studying his face.

My father gives him a sad grin. "It's been a long time, Maxumus." His skin color darkens to a reddish hue and there's a subtle change in his appearance, but his red is not as deep as Maxum's crimson. His eyes become the palest green I've ever seen. His silver hair remains the same and I realize it's the same as mine.

My jaw drops open. "You two know each other?"

"I suspected Erwald was your father," Maxum confesses. "But didn't think he was still alive. When you mentioned you didn't want to drag him into our problems, I planned on hunting down what happened to him, but only after we eliminated Galiana and Rob."

"I've been incognito since your birth," my flipping *father* says to me.

"The last time I remember seeing you was almost three hundred years ago," Maxum adds.

I'm still in a daze when my father opens a portal for us to keep moving. Maxum clasps my hand and guides me through.

We rush through the protocol I've become familiar with when portal jumping and finally we end up outside a simple house in the mortal realm.

Erwald (it's too weird to think of him as my dad) ushers us inside the quaint cottage. The outside reminds me of a gingerbread house. The inside is painted dark reds, grays, and black and has gothic style furniture and artwork.

I realize he's brought me to his actual home. Although if he's a double spy, he likely has many hidden safe houses.

"I'm sure you have a myriad of questions for me." Erwald stands rigid as if he's facing a firing squad, waiting for what he expects to be a brutal interrogation.

I don't really have questions, not right now. I give him a once over now that we've stopped moving. He's handsome, but that's a common trait in the supernatural realm from what I've seen. If I were to guess his age by appearance alone, I'd guess he was younger than I am, perhaps thirty, but with a blend of confidence and weariness that reveals his true age, which apparently is hundreds of years old.

When I look for similarities to confirm that he's my bio daddy, I find little, except for our silver hair. Even his eyes are a different shade of green. I'm definitely my mother's daughter in appearance.

"How did you find me?" I ask instead of the thousand other things I could inquire about.

"I was able to pinpoint your location through your mate bond with a demon. I was already on alert after I sensed your concealment spell was broken recently. I have been searching, but I couldn't get a reading on where you were located. I assume some powerful magic was hiding you."

My mind swings back to what I've been worrying about since my pack split up. Sure, it's fine and dandy to meet my father, but I need to address what's really important.

"We need to find the others," I say to Maxum.

"That is unwise." Erwald steps closer, as if to prevent me from leaving.

I glare at him with the force of forty years of abandonment. "I'm sorry. But are *you* telling me how to treat *my* mates?" I ask with a snarky tone, making up for him missing my angsty teenage years. He left his own mate and *me*, his daughter, so no, I'm not taking his fucking advice.

"*Mates?*" His eyes dart to Maxum, then back to me. "You have more?"

"Yes, five total. The last I saw them, they were being attacked by Galiana's main bitch witch. The same asshole who tortured and killed one of them."

"One of your mates is dead?" His tall frame collapses onto an elegant chair with an expression that speaks of his own grief about losing a mate.

We don't have time for catching up, and my tone suggests that as I answer him, "He's a phoenix and not dead, or I hope he's not, but that isn't the point right now. We need to rescue them if they have been captured."

"I'll go see if they retreated to our fallback location," Maxum says and brushes his thumb across my cheek in a goodbye.

I grasp his hand and hold it firmly. "I'm coming with you."

"I won't have you captured again." Maxum presses his body up against me as if it's betraying his idea to separate.

"If you will allow my presence, I can help retrieve your mates," Erwald offers.

Maxum's eyes snap up to take him in, finding him wanting. "I didn't think you'd want to get involved. Don't you like to lurk in the shadows?"

"How dare you?" Erwald growls, standing up from his chair. "You know nothing of what I've been through or what's happened."

"I know enough," Maxum throws back at him. "You didn't take care of your daughter."

"I did the only thing I could do to keep her safe." Erwald takes a few steps forward and I'm pretty sure this is about to devolve into a demon brawl.

"Enough!" I shout, stepping in between them with my hands out. "I need to find my pack. Now! So stop whatever the fuck this is and make me a portal before I zap your asses."

Erwald's eyebrows shoot up to his silver hairline, and he says in a wry tone, "I see you definitely inherited my demon side."

Maxum only smirks at that comment, looking oddly twitterpated with me over that. Then he clears his throat and opens a portal. "We'll drop out a few hundred feet away from the house and assess if there are witches in the area."

Erwald huffs but squares his shoulders and gives us a nod. "I'll stay close to Jadeana so you can focus on our surroundings."

With a grunt, Maxum grabs my hand and we jump through to the fae realm. We land close to the small home we stayed in last, and the portal snaps shut behind us.

Crouching down, we peer through the vibrant foliage but find no one wandering around.

"I sense brainwaves in the cabin." Maxum points toward the house. "But it feels muddled. I can't tell if it's our pack."

"Witch magic, if I had to guess," Erwald adds.

We hear a shout of pain coming from the direction of the house.

In my chest, my bonds yank hard. I bite back a screech of my own agony.

I know it's them inside.

My mates are in pain.

39

DESPERATE TIMES

CALDER

I knew this plan would devolve into a shit show, but I had no clue how horrendously this would go.

Our beautiful, loving mate has been ripped away from us.

The sheer terror and rage that pulses within our pack makes it nearly impossible to think. Not that we have time to.

And now?

My torturer and murderer stands before me, and I can only see red.

The evil witch has the gonads to offer me a smug grin. "Miss me?"

I'm so insanely enraged I can't even reply to the taunt.

At my side, Osen snarls. Then he swings a shadow tentacle into *Minerva*. What a fucking name… It's an insult to the Roman goddess of wisdom.

My tormentor sails through the air and crashes against a tree with a loud crack, and Osen's shadow pins her to the ground.

"Go. Kill her," Osen says with a jerk of his chin.

I fly over, lighting my wings ablaze and towering over the witch as she comes to. After a hard blink to shake away her dizziness, she gasps as she catches sight of me. But Osen's shadows gag her and ensnare her wrists before she's able to unleash a spell to harm me.

I remember that fateful day when she had captured me and blocked my magic. The haunting memories fill my mind of how she tortured me and how she shattered my soul.

Thankfully, as I stand before her now, I'm whole again. More than just whole... I'm bonded to an amazingly magical woman and my powerful incubus.

My body lights up with my phoenix fire, making her eyes widen with fear. Good. I'm happy she's witnessing her karma come to pass.

I block out the shouts of battle behind me, trusting Osen will do his best to protect me while I sort out my vengeance.

"Your disgusting plan to permanently break me has failed," I inform her. "I'd love for your soul to experience the torture I faced. I should rip it out and tear it to shreds so you never find peace, even in the afterworld, but I'm not that cruel."

I don't say that it's my mate who could destroy a soul with a thought. If anyone else overheard the nature of her abilities, that would be disastrous.

The heat from my body's fire makes her sweat. Her skin is blistering. Osen's shadows muffle her screams from the intense pain. Thankfully, they are immune to my flames.

I shift my fingers into talons to plow gouges in her flesh. Her eyes finally reflect the dullness of acceptance. She knows that this is her end.

Normally I don't revel in killing, but this is a special case. I lean down and whisper, "I hope the abyss swallows you up and you're never thought of again. That is the final death, when no one thinks of you or mourns your absence. Though I doubt anyone will truly miss you. It will be instantaneous. You'll be snuffed out, and the realms will be better for it."

The increasing vibration of the call of death crashes over me, and I know it's time.

I slash my talons over her throat, and she is silenced forever.

But I cannot stop. I slice over and over until she's a heap of meat, no longer identifiable as once having a human form.

"Calder!" Osen shouts, bringing me back from my crazed killing.

I spin to see Flint on the ground, eyes closed. Arran is stumbling in his berserker form and falls as he swipes to take out another witch.

Osen is on his knees, his shadows flailing wildly. But his magic is dwindling, since it wasn't properly replenished for a battle like this.

He's panting with effort but holding on.

I use my magic to open a portal behind me. Not as fast as Maxum can make, but I'm grateful to have the ability right now, although it's draining what magic I have left.

A warlock holds out his hands over Arran's prone form, threatening. "I'll kill him if you step through."

He expects me to abandon my pack, but I have no intention of leaving them behind.

Osen glances at me and reads my plan from my eyes alone.

I throw a fireball at the warlock and blast him backward.

At the same moment, Osen uses his last bit of magic to snatch up Flint and Arran and fling them through my portal.

I drop my flames and grab Osen, throwing his arm over my shoulders and dragging him through.

As I turn to close the portal door, I find I'm too late to block my enemy's path.

I release my hold of Osen and throw fire at the five witches and warlocks who charge through, but I only take out one of them.

A warlock casts a spell at me, binding me in iron chains. I scream out in blinding pain. I'm hit with another spell, and my world goes black.

When I come to, I find Flint, Arran, and Osen are all bound in irons and passed out around me in the living room of the small house we used recently. Flint looks to be frozen in stone by a curse. Arran and Osen are bloodied and bruised, but still breathing.

This was supposed to be our place to retreat if things went sideways. Now we are fully upside down, asses up, and fucked hard.

I don't know how long we've been unconscious, but it's dark outside.

The witch, Galiana, steps in front of my line of sight and glowers at me. "Your little rat pack has been more trouble than I originally estimated."

"Same goes for your pathetic organization," I sneer back at her.

"Pathetic?" Galiana scoffs. "I was the one who cursed your rabid pet wolf. I gave Minerva the tools to shatter your soul. I've already killed your fuck buddy incubus once. And I'm going to make sure your death sticks this time, along with the rest of your pack."

That shuts me up. She's responsible for Arran's berserker curse? She's behind my soul shattering? This witch was behind almost all our trauma. Jade's mother's death. Osen's. And who knows how many other supes have suffered by her hand?

My jaw tightens to the point I expect to crack a tooth.

This doesn't look good for us. If Jade and Maxum escape whatever situation they found themselves in, they'll come here and get caught as well.

Then it dawns on me why we are still breathing.

Jade *is* free.

We're bait.

Galiana wants her prize—Jade's unique magic.

The bit of hope that glows in my heart with the thought of Jade being free dies with the realization that she'll risk everything to save her mates.

I have no doubt she'd rather sacrifice herself than allow us to die.

Galiana is without honor and even if Jade negotiates her surrender for our release, the witch wouldn't hesitate to go back on her word and slaughter us all.

I must have faith that Maxum will keep Jade away and safe.

Just as I'm convincing myself he will, I sense my mate is close by. Osen and Arran stir as if they sense her too.

Goddess, no.

Run, my love.

Run and save yourself.

40

NOT TODAY, WITCH

JADE

*M*axum grimaces as he stares at me. He's itching to demand I stay behind, but knows I'll refuse.

"We have back up now. And I can help," I argue before he can say anything.

My demon glances up and looks at my father. Then his gaze lands on Amira, Darius, and Raithe. They didn't want to help at first, but when they heard about our odds, they agreed to take down the leader causing the most damage in the Anti-Supernatural Organization.

Amira admits she has her own beef with Galiana from back when she was an active member of the ASO. But the powerful witch on our side no longer uses destructive magic. So she'll be assisting us by laying down a suppressant spell to prevent our enemies from creating an escape portal or leaving the area. No one can come in or out unless Amira dies or releases her heavy-duty ward.

Fortunately, Raithe and Darius have no hangups about using their magic to attack and kill these asshole witches and warlocks.

We go over our plan one more time, then Maxum gives Erwald a nod to set things into motion.

My father draws his electric magic, wrapping it around his body in what appears to be a shield. It crackles like one of those science globes you find in novelty gift stores.

We all race into position, surrounding the house. Since Maxum insists on staying by my side, we approach together from the opposite direction from my father. Raithe and Darius advance from the other two sides.

I send out a plea to the universe to protect my friends and loved ones.

"*Galiana!*" My father's voice booms, and I suspect he can be heard for miles. "You killed my mate, Patricia Rosethorne. Now, come and meet your end," he challenges.

I'm shaking with nerves. My father is risking himself for me and my mates. If our plan fails, my chance to get to know him might have come and gone in a blink of an eye.

Maxum tugs me closer to his side, sensing my anxiety.

There's a stirring in my bonds, and I reach out with my mind. "*Flint?*"

"*Jade?*" he asks, sounding confused.

"*Hang in there,*" I say. "*We're getting you out.*"

"*No. Leave, Heartstone. It's a trap.*"

"*We know. And it's okay. That's my father outside, calling to Galiana. Raithe and Darius are here too.*"

"*Jade, it isn't worth risking you and the others. Arran and Osen are egregiously injured. They may not make it.*"

The horrific news that my mates are dying takes me to my knees. I clutch my chest and already feel the pain of their loss.

Maxum falls to my side and pulls me into a crushing embrace. "What is it?" he whispers.

"Flint doesn't think they'll live."

"Fuck him. He's being a martyr to make sure you turn around. To keep you safe." Maxum kisses my forehead. "We're going in."

I nod violently, my tears flying from my cheeks. "Yeah, fuck him. I'm saving his rock-hard ass."

Maxum smiles sadly, then gives me a kiss that feels too much like a goodbye.

"Witch!" Erwald commands with the force of someone who is accustomed to getting their way.

"Lord Erwald Krathion, so good of you to join us," Galiana says with an airy tone, as if he's a delightfully unexpected arrival at a cocktail party. "I'm about to kill off one abomination. Might as well kill off two. I'll finally have the father and daughter in the set."

Lord? That's something I'll have to inquire about when this is all over.

Maxum snatches up my hand, and we snake through the brush toward the house.

Arran's mate bond stirs in my heart. He's awake, hurting, and frantic with worry. I desperately wish I had telepathy with him. Instead, I send an emotion—hope—letting him know I'm alive and nearby.

I hear a blast go off at the front of the house, and the air vibrates with magic.

We make it to the outer wall of the house without incident.

Maxum stands up and peeks into the building's back bedroom window. He hovers his hand over the glass. His eyes close to concentrate on disabling the ward. After a moment, he smirks and gives me a wink.

I don't care if his saucy behavior is all false bravado. It helps me keep my wits as he swings open the window and jumps through the opening like a fucking acrobat. He somersaults in and bounces lightly to his feet. Dang. I wish I were half as graceful as I clamor up to the high sill. Maxum gives in to his need to help and pulls me through like I weigh nothing and sets me behind him as he faces the door.

Foot falls coming from the hall reveal our enemies moving about as they chant spells under their breath.

Maxum holds up two fingers to give me a head count. Closing his eyes again, he checks for Darius's and Raithe's brainwaves. Then he gives me the signal that they're in position. Raithe at the kitchen entrance. The hellhound should be waiting by the smaller bedroom.

I frown as I stare at the bed where I first kissed Osen. Will my incubus die again? Will any of us live? I'm under no illusion that the whole harem survives like they do in my romance books. In real life, we lose people we love.

Maxum captures the back of my neck and sweeps me in for a bruising, claiming kiss, and presses his forehead to mine. I can almost feel his words press into my soul. "We got this. Believe."

I want to believe.

I *have* to believe.

I pull back and glare at the door like it's stopping me from my happily ever after.

Maxum waits a beat as our enemies in the hallway move closer. He throws open the door and captures the first witch in his mind melting gaze, gripping her head.

She collapses and the warlock behind her is ready with a spell, but my protective electric magic flares inside me and shoots out of my palms before the asshole can hurt my demon, and the warlock crumples to the floor.

Shouts erupt as the rest of the ASO creeps are alerted to our presence inside the house. Mayhem ensues with magic zipping through the house.

I hear Darius's snarl coming from the other room.

Maxum blocks the way and is blasted with magic. As he moves into the hallway, I try my best to remember he's mostly resistant to witch magic. A powerful spell hits him square in the chest, and he's thrown backward, landing on the floor. He's stunned but appears to be alright.

Arran's howl fills the house with an eerie energy and worry fills me that either he or one of my mates are being injured.

Without a care for myself, I launch into the hallway on my way to save my guys.

Maxum scrambles to his feet behind me, and curses. "Jade, no."

That only spurs me more. What's happened to them that he doesn't want me to see?

Racing into the living room, I discover my guys all bound by toxic iron. Osen doesn't even have his eyes open. Calder's flames are sputtering, unable to light. Flint seems to be half stuck in a freezing spell, struggling to break free of its hold. Arran is in his berserker form and snarling at someone walking in from the kitchen.

With four other witches, Galiana comes into view and grins wickedly at me. "There you are."

The house rumbles with what feels like an earthquake. Flint's affinity is breaking through, even in his weakened state.

The witches stumble but remain standing.

Maxum darts around me, but Galiana is ready for him and, with a spell, he disappears, likely by a demon summoning circle.

"Fuck!" I shout. Hopefully, he's only been transported to a demon trap, and my father can get him out. "Erwald! She sent Maxum away."

I hear his curse and the firefight in front of the house dies off.

Raithe appears in his phoenix bird form, screeching as he snatches one of the witches and drags her away.

With a thunderous roar, Darius charges into the living area from the hall. He's an epic creature that looks more like a feral horse than a hound. His skin crackles with fire as he chases another witch from the house.

It's me against three witches. One of them being Galiana.

She's not to be underestimated. Not only is she powerful in her own right, she has stolen magic on her side. My magic, and who knows what else.

But will she show off her incubus shadows she uses to kill supes in front of the other witches? Or does she wish to keep that a secret?

The spell she uses to steal magic and souls with my power comes to the front of my mind. I hadn't planned on wielding it against her.

Then I remember the innate power I have. Time to see if I can use it on all three witches at once.

I call upon my soul sucking power and visualize yanking the souls from all three. The two witches by Galiana's side scream. Their eyes widen as they sense their essence being ripped from their bodies.

They fall to the floor. I'm a bit dazed. Did I just kill two people so easily? Without a second thought. Without remorse.

I cannot linger on that. I release their darkened souls to the ether for the universe to do with them as it will.

"Wretched abomination!" Galiana unleashes her power on me in retribution. She unravels my hold on her soul and attempts to do the same to me.

She wanted to take my power from me with my willingness. Likely so she could keep it for a longer duration. But she's given up on my compliance and is going for brute force instead.

We're locked in a standstill, both matched in magical strength. Unless someone comes along to take her out, it will be a battle won by endurance alone. She has practice and experience. I don't.

"Your mother was a traitor and a whore," she taunts.

"You sent her on the mission to seduce my father. What the fuck did you think was going to happen?" I demand, while fighting off her hold on my magic.

Galiana's attention snaps to my mates. I see the glimmer in her eye that shines with the desire for their deaths.

A bolt of electricity shoots out from my body and knocks her backward. Her focus falls back onto me, and she sneers. I've gained a bit of an advantage and I feel her faltering.

Raithe's and Darius's shouts carry from the outside, fighting our enemies.

A warlock slips inside and charges for me.

Fuck. I'll need to divert my magic and I can't afford to do that.

Somehow, bound in iron chains, my berserker gathers enough strength to get to his feet. He tackles the man and clamps his vice-like jaws onto the warlock's throat, ripping it out.

I'm distracted though. Galiana takes advantage, wresting me with her soul stealing power until I fall to my knees.

"You're stronger than her, Heartstone," Flint encourages me through our bond. My heart cracks seeing him still cursed and locked in his stone form.

My eyes slide over to Osen and Calder, barely conscious, but they seem to have been stirred by my presence. In their eyes, I see the echo of what Flint said, as if they've heard him.

I have to beat her, if only to save them.

A wave of power flows into me as if the idea of protection empowers me. Like I'm a momma bear.

Focusing back on Galiana, I tug hard on her soul, and she jerks forward. Her eyes go wide in surprise.

I only wish Erwald was here so he could help me kill her and avenge his mate.

As if being summoned by my thoughts, my father appears behind Galiana, stepping out from a portal. "Patricia and I had something you will never know, Galiana. *Love.*"

She flinches when she hears his voice at her back, and I yank at her soul.

He grasps her by the throat and wrenches her head clean off her shoulders as I simultaneously rip her from her mortal coil.

"That is for my mate and my daughter," he snarls, looking like the demon he is.

I gasp in shock at the pure graphic nature of witnessing something so bloody and violent.

Maxum jumps through my father's portal and gives me a look of relief when he sees I'm okay.

Amira rushes into the house with Raithe and Darius by her sides. Since she, Darius, and Maxum are the only ones who can handle iron, they work my mates out of their bindings.

Osen is first as he's the most affected. When he doesn't stir at all, I fall to his side, place my hands on his chest, and pour healing energy into him.

Calder yells to let him out next. He needs to be next to me, helping me. Yet, I don't know how he can assist.

But when his hands land on my waist and he holds me close, pouring his love into me, I know. My power magnifies, and Osen is coughing and opening his eyes within moments.

"What?" Osen sputters and sees the carnage that surrounds us.

Flint crashes into me next, like a freight train, knocking Calder and me over in his need to be near me.

I wrap my arms around him and kiss his beautifully monstrous face with horns and heavy brow. His tusks scrape against my cheeks roughly as he claims my mouth.

Serky-Arran leaps on top of us and officially makes it a dog pile. The berserker werewolf licks his huge, sloppy tongue over my face, and I shriek.

"*That's* what makes you yell out?" Maxum says with a smirk and a shake of his head. But I see the love and relief in his eyes, knowing his pack is okay.

I wave him over.

He drops to his knees beside me and crushes me to his broad chest. "I'm so happy you're alright, my mate."

"Mate?" Calder then glances at Maxum's chest and sees the new marking over his heart. "Thank goddess. It's about time, brother."

"Perfect timing," I say with a wink at my demon.

"Uh, Jade?" Amira calls out, breaking the moment of our reunion. "We should all leave, just in case Galiana's people send reinforcements."

We untangle ourselves from the ground, and it's clear that my mates are *not* okay.

Before I can race to check on my battered mates, I freeze as a presence presses up against my mind. At first, I panic, thinking it might be Galiana's soul trying to possess me.

But then I recognize the energy. My real mother.

"*May I speak to him before I move on?*" she asks me, sounding far away and so destroyed.

"*You're leaving?*" I ask, blinking back the tears because I thought she'd be a ghost forever, and I could get to know her once my anger at her betrayal dissipated.

"*Yes. I was only tied to the world because I needed to see you safe from Galiana. And now I know you will be happy with your mates.*"

"*I didn't know you'd leave so soon. I wouldn't have pushed you away.*"

"*I understand. And you were right. I should have been there for both you and your sister, but I didn't know how to be a good mother.*"

I don't have a response to that. From what Amira told me before about lust witches is that they didn't have a strong maternal instinct. It wasn't in her nature to be there for me.

"*I know you did what you thought was best. I hope you find peace.*" Then I suck in a breath.

"Erwald, my love. Thank you for avenging my death and protecting our precious daughter," she says through me.

My father's eyes widen. He races forward and grasps my shoulders, studying my eyes. "Goddess. With your spirit behind Jade's eyes, it's like seeing you again. She looks so much like you, my love."

"And she has your loving, compassionate heart. She would attempt to heal the realms by sacrificing her life, just as you tried to do," my mother says.

Is that what my father tried to do? There's so much I don't know.

"But I see a passion for experiencing life that you had," my father says.

"I have to go now. My soul is being called."

"No, please stay," he begs, pressing his forehead to mine.

"If I stay any longer, I will become a wisp, an echo."

My father kisses my forehead. *Thankfully.* I don't need that memory of kissing my dad.

"I've never stopped loving you, Patricia."

"Even in death, I've loved you."

A breeze moves through the room, and I whisper to my mother. "I love you."

I feel her embrace around me and the longing of being there for me for forty fucking years slams into me and cuts me down to my knees as I sob with the loss and pain of it.

My father catches me, and after a hug of his own, he hands me over to Maxum.

As my demon lifts me into his arms to carry me, I give my guys a worried glance, taking in their rough condition.

Erwald, Darius, and Raithe help to get my recovering mates through the portal.

By the time we go through protocols of various realm hopping and reach the boundary of Amira's property, we're all exhausted.

Darius has already done his 'hellhound sniff test' of my father, and Erwald's formally allowed inside the sanctuary under the old customs.

We place Osen, Calder, Flint, and Arran in the huge bed and, with their encouragement, I lay over them, giving them my healing energy. I only hope it will hold out and supply them with what they need.

Thankfully, my father is invited to stay on Amira's couch for the night.

With a lingering look, he reluctantly leaves me with my mates. It's so strange to meet this male who is at the very source of who and what I am, yet I know nothing about him.

When I wake in the mid-afternoon, I grunt with the stiffness and utter fatigue that wracks my body.

Fortunately, my mates seem to be recovering.

Maxum left early this morning with Arran to get intel on Galiana's coven and find out if we have to worry about any more of her followers in the ASO.

They return moments after I wake, and I wonder if it's the mate bond that has me so tuned in that I sense when they are nearby.

"So? What's the verdict?" Calder asks, yawning and combing his hand through his messy auburn hair.

"My hackers and informants tell me that Galiana's faction is decimated," Maxum reports with a satisfied grin. "None of the witches know who did it, either."

"That's good," Osen grunts out and labors to sit up. "We won't have to expect fallout later."

"And that means Jade's secret is safe," Flint adds and squeezes my hand happily.

A knock at the door has all of us tensing, expecting the worst. Maxum is closest and opens the door, revealing my father's grim face. He's returned from his own reconnaissance mission.

"Jade's been summoned to hell," Erwald says in a tone that chills me to my bones.

41

HELL FREEZETH OVER

MAXUM

*M*y worst fears have come true. The lords of hell have discovered Jade's existence.

"I will *not* hand you over to them!" I bellow, all the while glaring at Erwald.

Flint tugs Jade to his chest. His wings unfurl from his back, wrap around them, and he turns to stone.

I'd do that too, if I could.

Jade yelps at the sudden cocoon around her. "Flint, my love, they aren't here to take me away." She pauses, then checks, "Are they, Erwald?"

Her father flinches at her use of his common name instead of a fatherly moniker of endearment. The bastard deserves no more since he abandoned her as a baby. I don't care if he thought it was the right thing to do. I could never imagine walking away from my spawn, who I created with my fated mate.

He should have been training her all these years so she could protect herself and understand the threats in the realms she would face.

Then I remember if he had been around, Jade might not be the loving woman she is now. I know she had a rough upbringing, but I highly doubt Erwald and Patricia would have been overly loving parents. It isn't in their natures. Jade would have likely grown to be a battle-hardened version of herself.

If they had raised her, Jade definitely wouldn't have fallen for our ragtag pack. She'd have caught on to our true natures long before we got close and never have invited Arran inside her home or gone on a brunch date with me. She would have never let her guard down if she knew about all the dangers ready to destroy her.

We might be cosmic mate matches, but that isn't a guarantee for love or a bond. For all my anger over her parents' abandonment, I'm glad she was innocent enough of the supernatural world to give us a chance.

Flint's wings soften, and he draws them away to reveal our mate. "Don't go," he pleads.

Jade strokes Flint's square jaw, then looks at her father. "Do I *have* to go? Can we hide?"

"I don't think you can hide from them... not forever. Believe me, living on the run and in hiding is not a happy life."

A frown pulls at her lush mouth.

"I will accompany you as your representative and guardian," Erwald states, brushing a hand down his expensive shirt.

"Do you think they'll hear you out?" I demand. "Will they give your voice any more weight than five fated mates?"

"I hope they take it all into consideration," he says in a quiet tone that turns my blood to ice. "I'll give you a few minutes with your mates to decide if you wish to live a hard life on the run or present yourself to the lords for their assessment."

Jade gulps at the thought of meeting the demon lords. After Erwald closes the door behind him, we converge on our mate.

We're all arguing for the case to run. Except for Osen.

I grab his collar and shake him. "Are you insane?"

"Are you?" He knocks my hand away. "You both have to face this, or we'll never be safe or at ease again."

I snarl at him. I didn't even want to return to face the lords. I'm afraid that my presence will only harm Jade's case for freedom.

"We are all mated to Jade," Arran says desperately. "Doesn't that mean anything to them?"

"It means they could kill us all to break any claim on her," I answer and step back, palming my face and wishing Jade didn't have a drop of demon blood.

"I don't sense our deaths," Calder says in a quiet voice. "Not that it's proof of that outcome."

That gives me a bit of hope. "Flint? What do you sense?"

"I can't say since my protection gauge is broken to full strength all the time for her."

There is only one person who can decide. If I don't allow her the choice, then I'm no better than the monsters I left behind all those centuries ago. "Jade, what does your gut say?"

She takes a moment to consider the question. "We go, but be prepared to escape."

"Erwald can portal even into the royal chamber, since he holds the title of a lord," I say. "We have to trust he will help us if it becomes necessary."

We say our goodbyes to Amira, Raithe, and Darius. No matter what happens in hell, this will be our last day to seek shelter here. I've already taken Jade's magical creatures somewhere safe, so they won't be harmed if things go fucking wrong.

Darius escorts us outside of Amira's boundaries. Jade's eyes well with tears for the surly hellhound, and he begrudgingly accepts a goodbye hug from her.

"Are you sure you don't wish me to come along?" Darius asks.

"No, I'd rather not bring any more attention to your coven," I tell him, appreciating his offer. He likes us more than he lets on.

"Thank fuck," he says with a sigh, then a smirk. "Be careful out there. And if you ever need help again, find someone else."

Jade pouts, but then gives him a wink. "I'll send you a Happy Yule card with hellhounds dressed up as reindeer on it."

Darius chuffs at her, then disappears.

We portal to a few places before Erwald turns to Jade and places his hands on her shoulders. "I want to tell you how proud I am of you. I've loved you all these years. I wish I made different choices so I could have been part of your life. Whatever happens when we go to hell, I will do everything in my power to get you out safely, but do not let them know about your unique powers."

"Um, I don't know what to say, but thank you for helping me with Galiana." She bites her lip, then regains her strength. "And I hope I get to know you in the future, if you're interested in that. *If* we get through this next hurdle."

"Of course, it will be my honor to do so."

With that out of the way, Erwald shifts to his demon appearance and Jade sucks in a breath, taking in his revealed horns. Overall, he looks the same as his human glamour, and his eyes are still an unusual green that now contrasts with his red skin, which is a lighter shade than mine.

He opens a portal to hell. My pack surrounds Jade, giving her soft kisses on her head, shoulders, and cheeks.

I step in front of her and give her a searing kiss on the mouth. "No matter what you hear about me in there, know that I love you."

Her eyes widen, and her mouth parts to ask me what I mean, but I grasp her hand and pull her through right after Erwald.

The rest of my pack follows, and we find ourselves in an elegant hall reserved for the high lords of hell. The air is warm with a lingering scent of smoke. The polished walls and floors are carved from black obsidian that shines like glass.

The circular royal meeting chamber is just over one hundred feet in diameter, with large pillars keeping the ceiling of heavy rock from crashing onto us. It's made this way to discourage battles since everyone would be crushed under the weight if they broke.

Well, maybe not Flint if he shifted. But his special gift with rock manipulation doesn't extend into hell and it definitely doesn't work in this room.

Seven dark lords sit on gilded thrones in front of us. Each of them rules their regions of hell with a brutal and ruthless hand. Yet, they like to appear as they are above their base, primal instincts and play aristocrats and kings. Their power is waning just as it is in the other known realms. This farce of ruling with civility is their attempt at control, but we're counting on them to play into it today... for Jade's sake.

Their dark eyes are locked on to my mate. I can practically see the drool from their lustful thoughts as they trail their gaze over her curves. I'm tempted to rip out their eyes for daring to looking at what is mine.

Lord Muldon, the menacing male in the center, makes my stomach turn, because it all hinges on him. I fear he will punish Jade to make me pay for our personal connection. My very existence offends him now.

"High lords, I am here to respond to your summons for myself and my *progeny*." Erwald bows his head, but it isn't deep or long.

Interesting that he didn't use the usual demon descriptor *spawn* but used the term 'progeny' as if to claim her in a more significant way—as his replacement or mentee.

"Come closer." The high lord waves Jade to step forward.

Both Erwald and I stay at her side as we stop ten feet from the lords.

He studies her for a long moment, then slides his gaze over to me. "This cannot be my long-lost Maxumus showing his traitorous horns here?"

I clench my jaw but nod. "Muldon," I say, insulting him by not using his honorific.

"You've finally taken a mate, then?" He smirks like he's a cat that's caught the last canary. "When I last saw you, you were telling me to shove the throne up my ass and that you'd never suffer a needy mate."

"Yes, well, apparently, I didn't know the bliss of finding my mate match who perfectly fit with my *chosen* family."

Muldon's eyes dart up to take in the rest of our party. "Quite a menagerie you have collected. Were you trying to befriend every possible tragic and obscure species?"

I shrug off his insult. "Seems fitting I should find acceptance with them since I never fit in amongst those in hell."

"No, you did not," he says with a weary sigh. "At least your brother proved to be a proper demon."

"Don't rub it in," I growl. "I didn't plan on being the white sheep of the family."

Jade snaps her gaze at me, her brow crinkling in confusion, and then perhaps she's figured out my secret. "Are you two related?"

I press my lips flat, but Muldon speaks before I can confirm. "Jadeana of Erwald, you were raised as a human. Is that correct?"

"Uh, yes," she says with surprise at the topic change.

"But it appears you have mated with five males. That is not common in the mortal realm, is it?"

"No, it's not."

"Were you coerced into bonding with these mercenaries?" he asks, as if he's concerned for her agency. "Did they give you no other choice?"

"No. I chose them on my own, after fate put them on my path. My soul was drawn to each of them and picked them as my mates," Jade says with conviction, allowing no doubt to seep into her voice.

"When you made your choice, you were obviously ignorant to all this realm has to offer a female such as yourself." He smiles, attempting to seem accommodating. "I could have the bonds dissolved, and you would have your pick of demons here to shower you with attention and meet your every need."

Jade cocks her eyebrow and her hip defiantly. "Oh? So you'd kill off my loving, chosen mates just so you can all knock me up with your spawn?"

"I don't *need* to kill them." Muldon waves his hand dismissively. "But yes, we'd like a chance to continue our race with your cooperation and in exchange, we'd keep you well fed and well fucked. And isn't that everything you need?"

Jade narrows her eyes at him, calculating how to deal with this situation. "I wish you luck in finding someone else who would appreciate that offer, but I already have everything with my mates, who offer me more than only food and cocks. Besides, I have no interest in accepting a breeding role in *any* realm."

Muldon clenches his jaw. He never did like the word no, and especially from a female.

"If I may interrupt," Erwald cuts in before Muldon can respond. His voice comes out with a commanding force. I can feel the room bending to his will. I suspect he's more magically powerful than those sitting on the council. "This court owes me a life debt. I claim my progeny, Jadeana, to remain free as that favor. All hellborn will leave her in peace, in all aspects, for however long she lives. Do you understand?"

Muldon's eyes bulge out of his head, and he shakes with rage. "This? This is what you call in your favor for? She could be the answer to the lords' dwindling numbers."

He rushes down off the dais and attempts to grab Jade.

I dart in front of him, and he crashes against my chest. I'd sacrifice myself for Jade's freedom. If I have to fight him, I will. He sees the call for an official challenge written in my eyes and I'm pleased as I see nervousness in his returning gaze.

We growl at each other while I sense Jade being pulled into Flint's arms for protection.

"She is mine!" Erwald snarls and seems to grow twice his size. "And I will not have her used for your power games and passed around like she is nothing but a hole to fuck and incubation chamber."

"Come now. She is obviously not opposed to fucking multiple males!" Muldon shouts and moves to look at her again, trying to circumvent me.

"Her *fated* mates!" Erwald steps closer to Muldon, and the lord shrinks back. "*This* is why demons are cursed. You did not value those offering us love and offspring and now you're paying the price with a dying species. We should have been cherishing and protecting our female counterparts, instead we turned against them and now they choose not to incarnate for your bidding and abuse."

I glance back to check on her, and Jade's eyes are wide with a genuine look of surprise and being impressed by her father's words. Finally, the bastard is some use in her life—first with Galiana and now here.

"And this is why I chose not to stay here in hell and sit on this council under your thumb," I add. "I could not claim a seat with someone who harms our precious females."

My stomach turns as I remember how Muldon abused his mate and when she failed to offer him more spawn, my mother was found dead.

"But now that I *have* a mate, I suppose I could challenge you for a seat on the council. Actually…" I wave my hand over to Erwald and Jade. "They are also of royal lineage, so perhaps they might also decide it would be easier to challenge you than to have you decide Jadeana's fate. Three of us on the seven seats sounds fairly tempting."

Muldon snarls at my comment. He knows we could easily be his end.

He turns to Erwald. "Fine. Keep your spawn. I doubt she could produce quality demons anyway, since she's a fucking mutt." He doesn't wait for us to leave and storms out of the chamber.

Another council member speaks up. "Lord Erwald, never mind his theatrics. Consider Jadeana safe from hellborn via your life debt favor, with the condition that none of you attempt to challenge for a seat on this council. And I hope your reappearance now means you're back to your regular visits and reports of goings on in the realms."

"Yes, it seems that since Jadeana's secret identity has been revealed, there is no reason for me to hide away."

"Since you have claimed her as your progeny, then we expect that to be the case. In the coming years, we expect her to be trained in diplomacy and in spy work. Perhaps because of her unusual blood lines, she can be a bridge to all three from her lineage. We all know magic is dwindling, and it's time we stop blaming and root out the source. I've heard a rumor that the Fae Queen is trying to find a solution. Perhaps Jadeana can be the bridge between the witches, the fae, and the demons, so we may all survive."

I sense Jade's anxiety skyrocket as she feels the implications of what Lord Krall is asking of her. But at least we already have a way in to the Fae Queen's court through me. Krall has always been the most sensible demon on the council, and I can see what he asks will benefit all the realms.

"Can you agree to this?" Krall glances between Jade and Erwald.

Jade glances up at her father, who stares at her proudly and nods. They both respond with a yes.

"Then I will see you soon," the demon lord says.

Hearing our clear dismissal, Erwald portals us out, and we quickly escape before they change their minds about letting us go.

Jade slumps against Arran, and he lifts her bridal style into his arms, clutching her to his chest.

I'm just happy he didn't let loose his berserker during that whole shitshow.

"Does that mean I am free?" Jade asks, fear coating her voice. She isn't ready to believe things are going to work out in our favor.

"Yes, my sweet child," Erwald says, true endearment in his tone. "I can report back any information or progress you make so you don't have to suffer Muldon's hostility."

Her mind is easy enough for me to read now that we're bonded, and she wants to scoff at her father calling her sweet or a child. Though another part of her secretly loves it.

She's been aching for love all her four decades. And that's exactly what I, and her other four mates, intend to give her until the end of her days. And beyond.

4 2

THE ANSWER

JADE

*M*y mind is still spinning with the revelation that Maxum and I are both demon royals. I always knew I could be a royal pain in the ass. Now it's official.

Maxum is a bigger deal in hell than he ever let on. No one in our pack knew. He begrudgingly confessed that he could have had his father's seat on the council if he had challenged him for it. But he didn't want a demon's life, especially one of a ruler.

The guys are being brats about it and calling him *The Prince of Morally Gray*.

All too soon, it's time to part ways with my father. He says he has a few things to take care of to ensure my safety.

"If any demons show up, fight with all you have," my father says, then gives me his secret demon name so I can summon him if I need him and asks Maxum to teach me how to dial-a-demon.

I give my father a shaky hug goodbye and a promise to keep in touch.

Maxum gives him our contact information so we can connect in the future since our pack intends on lying low for a while.

Osen has hinted it's a mating honeymoon.

. . .

I'm a bit surprised when Maxum portals us back to his lake house as the sun sets behind the rolling mountains.

"I thought this place was compromised and not safe anymore," I say, taking in the beautiful sight. This house was the first place to truly feel like a home.

"We're free to return now that Galiana and Rob are no longer a threat, and it seems her minions are dead, too," Osen explains.

"Amira also gifted me the secret of her powerful wards so I can create them around the property," Maxum adds.

Happiness bubbles out of me that my pack has their home again. It was always meant to be their permanent retreat. I nuzzle into Calder's chest, and Osen presses behind me and kisses the top of my head.

"Stop hoggin' her." Arran grasps my hand and pulls me free from the love sandwich. He turns to rub it in their face that he now has me and sticks out his tongue.

Flint uses the moment to sneak attack, snatches me up, and runs toward the house. He has the widest grin I've ever seen.

"Hey!" Arran whines and gives chase.

Maxum races ahead like a bullet. It's stunning how powerful they are. My demon prince unlocks the front door and flings it open.

I peek over Flint's massive shoulder to see the others clamoring and shoving to be the next through the door.

Their faces are filled with joy and childlike excitement. My heart glows seeing them drop all their past suffering to play.

Flint slides me down his rock-hard body, but with just enough give in his flesh to remind me what I gifted him during our mating. He turns me to face the open plan living area with the attached gourmet kitchen.

The entire place is filled with a hundred fae wildflower arrangements, comprised of species I came to adore during our travels. A few dozen candles light up with magic to romantically illuminate the space. A banner hangs above the glass patio doors, reading "Welcome home, our beautiful mate." The sign is inexpertly hand painted, but I think I love it even more because of its rustic, heartfelt style.

Home.

My eyes fill with happy tears as my guys crowd around me.

I have a home, not just a house with my stuff inside it.

My guys are that home. No matter where I go, as long as they are with me, I have all I need.

Something zooms past us, and I jerk back, quickly realizing it's Sage as she does a fun kick in the air and spins like a furry ninja.

"You licked them all!" she says like it's her victory cry.

I bark out a laugh. "Yes, I licked them all. They're mine now."

"About time," Trouble snarks. "What took you so long?"

"Hey!" I argue. "It was pretty fast for human standards."

"Well, you aren't a human, are you?" he huffs.

"Touché." I roll my eyes and mutter. "I have the sassiest familiar ever."

"Believe it or not, I've heard others can be more obnoxious," Arran shrugs.

Maxum leads us to his old bedroom that Arran and I shared with him the last time we were here. When he opens the door, there is a gigantic bed that will fit all six of us. My eye travels around the large room to find various sex furniture like leather chaises for hitting the perfect angle, harness swings, and dungeon apparatus with tie downs.

"Fuck, yes." Osen runs a hand over the leather and grins wickedly. "This is perfect."

And I have to agree. We'll have a lot of fun in here. But I will also want quiet, snuggle time with each of them, and the soft bed looks just as inviting. He shows me the closet full of comfy clothes and sexy underwear and a few costumes for play time.

I give Maxum a hug and look up into his glowing obsidian eyes. "Thank you."

"Jade needs to eat." Flint places a kiss on my cheek and rushes back out to the kitchen to cook. He's such a caretaker, and my heart warms with the realization that this is the first time in all my years that I have not only one person to keep me safe and happy, but five.

We follow Flint into the beautiful spacious kitchen, asking how we can help.

When I study the living room and kitchen, I notice that somehow the damage created by the magical fight with Rob, Floofer, and Galiana has been completely erased. Maxum must have had people repairing our home this whole time.

Maxum puts on some music with a beat, and we burst out in laughter when we recognize the song *Monster Mash*. We have an impromptu dance party as we make dinner. I find myself laughing, grinding, and swaying with all of them at some point.

Flint has some secret dirty moves that have all the guys nodding their approval.

"Dang," Osen says with interest. "I can't wait to watch Flint fuck you. I bet he *rocks* your world."

My face and core heat with that image. "Yes, he does *rock* me hard and makes the *earth* quake," I say with a wink. "But you'll need to ask him if he wants an audience."

Flint lifts my chin so I'm looking up at his bold and masculine face. He sees the flush of my cheeks. "Does that excite you, Heartstone? To have me show them how I take care of your needy little pussy?"

"*Fuuuck,*" I hiss and my knees give out. My innocent gargoyle is developing a naughty vocabulary, and I'm here for it. "You can't just blindside me, talking dirty like that, Flint. My heart can't handle it."

He holds me to his bare chest, and his pronounced bulge presses into my stomach through his pants.

"I've been reading your books," he confesses.

I blush, remembering some of the things I've written. Will he recite dialogue and reenact the scenes for me?

"Screw dinner. I want to take care of our mate, and properly anoint this entire house with our mate's orgasms and our cum," Osen announces.

The rest of my mates crowd around me, and I'm overheating with their rapt attention. Dang. It's one thing to write or read this stuff, but it's intimidating as fuck when five insanely hot and large males devour me with a hungry look.

"I don't think I'm going to survive this," my voice pitches high with nervousness.

"My phoenix senses don't foretell a death, so you'll live… happily," Calder says with a wicked grin. "We're going to fuck you until you pass out from bliss and then rouse you again so we can give you another round of pleasure."

Flint lifts me so I'm sitting on the kitchen island, and instantly the other guys clear the surface. He kisses me slowly, pouring his love for me into such a simple act and I feel treasured, like the most precious gem.

Multiple hands caress every inch of my body as they strip off my shirt and bra. I'm guided to lie back against the cool tile and Flint slides my pants off. Claws drag against the rise of my hipbone and then slice through my underwear.

I gasp with the sudden breeze of air against my soaked pussy. He lifts my legs and stretches me open for their viewing. My feet are set out as far as possible on the edge of the counter.

I cover my face, slightly embarrassed at my being on display. I hope I don't look like an uncooked turkey like this.

May the stuffing commence!

It's one thing for one or even two of my guys to take a gander at my nether regions, but when I glance down and see five sets of lust-filled eyes devouring the sight of me, I have the urge to either have one of them inside me or to snap my legs shut. I vote for option one.

Both Osen and Calder lean in and their tongues battle over my folds, spearing me. My back arches off the cool tile with the incredible sensation.

Maxum appears over my head from the other side of the island, leaning down and claiming my mouth with his forked tongue. His warm hands brace the sides of my face and then one hand slips down to clamp over my throat. He squeezes just enough to light my body on fire with need. "I know what I'm craving for dinner."

Arran and Flint massage and suck on my tits, drawing the pebbled nipples into their mouths. Osen's thick fingers slide into my channel, and my clit aches as Calder bites down just enough to make me come undone.

My whole body vibrates. My magic electricity crawls over my flesh. I buck, almost sending me flying if I weren't being grounded by five gorgeous monsters.

Osen places light kisses over my low belly and moves upward to finally place his lips on mine. "Are you ready for us, our shadowflame?"

The combination of their mating nicknames is perfect to represent the love we share.

"Yes," I whisper against his lips. I know he's only asking about sex, but when I answer, it means more than that. I'm ready for all of them, for our lives to truly begin with each other.

His eyes swirl with shadow and the promise of making my fantasies come true.

One of his shadowtendrils brushes up against my tight hole and slides inside.

Then I feel the cool liquid move alongside, using his fingers.

"Where the hell did you get that lube?" Arran asks in confusion.

"What? I keep some in every room," Osen says flippantly, like that's what everyone does.

"You gonna plow my back forty?" I joke, using ranching terminology because I've read a cowboy romance.

Osen teases back. "Nah, I'm going to drill for cum. Pretty sure I'm going to stroke my payload."

I'd chuckle, but I'm being lifted by his shadows and positioned with my back to him. Calder steps in front of me and admires Osen's shadowtendril-rigging as I'm harnessed upright so they can both have their way with me. My legs are spread and Calder's hand cups my mound and he slips two fingers into my cunt. All the while Osen makes me ready to take him in my ass.

Dipping down, Calder licks and nibbles along my neck until he bites my nipple, and I cry out with a delicious mix of pain and pleasure.

That's apparently Osen's cue to place the head of his cock at my back entrance. The slow stretch as he sinks me down onto him has me sweating and moaning.

Once he's fully seated, he stills inside me, and Calder notches his cock and presses inside my pussy.

"So full. I… I… please, move," I beg.

And they do. They both work in tandem like this is some dance. Their hot mouths are on my neck. They kiss each other over my shoulder as I watch and clench around their shafts.

They groan and become frantic in their thrusts, as if this is a race, but we are all going to win. Osen wraps his shadow around Calder's balls and the base of his cock, squeezing and stroking. Another shadow flicks and rubs my clit until I'm fluttering around them.

Calder's wings unfurl and light on fire as he cries out, "I'm coming. Goddess, I love you, Jade, Osen." He bucks into me and spasms.

His hot seed fills me. My orgasm hits me hard, and it prolongs his release. Our pleasure triggers Osen, and he unloads in my ass.

Osen peppers kisses over my neck and shoulder, murmuring his gratefulness for having us in his life.

As soon as they slip out of me, Maxum has me in his arms. I wrap my legs around his waist, but don't have enough strength to keep them there. Arran and Flint come to my rescue, and each holds a leg and supports my back as they lift me high enough so Maxum can fuck me.

Maxum's tail presses in my ass, using Osen's release as a lube. His textured cock rubs against my cum covered pussy, making my toes curl with the wicked sensation. "You will have no doubt who you belong to by the time this night is over."

"And you're all *mine*!" I growl back, feeling every bit the demoness that I am.

"Yes, we are, our beautiful monster fucker," Maxum says with a smirk as he thrusts into me, and I cry out with the invasion. His tail and cock claim me all over again. He fists my hair and tilts my head backward as he clamps his sharp teeth over my delicate throat. If I didn't have complete trust in him, I'd freak out with this move, but I'm turned on. He's part crazed, perhaps just as much or more than Serky like this.

Maxum is ramming into me with such ferocity that if I were a mere human, it would leave bruises. Maybe a broken bone. But I'm no longer fragile. With his rhythmic pounding against my clit and how he's stimulating all the right spots inside me, I scream with the orgasm that hits me like a freight train. He plows into me just like one too as he chases his own bliss. His cum fills me with a groan and a shout from his mouth still around my neck.

I must lose consciousness briefly, because the next thing I know, Flint is carrying me over to the living room. He clutches me to his chest as he places a soft throw on the couch and sets me down gently.

My gargoyle stands and shifts to his huge true form. His pants are still on, but I can see the giant bulge pressing against the fabric.

"Do you need a break, Heartstone?" he asks via our mind link.

I shake my head no. I want all of them, and I want them *now*. I need this to remember we survived. We need to celebrate that we are all together.

Digging into my supernatural side, I find the strength to sit. My face is level with his groin, and I stare up at his pale gray eyes that shine with love.

My fingers hook on his waistband, but I don't reveal him. "You don't have to hide. You're perfect and gorgeous. And I wouldn't want you any other way."

The other guys glance at each other with intrigue glinting in their eyes.

Flint sighs and nods for me to pull his pants down.

Once his fully erect double cocks are revealed, there are gasps.

"Go ahead." He mutters, appearing resigned to the ridicule he expects. "Make your jokes now."

"Are you fucking kidding me?" Calder almost shouts his awe. "I'm jealous as hell."

"Me too, and I have shadowcocks," Osen adds, but he knew about Flint from when he was possessing me.

"Yeah, buddy." Maxum pats him on the shoulder. "I expected you were packing, but damn, that's impressive."

"And his cum tastes like candy," Arran grins.

Flint's hunched shoulders straighten, and he smiles shyly. "Jade likes them, and that's all that matters."

"I love everything about you," I correct and lean for to lick over the heads of his two cocks, humming when his sweet taste delights my tongue.

Flint moans. "Suck my cocks like a good girl."

I almost choke at his naughty order. I want to argue that I'm hardly a girl, but fuck, compared to his four hundred years, I am.

Besides, he's owning his sexiness right now, and I encourage it by taking one of his cocks down to the back of my throat, while I stroke the second one.

"I need to be inside you," he growls, the floor below us rumbling with his power. He pulls out of my mouth, drops to his knees. Taking my hips in his firm hands, he draws me to the edge of the couch, my back hitting the cushions with the force of his need. He lines up his cocks with my cunt and ass. Without warning, he plows inside me.

I cry out with the sheer pleasure of feeling him inside me.

Flint is a fucking machine, thrusting with a speed that defies his bulk. The fullness and friction are driving me wild, and I'm thrashing under him. His huge wings expand, but instead of blocking the other guys out, he pulls them all closer.

"Holy shit," Arran whispers. "I'm going to come just watching this."

"Fuck her mouth, Arran," Flint orders.

"Stars and stones, is Flint a secret dom?" Osen squeals with glee. "I might be falling in love."

Calder grabs the back of Osen's head, fists his hair, and kisses the ever-living fuck out of him. "*I'll* dom you. Get on your knees and suck the taste of our mate on my cock."

"Yes, sir." Osen drops to his knees. Like a man possessed himself, he swallows Calder down to the root.

Damn, they are beautiful together.

Half shifted and in a lusty daze, Arran finally registers that Flint gave him an order. He leaps up on the couch and presents his aching cock leaking pre-cum.

I lap up the slippery fluid, and he slips his shaft into my mouth to the flare of his knot.

Flint's consistent motion becomes jerky as he gets closer to falling off the edge of bliss. "You're so gorgeous. Magnificent. A perfect fit for our hearts. You take our cocks so well. Made for us." He grunts out the last words. "I love you, Heartstone."

Our bodies arch together and my pussy and ass squeeze down on his shafts, milking them. His cum fills me, his cocks pulsing inside. I cry out around Arran's cock.

My body is a puddle of noodle limbs, and Arran pulls from my mouth.

A tongue licks the cum from between my thighs and works its way to my tender pussy. When Arran swipes over my clit, I buck into the air and then collapse again.

"Sloppy fifths." Arran smirks and licks his lips. "And it tastes so good."

I stare down between my thighs to watch my werewolf. He's part Serky and part Arran, in a sexy blend of man and monster. Serky's wildness shines in his golden glowing eyes, but I sense Arran feels just as wild with the need to claim me now.

He pulls back and flips me over onto my stomach, and my chest lands on the seat of the couch. Arran leans over my body and wraps his hands around my waist and plunges his cock inside me. His knot slams against my clit and labia. I moan, anticipating the glorious stretch I'm about to experience.

I idly realize why he's last, because his knot will lock inside me and keep me as his for however long his knot remains engorged.

Arran's hand slides down and his clawed fingers drag over my clit. The thrill of danger races up my spine.

Calder shouts, spilling down Osen's throat.

The pure debauchery of the night has me coming on Arran's cock. When he feels my pussy spasming around him, he snarls and pushes his knot all the way inside.

I shout with the overly full feeling, and the sensation cascades into another orgasm on the heels of the first. Arran howls as he releases his load.

All four of my other mates howl with him, and I do too.

It feels like we're a true pack in that moment. Wild and bonded beyond anything I ever believed possible for me.

Everyone collapses onto the couch beside us. Serky doesn't take issue with all of them touching and kissing me as we wait for his knot to empty and deflate. I don't think I've ever been so relaxed and contented in all my life.

Osen breathes out. "I'm officially *dead*."

We all grumble at his horrible joke.

"Too soon?" He laughs as we agree. "Well, I am, because this is heaven."

A smile slides over my face as I understand what he means. I *am* in heaven and heaven is being in the arms of my loves.

EPILOGUE

A FEW WEEKS LATER…

"You're the only monster for me," she whispers over his feline ears.

The ears twitch, but his purring gives away how much he adores her words.

No one else would ever come between them again.

THE END

*I*n my office chair, I brush my hand over my magic containment pendant, thanking it for allowing me to work on my computer as I write. I stretch, grinning at the screen. I've finally finished my novella just in time to send it to my editor. This isn't exactly the full-length novel I had hoped to give readers, but it should satisfy them for the time being.

My mind is already planning my next series based loosely on my monster mates.

I race out to the living room and find Flint reading my older novels on the couch. I launch myself into his arms.

He reacts supernaturally fast and catches me, easing me into his lap.

"I finished!" I kiss his luscious lips and smile.

My gargoyle squeezes me to his chest. "I'm so proud of you."

"What would you like to do to celebrate?" Osen asks as he saunters into the room. "I have some suggestions."

Calder appears next to him and winks at the incubus. "I suspect most are clothing optional."

In his wolf form, Arran races into the room and crashes into me, knocking me out of Flint's arms. He licks my face like he hasn't seen me in a year.

"Be careful with her!" Maxum shouts as he storms into the room.

Instantly, he shifts into a very naked Arran, pinning me down over Flint's lap. "We missed you."

I roll my eyes. "It was only a three hour writing session."

"An eternity," he whines, then kisses me.

Maxum yanks Arran off and claims me for himself, lifting me into his arms. "I'm happy for you. We should celebrate."

"No reason to make a big deal. It's just a novella." I wave him off.

"Never diminish your victories," he reminds me with a firm voice. This isn't the first time, and I doubt it will be the last time he nails me on this behavior. "You were at it for weeks. And with everything that's happened, I'm surprised you could focus on writing at all."

"All cock access all the time has been mighty *dicks-tracting*," I joke.

Osen slides up behind me, making me the meat in the Maxum-Osen sandwich. "I haven't been able to focus on anything but our mate bond."

"Poor incubus needs more sexy time?" I coo.

He swats my ass. "And I'm severely deficient in the snuggle department."

"Hug attack!" Like a wild monkey, I jump from Maxum's hold and swing over to grab onto Osen. The guys accommodate my awkward fumbling and help transfer me over so I can crush Osen in a big hug.

He hums in my ear, desperately holding my clinging body flush against his muscular chest. "Never gets old."

"My turn." Calder taps Osen on the shoulder.

Instead of giving me up completely, Osen only allows a three-way hug. But I love it just as much. The love that thrums between us swells in my heart.

Maxum, Arran, and Flint join us, wrapping their arms around me, creating the world's best group hug.

Arran's bite mark tingles happily. Flint's mind caresses mine. Calder's talon marks at my back simmer with his warmth. The shadow and light in my chest stir with Osen's bond. The marking over my heart that represents Maxum's bond pulses with light.

I am exactly where I belong.

There's one tradition I have when I complete a book. I have a drink to celebrate down at my old neighborhood bar.

The guys wanted to go with me, probably to protect me, but there wasn't a threat anymore.

The server, Lora, squeaks when she sees me walk in. "Oh my god, Jade. Where have you been? I've been worried sick."

"Sorry. I had a family emergency and had to leave town."

Not completely untrue…

"Everything okay?"

"It is now. And I managed to get a book done," I say with a grin.

"That's wonderful news!" Lora gives me a hug. "I'll want a copy as soon as you're ready to share." She guides me over to the table I often sit at—the one where I first saw my guys. "I'll bring out your signature drink right away."

It only takes a few moments, and Lora appears with my wild cocktail loaded with fruit on a stick and umbrellas. It's obnoxious as hell, but was created in a pouty moment when I needed something fun to celebrate by myself.

Lora had chatted with me that night years ago for hours. It was nice to share a success with someone, even if she was mostly a stranger.

I catch Lora up on a bit of what's happened, a *normal's* version of events and leaving out my monster harem.

"Wow. That must be so weird finally meeting your father when you're forty."

"Yeah, but he seems like a nice enough guy. We plan to meet up regularly now so he can make amends."

Just then, the door opens and five of the most gorgeous males I've ever seen walk through the door. Their handsome leader looks to Lora and points to the empty corner booth. She nods and then her eyes go wide.

"Holy shit," she hisses at me. "Those are the same hot guys you were drooling over the last time I saw you."

"I believe you're right." I grin ear to ear when Maxum gives me a flirty wink.

I should've known these possessive and protective brats would follow me.

"They keep glancing at you," Lora says excitedly.

"Send them a round of my celebration drinks," I say with a smirk.

Lora runs off giggling and within minutes, delivers my ultra girly drinks to the guys and points to me as the gifter.

They all raise their glasses up and toast me with sassy smiles. But as they lift the glasses to their divine lips, they are poked and jabbed by the ornamentations. I can't help but snicker at their fumbling. Flint gives me a shy grin as he pulls all the fruit and umbrellas out and guzzles the drink in one go.

Osen crooks his finger to invite me over. Then they all do it. A thrill runs down my spine. I'm so gone for them.

Lora looks like she might pass out from the excitement. To be honest, seeing them here in my old stomping grounds, at the same place and the same booth that I first set eyes on them, makes them all seem like a beautiful dream. Like a story out of my books.

I pick up my drink and saunter over. "Hello," I say with a sultry voice. "Are you enjoying your *cock*-tails?"

"We'd enjoy them more if you'd joined us," Osen says like the smooth player he is.

Flint and Arran stand up so I can slide down the corner booth and sit in the middle. With my huge, hulky mates surrounding me, I glance around the mundane bar and almost laugh that my guys could be seen as anything other than the supernatural gods they are.

We flirt and finish our drinks, pretending this is the first time we've met. A do-over of sorts. Last time, I was an embarrassed mess when they caught me ogling them. Now, they are doting over me.

We get up to leave together, each of them giving me a seductive touch while Lora's eyes nearly pop out.

She pulls me aside. "Are you sure you should go with them?" she asks, concerned as a good friend should be.

"Yeah, I have a good feeling about them," I say, looking back over my shoulder at my perfect mates.

"Are you... going to... with *all* of them?" she gulps.

"It's research for my books." I give her a wink and slide back between my mates.

"Let's make this beautiful woman ours," Arran says loud enough for Lora to hear. Then he whispers, "Again."

THE END?

Continue on for my extra spicy bonus novella where Jade checks off some wild fantasies on her monster bucket list in ***Possessing Her Monsters.***

A NOTE FROM JADE

Dear Monster Fucker Reader,

I hope you enjoyed the slightly fictionalized story of my life. I've written this under my pen name Yve Vale to conceal my real identity.

The names and places have been changed to protect my harem and all my sweet monsters.

If you'd like to know more about proper monster harem care and handling, you can follow me via Yve Vale's newsletters, Facebook reader group, or even reaching out through email.

I'm available for questions and comments, or if you found an error in paranormal creature representation.

And I hope all of you find the supernatural loves of your lives (whether it's in the books or in real life).

Oh, and please keep an eye out for Amira, Darius, and Raithe's story.

With all my supernatural love,
Juniper Jade

POSSESSING HER MONSTERS

BEWITCHING MONSTERS
BONUS NOVELLA

YVE VALE
AREN VALE

1

THE LIST

"*W*hat's this?" Arran picks up my notebook on my writing desk that's opened to a particular page where I've been logging my ideas for a monster fucking bucket list.

A few of them have been checked off already such as primal chase and fucking—a la his berserker werewolf side, Serky.

His grin widens as he peruses the naughty list of sexual acts.

I lean back in my chair and watch his reaction with amusement.

When his eyes dart up to mine, I give him a wicked smile. "Obviously, it's an incomplete *fucket* list."

"You mean bucket list?" he asks with an arched brow.

"I do not. I stand by my perfect name for it."

"Heartstone?" Flint says from the open door. "Lunch is ready." He looks at Arran and the notebook. "Bring the list."

Experiencing some unexpected shyness or perhaps protectiveness over my intellectual property, I try to snatch the list from Arran's grasp.

He barks out a laugh and holds the dang notebook high above my head in the extremely mature game of keepaway.

"No fair," I huff.

Arran doesn't succumb to my bratty charms.

I make one more attempt to grab it, jumping as high as my short legs can launch me, but to no avail.

I throw out a pouty lip.

"And bring that luscious lip with you so I can have it as an appetizer," Flint says with a broad smirk and walks down the hall toward the kitchen.

My heart flutters for my gargoyle's assertive side.

I turn back to Arran, and it's a matter of principle to get my list back now. Besides, I wasn't ready to share it yet. I have so many more ideas to add.

"Babe, gimme that."

"Nah," he says, backing away toward the door and keeping a keen eye on me. "Got to share with the whole class." Then he bolts down the hallway like a playful pup. "Guys! Family meeting!"

But there's no need to call them, they're already filling their plates, expecting me to join them for lunch. My usual spot at the dining table has a filled plate waiting for me.

No matter how many times they do these sweet caretaking acts of love, I choke up with gratitude.

"Thanks for the food!" I shout to the room in general and chase after Arran.

The guys set their plates down, expecting me to collide into them. They stand still while they watch, amused by our antics.

At this point, it's a game neither one of us wants to stop playing. We're both competitive and don't want to lose.

Arran darts around Osen and behind Maxum.

I circle around our demon, but Arran stays just out of reach as I try my best to catch my fast wolf shifter.

Maxum sighs heavily then plucks the notebook right out of Arran's hand. He lifts it up, out of Arran's reach, and dang, he's tall. He glances at the contents. "Ah… finally. I was wondering when we'd get to this important and enjoyable undertaking. The Mighty *Fucket* List."

I jump right onto Maxum's body, and he grunts as I knock into him full force. His strong arm grasps and holds my ass, keeping me up on him. But even with the height I've gained with my thighs wrapped around his waist, it isn't enough to get the notebook.

His obsidian eyes drop down to study my face. "I thought you'd want us to fulfill every fantasy. So why are you fighting this, my little demon mate?"

Biting my lip, I realize he has a point, but there *is* something troubling me. "I don't know. Maybe I worry that if I do everything I won't have anything to look forward to?"

Maxum nods with understanding. "How about we always leave one thing unchecked?"

"And we might have to try some things more than once to get them right,"

Calder says to soothe me or tantalize me... I'm not sure yet. "We might take years to get through them to our satisfaction."

"Besides, I'm sure you'll keep adding to the list," Osen reasons.

Maxum sets my ass down on the island's counter top and wedges his hips between my thighs. He hands me the crumbled notebook. "What do you say?"

"Okay. We can start checking these off." I scan the list, but I'm unsure which fantasy to leave unchecked. "Maybe you can surprise me. Don't tell me which scenario you're saving or what you are about to do."

Osen leans against the counter and skims his hand up my thigh. His lips brush over the shell of my ear, sending shivers down my spine. "That's a brilliant idea."

Flint pushes both of them aside, carries me to the table, and sets me on his lap. "Jade needs to eat, then we can have a meeting about how to conquer her list."

I hold back a chuckle because I know he's going to treat it like a flipping mission from the Goddess herself. This is now a *take no prisoners and my vagina won't survive the situation.*

My gargoyle gives me a kiss on the cheek and then hand feeds me the sandwich he's made. FYI, not all foods are great for hand feeding. Small, bite sized items, no problem. Sandwiches not so much. I'm trying my best to use my dull teeth to rip into the chewy bread. I make it work, since I'm concerned Flint will try to baby bird feed me if I can't.

My protective giant's favorite thing is to hand feed me, so I do my best to play along. I can't stand to see his pouty lip, not in combination with those sexy tusks. My heart literally crumbles, and I give in to whatever he wants.

I'm starting to suspect he knows I'm a sucker for it, too.

No one else argues with him when he's determined to take care of me either. Probably because they're just happy he's finally over his touch aversion after four hundred years. He's got a lot to make up for.

After we're done eating, I give them all a quick kiss on the cheek and run off to write some more today. I hear their excited whispers and the rustling of the list, and my lady bits tingle with anticipation.

2

HERE COMES THE QUEEN

I wake up to an unusual sensation…

No one is in the bed with me.

Huh? There's always one, if not two, if not all of them, lingering in bed with me when I wake up. Even if they're all awake, they'd rather be near me than not.

Where are they? And what are they up to?

I throw on a robe and shuffle out to the kitchen to see if Flint has made me some *morning bean tea* as he likes to call it. I'm blessed with the smell of brewed coffee while I'm still in the hallway.

When I enter the large open floor space that includes a living room, dining area, and kitchen, I find all five of my mates on the couches and chairs —reading.

Not reading just anything. No, they're all reading my books.

"What are you doing?" My voice comes out hoarse because they all have tented pants from whatever scene they're reading.

Calder's eyes go wide. "Dang. I was so into this scene that I didn't even sense you coming into the room."

"Got to a good spot, huh?" I waggle my eyebrows and eye the outline of his engorged dick against his pants.

"You could say that," Osen jumps in. "But you have quite a few good scenes in this one."

I glance at the covers. "Wait. Are you all reading the same exact book? Is this a Monster Book Club?"

Arran lifts a notebook. "We're taking notes."

I notice there are several post-it tabs marking passages in each guy's book.

"Is this a critique group?" I ask, my throat going dry. I don't think I could handle them ripping apart my work.

Maxum chuckles and pats his lap for me to sit, and I do. "Not at all. We're interested in how you describe certain... acts. Then we can give you some live action experiences."

My eyes light up with mischief. "I'm finally have my own stunt men for research?"

A little later, I hear their voices carry down the hall to my office. The guys are still going over ideas about how to satisfy me. The debate is starting to get heated.

"She wouldn't like that." *Flint.*

I'm guessing the scene is a bit rough for his delicate sensibilities. Degradation maybe?

"Don't be so sure she won't like it. You don't know everything just because your minds are linked. *I* was in her actual brain." *Osen.* Such a petty brat sometimes.

"Might need some modifications." *Maxum.* Always the planner.

"Hey, guys. Check out page forty two. Uh, yes, please." *Calder.* He's becoming the happy-go-lucky optimist in the group, to everyone's shock.

"The cupcakes?" Arran asks.

I can almost hear him licking his chops because of his sweet fang.

"No, dude," Calder scoffs at the werewolf and chuckles. "Check out what they do at the bottom of the page. That would be hot."

My mind reels, trying to remember what I've written that has cupcakes in the scene. I'm not sure if knowing they're working on this together is the greatest thing in the universe or the most agonizing.

I'll admit it. I have no patience as illustrated by how fast I claimed the loves of my life—my monsters. I'm barely okay with not knowing what's going to happen—otherwise known as surprises. It's why I enjoy writing. I'm in control... *mostly.*

Calder and Flint are cooking dinner when I emerge from my writing cave.

"Where have the others gone?" I sneak a slice of zucchini, freshly picked from Flint's vegetable garden, and lean against the counter, wondering how I can help out. But they already have the table set, so there's nothing left for me to do.

"Research and development," Calder says with a saucy wink.

"You all are ridiculous," I chuckle.

"No. Dedicated," Flint states firmly. "With the ASO's hostile faction decimated, thanks to you, we can finally take the time off we've needed to tend to your needs properly."

"Yep," Calder explains. "But we aren't great at relaxing, so you and your kinky fantasies are our next mission."

"They aren't *that* kinky," I balk. When they give me an incredulous look, I add, "Well, maybe I'm a *bit* desensitized. All I read is smut. Hell, I'm even tame compared to some!"

Calder whips out his notebook and waggles his eyebrows. "Any book recommendations?"

Through the front door, Arran, Maxum, and Osen saunter in, laughing and joking around.

"I'll get back to you." I tap Calder's notebook and try to spy at some of the notes on the page.

He quickly hides his work and tucks it in his pants pocket.

"That's not safe in there," I say while running my hand from his chest to his waistband.

"Down, witch!" he commands teasingly.

But I take the order literally and slip my hand down to grab a handful of his junk.

"We aren't getting dinner if you keep poking the phoenix like that." Osen's voice suggests he's absolutely fine with that outcome.

"I'll poke whatever I feel like," I taunt. "A phoenix, a demon, a werewolf, a gargoyle, or a naughty incubus." I stick out my tongue to emphasize my point.

"I'll poke whatever I feel like too." Osen walks up and grinds his hardening cock against my ass. "And I'll take that tempting tongue hostage as well."

"But no, seriously. I'm hungry." I swat him away. "What were you all doing just now?" I eye them, trying to search for clues down the bond, but the three shut me down so I can't get a hint of what surprises they have in store for me.

"You'll warn me, won't you, my Heartstone?" I ask Flint with my sweetest, coquettish voice.

"You aren't going to sow dissension amongst our ranks, vixen," Maxum growls, but the sound makes my toes curl instead of making me shiver with fear.

"You make me sound like the enemy!" I grumble.

Arran sneaks up and wraps a hand around my throat, holding me to his strong body. Then he nibbles down the side of my neck. "No. You're our target, witch."

Even though I freaking love his attention, I spin, using the self-defense training they've been teaching me the last few weeks, and I break free.

I evade Maxum next. I'm feeling pretty freaking smug until Osen ensnares me in his shadows and yanks me to him.

"We should punish the lusty wench." With his shadowtendrils, Osen pins my hands behind my back, squeezes my breasts, and plays with my nipples into peaks as he carries me down the hallway to our shared bedroom. He whispers in my ear, "I've been worked up all day, thinking about how we're going to satisfy all your fantasies."

"Osen!" Flint shouts. "What about dinner?"

"I know what I'm eating." Osen drags his sharp canines down my neck and palms my mound.

Food, what's food?

Maxum is right behind us and nods to the cushy rug at the foot of our bed.

Osen sets me down on my knees but doesn't loosen his shadow's hold on my wrists.

Maxum and Osen tower over me as I stare up at them.

With a grin, Maxum says, "I know Flint and Arran have a strong need to nourish you, but I'm going to feed you something else. Make you our little sex toy." He drops his pants and his hard cock springs free. "Open up like a good cumslut, or you don't get to come later."

My skin heats and my pussy pulses with his dirty talk. His bossiness is exactly like one of my fantasies, and they're playing it out...

Being used for their pleasure.

I watch as Osen slides off his pants, unleashing his beast too.

I open my mouth as instructed.

Arran, Calder, and Flint all walk in and their eyes instantly heat when they see me ready to swallow down Maxum's cock.

"Lovely, but I need her naked," Arran says, then drops down behind me and unleashes his claws, tearing my shirt from my body.

I didn't even bother with a bra today, so my breasts are on display and my nipples are hard as rocks.

Arran slides his hand down the front of my pants as his claws drag over my sensitive skin.

"Oh, fuck," I hiss when the sharp point skims my clit.

Arran's patience ends, and he rips my pants and underwear to shreds.

Maxum runs his fingers through my hair and then grips the back of my head. "Open those slutty lips now. I'm done waiting." He takes my hair like a handle and guides my mouth down onto his shaft. "Good, little monster fucker. Take me all the way."

Calder drops down to his knees and slides two fingers into me. "You should feel how wet this needy pussy is for us already. How many cocks do you think we can stuff into it at once?"

"Oh, god," I mutter around Maxum's thick shaft, feeling myself clenching around Calder's thick fingers.

"Look at this pretty mouth choking on my cock."

"We're going to ruin her," Osen says like a promise. "I'm not sure what hole I want to take. Might take them all."

Maxum fucks my face, and I love the feral look in his eyes. His head finally falls back, and he shouts as he comes down my throat. "Fuck, yes! Take all of it, little slut."

I guzzle him down as fast as I can.

From behind, Calder pulls me to my feet and then nudges my legs farther apart. The head of his cock notches at my opening. "Who owns this pussy?"

"You do."

"And?" He demands my obedience.

"You all do, sir."

Osen steps in front of me and cups my mound, circling my clit with his fingertips. "Let's see how full we can fill her."

I moan, and he captures my mouth, commanding my attention as his tongue thrusts past my lips.

Calder jerks his hips and slams into my pussy.

I cry out with the sudden stretch.

He doesn't relent, but he does feed me his special power—to echo in my mind what he feels. I can experience what it feels like for my cunt to be fluttering around his cock. My body tingles with the magically combined pleasure.

Osen drops to his knees and licks my pussy while Calder fucks me from behind, I can feel his tongue sliding over Calder's shaft too.

My orgasm hits me hard and fast.

Osen stands up and presses the head of his cock against Calder's. "Let's see if this hole can take both of us at the same time."

I grunt as he slides alongside Calder and fills me to the freaking hilt.

"Damn. That's hot," Arran hums, his clawed hand grips my breast.

I'm sweating and whimpering as my pussy begins to accept the double invasion. Glancing over at Arran, I see he's partially shifted. His golden eyes study me, making sure I'm okay. When he sees that I'm still enjoying myself, he gives me a smirk and squeezes my tit harder.

Flint grabs my other breast and my attention snaps to my other side. His pale gray eyes lock with mine. "Now I know I can shove both of my cocks into one hole."

I whimper with the need to feel him inside me like that.

Maxum's tail slinks over my open mouth and dives inside. "Suck."

With Calder's bond and magic, the intensity amplifies as I sense Osen's and Calder's approaching their climax. Their release fills my stretched pussy, and I'm undone once again.

When I return to my body, I slump back into Calder's arms. Osen and Calder slip free.

Flint's strong hands position me, bent over the side of the bed, my ass presented for his pleasure.

My gargoyle leans down, boops my clit, and whispers to it, "You gonna be a good girl?" Then he sinks three fingers in me without any warning. I buck into the mattress, but thankfully, I've been opened up by my phoenix and incubus combined efforts.

Flint then uses their cum on his fingers to slick his dicks, and I feel him notch both of his cocks at my opening. "I'm going to fill this naughty witch and then the werewolf can lock it inside with his knot."

"I'm going to claim her pussy before the wolf does," Maxum corrects. "She'll officially be our dirty little slut."

A rush of air leaves my lungs as he slams his cocks inside me. I feel Osen and Calder's combined seed leaking out of me, and I feel like their little play thing. And I love it.

Maxum rubs my clit as Flint unloads inside of me.

Then my demon takes his place with his tail sliding along inside me with this textured cock.

I grunt with the force of his thrusts and he says to Arran, "Fill that mouth with something, will ya?"

Arran lifts my head from the mattress and slips his dick past my lips up to his swelling knot.

Osen and Calder smack my ass as Maxum plunges inside me. The sensations over power me. I spasm around his dick and tail which catapults him into his release. "Yes, you're going to take every drop."

I'm a sloppy, floppy mess when Arran flips me over and hooks my ankles over his shoulders. His werewolf ripples over his skin as he thrusts into me, his knot slamming against my clit. "I'm going to lock all this delicious cum in this abused pussy, and you're going to keep coming on my knot. Understand?"

I whimper and moan, thrashing as another orgasm threatens to decimate me.

"Understand?"

"Yes! I will."

"Such a good slut." Arran growls with pleasure. "Our perfect mate."

He fills me up with his release and knots me. His thrusts become shallow as he teeters me on the edge of bliss, making me fall off over and over.

I'm in a daze for who knows how long.

Then Arran carries me to the shower and his knot finally slips free.

Maxum was smart enough to have designed a gigantic shower stall with multiple shower heads so we can all wash up.

All five of my mates make sure to give me gentle kisses and touches, murmuring sweet things in my ear.

"Are you okay, Heartstone? You're our queen. I don't want you to feel we don't honor you," Flint says to me via our mind link. *"We didn't hurt you, did we?"*

"I know it was all in play." I brush my hand over his square jaw. *"And I loved it."*

3

CLOSE ENCOUNTERS

"*W*here the heck are we?" I ask as I step through a portal with Maxum. It looks like a stage set for a science fiction movie. Not a high budget one, but it's definitely a spaceship command center. There are leather captain's chairs and the 'windows' feature a backdrop of stars and nebulas.

For half a second, I wonder how far Maxum can portal. Could he portal to space? But when I throw my physical and psychic senses out to assess where I am, I feel like I'm on earth by the gravitational field and the taste of magic in the air.

I'm in the strange, silver latex dress and thigh high boots he insisted I wear which makes sense to me now. My demon even wanted me to do my makeup with an otherworldly vibe with smokey eyes and silver rhinestones.

He's wearing black slacks and a simple golden, v-necked, long sleeve shirt that looks striking against his crimson skin. It was odd enough to notice, but I hadn't considered it to be a costume for a space themed adventure.

The place feels like an amusement park ride. And a soft whirling, breezy hum suggests we're flying through space.

"Crew!" Maxum calls out.

My guys parade out from behind a partition as the theme from *Close Encounters of the Third Kind* chimes.

"Reporting for duty, Captain Magnum." Arran wears black pants and a shirt like Maxum's, but blue.

"Very good, Lieutenant Starseed." Maxum nods, and I snicker with the name.

Flint is shirtless as per usual and looks almost the same. But he's in tighter pants and covered in shimmering body paint that makes him iridescent. Instead of his usual travertine appearance to his skin, he looks like he's made out of moonstone.

Maxum greets him, "Ensign Asteroid."

Flint grunts and smiles at me.

Osen is wearing all black, and Maxum greets him, "Doctor Blackhole."

In a red shirt, Calder has a phaser at his hip, standing at attention by the door.

"Security," Maxum simply says with a nod.

He didn't... Oh, yes, he did.

I glance over at Maxum, smirking. "You're an OG Trekker, huh?"

Maxum shrugs. "I might have had a hand in inspiring Gene."

I'm going to have to ask all about this later. I shake my head, wondering what other surprise life experiences my demon will spring on me. "But a red shirt? For him?" I grin.

"Funny, isn't it?" Maxum nudges me.

"What?" Calder grumbles at Capt. Magnum. "You said she would like it."

"I do." I suppress a chuckle, thinking about how the Star Trek's red shirt officers die on every away mission, it's too on the nose for our phoenix to be dressed like that. "It's perfect. And you look flaming hot."

Calder preens with my praise, and to be fair he's hot no matter what he wears.

"Well, we seem to have an intruder amongst us, masquerading as one of the crew," Maxum says as he walks behind me. His large hands clamp down on my upper arms. He leans down and whispers in my ear. "Did you think that I wouldn't notice?"

"I don't know what you're talking about!" I say dramatically. "I'm one of you."

"We can't take your word for it," Dr. Blackhole (Osen) says. "We will need to run thorough tests. And we'll all have to be present so you can't shapeshift to trick us."

"Tests?" I struggle in Maxum's hold.

"A full body examination to start," the doctor says. "We need to discover what sort of species you are."

"Lt. Starseed, can you remove her clothing?" Maxum asks Arran. "Ensign, a little help?"

"Yes, sir," the lieutenant steps up to me.

Ensign Asteroid (Flint) takes over holding my arms behind my back.

My breasts are shoved forward with his hold, presenting them with my ample cleavage. Soon to be revealing more.

Arran's fingernails become claws. He uses one claw to slowly slice down the front of my skin tight dress, leaving behind a fine red line but never breaking my skin.

I'm breathing heavily by the time he reaches my pubic bone. When the hem snaps apart, the dress falls to the floor, and I'm exposed except where my bra, underwear, and knee high boots cover.

Lt. Starseed hums in appreciation. "This creature has done a fine job creating a seductive body."

"Remove her underwear, too," the captain orders.

"No!" I overdramatically place the back of my hand to my forehead. "Please, don't!" I gasp in mocked dismay.

Arran steps closer, a breath away, staring into my eyes like he's going to eat me alive. My blood thrums in my body, collecting down in my low belly. "My pleasure, sir."

In one swipe, Lt. Starseed's deft claws shred my panties, and they fall to the floor. With one hand, Ensign Asteroid easily unfastens my bra, and my breasts break free of their restraints for all to see. Impressive—my previously shy Heartstone is becoming an expert at the art of foreplay, not to mention the main play. He's got game.

Captain Magnum eyes me up and down slowly. His hungry gaze lingers at my sex. "Hmm. So far, she looks like one of us. A *very* sexy one of us, I should add. But that could be all a deception to lure us into her trap." He strokes his chin with narrow eyes. "Examination table!" the Captain barks.

Security (Calder) wheels out a doctor's exam table with stirrups. Lt. Starseed and Ensign Asteroid hoist me up onto the reclined table as Security restrains my arms and legs in straps.

Dr. Blackhole (Osen) wheels a medical cart over that's covered with a cloth, and I wonder what's underneath.

"What are you going to do to me?" My voice cracks and my heart races.

I'm not sure if I'm anxious or aroused. Maybe both. With all that we've been through, I completely and absolutely trust my monsters with my life. But I'm totally pinned down to the table and at their mercy. It's a little intimidating.

Dr. Blackhole, whips the cloth off of the cart for dramatic effect, revealing a numerous assortment of various dildos of all sizes and varieties. There are some I have never seen before. And I should know, being a romance author I have logged many hours into *research*.

Are dildos not exclusive to the mortal realm? I'm going to need to investigate this. My imagination excitedly jumps for joy with all the new possibilities that I'll be able to use, in my books, of course.

"Doctor, begin the scan." Maxum grins wickedly.

The doctor picks up a simple vibrating dildo and turns it on. "This should give us an understanding of how the specimen reacts to tactile stimulation."

He drags it back and forth a few inches over my body from my breasts to my sex. Even though I know how silly this setup is, I can't help but get caught up in the fact that I'm strapped down and five otherworldly males can do whatever they wish to me. I quiver with goose bumps with just the thought of what's going to happen next.

"Sir! Her body seems to be responding to the sound of the vibrating scanner. Look!" Security points to my exposed flushed skin, placing his hand on his phaser. "I'm ready if she attacks."

"Take it easy, Security. *We* are in control here. "Lieutenant, Security, assist the doctor with the breast exam," Captain Magnum orders.

From their hip holsters, Lt. Starseed and Security each take out their *phasers* which are actually nipple suckers

My nipples pebble with anticipation as they approach my breasts with caution.

They both massage my tits and then each lick a nipple to assure a tight seal before applying their devices.

I moan from the divine, pulling sensation.

Dr. Blackhole grazes his vibrating *scanner* over my clit down to my rosebud and then picks up a rather large butt plug with a bullet vibrator. With the sight of it, my puckered hole clenches tight. The ever observant Dr. *Osen* notices and applies ample lube over his *device*, thank goddess.

"It's time to digitize your pussy," Maxum rumbles in a gravelly voice that vibrates my sex all on its own. He rubs his finger *digits* over my folds and discovers I'm drenched, bringing me painfully close to an orgasm. He then holds up an alien looking tapered tentacle dildo and turns it on. He nods with a lustful smirk as it swirls and undulates.

He hums with his approval as he turns the dildo off.

But I'm not denied for long as Captain Magnum and Dr. Blackhole line up their *devices* to their respective holes.

"Doctor, begin your probe." Maxum glances at the doctor and they both begin to insert their vibrating *scanners* into me.

My breath hitches as I gasp, and I almost come.

"The doctor is in… The doctor is out… The doctor is in…" Osen slowly pulls the vibrating butt plug in and out.

Once Captain Magnum's *device* is fully seated, he turns it on. As it vibrates, he controls the speed of the swirling motion and edges me to the point of climax before slowing the mind blowing sensation down. I pant with need.

"Doctor, what's your assessment?" The captain asks, "Is she an invading alien threat?"

"I've never seen her species before. Her body seems to be designed for our attention, and I'm being driven to madness not giving into my urges."

"Ensign Asteroid, establish a mind meld and ascertain what she really wants from us."

"No!" I playfully protest.

Flint moves behind my head and places his fingertips on my temples. *"Are you okay, Heartstone? Is this too much?"*

My heart melts a bit with Flint checking in on me. *"I'm good. More than good. This is so much fun,"* I reassure my sweetheart.

"Mind link established, sir," Ensign Asteroid reports.

"Good. What are you getting from her?" the Captain asks.

Flint relays my thoughts, "She wants to sample our procreation fluids to find the best male specimens in our galaxy. And she believes we're the males she's been searching for all this time."

"You desire our seed?" Lt. Starseed asks, his voice raspy with need.

"I must have what you call your *seed* to sustain my life force. I *must* have it."

"I don't wish for a sentient being to die, maybe we should give her what she needs," the doctor suggests.

"Ensign, does the little female need us as badly as she suggests?" Captain Magnum asks as he plays with the dildo.

"She does."

My goddess, I'm going to explode. With our mind connection, I tell Flint, *"Ensign, I want to eat both of your hard cocks. Get your rock candy over here and into my mouth. Now!"*

"Sir! The subject is overpowering my mind! She's demanding I... No, I can't... I can't," Flint overdramatically cries out.

I never knew my gargoyle had such a silly side to him, but I'm here for it!

"Go on, tell us, Ensign," Captain Magnum encourages as he works the dildo in and out of me.

"She wants to eat my cocks!" Flint yells.

"Ensign, do what you must. Your sanity is worth more than your two cocks. Give them to her, man! This vixen is in control here! The power she wields over us is too strong to deny," Maxum bellows and raises his hand in surrender.

Flint kicks off his boots and drops his pants. He plucks off the nipple suction cups and blood rushes back to them, and I whimper with the sensation.

"Ensign, attach them to your own nipples," I order.

The ensign complies and then climbs up onto the table, straddling me over my chest. His rock-hard, bobbing cocks are bouncing off my chin. He tries to control them to enter my mouth with one hand as he lifts my head with the other.

"Muahaha," I cackle like the witch that I am.

"Wait… you're not actually going to bite and eat my cocks, are you?"

"Oh my goddess! Sweetie, no."

He sighs in relief.

My Heartstone is so amazing, so giving. Maybe he really would let me eat them if I wanted to. He slides his cocks into my mouth, and I do my best to take them both as far as I can, which mostly just past the tips. He groans from the tickling of my tongue along his shafts.

"Sir!" Ensign-*Flint* babbles out. "She's commanding all of you to strip."

"Yes, I feel the compulsion to do as she desires. She's able to control us through you. Alas! What will *be-come* of us!" Maxum feigns his resignation.

All four of the other guys are naked in a split second.

I'm impressed. Flint has really come a long way in our sex play.

I take his lead and command, *"Tell Security to bend over and grab his ankles,"* I mischievously tell Flint through our mind connection. "It's time for the red shirt to get *fucked*."

"Security, bend over. Grab your ankles. Doctor, line your cock up with his…" Flint suppresses a chuckle. "…his *blackhole*."

Security (Calder) obeys my command as the Doctor (Osen) leaves the vibrating butt plug in my ass and happily obliges.

"Now proceed to fuck your crew mate," Flint relays my order. "Security, you may pleasure yourself as your last act of duty."

Fortunately, Osen and Calder are in my field of vision as I watch this hot sex role play.

The good doctor slowly penetrates Security's *blackhole*. Security cups his own balls and strokes his flesh *phaser* while the doctor lends a hand, or I should say, *shadowtendril*. The sight of their passion for each other makes my heart swell, not to mention my pussy pulse with need.

"I'm being sucked in. I can't stop! I've just passed beyond the event horizon. I'm done for!" Osen hams it up. But I know he really is getting off on this.

"Attention! Captain Magnum! Lieutenant Starseed! Proceed to the medical cart and pick a flared-based vibrating instrument. Choose wisely..." Flint barks my commands.

Maxum leaves the vibrator in place in my pussy, and they both pick up a weapon of mass destruction. Of course, like I hoped for and predicted, they select the biggest ones on the cart. *Haha*, little do they know...

"Turn them on and..." Flint breaks character. "I can't... I just can't..." He stifles his chuckle.

Both Maxum and Arran give each other nervous looks.

"What is it, Ensign?" The captain narrows his eyes.

"Now lube them up and insert them in each other's ass! And make sure they stay there by holding them in place." He busts out into a full belly laugh and his cocks bob in my mouth with the movement.

They both do as I say, taking turns sinking the probes in slowly.

Through Flint, I add, "Now watch the doctor take Security's ass while Security jacks off until completion."

Captain Magnum disobeys my order and stares me dead in the eye, spitting in his hand to lube his thick cock. He slowly strokes his long shaft from the tip to the soft spikes at the base until his cock is so taunt that he looks ready to explode. His bulging veins and soft spikes pulse down the sides of his deliciously engorged member. Preparing to shoot his load, his large balls are tucked up tight against his body. Then he finally turns his gaze to watch my phoenix and incubus fuck. Damn, this is so fucking hot.

To outdo Maxum, Arran shifts into his wolf and... Oh my fucking goddess, what the hell?

He licks his own junk for lubrication. Well, I guess most guys would love to have that ability.

He shifts back into his human form and strokes his stiff rod with one hand, then he squeezes his plump knot at the base of his shaft. His precum glistens and a drop falls to the floor. As his arousal builds, he vigorously works his cock and suddenly, he shifts into his berserker.

"Serky!" I shout with surprise.

The sexual energy in this room is just too much. I'm about to go supernova. With the bonds through me, we crescendo together and explode into bliss simultaneously.

The blast leaves my ears ringing as a white-hot, bright light fills the room and blinds me. Time stops as we all tremble with everlasting orgasms that seem to be flying at us from the edge of the universe faster than the speed of light.

The speed of lust?

I do my best to gulp down Flint's double barrel load, but much of it runs down my chin and onto my chest.

Osen fires his shot deep into Calder's ass as Maxum, Calder, and Serky paint me with their release. My slick drips down my center and onto the exam table. It's a verifiable cum-fest, and the receipts are all over me to prove it.

Due to the intense force of my climax, the walls of my pussy are clenching down so hard that Maxum's sex toy pops out of me. Other than our panting breaths, it's the only sound in the room as it vibrates and swirls across the floor.

"Serky, fetch," I command.

My reluctant, but obedient berserker trots over to retrieve the dildo. I gasp as he first administers an oral *examination* with his long tongue deep into my sex. After he has his fill, he licks the dildo clean. Then he re-inserts it while staring in fascination as it enters my pussy.

"Good puppy." I would pat his head if my hands weren't restrained.

To make my point absolutely clear that *I'm* the one that's actually in control, I say, "Now, each of you will enter my *wormhole* until you launch me into other dimensions. Understood?"

They all snap their heels to attention and their cocks salute me as they all say in unison, "Yes ma'am!"

4

CHASING TAILS

"$\mathcal{Y}$ou get a five minute lead, little witch," Maxum tells me as we walk out to the shore by the lake behind our pack house.

"What?" I glance down at my sneakers and athletic short-shorts and sports bra that barely qualifies as one since it barely covers the girls. "What do you mean... *lead*?"

"We're chasing you, and if we catch you, we get to fuck you anyway we'd like," Osen licks his canines as if he's the wolf shifter.

"I don't remember signing up for a free-for-all chase with all five of you," I say, nervousness swelling in my belly. I mean, I like the idea in theory, but they all have a feral sparkle in their eyes. Even Flint, and he's usually the sane one.

"So this is why I'm dressed like the first female victim in a horror movie? I'm not training?" I ask.

"Oh, it's training alright, but not like you expected." Arran smirks. "Endurance. *Hole*-istic training."

Unexpectedly, Calder smacks my ass from behind.

I yelp and spin on him.

Maxum takes advantage of my distraction and grabs a large handful of my butt and squeezes. "Ready to be hunted, little monster?"

I gulp. Eyeing them, I'm intimidated by their strength and skills. But then a wave of determination emboldens me. "Five minutes?"

"Starting now." Calder smiles with an edge of menace.

Arran snaps his elongating jaw at me.

I bolt for the treeline.

I'm much faster and stronger than I was when the guys first met me, since I was pretty much human with all of my supernatural nature suppressed. My witch magic was only able to channel ghosts. Not a very proactive power.

My fae magic was non-existent until Arran's mating bite broke the containment spell. Now I have accelerated healing and electric mage abilities. Call me Lady Thor.

My demon side is a bonus, but other than enhancing my speed and healing, as far as I know, the only special power is that I can manipulate soul energy. Not great when evading my mates in a primal hunt because I don't want to hurt them.

I glance back as I enter the thick cover of the forest. Every one of my guys is watching hungrily, their hands clenched and their bodies straining as they hold back from chasing too soon.

I still have four minutes now before they follow. Through the bond, I sense they're itching to come after me now.

Running down a dip in the land, I'm now out of their sight. I pull out my literal ace in my pocket—Amira's new concealment pendant. I hadn't told my guys about receiving this unique item the last time we visited her. I knew eventually they would want to tackle this fantasy on my bucket list and it's a perfect time to give this charm a test run. Amira also taught me a few tricks in evading detection.

I throw the necklace on and feel its magic wash over me. I tuck the pendant under my bra to make sure it keeps contact with my skin so it works.

Then I make a sharp right in my trajectory to throw off my pursuers.

They likely think I'm heading straight for the caves that Flint made with his earth magic not long ago. But I don't intend to be obvious or predictable.

I keep light on my feet, trying not to leave any physical imprints behind. My magical and scent trail is now suppressed by Amira's magic pendant. I have to concentrate, using my own magic to make it work to its full effectiveness.

I skip over the shallow creek by stepping on the stones, keeping my shoes dry. Scrambling up a small ridge, I perch at the top where I'm able to watch as the guys start the chase. I have a great vantage point up here as they rush past my hiding spot and the path I took.

With my supe hearing, I pick up what they're saying below.

"Where the fuck did she go?" Arran growls with worry. "Can she portal?"

"I didn't teach her how… not yet anyway," Maxum says.

Then I sense someone coming closer.

Flint appears not far in front of me, scanning the area where I've squatted down to hide. I'm almost certain he sees me, but his gaze moves right past me.

Arran is right behind my gargoyle. He's sniffing the air, but nothing is pinging his senses. "Anything?"

Flint grunts and frowns. "I feel her close, don't you?"

"Yeah. But I can't believe she's gotten this good at hiding. We haven't had a chance to teach her much yet."

"We should have made time," Flint growls. "I don't like this. What if she's hurt or abducted?"

Maxum joins the fray and adds, "The threats are gone, and we're her protection now."

Osen and Calder crest the ridge.

"She can suck a soul right from someone's body," Osen says. "She shouldn't be underestimated. I wouldn't go up against her in a fight."

The guys all hum their agreement, and I want to pump my fist in the air that they think I'm a badass.

"Yeah, but she might not want to resort to just killing someone to get away," Calder adds.

"Where the fuck is she?" Arran snarls and runs off in a desperate need to find me.

The others run after him in their search.

I'm feeling victorious that my ability to mask my magic and scent to hide worked so well. Then I realize my happy ending is running away.

I'm going to have to go after them.

The tables have somehow turned.

I don't want to make it obvious I'm behind them, so I circle around and hope to get ahead of them on their path.

I scurry down the ridge and see that they're pausing to assess their plan. They probably thought this would be an easy victory since they thought I had no training in eluding a predator. A bit of pride hits me again that I've surprised them.

"Flint, if you are worried, use your mindspeak with her," Maxum suggests. "I already know you use it to secretly check in on her during our more intense moments."

Flint huffs that he's been caught. *"Heartstone?"* he asks via our mating mind link. *"I just want to know if you're okay."*

"I'm good. Just playing the game... too well apparently."

"She's alright," Flint tells them, and Arran releases a sigh of relief.

Aw. My gargoyle and wolfie are so sensitive and protective.

I'm ready to be caught and have them give a proper primal chase and rutting. Thank the goddess for accelerated healing.

About thirty yards from the guys, I pull off my invisibility charm and tuck it in my pocket. I begin my race away. The leaves and sticks under my feet alert them to my location.

"Fuck, yeah," Osen shouts, and they all give chase again.

My heart rate spikes. I'm out of breath as I run like my life depends on it.

It's a strange phenomenon. I know I'm safe with them. I know they would die rather than hurt me, but they *are* predators.

And my primal lizard brain aka cerebellum knows my guys are dangerous. It's screaming, *flight*.

I sense them fan out to flank me. Shit. I forgot they are essentially a hunting pack and most of them have kept supernatural beings safe for at least decades. Maxum and Flint for even longer.

I'm toast.

My undeveloped speed is nothing compared to their trained talents. Maxum and Arran (now in his berserker form) close in on me from the sides, and I hear Osen and Calder at my back. Flint's wings flap overhead and then he lands with a loud thump ahead of me.

I try to slip through the narrow path between my demon, werewolf, and gargoyle, but Maxum snatches me right off my feet.

With my legs pinwheeling like a cartoon character, I wiggle to get out of his hold.

The next thing I know, I'm upside down, slung over my demon's broad shoulder, and we're racing closer to the lake. Maxum slides his fingers under my shorts and panties and dives inside my wet pussy.

Unceremoniously, I'm tossed to the ground and land on a thick bed of moss. I have a sneaky suspicion one or more of them made a soft place for me to be fucked.

I'm about to protest their softhearted gesture, when a swarm of hands and claws rip away my clothes.

"What's this?" Maxum snarls, holding up Amira's invisibility charm. "Thought you could hide from us?"

His possessive tone sends a thrill through me.

"You can never hide from us again. We are going to fuck every hole now over and over until you understand this is our body, our mouth, our pussy, our ass to use for our pleasure."

I'm flipped over onto my hands and knees, my ass lifted into the air. A smack, then several, rain down on my full ass. I shout, but I know it's only for my mates' ears since there isn't anyone around for miles.

My soaking wet pussy is slapped. I yelp and a cock is at my entrance.

It happens so fast, I don't even know who is driving into me until I hear Osen groan with pleasure. His shadows shove my face down into the mossy ground as he pumps hard into my cunt. The slaps of his hips are vulgar.

Calder kneels down in front of me and lifts my head enough to power into my mouth.

Maxum slaps my tits and squeezes my nipples.

I hear the tell-tale sound of males jerking off, and I glance up to see Flint and Arran stroking their hard dicks as they eat up the scene.

Osen slides one of his shadowtentacles into my back entrance, slowly thickening his shadows, readying me for someone's cock.

Another tentacle slides around Calder's balls and then enters his ass. Our phoenix moans as Osen sinks inside him. Then his thrusts into my mouth become more urgent.

"Don't swallow," Calder warns. "We're going to use it for lube." With his next few pumps into my mouth, he grunts, "I'm coming."

I do my best to keep all his release inside my mouth. When he pulls away, Maxum leans forward and cups his hand for me to spit.

"Goddess dammit. That's too fucking hot." Osen grunts and unloads inside me.

As the incubus moves away, Maxum ensnares my waist. His soaked fingers probe my back hole. He pulls my against his chest and whispers over my ear. "I'm not going to be gentle, little witch. So if you want to run, you better try now."

His hold loosens ever so slightly, and I use one of the self-defense moves and twist away. I only get a few feet, my toes digging into the dirt before he's on me.

"Nice try," he growls and my core clenches with need. Knowing that Osen has already loosened me up, he slides his girthy, soft spiked, lubed dick into my ass. With every spike that pops inside, I whimper.

Once he's seated, he pumps into me a few times, then lifts me until I'm flush against his chest and vertical. Arran kneels in front of us, Serky on the surface, but I see that both are in control right now. His golden eyes flash with their power.

His clawed hand circles around my throat, holding me in place. His other hand slips down between my legs and his claw threatens my clit while Maxum continues to thrust into my ass.

Arran moves forward and notches his knotted cock at my entrance. He works inside me in tandem with Maxum's efforts. Once fully seated down to his knot, Flint presents his members for me to suck. I lick the heads and suck the best I can as Arran and Maxum jostle me with their punishing thrusts.

Maxum's tail snakes around and alternates in stimulating my clit, between Arran's knot knocks against it.

I'm rocketing higher and higher, and I cry out as my orgasm takes me.

My body clenches and milk my guys, and they shout as they follow me into bliss.

"Heartstone!" Flint warns before he pulls away and releases his delicious, candy flavored release over my tongue.

We all collapse into a heap on the forest floor and pant. Our breaths begin to unify into one rhythm.

I reach out and touch each of them. "I love you."

"And we love you."

A NOTE FROM YVE

ear Reader,

I hope you enjoyed this extra spicy bonus novella.

My husband, Aren Vale and I are excited about our new upcoming series. We're currently writing a Shadowcraft Academy spinoff series with all new characters and a cameo or two from the original series!

Our next project is about a water mage who has no idea there's a magical world until her latent powers manifest on an ill-fated swim in the ocean.

Her unique love interests will include: A sweet and protective 6'5" Cinnamon Troll (well, half-troll and half-bear shifter); An alphahole, sexy badger shifter who is her class rival and frenemy; and a suave, rockstar vampire who is participating in the school trials for one reason only—and it isn't for school.

To pass the school trials, they're abandoned on a fae island with only their magical skills to survive.

Will they help each other out? Or will they each focus on winning the scholarship prize so they can achieve their dreams?

With all my supernatural love,
Yve Vale

ALSO BY YVE VALE

SHADOWCRAFT ACADEMY:

(Dark Paranormal Academy Trilogy + Bonus Novella)

Hexed ~ Jinxed ~ Cursed ~ Blessed

BEWITCHING MONSTERS:

(Grown-Ass Woman & Monsters Trilogy)

Bewitching Her Monsters

Charming Her Monsters

Enchanting Her Monsters

Possessing Her Monsters

SHADOW MYTHS:

(Science Fantasy Standalones)

Chained Fates ~ Rebel Fates

FAE HEARTED:

(Fantasy / Shadowcraft Universe Origins Prequel)

Between Realms

Tangled Secrets

Chaos Tempted

Bonds Eternal

GODS ARE HIRING:

My Karmic Destiny

A Why Choose / RH continuation of

My Instant Karma by Raven Vale

ALSO WRITING AS

WRITING AS RAVEN VALE

GODS ARE HIRING:

M/F PNR Standalones

My Instant Karma

Cupid's Last Arrow

WRITING AS JADE VALE

CAGE BROTHERS:

M/F Dark Billionaire Contemporary Interconnected Standalones

For more book details, visit:

ValeRomances.com

THANK YOU FOR READING!

If you enjoyed this book, consider leaving a review on Amazon.

I would like to thank my readers and fellow authors for all your support.

Check out some of my other books and series below:

If you love Maxum, he has an appearance in
Shadowcraft Academy Completed Series
I didn't want magic. I was supposed to escape.
I'm forced to attend a magic academy with five males
who won't leave me alone—my fated mate dragon,
a dangerous vampire, a protective druid, a seductive incubus, and a hot
professor wolf shifter.
https://books2read.com/ShadowcraftAcademy1

Fae Hearted Series
A human servant with a secret.
A tempting deal with an Elven prince.
Three elves willing to break all the rules for her...

https://books2read.com/faehearted1

Chained Fates: Shadow Myths Book 1:
Four Demon Warriors. The last Serafim. One dark cell.

I find myself imprisoned with four gorgeous males
from a violent warrior species.
With their massive size, horns, and tails, I worry they will seek revenge for
my reluctant part in their torment.
When my healing hands wander, their growls turn to purrs.
Will they take me with them if we can escape?
Will they give me what I crave—their touch?
https://books2read.com/chained-fates

Rebel Fates: Shadow Myths Book 2
The Egyptian gods were aliens, and their people still exist...

I'm done with Earth. The moon base has to be better.
Famous last words…
However, my plan didn't go as I had hoped.
I end up on a ship with three intense warrior aliens who look like gorgeous
Egyptian gods—all who I begin to crave. They have heads of animals and
bodies of men. They look like Anubis, lion man, and a minotaur.
And they're furious I'm a stowaway.
I'm not out of trouble yet...
https://books2read.com/rebel-fates

Need bonus content? News on new releases?
https://yvevale.com/newsletter

ACKNOWLEDGEMENTS

A special thank you goes out to my husband, Mr. Vale, for supporting me. Thank you for being my sounding board, catching any rogue plot points or typos, and now writing alongside me.

Thanks to all my author and reader friends for their great advice, support, and friendship.

Also, I appreciate all of my wonderful fans! I love reading the lovely reviews you leave or when you reach out to talk about my books. They are gifts to my heart and soul.

And my deepest gratitude goes out to all of you who have encouraged me in my life.

ABOUT THE AUTHOR

Yve Vale loves spicy romance, fated mates, and redeemable supernatural bad boys who end up as cinnamon roll alphas for their woman.

She writes about strong females and their magical males, all set in paranormal worlds.

She is a lover and a fighter. This is why her books feature a fair amount of action, both in romantic endeavors and in battle.

Stalk me here: https://yvevale.com

www.ingramcontent.com/pod-product-compliance
Lightning Source LLC
Chambersburg PA
CBHW020604040726
47498CB00003B/621